Ellis Peters has gained universal acclaim for her crime novels, and in particular for *The Chronicles of Brother Cadfael*, now into their eighteenth volume. Here she takes the reader from the mountains of Czechoslovakia to the colourful landscape of contemporary India as her amateur sleuth, Dominic Felse, investigates a series of mysterious murders. Originally published in three volumes, each novel is further proof of Ellis Peters' extraordinary storytelling talent:

The Piper on the Mountain:

'Brother Cadfael has made Ellis Peters' historical whodunnits a cult series. Versatile as well as prolific, she comes up to date in *The Piper on the Mountain*' *Daily Mail*

Mourning Raga:

'The rich setting and colourful descriptions of life in the Indian city make absorbing reading' *Woman & Home*

'Ellis Peters turns her dexterous hand to the mysteries of India, where murder and kidnapping . . . are unravelled with her usual elegance' *Hello!*

Death to the Landlords!:

'Another of her enjoyable India-based stories. Miss Peters writes extremely well, and her vivid, loving descriptions of the Indian scene are a delight' *Daily Telegraph*

The Dominic Felse Omnibus

Ellis Peters

Comprising
**The Piper on the Mountain
Mourning Raga
Death to the Landlords!**

HEADLINE

First published in this omnibus edition in 1991
by HEADLINE BOOK PUBLISHING PLC

This omnibus edition was originally published in three volumes in
hardback: *The Piper on the Mountain* in 1966 by William Collins
Sons & Co Ltd; *Mourning Raga* and *Death to the Landlords!* in
1969 and 1972 by Macmillan London Ltd; and in paperback in
1989, 1988 and 1988 by HEADLINE BOOK PUBLISHING PLC

10   9   8   7   6   5   4   3   2   1

ISBN 0 7472 3771 9

Typeset by St George Typesetting, Redruth, Cornwall
Printed and bound in Great Britain by Collins, Glasgow

HEADLINE BOOK PUBLISHING PLC
Headline House, 79 Great Titchfield Street, London W1P 7FN

Contents

The Piper
on the Mountain

The Man who fell off a Mountain

Herbert Terrell went to spend his annual summer leave climbing on the Continent, and fell off a mountain in Slovakia. He was traversing a fairly steep rock face by a narrow path at the time, and it seemed that he must have missed his footing at a blind turn where the rock jutted abruptly. They found him fifty feet below, lying on a shelf at the foot of the slope. The shelf, being of white trias limestone, had predictably got the better of the collision. Terrell was impressively and conclusively dead.

Since there was nothing else they could well do for him, the local police did the obvious things. They took a long, cool look at the circumstances of his death, made a full report in the right quarter, popped the body in cold storage, and settled back to await instructions.

In due course, and through the appropriate channels, the news made its way back to all the interested parties in England; and between them, after their own fashion, they compiled Herbert Terrell's obituary.

Sir Broughton Phelps, Director of the Marrion Research Institute, received the news on a Sunday morning in his London flat. Immaculate from church, he sat at his desk and ploughed his way with disfavour through the surplus of work that had kept him in town over a fine week-end, when he would very much rather have been in his garden in Berkshire, sunning himself in a lawn chair. However, he was a hard-working, serious minded and efficient public servant, very well aware of the responsibilities of his office, and the sacrifice of an occasional Sunday was something he accepted as part of the price of eminence.

For one moment, as he cradled the telephone, his whole mind was concentrated upon Herbert Terrell. He saw him more clearly than he had ever seen him in the flesh: forty-five or so, middling tall, even-featured, obstinately unmemorable; a useful, reliable subordinate, thorough, valuable, arid and uninteresting. He saw again the dry, tough methodical body,

3

the austere face, the humourless eyes. Can there be such a thing as a civil servant who had ceased to be anything separate from his office? Where the human qualities are feeble and ill developed, perhaps the function eats them. Phelps saw his Chief Security Officer clearly as never before, but he saw him for only a moment. The features began to fade at once, until all that was left was the empty outline of a man, the vacancy that would have to be filled immediately.

The Marrion Research Institute was one of those hybrids so frequent in English public and social life. Old man Marrion had founded and endowed the place out of his oil millions, to prospect in dynamics and fuels for the future. The government had taken advantage of an optimistic director's over-spending to muscle in on this profitable field, and propped up the Institute's temporarily shaky finances in exchange for a watching brief and an option on all the results the Marrion computers, drawing-boards and laboratories produced. And this uneasy and contentious engagement had culminated in a slightly embittered marriage a year later, when the Ministry assumed the husband's role, and the Institute's scientists and mechanicians found themselves islanded and fenced in by considerations of national security, who had ingenuously considered themselves, up to then, as dedicated to human advancement. They had felt, some of them, like the children of an autocratic Victorian household, strictly confined in a world where the cheerful and ungifted ran free. And some of them, Sir Broughton remembered, had rebelled. For a little while.

Circumstances had exalted Herbert Terrell's office, as circumstances had placed him in it. Where security precautions are so tight and vital, the sudden death of one man cannot be allowed to disrupt essential services. Today only a skeleton office staff and the maintenance men were in, tomorrow someone else must be securely installed in Terrell's place, that man-shaped outline, faint as a wraith now, solidly filled again, another hand on the curbs, another sharp eye on the most secret of files, the private personnel file.

He supposed he'd better contact the Minister, and ensure that his authority to appoint could not be questioned. The old man didn't care a damn, if the truth were told, but could be awkward if his perquisites were infringed or his nominal authority by-passed.

Sir Broughton Phelps picked up the telephone again, and

switched on the scrambler before he asked for the number of the Minister's country house. No doubt where *he*'d be on a fine Sunday in July.

'Just a few minutes, darling,' he said across the desk to his decorative and influential wife, who had put her head into the library to call him to lunch. 'Something's come up unexpectedly. I won't be long.'

She made a face at him, not entirely playfully. Not even on Sundays did his time belong to her, but she still considered that it should. 'Something bad?'

'No, no,' he said soothingly. 'Nothing serious. Just a vacancy that's cropped up and has to be filled, that's all.'

The Minister's private secretary was a dashing young man whose native flippancy was held in check by his unerring sense of occasion. He had more respect for Sir Broughton Phelps than for most people, but even that wasn't saying very much. He intended, however, to rise in his profession, and he was good at official languages. It didn't matter that Sir Broughton could disentangle his utterances at the other end of the line just as effectively as the scrambler could unscramble it. What is said, not what is meant, goes in the records.

'I'm extremely sorry, Sir Broughton, but the Minister's just gone out for some urgently needed air and exercise. He's been hard at it all morning. Is it anything urgent? Should I try to find him? Or can I convey a message, and get him to call you back later?'

Fishing, thought Sir Broughton, mentally translating. Slept all morning, and won't come in until dusk. Could be over at Patterson's with his horses, but more likely fishing.

'I'd be obliged if you could get word to him. I just heard from Prague that the Institute's Security Officer has had an accident on holiday there, climbing in the mountains. I must make some arrangements to fill his place at once. No, it won't be a temporary appointment. Terrell's dead. If you could reach the Minister, I should be glad. My own nomination would be Blagrove, but of course I defer to his judgment.'

The secretary unscrambled that into: What does the old devil care, as long as the job's done properly? Go and get his OK for me, and he can doze off again.

So he went. His thoughts, as he walked down the fields towards the river, were speculative and pleasurable. He had his eye on a certain promotion job himself, but unfortunately the most hazardous thing the present incumbent ever did was to play a moderate game of golf. A pity!

The Minister was flat on his tweedy back in the lush, vivid turf by the river, his rod carefully propped beside him. He opened one speedwell-blue eye, startlingly young under its thick grey brow, and trained it forbiddingly on his favourite assistant.

'No touts, no hawkers, no circulars!' he said, in the buoyant and daunting voice he had only acquired in his old age, after a lifetime of watching his step, and one liberating instant of abandoning every such anxiety.

'No, sir, I promise you needn't move. It's Phelps on the secret line. I wouldn't call what he has a problem. It could be a slight jolt. His right-hand man's died on him – Terrell, his Security Officer.'

'Nonsense!' said the Minister, closing the eye again. 'Terrell's out of England somewhere, the Caucasus, or some such outlandish region. Climbing. Does it every year. Never could understand people taking up such unintellectual hobbies. What's in a lump of rock? What does he get out of it?'

'A broken neck, sir, apparently. It seems he fell off one of his pitches this time. They picked him up dead. No, sir, there's no doubt. Sir Broughton's had the official report. He's concerned about the vacancy, and would like your authority to appoint.'

'Hmm, yes,' owned the old man after a moment's thought, 'I suppose we shall have to be thinking about that. Did for himself finally, did he? I always said it was an idiotic way of passing one's time. Why do they do these things? I take it Phelps has someone in mind for the job?'

'He mentioned one Blagrove, sir, if you approve.'

'Old Roderick's boy. Might do worse. Used to work with Terrell before his promotion, I remember. All right, tell him he can go ahead, I approve.' He closed both eyes again, and lay soaking in sun. Not fishing weather, of course, but you can't have everything. 'Oh, and, Nick . . .' He opened one eye again, reluctantly.

'Sir?'

'There's a wife. Widow, rather. Terrell's, I mean. Seem to remember they separated, about a year ago. If Phelps knows where to contact her, perhaps he should break the news, otherwise they may have trouble locating her.'

'Of course, I'll suggest it to him.'

'Good boy!' said the Minister vaguely, and closed his eye again, this time with unmistakable finality, having taken care of everything. 'Not that I think she'll be fearfully interested,' he said honestly, and returned his mind gratefully to his own intellectual and productive hobby.

Chloe Terrell, formerly Chloe Barber, born Chloe Bliss and soon to be Chloe Newcombe, turned her key in the door of her Chelsea flat about eleven o'clock that night, and heard the telephone buzzing at her querulously. She towed Paul Newcombe across the hall after her, and plunged upon the instrument eagerly. One of the most disarming things about her was that even at forty-three she still expected only pleasant surprises. Telegrams, sudden knocks on the door at late hours, letters in unknown hands from unknown places, all the things that make most people's blood run cold, merely made Chloe's eyes light up, and had her running to meet benevolent fortune half-way. Fortune, hypnotised like the audiences from whom she conjured applause simply by expecting it, seldom let her down.

'Oh, Sir Broughton – how very nice! Have you been calling me earlier? I'm so sorry! Such a lovely day, we ran out to Windsor.'

She hoisted brows and shoulders at Newcombe across the pleasant, pastel-shaded room, to indicate that she couldn't make out what this caller could possibly want with her. Off-stage and on, her voice had made such a habit of intimacy that she never could remember to moderate the tone, whether for dukes or dustmen.

'Get yourself a drink, darling, and make yourself comfortable. One for me, too, please, and I'll be with you . . .' The telephone clucked at her, and she took her smooth, cool palm from the mouthpiece again. 'No! But *really*? Oh, no, it's impossible!'

She was a *belle laide*, brown, slender and sudden, with an oval, comical, elf's face, a blinding smile, and huge, purple-brown eyes. The eyes grew larger and larger now, dilating in pure astonishment, without, as yet, any suggestion of either consternation or delight. You would have been willing to hazard, however, that she enjoyed being astonished. A blazing smile touched her parted lips and lingered, but that could have been the reflex of disbelief.

'You've taken my breath away. I don't know what to say.

Well, that's very understanding of them, and very kind. I think I *should* like to go out there, yes. I do think I ought to, don't you? Where was it you said? Just let me write it down.' She scribbled indecipherably on the margin of the telephone directory, and whistled soundlessly at the outlandish spelling involved. 'Thank you so much for letting me know, Sir Broughton, and for your sympathy. So kind of you! So very kind! Good-bye!'

She put down the receiver, and stood staring at Newcombe over it, wide-eyed, bright-eyed, open-mouthed.

'Paul, the maddest thing! Herbert's gone and got himself killed!'

Paul Newcombe spilled his whisky. A few drops flicked from his shaky fingers and spattered the large photograph of Chloe Bliss as Viola, which stood on top of the cabinet. She made a delicious boy.

'What did you say? Terrell *killed*?'

'Yes, darling! Had a fall, climbing somewhere in some impossible place.' She spelled out from her own hieroglyphics, not without difficulty, and with a very engaging scowl: 'Zbojská Dolina – can that be right, do you think? In something called the Low Tatras, in Slovakia. He'd worn out all the ordinary Alps, you know. He was quite good, so they said. But this time he fell off a traverse, or something. Anyhow, they picked him up dead.'

'Look, honey, are you quite certain? Who came through with this? Can you rely on it that it's true?'

'Of course it's true. That was the head of his Institute on the line, and he had it officially. Poor old Herbert, who'd ever have thought it!'

'*Dead*! Well, I'm damned!'

'I know! And, darling, there's another thing, he says the Czechoslovak authorities are prepared to make it possible for me to go out there immediately, if I like, and see about the arrangements for bringing him home. Isn't that something? And I've never been to Czechoslovakia, so why not? After all, they've asked me . . .'

'Chloe,' he said, appalled, 'you don't realise what this really means.'

'Oh, yes, I do. But *I* didn't do it to him, you know. I didn't do a thing, it just happened. I can't make it un-happen. So what's the use of being hypocritical about it? In a way it's very convenient, you can't deny it. Now I shan't have to bother about trying to get him to agree to a divorce, we can get married whenever we like. And he did have a certain amount of money, besides being insured. Not that I'd have wished anything bad to happen to him just for that – or even at all. But why not admit to being interested in the results, now that it has happened? I hate humbug. Money's useful, and being a widow makes it easy to be your wife. And I want to be your wife, and you want me to – don't you?'

Newcombe put down his whisky, tilted her head back gently by a fistful of her thick, dark, straight hair, and kissed her vehemently. She emerged smiling.

'Well, then! And you will come with me to this place in Czechoslovakia?'

In a couple of weeks more he had, in any case, to undertake a protracted buying tour on the Continent – he manufactured and imported gloves, handbags, brief-cases and other small leather goods – but of course if she wanted him to he would go. She always got what she wanted out of him.

'Darling, this won't be business, not exactly. And I'll be there. It's fashionable to go behind the Iron Curtain this year, everybody's doing it. And it's the least we can do for poor old Herbert. The most, too,' she added reflectively.

'I thought you hated humbug! Oh, all right, of course, if you want to go . . .'

'Darling!' murmured Chloe, hugging him happily. 'It'll be wonderful! I must get lots of beautiful black. I look well in black, and they're sure to be rather conventional in Central Europe. But I'll be a *fiancée*, as well as a widow! What superb timing!' She held him off for a brief instant to get a good look into his swarthy, self-confident, faintly wary face. 'Are you sure you didn't pop over and *push* poor old Herbie off his mountain?'

He took it that she was playing games of fancy with him, and stopped her mouth the easiest and pleasantest way; but afterwards, on his way out, he had a queasy feeling that she might not have been joking. Either she was an immoderately silly woman with pockets of cleverness, as most people supposed, or she was an inordinately deep one who enjoyed appearing naïve. He could never quite make up his mind. Possibly she was both at the same time, or both in alternation. Whatever she was, she was irresistible, so he might as well give up speculating.

It was he who remembered, as he was leaving, that there

was one more person who ought to be notified. The girl wasn't Terrell's daughter, of course, she belonged to Chloe's first marriage, and her father had been a quite distinguished scholar in his provincial way, Professor Henry Barber, the sort of middle-aged, shabby, eccentric, companionable wit for whom young and ambitious actresses fall with a resounding but transitory bang. He'd died when his daughter was twelve years old, which meant she was turned eighteen now. She hadn't, by all accounts, got on at all well with her first step-father. Took herself off to Oxford, so Chloe said, largely to get away from him; after old Barber's unpredictable and exciting vagaries, this one's cool, correct orthodoxy had infuriated her. Newcombe hoped profoundly that the second step-father was going to be more of a success with her, but the thought of confronting a self-possessed and hypercritical eighteen-year-old frightened him more than he would have liked to admit.

'I suppose we ought to let Tossa know as soon as possible,' he said. The 'we' was partly a deliberate assumption of Chloe's responsibilities, and partly a pious prayer for harmony.

'Yes, of course, I'll call her in the morning. It's much too late tonight. *She*'ll take it in her stride,' said Chloe sunnily. 'She never could bear him.'

Adrian Blagrove came back from his leave on Monday morning, clocked his mechanical way through the Marrion Institute's defences in depth, and reported prompt at nine to his own office in the secretariat. He had been there no more than three minutes when he was sent for to Sir Broughton Phelps's office in the most august and sacred recesses of Building One, and acquainted first with the fact of Herbert Terrell's demise, and then with the probability of his own permanent appointment to the vacancy thus created. Both pieces of information he received with the appropriate awe, gravity and gratification, nicely tempered with a modesty which was far from native to him. Bursting with health and lightness of heart after his fortnight's holiday, he felt capable of virtuoso performances. This job was what he had wanted for years. The frivolity with which he played his graceful little comedy of accepting it was entirely unconnected with the tenacity with which he would hold fast to it, and the intensity with which he would perform it.

'The appointment is at present temporary, pending confirmation. You understand that, of course.'

'Of course!'

'But if you acquit yourself as well as I believe you will, I can say there's very little probability of confirmation being withheld. You've worked with Terrell, you know his methods and you know the organisation of his office. It's vital that someone shall be able to step straight into his shoes without a falter in the apparatus or its working. Can you do that?'

'I think I can. I'll do my best.'

He was a lanky but graceful fellow, not as tall as he appeared, but marked everywhere by noticeable length; long hands, long feet, long neck, long face in the best aristocratic tradition. A little like a well-bred horse, but with certain indications that the horse was by a sire with intelligence out of a dam with devilment. He was forty-one, and still a bachelor, in itself a diplomatic achievement, especially in view of the social life he led, and the fact that he was, as the Minister had remarked, old Roderick's boy, and old Roderick's only boy, at that.

'Then you'd better move in at once, and take over. The secretariat is geared to carry your absence a week longer, by which time we shall have made a new appointment there. Well, good luck, Blagrove!'

'Thank you sir!'

He left the presence very demurely. In the long, soundless corridors of Building One he danced a little when there was no one else in sight, but it was a sarabande rather than a jig, and his face remained bland, intent and fierce with thoughtfulness. He knew exactly what he would do with the Security Office; he had had his own ideas ever since he had worked with Terrell on a certain dossier, and found the differences between their minds sharpening at every contact. It was that dossier, he remembered, that had put Terrell in charge of security at the Marrion in the first place.

He moved his own personal things into the office which had been Terrell's. Temporary the appointment might be, and pending confirmation, but Blagrove spent a coolly happy hour rearranging things to his liking, taking down Terrell's few mountain photographs from the walls, installing his own yachting colour pictures in their place. The beautiful Chloe Bliss – he'd kept her picture in its place even when she left him – went into a desk drawer with the rest. Of Miss Theodosia

11

Barber, Tossa to her friends and contemporaries, there were
no pictures, or he might have been tempted to secrete one for
his own private pleasure when he had his predecessor's effects
packed up for delivery to the widow.

By noon he had made a clean sweep. As far as the Marrion
Research Institute was concerned, Herbert Terrell was not
merely dead, but buried, too.

Chloe spent the whole of Monday shopping for glamorous
mourning, and quite forgot about telephoning her daughter
until late in the evening. While she waited for the operator to
get the number of Tossa's Oxford digs she practised looking
appropriately widowed and murmuring: 'Poor Herbert!'
There was a mirror suitably placed opposite the telephone for
this exercise, so it wasn't time wasted. Shopping had acted as
a tonic; she was looking blooming. Pathetically blooming, of
course, but blooming. A pity about the name, though. What
could you possibly do with 'Herbert'? And yet how like him,
how decorous and dull. Even death, even a sudden death like
this, couldn't get such a name off the ground.

The telephone sputtered in her ear, and Tossa came on the
line, sounding defensively grim, as usual. Unexpected calls at
this hour of the evening could only be from home.

'Tossa Barber here. Mother?'

Where did the child get that gruff voice, like a self-
conscious choirboy just stricken by puberty? She might make
a hit on television some day, if she could learn to use her
natural oddities, but she'd never make it on the stage. You
couldn't fill a theatre with that bashful, suppressed baritone
stammer.

'Darling, yes, of course it's me. Did I interrupt something
for you?'

'No, nothing much, we were just planning this foreign
route. And arguing a lot, of course. The boys want to drive
and drive, they don't see any point in stopping at all, really.
But it doesn't matter, once we're across to Le Touquet we
can go wherever we like, and change the plans as much as we
like. We've got the car, that's the main thing. It's a VW van,
third-hand, but it's been looked after. And you won't have
to worry about us at all, because we've got two first-class
mechanics.'

Trot out at speed all the mitigating circumstances, and pray
that she isn't feeling maternal, or you've had it. Tossa and
her fellow-students had been planning this holiday abroad

all the term, and shelled out the money already for the air passage across the Channel, but one unpredictable impulse of mother-love on Chloe's part could still wreck it. Well, even if she quashed their plans, Tossa was determined she wouldn't go with her to Menton, to play chaperone for her and her next-man-in, before she'd even shucked off the present incumbent. She couldn't help it, and Tossa knew she couldn't, and didn't hold it against her. But, my God, how it complicated things!

'Tossa, love, there's something I've got to tell you. Darling, I have to go abroad, very soon, tomorrow if we can get a passage. You must try to be brave for me. I know you can. It's Daddy . . .'

Christ! thought Tossa, she *is* coming over all cosy and motherly. She can't have made it up with him? Even for her that would be an all-time, way-out crazy reaction. Even when she was gone on him she never tried this 'Daddy' business before – never in life!

'. . . something happened to him on holiday. He had an accident. He's dead, sweetheart!'

Never in life, no, just in death. That made sense, anyhow. Death called for a gesture, and Chloe Bliss wasn't the one to turn a deaf ear. Tossa stood frozen, clutching the receiver to her ear like some cosmic seashell bringing in the wavelengths of other worlds. And after a while she croaked faintly into the wood-dove's muted cooing: 'You mean it? He's *dead*?'

'Yes, darling. He had a fall in the mountains, and was killed. Everybody's being terribly sweet to me, his chief rang me up himself to break the news, and the Czechoslovak authorities have offered to give immediate clearance if I want to go out and arrange about bringing him home myself. And I do think I ought to, don't you, dear? I've said yes, and Paul is arranging everything, and coming out there with me. I should feel so inadequate, alone. You do understand, darling? You mustn't let it spoil your holiday, you know, I shouldn't like that.'

'No! I see,' said Tossa numbly, and fumbled for the nearest available exit. 'I'm sorry, Mother! It's quite a shock. How long do you think you'll be away?'

'Only a few days, I expect, maybe a week.'

'And you don't mind if I go right ahead with this trip with Chris and the boys? It won't be immediately, there's ten days or more yet.'

'Of course, go darling. I know you'll be all right with Christine and her brother. Just take care, that's all I ask.'

'Mother, I *am* sorry! About Mr Terrell – Herbert . . .' There wasn't anything, not one single thing in the world, she could decently call him. The field between them had been as arid as that. And whose fault was it?

'Yes, sweet, I know you are. But there it is, these things happen, that's all. Now, promise me you'll get a proper sleep tonight, and not brood about anything?'

'No, I won't brood. You know we weren't close. I'm just sorry it had to happen to him. Mother, where *did* it happen?'

Chloe repeated punctiliously the names she had to spell out carefully each time from her own cramped handwriting. Zbojská Dolina, Nizké Tatry, Slovakia. Strange, far-off places. But not really so far-off, in these days of circling the globe, like Puck, in eighty minutes.

'I'll send you a postcard, darling. Now good night, and God bless! Don't stay up too late!'

'I won't, Mother. Good night! I'm terribly sorry!'

She was the first and last to say that about the death of Herbert Terrell, and mean it. She stood for a long time with her hand still pressing the telephone receiver down on its rest, and she knew what she had said for truth, but still she didn't know why. They had never come within touch of hands or minds, she and the dead man. He had been everything she hadn't been used to and couldn't get used to, precise, cold, methodical, thorough, pedestrian. He had courted her doggedly in ways that had only succeeded in alienating her still more implacably. But whose fault was it? Whose? A little more effort, no, a little more willingness, and she might have met him and achieved contact, she might have tapped unsuspected warmths in him. And now it was too late, he was dead. You couldn't make new discoveries about people when they were dead, and you couldn't make amends to them either.

Well, no use dithering here like a wet hen, there was nothing she could do about him now. She marched back doggedly to her own bed-sitter, where her friends were sprawled happily over an outsize map of Europe spread out on the floor, the Mather twins in full cry. Tossa coiled herself once again in her place in the circle, and propped one elbow in the Aegean, and the other in the sea off Rimini. The soft, heavy wings of straight, dark hair swung forward and shadowed her face.

'Anybody interesting?' asked Christine, returning with capricious suddenness from Dubrovnik.

'No!' It came out so abruptly that it sounded like a snub, and she hastened to soften the effect, and made a mess of that too. 'Only my mother.'

It was simply that she didn't want to talk about it, not yet, perhaps never. Think, yes, but talk, no. But to her own ears, and especially when she considered the fourth person present, who had never met her until this evening, it sounded distinctly ungracious, even a little shocking. Why did she have to be so maladroit? Chloe Bliss could and did put her foot in it right, left and centre, but always in the drollest and most disarming ways. Her daughter, it seemed, had to trip over everything, even the simple answer to a straight question. This friend of Toddy's wasn't going to find himself charmed or disarmed by rough cracks like that.

She cast a side glance at him from under the protective shadow of her hair. His name was Dominic Felse, and he was reading English literature. She didn't know much more about him, except that it seemed he was a useful man in a boat, and Toddy thought well of him. He came from some river town somewhere in the Midlands, where all the grammar schools crewed racing eights, fours and pairs as a matter of course, hence his prowess. He was in his first year, like herself, and probably within a couple of months the same age; rather tall and a little gawky still, with a bush of cropped, reddish-brown hair, hazel eyes that didn't miss much, and a fair skin that freckled heavily across the cheekbones and the nose. What he was thinking of her was more than she could guess.

His reaction, if she could have known it, was not one of shock, but of honest surprise. His own mother was a gay, sensible extrovert, who caused him nothing but pleasure, satisfaction and security, so all-pervading that it had never even occurred to him to notice them at all. The revelation that this sullen, bright, brown imp of a girl had no such serene relationship with her mother came as an eye-opener, no matter how open eyes and mind had always been, in theory, to the infinite variety of humankind.

She might, he conceded, studying her covertly as she scowled down at Central Europe, be quite capable of contributing her fair share to any friction that was hanging around. He wasn't sure yet whether he was going to like her, though any friend of the Mathers was practically guaranteed in advance. But he was quite sure she was the most delightful thing to look at that had come his way since he'd arrived in Oxford.

Tossa would have been staggered to hear it. Brought up on the legend of her mother's charm, she had never been able to see anything in herself but the *laide*, and nothing at all of the *belle*. That hadn't soured her, she had sighed and accepted it as her fate. She had even convinced those of her friends who had known her from childhood, like the Mathers, that her view of herself was a true one. But you can't fool a young man you are meeting for the first time, without a preconception in his head about you, or any predisposition to take you at your own valuation.

So Dominic Felse saw Tossa as *belle*, and not at all as *laide*. Chloe's pale golden complexion became olive-bronze in her daughter, and smoother than cream. Chloe's rounded slenderness was refined in Tossa to the delicate, ardent tension of something built for racing, and anguished with its own almost uncontainable energy. Tossa still was like a coiled spring. It would be nice to teach her relaxation, but it was nice to watch her quiver and vibrate, too. Her face was a regular oval with wonderfully irregular features, lips thoughtful and wry, so that you missed the sensitivity of their moulding unless some sudden change in her caused you to look more closely; huge, luminous, very dark brown eyes. Her hair was a straight bob, just long enough to curve in smoothly to touch her neck; very dark brown like her eyes, heavy and soft and smooth, with a short, unfashionable fringe that left her olive forehead large and plaintive to view, an intelligent child's knotty, troubled forehead, braced squarely against a probably inimical world.

No, Dominic was in no doubt at all about Tossa, she was beautiful enough to stop any sane man in his tracks for another look, before she vanished and he lost his chance for ever. All the more effective because she didn't even know it. She might have a pretty good opinion of herself in other ways, for all he knew, but she hadn't the faintest notion that she was lovely to look at.

'She won't go and muck this trip up at the last moment, will she?' asked Christine, suddenly sitting bolt upright and abandoning the map, her grey eyes narrowing with suspicion.

Well, that was sound evidence, in its way. Christine had known Tossa's family almost since her infant school days.

'Oh, no, that's all right! She gave me her blessing. Don't

worry about her, she's going abroad herself, anyhow.' Tossa scowled even more fiercely, and stooped her weighted brow nearer to the map, only too plainly annoyed, thought Dominic, that she had volunteered something she needn't have volunteered. 'How far did we get?'

'Oh, we needn't plan all that closely. As long as we've got all the papers we even *may* need, we can go where we like, and see how the time works out.' Toddy drew up his long legs and hugged his knees. He was his sister's senior by an hour, and a good year ahead of the other two, and inevitably, or so it seemed to him, he was cast as the leader of the expedition. 'Everybody's got valid passports, and I've applied for the insurance card. Anything else we need?'

Tossa stooped her head even lower towards the map. The heavy curtain of hair swung low and hid her cheek, drooping like a broken wing. She followed the west-east road through Nuremberg, and on towards the border, over the border and on through Pilsen and Prague, until the edge of the map brought her up short of the Slovak border, baulked of her objective. What was the use, anyhow? His death was an accident, and no fault of hers. If she'd somehow failed him, that was incurable now.

But if she'd only given him a chance to be liked! Not everybody can do that by warm instinct, most of us have to be helped.

She hadn't done much to help him, had she?

With a sense of wonder and disbelief, as if her mind had taken action without her will, she heard her own voice saying with careful casualness: 'It wouldn't do any *harm* to have a carnet for the van, would it? Just in case we wanted to go farther afield? After all, we might – mightn't we?'

Two

The Man who wasn't Satisfied

The person who was to put the cat fairly and squarely among the pigeons presented himself at the gatehouse of the Marrion Institute on a Thursday morning, just two days after Chloe Terrell and Paul Newcombe had flown to Prague. He was of an unexceptionable appearance, somewhere between twenty-five and thirty-five, and carried upon him the indefinable stamp of the public servant. The ex-sergeant-major in command of the Institute's blocking squad used towards him a manner one degree on the friendly side of his normal one, recognising him as one of *us*. That didn't help him, however, to penetrate even the outer defences.

He asked to see Sir Broughton Phelps, and in his innocence really seemed to expect to be haled through the barriers on sight. He would not state his business, except to stress that it was urgent. When he was told that no one got to see Sir Broughton without a Ministry permit, he adjusted promptly and without undue surprise to this check, but he did not go away, nor did he withdraw his demand. Instead, he asked if a message could be taken in to the Director or his Chief Security Officer, so that they might make up their own minds whether to see him or not. The ex-sergeant-major saw nothing against this; and the stranger scribbled a few words on his visiting-card, sealed it down in an envelope, in a way which might have been slightly offensive if he had not just had it impressed upon him how stringent security arrangements round here were, and handed it over.

The messenger delivered this billet to Adrian Blagrove's secretary, who preferred, understandably, to hand it over to his chief unopened. So it happened that Blagrove was the first to withdraw the card and read what the stranger had written.

> Robert Bencroft Welland (said the card)
> Assistant Commercial Secretary
> British Embassy, Prague I,
> Thunovská 14,
> CSSR.

And above the name was scribbled in a vehement, cornery hand:

Terrell's accident was no accident.

Robert Bencroft Welland came in gravely, displaying no signs of elation at having penetrated the first protective layers, and no haste about completing the feat. He accepted a chair and a cigarette, and settled his brief-case conveniently on the carpet beside his feet. Shut in together, they contemplated each other across the desk which had been Terrell's

'Mr Welland,' began Balgrove very soberly, 'you appear to be suggesting something which doesn't seem to have occurred to anyone else, even as a possibility. The Slovak police were quite satisfied of the facts of poor Terrell's case, and made very full and correct reports which apparently convinced our authorities just as completely. I take it this is an unofficial approach, or you would have been sent here already provided with the means of reaching me, and wouldn't have had to write me – this little billet.' It glanced coyly between his closed fingers for an instant, and vanished again. 'May I ask if you've confided your doubts to anyone in Prague? Any of your superiors?'

'No, I haven't. I came to the Marrion Institute because it seemed to be the party most affected by Terrell's death, and what I believe to be the facts about it. I came over only yesterday, on a week of my leave, and I had some enquiries to make before I was ready to come to you.'

'Presumably, since you're here,' said Blagrove drily, 'your enquiries produced positive results. You realise you're the *only* person who has questioned the circumstances of Terrell's accident?'

'I could hardly let that influence me, could I?' said the young man mildly, with such simplicity that Blagrove took another and closer look at him. Under thirty, probably, of medium height and lightly built, neat, tow-coloured hair, all very presentable, all very ordinary. Put him among an office-full of civil servants, and you could lose him in a moment. Except that the good-natured face, earnest and dutiful to the point of caricature, had a little too much jaw for comfort, and confronted his seniors with a pair of wideset blue eyes of startling directness and obstinacy. He looked, at first glance, like all the others of his class and profession; but at second glance it was clear that being on

19

his own wouldn't stop him from doing whatever he felt he
had to do.

'Perhaps,' suggested Blagrove carefully, 'you'd better tell
me just why you're not satisfied.'

'In the first place, because I knew Terrell, and I've seen
the place where he was found. Oh, I didn't know him
well, but it so happens I've climbed with him, last year
in the Zillertal, so I know his class. He was an excellent
climber, on a rope or alone. The Zillertaler Alps were his
proper league. But the Low Tatras, where he was found,
are walking country. Not alpine stuff at all, but open,
grassy slopes and rounded summits, with wooded valleys.
You could find a few practice pitches there, rock outcrops,
scrambles, that kind of thing. But nothing to tempt a man
like Terrell. So the first question, even if I'd known nothing
more, is: "*What was he doing there at all?*" '

'I see nothing to prevent even a climbing man from
fancying a walking holiday now and again, for a change,'
objected Blagrove reasonably.

'Nothing whatever. Except that they just don't do it.
Hardly any of them, and certainly not Terrell. Once you're
as proficient as he was, you lose interest in the mild stuff. The
climbs have to get harder all the time, and higher. Failing that,
you just go somewhere new, where at least they're different,
unknown. But you don't go back to walking and scrambling.
And for that matter, even if you did go back, you certainly
wouldn't fall off a perfectly good traverse path, even at a
blind corner, like the place where they found him.'

'I shouldn't like to be so sure it couldn't happen. The skilled
and experienced sometimes fail to give all their attention to
the easy bits.' Blagrove was playing somewhat irritably with
the card he held in his fingers. 'Unless you have something
more than that to go on . . .'

'Oh, I have. You see, Terrell got in touch with me early
this year, and asked my advice about good climbing country
in the *High* Tatras. You don't know that part of the world?
There's this great, open valley of the river Váh, running
east-west, and to the south of it these broad, rolling crests of
the Low Tatras. Then to the north, sickle-shaped, like this,
and much more concentrated, there's the cluster of the High
Tatras, the highest peaks in the whole Carpathian range.
These are for climbers. Anything up to nearly nine thousand
feet, granite, three hundred or so peaks packed into about
fifteen miles length, and magnificent country. I advised him

to book in at Strba Lake, or at Tatranská Lomnice. And he did. He booked for two weeks at the lake. So what was he doing across the Váh valley in the *Low* Tatras?'

Blagrove raised his brows. 'He could surely have changed his mind. How do you know he went ahead with his booking?'

'For the best reason in the world,' said Welland flatly. 'Because *I* made the reservation for him, as long ago as April. And I know he turned up on time at the hotel, because he dropped me a card on arrival. He said nothing then about moving. On the contrary, he confirmed the arrangement we'd made by letter earlier. I was supposed to go along and spend the week-end climbing with him on Kriván. Only, you see, before the week-end came we got the news at the embassy that he'd been found dead – fifty kilometres away across the valley, in the Low Tatras, where he'd never intended going. He'd checked out from Strba Lake on the third day, and gone away to a small inn in one of the valleys in the other range. No mystery about *what* he did, up to that point. The only mystery is *why*?'

'And you think,' said Blagrove, his hands still and alert before him on the desk, 'that you know why?'

'No, not yet. All I have is certain indications that may suggest reasons. As, for instance, that at some time after his arrival at the lake, something happened within his knowledge, something that caused him to pay his bill there and then, and go rushing off across the valley. No one at the hotel could account for it. He just left. But something happened that made him leave. If it had been simply something that disinclined him to stay where he was, made him dislike the place or feel uncomfortable there, he'd most probably have transferred to another hotel, somewhere along the range, or come back to Prague. Instead, he made his way for some reason to this one particular valley in the Low Tatras, not even a very frequented place. Whatever it was that happend didn't just drive him away from Strba Lake – it led him to Zbojská Dolina. And believe me, it can have had nothing to do with climbing. Do I interest you, Mr Blagrove?'

'You interest me, yes, up to a point. You didn't say any of this to your superiors in Prague?'

'No, I didn't. One doesn't like to start hares of that kind without making sure first of as many facts as possible. I had some leave to come, and I used it to come over here. Whatever drew Terrell to the Low Tatras, it can't have been something private and personal from his own past, because he had no connections there, this was his first visit. He knew nothing of the country, he knew none of the people. I thought, knowing what his work was, and what it might sometimes involve, that there might be a link with something he'd handled or known about in the course of his duty. I hoped to get an interview with his widow, but she wasn't in when I called at her flat.'

'She's in Slovakia at this moment,' said Blagrove, 'seeing about having her husband brought home.'

'Ah, so that's it, I see. Well, since I could get nothing from her I spent the afternoon and evening among the press files, going back over the details – only the published details that are open to everybody, of course, but you'd be surprised how much that covers – the details of any reportable work handled by Terrell during the last few years. I have friends among the pressmen. I didn't tell them what I wanted, I didn't know myself. I just picked over their memories and then worked backwards through the files. I thought somewhere there must be something to dig up, something that would tie in at one end to Terrell, and at the other end to Slovakia – with a lot of luck, even to that part of Slovakia.'

Blagrove let out his breath in a soft, cautious hiss, and braced his shoulders against the back of his chair. 'And you found something?'

'I found,' said Welland with deliberation, 'the unfinished case of Charles Alder.'

In the moment of silence they stared steadily at each other.

'Or of course,' said Welland, 'if you prefer it, the case of Karol Alda.'

It was a pity. It was really a pity. To have the whole affair tucked away peacefully in its coffin as an accident would have been so much simpler and more satisfactory; but there were two good reasons for abandoning, here and now, any attempt to dissuade this young man from pursuing his enquiries further. First, he wouldn't be dissuaded; the supererogatory jaw was set, and the uncompromising eyes expected and would countenance only a zeal for justice the equal of his own. And second, to assume the responsibility for smothering a matter as serious as this was too great a risk. It would have to go to higher authority, however vexatious the results might be.

'I think,' said Adrian Blagrove, pushing back his chair, 'I

really think you'd better come with me to the Director, and tell him the whole story.'

Sir Broughton Phelps sat forward at his desk with his lean jaw propped broodingly on a closed fist, and scarcely took his eyes from the visitor's face as Welland repeated the tale of his reservations and his discoveries, until he reached Charles Alder's name.

There was an expectant pause there. Welland looked a little pale and a little anxious when it prolonged itself beyond his expectations. He would have liked someone else to contribute something, a hint of appreciation, or at least belief; better still, a grain of confirmation. But when no one obliged, he did not look any the less convinced or any the less obstinate.

'I know you must be much better informed than I am, sir, about this case of Alder's. But if you want me to sum up everything as I find it, I'll willingly go on.'

'Please do,' said the Director, fingering the clipped silvery hair at his temple. 'I assure you you have my very serious attention.'

'What I found, of course, was the dossier – or the published part of it – compiled by Terrell after Alder's disappearance. Otherwise I wasn't conscious of ever having heard of the man before. So my information comes, virtually, from Terrell himself. Alder was a refugee who came over here with his parents in 1940, and settled in England. He was then fifteen years old, and already something of an infant prodigy, musically and mathematically. I believe they often go together. His father was a physicist, and after a probationary period he was allowed to work here. He proved valuable, and before the end of the war all three of them were naturalised. The boy had studied physics, too, but soon began to distinguish himself in his own special fields, as composer and performer, and in the world of pure mathematics. Perhaps he was even a genius. After the war he did quite a lot of experimental flying, and originated some minor improvements in aircraft, ending up in this Institute, where he was associated with a number of important modifications in aircraft and car design. Also, it seems, he sometimes had differences with the government and his superiors. He objected to the exclusively military use of innovations which he seems to have considered could be beneficial in civil life. And he didn't like techniques of his evolving to be kept under wraps, when he believed they could be adapted to help with necessary processes in under-developed countries. He seems to have been a difficult colleague of individual views, insubordinate, unwilling to conform against his judgment. And he must have been really brilliant, because according to a *Guardian* article I found, about the time he vanished he was definitely in the running for the directorship of this Institute, and at his age that was fantastic.' The young man raised his direct and daunting eyes, and looked the present Director full in the face. 'Can you confirm that, sir?'

'I can and I do.' Phelps committed himself without hesitation. 'The man was brilliant. He was a computer that thought and reasoned. No programming, no minding, no servicing necessary. We spend millions trying to construct an Alder, and then wear out bright young men feeding it. When we get a genuine one as a free gift from heaven we usually fail to recognise him. But difficult he certainly was. Go on, finish your exposition.'

'Finally, after both his parents were dead, Alder wished and offered to resign from here. I don't know exactly why, I suppose he was disturbed by a feeling of alienation from the aims of this place, and maybe he felt out of sympathy with policy in general. Anyhow, he was obviously valuable, and he was persuaded to think it over while he took some leave that was due him. I take it the authorities here hoped he would change his mind and stay on. He went off into Savoy alone. And he never came back.

'When he failed to return on time, there were rumours and an alarm, and Terrell was sent to France to follow up his tracks, until they ended without further trace in Dauphiné. It was automatically assumed that he'd departed behind the Iron Curtain, but no more was ever heard of him from any quarter. He *could* have come to grief somewhere in the mountains, being alone there. But the obvious inference was that he'd turned traitor. And Terrell was the man who followed up his case, and compiled a very damning dossier out of all those small unorthodoxies in Alder's professional life and attitudes. I'd say that that dossier made it impossible for him ever to come back – supposing, of course, that he'd wanted to change his mind.'

'Happily we have no reason to suppose anything of the kind,' said the Director tartly. 'You don't seem to have wasted your time, Mr Welland. You find all this relevant?'

'I think it becomes very relevant, sir, when you remember that Charles Alder was born Karol Alda, of a Czech father and a Slovak mother. Especially when you add to that the fact that the mother's birth was registered at Liptovský Mikuláš, not twenty miles from Zbojská Dolina.'

'Let me understand you clearly. You are suggesting, I take it, that Alda may be there in those parts now – that he may have gone back to his old country and his old allegiance?'

'I am suggesting that it is more than a possibility. I should also hazard that that is exactly what you must have believed he would do.'

'And you'd be right, naturally. But the fact remains that there has never been any indication, not the slightest hint, that he did so.' He got up abruptly from his desk and began to walk the room, not restlessly, but with a controlled, energetic step, like a man starved of proper exercise making the most of cramped quarters. The two younger men followed his pacing with alert eyes, and waited. 'You think Terrell may actually have *seen* Alda?'

'Something unexpected happened to him, something that drew him across the river valley to Zbojská Dolina. It could be connected with Alda. I don't claim more than that.'

'But you imagine more, much more. You think, don't you, that either he saw Alda, or picked up somehow a clue to his whereabouts? And that he followed it up, and got himself pushed off a mountainside when he got too close for comfort. That's what you think, isn't it?'

Welland paled a little at seeing it posed before him in this pointblank fashion; even he had a trace of the diplomat's dislike of formulating anything too exactly. But he stared back gallantly, and said emphatically: 'Yes.'

Blagrove stirred protestingly. 'But, good lord, the case is six years old now! It's no longer important. Times have changed, the cold war's a dead issue, or dying, trade's developing. Even if Terrell did turn up unexpectedly on his trail, why should Alda even care any more? Neither Terrell nor any of us could be any threat to him there. And would it be worth killing the man just for plain spite?'

'But isn't that missing the point of what Sir Broughton said a minute ago?' argued Welland intently. 'You expected him to turn up in Czechoslovakia. Word of where they are always leaks out eventually, doesn't it? But not a word ever leaked out about Alda. So wherever he is, secrecy is vital – to him, and to whoever is cashing in on his work now. Six years of successful concealment argues it's important enough to murder for. I believe there's something going on right now, right there in the Low Tatras, that has to be kept absolutely secret, and that Alda is at the heart of it. I believe Terrell found out, or they thought he had found out, what he couldn't be allowed to report.'

'If there is anything in this,' began Phelps, after a long and pregnant pause, 'and I'm not admitting yet that there necessarily is, but *if* there is – then you realise it's happened in a place and in circumstances which practically put it out of our power to investigate. If he *is* there, and if he is being kept as tightly wrapped as all that, then we must assume that this is national business. In which case we must also assume that the Czech authorities, if not the police on the spot, know all there is to be known about this death.'

'I'm convinced,' said Welland vehemently, 'that they do. The local police know about mountains, they can't have failed to see what a queer sort of accident it was for an experienced man. Yet within a day they'd closed the case. I think they've had their orders.'

'Even if you believed in their honesty,' said the Director drily, 'our position would be the same. I can't impress upon you too strongly, Mr Welland, that everything to do with this Institute is top secret. In this case or any case that involves us in any way, nothing whatever may be confided to foreign authorities, friendly or otherwise. There can be *no* overt enquiries.'

'No, sir, I realise that. But I'm there on the spot. I week-end in the mountains quite frequently, they're used to me. I move about quite freely, I speak the language a little. I could look into it myself, without alerting anyone.'

He offered them a dutiful silence, but neither of them, it seemed, had anything to say. They looked at him narrowly, with unwinking concentration, and he found it unnerving that he had not the least idea what either of them was thinking. They were the product of the closed establishment, closed men, each in his own air-tight, suspicious, ambitious, narrow world, specialising in ever more attenuated expertise. The horrific thought visited him that he might live to be like them. He found it absolutely vital to give utterance again to the realities that still existed in him, while they existed.

'I intend to find out if Terrell was murdered. I can't help it. If he was killed for activities that seemed to him in line of duty, then I believe we owe it to him to investigate, and to see that justice is done. He's entitled to justice. Quite apart from the possibility that something is going on there that affects our national interests and security. We can't just let murder go by default. It isn't right.'

He produced this final simplicity with an authority that restored its lustre. He said with dignity: 'I would much rather proceed with your approval, of course. I hope I have it.'

But he would proceed with or without it. He was committed by his conscience. An interesting survival, but there he was in the flesh, determined and distressed, perfectly conscious of what he was saying and doing, and prepared to be judged by it.

'My dear boy!' said Sir Broughton, for the first time warming into the charming smile that transformed his professionally austere face into something human and likeable. 'Proceed with our blessing, of course, but with our warnings, too. One man, according to your theory, has already been killed. I beg you to take care of yourself. That's the first essential. The second is the preservation of complete secrecy for this establishment. That I can't over-stress. And the third thing is something I feel I ought to tell you. If you're going into this at all, you must go with your eyes open. Nobody knows this, outside this Institute and its parent Ministry.'

He came back slowly to his desk, and leaned on his hands there, pondering. For a moment he looked more than his age, an elderly man bowed by his responsibilities.

'When Charles Alder vanished, his current working notebooks vanished with him. They contained all his projects at the experimental stage, and at that stage they were so completely his own brain-children that no one could continue his work on them. No other sketches, no other outlines existed. We don't know, apart from a few preliminary ideas, what was in them. But he was at the height of his powers, and working like a demon, mainly on problems of aerodynamics. If he's been pursuing the same lines of research elsewhere, there could be sensational developments. There could be more than enough at stake to invoke murder. You understand that?'

'Yes, sir,' said Welland, weak with relief and gratitude, 'I understand.'

'And you understand the absolute need for secrecy? You must not say one word to anyone about this. You haven't taken anyone into your confidence? The press men, your friends?'

'I didn't tell them anything, beyond showing curiosity over Terrell's record. Knowing I'm stationed in Prague, they wouldn't wonder at that.' He was all eagerness now, dazzled and exhilarated by the Director's energy.

'And no one else, either?'

If Welland hesitated at all, it was so briefly that the instant passed unnoticed. 'No, sir, no one knows anything about this from me.'

'Good! Then go ahead, but take care of yourself. If you do hit upon a lead to Alda, you must report at once to us. Don't go on alone and take risks, just report back and wait for orders, you understand? I'll see that the Minister is kept informed, otherwise no one must know of this except the three of us here. I'll arrange with the embassy in Prague, and have any message from you transmitted direct to us here by telephone. We'll have a code signal agreed before you leave here. If you locate Alda, then send it. When we receive it, it may be advisable for Mr Blagrove to come to Prague on some pretext, to be on hand – and to help you,' he said, the human smile reappearing for one abstracted instant, 'in case of need. Even you may need help sometimes, Mr Welland. Who knows?'

'I'll be very careful, sir. You can rely on me.'

'We are relying on you, my boy. You'll report to nobody else but this Institute. Not even our people in Prague. You understand? *Nobody else*!'

He had accomplished all and more than he had hoped for. At the edge of an adventure, with the water cold and mysterious before his plunge, Robert Welland was a vindicated, even a happy, man.

Or he would have been happy, but for one small scruple.

As soon as he left the conference in Sir Broughton's room he hurried to the Underground station, and made his way back into London, to the Chelsea street where Chloe Terrell had her top-floor flat. It hadn't, of course, been absolutely honest of him not to tell Sir Broughton about the note he'd dropped through Mrs Terrell's letter-box, when he found her out. The note certainly did confide something, more than he should have said, even to the suggestion of murder. But there was no harm done, after all, because Mrs Terrell was not merely away from home, but out of the country. He had Blagrove's own word for that. So no one would have read the note he should never have been so indiscreet as to write, and what he had said was not, in fact, a lie. No one knew anything about this affair from him. And no one would.

There wasn't even any hurry about it, his sense of anxiety and impatience was folly. She was in Czechoslovakia, and she wouldn't, couldn't be back yet. He had plenty of time to dig out the porter of the service flats, explain that he'd left a vital paper by mistake, not knowing Mrs Terrell was out of the country, and must recover it and get word to her elsewhere at once. The porter would have keys, and it wouldn't be difficult to establish his own good faith. When he'd burned that note he would feel better, because his shadow of a lie wouldn't exist, then, and there would be no leakages through him. He liked to have everything above-board, and that was how it would be.

All the same, his mind was not quite easy. Better just have a look at the top-floor flat first, before he tackled the porter, and make sure that it was still closed and empty. Just to reassure himself.

The lift was creaking its way slowly upward as he stood in the hall; he had caught a glimpse of the door closing upon a dark, slender girl with her arms full of parcels, and to judge by the time that elapsed before the lift-cable was still and the door clashed open, high up the shaft, she was disentangling her purchases at least four floors up. He pressed the call button, and nothing whatever happened. A woman with both hands full doesn't stop to close the lift doors after her. He would have to walk up.

He didn't know why he was hurrying as he tackled the stairs. Hadn't he already told himself that there was no haste, no possibility that Mrs Terrell would have returned and read his note? But he began taking the steps two at a time before he reached the second landing, and by the fourth he was running, his heart pounding and his breath short. He came to the corner from which he could see Chloe Terrell's door, and baulked as if he had run his nose into a brick wall. For the outside door of the flat stood open. And the pretty girl with the parcels stood in the hall with her burdens dropped unceremoniously about her feet, and his letter open and unfolded in her hands.

She was still as a statue until his rush of movement ended in abrupt stillness, and then she was aware of him, and looked up at him over the spread sheet of paper with great dark eyes blank with horror. For a moment they stared at

29

each other in fascination and dread. He didn't know what to say to her. He didn't know what to think.

She couldn't possibly be, she wasn't more than eighteen or nineteen! But women did marry as young as that. How was he to know that the wife would be a mere child? Horrified, he lifted his leaden feet up the last few steps, and moved towards her like a hypnotised rabbit, utterly helpless.

'Mrs Terrell . . .?'

She stared back at him as if she had heard nothing, following her own fixed channel of consciousness. She looked down at the sheet of paper in her hand, and back at him.

'You're Robert Welland? It was you who left this note?'

She had a voice that startled, an octave deeper than anyone would have expected; a gruff whisper, like an adolescent boy not yet used to his new instrument. She took a small step back from him, warily and wildly, and stumbled over her own parcels discarded on the floor.

'Yes, I'm Robert Welland. I didn't mean . . . I didn't realise . . . Mrs Terrell, I must apologise and explain . . .'

'I'm not Mrs Terrell,' said the girl, shrinking. 'I shouldn't have opened it, but I thought it might be something I ought to send on. I'm Tossa Barber. Sorry, that won't mean a thing to you.' She put up her hand dazedly, and pushed back the fall of dark hair from her brow. 'I'm Mrs Terrell's daughter. I came up to do some shopping for the holidays, and I use her flat when I'm in town.' It was extraordinary that she should feel she had to explain to him, when it was he who had so much to explain, the letter, the implications of the letter, his presence here in such a hurry. Suddenly she was calm for both of them, because it was too late to take back anything, and there was no way to go except forward. 'You say here,' she challenged pointblank, 'that my step-father was murdered.'

In what he had written he had not, he remembered, used that word. He thought of a hundred ingenious evasions, and confronted by Tossa's large, unwavering eyes, rejected them all. 'Yes,' he said helplessly, 'that's what I believe.'

'Come in,' said Tossa. 'You may as well. Now I have to know. You can see that, can't you? I've *got* to know.'

He made one convulsive attempt to extricate himself, even as he was stepping forward into the flat and closing the outer door behind him. He couldn't possibly confide in a child like this, even if he hadn't just sworn secrecy under awful warnings; but neither could he stand in an open doorway close to the echoing well of the stairs and the lift-shaft, and make his excuses for all the house to hear.

'Miss Barber, I'm very sorry I've alarmed you for nothing. Since I left this note for your mother I've had an opportunity to consult the people who're best-informed about your father's . . .' These relationships were confusing him, he didn't quite know where he was with them. '—about Mr Terrell's death. I should be glad if you would try to forget about the whole matter, I did have my suspicions, but they're not shared by others who should know best, and it may be that I was quite wrong.'

'You just said: "That's what I believe",' she reminded him, 'not: "That's what I *believed*".' She slipped by him very quickly at the slight movement of retreat he made, and put her back against the door. 'No, you can't! You can't go away now and leave me like this.'

And he saw that he couldn't. Not simply because she already understood too much, and could make his escape impossible, but because her face was so desperately resolute and her eyes so full of an acute personal distress for which he was responsible. It was already too late to undo that; all his disclaimers wouldn't convince her now, all his reassurances wouldn't restore her peace of mind. His own little indiscretion had trapped him. It wasn't enough even to plead that he had promised secrecy, since his promise had been breached by accident almost as soon as he had given it.

'Miss Barber,' he began earnestly, 'I did come here with certain information that disquieted me, and I wanted to consult Mrs Terrell before I took the matter any further. I've now had it impressed upon me that this whole affair is urgently secret, and I'm bound by that. It was foolish of me not to have realised it for myself, and I'm deeply sorry that my mistake has now caused you distress. I wish I could undo it.'

'You can't,' said Tossa fiercely, 'and you can't leave it like that. Maybe I shouldn't have read it, but I did, and he was my step-father, even if we weren't at all close, and do you expect me just to sit back and live with the thought that somebody murdered him, and not do anything at all about it?'

'I sincerely hope there's going to be no need for *you* to do anything about it. That's a job for others.'

'No!' she protested passionately. 'That isn't good enough. That doesn't help me.'

He had already reached the point of knowing that he was going to tell her everything. Maybe he was a good judge of human nature, and maybe he wasn't, but it seemed to him that there was only one way of ensuring that secrecy should indeed be complete. She had the passion to demand her rights from him, maybe she had also the generosity to meet him half-way when he piled the lot into her arms without reserve.

'Miss Barber, I gave my word. There's no way I can satisfy you, except by extending that promise to cover you as well as myself. If I tell you everything, then I shall be vouching for you, too. Staking my reputation on you. Maybe my life.'

She opened her eyes wide to stare at him in wonder and doubt, but she could find no hint of anything bogus in his face or his tone. It seemed people still existed who talked in those terms, quite without cant.

'Do you want to know on those conditions? Remember, I shall then be relying upon you absolutely.'

'You can,' she said. 'I won't breathe a word to anyone, I promise. Yes, I want to know.'

'And you understand that it's a matter of national security that what I tell you should go no further?'

'Yes, I understand. You have my word.' Her face was earnest with the terrible solemnity of youth. Yes, he thought, she had the generosity and imagination even to be able to keep secrets. And he stopped being afraid of her, just when he should have begun to be afraid.

He sat down with her on the antique bench in Chloe's hall, and told her the whole story, suppressing nothing, not even the significance of the notebooks Alda had smuggled out of the country with him when he vanished.

For a moment, at the end of it, her sceptical mind revolted. Spies, counter-spies, defecting scientists, all exist, of course, but as sordid professionals fumbling grimy secrets of dubious value, for which governments must be crazy to pay out a farthing in bribes or wages. Not like this, not with ideals mixed up in the squalor, and patriotism – whatever that ought to mean, in these days of supranational aspirations – and honest, clean danger. It couldn't be true! Robert Welland was a romantic who had constructed a romantic's ingenious theory out of a few chance facts, and all he was going back to was the long, slow let-down into the untidy world of reality. He wouldn't find anything; there was nothing to find. Herbert Terrell had simply made a mis-step at last, the one that waits for every expert somewhere along the way, and fallen to his death.

Just for a moment she held the facts away from her, and saw them thus distantly and coolly; and then the whole erection of evidence toppled upon her and overwhelmed her, and she believed with all her heart, and was lost. She had no longer any defences against Terrell. He was dead, murdered, killed as the result of something he had undertaken out of his sense of duty to his profession and his country. He was more than she had ever given him a chance to show, and she owed him justice all the more now, because she had denied it to him living.

'So you see that everything possible will be done to find out the truth. And you will be very careful, won't you, not to let anything out even by accident? Remember I've vouched for you as for myself.'

'I won't forget. I'm very grateful for your trust, I shan't betray it.' She was staring before her with stunned eyes, seeing herself suddenly drawn, almost against her will, into a world of noble clichés, which she vehemently distrusted, but for which there existed no substitutes.

'And you'll try to set your mind at rest, and leave everything to us? I'm sorry that I've troubled your peace at all.'

'Oh, no!' she said positively. 'It's better to know.' And to his question, with only the faintest note of reserve: 'I know you'll do everything possible. And thank you!'

But he hadn't her personal obligations, and he hadn't her sense of guilt, and how could he expect her to sit back and let him lift the burden of her conscience and carry it away with him?

The first thing she looked round for, when he was gone, was the large-scale map of Central Europe she had just bought at Hatchards.

'Czech visas,' said Toddy thoughtfully, 'cost money.' He sat back on his heels and pondered the delectable roads racing eastwards across the map, and his expression was speculative and tempted. 'Not that I'm saying it wouldn't be a nice thing to do, mind you.' He added ruefully: 'Rather a lot of money, if you ask me!'

'I know they do, but look at the tourist exchange rate! We should more than get it back. And if we did decide on it, we could be through France and Germany in a couple of days. Eating in France is damned dear unless you picnic all the time, and who wants to do that? I bet we'd save by running through as quickly as possible, and surely Czechoslovakia would be a whole lot more interesting.'

'I always did think you had a secret urge to live dangerously.' Christine swung her legs from the edge of the table, and drew the crumbling Iron Curtain thoughtfully back into position with one toe. 'Quite apart from prison cells, secret police, and all that guff – supposing it is guff, we could be wrong about that, too! – who does the talking?'

'We all do, in English. I'm told the Czechs are marvellous linguists, now's their chance to prove it. And if we do get out of bounds for English, I bet Toddy's German would get us by well enough.' Tossa withdrew a little, to leave them with an idea they would soon be able to persuade themselves was their own. 'Whatever you think, though, I'm easy. But I'll write for visa applications if you like. They say it only takes a few days. I'm going to make some coffee,' said Tossa, judging her moment nicely, and left them holding it.

'Maybe it does seem a pity not to use the carnet, now we've got it,' said Christine reflectively.

'Quickest route on the map,' reported Toddy, sprawled largely across Europe, 'is Cassel – Brussels – Aachen, and straight down the autobahn. It takes you right past Wurzburg now, and part-way to Nuremberg. Might have got a bit farther, too, since this was printed.'

'It's faster travelling through France than Belgium,' warned Christine. 'We could just as easily run through to Saarbrücken, and get on to the southern branch of the autobahn, and then go north to Frankfurt.'

'It's miles longer.'

'Yes, but hours faster.'

Dominic, who had never yet driven on the Continent, said nothing, but sat back and let them argue it out. So it happened that he was the only one who did not miss the look on Tossa's face when she re-entered the room with the coffee tray, to find the twins deep in discussion of the various ways of reaching the Czech border quickly, and the possibilities presented once they had crossed it. He saw the small, fevered spark that lit in her eyes, the brief vindicated smile that touched the corners of her mouth, and ebbed again even more rapidly, leaving her fixed and sombre.

Tossa had what she wanted. But what it gave her was not

pleasure, it seemed to him, only a brief and perilous sense of accomplishment, as if she had just taken the first step on a very uncertain journey.

Three

The Man who Thumbed a Lift

They came spiralling down over France at about nine o'clock on a fine Thursday morning, craning to see the bewildering expanses of the blown sand-dunes revolve below them, starred with little salt pools and furry with pines. The estuary of the Canche dipped under one wing and vanished, the bridge and its crawling beetles of cars disappeared. By dazzling glimpses the white, urbane, anglicised villas winked at them from among the trees, and the long beach trailed a golden ribbon along the lacy edge of the sea. Le Touquet would never be so beautiful again.

Twenty-five minutes after they had left England they were creeping gingerly round the snack-bar called 'L' Aubette,' and into the groves of pines, round whose braced feet the waves of sand broke like a patient and treacherous sea. The first gendarme eyed them warily as they rolled decorously round his concrete bollard, and bore away towards the golf links. Left turn after left turn, until you cross the bridge over the Canche, and then sharp right. And you've started. You're heading for Montreuil-sur-Mer and the main Paris road; for Brussels and Aachen and the Cologne-Frankfurt autobahn, and all points east.

'We're in France!' said Dominic, shattered and transported, for the first time relaxing the grim concentration with which he was keeping to the right. 'We're abroad!'

They ran off the autobahn for their first night at the resthouse at Siegburg, and thwarted of a bed there – it seemed one must stop at about four o'clock to be sure of a room anywhere immediately on the motorway – cruised down the hill into the town, under the Michaelburg, and fetched up in an embarrassingly narrow and difficult yard off the glittering main street. Toddy parked the van gingerly in a cramped corner, and hugged himself at the thought of Dominic manipulating it out into traffic next morning. Every man for himself!

They strolled through the surprising glitter of the streets, still lively at past eight in the evening, and climbed the Michaelburg in the dusk to the fortress church.

And out of the blue Tossa made her next move.

'Wouldn't it be fine to go all the way east into Slovakia?' she said suddenly and fondly, as they sauntered down again through the silent gardens. 'As far as the Tatras, anyhow. We *couldn't* go back without seeing the mountains.'

'If we have time,' agreed Toddy accommodatingly, willing to entertain all suggestions. 'We've got to see Prague first.'

The twins had known her for years, perhaps that was why their thumbs didn't prick. They knew her so well they'd stopped being sufficiently aware of her to question her attitudes and motives. What she offered, they accepted at its face value. Dominic had no such insulation. He walked beside her in the deepening dusk, her long, impetuous step almost a match for his, and felt some inexplicable tension drawing her taut as a bow-string.

It was at that moment that Dominic grasped, without any adequate grounds for his certainty, that she was steering this expedition carefully and patiently towards some end of her own. Hadn't she been the one who had suggested providing the car with a carnet? Wasn't it she who had thought of the Czech visas? Now, if he was right, she was making the next move, prodding them to hurry on eastwards into the Tatras; and *if* he was right, she would gently but doggedly persist until she got her own way.

'Why don't we just steam ahead right to the mountains,' said Tossa, in the same brightly eager voice, 'and take it easy on the way back? I've been had too many times, with the days running out because some gourmand for Gothic couldn't be dragged away from some cathedral or other. Make sure of the remotest bits first, *I* say. We know we've got to get back, let's make a point of getting *there*.'

'Toddy!'

'Hallo?' mumbled Toddy sleepily, across the bedroom window silvered down one edge with moonlight. 'What's up?'

'You know you told me Tossa's step-father got killed, climbing somewhere?'

'Hmm, yes, what about him?'

'Was she fond of him at all?'

A snort of laughter from the other bed fetched an answering creak out of the pale, scrubbed wood of the bedstead. 'Are you kidding? She couldn't stand him. He was so correct he made her want to throw things. Tossa left home, didn't even see much of her mother until she left this fellow for good. Why, what about him?'

'Oh, nothing. Just wondering if she had him on her mind, or something.'

'Tossa misses him like you'd miss a rotten tooth. No, that's a lie, too, because since her mother left him she hasn't even felt any twinges. Even before he kicked off, he just wasn't there any more.' A rustle of bedclothes and a lift in the sleepy voice indicated a quickening interest on Toddy's part: 'Hey, Dom, you getting to like our Tossa?'

'She's all right,' said Dominic sedately. 'Bit prickly sometimes. Tod, where did this fellow kick off?'

'Oh, abroad, somewhere. Austria or Switzerland, or somewhere. Didn't check, actually. Does it matter?'

'Not a lot, I suppose. If you're dead you're dead. Good night, Tod!'

'Good night, Dom! That's final notice!'

'OK! Pass out, I've finished.'

Toddy passed out with the aplomb of an exhausted child. They had had to rise in the middle of the night to drive down to the airport. Dominic, however, lay awake and alert. Toddy might not know where this chap Terrell had got himself killed, but according to Dominic's pricking thumbs Tossa knew. Tossa knew, and stage by stage she was taking them there, to the very region, to the very spot. What did she know of the Tatras, unless that Terrell had dived to his death somewhere round their granite planes? Why mention them, unless of fixed intent?

Dominic's father was a C.I.D. Detective-Inspector in a county force on the Welsh borders. Maybe there's something to police parentage that sets you nosing for mysteries wherever you go. Or maybe there was really something about Tossa's shuddering anticipation that justifiably set his flesh crawling. Whichever it was, Dominic was a long time falling asleep.

They camped the next night, a little way short of the Czech border, in the beautiful, rolling, forest-and-meadow land of the Palatinate. And in the morning they crossed the frontier.

Waidhaus was quiet, efficient and polite, the Customs house poised on the edge of a sharp dip. Beyond the barrier the road curved away into Czechoslovakia, straightened again, and immediately began to climb; and there before them, on either side of the way, were the white buildings of the Czech Customs offices; and drawn up in the roadway on the near side of the barriers were at least a dozen cars, buses and caravans, from which at least fifty people had spilled out to flourish carnets and passports at harassed but amiable Czech officials.

It took them an hour to get through. There were more papers to be dealt with here, passports and visas, the carnet, the insurance document, as well as a polite and good-humoured pretence at examining their baggage, and a genuine scrutiny of the car.

'For the first time,' said Christine approvingly, 'I feel as if someone cares whether we've arrived or not. It got almost insulting, being waved from one country into another like tossing the morning paper over the gate.'

'Not so cynical as the French,' Toddy allowed judicially, in an undertone, distributing their cleared passports. 'Not so disdainfully efficient as the Germans. I like to see officials who sweat over the job, and aren't past getting excited. That immigration chap took a liking to your passport photograph, Tossa – even showed it to his mate at the other table. Come to look at it,' he admitted, studying it impartially, 'it isn't at all bad.'

'Thank you!' said the saturnine young Czech who had been feigning to examine Tossa's suitcase, without so much as disarranging the one tissue-wrapped party dress she had popped in at the last moment 'in case.' 'Everything is in order. You can proceed.'

They piled eagerly into the van again, Dominic at the wheel. The Customs man signalled to the young soldier who held the chain of the barrier, and up went the pole. Gravely they acknowledged the salutes that ushered them through into a new country, and wormed their way through the congestion of cars and under the quivering pole.

'We're in!' breathed Christine, staggered to find it so easy.

'No iron curtain, no nothing,' agreed Toddy, astonished in his turn. 'A bit like crashing the sound barrier, though.'

The van climbed out of the frontier hollow, between slopes of silver birches, under the distant shadow of the first of many castles, a gaunt ruin on a lush, wooded hill. They were surging merrily into full speed, when a second barrier loomed in sight, barring their road, and a tall wooden watch-tower beside it. The very young soldier on guard there glared with a solemnity beyond his seventeen years, as Dominic slowed to a discreet halt before the bar, and waited dutifully to see what was required of him.

With unshaken gravity the boy lifted a telephone from its stand in the box beside him, and consulted some unknown authority.

'No iron curtain?' whispered Christine, between apprehension and the giggles.

'Shut up, idiot!' hissed Toddy. 'He's only doing his job.'

The boy replaced the telephone with deliberation, walked round them, eyeing the girls with a curiosity that brought the transaction down to a completely human level, and hoisted the pole, motioning them through with only the most austere inclination of his head. He was very young, and took his duties seriously.

They saluted this gateman, too, but apart from a quickening spark in his eye he preserved his motionless dignity. Possibly he treasured the girls, acknowledging his services decorously from the rear windows; but if he did, he wasn't admitting it. Only when they were well away from him, soaring up the slope, did he suddenly lift one arm above his head, in a wave as impersonal as the hills.

They never even saw it; all their attention was fixed eagerly ahead, as Dominic accelerated happily towards the crest of the rise, among the shimmering birch trees.

A man's figure rose suddenly and joyously out of the ditch beside the road, and stood on the verge, energetically thumbing them to a standstill. A young, round, glowing face under a sunburst of blond hair beamed at them confidently, and had no doubt whatever of its warm and friendly welcome. A small rucksack swung from the cajoling arm that flagged them down. In the other hand he held a large open sandwich, which he balanced expertly as he ran alongside them and signalled, from ingenuous blue eyes and beaming mouth, his pleasure in having hooked so interesting, so rewarding a ride. The GB plate, the number, the girls, one glance and he had them all weighed up.

Dominic wound the window right down, and said: 'Hallo!' As an obvious greeting he didn't see why it shouldn't do just as well as any other; but in spite of Tossa's predictions he was hardly prepared to be addressed promptly and fluently in his own language.

'Good morning!' said the beaming young man, tilting his open sandwich just in time to retrieve a slipping gherkin.

'Please excuse that I trouble you, but if you go to Prague, may I ride with you? If you have room?' He knew they had room he had practically measured their cubic content with that one expert flick of a blond eyelash. 'I could be of help, if you do not know the road. To work my passage, I shall be the guide, if you permit?'

Toddy not only permitted; he applauded. He enjoyed driving, but to him navigating was a chore. He cast a glance behind him at the empty road, and was out of the front passenger seat like a greyhound from its trap.

'It's all yours! Here, give me your rucksack, I'll stow it in the back with our stuff, and you take this seat.'

'But you are sure? The ladies will not mind if I ride with you? I should not like to be a burden, and some people do not approve of auto-stop.'

They assured him that this method of travelling was well-established even in England, and that they had no personal objection to it, had even used it on occasions. They installed the young man, his sandwich, and his rucksack. Christine, rendered thoughtful by the last glimpse of the gherkin as it vanished behind strong white teeth, reached into the food-box and began to compile a mid-morning snack.

'You are also students?' asked their new passenger, as they drove through Rozvadov, a nondescript street-village hardly different from those they had left on the other side of the frontier, except that, lacking the exact German tidiness, it appeared a little shaggier and dustier. 'My name is Miroslav Zachar. To my friends Mirek – you will find it easier to remember. I am student of philosophy.'

They told him freely who they were, and what they were reading, and he overflowed with uninhibited questions, produced so naturally and confidently that it was impossible to find any of them offensive. They were on vacation, of course, like him? Was it their first visit to Czechoslovakia? Where were they going to stay in Prague? And where else did they intend to go? He was full of helpful suggestions. Castles, lakes, towns, he knew them all.

'You must do quite a lot of auto-stopping,' said Christine, busy with cheese and crackers. 'You seem to have been everywhere.'

'I do it a lot, yes. Every holiday. Sometimes I go with friends, sometimes alone. It is better alone. For one person it is easy to get a lift.'

'And what made you come all the way out here? You *do* live in Prague?'

'I have been walking in these hills of the Bohemian Forest. Now I come back to the road, hoping to get a lift back into Prague quickly. This is a good place, foreign cars coming in here, naturally they rush straight to Prague. But I am lucky to meet some more students. That's nice! I'm glad I time it so good. No, in Prague I have an uncle and aunt, if you will kindly take me so far I can stay with them, and afterwards stop another car,' he said serenely, 'to take me on eastwards. Because of course you will be staying in Prague.'

'Perhaps only for one or two nights,' Tossa said suddenly, in that gruff boyish croak of hers, that could be so disconcerting to the unaccustomed ear.

They were on a stretch of road complicated by many climbing bends among trees, but without forks where Dominic could possibly go wrong. Miroslav Zachar abandoned his navigating for a moment to turn his head and study this dark-brown girl seriously. His amiable moon-face shone upon her approvingly.

'You will be going on so soon? But where?'

'Into Slovakia,' she said quite positively, asking no one's agreement.

'No, really? You go to Bratislava, perhaps?'

'No,' she said, with the same authority; and if no one took her up on it now they were quite certainly committed. And no one did. 'No, we want to go the Tatras. We can make a longer stay in Prague on the way back. Is that the same way you wanted to go? You did say eastwards. Where is your home?'

'My home,' said Mirek, delighted, 'is in Liptovsky Mikulás. That is very near the Tatra range. If you are really going so far, and if you would like to have a guide, believe me, I will make it easy for you, I will take care of everything. You have rooms in Prague? No? I can arrange it. The Students' Union will manage it for us, you'll see. And I will show you the city. I know it like my hand. How long you would like to stay? One night? Two nights? I shall make a programme for you. And then you will take me with you to Slovakia? I know the best camping-ground on the way, in Javorník, in the most beautiful hills. Oh, I shall work my passage, you will see!'

It sounded like the answer to everything. The others might have demurred at leaving Prague so soon in other circumstances, but with a heaven-sent guide added to the party, gratis, it seemed much the most practical and economic solution to run right through, as Tossa had urged, spend as long as possible in the east, and then make their way back, without a guide, over a road already travelled once. Even if they saw fit to vary it, they would at least know the lie of the land.

'It's a bargain!' said Tossa, incandescent with eagerness. 'One night in Prague, if you can really work it for us . . .'

'Two!' Christine demurred.

'One! We shall come back, and we shall know the basic lay-out then, we can easily find our way around. And then we go on to the Tatras. Mirek, you must know those parts awfully well, if it's your home. Do you know a place – not in the High Tatras, actually, in the Low Tatras – called Zbojská Dolina?'

'Dig that!' said Toddy, impressed. 'The girl's been studying the map.'

'You have so good a map?' Mirek was astonished and respectful. 'It is only a small valley. I think it is not marked on any map I know. We do not have many such large-scale maps for walking, like yours.'

Tossa fortified herself with a large bite from her cheese cracker, and made the most of the muffling noise. 'No, it isn't on the maps. I knew somebody once who stayed there, and they – she – said it was lovely. I always thought I'd like to go there.'

Geese, parading the dusty open green of the small town of Bor, scuffled with indignant shrieks from before the wheels of the van. The small, dilapidated castle mouldered peacefully among its trees on their right, as they curled through the single deserted street. Everything was coloured a faint, neutral brown. New pastel paint would have shattered a sacred silence. Border Bohemia drowsed, veiled itself, and let them pass by.

'Hey!' reminded Dominic peremptorily. 'Which way at this fork? I can't see any "Praha".'

Children at the crossroads, in diminutive shorts and faded cotton sweaters, bounced, smiled and waved at them energetically. Of the welcome extended to foreigners, on this level, there was no possible doubt. They were the glitter in the children's world.

'To the left,' said Mirek, sliding hastily back to his duty.

'This friend of mine,' Tossa's voice persisted, doggedly offhand behind Dominic's shoulders, 'stayed at a little inn somewhere in this Zbojská Dolina. It was called the Riavka hut. Do you know it?'

They cruised down into a river valley, level green meadows on the near side of it, a sharp escarpment beyond, and climbed out again by a winding road, glimpsing silver on either hand as they turned.

'Why, yes, surely I know it,' said Mirek.

'My friend said it was lovely walking country there. We like to walk. Do you think we could get rooms at this Riavka hut? Do you think the Students' Union would try to arrange it for us?'

They were climbing steadily into the little town of Stríbro.

'It means silver,' explained Mirek, as they wound their way into the square, and turned sharp right out of it, to uncoil in a long spiral down the mount on which the town was built. 'Here there were silver mines.' And to Tossa, without turning his head, he said cheerfully: 'Yes, they can arrange it. I shall do it for you. For you I shall do everything you wish.'

And not one of them had questioned this sudden detailed knowledge she had displayed of the region to which they were bound; no one had marvelled, and it was too late to marvel now. She had the whole expedition in her hands. They were going where, for her own inscrutable purpose, Tossa wished to go.

Mirek showed them Prague. Seeing they had tamely submitted to staying only one night in that delectable city, it was amazing how much he did manage to show them. The shopping centre, based firmly upon the great, broad thoroughfare of Wenceslas Square and the two streets forking from its massive foot, was concentrated enough to be viewed quite easily and quickly. But how did he manage to get them to Hradcany, that magical castle-quarter walled like a town within the fortress ramparts high above the Vltava river, and also out to the Mozart Museum in its lost, enchanted garden south of the town? It was impossible in the time, but Mirek did it. He showed them the little monastery of Loretto, long monkless, with its honeyed carillon of bells and its blinding treasury. He showed them the eleventh-century hall deep beneath the castle, austere, imaginatively restored and imperishably beautiful, after which all the loftier and later layers were anticlimax. And late in the evening he showed them a very handsome dinner, and two tiny night-clubs, each with an incomprehensible but apparently sophisticated cabaret.

They fell asleep in the beds Mirek had found for them, with a picture of Prague behind their eyelids, shabby, neutral-tinted, mouldering, gracious, imperial, drab, flamboyant, invulnerably beautiful; so old that it was indifferent to criticism; so assured that it turned a deaf ear to praise. The dirty industrial quarters hanging on its skirts were merely the soiled ruffles of an empress, dulled by one day's wear. The fall of the tumbling terraced gardens beneath the castle, encrusted with stone statuary and grottoes and galleries, was a cascade of lace on the imperial bosom, heady and fresh as the acacia sweetness that hung on the night air.

And the next day they headed eastward for Slovakia.

They drove down out of the Javorník hills at leisure from their night camp, and into the town of Zilina. Beyond the civic buildings in the town square the crests of farther hills hung in the sky, pointed, shaggy, forested, the cones and pyramids of the Little Fatras. Mirek, moved to ecstasies of local patriotism as soon as he stood on Slovak soil, had whiled away the miles by telling them the story of Janosík, the Slovak outlaw-hero, who took to the hills here with his eleven mountain boys, in revolt against the feudal tyranny that kept his countrymen serfs. Born in the Fatra Hills, he died at last on a gallows at Liptovsky Mikulás, and after him all the mountain boys died tragic deaths. No happy ending for them; the usual comparison with Robin Hood, said Mirek a little didactically, foundered on that rock of martyrdom. There were may songs about Janosík, and Mirek knew them all. It took the waft of coffee from the foyer of the hotel to silence him.

'You'd like the second breakfast here? We're not in a hurry today, and the next stretch is wonderful. You will want to stop and take pictures.'

They agreed that they could do with coffee. Toddy turned the van from the road, and let it run gently into the parking-ground along the hotel frontage.

'Look! An MG!' Christine halted them delightedly to admire a car from home. 'No GB. Diplomatic plates! Somebody from the embassy must be here.'

'Idiot!' said Toddy amiably. 'It doesn't have to be an English owner. Probably United Arab Republic, or something. Half the world buys British when it comes to cars, especially semi-sports jobs like this.'

'There's a suitcase on the back seat, anyhow.' Christine had already caught the Czech habit of walking all round unfamiliar cars and examining them closely, without the least embarrassment or offence. 'So he's not staying here, only halting like us. Maybe he smelled the coffee, too. What'll you bet I can't pick him out in the kavárna?' She had adopted the Czech word for café, it came more naturally now than the French; and since in English both were borrowed, why not use the native one?

'If you know the code,' said Toddy, 'you can tell by the registration letters which embassy it belongs to. Do you know, Mirek?'

'It is someone from the British Embassy,' said Mirek at once.

Tossa's warm, rose-olive complexion protected her from betrayal by pallor or blushing, and her silences were quite inscrutable. She looked the MG over, and dismissed it from her notice. 'Come on,' she said impatiently, 'I'm famished for that coffee.' And she led the way in through the cool, dim foyer, shoving the kavárna door open with a heave of her shoulder, and marching across the room to appropriate a table by the window.

'Mostly Czechs,' reported Christine confidently, looking round with interest as she sat down at the marble-topped table, scaled to allow half a dozen people to spread their elbows comfortably.

A white-aproned waiter came bustling to take their order. They left the talking to Mirek. Their only complaint against him was that he made everything too easy; but the time was coming when he would leave them to their own limited resources.

'Got him!' Christine proclaimed with satisfaction. 'Don't look round yet, he's looking this way. In the corner away to the left, close to the mirror. Wait a moment, I'll tell you when you can look. But that's him! He couldn't be anything but English. Mirek, do *we* go around looking as conspicuous as *that*?'

'Hurry up!' protested Toddy. 'I'm getting a stiff neck, trying not to turn round. Can I look yet?'

'Not yet. I'll tell you when. *Now, quick*! He's just talking to the waiter.'

She was right, of course. There was only one person there

who had to be English. You could almost say he had to be an English diplomat. Quite young, about thirty, dressed for the country, but so correctly that he retained a look of the town. Nondescriptly fair, rather lightly-boned among these solid square Czechs and gaunt, rakish Slovaks, withdrawn, gentle, formal. The cut of his sportscoat gave him away, and the Paisley silk scarf knotted in the throat of his open shirt. Even the way he drank his coffee was unmistakably English.

'Funny!' sighed Toddy. 'You never notice anything special about people when they're at home. Man, does it stick out here!' He plumped his chin into a resigned palm, groaning. 'I give up! I bet from over there I look just like that!'

'Oh, not quite,' said Mirek, comfortingly. 'One could say, perhaps, English on sight, but not *embassy* English. More student English. It is a distinction.'

'Thank you! Thank you very much! I don't *want* to be identifiable at a hundred yards.'

'Why not?' said Mirek disarmingly. 'Are you ashamed of it?'

'He looks lonely,' said Christine. 'Shouldn't we pick him up? It would be quite easy. He's giving Tossa the eye, anyhow.'

Tossa turned and gave the distant customer a long, considering look. Not a muscle of her smooth oval face quivered. 'Not my type,' she said, after a merciless scrutiny, and turned back to her coffee. 'Anyhow, he's probably heading the other way, back to Prague.'

Christine shut her eyes for a moment to reckon up the days since they had left England. 'Monday! Yes, I suppose he could be. Back to the grindstone after a week-end in Slovakia. But the way the car's parked, I'd have thought he was going our way.'

Dominic had been thinking the very same thing, and was thinking it still; and the thought had first entered his mind in the instant when Tossa's eyes had encountered those of the Englishman in the distant corner, held his gaze just long enough to register detached and unrecognising curiousity, and moved on just in time to avoid any suggestion of rudeness. For the man hadn't been quite so adroit. He hadn't the kind of face that gives much away, but for one instant there had been a kindling of his eyes, a sharpening of his attention, the unmistakable, instantaneous light of recognition. It was gone in an instant, too, without trace.

He looked at her now with interest and approval across the room but as if he had never seen her in his life before.

Because he had recovered himself, and suppressed what she must not be allowed to see? Or because he had taken a hint from her cool, impersonal glance, and responded in kind as soon as he had grasped what she wanted? If the second, then they were in this curious affair together, and yet separately, for plainly he hadn't expected Tossa to show up here in the middle of Europe, but equally plainly he had hastened to conform to what she desired when she did inexplicably appear. And if the first? Then Tossa wasn't acting; he knew her but she did not know him, and there was something in the air important enough – or sinister enough – to make it expedient for him to dissemble his knowledge.

Dominic drank his coffee, and let their chatter ricochet round him; he was beginning not to like this secrecy at all. Tossa's affairs were her own, but after all, here they were seven hundred miles or more from home, in an alien, and some would even have said an enemy, country. There had been one death, a death which began now to look more and more suspect. Beyond question Tossa was up to something, biting off, perhaps, much more than she could chew. And what could he do? nothing, not even question her or offer help, unless she showed a disposition to want it, and that was the last thing he expected from Tossa. Nothing in the world he could do, except, perhaps, stay close to her and keep his eyes open.

When they paid for their coffee and left, Tossa walked out without so much as a glance in the stranger's direction; but Dominic, looking back quickly from the doorway, saw that the waiter was just threading his way between the tables towards the Englishman's corner.

In the foyer Tossa halted, rummaging like a terrier in the depths of her overcrowded handbag after powder and comb. 'You go ahead, I'll be with you in a minute.' She wandered off questingly towards the back of the hall, and left them to make their way out into the sunshine without her.

Dominic let the others go on ahead, and halted on the pavement a step aside from the doorway. The wide glass door was fastened fully open, and the dimness of the wall behind turned it into a very passable mirror. It showed him, darkly but distinctly, a segment of the foyer which included the door of the kavárna, just swinging back after the passage of a waiter with a tray of beer-tankards. A moment more, and the door swung again, more sedately, and the solitary young man came out into the hall, looked round him quickly, and began to read the cinema posters on the baize notice-board.

The clack of Tossa's sandals echoed lightly from the rear corridors, and she came into sight, first a pale shadow in the glass, then rapidly growing clearer and closer. She passed by the young man without a glance, busily stuffing her powder compact back into her bag. Something oblong and small dropped out of the bulging outer pocket just before she snapped the catch.

Dominic ought, of course, to have turned in at the doorway to meet her, and called her attention at once to whatever it was she had let fall. Instead, he leaped away from the wall like a scalded cat, and by the time she emerged he was strolling round the corner after the others, looking back at the turn for her, and waiting to be overtaken. She came up with him brisk and smiling, and even slipped her hand in his arm as they fell into step together, a thing she had never done before.

He had hardly understood what he himself had just done, and why, until he felt her fingers close warmly on his sleeve, and realised with a startling surge of bitterness that even that touch was merely a part of her camouflage. It wasn't that he blamed her for making use of whatever came to hand, if she had such an urgent need to cover her secret; but he did resent being made the recipient of a first small mark of intimacy for so humiliating a reason. It hadn't dawned on him until then that she might be going to matter very much indeed in his life. And this, he thought bitterly, counting the seconds before the MG man should come hurrying after them, is a fine time to realise it!

Toddy and Christine had the map spread out against the side of the van, and were tracing the next stage of the drive.

'We are about to enter,' proclaimed Toddy, turning from his explorations to report to the late-comers, 'the spectacular gorge of the Váh, clean through the Little Fatras, passing close by the romantic ruins of Strecno castle and Stary Hrad – to name but a few! Come on, pile in. I'm driving.'

The young man from the MG came bustling round the corner at that moment, and seeing them already embarking, broke into a light run, and waved an arresting arm.

'Excuse me! Just a moment!'

Nearly two minutes, thought Dominic. Time to read a few

words, or write a few words, or both. Provided she passed him something a message could be hidden in properly.

She had. What the young man held out, as he came up panting and smiling, was her little leather comb-case, an ideal receptacle for a folded slip of paper.

'Excuse me, I was in the hall just now, I believe you dropped this as you were leaving.'

She took it, astonished and charmingly vexed at her own carelessness, and voluble in thanks to him.

'Not at all! I'm glad I caught you in time.' He withdrew a step or two, making it clear he had no wish to detain them. 'You're on holiday?' He looked round them all, memorising faces, his smile a shade too bright, but then, he had every mark of a naturally shy and serious young man. 'You're going on into the mountains?'

They made dutiful conversation, as one does when the encounter can be only a couple of minutes long, and probably will never be repeated. There is an art in touching deftly and graciously, and leaving a pleasant warmth behind on such occasions. On the whole, the young do it better than anyone.

'I'm sure you'll like it in Slovakia. There's lovely country to be explored here. Well, *bon voyage*! Have a good time!'

He drew back a few more steps, and then wheeled and walked smartly away from them. Tossa, with admirable calm, shoved the comb-case into her bag without a glance, and climbed into the van.

And no one else, thought Dominic, handing Christine in after her, had noticed a thing amiss with that little scene. Or could he really be sure of that? The twins would have given tongue at once, almost certainly. But who could be sure how much this pleasant fellow Miroslav noticed, or how deep he was? Or, for that matter, he thought for the first time, and with a sudden sickening lurch of his heart, who or what he was?

'Didn't play that one very well,' said Christine critically, as they took the road eastwards out of Zilina. 'After hooking him so neatly, too.'

'Too little!' responded Tossa automatically. 'I threw him back. Anyhow,' she added wickedly, with a smile of pure defiance, 'I got my bait back, didn't I?'

The oddest thing in their three-day acquaintance with Mirek happened when he took his leave of them. And of all people, it was Tossa who precipitated it.

He brought them safely to Zbojská Dolina by mid-afternoon, himself driving the van up the last two miles of rough and narrow mountain track to the Riavka hut, and there confiding them to the care of the Martínek family. He fulfilled, in fact, everything he had undertaken for them, and everything he had claimed for himself was proved true. Clearly he was indeed a local man, well known here, for Martínek senior hailed him from the open cellar-flap of the inn with a welcoming roar as soon as he blew the horn at the log gate, and Martínek junior, higher up the incredibly green valley pastures with two rangy dogs, whistled and waved. Mrs Martínek came hurrying out from the kitchen to the bar, the scrubbed boards creaking to her quick steps, and shook Mirek by the hand warmly but casually, as a crony's son from the next village rather than a rare and honoured visitor. Any friend of Mirek's, clearly, was welcome here.

All the doubts and suspicions that had been haunting Dominic's mind since morning were blown away. He felt ashamed and confounded. There were, it seemed, still people in the world who had nothing to hide, and were exactly what they purported to be.

'I leave you now,' announced Mirek, beaming at them over the pile of luggage he had assembled on the bar floor. 'You will be all right with Mrs Martínek, she has two rooms for you, and everything is prepared. You can talk to her in German, she understands it a little. And Dana – she speaks English, enough for everyday. So now I shall go home. I thank you very much for such a pleasant ride, and I hope we shall meet again some day.'

It was an honest farewell speech if ever they'd heard one. He shook hands all round, his rucksack already hoisted on his shoulder.

'But how far have you to go?' Toddy demanded. 'After all you've done for us, you must let us drive you home. Or at least down to the road. Oh, nonsense, you must! We know this road now, we're home and dry, now let's see you home.'

But Mirek wouldn't hear of it. He laughed the offer out of the bar window. 'All this time I have no exercise, these few miles to my home I must walk. Often I walk the length of Slovakia on vacation. No, no, no, you will have your own walking to do.' He held out his hand to Christine. 'I have been very happy, getting to know you all. It was for me a great pleasure.'

When he reached Tossa, she was gazing up into his face

Ellis Peters

with the most curious expression, half sullen and half guilty;
and Dominic saw with astonishment that there were tears
in her eyes. As they shook hands she suddenly reached up
on tip-toe, and kissed Mirek's round brick-red cheek very
quickly and awkwardly.

'Mirek,' she said impulsively, 'you've been absolutely
everything some people at home would like to think Czech
people *aren't* – so kind, and warm, and *sincere*. I can't tell
you how much I've appreciated it.'

This extrovert behaviour was staggering enough in their
moody, insecure and sceptical Tossa; but before they had
time to wonder at it, something even more surprising had
manifested itself in Mirek. Out of the collar of his open-
necked shirt surged like a tide the most stupendous blush they
had ever seen, engulfing muscular neck and tanned cheeks,
burning in the lobes of his ears, and washing triumphantly
into the roots of his blond hair. He stood looking down at
Tossa from behind this crimson cloud, his pleasant features
fixed in mid-smile, and his blue eyes helpless and horrified.
He couldn't even think of a joke to turn the moment aside,
it was Toddy who had to prick the bubble of constraint and
set him free to go.

'You know what the English are,' said Toddy indulgently,
'well-meaning but imprecise. The girl means *Slovak* people,
or course!'

Four

The Man who kept the Score

The Riavka hut took its name from the brook that came
bounding down Zbojská Dolina from its source in the topmost bowl of the valley, 'riavka' being a Slovak diminutive
for just such an upland river. It looked very much like any
other mountain hut in any other high range anywhere in
Europe, a large, rambling, two-storied house, part stone,
part wood, with heavily overhanging eaves, railed verandas,
and firewood and logs stacked neatly beneath the overhang all
along one wall. Besides being an inn for the herdsmen and the
occasional rambler, it was also a farm and a timber-station,
and a whole conglomeration of low wooden buildings clung
to the outer log fence that bounded its garden and paddock.
It stood in lush green meadows, a third of the way up the
valley, and cows and horses grazed freely to the edge of the
conifer belt that engulfed the path a few hundred yards above
the house.

Beyond was deep forest, the brook purling and rippling
away busily somewhere on their left hand, until they crossed
it by a log bridge, and walked for some way on a rock
causeway poised high above it. The pines and firs absorbed
the heat of the sun, and transmitted it to earth as a heavy,
intoxicating scent as thick as resin. The padding of needles
under their feet was deep and spongy, and there were huge
boletus mushrooms bursting through it here and there, and
colonies of slim yellow 'foxes' like pale fingers parting the
mould. In the more open places, where the heat of the sun
poured through upon them suddenly like laughter, and the
ripe August grass grew waist-high, the air was rich with
a spicy sweetness that would always thereafter mean hot
summer woods to them, the scent of raspberries. The wild
canes grew in thick clumps among the grass, heavy with
fruit. They picked handfuls, and walked on, eating them.

Beyond the belt of woodland there were broken areas of
outcrop rocks and boulders, the interstices of the rocks full
of flowers, heaths and stonecrops and alpine roses. The
path, partly natural, partly laid with flat stones, wound

bewilderingly through this miniature rock town, taking the easiest way. They had lost the brook now, it ran somewhere in the deep cleft that fell away on their right; but beyond the point where the rocks gave place again to higher, drier meadows they kept company with it again for a while, and crossed it again. In the greener, moist patches here there were gentians of several tints and sizes, and the colours of quite ordinary flowers, as is their way in the mountains, had darkened into glowing brilliance, the scabious royal purple, the coltsfoot burning orange.

They were overshadowed now on either side by scree slopes and striated faces of rock. If a climber wanted a little practice in Zbojská Dolina, this was where he would have to come. There were a few nice rock pitches leaning over them here, a few limestone needles of the kind experts like to play with when the snow-peaks are out of reach. Ahead of them, on a low shelf on the right-hand side of the valley, and almost thrust from its precarious perch by boulders settling at the foot of the scree, sat a small white building, its squat walls leaning inward with a heavy batter, a tiny lantern tower crowning its roof. The door, as the sunlight showed them, leaned half-open, its upper hinge broken.

'Wonder what that is?' Christine said.

'It's a chapel,' said Tossa. 'Some people got snowbound here once, and died of exposure, so they built a little refuge in case the same thing happened to somebody else. That sort of chapel, not one for holding services.'

'How did you find all that out?' demanded Toddy. 'It isn't in the guide-book.'

'Dana told me. I was asking her about the valley just before we came out, that's all.' Tossa took a wide, measuring look round her, at all the exposed faces of rock, and her gaze settled with a swoop upon the pallid scar of a path that crossed the mountainside on the opposite slope, on a level slightly higher than the roof of the chapel. Above the mark the oblique, striated rock rose steeply, below it was almost sheer for fifty feet or so. But for one excrescence where a harder stratum had refused to weather at the general speed, it would have been a perfectly straight line that crossed the cliff, from the crest on one side to a fold of bushes and trees on the other, descending perhaps fifteen feet in the process. But at the nose of harder limestone the path turned sharply, making a careful blind bend round the obstruction. The result looked, from here, like a large, bold tick slashed across a slate.

Tossa hitched her camera round her neck, and left the path. Without a word she turned towards that face of rock, studying it all the while with drawn brows and jutting lip as she went, and set a straight course for the foot of it across the strip of meadow and into the fringe of bushes.

They all followed her docilely. Dominic would have followed her in any case, and the twins didn't care which direction they took, where all was new and the sun was shining. Almost imperceptibly, for these very reasons, they had arrived at an arrangement by which Tossa constantly set the course, and the others fell into line after her; for Tossa did care where she went. Tossa was a woman with a purpose. Through the trees she led them, following her nose blindly now, or perhaps drawn by the invisible thread of tension that had compelled her across Europe. Her navigation was accurate enough. She came to the spot where the trees fell away, then to the first slanting tables of outcrop rock, tilted at the same angle as the strata in the exposed face above. The cliff hung like a pale grey curtain over them, the heat of the sun rebounding from it into their faces. A broad limestone shelf, moving upward in three irregular steps, jutted from the foot of the pleated folds.

'Where are we going?' asked Christine idly, not greatly concerned about the answer.

'Oh, we'll go on up the valley in a minute.' Tossa squinted experimentally and almost convincingly into the view-finder, and backed a little from the cliff. 'I just thought this would make a fine backcloth for a picture.'

If it was simply an excuse for her detour, it wasn't a bad one. The light was fingering every pleat in the rock curtain like the quivering strings of a harp, and she had space enough to get plenty of contrast and scope into her picture.

'Would you mind disposing yourselves nicely on the seats so thoughtfully provided for you? One on each step. A little more to the left, please, Chris. *My* left, you nut! Yes, that's fine! Hold it!'

They clambered obediently up the shelf of limestone, and sat down where she directed, while she made two exposures, and took her time about it. As she lowered the camera for the second time, Dominic saw her raise her head and cast one rapid glance at the cliff directly above the spot where he was sitting; and because she had just uncovered her face it was for once a naked and readable glance, fierce and doubtful and afraid, and aching with a dark, suppressed excitement that disquieted him horribly.

It was gone in a moment, she was winding her film on and waving them down. The others had noticed nothing, because they were looking for nothing. But Dominic cast one quick glance upwards, where she had looked, and saw that he had been sitting right beneath the jagged nose of rock that jutted to form the angle of the path above.

He felt a light sweat break on his forehead and lip, as understanding broke like a flush of sudden heat in his mind. Tossa on a trail was single-minded to the point of ruthlessness. That projection of rock up there, making a blind cross with the face of the cliff against the sky, was the cross that marked the spot where the accident occurred. He was sitting in the very place where Tossa's step-father had crashed to his death.

Dana Martínek was alone in the bar when Dominic went in to order their coffee that evening. He had hoped she would be. His friends were sitting on the little front terrace under the stars, well out of earshot. If he was making a fool of himself, concocting a melodrama out of a few trivial incidents and Tossa's moodiness, now was the time to find out and alter course.

'Miss Martínek, we've been up as far as the chapel this afternoon. Just opposite there, on the other side of the brook, there's an almost sheer rock face, with a path crossing it. You know the place I mean?'

She turned from the washing of glasses to look at him curiously; a tall girl, not pretty, but with the composed and confident carriage which was common among young women here, and a cast of face to which he was becoming accustomed, wide-boned but softly and smoothly fleshed, widest across the eyes, which were themselves rounded and full and clear. Eyes that could conceal with perfect coolness; but what they did choose to confide, he thought, would be the truth.

'Yes, I know it,' she said, volunteering nothing.

'Wasn't somebody killed in this valley only a couple of weeks or so ago? An Englishman who was staying here?'

She said: 'Yes,' without any particular reluctance or hesitation, but that was all.

'And was that the place where it happened? He fell from that path on the rock?' His spine chilled at the thought that he had been sitting there posing for a photograph. 'Miss Martínek . . .'

Burningly candid faces like hers could withhold smiles, too, their assurance made it possible to be grave even at close quarters and with strangers. But she smiled at him then, not without a touch of amusement in the goodwill. She was twenty-one, two good years older than Dominic.

'You may call me Dana, if you like. It is quicker. Yes, you are right, it was there that he fell.'

'From that bend in the path?'

'So it seemed.'

'Would you mind telling me about it?'

'What is there to tell? Mr Terrell came here and wished to stay, and the room was free, because one couple who should have come had illness at home. So of course, we took him. He was out alone all day. That's normal for people who come here, at least when the weather is good. So we were not worried on the third evening, when he did not come back until dark. But by ten o'clock we grew anxious, and alerted the mountain patrol, and went out ourselves with lights, to search in the head of the valley. But we were not the first to find him. When we got there the police from Liptovsky Pavol were already there. He was dead when they found him.'

'The police? But you hadn't notified the police, had you? Only the mountain rescue people.'

She shrugged. 'The patrol must have called the police, I suppose. They were there. It was they who found him.'

'And his injuries? Did it seem as if they *were* the result of a fall like that?'

She looked him in the eye for a moment, very gravely. 'Mr Felse . . .'

'You may call me Dominic,' he said, with a grin that managed to be unwontedly impudent because of his nervousness. 'It takes longer, but it's more friendly.'

'Dominic,' said Dana, her smile reappearing for a moment, 'you should ask the police these questions. I did not have to go and look at that poor man broken on a slab of limestone, and so I did not go. All I know is what my father said, and he helped to carry him. You know what such a fall on such a surface could do to a man's bones, how many fractures there would be, what sort of fractures? Yes, he was like that. Yes, he fell. You do not get like he was in any other way. They say he died within a few minutes, maybe almost instantly. And I

57

think you have too romantic an imagination, you should curb it.'

'Not me,' said Dominic, taking his elbows from the bar with a sigh. 'It isn't that easy. Well, thanks, anyhow. I'll take the coffee out, shall I, and save you a journey.'

While she was making it he thought of another question. 'What sort of equipment was he carrying, this Mr Terrell?'

He had hardly expected very much from that, but she turned and looked at him with interest. 'Yes, that was perhaps odd. He had with him ice-axe, nylon ropes, *kletterschuhe*, everything for climbing. Naturally he did not carry or need them here. But perhaps it is not so strange, because he came here from the High Tatras. You know them, the big mountains, you must have seen them across the valley as you came from Ruzomberok.'

'Yes,' he agreed eagerly, remembering how abruptly that sickle of icy heads had appeared in the sky on their left hand, like a mirage of snow-fields and honed blue slopes and trailing banners of cloud beyond the green, lush flats of the Váh, fifteen miles wide. 'Yes, *there* he'd want his kit.'

'I asked him how he could bear to leave Strbské Pleso, but he said he had pulled a muscle in his arm, so he came away where he could walk, and not be tempted to use it too soon.'

'Strbské Pleso? That's where he was staying, over there?'

'It means the lake of Strba. It is at the western end of the Freedom Road, that high-level road that runs along the range. Hand me that tray, will you, please? So, and there is your coffee.'

He thanked her, and lifted the tray, balancing it carefully. He had reached the doorway, encrusted with stars, when she said quietly behind him: 'Dominic . . .'

'Yes?' He turned his head alertly.

'Do you know you have been asking me all the same questions your friend asked me this afternoon? The little dark girl – Miss Barber, I think she is called.'

'Yes . . . I thought she might have,' said Dominic, and wavered in the doorway for a moment more. 'Did she ask what hotel he was staying at, over there?'

'No, she did not. But in any case he did not tell me that, and I did not ask him.'

'All right. Thanks, anyhow!'

He carried the tray of coffee out to the terrace. It was not at all surprising that he should arrive just in time to hear Tossa saying, with the sinister, bright edge to her voice that he was beginning to know only too well: 'How about making a sortie over into the High Tatras, tomorrow?'

All the way along the winding road that brought them out of the range, with the enchanting little river bounding and sparkling on their left hand, and the firs standing ankle-deep in ferns along its rim, Dominic was waiting with nerves at stretch to see how she would manage to direct their movements exactly where she wanted to go, and how much she would give away in the process.

'To the right,' Tossa instructed him, poring over the map as though she had not already learned it by heart, 'and keep on the signs for Poprad.'

At Liptovsky Hradok there was a promising fork, where the left-hand road seemed to set course directly for the roots of the mountains.

'Don't take it,' warned Tossa, 'keep on towards Poprad. It doesn't join the Freedom Road, it goes straight over into Poland, and we can't go, and anyhow I think the frontier's closed there. It's a broken line on this map. There's a left fork from this road, oh, twenty kilometres on, that takes us up on to this Freedom Road, and then it runs on along the range all the rest of the way.'

All of which Dominic knew as well as she did; he'd been doing his homework even more industriously. He also knew that the first-class route up to the Freedom Road was nearer forty kilometres ahead than twenty, and joined the shelf highway in mid-course; but the turning to which she was directing them, short, second-class and quite certainly extremely steep to make the gradient in the distance, would lead them to the western end of the upper road, and straight to the lake of Strba.

That didn't take much accounting for, of course; so much she had learned from Dana. What he was waiting to see was what she would do and where she would lead them when they got there. Because she wouldn't know precisely where to look for her step-father's traces in the lake resort, unless she had information Dana didn't possess.

The road streamed eastward along the floor of the great valley, threading the cobbled streets and spacious squares of small towns, and emerging again into the empty, verdant fields, that fantastic back-drop of peaks still unrolling steadily beside it.

Two main streams combine to form the river Váh, the

White Váh the white mountain water from the High Tatras, the Black Váh from the district of Mount Royal in the Low Tatras. Their road crossed the White Váh for the last time, not many miles from its source, and they were over an imperceptible water-shed, no more than the heaving of a sigh from the valley's great green heart, that separated the westward-flowing Váh from the eastward-flowing tributaries of the Poprad, which is itself a tributary of the Dunajec, and joins it to wander away northward into Poland beyond the Tatra range. Those tiny streams they were leaving were the last of the Danube basin. This new and even tinier one, crossed soon after they turned on to Tossa's climbing road and headed precipitately towards the foothills, was the first innocent trickle of the vast drainage area of the Vistula. A couple of miles and a slight heave in the level of the plain determines their eternal separation.

The van climbed dizzily, on a roughly-surfaced but adequate road, left the viridian levels of the river plain, and wound its way between slopes of forest and cascades of rock rich with mountain flowers. The gradient increased steadily. The peaks had abandoned them, they were tangled in the intimacy of the foothills, and there were no longer any distances before them or behind.

They emerged at last on to a broad, well-made road that crossed them at right-angles, and went snaking away left and right along the shoulder of the range.

'Which way now?'

'Whichever you like,' offered Tossa with deceptive impartiality. 'This must be the Freedom Road. Left is the highest end, and we're quite near it here. How about going up there to Strba Lake for lunch, and then we can drive the length of the road to Tatranská Lomnice at the other end, and see if we can go up the funicular?'

It sounded a reasonable programme, and they accepted it readily. The great road climbed still, between slopes of noble pines, until it brought them out suddenly on a broad, open terrace, and the whole panorama of the plain below expanded before them, an Olympian view of earth. They parked the van in a large ground thoughtfully provided opposite the terrace, and rushed to lean over the railing, and marvel at the pigmy world from which they had climbed.

The whole flat green valley of the Váh lay like a velvet carpet beneath them, shimmering coils of cloud drifting between. Through this wispy veil they could see clearly the white ribbon of the road, and the silver ribbon of the river, threading the emerald field, and the little towns splayed like daisies in the grass of a meadow.

'But wait till we go up to the Lomnice Peak!' Tossa promised them, and the magic of joy had penetrated even Tossa's absorption, and made her eyes shine and her voice vibrate. 'This, and another leap on top of it – an enormous one, it looks in photographs. Quick, lock the van, and let's go in to the lake.'

The snow-peaks, exquisitely shaped, bone-clean, polished granite and gneiss, reappeared as soon as they turned inward to the heart of the range, head beyond beautiful head materialising as they walked the curves of the road towards the blue gleam of the lake in its oval bowl. First there were white villas and large modern hotels, and then as the water opened before them broad and gracious, the older hotels, partly timbered, marking their age by their wooden towers and little lantern turrets, an element of fantasy that turned out later, surprisingly, to be traditional; for these towers for tourists were the lineal descendants of the timber churches and belfries of Slovakia, some as old as the thirteenth and fourteenth centuries.

There were hotels round almost a quarter of the lake shore, but above and beyond rose the mountains, forested in their lower reaches, sharpened to steel above, etched with piercing patterns of ice, and snowfields radiant as flowers. Across the water, not far from the shore, towered the timber structure of a ski-jump, like an out-of-season shrub barren in summer and simulating death.

They walked the whole circuit of the lake, staring, exclaiming, photographing, as hordes of other holiday-makers, probably of a dozen nationalities at least, were also doing all round them. And Tossa took stock of every hotel they passed, and gave no sign of seeking or finding.

Not until they came to the Hotel Sokolie, built out to the very edge of the lake, with a terrace overhanging the clear, chill shallows, a sunken garden between its walls and the road, and its name on a wooden sign by the gate.

'This looks nice,' said Tossa, loitering. 'And not too posh, either, so it won't be frantically dear. Anybody but me hungry yet?'

She was learning how to do it. She had the tone just right, happily casual, attracted but easy, willing to go along with the general vote. She had known all along which hotel she was looking for; and that was information she could not have got from Dana.

Not one of the luxury models, just as she had said. Not even new. Half its structure was in wood, with a shingled steeple on one corner. But it had a pleasant, welcoming foyer, and a pine-panelled dining-room with a view over the terrace and the lake. And it was very easy to get the twins compliantly through the swing doors after her, and heading, on the head waiter's prompt and agile heels, towards a table near the window, where the mountains leaned to them in silver outline against a sapphire sky, and the ice-cold mountain water mirrored that blue with a deeper, gentian tone, drowning their senses, soothing them into hungry complacence.

There wasn't a hotel anywhere round the lake that couldn't have provided them with an equally wonderful prospect and a comparable menu; but only this one would do for Tossa. For this was undoubtedly the hotel where Herbert Terrell had stayed for his few meagre days, before he removed to the Low Tatras, to Zbojská Dolina, and the death that was waiting for him there.

'I knew it!' said Toddy, groaning. 'We're going to get the English expert let loose on us wherever we go, I can see that. And I'll swear we never actually said a word in the head man's hearing, he just looked us over. How *do* they know?'

'You'd be even more annoyed,' said Christine with certainty, 'if they took you for something else, instead. Like all the English!'

The head waiter had led them to their table himself, but having weighed them up in one shrewd glance he had thereupon withdrawn, and despatched to them a short, square, good-humoured citizen who greeted them, inevitably, in very competent English. Pretence was useless; they were immediately recognisable, it seemed, wherever they went.

Tossa followed the waiter's bouncing passage through the service doors with a narrowed and speculative glance, the gleam of purpose in her eye. She was here after information, she had an obvious use for an English-speaking waiter. The chief difficulty confronting her now must be how to slip her three companions long enough and adroitly enough to be able to talk to the man alone.

'We could have our coffee on the terrace,' she suggested, her eyes dwelling dreamily on the blue, radiant water outside.

Of course, coffee on the terrace! And then, when they were comfortable and somnolent in the sun, half drunk with mountain air even before they succumbed to the 'Diví Hrozen,' Tossa would begin delving into that all-purpose bag of hers for her powder compact, and wander off demurely into the hotel, ostensibly in search of a mirror and privacy, but in reality in pursuit of the English-speaking waiter.

Everything happened just as he had foreseen. At the edge of the terrace, leaning over the brilliant clarity of the water, Tossa was the first to finish her coffee, and first to excuse herself.

'Oh, lord, what do I look like?' She peered into an inadequate mirror, and scowled horribly. 'You might *tell* a girl!' She gathered up her bag in that armed, belligerent way women have, and pushed back her chair. 'I'll be right back.'

He gave her three minutes before he followed her in through the now almost deserted dining-room, and into the foyer. The sunken garden must, he calculated, continue past all the rooms on the landward side of the house, including lounge and bar, and not a window would be closed on a day like this. The English-speaking waiter was not in the dining-room; he might be in the bar, he might be in the kitchen, he might be almost anywhere, and out of Tossa's reach, but at least the available rooms could be covered. Dominic was launched on a course from which he could not and would not turn back. If he had to listen from hiding he would do it, yes, or at keyholes if necessary; anything to feel that he had the knowledge to help Tossa when the need arose. If it never arose, so much the better, she need never know; and nobody else ever should.

The garden was green, shrubby and wild, its lawns scythed instead of mown, as was the custom here. The thick, clovery grass swallowed his footsteps, and the level of the windows just cleared his head. He walked softly the length of the wall, listening for Tossa's voice; and suddenly there it was, clear, urgent and low, sailing out from the open window above him.

'But *why* should he leave like that? *Something* must have happened. Didn't he say anything to account for it?'

'No, madame, nothing at all.' A slightly beery bass, rich and willing to please. 'All was as usual with him that morning, only the rain kept him indoors. Here he sat and waited, and read the English papers. There was nothing.'

'But there were other people here. Did he talk to anyone?'

'Only to me, madame. I was on duty here.' The waiter's voice was patient, puzzled and reserved. Did she really think she could run round the district like this, asking fierce questions about the sudden death of a foreigner, and not call attention to herself? 'We had not many callers, because of the rain. Only residents. There were a few, of course. Some herdsmen came in, local people, and drank coffee. They were playing cards, the English gentleman went over and watched them for a while. He was asking me about the pack they used, and the game they played. You have other games, this was strange to him. When the man left he picked up the paper on which they had been keeping the score, and examined it. But what is there in that?'

'But then very soon he packed and left?'

'About half an hour afterwards I saw him come down with his bag, and go to pay his account. He asked me about getting a car.' The note of constraint had become a softer, more deliberate intonation of wonder and interest. He went on answering questions almost experimentally. To see what she would ask next?

'But he was interested? In these herdsmen and their game? Did you see this paper with the score on it? Was there anything special about it? But how could there be!' said Tossa hopelessly, and heaved a long, frustrated sigh.

'I did not see it, madame. He put it in his pocket and took it away with him.'

The silence was abrupt and deep, like a fall down a well, but not into darkness. After a moment Tossa said, in an eased voice: 'I believe his widow came and collected all his things. You don't know . . .' She drew back suddenly and warily from what she had been about to ask him, and said instead: 'He asked you about the men, too? What about them?'

'Simply who they were, from what place they came. I think he was interested in the dress. The two older men wore the old, traditional dress from Zdiar.'

'And which of them was the one keeping the score?'

'Oh, that was a young man I know well, but not from here, he comes from across the valley.'

'Did you tell Mr Terrell about him, too?'

'I think he asked me his name, and where he came from, yes.'

In the same muted voice, but now curiously slowed, as

though she had reached the end of one stage of her journey, Tossa asked: 'And what *was* his name?'

'His name,' said the English-speaking waiter simply, 'is Ivo Martínek. His father keeps a hut, over there in the Low Tatras.'

Dominic reached the hall in a frenzied dash, just in time to saunter convincingly into Tossa's sight as she emerged from the deserted bar. He hoped she wouldn't notice his slightly quickened breathing. Looking back from the doorway as they went out to join the twins on the terrace, he caught a glimpse of the English-speaking waiter gazing after them with a wooden face and blank eyes. He was glad to let the door swing closed between them, and hustle Tossa almost crossly away from that look.

He did not, therefore, linger to take another quick glance into the hall, or he might have seen the waiter shut himself firmly into the telephone box and begin dialling a number. But even if he had been within earshot he would not have learned much, for it was not in English that the English-speaking waiter began:

'I am speaking from the Hotel Sokolie. Comrade Lieutenant, I think you should know that there is a young English lady here who is asking many questions about the dead man Terrell.'

They drove back to the Riavka at last, drugged with mountain air and bemused with splendour. Even though the highest leap of the funicular to Lomnice Peak had been out of commission – as it so often is by reason of its extreme height and free cable – they would never forget the bleached, pure, bony world of the Rocky Lake, half-way up, and the far-away, sunlit view of the valley five thousand feet below them, or the steely, shoreless waters of the lake with the clouds afloat on their surface, incredibly clear and still in a bowl of scoured rock, its couloirs and crevices outlined in permanent snow. The mirror of winter in the dazzling sunlight of summer remained with them, a picture fixed and brilliant in the mind's eye, all the way home.

Tossa had taken a great many photographs, and talked rather more than usual. The twins had hopes of her. The time would come, they felt, when they would even cease to think of her instinctively as 'poor Tossa!' After all, with a mother like she had, she'd be doing extremely well if she managed to be normal at twenty. Even better, Dominic showed distinct signs of being interested, which was exactly what Christine, at least, had had in mind. And what a day! The stone-pure, sunlit, withering summits, and then this soft but lofty valley to cradle them at the sleepy end of it!

'I have to write to my mother,' said Tossa resignedly, over dinner. 'At least a postcard, otherwise there'll be trouble. Stick around, I won't be long.'

Whatever she did now, whether she went or stayed, talked or was silent, Dominic couldn't help finding some hidden significance in it. He was uneasy in her presence, but he had no peace at all when she was absent. After a few minutes he left the others in the dining-room, and went out to the bar to buy stamps. That, at least, was his excuse; what he really wanted was to be where he could keep a silent and unobtrusive guard on Tossa.

He could not quite bring himself to follow her upstairs; things hadn't reached that pass yet. But from the bar, with the door standing wide open on the scrubbed pine hall, he would hear her if she called. Crazy, he fretted, to be thinking in such terms; and yet she was certainly meddling in something which was of grave concern to other and unknown people, and they were all these miles from home, in territory the orthodox Briton still considered to be inimical.

Dana turned from her array of bottles behind the bar, and gave him his stamps. She looked at him in a curiously thoughtful way, as if debating what to do about him. He was turning away when she said suddenly: 'Dominic!'

'Yes?' He turned back to her, shaken abruptly by the recollection that she and her family were directly involved in this mystery of Terrell's death. Her brother, that tough, stocky young forester, burned to dull gold by the yellowing mountain sun, was the man who had kept the score in the card game at the Hotel Sokolie, and left behind him, apparently quite light-heartedly, a scrap of paper which had drawn Terrell here to his death.

'I do not know,' said Dana very gravely, 'what it is that is troubling Miss Barber, but I think I should perhaps tell you that today she thought of one more question to ask me.'

'Since we came home?' His choice of phrase astonished him, yet it had come quite naturally; he couldn't think of any people in Europe with whom he'd felt so quickly at home, if it hadn't been for this distorted shadow in the background.

'Yes, since then. She asked me which room Mr Terrell occupied while he was staying here.' Her eyes were searching his face closely; he felt almost transparent before that straight, wide glance.

'And which room *did* he occupy?' His throat was dry and tight with the effort to keep his voice casual.

'The one in which you and your friend are sleeping,' said Dana.

He had a feeling that she knew exactly what he was going to do, and that there was no point whatever in attempting to dissemble it or postpone it. He said: 'Thank you!' quite simply, not even defiantly, and walked out of the bar and straight up the stairs. The pale, scented treads creaked; she would know every step he took. Tossa, very busy upstairs, might hear the ascending footsteps, but would not recognise them; he was only too well aware that she hadn't had any attention to spare for learning things about him. None the less, he approached his own bedroom door very softly, and turned the handle with extreme care, pushing the door open before him suddenly but silently.

Tossa, on her knees at the chest of drawers, the bottom drawer open before her, brushed the lining paper flat and shoved the drawer to in one smooth movement, swinging to face him with huge eyes wary and challenging. He saw in the braced lines of her face excitement and consternation, but no fear, and that frightened him more than anything. Then she saw who it was who had walked in upon her search, and something happened to her courage. It was not, perhaps, fear that invaded her roused readiness, but a trace of shame and embarrassment, and a faint, formidable glimmer of anger.

'Oh, it's you!' she said, too brightly. 'Maybe you know where Toddy's put the big map. I thought it was here somewhere. I couldn't remember how to spell some of the names.' Her breathing wasn't quite in control, but the solid, sensible note was admirable, all the same.

'It's still in the van,' said Dominic, in a tone to match hers.

She got up and dusted her knees, unnecessarily, for the floor was spotless and highly waxed. 'Damn! It would be. Where's the road map, then, the pocket one?'

There was no way past that solid front. He found the map for her, and let her walk out with it, and with all the honours. But when she was gone he closed the door carefully, and took the room to pieces. For whatever it was she was looking for – and he was reasonably sure of the answer to that – she certainly hadn't yet had time to find it. If, of course, it was here at all. And if it was, he wasn't going to miss it.

Nothing under the linings of the drawers; she'd reached the last one, no need to look there again. Nothing under the rugs; the crevices between the pine boards were sealed closely and impermeably. No chimney, of course, except the stack of the tiled stove in the corner. He explored the accessible area inside the metal door, and found nothing. Nothing under the pelmet of the heavy curtains. Nothing in the huge, built-in wardrobe; he examined every hanger, every board of the floor. One side of it was for hanging clothes, the other had six shelves, ingeniously and improbably filled with Toddy's few belongings. Dominic stood and looked at them glumly for a moment, and then began at the top one, and tested them all to see how tightly and immovably they fitted.

The third shelf, just at shoulder-level, stirred ever so slightly in its place.

With his left hand he eased it carefully out as far as it would go, no more than a fraction of a fraction of an inch, and with the finger-tips of his right hand he felt along the rear edge of it, running his nails deep into the crevice. Two-thirds of the way along, something rustled and stirred, dislodged a centimetre from its place. A corner of something white showed beneath the shelf. He edged it gingerly lower, and drew out a long slip of paper, carefully folded to be narrower than the thickness of the shelf, and perfectly invisible when inserted behind it.

And there it was in his hand, when he had unfolded it; four columns of figures, headed by initials, broken by periodical tottings-up, the score of an unknown card game. Nothing at all odd about it that he could see, until he realised that it was scribbled on good-quality manuscript music paper, and suddenly holding it up to the light, found the upper half of an English firm's water-mark glowing at him from the close texture.

Even then it took him a full minute to think of turning it over. On the other side was noted down, in slashing strokes by a ball pen, a few bars of music, that rushed across the paper impetuously, only to be scored through impatiently a moment later, and left hanging upon an unresolved chord.

Dominic hadn't worked very hard at his piano lessons when he should have done, but he could decipher enough of this to see that it was the opening of what seemed to be a rather sombre prelude for piano. Maybe a nocturne: or maybe he was merely rationalising from the few lines of verse that were scrawled above the abortive essay, in a passionate hand and in good English:

Come, shadow of mine end, and shape of rest,
And like to death, shine through this black-faced night.
Come thou, and charm these rebels in my breast,
Whose raving fancies do my mind affright.

Dominic stood staring at it for a moment, recognising Dowland, and frozen to a stillness of pure wonder at finding him here in this vehement and impersonal landscape; those poignant, piercing words of loneliness among these aloof and unmoved mountain outlines startled like frost at midsummer.

Then, without stopping to reason or doubt, he marched out of the room with the wisp of paper in his hand, and straight to the room the girls shared. Tossa was feverishly writing her postcard there, to have something to show for her absence. She looked up at him warily and coldly, as at an enemy. Whoever pursued her now was her enemy, and must simply be prepared for the hurt, and contain it, and go on doggedly, if he wanted to help her. Dominic laid the slip of paper on the table in front of her, and said in a flat, detached voice:

'I think this may be what you were looking for.'

Five

The Man on the Skyline

She gave him one flaring glance, bright and tense at the edge
of panic, and then dropped her gaze to the torn half-sheet of
paper, and sat staring at it with painful concentration for a
long minute. Once she read through the few scrawled lines of
verse and scanned the twenty bars of music without taking
in a word or note. The second time, frowning fiercely, she
grasped at least the sense of the words, and in a moment she
turned the page, and surveyed the columns of figures. With
no change in her expression she looked up at Dominic, and
stared him fairly and squarely in the eye.

He expected her to say flatly: 'What is this, a joke? I
wasn't looking for anything except the map. I don't know
what you're talking about.' For a moment, indeed, she had
intended to do just that, but when he stared back at her with
that intent and sombre face, waiting for her to lie to him,
disturbed and disappointed in advance, she found that she
couldn't do it. What was the use, anyhow, if she couldn't
be convincing? She couldn't guess what he knew, but it was
enough to make him quite sure of himself. She hadn't been
aware of pursuit until now, and suddenly it seemed as if she
had been running to evade him ever since they left England.

'Thank you!' she said, and with a deliberation somewhat
spoiled by the unsteadiness of her fingers she folded the
paper away into her writing-case. She waited, and there was
silence, but he didn't go away and accept his dismissal; she
had never thought he would. 'Now I suppose you're going to
ask me why I was looking for it, and what it is?'

'I know what it is,' said Dominic bluntly. 'It's the paper
Ivo Martínek happened to have in his pocket the day your
stepfather watched him and his friends playing cards in the
Hotel Sokolie. He used it to keep the score on. And I know
why you were looking for it. Because your stepfather picked
it up afterwards in curiosity, and got so excited about it he
left the lake and came over here, to find out more about it.
Where it had come from, or who owned it, or who wrote
those few lines of "Come Heavy Sleep" on it, and the few

bars of music. Not Ivo, that's certain, but somebody Ivo rubs shoulders with pretty casually. Or was it that he *knew* who was involved, as soon as he saw the handwriting?'

Tossa closed her writing-case with a slam. 'Have you been spying on me long?' she asked in a viciously sweet tone.

It didn't hurt as much as he'd expected, because he was ready for it; he knew how she felt, and was even disposed to be on her side. He couldn't afford to stand on his dignity, since he'd kicked it from under him, perforce, the moment Tossa's safety and well-being became more important.

'Quite a time, ever since Siegburg, when you first gave yourself away. Call it spying if you want to, I don't mind. I don't care what you call it, or how badly you think of me for it, just as long as it's effective when the pinch comes. Because if you can't see that you're running head-down into trouble,' he said urgently, 'for God's sake wake up! Whatever you've got on your mind, quit trying to carry it alone. What do you think friends are *for*?'

'I can't tell you anything,' she said defensively, shaken by the warmth of his tone.

'All right, I'm not asking you to, not yet. I'll tell you, instead. Ever since your stepfather got killed, you've been steering us steadily towards this place. First you suggested a carnet for the van, then Czech visas, then at Siegburg you started talking about coming straight into Slovakia, here, to the Tatras. That was when I began to get the idea, and after that it wasn't so hard to follow up the later developments. Suddenly you knew about a wonderful little place in Zbojská Dolina, that you'd never mentioned before. And when we were here, you took us off the path up the valley, just at the right place to locate the spot where Terrell fell and was killed. I know, I asked Dana, last night, and she told me just what she'd told you. And then you suggested a trip over into the High Tatras, and took us straight to the right resort, the one where Terrell was staying before he moved here, and even to the right hotel. And that's something you didn't get from Dana, because she said she didn't know, and I believe her. But *you* know. You had it from somebody else, before we ever came here.'

'Dana must have known,' Tossa said involuntarily. 'It was her brother who . . .' She caught herself up too late, jerking her head aside to evade his eyes.

'Who was there playing cards in the Hotel Sokolie, and left behind that bit of paper? Yes, evidently Terrell noticed him, all right, but that doesn't prove he ever noticed Terrell. He was with three friends, drinking coffee and playing cards, he wasn't bothered about the foreigner who came and looked on. And in any case, you didn't ask Dana about the hotel. You didn't have to, you knew it already.'

'You seem,' said Tossa with a tight smile, 'to be pretty well-informed yourself.'

'I listen at windows. Toddy ought to have warned you.'

They were beginning to hate and blame each other for the stone wall between them. He was catching her tone, and that wouldn't help anyone. He dragged the dressing-table stool across the room and plumped it down close beside her chair, and leaning forward with desperate earnestness, closed his hands hard over hers. She quivered, but she didn't draw away.

'Look, Tossa, you've got to listen to me. We're not in England now. We're in Central Europe, in a Communist country. If our people think we haven't all that much reason to trust the Czechs, how much reason do you think the Czechs have to trust us? Historically, a hell of a lot less! How do you think it would look at home, if a chap with a Czech passport came poking around one of our small towns, asking a lot of nosy questions about a death that was officially accidental, cornering waiters in hotels and trying to pump them, and searching rooms for hidden bits of paper? Just give it a thought! Yes, I *was* listening under the window, I heard you talking to the waiter. That's the only time, but I don't give a damn, anyhow, you can call it what you like. What I want is for you to stay out of trouble. The way you're going on, you're going to end up in gaol. No, wait a moment!' he checked abruptly. 'Let's have it quite straight. There was one other time when I spied on you. At Zilina, when we were leaving the hotel. I saw you drop your comb-case for that fellow with the MG to pick up and return. You sent him a message that way, didn't you?'

Tossa's hands lay still in his. She looked at him helplessly, and shook her head, without vehemence this time, but no less conclusively. 'I'm sorry, I can't answer questions. I can't tell you anything.'

'No, I beg your pardon, I said I wouldn't ask. All right, I think you did send him a message. And he sent one back to you the same way. I know you knew him before – or at least that he knew you. Maybe he's the one who started you on this hunt. The one who told you where your step-father stayed in Strbské Pleso. The one who told you there was something wrong about the way he died. X with diplomatic plates. And then you begin drawing attention to yourself here by asking questions all over the place! Do you seriously think an English diplomat can make a move in this country without the authorities knowing all about it? It works much the same way in any country, they *have* to know where these people are and what they're doing. Don't you see, Tossa, why you frighten me to death? If you have to go on with this, why alone? If we knew what you were after we could try to help you at least, and you wouldn't have to expose yourself even further, and make yourself more conspicuous, by having to evade us, too. Wouldn't it be better?'

'I'm sorry,' she said again, her voice a little unsteady. 'I can't tell you anything. I haven't said yes to any of this, you're only guessing.'

'All right, I'm only guessing, but they're pretty safe guesses.'

'I'm sorry, I really am sorry . . . but I can't tell you. Not won't – can't.' Her hands turned suddenly in his, warmly returned his grip for a moment, and then struggled free in outraged shyness. 'I don't admit to anything. You'll just have to let me take my chance.'

'That's something *I* can't do,' said Dominic, letting her go regretfully but hastily. He caught her eye, and the gleam of a smile passed between them, and foundered in the sea of their gravity. 'Not won't – can't. I'm sticking close to you, and if you ever do want me, I'll be around.'

'I shan't need you. Nothing's going to happen to me. Do the others . . . I mean, they haven't noticed anything, have they?'

'No, I'm sure they don't realise there's anything going on. And I shan't tell them. Only you can do that.'

The air between them had cleared, they could look at each other again almost hopefully, and with a new curiosity. 'There isn't anything going on,' she said firmly, presenting the formal untruth with the assurance that it would be understood as it was offered. 'Thanks, Dominic, all the same.'

'Then, look, is there anything I can do to help you? Without asking any questions? You don't have to tell me why, just what I have to do.'

She looked up at him intently for a moment, a deep spark kindling in her eyes. Then she ripped open the zipper of her writing-case, and drew out from the rear pocket a four-inch square of newsprint.

'Yes! If you really mean that, there is. You can help me to find this man. He's here somewhere, in this valley or near it. Take a good look at him, so you'll know if you do see him around. And if you do, tell me.' She pushed the newspaper clipping across the table to him. 'I stole it from the files,' she said, 'the day before we left England. It was the best I could find.'

Dominic noted, even before he looked at the face, that the caption had been cut off. It was sharply printed for a newspaper photograph, almost certainly from a studio portrait. A man leaned forward across a desk, his jaw propped on linked hands. He might have been about thirty-five years old; a tapered face, broad across eyes and brow, lean of cheek and long of chin, with a thin, high-bridged sword of a nose, and a cool, long-lipped, sceptical mouth. The hands linked under his chin were large, broad-jointed and calm. They looked capable of anything. Light-coloured hair drew back at high temples, duplicating the arched, quizzical line of his brows. The eyes were deep-set, probing and lonely, and looked out from the page with an aloof, almost a hostile, composure.

Dominic forgot for a moment his promise to ask no questions. 'Who is he?' he asked curiously, looking up across the photograph into Tossa's face.

'By all the indications,' said Tossa, grimly and quietly, 'he's the man who murdered my stepfather.'

Above the chapel on its shelf of rock there were sudden moist meadows, and a wealth of brilliant green pasture. Beyond, again, lay the final great, irregular bowl, green in the base, rimmed round on all sides with paling slopes of grass and ashen slides of scree. Laborious zigzag paths climbed to two cols, where the snag-toothed rim of rocks dipped to let them through; and all the sides of the bowl were circled by contour paths, along which the hill sheep trotted confidently, and sometimes dark-red, handsome goats, chestnut-coloured like Dominic's hair.

They had probed every corner of the valley itself, and discovered every cottage. They were known, now. One of the herd-boys brought Christine edelweiss from some secret place on the summits, and a woman at the highest cottage below the huts gave them an armful of flowers from her garden. Many of the faces were becoming familiar. But they had never yet caught a glimpse of the face in Tossa's stolen photograph.

They climbed the more northerly of the two cols, and emerged among high, windy wastes of pale turf, billowing away towards more folded valleys beyond. There were no houses in sight here, only the true open, rolling, rounded crests of the Low Tatras.

They climbed the more southerly col, and beyond the crest the path traversed a broken slope of rocks, and brought them down into a high green bowl not unlike the one they had left, but smaller and more sheltered. There was a single, isolated farm here, too remote to be incorporated in any collective, and therefore still operated privately. There were smoky brown cows in the pasture, and poultry in a paddock behind the house. A handsome old woman, tall as a man, and coiffed elaborately in lace, was scything clover in a meadow. A middle-aged man came striding through the yard with two large milking pails; but he was short and gnarled like a mountain tree. A plump woman shrilled at him from a window of the house. They saw no one else there.

Two of them, of course, were not looking for anyone in particular. Toddy and Christine walked and scrambed and bathed, and sunned themselves, and saw nothing constrained or secretive in their companions. Everything was as open and candid as the day to them.

They were on their way back into the highest bowl of Zbojská Dolina, lunging down the scree, when the first heavy, solitary drops of rain fell. Ten minutes previously the sky had been clear and blue, now a curtain of heavy purple was being drawn slowly over the crests behind them.

'We're going to get caught,' said Toddy, and paused to look round for the quickest way to shelter. The huts lay nearer to the path from the other col. 'Let's cut a corner. If we traverse from here to the other track we may make it to shelter. There's a contour path, look – it cuts off a long run in the open.'

The thin grey ribbon danced its way round the side of the bowl, threaded a few clumps of stunted bushes at the edge of an outcrop of rock, and balanced along the rim of a fifty-foot face of sheer, fluted cliff. At the foot of this expanse a shelf of rock jutted out irregularly, some twelve to fifteen feet wide, and below that the level dropped again,

though less abruptly, sliding away down open rock and
rubble and scree into the bottom of the bowl.

They saw, when they had tramped smartly along the
sheep-path in single file, and brushed through the bushes
suddenly fragrant with the first spurt of rain, that this whole
face of the bowl, the only one scoured clear of vegetation
from top to bottom, formed a slightly hollowed channel, a
groove not much more than twenty yards wide down the side
of the basin. Where they stepped out on the rock itself, the
path was solid and not even very narrow, but polished and
sloping, so that they checked and trod carefully. Looking
up on their left hand towards the crests, they could see
the reason. Two or three pale slides of rubble and scree,
chalk-lines on the greyer rock, converged upon this ledge,
and for centuries had been sending the detritus of their
weathering slithering down by this route into the valley.
The ledge on which the path crossed, too narrow to check
the slide, had been honed into steely glossiness by its onward
passage. The broader ledge below had collected the rubble as
in a saucer, stacking it up neatly in a talus against the cliff.

Toddy peered respectfully over the edge. The declivity was
not sheer, after all, when seen from above, nor quite without
vegetation. Apart from the centre of the slide, where the
polishing of friction had smoothed away all irregularities, it
would not have been impossible to climb down the slope. And
there below, a pie-crust of heaped boulders and stones and
dust, the talus leaned innocently against the mountainside,
while its accumulated overspill of years lay desultorily about
the bottom of the valley, a hundred and fifty feet below.

'Look at that!' Toddy forget the ominous, slow slapping
of the rain for a moment, and hung staring in fascination.
'Wonder how long it took to build up all that lot?'

Christine took one quick glance below, and withdrew to
the inner side of the path. 'Longer than it'll take to shift it,
my boy, if you miss your step.'

'And do you realise the process grades all that stuff down
there? Piles it up with the boulders as a base, and the finer
stuff above. I read it once in some book by Norman Douglas
about the Vorarlberg. And it builds up at the steepest angle
maintainable. It looks as solid as a wall, and if you blew on
it the whole lot would go.'

'Then don't blow. Come on, the rain's coming.'

In single file they paced cautiously across the level of the
rock, and came thankfully out on to terraced, coarse grass

and a milder slope, where they could take to their heels and go bounding towards the huts. A soft crackle of thunder and a lipping of lightning along the crests, beneath the spreading purple cloud, nipped at their heels and drove them as corgis drive cattle. The plunge of their descent carried them lower than the highest hut, and towards the cluster below. They were still a hundred yards from them when the cloud parted with a sound like the tearing of rhinoceros hide, and the rain came down in a slashing fall.

They ran like hares. The nearest door was held wide open before them, and a long brown arm hauled the girls in. In the dark, warm, steamy interior, with the fodder-loft above one end, and rough wooden benches round the walls, six of the herdsmen were gathered already, and others came running hard on their heels, scattering water from their black felt hats and frieze capes as they shed them inside the doorway.

Broadly smiling faces loomed at them through the steamy air, weather-beaten faces of large-boned young men, seamed, teak faces of hawk-nosed old men. The entire upland population of Zbojská Dolina was gathering into shelter from the first thunderstorm of August. There could not be a better place for studying them, or a better time.

They made room for the foreigners on the most comfortable bench, close to the small iron stove. An old man with thin metal chains jingling round his hat, and the traditional cream-felt trousers still worn without affectation to his daily work, embroidered thighs and all, offered them mugs of coffee, and a young fellow brought out of his leather satchel soft, light buns filled with cream cheese and poppy-seed. The air was heavy with scent of clover and damp felt and garlic breath, and it began to feel like a party. Except that at a party you do not look steadily round at every face in the company, as Tossa was doing now, memorising their lines and measuring them against a remembered face that is not present.

They had now seen, surely, every soul who habitually frequented Zbojská Dolina. But they had not seen the man Tossa was looking for.

The rain stopped as abruptly as it had started. In a matter of seconds, before they had realised that the drumming on the roof had ceased, a finger of sunlight felt its way in at the open door, and the tatters of cloud melted magically from half the sky. They emerged into a washed and gleaming world, withdrawing themselves almost reluctantly from a discussion conducted in mixed German and Slovak, with an English word thrown in here and there, notably the now international word 'folk-lore,' which the herdsmen batted about among them with a note of tolerant cynicism in their voices. The party clamour fell behind them, with their own thanks and farewells, and the hut emptied.

The four of them walked in silence in the wet grass, the eastern sky pale and clear as turquoise before them, the ring of crests picked out with piercing sunlight beneath a still ominous darkness to westward.

'Listen!' Christine halted, head reared. 'What's that?' She looked round the slopes of the bowl, and back towards the huts, but the sound that had caught her ear seemed to have no source.

Then they heard it, too; a sudden rippling, vibrating entry on a high note, that shook down a scale into a deep, still, slow melody, breathy and hushed, like a bass flute. Soft and intimate, and yet from no visible source, and therefore as distant as the summits, at least, and perhaps from beyond them. There are sounds that can whisper across ten miles of country, especially in mountain air, where slope gives back the echo to slope, and even a flung human voice can span valleys as lightly as the wind. This tune – it was a full minute before the procession of sounds became a tune to their unaccustomed ears – was muted and wild and sad, and the nature of the instrument, whatever it might be, seemed to determine that it must be slow.

'Some sort of a pipe,' said Dominic. 'Maybe they've got a local version of the alphorn here. That's modal, surely, that tune?'

'Mixolydian,' said Christine. 'I think! I never heard anything like it before. That entry! Listen, there he goes again!'

Down from its first reedy, impetuous cry span the thread of sound, and settled low and softly, like a lark dropping. Full and deep the lament sang itself out, and was gone. They waited, but it did not come again.

'That's all. What a pity!'

Tossa turned back once more, before they began to descend the valley path, and halted them again with an exclamation of delight. 'Look, there go the goats!'

Sleek and dark and brilliant with rain, the chestnut goats minced daintily out of the grey of rocks along the skyline, into the beam of stormy sunlight, that turned each one into a garnet on a chain for a moment, out of it again through the narrow cleft of the southerly col, and so out of sight. Gaudy as players in a spotlight, they gleamed and passed. And after them, abrupt and tall and dazzling against the dark, a man walked into their vision.

Tiny and distant as they saw him, he filled the sky for a moment. A long, rangy figure, like most of them here, in the modified local dress that made them all look like Mirek's brigand-patriot Janosík and his mountain boys. The brief glitter like a crown on his head must be the fine chains that ringed his hat, the light streaming down his body was the sheen of his rain-soaked frieze cloak. His swinging stride carried him into the gleam and out of it without pause; and they saw clearly, bright and ominous against the dark sky, the stock of the rifle projecting over his shoulder, and the inordinately long barrel swinging momentarily into sight below his hip as he turned through the col, and vanished in a swirl of his wet cloak, leaving the stage empty.

Below, near the Riavka hut, it had not rained at all. The meadows were dry and bright, the cloud had passed, torn its skirts on the summits, discharged its rage there, and dissolved in its own tears.

They lay in the blonde grass at the edge of the paddock, half asleep, reluctant to go indoors. And it was there that they heard the far-off pipe again. The notes came filtering into their consciousness like music heard in a dream, so distant they were, and so faint. If they had not heard them already once that day, they would probably not have been aware of them now; and even as it was, they had been listening to them inwardly for some minutes before they realised what it was that was stroking at their senses.

Dominic lay stretched out at ease, the breeze just stirring Tossa's dark hair against his shoulder, and let his mind drift with the elusive sound rather dreamed than heard. That abrupt, cascading, improvised opening, hardly loud enough to be heard at all, and yet startling, and then the full, deep, remote air. He wondered how well Christine really knew her modes? 'And ever against eating cares, lap me in soft Lydian airs.' Or Mixolydian, what's the odds? To follow the tune you had to relax and let it take you along with it, for its progress was deliberate and abstracted, running line softly into line. Not until he stopped consciously listening did he catch the form of it, and fall into the loose, plaintive cadence so smoothly that the words came of themselves.

Curious how the simplest doggerel folk-songs have a way of making themselves applicable everywhere.

> *Sometimes I am uneasy*
> *And troubled in my mind . . .*

Like Tossa, with her tender conscience, and her sense of obligation to a man she had cordially disliked. He turned his head softly, to study through the seeding grasses her unconscious face, turned up to the slanting rays of the sun with eyes closed, half asleep, but still anxious in her half-sleep, and still vulnerable. Her eyelids, loftily arched and tenderly full, were veined as delicately as harebells, and her mouth, now that she wasn't on guard, was soft and sad and uncertain as a solitary child's.

> *Sometimes I think I'll go to my love*
> *And tell to her my mind.*

He was leaning cautiously over her on one elbow when she opened her eyes, looked up dazedly and blindingly into his face, and smiled at him without reserve or defence, out of the charmed place of her half-sleep. And suddenly, in the same instant that her open acceptance of him made his heart turn over, the true significance of his own ramblings stung his mind. He rolled over and sat bolt upright, his fingers clenched into the grass.

> *Sometimes I am uneasy*
> *And troubled in my mind . . .*

He wasn't mistaken. That was the air he'd been hearing now for two minutes at least, and he'd known it, and never grasped what it meant, or how downright impossible it was. The pastoral mood was right, the loose form was right, and the music was certainly modal; but how could some shepherd piper here in the Low Tatras, in the heart of Central Europe, be playing an unmistakably English folk-song called 'Bushes and Briars'?

The Man in the Chapel

The astonishing thing was that no one else had noticed anything odd; they lay placidly chewing grass-stems on either side of him, and gave no sign. Nobody but himself had caught and identified the air; and in a moment more it was gone, and even the distances were silent.

He debated uneasily whether he ought to call Tossa's attention to his discovery, but the decision was taken out of his hands. He had no opportunity to speak to her alone before they were called in to their early supper; and midway through the pork and dumplings Dana appeared in the doorway to announce in a flat, noncommittal voice: 'Miss Barber, someone is asking for you on the telephone.'

Tossa dropped her fork with a clatter, suddenly jerked back into her private world of pitfalls and problems. Her face was tight and wild for an instant.

'*Telephone*?' said Toddy incredulously. 'What, here? What secret contacts have you got in these parts, Operator 007-and-a-half?' Dominic was beginning to marvel and chafe at the insensitivity of Toddy; he'd known the girl for years, he should have felt some response to her unbearable tension.

'Don't be an ass,' said Tossa with a sigh, getting to her feet with a creditable pretence of boredom and resignation. 'It'll be my mother, of course.'

No one, fortunately, thought fast enough to observe that they had come to Zbojská Dolina only on the spur of the moment, and their address certainly could not be known to anyone in England, since Tossa's card home had been posted only yesterday.

'I never thought your fond mama was fond enough to spend a guinea a minute, or whatever it is, talking across Europe to her darling daughter,' said Christine cynically.

'Don't be silly, Paul will be paying the bill, of course.'

Dana, hovering in the doorway, said clearly and deliberately: 'It is a man calling.' She cast one brief glance at Dominic, and hoisted her shoulder in a slight but significant shrug. She was a little tired of secrecy, and not altogether disposed to go on being discreet. Dana was taking no more responsibility for anything or anyone. It was up to him now.

'What did I tell you? Paul getting paternal!' Tossa walked away to take her call, the back view almost convincing, resigned and good-humoured, ready to report faithfully to her demanding family, and extricate herself from any further enquiries. Though of course, she knew, none better, that it was not Chloe Terrell on the line, or Paul Newcombe, either or anyone else in far-off England, but somebody here in Slovakia, somebody from whom she had been half expecting a message all this time.

She came back a few minutes later, still admirably composed, if a little tense. She sat down with a sigh, and resumed operations hungrily on her pork and dumplings.

'Everything all right?' asked Christine cheerfully.

'Oh, sure, everything's all right. They're home, and no troubles. Just felt they ought to check up on the stray lamb.' She wasn't too loquacious, because she never talked much about her relationship with her mother, and it wouldn't ring true now. 'Paul mostly, of course, they're always like that. He means well.'

When she was lying with every word and every motion of her body she could still, it seemed, keep the secret from the Mather twins, but she couldn't keep it from Dominic. A private geiger-counter built into his deepest being started a pulsating pain in response to the rising of the hackles of her conscience, and halved her pain. And she was aware of it, for she flashed one appraising look at him, and then resolutely evaded his eyes.

But repeatedly, he noticed, his senses perhaps sharpened by the pain, she was glancing now at her watch. She had an appointment to keep. Or she was counting the minutes until she could be alone and stop lying? It wasn't her natural condition, it hurt her badly, she might well look forward to a respite from it.

But no, she had an appointment! She drank her coffee quickly, though it was scalding hot. She had one eye constantly on the time, and was calculating something in her mind, and frowning over it.

'You won't mind if I run off and write a proper letter home?' she said deprecatingly, pushing her chair back. 'It's the one sure way to keep 'em quiet for the rest of the trip.'

'You could do it down here,' suggested Toddy obtusely, 'and nod our way occasionally.'

'What, with television around? You don't know how much concentration it takes. I'll be down in an hour or so.'

She made her escape in good order; only the back view, as she left the room, somehow conveyed a sense of brittleness, excitement and tension. But she was right, they had television to divert their minds, compulsive here even before the sun was down, because they were on holiday from all cerebral engagements, because they had been out in the fresh air all day, and because, when it came to the point, the programmes were rather better than at home, and the picture very much better. They wouldn't begin to miss Tossa for an hour or so, and they wouldn't miss him, either.

He gave her two minutes' start; he was afraid to make it longer. Then he made an easy excuse about bringing down the maps and surveying the route into Levoca, where there was a notable church and some splendid carving by Master Paul. They agreed cheerfully; they would have agreed to anything, provided it made no claim on them tonight.

He walked straight through the bar, across the terrace, and out to the edge of the trees. There he waited, because the light was still on in the girls' room. If she didn't come in a few more minutes, he would assume he could relax, and think about fetching the maps. And he would feel crazily happy to be owing her an apology; as though she wronged him by going her own way, and he injured her by feeling injured. The relationship between them was growing more and more complex and painful.

The light in the girls' room went out.

He counted the seconds, hoping she wouldn't come, ready to blame himself for all sorts of suspicions to which he had no right. Then he saw Tossa's slight, unmistakable shape in the doorway, saw her close the door behind her and slip away from the house, heading towards the climbing path.

He stood motionless among the trees, and let her pass. It was still daylight, though the direct rays of the sun had forsaken the valleys, and were fingering hesitantly at the heights. In the bowl among the summits, where the chestnut goats habited with their elusive bandit-herdsman, it would still be broad day; here among the trees it was almost dusk already. She had the evening world to herself; she moved through it like a wraith.

Dominic stole out of his hiding-place and silently followed her.

Among the trees it was easy to keep relatively close to her, and still escape notice; but afterwards, when they came to the heath land and the scattered rocks, through which the track threaded bewilderingly, he had to hang back a little and slip from cover to cover with care. If she looked back at a turn of the path she might easily glimpse him, and he was reluctant to be caught shadowing her, however illogical that might seem. She hadn't made any concessions, hadn't invited him into this secret affair of hers, hadn't asked him for anything. She had given him her commission without her confidence, and only when he asked for it; and his acceptance of it had given him no rights whatsoever, because he had bargained for none. But neither had he made any promises to withdraw, or cede any of his rights to act on his own. Principal and shadow, they maintained each his station. But he felt that there was, in a way, an obligation on him not to obtrude.

The bruised grasses underfoot, rich with dwarf heaths and wild thyme, sent up a heady sweetness in the cooling evening, and the small breeze that came with the change brought back to him the occasional light rustle of Tossa's shoes on the loose stones. The most difficult bit was going to be the belt of open meadows, before the valley closed in on both sides in broken rock faces and drifts of rubble and scree, mingled with scattered copses and thickets of bushes. How far could she be going? Not up to the highest bowl, surely, where the huts were? At this hour, and without a coat?

She was out of the rock belt now, she set off boldly across the meadows, and he hung back in cover, and let her go. Once she looked round, and stood for a moment with head reared, watching and listening to make sure she was alone. Then, satisfied, she turned and hurried on, breaking into a run.

He dared not step into the open after her until she had vanished at the first turn of the path, where the outcrop rocks closed in upon it and twisted it, like fingers snapping off a thread. But then he set off across the thick, silent turf at a fast run, to make good the distance he had lost. Even if she looked back, now, she could not see him, and with this springy carpet under his feet she would not hear him. He reached the rocks, and began darting after her from bend to bend of the cramped path, until he heard a stone roll away from under her foot, somewhere ahead of him and not far away.

She had left the path; though narrow and winding here, it was almost level and partly grassed, a stone would not roll like that unless she had begun to climb again. By the sound, she had turned to the right from the track. That way there was at least one possible goal; he could see the roof of the little refuge, rose-coloured tiles against the backdrop of ashen scree. It was still in sunlight, a long ray pierced the open lantern tower like a golden lance. They had climbed a considerable distance already, and for a little while, at least, had outdistanced the twilight.

Yes, she was heading for the chapel. Quiet as she was, the small sounds she did make came down to him clearly, and he could trace her progress by them. The pathway up to the shelf had been laid, at one time, with flat stones, but many of them were unsteady now. And here there were thick bushes and even trees, encouraged by the shelter of the little promontory. Stones from the encroaching scree-slope behind had rolled right down among the bushes, and lay raw and pale in the grass. Then, as the track reached the edge of the level shelf, the trees fell back, and Tossa stepped out on to the plane of rock before the chapel door. Rubbish of scree had reached the wall on the inner side, and begun to pile up against the footings.

Tossa never hesitated. She walked quickly across the few yards of open space, towards the door that sagged sideways on its broken hinge. Dominic wormed his way to the edge of the trees, and watched her go. The place seemed private, silent and abandoned, surely safe enough. He found himself a secure spot in cover, and settled down to wait until she should reappear.

Tossa reached the door, laid her hand on the leaning timbers, and slid round them into the chapel. It seemed she might be a few minutes late for her appointment; at any rate, it was three minutes past eight by Dominic's watch. She vanished. He began, almost unconsciously, to count seconds.

Four seconds, to be exact. Four seconds of silence from the instant when she disappeared round the sagging door into the dark interior. Then the sharp, small crack, that he took first for a dry twig snapping under a foot, and knew next moment for a gun-shot.

He discovered that he knew it when he found himself flat

on his face, writhing like an eel out of the bushes and on to
the grey, striated face of rock, wriggling frantically towards
the door of the chapel. And it seemed that his senses were
capable of splitting themselves into action squads, where the
need was sharp enough, for he was simultaneously aware of
recording the dull sound of a fall, and the faintest of muted
cries, while his conscious hearing was busy with the sound of
the shot, struggling to sort out its direction, and baffled by
a multiplicity of echoes. Here in this confined and complex
valley every explosion of sound ricocheted from plane to
plane, repeated endlessly along the gorge, out to the open
bowl to westward, and the lowland spaces to eastward.

Tossa had walked into the chapel erect and innocent.
Dominic crawled, drawing up his feet behind him into the
grateful shade of the doorway, and dragging himself up by
the great iron latch. He scrambled round the obstruction,
and the first thing that hit him was the slanting shaft of
sunlight through the empty window-frame on his left hand.
It blinded him for a moment, and then, before he regained
his sight or took his sheltering arm down from his eyes, he
grasped the significance of this late radiance, and dropped
to the floor again in a hurry. His outstretched right hand hit
upon something warm and rough-textured, a tweed sleeve,
the roundness of an arm limp and still within it.

A yard before his face, and on the same level, Tossa's
face hung frozen and blank with shock, lips parted, great
eyes stunned into dullness. That was the first thing he saw
as his vision cleared again. The second was the young man
who lay sprawled between them half on his face, one arm
doubled under him, one flung out towards the doorway, with
a blue-black hole oozing a sluggish glue of blood just to the
right of the base of his skull, in the neatly cropped fair hair,
and a small pool gathering underneath his throat, in the dust
of the paved floor. A well-dressed young man, in good grey
slacks and sportscoat, as English as brown ale. It was hardly
necessary to stoop and examine the motionless, astonished
face pressed against the dirty flagstones, but Dominic did it,
all the same.

The man who ran the MG, the man who had drunk coffee
in a corner of the kavárna at Zilina, and exchanged messages
with Tossa by means of her comb-case, was never going to
report on his mission, whatever it might be. There was no
pulse detectable in the wrist on which Dominic pressed his
fingers; there was not the faintest misting discernible on

the watch-glass he held to the slack lips for want of a mirror.

X with diplomatic plates was unmistakably and irrevocably dead.

Tossa came out of her daze with a violence that almost shattered them both, broke into rending, tearless sobs, and tried to get to her feet, in a horrified recoil from the poor creature on the floor. Dominic dropped the heavy hand he had been holding, and caught her by the shoulders roughly, pulling her down again.

'Don't get up! Don't you understand? The window! The light!' He reached across the dead man, and drew her close to him, kneeling upright and holding her tightly in his arms. His back ached with her weight and his own, but that didn't matter. Neither, for the moment, did the dead man over whom they leaned to each other thankfully and fearfully. 'I'm here, I'm with you, I won't leave you. Keep down, and keep hold of me. You'll be all right. Tossa, you know me – Dominic. Now, take it easily, and we'll pull out all right. I came to look after you. I said I'd be around.'

'He's dead!' whispered Tossa, shivering with shock. 'He *is* dead, isn't he? There's nothing we can do for him?'

'No, there's nothing we can do. He's dead.' It disposed, he saw, of the first urgency. He felt her relax in his arms. Now they were two, burdened with the responsibility only for themselves. It was no comfort at all, but it simplified things. It even accelerated understanding.

'I came here to meet him,' she said numbly. 'He telephoned me. It wasn't my mother.'

'I know. Never mind that now. What happened? When you came in here? Tell me what you can.'

'He was standing over there,' she said in a dulled but obedient whisper, 'beyond the window, where it's dark. When I came in, he started across to meet me. He stepped right into the sunlight, and then he suddenly lurched forward, and fell past me. I couldn't understand what had happened to him, all at once like that.'

'Somebody shot him,' said Dominic. 'Somebody's outside with a rifle. I heard the shot. He was covering that window, waiting for his chance, and he got it when this chap stepped into the light. So keep down here in the shadow, whatever you do.'

'He may have seen us come,' she said, shuddering in his

arms, 'you or me or both. Especially me – I didn't hide. Suppose he thinks Mr Welland may have told me something before he was killed? He *came* to tell me something!'

'Somebody out there was damned determined he shouldn't get the chance. *Did* he manage to say anything to you? Anything at all?'

'When I came in he started to say: "Miss Barber, there you are." Something like that. And then he pitched forward and fell down.'

'And afterwards? When you were kneeling by him?'

'He did try to say something. It sounded like: "But he couldn't have known – nobody else knew!" And then he said? "Impossible!" quite clearly, sort of angrily. Just: "Impossible!" And then there wasn't anything else. And now he's dead!'

'And on the telephone? He didn't tell you anything then?'

'He only said he must see me, and would I meet him here. It's my fault. If it hadn't been for me, if I hadn't interfered, he'd still have been alive. I never wanted to break things, but I do. I break everything!'

She was shaken by a momentary gust of weeping, but she pushed the weakness away from her indignantly, and clung to Dominic's sweater with convulsive fingers, as to the anchor of her sanity.

'If the man outside – the man with the rifle – if he knows we're in here, if he knows we're defenceless, we're as good as dead, too, aren't we? Because he can't afford any witnesses.'

'He may not know. And even if he does, he can't be all sides of us at once. Listen, Tossa! You stay here, and stay down. You understand? I want to take a look out of the window.'

'You can't! He's that side, he must be. He'll fire again.' She kept her hold of him fiercely, and it was not a hysterical grip, but a very practical and determined one, meant to secure what she valued.

'Don't worry, I'm not going to show myself, I'm not such a fool. I've got to see where he could be, and how much ground he can cover.' He detached her hands from his person firmly, and slid away from her along the dusty floor, to draw himself up cautiously on the dark western side of the window.

With his cheek flattened against the wall, he could peer out with one eye over the range of country which must contain, somewhere, the man with the rifle trained on this spot. He found himself looking out, as he might have realised before if his mind had been working normally, over the full width of the valley, for below him the ground fell away to the path and the brook. Only a long segment of the opposite wall of the valley was presented to view. That was comforting, for it meant the marksman must be some considerable distance away, too far to change his ground quickly. His field of fire was more or less determined. Dominic recollected the way the bullet had entered, slightly to right of centre near the base of the skull. That seemed to indicate that the rifleman was somewhat up-valley from their position, undoubtedly somewhere in cover on the far side, and approximately on a level with the chapel.

Right opposite the window where he stood, and on a level perhaps a few yards higher, was the scarred face of rock where Herbert Terrell had fallen to his death. There were plenty of bushes at the up-valley side of that cliff-face. The position was approximately right. Murder, it seemed, clung very close to this spot.

What could the distance be? Nearly half a mile, surely. Did that mean telescopic sights? If he couldn't sight them from where he was, he certainly couldn't change his position and shorten the range very quickly. And if he was covering this window from over there, he couldn't even see the doorway, it was round a good, solid corner of masonry. So with a lot of luck he might not have seen them at all. In that case he could only feel uneasily certain that the young man who knew too much must have come here to meet someone, and he might, just might, know enough to feel sure who that someone was likely to be. But he couldn't *know*, at this moment, and he couldn't break cover and show himself, *in case* someone escaped to tell the tale. Secrecy was of the essence. When he killed it had to be anonymously, unless he could be absolutely sure of killing *everyone* who might be able to connect him with the affair.

There was cover for most of the way back to the Riavka hut; only the thirty yards of open rock here outside the door, and the expanse of meadows well below, presented real hazards. And the first was surely the worst, just the getting out of this stone box, and into the bushes. It was all very well calculating hopefully that the enemy must be in a position from which he ought not to be able to see the doorway, but even so he might be able to see the last few yards of that rock shelf before the path dropped from it into the trees.

And it appeared that he was an excellent shot, too good by half. Could he command a view of the lower meadows from his perch? And would a target crossing them be still within his range?

If they waited a little while the abrupt dusk would fall, and make it easier to move unseen; but easier for their enemy as well as for them. And in that same little while he could be down in the valley, if he knew enough to be sure who they were and where they must make for, and slicing diagonally across rough ground to get to the meadows before them and cut them off there.

Dominic licked sweat from his lip, and hung irresolute for a moment. The slanting shaft of sunlight, narrower and narrower every moment, had begun to tilt steadily now. The globule of brightness where it struck the far side of the window-frame was climbing upwards, accelerating all the time. He understood; the sun had reached the point of dropping behind the crests, and when the last sliver of orange-red vanished it would suddenly be half-dark. If there was going to be one moment when it would be safe to run across the shelf of rock and into the trees, that would be the moment. The valley dusk fell like a stone; even eyes braced and trained to watch steadily must be blind for a second or two.

He looked down at Tossa, coiled in the dust of the floor and watching him unwaveringly. She had on a heather tweed skirt that could vanish against almost any indeterminate background, but her sweater was cream-coloured. Dominic peeled off his dark-red pullover, and tossed it across to her.

'Put this on. And for God's sake do just what I tell you, and don't give me an argument. We've got to get out of here intact, that's all that matters.'

She looked at the dead man, and said faintly: 'We can't leave him here like this.'

'Don't be an idiot! We can't take him with us, and if we get knocked off ourselves we can't even report his death. Do as I tell you. Put that pullover on, and get over to the door. Stay inside until I give you the word, and then run for the trees. And I mean *run*! And keep running. Stay in cover. When you come to the open bit, I hope it'll be dark enough to cover you, but run like a hare, anyway. Don't stop till you get home. I'll be following you.'

The globule of gold, redder and angrier now, was halfway up the window-frame, and gliding upwards always a shade more rapidly. Tossa scrambled into the dark pullover, and slid like a cat along the flagstones, but towards him, not away from him. Before he knew what she was about she was on her feet close to him, trembling against his shoulder.

He turned on her furiously. 'Get the hell over to the door, I told you! . . .'

He broke off there, confounded. In the half-darkness her soiled, strained face was only inches from his own, and not fixed in ill-judged obstinacy, as he had expected, but utterly grave and calm. It was as if he had never seen her eyes fully alive and conscious before, because what she was looking at now was the intimate prospect of death.

'Yes, I'm going,' she said placatingly, and leaned forward suddenly the last few inches, stretching on tip-toe. Her mouth touched his hesitantly, fixed and clung for a staggering instant. 'Just in case!' she said in a rushing whisper, and she was gone, stooping and darting under the wasting finger of light, and crouching alert and still just within the doorway.

The circle of gold reached the top of the window-frame, and collapsing together like a punctured balloon, vanished. The glow went out, the dusk came down like a lid.

'Now!' urged Dominic hoarsely. '*Run!*'

She was off like a launched arrow. He heard the light, rapid flurry of her footsteps racing across the smooth rock, heard them recede, vibrating away into silence. He held his breath until the blood thundered in his ears, waiting for the shot, but it didn't come. She was away safely, she hadn't been seen.

His knees shook under him with relief and reaction. He clung to the edge of the window and leaned his forehead against the chilly, flaking whitewash of the wall for a moment. Now give her time, don't follow her too soon, in case *he* makes some move to case the chapel more closely. Because he must be wondering desperately how successful he's been, whether this poor devil's mouth is securely closed, and whether it was closed in time. There must be no more disturbances, here round the chapel, until Tossa's clear away and safely out of it.

He laid the back of his hand against his lips, carefully and wonderingly, pressing the lingering warmth and stupefaction of her kiss more intimately into his flesh. It would be a mean thing, as well as a stupid one, to attach too much significance to it. She'd kissed Mirek when he left them. Dominic was beginning to understand that action of hers very well now;

it was an act of atonement for the distrust she had felt of Mirek's disinterested kindness. And she'd kissed him now out of gratitude just for his being there, and as a symbol of human solidarity, in the face of the threat to their lives. And that was all. An impulse, like the other one, because she was not very articulate, even if there'd been time for words.

Five minutes, at least, before he ought to move to follow her, and nothing now he could do, except watch that darkening expanse of mountain-side across the valley, and listen with strained ears for any sound. She would be among the rocks now, near the edge of the meadows. Thank God she could run like a deer. And the man with the gun was half a mile away, even as the crow flies, and nearer a mile on the ground. Out of his sight was out of his reach.

But what had she meant by: 'Just in case!'? The words penetrated to his brain only now, and shook him with a new astonishment, and a new and illuminating recollection of her face, half out of focus because of its nearness, reaching up to his. He had never seen her utterly relaxed and at rest until that moment; as though she had only just seen clearly what it was all about, and what was of value in it, and what of no value, and dropped all the non-essentials, like worrying about her own conscience, to concentrate on what really mattered. And kissed you, he said to himself sardonically. My boy, you fancy yourself!

Detail was lost now in a dimness which was not yet dark – the afterglow was something for which he hadn't, in fact, made sufficient allowance – but which did confuse vision over any distance. The five minutes were up, surely he could risk leaving now. If he attracted notice, at least she was clear of it, there was one safely away to raise the alarm. And since Tossa had crossed the open space without producing any reaction, the odds were that his original calculations had been accurate, and that whole shelf of rock before the doorway was out of the murderer's range. No harm, though, in making a run for it.

He stepped wincingly round the body stretched on the dusty floor, and for a moment the thought of leaving him here alone was almost unbearable. Death is lonely enough in any case. He had never seen it quite so close before, and never so crudely, only in its tamed and mitigated state, ringed with rites and sympathisers. Dominic stood shivering for a moment in his thin sweater-shirt, irresolute over the dead man, and then turned his head aside with determination, and made for the door. The only thing he could do for this poor wretch was not to be done here. He slid round the leaning door, stepped out gingerly on to the rock, and ran.

Half-way across the open space a stone rolled under his foot, and brought him down in a heavy fall, knocking the breath out of him. The noise seemed enormous, and set echoes rolling from side to side of the valley. He lay half-dazed, but already groping forward with his hands to thrust himself to his feet again; and suddenly a second sharp, dry crack sent sharper echoes hiccuping down the rocks, and something hit the ground close beside his right ear with a horrid leaden plunk and a sharp, protesting whine.

Every nerve in him curled wiltingly in upon itself, struggling to make him smaller and less vulnerable. Every particle of energy he had left in him gathered him to his feet in a wild leap, and hurled him forward towards the shelter of the trees. He knew very little about guns, but he knew the whimper of a bullet ricocheting. Not an inch of this shelf was out of the marksman's range now, and a racket like that fall, to a true ear, made almost as fair a target as a proper sighting. He *had* changed his position, but he was still up there on the hillside, he'd merely worked his way down-valley on the same level, to cover the doorway. By the only route, then – by the traverse path across the cliff, from which Terrell had fallen to his death.

Dominic reached the edge of the trees and half-fell into their shelter; and something flew out of the green shade to meet him, and folded thin, straining arms about him with a sob of thankfulness and desperation. The shock fetched a gasp out of him. He clasped the embracing fury tightly, and hissed at her in confused rage:

'What the hell are you doing here? I told you to keep going!'

'Without you?' Tossa spat back at him indignantly. 'What do you take me for?'

'Well, come on now, damn you! Get out of here, quick!'

'My God, I like that! I've only been waiting for *you*!'

'Shut up, just *run*!'

He caught her by the wrist, and dragged her at a frenzied, slithering run down the steep path. Speed was better than silence, now that they were in cover. Whatever noise they made they could out-distance, and the man with the gun, whatever his powers as a shot, had just demonstrated that he was still up there on the opposite mountainside, and could not possibly out-run them on their way down to the hut. Behind them they heard the sound of stones rolling, the faint slither of scree. Perhaps the spent bullet had started a minor slide. They didn't stop to investigate. Hand in hand they ran, untidily, blindly, bruising themselves against rocks, slipping on the glossy grass, until they reached the main path, and settled down to a steady, careful run. Across the meadows they could race silently, the thick turf swallowing their footsteps; and beyond, through the broken heathland, they relaxed their speed a little, feeling themselves almost safe, almost home.

'Dominic – he didn't hit you? You're sure?'

'No, I'm all right, he didn't hit me. But, Tossa . . .'

'Yes?'

'We can't keep quiet now. This is murder. You'll have to tell everything you know.'

'I can't! You don't understand.'

'You'll *have* to tell how this happened. If you don't I shall. And it was to him you promised not to tell anything – wasn't it?'

'Yes,' she said faintly. They were in the darkness of the forest now, above the brook, and they had to go gently, partly because they found themselves suddenly very tired and unsteady, partly because the path was narrow and the night deeper here. He folded his arm about her, and they moved together, warmly supporting each other.

'He's dead, Tossa. It's for him you have to tell the truth, now. That releases you.'

'No,' she said, shivering. 'You don't understand. I'll tell *you* but I can't tell people here. I can't! You'll see that I can't.'

'Never mind, don't worry now. Let's get home and find the twins. We'll talk it over, we'll see how best to handle it.'

Touching each other in the darkness, holding fast to each other where the path was tricky, confounded them almost more than their momentary head-on encounter with death. They were close to the deep green basin where the hut lay; the lighted windows shone upon them through the trees. Hand in hand they stumbled across the open grass towards the door of the bar.

Seven

The Man who wasn't In Charge

The first look at their soiled and shaken faces effectively cut off all questions and exclamations, shocking the twins into silence. The significant jerk of Dominic's head drew them after him up the stairs, unresisting, to an urgent council of war.

In the girls' bedroom, secure from surprise at the far end of a creaky wooden corridor, Tossa sat down on her bed and unburdened herself of the whole story at last: how she had blundered into the affair by accident, through reading Robert Welland's note left for her mother, how he had come back to reclaim it, too late, and made the best of it by telling her everything, and so putting her under the sacred obligation to keep it secret. She told them everything she had learned about Karol Alda, why he must be somewhere here, close at hand, and why it was almost certain that he was a double murderer. The newspaper photograph, the half-sheet of music paper, passed from hand to hand in a stunned silence.

'I believe my step-father recognised this handwriting as soon as he saw it in the Hotel Sokolie. He must have seen it regularly when they were both at the Marrion Institute, and it was his job not to forget things like that. I think he followed Ivo Martínek over here to look for Alda. I don't suggest the Martíneks know anything much, or even that they're particularly close to Alda. This place is an inn, the local people do use it, and that piece of paper could easily have been left here some time when Alda was here, maybe sitting over a beer, playing with an idea he had in his mind. He's a musician, too, it seems he was a very good one. He didn't get this right. He tore off the false start and left it on the table. Maybe Ivo just picked it up out of curiosity, and felt interested enough to pocket it. Something like that, something quite casual and harmless, because he didn't think twice about making use of it when he wanted a paper to score their card game, and he didn't bother to take it away with him afterwards. But it did prove Alda was somewhere in the vicinity of the Martíneks, known and accepted there. So my step-father came to look for him here. And he was killed here, up the valley where we went the first day. Opposite the place where Mr Welland was killed tonight.'

'And for the same reason,' said Toddy positively, his face sharp with excitement. 'Because they both located him! Isn't it plain? This chap Welland was to try to trace him, and report back to the Institute through the embassy in Prague. And he'd done it! He was in Zilina when we came through, and saw you there, and you tipped him off where he could find you. And three days later he turns up on the telephone, asking you to meet him. He'd found him! He'd been to Prague to send the notification they'd agreed on, and he came back here to keep an eye on event in the meantime. *You* were a complication.'

'My guess is,' said Christine, gnawing her knuckles furiously, 'he was worried about you turning up on the scene. He'd been thinking it over, and he wanted to have a word with you tonight to get you to lay off. Maybe to tell you whatever he knew, as the best way of satisfying you. But certainly to warn you not to start anything.'

'Whatever he had to say to me,' said Tossa, 'couldn't be said over the telephone. Maybe he was going to tell me where Alda was, maybe he wasn't. What difference does it make now? Whoever killed him was taking no chances. And now what do we do?'

'We report the death,' said Dominic forcibly, 'and co-operate with the police.'

Toddy gaped between the fists that clutched his disordered hair. 'Are you crazy? Can't you see this is a hand we've got to play *against* the police? Against the Czech authorities, against every soul round us? Can't you see there's a little matter of national security involved? Tossa's told you, the affair's top secret, and big enough to kill for. She's pledged to keep everything to do with the Marrion Institute secret, and that goes for us, too.'

'You're seeing this as a real-life spy thriller,' said Dominic without heat. 'I'm seeing it as a murder. Murder is something I don't play spy games with. Odd as it may seem to you, I believe that the professional police everywhere are dead against murder, and when they run up against it their instinct is quite simply to try to find out who did it, and get him. If you ask me, do I think that goes in a Communist country, yes, I think it goes in every country, and always will, as long as people are people and professionals are professionals. It's a queer thing about police – by and large, in spite of a few slip-ups, *they don't like crime.* And I come from a police family, and I don't like it, either. So either *we* go to the police or *I* go to the police. Whichever way you like.'

'*We go*,' said Tossa, faintly but finally. 'We have to, I do see that. We owe it to him *and* to them. Only I can't tell everything, I can't tell about the Institute, or anything that's mixed up with security. You may be right about the police, Dom, they may be absolutely on the level. Only I'm bound, don't you see that? I'm not entitled to take any risks, it isn't for me to judge.'

'You can tell them about the shooting,' urged Christine, 'without mentioning the background. You could say you went up the valley for a walk after dinner, and heard the shot, and found him in there. There's no need to say you went there to meet him.'

'That's it! You'd be giving them everything that could possibly help them over Welland's murder. *If* they're genuinely interested in solving it,' said Toddy sceptically, 'though that's a laugh, if ever I heard one. You were out together, you two, you blundered into it without meaning to. That's all you need say.'

'Even just to cover ourselves,' admitted Christine, frowning over the perilous tangle that confronted them, 'we'd have to go that far. But there's no need to go any further. What are we supposed to do, go there and say: "Please, some of your confidential agents have wiped out two of ours because they got too near to something hot. Do something about it!"? I like to think I'm honest, but my God, I don't take it to those lengths!'

'And supposing there's nothing whatever official or approved about this murder?' demanded Dominic. 'Supposing it's a completely private act, and the police are just as interested in catching the criminal as you are. You think it'll make no difference to their chances, our keeping back nine-tenths of the facts?'

'You can't,' protested Toddy savagely, 'be as simple as you're acting!'

'Wish I could say the same for you, but apparently you can. All right, we can't drag the Institute into it, but we could still tell the truth about tonight, we could still say he telephoned Tossa and asked her to meet him, we could even say why – that she didn't feel satisfied about her step-father's death, and came here to see for herself, and Mr Welland was in her confidence and wanted to help her. Half of which,' said Dominic, scrubbing at his tired forehead, still pallid with dust from the white-washed wall of the chapel, 'they'll know already, and if you doubt that you're even simpler than I thought. But make up your minds, and let's get going. I'm for telling as much of the truth as we can.'

'And I'm for using our gumption and telling as little as possible.' Toddy set his jaw obstinately. 'Didn't you hear, there are plans of secret work involved, valuable stuff, dangerous stuff. Of course it's no private murder. You just heard the shot, and went in and found him. For God's sake, whose side are you on?'

'Christine?' appealed Dominic, ignoring that.

'I'm with Toddy,' said Christine, roused and belligerent. 'Let's face it, we're in enemy territory over this, we *can't* co-operate.'

Dominic looked down at Tossa's tormented face, and gently touched her hand. 'It's up to you, Tossa. Whatever you say, I'll go along with.'

She shook her head helplessly, and didn't look up; after a moment she said huskily: 'I can't! I'd like to. I'd much rather, but I can't. I'm with them, Dominic.'

'All right, we'll do it that way.' He looked at Toddy, who alone had enough German to be sure of communicating, where none of them had Slovak, and English was somewhat less common an accomplishment than in Prague. 'Will you telephone, please, Tod? You'll have to ask Dana which is the right place to call, but all you have to get over is that we're reporting a death, and where they'll find him, and that we're coming in with our statements. We shall have to, so why not now? Find out where we should check in, and I'll be getting the van out.'

Liptovsky Pavol, St-Paul-in-Liptov, turned out to be a small town of perhaps five short streets, all of them converging on the vast cobbled square in front of the church. Two of the streets, which were a yard or so wider than the others, conducted the main road in and out of this imposing open space, which in fact was not a square at all, but a long wedge-shape, inadequately lit, completely deserted except for two or three parked Skodas and an ingenious home-made body on a wartime Volkswagen chassis, and scalloped on both long sides with deep arcades, beneath which the van's lights fingered out the glass of shop windows. The short side of the wedge was the municipal buildings, the only twentieth-century block in sight; and in the rear quarters of this town hall there were two rooms which did duty as the police office for the sub-district.

It was past ten o'clock by the time they found it, and locked the van on the cobbles outside; but they were not surprised to see the door open and the lights on inside the dingy passage-way, since their telephone call would obviously have alerted the local force, and presumably sent someone clambering and cursing out to the chapel in Zbojská Dolina long before this. In such a quiet little place the police office would surely be closed and abandoned around five o'clock, at normal times.

They had agreed on the way that Dominic was to do the talking. Of the two who had been on the scene, presumably the Slovaks would expect the man to act as spokesman, the girl to confirm what he said. Even such small points affect one's chance of being believed without question.

The passage was vaulted, with peeling plaster, and belonged to some older building, now largely replaced. There was an open door at one side of it, and a steep wooden staircase within. Dominic climbed it slowly, his throat dry and constricted, every step carrying him deeper into a strange land. What if Toddy was right? What if the damned cold war was still almost at freezing point, and he was in enemy territory? He had felt nothing but friends round him here, but suddenly he was a little afraid. 'He speaks English,' Toddy had reported, coming back confounded from his telephone call. '*Good* English!' It had frightened Toddy more than anything else, when it ought to have reassured him and made things easier; and it was frightening Dominic now. With an interpreter you have also a protective barrier, you can plead misunderstanding, you can be inarticulate and still credible. With this man he was deprived of any insulation. But at least he was warned.

'*Pod'te d'alej*!' said a leisurely, rumbling bass voice, in reply to his tentative knock on the door at the top of the stairs. And next, in the same easy tone: 'Come in, please!'

He spoke excellent English, almost unaccented. Learned from records? Certainly not only from the book.

Dominic opened the door and went in, the other three filing closely behind him. Toddy closed the door after them. The room was small, twelve by twelve at most, and bare, furnished with a couple of chairs in front of the desk, and two more behind, a battered typewriter, two tall, narrow filing cabinets, and a small, iron stove. The walls were painted a dull cream, and scaling here and there. Behind the desk somebody had used the wall as a convenient tablet for notes, calculations, and pencilled doodlings, perhaps while hanging on the telephone, or filling in very dull duty hours with nothing to do. It would be very surprising indeed if there was much crime in Liptovsky Pavol.

'*Nadporucík* Ondrejov?' asked Dominic with aching care. To the best of his knowledge the correct translation of the rank was 'lieutenant,' like an army rank, but he didn't feel certain enough of his facts to use it. He preferred at least to pay his host the compliment of attempting to pronounce his Czechoslovak title.

The elderly countryman behind the desk took his broad behind off the office chair, and rose to straddle the floor like a farmer his lands.

'Come in, come in! Yes, I'm Ondrejov.' The younger man who had been sitting on the rear corner of the desk rose, flicked an eyebrow at his superior, intercepted and recorded the answering twitch of the grey, bushy head, and walked away into the inner room, closing the door gently after him 'Please, Miss Barber, take this chair. Miss Mather? Be seated, please! And you are Mr Felse? Yes, we were waiting for you. It was good of you, it was right, to notify us at once.'

He might have been sixty, or five years less or more, there was no dating him. He had probably looked much the same for ten years, and wouldn't change for twenty more. Grey at fifty, and still sporting curly, crisp grey hair at eighty-five. No, ninety, he looked remarkably durable. He was not the long, rangy Slovak shape, with great, elegant, shapely bones, but short and sturdy and running to flesh, broad-beamed and broad-breasted, broad-cheeked and wide-eyed, broad-jowled and stubble-chinned, with a bright, beery face. Perhaps of mixed blood, the most inscrutable product in the country, looking now Czech, now Slovak, almost at will. In the high-coloured face the blue, bright, knowing eyes were clear as sapphires, and limpid as spring-water. He was in his shirt-sleeves, his tie comfortably loosened round a bull-neck. Dominic felt better; this was what Mirek Zachar, of fond memory, would have called a 'country uncle.' He warned himself vainly that what he felt might be only a false security. He was so tired that it would be dangerous to relax.

'We were grateful for your call. You may rest assured that everything is in hand. Now, naturally, I should like to hear the story directly from you. Please, Mr Felse! You may speak quite freely. For the moment this is not official.' He smiled benevolently into Dominic's tired, drawn face. 'You are wondering about my English. It is not so strange. People of my generation here learned English because we had relatives in England or in America. In America especially. We learned English in the hope of going there some day to join them. I was there for five years, before the war, and now I keep up my English from books. My children have forgotten it, my grandchildren do not learn it. They speak excellent Russian, and I am out of date. Times change. It is not matter for regret, only for interest. But I like to use my assets. You need not be afraid that I shall not understand you. Please, speak!'

They were as tongue-tied, after that, as if they had really been confronted with the grim, smooth police official of cold-war fiction, and a good deal more at a loss. Nevertheless, Dominic set to work and ploughed his way doggedly through their agreed story, disliking it more with every word, but making a good job of it.

'Miss Barber and I were out for a walk this evening, after dinner. We ate rather early, I think it must have been about twenty minutes to eight when we went out. We took the road up the valley, and when we got near that small chapel on the hillside there we thought we'd go up and have a look at it.'

Lieutenant Ondrejov, a model listener, did not once interrupt, not even with an intelligent and helpful question, but neither did he leave the narration to plod along unencouraged. His round, good-humoured face was encouragement itself, he helped the story along with an occasional sympathetic nod of understanding. They could hardly expect much excitement from him, since he knew already the crucial fact of the murder; but no one could complain that he wasn't responsive. At the end of it he leaned back in his chair with a gusty sigh, and looked from one to another of them thoughtfully, scrubbing at his bristly chin with thick, adroit finger-tips.

'I understand, yes. You went up the valley together, you and Miss Barber?'

'Yes,' said Tossa gruffly, lifting the lie from Dominic's shoulders this time. It was the first time Ondrejov had heard that odd, touching little voice of hers, and it made him cock an eye at her with twinkling interest, his grey head on one side.

'And you were together when you heard the shot, and entered the chapel?'

'Yes.'

'Tell me, did you know this man at all? The dead man?'

'Not know him, exactly. But we'd seen him once before,' said Dominic firmly, 'when we were driving through into Slovakia.'

'In the hotel at Zilina?' suggested Ondrejov affably.

Four hearts lurched sickeningly towards churning stomachs. He had tugged the ground out from under them like a mat, and the fall, though they sat still and kept their faces obstinately blank, knocked the breath out of them, and the invention with it. He was guessing, with preternatural accuracy, but guessing. He *couldn't* know. They stared polite, patient, uncomprehending enquiry.

'In a hotel somewhere on the way,' said Dominic. 'We came through so many places, I forget names.'

Ondrejov leaned over his desk and wagged a finger at them admonishingly. 'Children, children, never try to deceive the old ones. It may be a long time since they were boys, but they have had two refresher courses with their sons and grandsons, and that is much more dangerous. Now, do you want to tell me anything more? Or to think again about what you have already told me?'

Dominic said: 'No!' for all of them. What else was there to say? However disastrously, they were committed now.

'Good! Then let us see if we can contribute something, too.' He tilted his chair back, and reached behind him to turn the handle of the inner door. '*Mirku! Pod' sem*!'

Into the room, as fresh and pink and blond as ever, walked Miroslav Zachar, and took up station solidly at his chief's left elbow, confronting with a heightened colour but a placid and purposeful face his four erstwhile friends.

'Mirek,' said Ondrejov heartily, slapping the young man resoundingly on the back, 'I think you should explain to our young guests exactly what you are doing here. Tell them everything, we have nothing to hide from them.'

'I am here,' said Mirek simply, 'because I discovered the body of Robert Welland this evening. I reported it by telephone from the nearest connected house, which happens to be over the north wall there, in another valley – you would not know the path. Then I waited with the body until the detail came out there, and returned here to report fully in person.'

'Perhaps,' suggested Ondrejov, 'it would help if you explained in full your connection with the affairs of these young people, and how you came to be on the scene tonight. From the beginning!'

'Certainly!' He looked from face to face round the four of them, looked them all fully and firmly in the eyes. Why not? He had nothing to be ashamed of, even if he had been cheated and startled into feeling shame when Tossa kissed him by way of apologising for reservations she should, instead, have respected and re-examined. He had had a job to do, and he knew he was good at it. Dominic, a policeman's son, gave him the ghost of a smile; they were all giving him their fixed and painful attention.

'I was detailed to pick up your party at the frontier, escort you as far as I could, and continue to keep an eye on your movements and your welfare afterwards.'

Toddy, hackles erected, demanded: 'Why?'

'Why? Naturally Miss Barber, like other visitors, was obliged to apply for a visa. With the recent events in mind, and certain diplomatic complications always possible, our police in Bratislava were hardly likely to have left Mr Terrell's background and circumstances unexamined. They knew that he had married a widow named Barber, with one daughter, now a student at Oxford. The connection was not beyond their ability. They therefore felt that it would be well to keep a protective eye on Miss Barber as long as she remained in this country, for her own good as well as ours. We do not want trouble. There seemed reason to suppose that Miss Barber and her friends were making for the Tatras. I was born here, I used to serve under Lieutenant Ondrejov before I transferred to the plain-clothes branch. As a local man, with good English, and as you see, quite well able to look like a student, I was seconded to this duty.'

'Then I suppose this means you've been spying on us ever since you pretended to leave us,' said Toddy bitterly.

'I have been carrying out my assignment. Without, I hope, interfering with your enjoyment. This evening I was in cover on the hillside above the chapel, near the crest. There is a place there from which you can cover, with glasses, almost the whole length of the valley. I have often used it. You were within view for perhaps half of your walk, and hidden from me only when among the trees. I saw you come to the chapel.'

'And were they together?' murmured Ondrejov innocently.

Into the momentary well of silence, while the four of them held their breath, Mirek dropped his: 'No,' very gently, but it fell like a stone.

'Did they enter the chapel together?'

'No. Miss Barber came first. It was clear from her manner that she thought she was alone, but I had already seen Mr Felse carefully following her. She climbed to the rock shelf, and walked straight to the door of the chapel. I had her within sight until the last few yards. The doorway itself was out of my sight. Mr Felse remained in the shadow of the trees, and did not attempt at first to follow her.'

'And then?'

'Then there was a shot. It came perhaps five or six seconds after Miss Barber passed out of my sight and into the chapel. I could not determine from which direction the sound came, it is very difficult in such an enclosed and complex place. It *could* have been fired from outside, even from some distance. But my immediate impression was that it came from within the chapel itself.'

Tossa's hands, linked in her lap, tightened convulsively, but she made no sound. It was Toddy who flared in alarm and anger: 'That's a lie! You're trying to frighten her! You know it isn't true!'

'Please, Mr Mather! Go on, Mirek, what next?'

'Mr Felse dropped to the ground and scrambled across to the doorway. They were in there for several minutes together. I was raking the valley for any signs of movement, but I found nothing. I therefore began to work my way down the slope towards the chapel, but as you know, it is rather a risky field of scree there, one must go cautiously. While I was still well above, I saw Miss Barber dart away from the doorway and run down the path among the trees. After perhaps five more minutes Mr Felse followed her. It was then beginning to be dusk. He had a fall on the rocks as he ran across the open ground. It was then I saw that Miss Barber had waited for him, just within the trees.'

'And by the time you got down there?'

'They were both well away. And when I entered the chapel I found Mr Welland's body there.'

'Mr Felse stayed behind, perhaps, just long enough to

go through the dead man's pockets?' suggested Ondrejov placidly.

Involuntarily Dominic let out an audible gasp of disgust, remembering that the idea had never even occurred to him. And Miroslav smiled.

'I don't suggest he did do so, but the time would have been sufficient, yes.'

'And did you hear a second shot, as Mr Felse says? When he fell?'

'I did not hear one, no. Admittedly I was coming rather quickly down the scree, and I was concentrating on my foot-work, as well as making a considerable noise of my own.'

Tossa raised her heavy eyelids just long enough to flash a glance at Dominic, and intercept his startled glance at her. They had heard the scree shifting, and never dreamed of looking up there for a witness.

'One more point,' said Ondrejov comfortably, stretching his broad shoulders back until the chair creaked. 'The encounter at Zilina. Did it appear to you that Miss Barber was acquainted with Mr Welland?'

'Yes, quite certainly she was.'

'And did she, then, behave naturally when meeting him there?'

'No, she affected not to know him. As I think her friends really did not. But she took occasion to pass a message to him, and he almost certainly passed one back to her.'

'Such as this folded scrap of paper, perhaps?'

Ondrejov produced it gently from his pocket, unfolded it with deliberation, and read aloud in his amiable rolling bass: 'I shall be at the Riavka hut. Please contact me!' He looked up over Tossa's note with twinkling blue eyes narrowed in an indulgent smile. 'If our young and chivalrous friend did go through the victim's pockets, he didn't make a very good job of it, it seems. Zachar has had more practice, of course,' he added by way of consolation to Dominic, and folded the paper carefully away again.

'So it seems we have a somewhat changed picture now. You are sure there is nothing you wish to add or alter?' Where would have been the point? All their lies were already demolished, and to think up new ones now would be worse than useless. They were silent, watching him with closed faces and apprehensive eyes. 'In that case you must see my predicament. And you should also take into consideration the fact that as yet the cartridge-shell has not been found, and since the bullet is still embedded in the dead man's skull, and only an autopsy can recover it for examination, so far as we know up to now it could as well be from a pistol as a rifle. Couldn't it?'

Tossa was the last to see where he was leading her. She stared from behind these serried facts as through bars, and shook her head helplessly, trying to shake away the sense of nightmare that oppressed her.

'None of us has a gun, or ever had one,' said Dominic quickly and quietly. 'Certainly Tossa couldn't have had one on her last night. I was following her every step of the way.'

'But at a safe distance. And certainly is a large word. A small pistol is not so difficult to conceal.'

'She was never out of my sight for more than a few seconds.'

'The few seconds when the shot was fired.'

'But this is fantastic!' cried Toddy wildly. 'For God's sake, how could she cart a gun about with her without my sister seeing it, sooner or later? How could she get it into the country?'

'Oh, come, Mr Mather! Are you really suggesting our frontier staff are so thorough? Did they even open your cases at Rozvadov?'

Tossa put up her hands wonderingly, and touched her throbbing temples and drawn cheeks as though to satisfy herself that she was still in her own day-to-day flesh, and not astray in a bewildering and terrifying dream.

'But I've never even touched a gun, not once in my life. If you really believe I had one, then where is it now? What did I do with it?' Her voice was so heavy that she could hardly lift the syllables. Like her eyelids, like her heart.

'Ah, that is an open question. The obvious thing to do with it would be to toss it out of the window immediately. But the valley is large enough, and the dusk by then was deep enough, to make it a very open question indeed. So no doubt you will realise, my dear Miss Barber, why I am obliged to keep you, for the present, in custody.'

The next ten minutes were confused, noisy and angry. Tossa sat mute and numb in the middle of the storm, too tired to distinguish voices any more, too disoriented to know friends from foe, too deeply aware of having lied, and forced Dominic to lie, to put up any fight for her own liberty. Christine had an arm clasped tightly about her shoulders, and was adding a soprano descant to Toddy's spirited impersonation of an Englishman at bay. Toddy raved about police states, conspiracies and frame-ups, and threatened everything from diplomatic intervention to gunboats. In the heart of her desperate confusion and solitude Tossa remembered inconsequently that Czechoslovakia had no coastline, and laughed, genuinely laughed, but no one noticed except, perhaps, Ondrejov, who noticed everything, whether he acknowledged it or not. He looked like a good-humoured, clever peasant, and he sat here behind his desk manipulating them all. She suspected that he was very much enjoying Toddy. There couldn't be much theatre in Liptovsky Pavol.

'Now, now, my dear boy, I guarantee that Miss Barber shall be well treated, and we'll take every care of her. And since it's too late now for the rest of you to think of going back to Zbojská Dolina tonight, I'll make arrangements for beds for all of you, and we'll call the hut and tell the Martíneks you're staying here.'

'That isn't good enough! You know very well that you've no right to detain Miss Barber. As the person in charge of this case, *you* will be held responsible.'

Pale with rage, Toddy stood between Tossa and her captors, his nostrils pinched and blue with desperation, as gallant as he was ineffective. Dominic, deep sunk in his own silence and doubt, stared hard at Ondrejov, and wished he could read his mind, but it was impenetrable. Did he really suspect Tossa? Or had he quite another motive for this move? He swung in an agony of indecision between two opinions. The one thing of which he was in no doubt at all was that it was his job to get Tossa out of this. Toddy could make as much fuss and noise as he liked, it wouldn't be done that way. If Ondrejov had been what Toddy claimed he was, he would have laid Toddy flat long before this. And let no one think he couldn't do it single-handed, as old as he was!

'In charge? *I* in *charge* of the case?' Ondrejov's blue, bright eyes widened as guilelessly as a child's. 'You think such cases as this are left to the uniformed branch here? No, no, I am waiting at this moment for the plain-clothes people to arrive from Bratislava. I am responsible to them. That is why I am compelled to hold you available, you see, *my* field of action is strictly limited. The men from Scotland Yard,' he said, pleased with this flight of fancy, 'will be here in a matter of a few hours. You may put your objections and make your statement to them.'

'Then at least,' said Toddy valiantly, hunted into a corner but still game, 'I demand that the British Embassy in Prague shall be contacted at once, and informed that Miss Barber is being held on suspicion.'

'The British Embassy,' said Ondrejov, dwelling upon the luscious syllables with sensuous pleasure, 'has already been informed. As a matter of courtesy, you understand, Mr Welland being a British national and a member of their staff. They will also be informed that Miss Barber is here, and may be held on suspicion of murder. By tomorrow morning, no doubt, someone will be flying in to take care of her interests, and I can assure you I shall make no objections.'

They fell back and studied him afresh in silence, with something of the embarrassment of people who have flung their full weight against an unlatched door and fallen flat on their faces, but with a residue of distrust, too. Did he mean it? It appeared that he did, for he wasn't even troubling to lay any great emphasis on the correctness of his proceedings; but what he intended should follow from them was another matter. Perhaps he was simply covering himself, and making sure that all the awkward decisions should be left to his superiors, when they came. That was human and credible enough, in any country, in any force.

'When it comes to the point,' said Dominic, on the heels of the dubious silence, 'Tossa has nothing to be afraid of.' He was curiously in doubt, himself, whether he was speaking for her or for Ondrejov. 'As soon as the bullet's recovered it will clear her completely. Because it will be a rifle bullet.'

'Now that,' said Ondrejov, fixing him with a bright and calculating eye, 'is a sensible observation. Tomorrow,' he went on briskly, dropping the pretence of harmlessness as blithely as he would have dropped a cigarette-end, 'I suggest you may all prefer to move to the hotel here, and remain near Miss Barber. When you have satisfied youselves that there are people present to take care of her interests, perhaps *you*, Mr Felse . . .' The blue eye dissected him again, with analytical detachment and interest. '. . . will be so good as to drive your van back to Zbojská Dolina to settle the bill and collect your luggage.'

He still sounded like a country uncle, but one you wouldn't care to fool with; and there was no mistaking that this was an order.

'It will be interesting,' said Ondrejov meditatively, 'to see who does turn up to take the responsibility for Miss Barber.' He smiled into the inscrutable distances of his own thoughts, which were certainly more devious than his bucolic appearance suggested, and repeated pleasurably: 'Very interesting!'

Eight

The Men who came to the Rescue

The man in charge arrived in Liptovsky Pavol at about four o'clock in the morning, having preferred to go directly to the scene of the crime and make his own observations on the spot, before taking over the office end of affairs from the local force. He brought with him a very smart police car from Bratislava, a driver, and two subordinates, which entourage was in itself a more signal recognition of Robert Welland's V.I.P. status than he had ever received in his lifetime.

The officer's name was Kriebel, and he looked like an alert, confident, athletic schoolmaster. He was two steps above Ondrejov in rank, six inches taller, and twenty-five years younger, and he weighed up his man in one long, careful glance, and then enthroned himself casually on a corner of the desk, and swung his legs. This move, which established their relationship while keeping it informal, also deprived Ondrejov of his own favourite chair without putting it into use for his superior officer. To Kriebel a tactful gesture, it seemed to Ondrejov merely silly. But he was adroit at handling young men who were ambitious, sensitive of their rights and advantages in the presence of the old and stagnating, and considered themselves to be handling him. This one wouldn't give him much trouble. He had never wanted to move into the plain-clothes branch himself, and not only because it would have meant moving from Pavol. He knew where his talents lay.

He planted himself squarely on his two sturdy legs, and made his report reasonably fully. The young people? They were all put to bed long before this, the girl Barber in the cell downstairs, the others at Pavol's single small hotel. Had they made formal statements? No, he had preferred to wait for the arrival of the detectives from Bratislava. He contrived to suggest that he had been a little nervous of pressing four English students very far, with the possibility of an international incident obviously hanging over them like a storm-cloud. He outlined the evidence against

Tossa, colouring it brightly and then slightly deprecating its brightness, even suggesting that it was not enough of a case to justify holding her. Kriebel, listening and frowning a little, found the tone too patronising on one hand and too timid on the other, and came to the considered conclusion that the girl should be held.

The body of Robert Welland was by then being manhandled from the chapel towards the ambulance that waited for it at the Riavka hut, on its way to Liptovský Mikuláš, where the experts were sleepily and crossly preparing its reception.

'And the other three?' asked Ondrejov, with hunched shoulders and dissenting face. 'None of them can possibly have been involved in the actual killing, only the girl Barber had the opportunity. I take it there's no need to interfere with their plans? We can reach them at Zbojská Dolina whenever you want them, there's no particular advantage in keeping them here.'

'On the contrary, I think it's essential to have them under our eyes. We'd better fix them up here in the town, and keep them under surveillance, at least until we get the medical and laboratory reports. Then we'll know better what we're handling.'

All very well being correct and courteous with foreigners, but Kriebel carried the responsibility, and this was murder.

'As you think,' said Ondrejov austerely, with a face so blank that a duller man than Kriebel couldn't have failed to deduce what it was concealing. 'Then after you've seen them, I'd better send the young man Felse off with their van to bring their things from the Riavka, and settle them in here at the Slovan.'

'I should be glad if you would,' said Kriebel, his voice noticeably thinning as the woodenness of Ondrejov's face thickened.

'Certainly, Comrade Major, whatever you say.'

If you want a superior, half your age, to keep things rolling your way, there's nothing like persuading him that the idea was his in the first place, and that you cordially disapprove of it. Ondrejov wasn't going to have the slightest trouble with this one.

'By the way, Comrade Major, I've notified the British Embassy of the girl's situation. Since they're concerned in any case, the victim being one of their own men, I thought it wise to forestall any criticism on that head. I hope that's all right? It won't, of course, affect your handling of the case in the least,' he hastened to add, with a nice blend of flattery and malice.

It wouldn't now, at any rate. Ten ambassadors threatening all the professional reprisals in the world couldn't have made Kriebel release his hold of Tossa Barber, after that.

It was some hours more before the rescue party began to gather. Even Kriebel had to sleep, after driving some three hundred kilometres from the Slovak capital, and then putting in an hour and a half of intensive work in Zbojská Dolina; consequently the four enforced guests of the establishment were also, by native standards, allowed to lie late, though not, to judge by the look of them when they were finally assembled in the police office, to sleep late.

Only Tossa, once stretched out on the cot in her small, bare room, had collapsed out of the world as though hit on the head with a blackjack; it was her only way of escape from a load temporarily too much for her to carry or comprehend. They dragged her out of her refuge too soon, but at least she had been able to withdraw for a few hours into the utter darkness and indifference of irresponsibility.

She came back to her distorted and frightening world drunken and stunned with sleep, but calm. She was glad, in a way, that they had kept her segregated even from Christine; the load was hers, and sympathy and advice would only have confused her. As it was, though she hadn't spent one waking minute thinking about it, she had a very clear idea of what she had to do. Last night there had seemed no point in correcting her false story, since Mirek had effectively established what was false in it; now it seemed to her essential that she should tell it herself as fully as she could. There were still things she could not talk about; but to admit that she had felt unsatisfied about her step-father's death, and set out deliberately to investigate it herself, need not involve the Marrion Institute at all. No lies this time. Truth and nothing but truth, if not all the truth. It might not help her out of her mess, but it would do something to put her right with herself.

'I want to make a statement,' she said, when Ondrejov came to fetch her up to the office.

'So you shall soon, but not to me. And don't be in too big a hurry.' He looked her over with shrewd and thoughtful eyes. 'Finish your coffee, there's plenty of time.'

She shook her head; it seemed to her an odd attitude. 'The men from Scotland Yard came, then?' she said, with a pale, brief smile.

'They're not the only arrivals. There are three gentlemen her to get you out of trouble.'

'Three?' She was impressed and amused, in a sad and private way, even very slightly curious, but she didn't care to ask him questions; in her position it didn't seem to her that it would be the thing to do. 'I don't think they can,' she said, after a moment's rueful reflection. 'Not for a day or two, anyhow, not until your people have found the bullet.'

'No,' agreed Ondrejov smugly. 'I don't think they can.'

'Are the others all right? Shall I see them?'

'They're all right, and you'll see them.'

They were already in the outer office when he followed her up the narrow stairs and through the thick brown door. Swollen-eyed and uneasy after a wakeful night, they sat silent, waiting to be interviewed, the youngest detective keeping a cool eye on them from behind the desk. Their eyes lit at the sight of her, and Dominic came eagerly out of his chair; but before anything could be asked or answered the inner door opened, and Kriebel leaned out.

'In here, please, Miss Barber.'

She turned one quick glance in Dominic's direction, and for an instant they stared helplessly at each other. Then she went on obediently into the inner room, and Ondrejov followed her in and closed the door.

'Miss Barber, my name is Kriebel. I am in charge of this investigation. Please sit down!'

The chair that had been placed for her was in front of a large table, and in the full light from the window. Beyond, the rest of the room seemed dim by comparison, and it was larger than the shabby little outer office, obstinately and characteristically preferred by Ondrejov, so that she did not immediately sort out the strangers from the plain-clothes men among those present. Her tired but competent mind could deal with only one thing at a time.

'I should like to make a statement.'

That brought the rescuers forward to declare themselves at once, as if she had sounded an urgent alarm. Three of them, just as Ondrejov had said, all suddenly revealed as English the moment they moved and drew her eyes to them. English with the ludicrous, staggering Englishness which, as Toddy had rightly observed, is never even detectable at home. And all of them willing her to silence and delay.

'Miss Barber, I advise you to think carefully about your position, and do nothing in haste.'

'We are here to take care of your interests, Miss Barber.'

The first of them was a middle-aged gentleman of immaculate appearance, smooth-faced, grey-haired, rounded and agile, with a lawyer's cagey face; the second a long, loose-limbed young man with a handsome, superior countenance, like a clever horse or a county dowager, and an alert and impudent eye. The third, who had stayed where he was and said nothing so far, looked at once the most truly concerned and the most likely to be effective. He was perhaps even more English than the others, but in a way which looked more at home here, with the fields only a stone's throw away, and the crests of the mountains bright in the distance outside the window. Almost elderly, tall and rather thin, with dark hair silvered at the temples, and a good-looking, well-preserved face that could have belonged equally appropriately to a retired military man or a high civil servant. He had on Bedford cords and a tweed jacket worn into the baggy shapes of comfort, with leather patches at the elbows, the sort of jacket that should be accompanied by a floppy tweed hat to match, preferably with flies stuck round it.

She had never seen any of them before in her life; but of course, they had to take responsibility for all sorts of strays like herself. No wonder the one with the lawyer's face, for all his smooth expression of reassurance, fixed his snapping legal eyes on her as if he detested her. As if it wasn't enough to have an English attaché shot, an English student had to get herself arrested on suspicion of having shot him!

'I beg your pardon, Major Kriebel! Miss Barber should know her rights, she should have time to think, but I realise that you have an urgent duty to do. Have I your permission to speak to her before you question her?'

'By all means! In my presence, of course, at this stage, but, I assure you, quite freely.' Kriebel was on impregnable ground, at least pending the medical and ballistic reports; he could afford to be generous. 'Miss Barber, these gentlemen are from the British Embassy in Prague. They are here to look after your interests in this unfortunate situation. Please, Counsellor!'

'My name is Charles Freeling,' said the lawyer. 'I am counsellor to the embassy. And this is Adrian Blagrove, who is assisting us with the preparation of some technical data for translation, in connection with the new trade agreement consultations. I brought him along because he used at one time to work with your late step-father, and naturally he'd like to assist you if he can. And here,' he indicated the man in the tweed jacket, who came forward with a sudden brief, kind smile, rueful and charming, 'here is Sir Broughton Phelps, whose name will be known to you, I'm sure. Sir Broughton happened to be on holiday in the White Carpathians, I took the liberty of passing on word to him about you when the news came in.'

Yes, that, at least, was a name she knew. So the Director of the Marrion Research Institute 'happened' to be on holiday here! And hadn't she heard the other name before, too? Blagrove? Hadn't Robert Welland mentioned him as the new Security Officer? The man who had stepped into Herbert Terrell's shoes? And suddenly he turned up here, 'assisting with the preparation of technical data for translation'!

The shock of enlightenment helped to brace her. Here to look after her interests? They were here, and here in desperate haste, to make sure she gave nothing away. That granted, no doubt they'd do their diplomatic best for her.

'Your step-father was on my staff, my dear.' Sir Broughton took her hand, looking down at her with his warm, worried smile. 'I shall be only too glad if I can do anything to help you. Freeling was trying to contact me most of the night, it seems. They managed to reach me early this morning at Topolcianky. I've been fishing down in that district.' She'd been right about the flies. 'I shouldn't worry too much, you know. You haven't done anything you shouldn't, have you? Then it's only a question of telling your story sensibly, and having a little confidence in the authorities.'

A beautifully ambiguous reassurance, but she correctly interpreted the warning.

'It was very good of you all,' she said dutifully, 'to rush to help me like this. I'm afraid you must have spent the night driving.'

'Blagrove and I came in to Poprad by air taxi, early this morning,' said Freeling. 'Sir Broughton drove up from Topolcianky. We were very grateful for such prompt notification of poor Welland's death and your situation, and for Major Kriebel's courtesy in allowing us to see you at once. Now, the main thing is that you should think carefully, both about your rights *and your responsibilities*, and do nothing in haste. No one can demand a statement from you, you must realise that.'

'No one is demanding it,' she said. 'I want to make it. I told Lieutenant Ondrejov some things that weren't true, last night. I want to put them right.'

She was saying, it seemed, all the things one should not say. Everything was topsy-turvy, only her enemies looked pleased with her, especially Ondrejov, who was beaming so brightly that his blue eyes were pale as aquamarines in his brick-red face. The embassy party looked painstakingly benevolent but inwardly frantic; even Sir Broughton, the most human of the three, was frowning at her admonishingly.

The pause of glee and consternation was abruptly interrupted by a loud, peremptory voice in the outer room, speaking unmistakably English. Tossa pricked up her ears apprehensively, unwilling to trust what they told her. She looked round for someone who would be quick to understand, and found herself appealing directly to Ondrejov.

'That's somebody else for me, I'm afraid. I know him, he's – he's a friend of my mother's.' How could she say, with these people still employing the mourning note when they spoke of Terrell: 'He's going to marry my mother.'?

Ondrejov got up and went into the outer room, closing the door between; and presently reappeared with a wooden face, ushering in before him a large, angry, black-avised man in an incongruous business suit, who descended upon Tossa like a perturbed thundercloud.

'For God's sake, girl,' demanded Paul Newcombe, 'what have you been up to? Here's your mother phoning me in Vienna to say she's had word from some chap called Welland that you're prowling round the regions where poor old Herbert got killed, and will I please find out what you're up to, and tell you to stop it. And when I come in from Austria to the address she says you put on your card home – and a hell of a job I had finding the place! – I'm told you and your friends have gone, and I'll find you here. *Here, at the police station*! What in the world's been happening?'

Tossa sat shaken and pale. It was going to begin all over again, every one of them worse than the one before. She was going to hate this one as she'd hated Terrell; there was no escape. She looked past the looming shape that was without authority, straight at the two Slovaks who were looking on with such narrow and considering interest.

'Major Kriebel, this is Paul Newcombe. He is not related to me, but as a friend of my mother's I suppose he feels responsible for me. Mr Newcombe, I was just going to make a statement to Major Kriebel and Lieutenant Ondrejov. It ought to answer all your questions. And with their permission I should still like to make it.'

'By all means.' Kriebel was moving now partly by guesswork, but not entirely; he had exchanged one rapid glance with Ondrejov, and though nothing appeared to be communicated, something had certainly been understood. 'Gentlemen, if you will allow Miss Barber to speak without interruption, you may remain. It is a concession I need not make, but I will make it.' Ondrejov's aloof expression and slightly raised brows had said eloquently: 'Please yourself, it's your funeral. But *I* wouldn't!' 'Comrade Lieutenant, will you take down Miss Barber's voluntary statement?'

'The reason I told some untruths last night, and persuaded Mr Felse to tell them, too, against his advice, was because I was afraid of becoming more deeply involved if I told the truth. I thought I could give you all the relevant details about Mr Welland's death, without coming right out and saying that I came here for a special purpose of my own. I persuaded my friends to come, too, and spend the holiday here with me, because my step-father had died in Zbojská Dolina, and I wasn't satisfied about his death, and wanted to see the place for myself. I met Mr Welland when he was on leave in London, and we talked about it, and he promised me to look into it himself. But I still wanted to come. I didn't tell him that, and he knew nothing about it until he saw us at Zilina, on our way here. Evidently he didn't approve, since it seems he notified my mother.'

She told it exactly as Dominic had suggested yesterday, faithfully admitting Welland's telephone call and her appointment with him, and describing the circumstances of his death. But everything that touched on the Marrion Institute, or national security, or the defection of Karol Alda, still had to be suppressed, and that effectively censored Welland's last cryptic words to her. Had they meant anything, in any case? They stuck in her mind curiously, but their suggestions were too enormous and too vague, she could not trust herself to make a judgment upon them.

There was too much at stake. There sat the Director, listening to her with an anxious and sympathetic face, and willing her to be discreet if it killed her; and the Security Officer, brightly inscrutable, taking her in with cautious approval as she skirted delicately round the establishment that was his charge. She felt it when they began to breathe again. Compared with the secret activities and preoccupations they had to protect, both she and Welland were equally expendable.

Carefully she covered from sight the whole background of the death she most sincerely wanted solved. Right behaviour, she thought sadly, is always a compromise at best.

Ondrejov took down her statement, and presently transcribed it briskly, still in English, on the typewriter in the outer room, and brought it back for her to read and sign. No one tried to prevent her from signing. They were unspeakably relieved by the content of the statement. Her predicament hardly mattered, by comparison; but they gave her to understand, by encouraging glances, that in return for her services they would exert themselves to deliver her.

'I'm only terribly sorry,' she said suddenly, her voice a muted cry of protest, 'for poor Robert Welland!'

'Of course, of course, so are we all. But I'm sure the affair will soon be cleared up,' said Freeling soothingly. 'It occurs to me, Major, that as you have no facilities here in Pavol, and it may not be very convenient to move her elsewhere, perhaps you would agree to Miss Barber's being discharged into my custody, pending further enquiries? On the strict understanding, of course, that she shall be made available to you whenever required, and shall not leave the town? I would pledge myself to produce her on demand at any time.'

'I hardly think,' suggested Sir Broughton Phelps rather drily, 'that such a proposition can be entertained if it comes from your people. But as one who had the greatest respect for Miss Barber's step-father, I should be very glad to abandon my holiday and remain here, if you'll allow *me* to make myself responsible for her? And for her friends, too, though they are not, I believe, in custody?'

Paul Newcombe bristled. 'I am representing Mrs Terrell here, and if Tossa can be released I think it should be into my care.'

Ondrejov thumbed through the stapled sheets of Tossa's statement, and hummed a little tune to himself, modal, like the pipe-tunes of Zbojská Dolina. He looked inordinately placid and content, like a fed infant.

'Her friends are quite at liberty, here within Liptovsky

Pavol, but I am restricting their movements to the town for the time being. Miss Barber, I regret, must remain my charge. She can be held available to you at any time which is suitable,' said Kriebel firmly, 'but she is my responsibility. You have heard for yourselves the grounds on which I think it necessary to hold her, and they speak for themselves. Only Miss Barber had the opportunity of committing the murder, so far as we yet know. Of the others, only the boy Felse was also present at the chapel, the others clearly knew nothing about it until afterwards. They will all be invited to record statements, but they will not be held. Miss Barber did have the opportunity, and as you have heard on her own admission, she gave a false account of what happened. She must be held. I have my duty to do.'

It was at this moment that Ondrejov chose to look up at his chief and say ingenuously: 'Perhaps, Comrade Major, it would be as well if young Felse made his statement next. Then I can start him off to collect their things from the Riavka, while the other two tell us what little they do know. They'll be wanting their clothes and night things.'

'Certainly,' said Kriebel. 'Call him in. And gentlemen, if you wish to remain . . .?'

Now why did he make them that gratuitous offer, she wondered? Not because he owed it to them, not because he felt pressed; on the contrary, he was more at ease every moment. He wanted to see what their response would be, whether they would jump at the chance of staying to make sure that Dominic's account would bear out Tossa's, and frowning him away from any undesirable revelations; and he wanted to observe their reactions if there were indiscretions – and indeed, even if there were none.

Three of them relaxed, cautiously but perceptibly. 'That's very considerate of you,' said Freeling. 'We have a duty to all four of these youngsters, we shall be glad to stay.'

Only Paul Newcombe got to his feet, thick and glossy and lowering like a prize bull. 'My job is to look after Miss Barber. Do I understand that she must continue in custody?'

'I regret that she must,' said Kriebel crisply.

'I would remind you that I've had no opportunity yet to talk to her, and that I'm here at her mother's request. May I have a quarter of an hour with her, at least?'

The glance that flickered back and forth between Ondrejov and his superior was almost too rapid to be visible, but Tossa caught it.

'If you go down with her now, you may have a short interview with her, by all means.'

Paul jumped at it, was even surprised into expressions of appreciation; they were being almost excessively correct. Tossa wondered about these concessions herself, until she had been led helplessly past the anxious three fidgeting in the outer room, and down the stairs to her cell. Then she understood. The plain-clothes escort who opened the door for them and followed them in was Miroslav Zachar; if Paul had anything of interest to say to her, it certainly wasn't going to be missed.

Ondrejov, ushering Dominic into the inner office, smiled fatly to himself, and sharpened his pencil with a leisurely, enjoying deliberation.

The twins, frayed into nervous silence, were admitted together into the inner room, and Dominic went down the stairs with Ondrejov's hand on his shoulder. Every step seemed to him to be on eggs; or else there was a slack rope under him. He didn't even know whether he'd said the right things, telling half the truth like that, suppressing the other half, with one eye cocked on the anxious, dignified, admonitory English faces, and the other on this gross, earthy, ordinary soul who tramped solidly at his heels. He hadn't even known who they were, those three hanging on his words. They couldn't all be from the embassy, could they?

Mirek had made it necessary to tell the truth about the actual circumstances of Welland's death, to admit that Tossa had gone there to meet him, and had expected him to have something to tell her about her step-father's accident. As for the rest, he had objected to answering for anything that wasn't known to him personally; hearsay evidence wasn't good in English law, anyhow.

The van was standing in front of the Hotel Slovan, a small, decrepit, gabled house, its portal withdrawn under the arcade of the square.

'Drive carefully,' said Ondrejov at his shoulder. 'You know the road?'

'I drove here. I know the road.'

'You'd do well to eat your dinner there, it'll be time. And on the way back, *drive briskly*. Understand? Don't stop for anything or anyone, keep going, and keep a good pace. Your friends will be waiting for you,' said Ondrejov soothingly.

'Don't worry about them, they'll be all right. Miss Barber, too. I'll take care of her.'

'Who was the other one?' Dominic asked abruptly. 'The one who went off with Tossa?'

'You don't know? A Mr Newcombe. It seems he feels himself to be in the place of a father. I assume her mother is thinking of marrying him.'

'Oh! I see!' His tone indicated that he did not see very clearly. He climbed into the driving seat of the van, and inserted the key. The engine quivered into life. 'She isn't alone, is she?' he asked, his mind suddenly very clear and very calm. 'She won't be alone?'

'She won't be alone at all. I have two daughters, my boy. I have a grand-daughter. You can be easy.'

The miracle was that he instantly felt easy. He started the van moving. It rolled across the cobbles of the square, towards the neatly patterned width of roadway, sailed decorously into it, and vanished between the step-gabled façades at the far end.

Mirek Zachar materialised at Ondrejov's elbow, large and placid from the shadow of the arcades, buckling his crash-helmet under his chin.

'This man Newcombe's booked in here, at the Slovan. All right, I can keep the kid in sight, don't worry. I know these roads better than he does. You'll be at the bend by Král's, in case?'

'Or someone else will. We'll be keeping constant watch there. If anything goes wrong, if there's anything even questionable, telephone.'

'Surely!' said Mirek, and straddled his Jawa and kicked it into life before it was out of the arcade.

'If you lose him,' threatened Ondrejov, raising his voice peremptorily above the din, 'I'll have your hide for a jacket!'

Nine

The Man who Reappeared

Now that he was on his own he could think; he had a lot of thinking to do, and seven miles of driving to help him to do it. The one thing he knew for certain was that everything rested on him. They might come running from all directions to Tossa's aid; the responsibility for her, nevertheless, belonged simply to herself and Dominic, no one else. And Tossa was a prisoner, and immobilised; so there was no one left but Dominic.

Unless, perhaps Ondrejov . . .? His actions were apparently orthodox, but there was something about him that continually indicated the possibility of deception, as though he enjoyed making all the signposts point the opposite way. But the trouble was that one couldn't be sure, and there wasn't time to wait and watch developments. So that left the answer the same as before; it was up to Dominic.

The details of Welland's murder had to make sense; every murder must make sense. A distorted sense sometimes, where a distorted mind is involved, but Dominic had a feeling that there was nothing in the least deranged in this killing. Therefore, if he had all the facts at his disposal, he ought to be able to work it out; but since he had not all the facts, he must be prepared to fill in some of the gaps with intelligent speculation.

Start with something positive: someone was prepared to kill in order to ensure that people from Karol Alda's English past should not contact him. First Terrell, then Welland, as soon as they got too near to finding Alda, and both of them within the same small valley. Therefore Alda was there to be found, either in person or in such strong indications as could not fail to lead directly to him elsewhere. But because of the urgency which apparently had attached to removing the hunters at short notice, it seemed to Dominic more likely that the man himself was there. Not certain, but for present purposes a reasonable assumption.

Was it therefore necessarily true that Alda himself had done the killing? He was wary of thinking so; if he and his

122

work were now vitally important to this country, and had to be kept secret, far more likely that the necessary killing would be undertaken by professionals experienced in the art, leaving the genius to work undisturbed. That was assuming that this was really national business, of course. If it was a personal murder with a personal motive behind it, then Alda was, presumably, taking care of his own privacy.

In either case, if it was as vital as all that, the next move was already implied. Because whoever had shot Welland had also got in a second shot at Dominic on that occasion. He knew, all too well, that there had been one witness there, probably he knew there had been two, and who they were. He could not know whether Welland had had time to give up his secrets to them before he died, and he could not afford to take risks. They were both dangerous to him, and due for removal. If he knew enough, Tossa would be his chosen target. But Tossa was safely out of circulation and out of his reach. And who had put her there? Ondrejov, that inscrutable, innocent countryman.

The striped fields under the hills danced by outside the windows of the van, and he was back at the enigma of Ondrejov once again. Was Tossa really being held because he – or his superior, or both – suspected her? Or because, like a true policeman, he refused to let her run free and be used for bait?'

Either way, that left Dominic Felse next in line; and Dominic Felse was not out of circulation; he was here in the van, driving along a mountain road, alone.

Was there anything else positive to go on? Too much speculation was only beginning to confuse the issue. Yes, there remained, if nothing else, the few words Robert Welland had left behind him in dying. Tossa had reported them as: 'But he couldn't have known – nobody else knew!' And then, furiously: 'Impossible!' Welland had almost certainly been convinced that Alda had killed Terrell. Therefore Alda must be the 'he' who couldn't have known, presumably, that Welland had actually located him. How, then, could he have acted on the knowledge? And then: 'Impossible!' What was impossible in Welland's eyes? Certainly not that Alda should attempt to kill him; that was something he could, by his own theory, have expected.

He had reached the curve of the road where the rutted track turned off to the right, into Zbojská Dolina. The van rounded the bend, and began to climb. Another mile, and the low roof and deep eaves of the Riavka hut budded suddenly like a mushroom out of the meadow grass, with the bluish, fragrant darkness of the firs behind.

Somehow he had arrived at a totally unexpected conclusion, and no matter how much he walked round it and looked for other ways, they all brought him back to this one need. In the tangle of secrecy, suspicion and subtlety they had all been hunting for one person, but without ever speaking his name, ever asking after him, ever pausing to consider that he might not even know they wanted him. Never had it occurred to them that he might not be hiding or avoiding them at all, but only quite oblivious of them, because they were too sure of their sophistication to ask their way to him, and let him speak for himself. It is the only thing the twentieth-century spy must not do, go straight towards his objective. But how if this wasn't a real-life spy story at all, but something at once simpler and deeper?

He still didn't know what he was going to do when he brought the van lumbering to a standstill on the stony level outside the Riavka gate. All he was sure about was that there was no time left for going roundabout. The police could hardly hold Tossa, once the ballistics report proved they had a rifle to hunt for, and how long would that be? Could he rely on more than this one day?

He needed immediate action; he needed an open, honest solution, however inconvenient to however many people, because only such a solution could deliver Tossa. Not simply free her from custody, but deliver her from her own complex captivities, and make her look forward into the world with the same wonder and clarity he had seen in her eyes just once, when she had believed she might be going to die.

What he needed, and needed desperately, was Karol Alda.

The Martíneks were a little constrained, but genuinely kind. Even Ivo came down from the pastures to hazard his few halting words of English. Dana helped by packing the girls' things, and her brother loaded the van, while Dominic ate the lunch Mrs Martínek laid for him on the corner table in the bar. He paid the bill, rather shyly contriving to avoid picking up the change; and Dana, ambassador for the family, went out to the doorstep with him to say goodbye. But the slight constraint was still there, and her words were still carefully chosen. He couldn't blame her. Nobody, in any country, wants to be mixed up with crime and possible treason. If he asked her, now, the questions that should have been asked at the beginning, she would not answer them.

He took the van far enough down the track to be out of sight, and then drove it aside at a relatively level spot, and parked it among the trees, where it would not be immediately noticed. Then, making a detour in cover about the Riavka clearing, he set out to climb the valley.

It was just past one o'clock, fine and clear and warm, with a fresh breeze that made walking pleasant. There was no one stirring but himself; Zbojská Dolina was not high enough to be fashionable, and at midday the herdsmen were eating and sleeping by turns, somewhere out of sight. It occurred to him, when he came to the defile where the chapel loomed on its shelf of limestone, that he was still wearing the dark-red sweater he had worn the previous evening, and that it was as conspicuous at noon against the greens of grass and bushes, as it had been unobtrusive in the dusk, where all dark things were parts of the general darkness. There might well be policemen working here, combing the tumbled, bushy ground below the shelf, for the non-existent pistol Tossa might conceivably have had about her and tossed through the window after the murder. But it was too late to do anything about it now. He drew aside into the trees wherever he could; but he saw no one, and heard nothing but the chirring of crickets and the vibration of the conifers in the breeze.

He came into the upper bowl of the valley, where the huts clustered at the edge of the brilliant bog grass. They were silent, too. On such a warm and settled afternoon everyone would be up in the high pastures, drowsing among the folds of crest-country where an army could scatter and vanish. It wasn't easy to distinguish sheep here, they fused with the pale, stony colours and sometimes refused to be detected even in motion. Only the chestnut goats burned like tiny, active jewels in the bleached grass.

He was ranging slowly up the slope, in an easy spiral, when he saw them dancing daintily along the contour path high above him, towards the outcrop rocks that contained the northern col. Behind him and a little below him lay the isolated hut, the highest in the valley; before him was the corrugated, sidelong fall of grass, and then the long grey scar of the rock chute that poured the debris of the heights down to the talus on the ledge. He stood on a level with the upper face of the talus, and not fifty yards from where its first spilled stones welled over into the grass and peppered the slope. It didn't look so terrible from here, or so steep; it looked almost like a very rough and irregular path, a replica of the one above, but built up ten feet high with stones. The sheep-path on which he stood led vaguely up to it, and there turned to the right, and climbed the staircase of terraced tracks, tread by tread.

And high above him, mincing delicately towards the col, the dark-red goats made a dotted line of colour, with the tall brigand-figure of their herd striding at the head of the line. This time there was no frieze cloak, and no hat glittering with a band of fine chains. But there were the cream felt trousers, the wide-sleeved white shirt, the dappling of embroideries, the length and looseness of that mysterious body, the only one in Zbojská Dolina he had not seen at close quarters. The only one!

Dominic cupped his hands about his mouth, and sent a high, yodelling shout up towards the crests. The goats bounded on, unperturbed. The man halted, two full seconds later, as though the sound had only just risen to him, and looked at leisure about the valley below him. Dominic knew the moment when he was seen. He was the only alien creature there to be found, and the practised eye could not choose but find him. He waved an arm, and an arm was waved casually in return, before the remote figure turned to climb higher.

He would go; there was nothing to keep him, and only fifty yards or so to climb before he slipped through the pass and was lost. And even if pursued, would he be found again? He had time to vanish utterly before Dominic could reach the crests.

There was no moment when he consciously chose what he would do. All he was aware of was of doing it, without hesitation and without argument. Afterwards he did remember feeling glad, after all, about the dark-red sweater that made him a land-mark; and he recalled a sort of logical thought-process which he had probably adopted after the event, to rationalise his actions. If he could not reach the stranger in time, then the stranger must be drawn back to him. Mountain men are for ever suspicious of the folly of visitors, and their unbelievable innocence in dangerous places. It is their instinct to pull novices out of trouble. They can no more ignore the challenge than a fireman can pass by a fire.

He was on the stony edges of the talus almost before he

realised it himself; straight ahead, from the dead end of the contour path that turned and climbed here sensibly on solid ground, straight on to the giant's causeway of boulders. And it was too late to yodel again now, and too late to look up and make sure that he was observed. It was suddenly a wonderfully simple world, and there was only one enemy, and only one issue, whether he survived or died.

If he had really been an innocent, it would have been an easy thing to start on that journey; but if he had been an innocent he would never have done it, because he would not have known that it could serve his purpose. And because he was no raw novice, he began to suffer even before the first solid boulder shivered like jelly under his foot, and brought him up in tense balance, his breath held, his arms spread for stability. It was even more difficult because he had to look sure of himself until he had gone far enough to drag the goat-herd down from his heights. If he looked a fraud, who would bother to come to his rescue, even when he really needed it?

He was still poised, waiting to take the next step, when he heard the long, peremptory shout above him, and his heart turned over and melted in crazy gratitude. He dared not look up. Sweat broke on his body as he raised one arm and waved briefly and precariously in acknowledgment, like a cheerful fool completely misunderstanding the warning. He had to go on. How long would it take the herdsman to drop down the slope to him? How much farther must he go on this quaking, lurching, insecure pathway, that led nowhere except, in a ruinous fall, down to the bottom of the bowl?

He couldn't look up, and he couldn't look down. He had read Norman Douglas, too; he wanted to take his grim advice, and drop sensibly on to all fours, to lower his centre of gravity as far as possible, and avoid the shifts of weight that would roll the first stone onward over the ledge, and set the whole appalling mass in motion. There wouldn't be much left to identify, if he went overboard with this lot. A coffee-grinder couldn't do a better job on the bean that slid down into its teeth, then these stones would do on his body.

And now he couldn't look round, either. Absolute balance was everything. One more step, short and steady, sliding the weight gradually from foot to foot, eyes fixed ahead. He felt like a beach-spider scuttling over a quicksand, but in slow-motion; his sense of proportion was suddenly invaded by the monstrous illusion that every honed rock under his foot was a polished grain of sand slithering away and sucking him under. The quiver of insecurity was everywhere, under him, round him, in the air that embraced him. The temptation to lean inward and clutch at the rock face on his right hand was almost irresistible, but he knew he must not do it. That was the quickest way to urge the first stone gently outwards, and loose the avalanche, himself one grain among the many, and the most vulnerable. The grained grey rock leaned to him invitingly. He drew his hand back fastidiously, steadied his breath, and felt with an outstretched toe for the next precarious and shuddering plane on which he could rest.

It accepted his weight perfidiously, and then at the last moment it lurched, and almost brought him down. He swayed and stared, afraid to close his eyes, fighting for balance, streaming with sweat in a sudden flood that scalded his eyebrows and eyelids, and burned bitterly on his lips. His supporting foot slipped, the stone under it rolled with agonising slowness between its fellows, and ponderously found a new equilibrium. He was down on hands and knees, quivering, toppling, wrestling with the air within him and without, fighting to balance his terrified flesh with the poised wings of his desperately calm mind. Under his spread, cautious fingers the stone felt like a ploughed field shaken by earthquake. Slowly, slowly the convulsions settled. He hung still, intact, amazed, running with sweat.

Through the thunder of blood in his ears, he heard a voice behind him saying very clearly and coolly: 'Don't be startled! Keep quite still. I'm here close behind you.'

And indeed the voice was close, steady and sourceless, like voices heard in delirium; and like those voices, it did not startle him, it was strangely acceptable, almost familiar; even the fact that it spoke in unaccented English did not strike him as surprising. The only thing he wondered about then was time. How long could he have been kneeling here sick and blind, fighting for his nerve and his balance, if the stranger had had time to drop down the slope to him and follow him out on to this vibrating man-trap?

'Don't move until I tell you.'

A hand, long, large-jointed and muscular, came steadily sliding past his shoulder, and closed over his right hand, holding it down hard against the stone. The hand's invisible fellow settled bracingly under his right arm-pit.

'Now! Turn inward towards the slope. Gently! I've got your weight.'

The hands holding him felt like the only stable things in the universe. He trusted them, and turned about the pivot of his own anchored arm. He could see nothing but the close, grained surfaces of rock, and the light on the side of him where the fall was; but now it had changed to his right side. When he had blinked away the sweat that stung his eyes, the range of his vision took in also the hand that gripped his own, a muscular, naked forearm, the edge of a wide linen sleeve, and a knee, cased in cream-coloured felt, drawing back slowly to a new position.

'All right?' asked the voice.

'Yes. I'm all right.'

'Keep still, then. I'm going to turn ahead of you. No, keep down!'

The hands withdrew from him. He drew breath cautiously, and through the interstices of his human and commanding terror intimations of reason and will came floating back to him.

'Good! Now follow me closely. I'll go slowly. Hold by my ankle as you move up after me.'

'I'm all right. I'll follow.'

But sometimes he accepted the offer, all the same, closing his fingers firmly on the lean ankle above the laced sheepskin shoe, partly for the comfort of another human being's solidity and nearness, even more with a sort of detached elation, because he had risked his life to draw this man down within his reach, and here he was now in the flesh, under his hand.

The way back seemed longer than the way out. They moved by careful inches, spreading their weight low and delicately, like cats. The sun was burning on the exposed nape of Dominic's neck, a new and almost grateful discomfort; the stones were warm under his palms, warm and shaking like live flesh, searing his skinned finger-tips. He felt for the places that had held firm under his guide, gripped the heel of the soft shoe, ...nd crawled doggedly on; until suddenly the shoe was drawn out of his grasp, and set its sole to the ground, and there were a few blades of bleached, seeding grass that fluttered beside the arched foot.

Dominic stared at them, and for a moment could not realise what they were doing there. A hand reached down to lift him by the arm. His companion was on his feet, on the pale, terraced hillside at the end of the talus. They were out of it, and they were alive. Dominic put foot to ground eagerly, and the ground held steady under him; now it was his knees that gave way and all but let him fall.

He could hardly stand. But for the arm that encircled him and hoisted him down the slope, he would have had to sit down in the grass and wait helplessly until the shock and reaction passed. Shamed and dismayed, he let himself be hustled into the highest hut, and dumped without ceremony on the camp-bed that stood in one corner of the single room. He sat with his head in his hands, drawing in deep, steadying breaths, his eyes closed.

A hand tapped him smartly on the shoulder, and he opened his eyes to find a glass being dangled in front of him.

'Here, put this down.'

The voice had abandoned its cool, unstartling detachment; it was peremptory, warm and formidably angry. Dominic took the glass meekly; he didn't know what was in it, but it was fiery and bitter, and burned into all the corners of him with a salutary shock. Everything shook into place again, sun and shadow and forms and thoughts. He realised for the first time the full implications of what he'd done. Apart from risking his life in that perilous passage, he had presented himself as a sitting duck for anyone who wanted to wipe him out. What could he have done in his own defence, quaking out there on a rolling heap of marbles, without even a hand free to throw stones, much less the possibility of running for cover? If he had miscalculated about this man in front of him, he would have been dead by now, and buried, and probably beyond identification if ever they recovered what was left of him.

But he hadn't miscalculated. He was here, alive; and this man had brought him here.

He looked up over the empty glass, the drink stinging his throat and eyes, and for the first time gave all his attention to his rescuer. He found himself looking up into a frowning face, broad across eyes and brow, lean of cheek and long of chin, with a scimitar of a nose, and a long, sceptical mouth. Light brown hair arched high at the temples, duplicating the line of his brows; and the deep eyes beneath stared hard at Dominic, and not precisely indulgently, or with any great liking.

'And now perhaps you'll tell me,' he said grimly, 'what the devil you thought you were doing, out there?'

'I was looking for you, Mr Alda,' said Dominic. 'And I've found you.'

Ten

The Man in Ambush

There was a moment of silence, blank and profound, while they stared at each other. Anger left the formidable, self-sufficient face, and something of wonder, interest and speculation came into it, but nothing at all of either understanding or disquiet.

'You know my name, it seems. Should I know yours?'

'It's Dominic Felse. But no, you won't know it. I'm English.'

'That I'd already gathered,' said Alda drily. 'Only an Englishman, and I should guess a Londoner, would go striding out on treacherous places with quite such aplomb. Do you realise now that you did your best to kill yourself? Or are you completely a fool?'

The *becherovka* had begun to burn in Dominic's cheeks. 'I'm not from London. I'm a countryman, almost a hillman. I knew what I was doing.' He was angry with himself the minute he'd said it; it sounded like a child's pique, though he had intended something quite different and very much more respectable. 'I've climbed quite a bit,' he said, almost apologetically. 'I know the sort of places where one shouldn't go.'

'Then you *are* completely a fool! Or else,' he said, narrowing his deep-set eyes intently, 'you wanted me very badly. Perhaps you'd better tell me why.'

'You *are* Karol Alda?' He knew it, but he wanted it said.

'They call me Karol Veselsky here. But yes, I am Karol Alda. Karol Alda or Charles Alder, whichever you prefer. And what do you want with him?'

'I've got a friend who's in trouble, and I want your help. It concerns you. But it's quite a story.'

'You'd better tell me.'

And Dominic sat with his hands gripped tightly together between his knees, and told him, almost in a breath. He was not afraid of not being understood. And now he was no longer afraid of any kind of evasion.

'There are four of us here together, I daresay you've

131

seen us around. One of the girls is Tossa Barber, and her
step-father was a man named Terrell, who was killed here
in this valley, about three weeks ago. It isn't that she was
fond of him, or anything, but she felt bound to him, and
she wasn't satisfied about his death, that's why she got us
to come here. She wanted to find out for herself. And what
she found out was that *you* were somewhere here, and he'd
picked up your trail and was looking for you. Tossa felt it
might have been murder. But the Slovak police had closed
the case and lost all interest in it.'

'Perhaps,' said Alda, eyeing him levelly, 'because for them
there was no mystery about his death.'

'You mean they *know* how he died?'

'They know exactly how he died.'

'How?' asked Dominic, moistening dry lips. 'I mean, how
do they *know*?'

'They know because I told them. I reported his death.'

'*You reported it*? I thought the Martíneks . . . They called
out the mountain rescue people . . .' He broke off there,
remembering Dana's account of that night search. The
Martíneks had notified the mountain rescue service, and
then gone out to hunt for their missing guest, but the police
had been first on the scene. Because the police, it seemed, had
known exactly where to go. 'Would you mind telling me about
it? This isn't curiosity, it's terribly important.'

'It's very simple. I was on my way home by the high-level
path that crosses the open rock there. Since you came to
investigate his death. I take it you've looked at the place. I
wasn't thinking of Terrell. I haven't thought about him for
five years at least, I've had other things to think about. I
had no idea he was within seven hundred miles of me. And
at the blind point in the path I met him, face to face.' He
caught the brief, fearful gleam of Dominic's eyes, the one
returning instant of doubt, and smiled wryly. 'No, I didn't
touch him. I had no time for anything beyond recognising
him. Because he'd recognised me, and his reactions were the
quicker and the deadlier. He shrank back from me. Jumped
back would be nearer the truth. And he went over the edge.
When I climbed down to him – it takes ten minutes or so
from there – he was already dead. Well, my own telephone at
home was as near as any other, so I went on there, and called
in the police from Pavol. There was never any mystery for
them about his death, except perhaps the mystery of what
he was doing there at all, in the dusk alone.'

'But do they know,' asked Dominic pointblank, 'about the connection there was between you before? Did you tell them he was the man who was put on your case when you left England?'

Alda's eyebrows rose. 'You're very well-informed, I see. I told them I had known him and worked in the same institute with him. That was necessary, they wanted him identified, of course. But as for the rest . . . why bother? It seemed to me irrelevant. I could and did tell them exactly how he fell to his death, and they didn't question my word. I didn't think our past connection had anything more to say in the matter. The man was dead. I took it for granted, then, that our meeting like that was pure chance.'

'It wasn't! He was looking for you, trying to find out what you were doing here, what you were working on. He'd found a piece of scrap paper, music paper, with your handwriting on it, and that brought him here to Zbojská Dolina, searching for you. I suppose it would have been another feather in his cap if he'd been able to bring home word of something sensational.'

He had got so far when he saw that Alda was leaning back against the wall in a convulsion of silent laughter. He sat staring, confounded.

'Forgive me! But how baffled he'd have been if he had found out what I'm working on! Do you know what it is? Do you know why my privacy was left largely undisturbed, why things were arranged so that I did not have to come into the limelight with my story? Because of my vitally important work! Because I am at work on an opera about Comenius! How many sinister codes he'd have read into every note! Especially into the evangelical psalms! That was his profession, and his occupational hazard. It seems he died of it.'

Every word rang true. Dominic believed him all the more readily because there was no attempt to convince; belief was taken for granted, as between honest men who recognise each other on sight. But he still did not understand.

'But *why* did he fall? Even if he was startled, even if the dusk was coming on, *why*? He was used to mountains, he climbed the big stuff. Why did he jump back like that? Did he expect you to attack him?'

'Possibly, though nothing was farther from my mind. If only he'd known how little ill-will I bore him, how little

I thought of him at all! But more probably he suffered a reflex of conscience, a superstitious recoil. Coming face to face quite inescapably, as he did,' said Alda softly, 'with a man he had, by his own standards and in his own way, murdered.'

Alda lifted the empty glass from Dominic's clenched fingers, and went and refilled it at the rough cupboard on the wall. 'Here, it won't hurt you. You still look as if you need it. How much do you know about myself and Terrell and the Marrion Institute? And how did you get to know? Security must be as tight as ever there.'

'Tossa had it from a man named Welland, some sort of secretary at the embassy in Prague, who knew Terrell as a good climber, and didn't believe his death could be an accident. He began poling into the past, and he . . . well, he found . . .'

'He found me. Quite! A Slovak, an enemy, a possible murderer. A defecting physicist-cum-mathematician on highly secret work. A little hackneyed now, perhaps, but to him convincing, I'm sure. Do you need to know the rest of it? How much do you know?'

Dominic told him, and blushed feverishly over the telling. It was like recapitulating the plot of a sausage-machine thriller; in this clear air he marvelled that anyone should be able to view motives and actions in such crude and unlikely ways.

'Yes, I think you do need to know everything. After your recent effort,' he said tolerantly, 'I think you've earned it. When I went off into Savoy for my leave, to consider whether or not I should resign, I went up alone into the highest routes I could manage, and kept in touch with no one, either at home or locally. I was trying to wear myself out, body and mind, in the hope of a revelation. And just at the end of my time I was cut off in a solitary refuge in Dauphiné by bad weather and a slight injury, and kept there for a fortnight. The place was well stocked, and I was glad of the extension. But when I got down into Briancon at last, with a fortnight's beard, burned dark brown, and much thinner than when I went up, I found out from the first English paper I bought that the hysteria of the times had turned me into a fugitive and a traitor. The main points of Terrell's dossier on me were already in print. They hadn't given me two weeks' grace.'

'You mean,' demanded Dominic, the glass shaking in his hand, 'you never ran away at all?'

'Never until then, certainly. After that you might say I walked away. The hue and cry was out after me as I sat reading the catalogue of my offences in the middle of it. All I did was to accept the omen. No, I didn't run, I walked to the nearest exit. It was a work of art, that dossier. No absolute lies, you understand, only double truths. Maybe it was only the work of a suggestible, ambitious mind bent on rising in his profession, and able to convince himself in the process. Maybe it was coldly and deliberately constructed, for the same personal reasons. I gather he got the Security Office on the strength of the job he did on me. He was a junior in the secretariat when I knew him. All I know is, when we ran headlong into each other he sprang back from me, and went over the edge. How do I know what he saw, and what do I care? Why go further into it now?

'I could have come back, of course, but it would have been to a shower of mud, and a hard fight ahead of me to clear my name. The times were against me. But that wasn't why I walked away. It was disgust I felt, not fear. And something else, too. A sense that a gate had opened before me for a purpose, and I mustn't hesitate to pass through it. So I simply turned, without haste, and walked away again into the blue.'

Dominic's teeth chattered faintly against the rim of the glass. 'But you must know that you left people in England convinced that you'd changed sides in the cold war. Even your coming back here would be interpreted as backing up that view.'

'Boy, I was born here. The old lady who has the farm just over the col is my grandmother. Her home is my home. I became English at fifteen because my parents became English, at a time when I was a minor, and went along naturally with them. Don't misunderstand me, I have nothing against being English. I have simply recognised the fact that in spite of the filling in of papers, I am *not* English. The process is more complex than that. I took my time over the decision, but in the end I came home.'

'But you did bring your gifts with you. To be used here.'

'Gifts are to be used wherever one goes. But what gifts? That attack on me was an oracle and an opportunity. For years I'd worked earnestly in government service, trying to keep my belief in the professed ideals of government, against

135

all the evidence, forcing myself into the mould of a life for which I was never intended. It took that crisis to make me realise I'd been using my energy in the way least suitable for me, and least effective. Every man must use his own tools for the re-shaping of the world. I've gone back to mine. Music, tranquillity, human affection, human dignity – they can all be used to state the political truths I believe in. Putting aside, of course, the narrower meaning of "political". I came home and asked them to take me back as what I am first and foremost, a composer. And they accepted me as a Slovak again on my own terms. I chose to take my grandmother's name, which is Veselsky, simply because I didn't want to be an international sensation or a bone of contention, in Czechoslovakia or England or anywhere else. I refuse to be used as ammunition against either of my two countries, and I need privacy and peace in which to work. They must have thought them reasonable requests – they've been almost too religiously respected.'

'Then you're giving *all* your time to music?' asked Dominic doubtfully.

'You think all my time is too much? This pastoral life is only part of the picture. For composition I find it ideal here in the mountains, but there are other aspects of my life, too. I give occasional piano recitals, I do a great deal of conducting. Oh, I assure you all my time is hardly enough.'

'No – I suppose not. But in England,' ventured Dominic hesitantly, 'you had other work as well, this work with aircraft design, and all that. And that was important, too. Tossa said Welland told her you could have been Director of the Marrion. Don't you miss all that ? Don't you ever want to get into it again here?' He had not quite the hardihood to add: 'And if you don't, why did you bring your notebooks with you?'

Alda smiled. 'I won't say it gave me no satisfaction. I may even take it up again some day, if I do it will be in a very different way. Meantime, with only one life to spend, I'm making sure of the first essential first. Nothing is going to elbow out music a second time. But I keep in touch,' he said, meeting Dominic's absorbed stare with faintly indulgent good-humour. 'I have a friend in America who keeps me supplied with technical magazines. If I ever do decide to get back into the field I shan't be starting under any great handicap. Not that I think it likely,' he admitted tranquilly. 'If ever I thought myself indispensable,

I've been cured of that. At least one of my undeveloped ideas went into commercial production this spring with a French company – and to better effect than if I'd worked it out for the Institute. What they'd have kept it for I daren't imagine. Prunières have incorporated it in a light helicopter for crop-spraying in tropical countries. No secrets, reasonably cheap production, and a sensible use. They're welcome to the profit. I'm content. No doubt somebody or other will happen on all the other ideas, too, given a few years. Simultaneous discovery in music is less likely. I'll stick to music.'

'Then, of course,' conceded Dominic, 'I suppose it wouldn't be liable to occur to you that Terrell might have been prowling round to spy on your work. And you couldn't guess – how could you? – that there was likely to be another death.'

'Another death?' Alda looked up sharply. 'I've heard nothing about a death. Surely the police would have contacted me?'

'They haven't had much time, it only happened last night. And then, the Terrell case would be closed for them, and they only knew the half of it, they wouldn't connect this with you. And we weren't as helpful as we might have been, because we didn't know . . . we thought that you . . .'

'That I'd killed Terrell, and might well kill someone else? Yes, I see your point. If you've given up that idea now,' he said grimly, 'you'd better tell me just what's happened.'

Dominic told him the story of Welland's death, and all that had followed it. Alda had risen, and was pacing restlessly and silently across the patterns of sunlight and shadow in the window of the hut, which faced down the valley, away from the doorway and the smooth grey scar of rock.

'So your friend is being held on suspicion? And you came to look for me! As a valuable witness, or as the murderer?'

'How could I know which, then? I hadn't met you or spoken to you, all we knew was the Terrell version. Didn't it seem the obvious thing to think at first, that you were picking them off when they got too close? We'd seen you up on the skyline there with the goats, we saw you carried a rifle . . .'

'A *rifle*?' Alda whirled on him with a face of blank, disdainful astonishment. 'I carry *a rifle*? I don't think I've ever even had one in my hands. You're dreaming.'

'But I did see you with it, up on the crests,' protested Dominic, shaken. 'A great long stock sticking up over your shoulder, and the barrel . . .'

He broke off, hopelessly confounded. Alda had flattened his wide shoulders against the shadowy wall of the hut beside the window, and was laughing his heart out.

'I don't understand.' Dominic was on his feet, his face burning, a little from the conviction that he had somehow made himself foolish, but much more from the *becherovka*. 'In any case I'd really stopped believing it was you doing the shooting, before I came up here looking for you, but I know what I saw . . .'

'But you don't! That's exactly what you don't know, but *I* do, now. This . . . this is what you saw.' He crossed the dim room in three vehement strides to the corner behind the iron stove, cluttered with tools, and draped with the black felt cloak he had worn in the storm, and disentangled from behind its veiling folds a long object, which he brought forward into the light from the window, and held upright for inspection, laughing still.

It was within three inches as tall as Alda himself, and about as thick as a child's wrist, a tube of pale wood polished by age and handling. To the back of it, at the upper end, was secured by closely plaited hemp cords a narrower pipe about two feet long, a small round mouthpiece jutting from the back of it at the lower end. It had the conscious irregularity of hand-made things, so that there could never be an exact duplicate. It varied somewhat in thickness from end to end, and was a little bowed and twisted; when Alda lifted it and set the mouthpiece to his lips the double pipe, projecting some fifteen inches above his head, curved very slightly over his left shoulder. He held it with his left hand at waist level, and fingered below at the full stretch of his right arm; and round the finger-holes carved and painted mountain boys circled, dancing.

A gust of breathy, rustling notes came cascading out of the pipe, twining and shaking downwards in an improvised flourish, to settle deeply and sonorously into a slow, plaintive tune. It was hardly louder here, but for the reverberations from the walls, than when they had heard it descending from the hills beyond the col, through a couple of miles of mountain air.

'This is my rifle,' said Alda, taking his lips from the mouthpiece and turning the pipe gently in his hands. 'We call it the *fujara* – not very portable, and a little ponderous to play, because of all the over-blowing, but the queen of the pipes, all the same. The nearest thing to a gun I've ever possessed, or am ever likely to. Did you never hear it, down in the valley?'

'We heard it, yes.' Dominic stretched out his hand and took the pipe, fascinated. The wood was silken smooth under his fingers. The little bandits, axes brandished above their heads, leaped like deer, legs doubled under them. 'But we didn't know what it looked like, we'd never seen one. How could we guess?' He fitted his fingers to the holes, and held the instrument against him; and it hung lightly enough, for all its bulk. 'What did you call it? A *fujara*? It's beautifully made.'

'My great-grandfather made it. For a *fujara* it's on the small side, most of them run close to two metres.' He laid it back carefully in its corner, cushioned by the folds of the heavy cloak.

'So it was you,' said Dominic. 'I wasn't imagining things, you *did* play "Bushes and Briars".'

'Very probably. Was that what brought you up here after me?'

'Partly that. A musician who lived somewhere in these hills and knew English songs seemed a fair bet for Karol Alda. And by then I'd begun to think that maybe the whole business wasn't quite so obvious as it seemed, even before I knew your side of the story. I know now that you hadn't got anything to fear, or anything to hide, so why should you want to kill Welland? But you see, somebody else *has* got something to hide, somebody else *is* afraid. And I don't think we were wrong about what he's afraid of. He's killed once to keep your case from being dug up again and re-examined, and he may kill again for the same reason.'

'Terrell's death was not murder,' said Alda, considering him thoughtfully.

'No, I accept that. But it started Welland off on the same trail, and Welland's death *was* murder. And now that we know where you stand, and there isn't anything treasonable about co-operating, there's nothing to prevent Tossa and me from telling the whole truth. Will you come down to Pavol with me, and tell your part of it, too? Between us all, we ought to be able to clear up this case, and get Tossa out of trouble.'

'I'm ready,' said Alda. 'We can go whenever you like.'

* * *

Dominic was the first to set foot outside the open doorway, on the sunlit stone under the deep overhang.

There was a sharp, small crack. Something sheered into the weathered wall just in front of his face, and flying splinters stung his cheek. He clapped a startled hand to the place, and brought a smear of blood away on his fingers. And in the same instant Alda flung an arm about him and hoisted him bodily back into the hut in one heave, slamming the door to between them and the second bullet, as it thudded into the thick timbers where a split second before Dominic had been standing.

'I brought him here,' said Dominic huskily, coming out of his moment of sickening shock with quickened senses. He wiped at his stinging cheek with the back of his hand, and stared almost disbelievingly at the minute smears of blood that resulted. 'I got you to come down out of your clouds to help me, and now look what I've done! Led him straight to you.'

'You don't know that. Does it matter, anyhow?' Alda drew breath cautiously, and looked the boy over in the warm wood-darkness within the closed door. All the lines of his face had sharpened and brightened, in what might have been merely tension, but looked strangely like pleasurable anticipation. He slid past Dominic to the small, single-paned window that let in light on this side of the hut.

'I do know. If he'd known exactly where to find you, he'd have come for you in the first place. It's *you* he wants suppressed. But he did know where *I* was, to a bit. All I've done is fetch you out of cover for him.'

'No, you've done something much more useful, brought *him* out of cover. And if he was following you, why didn't he pick us both off while we were out on the talus?'

Dominic's mind was groping its way with increasing certainty through shadowy places. 'He couldn't have been following me, not closely. But he knew where I'd gone. I think . . . I think he was betting on picking me up on the way back, but when I didn't go back promptly enough he came looking for me. He must have found the van. He'd know I was still up here, somewhere. If he'd arrived while we were exposed out there, we should both have had it. Therefore he didn't. He didn't reach these parts until we were inside here. And he didn't know there was anyone in here until he heard the *fujara*. What else could it be? That would be worth investigating, wouldn't it? He was looking for a musician. He only had to wait and see who emerged, to find out if he was wasting his time. Now he knows he wasn't. He knows we're both here. He's seen us.'

'You're taking it for granted,' said Alda equably, his lean cheek flattened against the wall beside the dusty pane, 'that he's someone who'll know me on sight.'

'He'll know you. I'm sure.'

'And that I'm critically dangerous to him. But I swear I know of no reason why I should be.'

'I don't understand why, either, but I'm sure I'm right. Welland was killed because he was determined to find you, and he looked like succeeding. Tossa and I are marked down because Welland might have told us what he knew. But you're at the heart of it. There's something in your past, in your connection with England, that can ruin somebody, and if he can silence you, the urgency's over. And I brought you and pinned you here for him!'

'Up to now,' said Alda, 'we are still alive. If he knows where we are, let's see if we can find out where he is. He must be on this side, since he has the doorway neatly covered.' He reached a hand out of shelter to rub away the dust from the window-pane. There was no shot. 'The sun probably reflects from the glass, it's directly on it. So much the better. Come here!'

Dominic came, slipping along the wall and pressing intently at his shoulder, to peer out at the pale corduroy hillside curving away from them round the side of the bowl, until it reached the talus. He looked down the broken, scoured, almost grassless fall below to the bottom of the basin, and again up from the talus by the bare, polished funnel to where the level of firm rock conducted the path across it. The whole bowl seemed, at first glance, to be void of cover, but when he considered it in more detail there was scattered and meagre cover everywhere.

'I am supposed,' said Alda serenely in his ear, 'to be somewhat of a prodigy at mathematics. Let's see how precisely I can calculate. I don't propose to open the door again simply to try and examine the bullet-hole, but I estimate that he was shooting obliquely into the doorway. The angle I should judge to be something like thirty degrees. And he's certainly on a higher level than we are. The scar makes things easier – at least we can write off the areas where he can't possibly be.' He was silent for a moment, his eyes roaming the exposed stretch of country intently, his hand on Dominic's shoulder. 'I make him approximately on the level of the rock path up there. Draw a line along from the distant end of it, say twenty yards. Somewhere within ten yards above or below that line, according to my estimate, he should be. You have that area fixed?'

'Yes.' There were low clumps of bushes there, and some irregularities in the folded ground; it looked a possible hide.

'Keep it fixed. Watch for the slightest movement there, when I give you the word. I'll see if I can draw him.'

It was extraordinary; his voice sounded gay, his step was elastic, there was no doubting his pleasure now. Dominic, faithfully fixing the oblong of ground he had marked down, longed to turn and look at his companion. Maybe it was true that they were all born Janosíks, venturers by instinct, even the artists.

'A hat wouldn't be convincing,' mused Alda cheerfully, somewhere behind him. 'A shirt-sleeve, perhaps. You're ready?'

'I'm ready,' he said huskily, his eyes already aching with concentration.

The shot made him leap and shrink inside his skin all the more violently because he was waiting for it with so much passion. Alda made a small, echoing sound on the heels of the impact, half hiss, half laugh, drawing in breath through his teeth. And in the low bushes at the very edge of the rock path, that were quivering faintly and constantly in the breeze, there was a sudden tiny convulsion for which the wind was not responsible.

'He's there! I've got him!' He could turn his head now, and he did, in a frenzy of anxiety, reaching a hand for Alda's arm as he came slipping back to him. 'You're all right? He didn't touch you?'

'I'm all right.' He was laughing to himself, a small, inward rhythm like a cat purring. 'Where was he?'

'Right at the edge of the scar, a yard or so above the path. It's all still there now, but I'm sure. I saw him move. Only he may not stay there,' he said, his heart contracting ominously. 'If we don't return his fire soon, he'll know we're unarmed. If once he gets the idea, he can come down at leisure and get us. We'd have to cross open ground every way if we ran for it.' He had got his companion into this, and he must get him out. 'Even if we could kid him we had a gun here,' he said, 'we might keep him frozen where he is.'

And suddenly it occurred to him that they were not totally defenceless. One man with a gun here on the door side of the hut, and the enemy would have to keep cover, and fix his attention upon that danger. There was the window at the back, and a sporting chance of reaching cover from it, and escaping into the valley. That fellow up there couldn't look everywhere at once.

He turned his head again and looked at Alda, who was scanning the rifleman's hide with narrowed, eager eyes.

'Would you mind terribly if I borrowed your *fujara*?'

Alda started, shortened his ardent stare, and looked with amusement and delight at his ally. He was very quick on the uptake.

'You won't take in a Slovak that way,' he warned indulgently.

'No, I know that,' acknowledged Dominic, gazing back at him with eyes wide and steady. 'But I haven't got to – have I?'

They understood each other perfectly. In some incomprehensible way they had borrowed from each other, and even words had become almost superfluous, so companionably did their minds confer.

'You know the lie of the land here better than I do. You speak the language, I don't. And you're the more essential witness now. I don't understand why, either, but you are. Let me hold his fire here, and you get out by the window and run for help. I'm awfully sorry,' said Dominic, picking his words as fastidiously as a drunk in his anxiety, 'to be cornering the safe job for myself, but it's quicker and easier this way. If you'll let me try to use the *fujara* for camouflage, I shall be safe enough. He won't dare rush me, if he thinks I have a gun.'

It was perhaps the most important speech of his life, up to that moment, and he had to get it right. He licked sweat from his lips. All that mattered now was Tossa, safe for a little while in Ondrejov's care, and safe for ever, even from baseless regrets for that bird-of-prey, her stepfather, once Karol Alda reached Liptovsky Pavol.

There was a brief and pregnant silence; then Alda said, with a soft ripple of contented laughter: 'A good idea! All right, I'll go. Take the *fujara*.'

Dominic didn't at first recognise the chill that budded so

curiously in his heart. It wasn't fear; he was too excited to be afraid. Fear comes more leisurely and deliberately, and grips the corner of your consciousness that isn't keyed up to resist it. It was a full minute before he recognised it as disappointment. He had what he'd wanted, but somehow he hadn't expected to get it so easily, without question. He took the *fujara* in his hands, the smooth, pale, polished, painted wonder that had to do duty for a gun.

'Say when you're ready, and I'll try to cover you.'

He heard the harsh sound of a rusty hasp yielding, the creak of the window-frame.

'When you like. I'm ready.'

'Good! Now!'

Dominic opened the door violently, took one rapid step out upon the stone, and on the instant recoiled, stiffening against the jamb. The shot smacked with unnerving aplomb into the opposite door-post; he stared at the hole in dreadful fascination. At least he knew the angle now. If the marksman had been at the opposite end of the rock crossing, Dominic Felse would have been as good as dead.

Vaguely, at the back of his mind, he heard the soft thud of Alda's feet on the ground outside the window, and their light, fleet running. This was the most desperate of all the moments left to him. He might have a long siege to withstand, but Karol Alda must get away safely. Dominic skinned off his red sweater, and swung it before him across the threshold.

Five! Another hole in the timbers of the wall, terrifyingly close, and two holes through his sweater at the shoulder. He leaned against the jamb of the door, and his knees felt like jelly. How many shots could there be in the magazine? And all he was armed with was a *fujara*; a beautiful, strange, mysterious musical instrument, the antithesis of every known instrument for killing, a whispering pipe that made itself heard over ten miles of country like a melody dreamed rather than heard, and other-worldly even in a dream.

The running footsteps were quite lost now. He strained his ears, and could hear nothing but the last light sighing of the wind under the eaves of the hut.

He pushed the door to carefully, leaving only a narrow chink open; and tenderly he raised his long weapon, and slid it forward through the crack, drawing a bead upon the bushes at the end of the rock path.

After that there was silence. Even the wind had dropped in the height of the afternoon hush.

He watched the clump of bushes where the enemy lay hidden, and lost count of time. He had no attention to spare for any other spot in all that arena of grass and rock and scree. That was why he failed to see Karol Alda until he lay some twenty yards above and behind the rifleman in the bushes, at the rim of the circle round which Dominic's feverish attention patrolled steadily and dutifully, all senses at strain. He froze, helpless and appalled.

So that was why Alda had accepted his rôle with such deceptive placidity, Alda with his adventurer's face and his far-sighted eyes, the bandit-artist out of the lawless past, with the old brigand-songs ready on his tongue. He had never had the slightest intention of going for help. He was patiently, calmly, happily circling round above his enemy, unarmed as he was, dropping now into the perimeter of Dominic's charmed circle, behind the gunman in the bushes.

And there was nothing, nothing at all, that Dominic could do to help him. Except, perhaps, show himself again outside the door, and that he could hardly do with conviction until the crucial moment. It couldn't go on being convincing indefinitely, he had to save it as his trumpcard. He held his breath, watching. The muzzle of the *fujara* sagged a little, and he jerked it back guiltily, his heart lurching and recovering in an instant.

How could he ever have thought that a man like Karol Alda would leave the sticky end to him? He might have known. He should have known.

The sun was still high, and shadows still short and black. There was only one way of moving in undetected from the south-west, and that was flat to the ground. Alda had a gift for this game, Dominic had to grant him that. He must have made a large circle to reach the place of vantage where he now lay. From the hut he looked as obtrusive as a lizard spread out in the heat on a sunlit wall, though he had rolled up the wide white sleeves of his shirt to his sunburned shoulders; but from where the enemy lay, equally flat to the ground in his thicket of gnarled bushes, Alda would be quite invisible. From here, too, cover looked pitifully thin between them; but he knew to his comfort that there was more of it than there seemed.

But the one man had a gun, and the other had only his

hands, and the odds were crazy. He shouldn't have done it. He should have made off down the valley to get help, as fast as he could. Dominic gnawed his knuckles and dripped sweat in an agony of helplessness. Even if he propped up the *fujara* here and made a run for it from the rear window now, he couldn't possibly reach either the nearest cottage or Alda in time to affect the issue. All he could do was stare until his eyes glazed, and wait for the single decisive moment when he ought to draw the enemy's fire again. It might all depend on his timing yet.

Another yard gained. Dominic caught the rapid, smooth movement as Alda flowed through the grass. Fifteen yards now between them, not more, and this afternoon hush over everything, not even a breath of wind to rustle the bushes and cover his advance. Nobody could be so silent as to leave that stillness undisturbed at only a few yards distance. The mystery was how he had got so close without betraying himself.

The bushes stirred stealthily, up there at the edge of the scar. A streak of brown slid out of cover beneath the silver-green branches, articulated, deliberate, grotesque, a man's body. The man with the rifle had caught that last movement, and awakened to the near and perilous presence of his stalker. He was leaving his hide, slithering downhill flat on his belly, with the clump of bushes between him and his pursuer, feeling his way backwards to the edge of the rock slide, and cautiously over it.

Of course! He didn't know whether his antagonist was armed or not, and he was taking no chances. He wanted rock, not bushes, between himself and Alda. He was easing himself down to a tenable hold, some five feet or so below the edge, where the stray boulders that fringed the broken ground would cover him.

The distant figure, featureless and anonymous, had turned its back now on the hut below, and paid no attention when Dominic, grasping with a revulsion of horror of what was to come, flung the door wide and ran out into the open. He was no longer interested in any target but the unseen enemy in the grass above him, closing in coolly and patiently on the abandoned bushes, and gathering himself now for the final long leap downhill.

Dominic made a trumpet of his hands and yelled wildly aloft. And at the same moment Alda made his leap, beautifully and vainly gauged to drop him upon the very spot from which the other man had so silently withdrawn.

The rifle, its barrel a bluish gleam in the sun, was already braced and waiting for him. Dominic saw it flung up to meet the hurtling body, felt the tension of the firing arm like a pain transfixing his own flesh, and set his teeth and held his breath, steeled for the shot. A small, distant, dry, bright sound. The slopes took it up and tossed it among them in innumerable echoes, ripple on ripple, to die in the depths of the valley below.

The bushes threshed beneath Alda's falling body, swallowing him from sight. Dominic drew breath in a wail of despair, and stood staring numbly, so sick with his own impotence that he saw what happened next only as an illogical sequence experienced in a dream, and for several seconds could make no sense of it in this disastrous daylight world.

The man braced on the rough rim of the rock chute hung quite still for a long moment. Then slowly his arms sank and spread apart, and the rifle slithered from his hold, and drifted away from him almost languidly, to lodge in a tuft of grass ten feet below, and hang there gently rocking. His outspread hands clutched at the rock and the thinning soil beneath him, and found no purchase or no strength to maintain their hold. His knees sagged gently under him, and his body began to slide, first with unbelievable slowness, then with gathering momentum, until it struck a projecting knuckle of rock, and was flung abruptly outwards towards the centre of the chute. It struck again, and rebounded, and came spinning and turning and bouncing downwards like a stone.

In the dwarf bushes above, Karol Alda gathered himself up nimbly, and slid hastily down the few yards to where the rock path began. He reached the edge just in time to see the rag-doll form strike the piled stones of the talus on the ledge below. A sudden convulsion shuddered through the whole laborious erection, running like a ripple from the shock, outward to either end. Particles of stone shifted, toppled, re-settled, and set their new neighbours shuddering in their turn. Then, with a sudden grinding roar, the whole unstable mass burst from its shaky moorings and exploded violently outwards over the valley, spitting rocks like chaff, and hurtled down with the body, in an earth-shaking thunder and a cloud of pallid dust, into the bottom of the bowl.

Eleven

The Man who Failed to Arrive

Down from the recesses of the northerly col Ondrejov came bouncing and rolling, that lumpy elderly body of his marvellously deft and rapid in movement, his rifle bumping vigorously at his hip as he ran. Hard on his heels came Miroslav Zachar, still in his leather motor-cycling jacket, and sweating profusely, and two young policemen in uniform. They descended upon the hut, where Dominic stood dazed and appalled, staring down into the cauldron below him, from which a thick, choking smoke of dust rose, and the last muted rumblings of the thunder.

Ondrejov turned him about by the shoulders, looked him over for damage, and found nothing worse than a scratched cheek.

'Well for you two,' he bellowed, clouting him boisterously behind in his relief, 'that I've kept my hand in with a rifle. And well for you I had Mirek on your trail. He was waiting for you below, and you never came. You cost him a fine hunt before he found the van, and a fine fright I got when he rang up to tell me. If you youngsters would only do as you're told! I had the road well covered for your sake, but we had to reorganise in a hurry. There'll be two of us on their way up the valley now, and the rest of us came over the quickest way from Král's inn. And lucky for you the first shot gave us our bearings. You're all right?'

'Yes. Thank you! I'm all right,' said Dominic, still staring down into the boiling eddies of dust below, beneath which the wreckage of the talus still slid and settled with sluggish, sated movements. He thought of a body buffeted and ground and slashed in that titanic disintegration, and the body became live, and his own. He would never play with those things again! He felt sick, but he was alive. For the moment that was all he could feel, and it was enough.

'Mr Alda . . .' he said. His tongue was slow and stupid, and his mouth dry with dust. 'Mr Veselsky, I mean . . .'

'Mr Veselsky is on his way down, look! Like one of his

own goats! Does he look damaged? *Nie*, there was only one shot – mine.'

Alda was dropping down the grass slope on the far side of the scar in long, sure-footed bounds, balanced like a dancer. They saw that he carried a rifle in his hands.

'Good!' said Ondrejov. 'The gun at least we have, if we can't have the man.' He laid his arm warmly about Dominic's shoulders, and turned him towards the descent into the bowl. 'Come on, let's go down. Let's see what we have there.'

What they had was a wilderness, a new desolation. They foregathered in silence in the safe, hollowed heart of the bowl, where nothing could fall any farther, and ranged the scattered fringes of a desert of tumbled stones, through a pall of acrid dust that still silted down thickly on every blade of grass between the rocks, until there was no green left. Somewhere under those piled cairns the body of Robert Welland's murderer was buried.

'There won't be much to identify,' said Ondrejov grimly, 'but I suppose we shall have to dig him out. We shall need heavy equipment on the job. You didn't, by any chance, get a proper look at him?'

'No, nothing. I saw only the end of his fall.'

'And we had no field-glasses. No telescopic sights, not even a diopter. Our best shots were covering the road.' Ondrejov nodded sombrely, looking down at the rifle in his hands, on which the dust was settling pale and fine as talc. 'He had, though. A Zbrojovka Brno gun, of course. ZKM 581 small-calibre rifle. Automatic. Light to carry, not too bulky to hide, and a man could run into them by the thousand here. That tells us nothing till we find out who applied for the permit to buy it. As we shall.' He shook himself like an experienced old dog making ready for action, and turned towards the downhill path, coughing. 'Let's get back where we can breathe. We'll work this out in Pavol.'

'Then we still don't know who he is,' said Dominic, swept along in Ondrejov's arm, shaky with reaction now.

Ondrejov hoisted an eloquent shoulder. 'We soon shall. We're in no hurry now.' He looked back once, briefly, at the murky desolation where the murderer lay buried. 'Neither is he,' he said laconically. 'Even for him, the emergency's over.'

'I'm officially off-duty,' said Ondrejov smugly, 'but as Major

149

Kriebel is at Liptovsky Mikuláš, examining Mr Welland's baggage at his hotel there, and enquiring into his movements, I shall take the liberty of presiding until he returns.'

And he did, and the wires hummed. First, the salvage operations in Zbojská Dolina; then a dutiful call, naturally, to Major Kriebel, so worded that he would, with luck, feel it incumbent upon him, in defence of his dignity, to go to survey the devastation in the valley before he came back to Pavol; and lastly, calls to the two hotels at Mikuláš where Freeling, Blagrove and Sir Broughton Phelps had installed themselves, and across the square to the Slovan, where Paul Newcombe had taken a room. None of them was actually in his hotel to be contacted personally, which was hardly surprising on a lovely August afternoon; it was a question of leaving a message in each case, asking them all to report at Ondrejov's office, in person or by telephone, as soon as possible.

That done, Ondrejov assembled his cast for the last act, the Mather twins from their forlorn and fruitless councils of war at the Slovan, Tossa from a long and blissful sleep on her solitary cot downstairs. And they all talked at last, fully and freely.

After that, Ondrejov talked.

'When Mr Terrell was found dead,' he said, 'I was already in possession of the facts about that death, but not of the background. I therefore knew from the beginning that this was not a case of murder. But there were certain curious features about it that interested me. And when you, Miss Barber, applied for a visa, with your friends, the authorities, who were also on the alert, contacted me. We supplied you with Mirek as an escort, and waited to see what would follow. And it was known to me, before the death of Mr Welland brought things into the open, that you were making enquiries about your step-father's movements. Movements which we already knew, but to which your anxiety gave significance. You even uncovered some points which were not known to us. For instance, at the Hotel Sokolie – you remember the waiter who spoke English? He was a very worried man, Miss Barber, very worried. He had thought nothing of the small matter of the card-game, and the paper on which Ivo Martínek kept the score, until you became excited about it.'

Tossa, refreshed and radiant, sat by Dominic's side, and smiled back at Ondrejov with all her heart. She had never looked younger, and never in Dominic's experience half so light-hearted. She was clear of suspicion, clear even of her suspicions of herself. Terrell had not been a hero or a patriot, but only an ambitious schemer bent on climbing in his profession, if necessary over other people's faces. She was free of him, she had her life back fresh and new, and she had Dominic tightly by the hand. She knew now, though imperfectly, how nearly she had lost him.

'Naturally I questioned the Martíneks about that incident; so already I had a picture of another kind of case, with its roots somewhere in the past, even before Mr Welland was killed. I knew from Mr Veselsky – shall I call him Mr Alda, for our purposes? – I knew from Mr Alda that he had known Terrell, and worked in the same enterprise with him in England. I knew from your activities that you suspected Terrell had been hunting for someone or something in the neighbourhood of Zbojská Dolina, and I knew from Ivo the nature of the lead he – and you after him – had found. Of Welland I knew only that he had known Terrell, and that he, too, was returning with marked persistence to the place where Terrell had died, also plainly in search of something there. It was as evident to me as it was to you that every thread led into the heart of that one valley, and that the person to whom all those threads were leading must be Mr Alda. The man who had known and worked with Terrell, and reported his death, the man who had an English past of some importance. Which, naturally, we, too, investigated.

'Now you, Miss Barber, have been so kind as to fill in all the gaps. It is very lucky for me that Mr Welland was forced by circumstances to confide in you. I had not this detailed knowledge then, but I had enough to show me that certain persons, *all English*, were very much interested in locating Mr Alda, and that after the death of the first of them those of you who were continuing the search obviously held that same death to be murder. I knew it was not; but it was interesting to think that there was somewhere, known to someone, a reason why it *could* have been murder. And the second death *was* murder. I was not altogether prepared for that, never having taken it quite seriously. Your secret agent game became real, quite suddenly, because it appeared there *was* someone who was desperate to prevent you from finding Mr Alda, someone who had killed and would kill again to keep the facts about his departure from England from being re-examined, or the case re-opened in any way.

'But where I had the advantage of you, of course, was in knowing beforehand that it *could not* be Mr Alda himself. We preserve his quietness here, but that is not the same thing as keeping his secrets. He lives a life in which not even an Englishman could find anything underhand or controversial, he had nothing to hide and nothing to fear, and he would not care how many English people came investigating him, provided they didn't hinder his work. For the same reasons, *it could not be any other Czech or Slovak*, official or unofficial.'

He had reached this point, when there was a knock on the outer door. Mirek got up from his place and looked enquiringly at his chief.

'Let him in,' said Ondrejov, settling his solid body more complacently in his wooden arm-chair, and his chin more contentedly into his chest. 'Let's see who's the first.'

Every head turned to watch the doorway; and into it, all the more belligerently for his considerable inward disquiet, marched Paul Newcombe. He looked quietly round the circle, caught the excitement that burned in them all, and was alarmed, caught the glow and animation of Tossa's face, and was reassured. He halted, uncertain what to make of them.

'You left a message for me at the hotel. I was only out for a walk.'

'Come in, Mr Newcombe, come in. Mirek, find Mr Newcombe a chair. You're just in time,' pursued Ondrejov amiably, 'to hear me conclude that the only person who could possibly have an interest in preventing an Englishman from finding Mr Alda was someone connected with the circumstances in which he left England, someone who had gained by that case, and stood to lose by any reappraisal. In fact, *another Englishman*.'

'I know absolutely nothing about this affair,' Paul said loudly and aggressively, his bull head lowered in an instant. 'I came from Vienna only because of Tossa, and that's all I care about. But I can account for every minute I've spent in this country.'

'Ah, but you need not, Mr Newcombe. Sit down, and be easy. You were never a very likely suspect. Now if it had been Terrell's murder, I might have wondered . . . But in any case you have accounted for yourself quite adequately,' said Ondrejov, grinning like a happy demon, 'simply by being here – and alive.'

* * *

'We have, then, our hypothetical Englishman. Can we give him any distinguishing features? A face? Not exactly, but an office or a status, perhaps, yes. He was connected with Mr Alda's life and work in England. He gained by his leaving England. That, at least, was my theory.

'Now, thanks to Miss Barber, I know much more about Welland, how he came into the case, what his motives were, what sort of man he was. We know that he went to the Marrion Institute, and proposed that he, being here on the spot, should investigate what he believed to be Terrell's murder. He saw it as something they owed to the dead man, and to justice itself. Now I ask you, how could any of those in authority openly deprecate his zeal? They could not. In any case it seems he would not have agreed to drop his quest. I invite you to look closely at Mr Welland, for I think he is worth it. There is every sign that he was a good, conscientious and honest man. And what follows? He would have insisted on investigating to the bitter end, and I think he would have made the truth known, no matter what that truth turned out to be. Which would not have suited X at all, for X alone knew exactly what was there to be uncovered.'

'I hope,' said Alda drily, 'that you can make that good. For I tell you plainly, *I* am still in the dark.'

'Well, let me theorise, it was all I could do then, and what Miss Barber has told me since fits in with my theory. As for you, you do not know only because you do not care. You will see!

'Given, then, a devoted avenger who means to know the truth, and will not be stopped by persuasion, and cannot for shame's sake be stopped by a prohibition, what is to be done? Use him! Let him find Alda, and then both he and Alda can be eliminated, and there's an end of it. Let him find Alda, yes, but only if it can be ensured that he shall report his whereabouts only in the right quarter. It seemed to me that X must be in a position to know all about that interview at the Institute, and also to give orders to Welland concerning this case, to say in effect: "You will preserve absolute secrecy, reporting only to me", and be trusted and obeyed. "Security" is such a useful word, and can blanket so many personal meannesses.

'Now see what Miss Barber has told us about the last words Welland ever spoke to her. "He couldn't have

known . . ." *He*? Obviously the expected he, the defecting
scientist, the one who was thought to have things to hide,
and had nothing, except his personal privacy. "—*no one
else* knew . . ." No one else but the one, or the ones,
to whom he had already reported, the ones who had the
right to know! He said it himself, and then he understood
what it meant, and he cried: "Impossible!" Impossible
that his superior, the person, or one of the persons, for
whom he was working, could also be his murderer. But
he knew then that it was not impossible, that it was the
truth.

'Such was my theory. And if this was true, then both Miss
Barber and Mr Felse were in danger after that death, simply
because they had been present, and he might have confided
something to them. Fortunately the circumstances made it
possible for me to place Miss Barber in safety by holding
her on suspicion. You would have made things much more
difficult for me if you had told the truth the first time, but
luckily you did not. And this, again, enabled me to inform
the British Embassy that she was being held. You will surely
understand how very curious I was to see exactly who would
turn up to take charge of her . . .'

It was not a knock this time, only the sudden, rather
high-pitched, imperious English voice in the outer room.
Ondrejov drew in a long, contented breath, knowing this
one, and knowing him the most expendable.

'Another chair, Mirek.' He rubbed his hands; how
convenient that he had been able to secure all the time
he wanted, simply by deflecting Major Kriebel's most avid
attention to the salvage operations already under way in
Zbojská Dolina. 'Ah, Counsellor! Come in, come in! You
received my message, then.'

Charles Freeling closed the door after him with quiet
precision, to show how perfectly he was in control of both
his own reactions and the right manipulation of inanimate
things.

'I should have been here earlier, but I had some trouble
hiring a car. I preferred to come in person. Am I to take it
that the matter is now cleared up, and Miss Barber no longer
under restraint? Or is it intended to charge her?'

He took his stand, significantly, at her side, even laid
his fingers delicately on her shoulder in reassurance. She
did not even notice; she was clinging to Dominic's hand,
but she was watching Ondrejov, with wonder and delight,

her newly released and exuberant senses sharing his slightly mischievous but utterly human pleasure in his game.

'No, there will be no charge against her, Mr Freeling. I am in process of uncovering the murderer of Mr Welland, by elimination. I hope you will join us for the remainder of my exposition. We had reached the point of demonstrating that the murderer must be an Englishman, and one in a position of authority.'

Freeling's eyebrows soared. Ondrejov was meant to notice them, and to appreciate, if it was not beyond him, the neat, satirical smile that accompanied their elevation. 'I hope, I do hope, Lieutenant, that I am not your man?'

It was an attractive idea, in its way, and even just barely possible. Was it too much to conceive that a devoted and orthodox public servant might feel called upon to wipe out a less devoted and less orthodox one, in order to keep a discreditable case from being reviewed to England's embarrassment? It would have made a nice ending. A pity!

'You have good reason to hope so, Counsellor,' said Ondrejov earnestly. 'My man is already very, very dead.'

'Well, as you know, there were four who ran gallantly to protect Miss Barber, and to argue eloquently that she should be released in their custody. I did not put her in that somewhat risky situation, naturally, since by then I was convinced that one of them had designs on her life. But I did, with planned safeguards, allow them a chance at Mr Felse. A chance which his own enterprise considerably complicated.

'We have now reduced our four to two. But we still have those two people to choose from, and the motives are surely taking form. Both of these men gained by ensuring Mr Alda's disgrace. One of them, as I have learned, assisted Terrell in the compilation of the notorious dossier, was advanced in his profession as a result, and has now stepped into Terrell's shoes. The other became head of the Marrion Institute, a promotion which would have been unlikely if Mr Alda had continued – I believe the word is "clean".'

'It isn't enough,' said Alda, suddenly and with authority. 'Neither motive is strong enough for murder. For his whole career, for his reputation, a man might take such desperate measure. But my return now, even my vindication, would not have unseated anyone or disgraced anyone. Even if they all conspired to produce that dossier on me, and so quickly, all they had to do was sit tight and plead that they had acted throughout in good faith. They wouldn't be broken for that, either of them. Believe me, I know my England. They would be supported and covered to the limit, short of something like murder. I might get my reputation back, a little finger-marked. They wouldn't lose theirs.'

'They do not discard their failures?' Ondrejov asked with interest.

'On the contrary, they promote them.'

'And we are too quick to discard ours. Somewhere there must be a workable compromise.' He scrubbed his chin with hard knuckles till the bristles rasped, and spared one twinkling glance to enjoy the lofty forbearance of Freeling's face. 'Well, I accept your judgment. Then there must be more.'

Dominic looked at Tossa, and she looked back at him with all her being open and happy behind her eyes, drawing him in. He closed his fingers on hers. 'Tossa, do you remember, you told us at the Riavka that there were note-books that vanished?' It was a detail she had forgotten to mention, in her haste, when rushing through her story to Ondrejov, an hour ago. 'Tell them about that. What Welland told you.'

She caught the glitter of his excitement without understanding it, and turned quickly to look at Alda. 'Mr Welland said they told him at the Marrion that you took all your papers away with you, when you went. All your notes, all your plans . . . They told him the potential value was enormous, that you had planned work with you that could easily account for murder.'

'Notes? Plans?' Alda met her eyes across the circle with a grey-blue stare of detached astonishment. 'I never intended to leave. I went on holiday with a rucksack, and when I got back to Briancon I found myself already a traitor. I took nothing with me. What I stood up in, a change of shirt and underclothes, some music paper, and a little money. Nothing more.'

'But you *had* projected work?' said Dominic intently. 'Ideas that might have worked out and been worth a lot? You had them there, in the Institute?'

'Oh, yes, several. Some might have foundered. Most would have worked out. But I give you my word I left them there.'

'Yet Robert Welland told me,' said Tossa, her shining eyes fixed eagerly on Ondrejov, 'that somebody there in the Institute – he didn't say who, but *one* of them – told him Mr

Alda had removed all his notes and papers. He said nobody knew it, except the Institute and the Ministry.'

'And, don't you remember,' Dominic took up just as ardently, appealing to Alda, 'up there in your hut you told me about the crop-sprayer? The helicopter adaption? One of your ideas, put on the market by a commercial firm in France? How many years' work would it have taken, to put it into production?'

'Three. Four, perhaps, without me. It was a completely new engine, driving a re-designed three-blade rotor. I was glad to see it produced for ordinary, human uses. But someone else must have hit on it. Why should my design turn up in France?'

'Because it was safer than selling it in England,' said Dominic. 'Are you even sure it's the only one?'

'No,' admitted Alda, startled. 'How can I be sure? There could be others. I shouldn't care, I shouldn't think myself robbed. Better they should be used in the open market than filed for Institute modulations. They were always military! And we were not even a military establishment.'

'And how many were there in all, in these notebooks?' asked Ondrejov. 'How many such marketable projects?'

'It's hard to remember. Perhaps as many as nine or ten, at this same stage. Some others merely conceived and sketched out.'

'A fortune!' said Ondrejov, and sat back with a long breath of fulfilment, spreading his hands peacefully on the table. 'Is it enough to kill for now? To keep this from being uncovered? Would they have kept their jobs then? Their reputations? Either of them could have done it. You are gone, your papers are there. How easy, if the idea dawns in time, to make away with them, and say: You see, his flight was premeditated, he removed everything! Who would doubt it? Who would stop to wonder? It is a time of hysteria, press and public would make enough outcry to cover one man's orderly retreat with a stolen fortune under his arm. Either of them could have done it. Either of them was a natural repository for Welland's reports – one the Director, the other the Security Officer. Both of them turn up here. Either of them could have followed Welland to his rendezvous and shot him, and then returned from the scene, the one by plane back to Prague, the other to the White Carpathians – three or four hours by car, what is that? – in time to be fittingly surprised and distressed when he heard of Miss

Barber's detention. Either of them could have acted on my hints, and followed Mr Felse this morning, waiting to pick him off and make away with another possible witness. Mr Blagrove could have hired a car in Mikulás – was that why *you* had difficulty, Counsellor? – Sir Broughton Phelps already had a car, hired in Bratislava. *One* of them had bought a ZKM 581 hunting rifle, with telescopic sights and the special sixteen-cartridge magazine. *Which*?'

The knock on the door and the abrupt burr of the telephone came at the same moment.

'Come in!' shouted Ondrejov, and reached for the telephone. *'Ondrejov! No, islo to! Dobre, dobre!'* Hanging upon the telephone with held breath, and watching the door with snapping, sparkling blue eyes, he saw Adrian Blagrove enter the room, his long face wary, his long lips faintly disdainful, his aloof eyes more than a little defensive.

'D'akujem, uz to viem,' said Ondrejov gently to the telephone. *'Viem, kto to je.'* He hung up. 'I know,' he repeated in English, more to himself then to them. 'I know now who he is.'

He pushed the instrument away from him wearily but contentedly, to the length of his arm. 'They have found the car from Bratislava, a little above the place where you hid your van, Mr Felse, but better hidden. He had more cause to hide. And in the head of the valley they have also found Sir Broughton Phelps. What remains of him.'

Twelve

The Man with the Fujara

The light in the room had mellowed into the fine, clear gold that came between the mountains at the onset of evening, and its clarity, sharp as wine, seemed to be the appropriate colour of the quietness that had descended after the young people were gone, marshalled away decisively by Karol Alda to his grandmother's farm by the southerly col; after Paul Newcombe had accepted his polite but firm dismissal with a shrug, between offence and relief, and gone off to see about his return to Vienna next day; after the young constable had withdrawn to the outer room to clatter out the transcription of his notes on the typewriter, and Mirek Zachar had taken his Jawa and gone thankfully off-duty, with a light heart and his job completed.

'Lieutenant,' Charles Freeling began very carefully and gravely, when the three of them were alone, 'on behalf of my embassy I want to express our appreciation and admiration of the way you've handled this very difficult matter, and the consideration you showed towards these young people. I needn't tell you what a great shock this has been to us. We shall take up the matter of the Alda plans, of course. Clearly my country has done a great injustice to him, which ought to be set right. But it seems that he does not wish his case to be brought into prominence again at this late stage. For that I am grateful. We are none of us free agents, and absolute justice would seem to be a luxury we cannot always afford. At a time when technical and cultural co-operation between our countries is making such progress, is it worth while to allow old irregularities to obtrude? Publicity could do so much harm. We are being obliged to admit to a wrong. But since, after all, the man is dead . . .'

Within one hour Sir Broughton Phelps had become 'the man,' an inconvenience, disowned, deprecated. This morning they would have been rolling out red carpets for him and listening enthusiastically to his fishing stories.

'Gentlemen,' said Ondrejov, leaning back in his chair and spreading his great arms on the table with a gusty sigh, 'I am merely a policemen, with a straightforward job to do, and I shall do it. I shall pass on the relevant information to Major Kriebel, and Major Kriebel will make his report in the proper quarter. After that it is out of our hands. But I think you need not worry too much. Here the newspapers do not go in for lurid reports of murders. And even if they did, you see the chief occasion for it is already lost. There will be no charge, there will be no trial. As you say, the man is dead.'

Freeling looked at Blagrove, and Blagrove looked at Freeling, and visibly they bit on the reassurance, and found it sweet.

'And as for what you report and publish in England, provided you do no further injustice to Mr Alda or to this country, that is no responsibility of mine. "Sir Broughton Phelps Dies in Landslip in the Tatras"! It's enough that I was able to put it there, and in time. England is your own house, gentlemen,' said Ondrejov. 'Set it in order yourselves.'

Outside the farmhouse windows looking westward, shadowed by the deep overhang of the eaves, the sky was smouldering in reds and yellows and livid greens, the flamboyant refractions from the dust of the talus, the funeral fires of Sir Broughton Phelps. In a high-backed wooden chair Mrs Veselsky presided, bolt upright, eighty-three years old, and as clear-cut as the steely profile of Kriván, her lace cap and embroideries formal as a queen's regalia, her face proud and serene as she watched her grandson. Toddy and Christine, most readily adjusted, least involved, least changed of them all, hung enchanted over the grand piano that filled one end of the room, where Alda had spread out for them, on an embroidered shawl, the assembly of the pipes of Slovakia.

They passed from hand to hand, smoothing them and marvelling at their intricate decoration, the six-finger-holed labial pipe, the double pipe, the end-hold *koncovka*, the transverse folk flute, the children's reed-pipes, the ragman's whistle, the whole complex family from the toy *fanfárka* to the great *fujara*. Not the same as they had left in the hut over the col; this one was at least six inches longer, and even more wonderfully painted and carved and inlaid.

'Well, anyhow,' said Dominic, with his sore cheek against the cool tiles of the empty porcelain stove, Tossa close beside him in the shadowy corner, and peace on his eyelids like the palm of a warm hand, 'you must admit that even when I got myself into a fight, I did find myself a genuinely defensive weapon.'

Alda laughed, stroking the long golden flank of his pipe gently. He raised the mouthpiece to his lips and the *fujara* shook out its strange, shimmering banner of notes, forked and flying, as his fingers vibrated on the holes. He drew out the improvisation long and lovingly, brought it circling down like a skylark from the wild heights of air into the nest of one lingering, full, fluting note, out of which the melody rose plaintively and slowly, unfolding with such deliberation that they followed it like creatures bewitched, feeling their way, knowing it before they knew that they knew it.

> *Through bushes and through briars*
> *I lately took my way . . .*

The incredible sunset was fading. Tomorrow there would be nothing left but the transient layer of dust on the stones in Zbojská Dolina, waiting for the first cleansing rain, the new rock town in the bottom of the bowl, and the almost-empty saucer at the foot of the scar. But there would still be the recurring springs, and the chestnut goats, and this music; as long as anything remained, these would remain.

> *Sometimes I am uneasy*
> *And troubled in my mind . . .*

No, that belonged to the bushes and briars of old distress. Tossa's mind, newly adult, embraced its responsibilities with awe but without fear. Chloe Terrell would be getting back from Slovakia a new daughter, out of her power, wiser, older, larger than she.

> *Sometimes I think I'll go to my love*
> *And tell to . . . her . . . my mind.*

But not yet, not here, not in this land, where they had bumped full tilt into death together, and she had been startled into mistaking a moment's human warmth and solidarity for something rarer and more personal. He mustn't touch her now, however much he longed to. She was hardly out of her chrysalis, she had to have time to try her wings.

> *But if I should go to my love,*
> *My love he will say nay . . .*

He'd almost forgotten that this was really a woman speaking, but Tossa had remembered it. She was singing the words in her husky whisper, close beside him, and her hand, hidden in the shadowy corner between them, felt for his hand, and closed on it warmly.

> *'If I show to him my boldness*
> *He'll ne'er love me again.'*

There was no urgency now, and no danger; and yet when he turned his head and saw her smiling at him in the dimming light, her eyes looked to him just as they had looked before she left him in the chapel, only to wait for him, against orders, at the edge of the trees: clear, assured, roused and glad.

'Wouldn't it be a marvellous world,' said Tossa, staring ahead into a future as uncertain and dangerous as the future had always been, and yet as attractive and promising, 'where we could go straight up to one another and ask what we wanted to know? Where all the secret formulae turned out to be songs, and all the rifles were *fujaras*!'

Mourning Raga

The whole affair began, as the unexpected and chaotic so often did, with Tossa's mother. And as usual, on the telephone.

Tossa's mother was herself unexpected and chaotic, though contained in as neat and trim a package as you could wish, slim and brown and perennially young, even after three marriages and two widowhoods. She had begun life – indeed, she still continued it, with unflagging verve and success – as Chloe Bliss, a perfect name for the stage though it also happened to be her own by the grace of fate; had been in succession Chloe Barber, until Tossa's professor father inconsiderately died in his charming prime, Chloe Terrell, until the infinitely less interesting and less suitable Herbert Terrell fell off a mountain in Slovakia and got the worst of it in the consequent collision with a slab of white trias limestone, and Chloe Newcombe, which after two years, rather surprisingly, she still was. Perhaps Paul Newcombe, on the face of it a depressingly solid and stolid type of business manipulator, was more durable than he looked; perhaps, even, there was more to him than met the eye. If he was to hold Chloe's vagrant interest much longer there would certainly need to be.

The enchanting creature who was such a problem to her husband was no less a headache to her daughter, with the rueful difference that there was only one daughter, and she could never shuck off the load on to a successor. It was late now for Chloe to produce a co-custodian, even if she did still look no more than thirty. In lieu of a son she had cheerfully set up a stake in a prospective son-in-law. In any case, Chloe could never resist putting on her maximum charm for any young man who was drawn into her orbit. Usually they succumbed; in Dominic Felse's case she was content to play it as a delicious game, and close her devastating purple-brown eyes to the consideration of whether she was winning or losing. After all, Miss Theodosia Barber was her daughter, and in her complex and evasive heart Chloe had a natural love for her, and – even better – a very healthy and wary respect.

They were in Tossa's rooms in a genteelly decaying corner of north Oxford when the call came through, and Dominic's recently-acquired third-hand Mini was sitting at the kerb outside, waiting to take them down for the Christmas vacation. They were looking forward to a peaceful celebration in the bosom of his family, and privately congratulating themselves on the fact that Chloe was frantically filming, well behind schedule, somewhere in Somerset, and hardly likely to give a thought to her daughter's activities while the panic lasted. Conscience prompted her to manifest mother-love from time to time, with an over-exuberance which was designed to make up for the long neglects in between; but conscience knew better than to interfere with business. Consequently the maternal interludes usually came when they could do the most devastating damage to Tossa's plans, and none whatsoever to Chloe's.

The phone rang in the hall below. Across the case on which Dominic was kneeling they looked sharply and speculatively at each other. Dominic's left eyebrow elevated itself dubiously. He said: 'Uh-huh!' in a tone Tossa was inclined to resent, though she herself frequently said very much more on the same subject.

'It may not be for me,' she said, convincing nobody.

But it was for her. Her landlady's voice called up to her with the promptness of a derisive echo, and she went down resignedly to fend off the inevitable. Distant and guarded, gruffer than usual with defensive tension, her miniature baritone eddied up the staircase:

'Tossa Barber here – Oh, yes . . . hullo, Mother! How are you? How is the shooting going?' Side-track her back into her proper sphere, that was the strategy; but Chloe could always talk twice as sweetly and three times as fast. 'Yes, well, darling, you know we were going up to Midshire . . .'

Were going! Dominic stopped wrestling with the recalcitrant lock of Tossa's big case, and conveyed himself across the room and halfway down the stairs in a hurry, to a position where he could sit and brood balefully over the conversation, and make entirely sure that his interests were not forgotten. Every time she raised her eyes she could not help but see him, shamelessly listening and willing her to harden her heart. Chloe had a particularly annoying way of erupting just when they were all set for a holiday.

Computing the total content of a telephone conversation from one end of it, and the passive end at that, is never easy. With a kingfisher mind like Chloe's at the far end of the line it was next door to impossible.

'Yes, I remember you said she had . . . terribly interesting! Well, but what can I . . .' A long interval of the distant purring, while Tossa's eyes took on a stunned and glazed look first of shock and then of total non-comprehension. Something fearful was going on. Dominic loomed threateningly, and she flashed him a helpless glance and shook her head at him to show she hadn't forgotten everything they had arranged between them. '*Where*? But . . . No, but you're serious? I . . . well, of course I do see how marvellous, but . . . So *far*! And I'd be scared, alone! Oh! . . . Oooohh!' she breathed in a long, awakening sigh, and a gleam came to life, far behind the glassy astonishment of her eyes, and grew and grew, like a moonrise. A hint of excited colour flicked her cheeks. Drat the girl, she was falling for it, whatever *it* was, after all her years of experience with that infuriating, lovely mother of hers. Dominic shuffled his feet and cleared his throat menacingly, and Tossa looked up and smiled at him with the eerie bliss of a sleepwalker. 'But would she really . . . for *both* of us? Well, of course, I do realise it's a once-in-a-lifetime chance . . . But, gosh, Mother, I don't know! I *would* love to . . . I bet he would, too . . . Look, let me talk to him and call you back . . .'

'Yes,' said Dominic grimly, just too quietly to be heard at the other end, 'you do that! Get her off there and give *me* a chance to get some sense into you. *That Chloe!*'

'A quarter of an hour, Mother, yes, I promise. Give me that number again . . .'

She cradled the receiver and came drifting up the stairs muttering it to herself, and Dominic gave her his ball-pen to write it down, before she lost herself among the digits. She looked a little drunk, on what manner of intoxicant he couldn't imagine. *She* was usually the one who had all the evasion ready when Chloe sent out distress signals. She, after all, could be as cynical as she liked about her own mother; Dominic knew better than to venture on the same terms. He had an instinct for the exact line where his privilege ran out, and he was light on his feet, and could always stop short of it. He took her by the hand and towed her back into her own room. Her knees gave under her; she sat down dreamily on the bed, staring through him into the pale December sky.

'Now, look, we were going to my parents in Comerford, remember?' Help, she'd got him talking in the wrong tense now! 'We *are* going!'

'Yes, of course! I haven't forgotten anything. If you say so, when you know . . . if *they* say so, that's where we're going. I wouldn't ditch them for anybody in the world. You know that. But wait till I tell you what she offered us . . .'

'Us!' Yes, give her that, Tossa had made sure that he was included.

'It isn't what you think, she doesn't want us to go to her for Christmas! Not a thought of it! She's totally taken up with this film, all they'll do about Christmas is throw a party right there on the set, and get as high as kites, and then go right back to work. That's the stage they're at, I've seen it all before. No, this is something that only happens once. That's why I didn't say no. I *couldn't*! I mean, with only one lifetime, and money not all that easy to come by . . . Well, what would *you* have said?' she challenged warmly.

'How do I know, until I know what you're talking about? What *does* she want us to do?'

'She wants us,' said Tossa, her voice growing faint with mingled wonder and disbelief, 'to take a little girl to India.'

Dominic sat down abruptly on the suitcase and the stubborn lock, as if electing itself a sign and portent for the occasion, clicked smugly into place, ready for off. Though it wasn't as simple as that; for India, at this time of year, you'd want . . . what? Not the winter casuals of workaday Oxford, at any rate. Cottons? Light sweaters? Good lord, what was happening? He was taking it seriously, and it could only be some sort of mistake, or somebody's idea of an elaborate joke. He sat staring at her warily, and pushed resolutely out of his mind visions of temples and royal palms, and the legendary beach at Kovalam, and . . .

'You did say "India"? And you're sure that's what *she* said?'

'I asked her again. She said it twice. She said "Delhi", too. There isn't any mistake.'

'And *both* of us can go?'

'She said so. I said I'd be scared alone.' That was a useful formula, and he knew it; what it meant was: 'Not without Dominic!' and he was duly grateful for it. There were many things of which Tossa was wary and suspicious, after her experiences with parents and step-parents, but very few of which she was scared.

'All expenses paid?' That was how it had sounded.

'Money's no object.'

'But *whose* money?' The only little girl Chloe had was sitting there on the edge of the bed, staring at him with eyes so wide in wonder that the highlights in them soared into silvery domes like the Taj Mahal. And in any case Chloe spent her money as fast as she earned it, not to mention making formidable inroads into her husband's as well.

'Dorette Lester's. It's her little girl we're supposed to escort to Delhi.'

'Who's Dorette Lester?' demanded Dominic, unaware of his blasphemy. Only Julie Andrews shed more sweetness and light, but then, the few films he did see never seemed to be that kind of film.

'She's the American star they brought over to play Marianne in this film Chloe's making. I told you. Everybody thought they'd fight like tigresses, and they fell into each other's arms on first sight, and have been as thick as thieves ever since. That's how it comes that Chloe's willing to lend me to help out Dorette over the kid. She wants us to drive down to Bath and hear all about it, and get fixed up about dates and everything. I suppose we could do that much, anyhow, couldn't we?'

'Today? Now?'

She nodded. The scintillation of desire, fever-white, was still in her eyes. You don't get offered India on a salver every day. 'We can still say no, if we want to.' But she didn't want to, and neither did he. Not if this was on the level. They eyed each other thoughtfully, still chary of believing in such luck.

'There has to be a catch in it,' said Dominic firmly.

She didn't argue; she knew her mother even better than he did, and it was a reasonable assumption that they would trip over a string or two sooner or later. 'It would have to be a big one to tip the scale much, wouldn't it?' she said honestly.

Dominic got up and hoisted the suitcase on which he had been sitting. The coy lock held, ready for any journey. 'You'd better call her back, hadn't you,' he said, rather as if it had been his idea all along, 'and tell her we're coming.'

Some youthful genius from down in the boutique belt, who hatched outrageous ideas on the side and sold them in much the same way as he did outrageous clothes, had come up with the improbable inspiration of making a big musical out of *Sense and Sensibility*, and with his usual luck had found suckers all round him ready to buy the notion that Jane was with it. He had besides – and it was his chief asset – a gift for concocting elegantly dry, agreeable and piquant music, so witty that it turned the most banal lyrics into epigrams, and it was an even bet that the film he had conned his less well-read contemporaries into making would turn out to be not merely a box-office bonanza, but also a surprisingly good film. They had gone the whole hog on casting it. Most of the money in the venture was American, and the producers had insisted on getting Dorette Lester to play Marianne, the 'sensibility' half of the two sisters. The English director, with equal certainty, had declared that no one but Chloe Bliss would do for Eleanor. Chloe's daughter might have cocked a quizzical eyebrow at the idea of her mother standing for 'sense', but it was what she could suggest before the cameras that mattered, not what she really was, and before the cameras or an audience there was nothing Chloe could not be, from an electrifying Ariel in *The Tempest* to an awe-inspiring grande dame in Wilde. Musicals were something new for her, but she took to the form like a duck to water. She sang the outrageously clever songs of the boy genius, half-pop, half-avant-garde, with such conviction that even the composer was startled. He had never taken them all that seriously himself. What he did was juggle the notes and words around a little, and the money came rolling in. He had never ceased to find it funny, but was a little unnerved when he found it could also be moving.

One of those ladies hired to play the youthful Dashwood sisters was turned forty, and the other was thirty-six, and there were plenty of genuine teen-age actresses to be found, what with half the pop singers taking to the boards or the screen or both as to the manner born; yet nobody seemed to find the casting at all strange. Only a year ago Chloe Bliss had added a superlative Peter Pan to her repertoire. And as for Dorette Lester, one of her most passionate admirers had once said that she couldn't sing, couldn't dance, couldn't really do very much in the acting line, and didn't have to; just looking at her was enough. But if she had to act, it had better be in some such part as the hypersensitive and emotional Marianne Dashwood, where over-acting, controlled by an intelligent director, wouldn't show.

Dorette had been married in her early twenties, before she became a star. Tossa told Dominic all about it, or as much as she herself had gleaned from Chloe's thumbnail sketch, on the way down to Somerset in the Mini.

'The way I see it, she can't have been much then, and apparently he was rich, and must have been no end of a catch. A couple of years later, and she probably wouldn't have looked at him. He was a graduate from the University of the Punjab, doing post-graduate work in research physics and chemistry over in the States. Anyhow, she married him. And they had this little girl. And then things clicked into place, the way they do at the wrong moment, and she made a hit and grew into a star. And I suppose she got very busy and involved with her job, and he was just as busy with his, and maybe they were too far apart ever to make a go of it. Anyhow, they didn't. She divorced him years ago, and gave herself wholly to her career. And he went back to India, and presumably devoted himself to his.'

'And the little girl,' said Dominic, after a pause for reflection, and in a tone of some wonder, 'is now about to be shipped off after him?'

'That's the way it looks.' And she aded doubtfully: 'Maybe just for a visit?' Dominic said nothing to that; he didn't think so, either. 'Well, it seems she's getting married again. Dorette, I mean. Maybe he doesn't react too well to the idea of a ready-made daughter nearly fourteen years old.'

'Or maybe she thinks he won't. I don't suppose she's ever asked him. Or asked the kid what *she* thinks about it.' A possible catch was beginning to appear, and he couldn't help wondering what they were getting themselves into. Still, if the case was as he was beginning to suppose, it could be argued that the little girl would be better off with her father. Or hadn't he wanted her, either? He seemed to have let her go without too much of a fight, and put the width of the world between them.

'Still,' said Tossa, mind-reading beside him, 'we shall have to go on and take a look at the whole set-up now, I've committed us to that. We can always back out if we don't like the look of it.'

She looked at Dominic warily along her shoulder; there was something in the acute care he was suddenly giving to his driving, and the look of almost painful detachment on his face, that told her he had found himself abruptly reminded how delicate might be the ground on which they were treading. For Tossa also was the child of an egocentric actress, and her early years also had been bedevilled by her mother's remarriages and haunted by her mother's wit, charm and success, which left her seedling only shady ground in which to grow. He needn't have worried, Tossa was very well able, by this time, to make good her right to a place in the sun. The amiable conflict between mother and daughter was fought on equal terms these days, and as long as Dominic was on her side Tossa had the secure feeling that she was winning. Still, all experience remains there in the memory to be drawn upon that need.

'When you come to think of it,' said Tossa practically, 'I might be just the right person for this job. If the kid is going to be flown off to her father in any case, it might as well be with somebody who's been in much the same boat, and knows the language.' And somebody else, she thought, but did not say, who's never had parent trouble in his life, and doesn't know how lucky he is, but manages to rub off some of the luck on to other people even without realising it.

'It might, at that,' agreed Dominic, cheered. 'Anyhow, let's go and see.'

By which time they were close to the turn that led to the Somerset studio, and the issue was as good as decided.

The Misses Eleanor and Marianne Dashwood sat side by side on a flimsy, gilded, Empire sofa like twin empresses receiving homage, pretty as new paint and something more than content with each other. 'Thick as thieves,' Tossa had said, but in this white, gold and pale blue elegance it seemed an inadmissibly crude phrase – even though the white and gold was gimcrack when you came close to it, and stopped abruptly twenty feet away, to give place to the hollow, cluttered chaos of any other sound stage, littered with skeleton fragments of booms and wiring and cameras and lighting equipment, and a miscellaneous assortment of frayed, bearded, distrait people carrying improbable things and using improbable words in several languages. 'Cheek by jowl' suggested itself, Dominic thought, in some underhand way, but could hardly be entertained in face of Eleanor's resolute and shapely little chin and Marianne's damask-rose cheek. In view of the late-Empire ball gowns of Indian muslin, the daintily deployed curls, dark brown and scintillating gold, and the white silk mittens that stopped only just short of the creamy shoulders, better settle for hand-in-glove. As sure as fate, that was what they were; and anyone around here who had plans that involved manipulating these two Dresden deities had better watch out, because he would be playing a formidable team.

It was an earnest of their sheer professionalism that even between takes they continued to look in character, Chloe gently grave and cool and exceedingly well-bred, Dorette sparkling and distressed by turns, as extrovert as a fountain. Neither of them put her feet up or lit a cigarette. They sat with one foot delicately tucked behind the other, to show a glimpse of a pretty ankle, as young ladies were taught to sit once, long before the miniskirt and the glorious freedom of tights. Dominic revised a half-conceived notion of what Dorette must be like; she might not be a gifted actress, but she was an intelligent diplomat who could make what gifts she had do just as well.

And talk! She could talk the hind leg off a donkey!

' . . . and then, you see, Tossa – Oh, forgive me! May I call you Tossa? You see, I feel I know you already, your mother has talked so much about you. And you're so *like* her, did you know that?' Tossa knew it, and could hardly fail to be flattered by it, even though she often looked in the glass to find the homely, reassuring outlines of her father's face, less obviously but just as surely there behind the delicate flesh, and the straight, bright, luminous gleam of fun in the eyes that could only have come from him. ' . . . and then, his family made it quite impossible, you know. Oh, Satyavan was simply the new India in person, travelled, educated, sophisticated, brilliant and already rich in his own right . . . he had a company making beautiful cosmetics, and another one running travel agencies all over the East and the Middle East. The family were rupee millionaires even before him, but that was all in textiles, cottons and silks, and they really looked down on anything else. An old family, too, and these Punjabis are very proud. So *I* was the undesirable one, you see. His mother was broken-hearted when he married me. She'd been widowed for two years then, and Satyavan was the only child, and of course, you know, *sons* . . . *Hindu* sons . . . Sometimes I think that if only Anjli had been a boy . . . But she wasn't, and then there weren't any more children.' She wiped away, discreetly and with great dignity, a non-existent tear. 'Really we never had a chance to bridge the gulf. And it *is* a *real* gulf, one would need a lot of patience, and love, and craft . . . and luck! And luck we didn't have.'

Dominic hedged his bet still more cautiously. Only a very

clever woman would have used the word 'craft' just there. Moreover, Chloe, delicately fanning, her wide eyes on her fictional sister with all the critical admiration of a second watching his expert principal in a duel (and without any qualms whatsoever about the outcome), had raised one eyebrow with a connoisseur's approbation, and the corners of her very charming and very knowing mouth had curled into an infinitesimal and brief smile of pleasure. What chance had any husband with women like these?

'And he didn't even try to get custody of Anjli?' Tossa had seen the omens, too, and reacted with a blunt and discordant question; simply, thought Dominic, to see what would happen.

Dorette's damask cheek bloomed into the most delicious peach colour, and again faded to the waxen white perfection of magnolias. Dominic was fascinated. The magicians of the world would go grey overnight, worrying how she did that in full view of her audience, at a range of a few feet, and in harsh film lighting.

'Tossa, you must be charitable, you must understand . . . Poor Satyavan, you mustn't think he didn't love her . . .' (Or why, thought Dominic ruthlessly, would you be shoving her off on to him now, you being the loving mother you are?) 'Yes, he did try . . . indeed he tried very hard. But you see, at that time we were so bitter, both of us. And I fought just as hard. Perhaps it was simply that I was American . . . for after all, there is an understanding, don't you think so? . . . of one's own people? They gave her to me. That was all that mattered then. I didn't think of him . . . of his mother . . . To an Indian woman sons and grandsons are everything, but even a granddaughter would be such joy . . . But it's only afterwards that one realises the cost to other people. You mustn't think I haven't thought about this for a long time, and gone through agony. All these years, ever since she was six years old. I've had the joy of her, and he . . . My poor Satyavan . . .' She made a little poem out of the name this time, the first 'a' muted to a throw-away sound almost like 'u', the second a long sigh of 'aaah'! Her wisp of an embroidered Jane Austen handkerchief came into brief, subdued play. No doubt about it, Dorette was an artist.

Tossa's dry little, gruff little voice said: 'Yes, I do see, he must have missed her terribly!' But Chloe's undisturbed smile said serenely that Dorette was doing very well, and could afford to hold her fire. Perhaps she even read her daughter's implacable motives; whatever the doubts about Dorette's brain, now rapidly being revised, there had never been any doubts about Chloe's. Dominic held his peace, and saw the Taj Mahal clear as in a vision.

'Tossa, there's a time even to give up what one wants and needs, a time to remember . . . not other people's wants and needs, but *theirs*. The children's.' Dorette turned her head and gave them the benefit of her full blue stare, radiant and dazzling; and her beauty, of which they had heard so much and thought so little, was absurd, agonising, irresistible. They understood her power, and being immune to it made no difference when the rest of the world was vulnerable. She looked eighteen, agitated, appealing, Marianne to the life. The Austen irony was missing, perhaps, but this was between takes. 'She had a whole family there, wanting and longing for an heir. She has a *kingdom*, you might say. What right have I to keep her from it? What can I give her to make up for it? In America she is just one little girl, not nearly a princess. And my husband . . .' She looked momentarily doubtful about the word, but shouldered it and went on: 'He has rights, too. She knows nothing of the world *he* can offer her, and she has a right to know everything before she makes a choice. When I marry again . . .' Oh, noble, that brave lift of her head, facing the whole world's censure for love! Or money. Or *something*! ' . . . she will be watching us from a cool distance, I know that. She knows who her father was, she knows he is far away, and almost lost to her. I want to be honest with her! I want her to go to her father!'

A pale person in an unravelling pullover and a green eyeshade leaned through the pump-room palms and called: 'Any time, Dorrie!' and Miss Lester, switching from emotion and sincerity to a note of sharp practicality which Tossa found almost insulting, called back in quite a different tone: 'Coming, Lennie! Give us three minutes more!' and as promptly returned to character. As though Chloe's two student stand-ins for a New England governess who declined to cross the world had been a couple of cameras trained on her. No more sales-talk was necessary, Chloe's brief, reassuring glance had told her they were sold already; still, for her reputation's sake she kept up the performance in a modified form and at an accelerated tempo.

'My husband is expecting his daughter. I wrote to him a month ago, before I left the States, to tell him that she would be coming. He will be so happy to see her, and so grateful to you.'

For one brief and uncharacteristic moment she looked back, remembering a thin, fastidious face set in the tension of distaste and disbelief as he argued his case in court, with the dignity he was incapable of laying aside, and which had passed for arrogance and coldness. He could hardly be expected to compete with such an artist in heartbreak and tears and maternal desperation as Dorette Lester; sometimes she wondered why he had even tried. And sometimes, too, she wondered exactly why he had waived his rights of access, resigned from his science chair, and left for India immediately after the divorce suit ended. Was it outraged love and implacable anger against his wife who had shucked him off - a broken heart, in fact? Or had he merely extricated himself in shock and disgust from a world he had suddenly realised was not for him, a jungle not denser than, but different from, his own? She knew better than to simplify his withdrawal; herself uncomplicated though occasionally devious, she was subtle enough to recognise a greater subtlety.

'I will give you his address in Delhi, and his mother's too - Mrs Purnima Kumar - just in case of any contretemps. There will be no difficulty, you'll see. And of course, *all* expenses will be my concern, I'll see that you have plenty of funds. No need even to hurry back, after all, you must see something of India while you're there. Satyavan will be glad to help you make the best use of your time, I know.'

She didn't know anything of the kind, she hadn't been in touch with her ex-husband since he left America, but the family eminence ensured that they would have to put on a show for the visitors; she had learned that much about the Kumars.

'When,' asked Tossa, with careful, measured quietness, 'is Anjli expected to arrive in London?'

'The day after tomorrow. If you could come with me to meet her at London Airport, we could have a night all together, and I could arrange your flight for the next day. Such luck, I have an old, good friend who is filming over there, quite near to Delhi, and I'll wire him to meet your plane and take care of you. If you need anything - but *anything*! - you can call on Ernest, there's nothing he wouldn't do for me. But the journey itself is just too much for a child alone. And we're so pressed, quite behind schedule, you see it's impossible for *me* . . .'

Yes, quite impossible. Not simply because it would inconvenience her, there was more to it than that. India was an alien world into which she had no wish to venture, and Satyavan Kumar was something more distant than a stranger, because he had once been so close. This much of Dorette at least was genuine, she would almost rather die than confront this part of her past again. That all-American marriage – they said this millionaire of hers was a disarmingly nice and simple person – was her life-line, she daren't let go of it for an instant to look behind her.

'You *will* take my little girl over there for me, won't you?' Knock off the calculated charm, and in its way it was still a cry from the heart.

'Dorette! You ready there?'

'Yes, Lennie! We're right with you! *Tossa, dear* . . .'

'Yes, Miss Lester . . . Yes, of course we'll take her!'

'Darling . . . so grateful . . . my mind at rest now . . . *Sure, Lennie, coming*! Day after tomorrow . . . Heathrow . . . I'll phone you the details . . . what was that Midshire number again?' And Chloe laughed, not aloud, just a faint purring sound of contentment, and hugged and kissed her own daughter briefly.

When they crept out of the sound stage she was singing, without a trace of irony, back there behind them in the furnished corner bright as a nova:

> '*When will you learn to moderate, my love,*
> *The ardour of a heart that can be broken* . . .

Tossa sat dour and silent in the Mini for some moments after they had made their way out of the lot and turned north for Midshire and Dominic's blessedly normal home. Then she said in a dubious voice: 'Of course, for all we know the father may be no better. But at least he ought to have his chance. And anyhow, *this* one's contracting out, so *somebody* has to do something.' And in a moment, with reviving optimism about the general state of man: 'We'll see what your people say about it.'

All Dominic said was: 'I still don't see where the catch is, but there has to be one somewhere.'

What Dominic's people said, almost in unison though they were tackled separately, was: 'Of course go! You'd be crazy not to. *Always* say yes to opportunity, or it may never offer again.' And his mother, viewing Tossa's grave face with sympathy, added: 'If the worst comes to the worst, *bring her back*. We can fight out the rest of it afterwards.'

So they were all there at Heathrow to meet Anjli's plane, Dorette in mink and cashmere and Chanel perfume, Chloe booted and cased in leather dyed to fabulous shades of purple and iris, with something like a space helmet on her extremely shapely little head and Ariel's formidable and lovely make-up on her clever faun's face, Dominic and Tossa top-dressed for the frost outside, but with their modest cases full of hurriedly assembled cottons and medium-weight woollens, mostly organised out of nowhere by Dominic's mother. Who now had her feet up at home, a drink at her elbow and a paperback in her hand, and only the mildest regrets at facing a quieter Christmas than she had expected. It was a long time since she'd had her husband to herself over the Christmas holidays. And what fools these children would have been to pass up India, upon any consideration, when it fell warm, aromatic and palpitating into their arms.

In the arrivals lounge the privileged crowded to the doors to see their kin erupting through passport control. Dorette swooped ahead in a cloud of pastel mink and subtle fragrance.

'*Darling*! Oh, honey, how *lovely* to see you!'

The girl turned an elegant head just in time to present her left cheek to the unavoidable kiss, adjusted her smile brightly and extricated herself more rapidly and dexterously than Dominic would have believed possible.

'Hi, Mommy! How have you been? Gee, what a flight, I'm about dead on my feet. Oh, hi! You must be Miss Bliss, Mommy's told me so much about you, and all about this darling film. My, that outfit's *keen*, you know that? It's just a *dream* . . .!'

If ever the selfconscious and phoney and the real and eager and young met in one voluble utterance, this was the time. But it took somebody Chloe's age to respond to all the nuances at once, and Chloe had relegated herself deliberately to a back seat, and didn't mean to be turfed out of it. Let Tossa, who prided herself so on her maturity, make her own way through the quicksands. Chloe smiled, kissed the pale golden cheek and made a cool neutral murmur in the small, fine, close-set golden ear.

'And here's my daughter Tossa, who's coming with you

to Delhi . . . And Dominic Felse, a friend of Tossa's . . . a
friend of all of us . . .'

'Why, sure,' said the clear, thrilling little voice, aloof as
a bird, 'any friend of yours! I just hope I get in as one of
the family, too.' She put a thin, amber hand into Tossa's,
smiled briefly and brilliantly, and passed on to Dominic with
markedly more interest. 'Hullo, Dominic! Gee, I'm lucky,
being so well looked after. I sure appreciate it, I really do.'

So this was the poor little girl! Little she was, in the
physical sense, well below average height for a fourteen-
year-old, and built of such fine and fragile bones that she
contrived to seem smaller than she was. She wore a curly
fun-fur coat in a mini-length, and a small round fur cap to
match, in dappled shades of tortoiseshell, like a harlequin
cat. Her long, slim legs were cased in honeycomb lace tights
and flexible red leather boots that stopped just short of her
knee, and the honey of her skin glowed golden through the
comb. A fur shoulder-bag slung on a red strap completed
the outfit. But the accessories of her person were every
bit as interesting. Her fingernails were manicured into a
slightly exaggerated length, and painted in a pink pearl
colour, deeper at the tips. The shape of her lips had been
quite artfully and delicately accentuated and their colour
deepened to a warm rosy gold. A thick braid of silky
black hair hung down to her waist, a red ribbon plaited
into it. Half her face was concealed behind the largest
butterfly-rimmed dark glasses Dominic had ever seen; but
the part of her that showed, cheeks and chin, was smooth
and beautifully shaped as an Indian ivory carving, and
almost as ageless. Sophistication in one miniature package
stared up at Domonic unnervingly through the smoke-grey
lenses. The obscurity of this view suddenly irked her. She
put up her free hand in a candid gesture of impatience,
and plucked off her glasses to take a longer, clearer, more
daunting look at him.

The transformation was dazzling. Thin, arched brows,
very firm and forthright, came into view, and huge, solemn,
liquid dark eyes; and the face was suddenly a child's face
as well as a mini-model's, eager, critical and curious; and
presently, with hardly a change in one line of it, greedy. No
other word for it.

She was at the right age to wish to be in love, and
to be able to fall in love almost deliberately, wherever a
suitable object offered. Dominic was a suitable object. He

saw himself reflected in the unwavering eyes, at once an idol for worship and a prey marked down.

Over Anjli's head he caught Tossa's eye, marvellously meaningful in a wooden face. They understood each other perfectly. No need to look any farther for the catch; they had found it.

Two

'I was here, once, said Anjli, unfolding the coloured brochure of Delhi across her lap with desultory interest. 'In India, I mean. But I can't remember much about it now, it's so long ago.'

'Your mother didn't tell us that,' Tossa said. 'Was she with you?'

'No, only my father. She didn't want to come, she was filming. It was the year before she divorced him. I was only just five. I used to know a little Hindi, too, but I've forgotten it all now.'

Her voice was quite matter-of-fact; she felt, as far as they could detect, no regrets over America, and no qualms or anticipation at the prospect of India. She had been brought up largely by competent people paid to do the job, and she was under no illusions about her own position or theirs. A child in her situation, intelligent and alert as she was, would have to acquire a protective shell of cynicism in order to survive, thought Tossa. Anjli knew that there was money on both sides of the family, and that however she might be pushed around from one parent to the other, that money would have to maintain her in the style to which she was accustomed. As for the cool equanimity with which she had parted from her mother at London Airport, who could be surprised by it, when she had spent most of her young life as isolated from her mother as from her distant and forgotten father?

'He brought me to see his mother, I think, but I don't remember her at all. I guess she must have been pretty upset at his marrying in America, like that, and staying away all that time. They're very clannish, aren't they?'

'Very much like the rest of us, I expect,' said Tossa. 'She'll be pleased enough when she has you on a more permanent basis, I bet.'

The Indian Airlines plane hummed steadily towards Delhi, half its passengers dozing, like Dominic in the seat across the gangway from them. Strange, thought Anjli, without resentment, almost with appreciation, how neatly Tossa had steered him into that place, though Anjli had designed that he should sit beside her, as on the long flight over. This small reverse she could afford to take in her stride; she had time enough, she calculated optimistically, to detach him from his Tossa before they left Delhi again. As yet they were only one hour inland from Bombay. The adventure had hardly begun.

'Oh, I haven't made up my mind yet about staying,' she said firmly. 'I don't know whether I'm going to like it here. It's kind of a corny country, don't you think?' She frowned down at the coloured pictures of the Red Fort and the Qutb Minar. 'All this old stuff, I mean, what's the *point*? In the States we've got everything *new*, and after all, I've grown up there. This will be an experience, but I don't figure I'm going to want to stay here too long.'

She was quite firm about it; and on reflection, Tossa thought, she was quite capable of demanding to be taken back again when India palled, and getting her own way, too. Dorette had made her plans; but so might Anjli, and there was a good deal of Dorette in Anjli, enough to make the struggle a dangerously even one if it ever came to that. And yet . . .

'Do you really think,' said Anjli suddenly, her cheek turned to the window, where the blinding light clung and quivered as it touched her lips, 'she'll be glad to have me? She's old, and she *hated* it when he married Mommy.'

'But you're not Dorette, you're you . . . partly her son. You're her only grandchild. She'll be glad,' said Tossa with certainty.

It was the nearest they had come, in all that long and tedious journey, to asking and giving sympathy; and even now Tossa felt herself to be on thin ice. Very aloof, very independent, this child; she'd be infuriated if you tried to mother her, when she'd managed for so long without any mothering. Not the clinging kind, Anjli; except of course, in a predatory fashion to Dominic's arm when the slimmest chance offered. Inscrutable, dangerous and to be respected, that was Satyavan Kumar's daughter. Tossa didn't know whether to be sorrier for the grandchild or the grandmother. Somehow, between these two, the face of the father eluded her imagination; for it had never entered Dorette's head to show her a photograph of Satyavan. Probably she hadn't even kept one, once the man himself was out of her life.

Anjli, her cheek against the sun-warmed glass, watched

the baked, thirsty land revolve beneath them, presenting a changing, circling pattern of white buildings, radiating roads, scattered green trees dispersed in a rose-red landscape. The palette of North India, apart from the hills, is a wonderful range of reds and oranges and browns, glittering with drought. In winter the green of foliage looks faded and silvery against it, and the violent crimsons and purples of early flowering trees explode like fireworks.

'Look, Delhi!'

Dominic awoke, and came to lean across them both and peer down with them at the fabled city, older than Alexander, eight cities superimposed upon one another, overlapping, showing faintly through like a palimpsest. The radiant light picked out minarets, domes, pompous white office blocks, the superb sweep of the King's Way, ruled across New Delhi in rose-pink, lined on either side with vivid grass and the embroidered mirror-glitter of water, clustering green of parks, the spinning wheel of Connaught Place with all its radial roads straight as arrows. For some moments they had a perfect sketch-map before them, then the plane settled lower and selected its way in to the international airport, and they were left with a narrowing circle of the south-western cantonment, ruled in rectangular blocks, gathering, solidifying, growing to lifesize.

Anjli, gazing dubiously down at the city of which she was mortally afraid, settled her brow artfully against Dominic's arm and counted, shrewdly, her blessings. Never look too far ahead; now is what matters. Because there isn't any tomorrow, and you can't make much capital out of yesterday, it slips through your fingers; but now is something there'll always be, even if it changes its shape.

Dominic saw the tense line of her mouth and cheek, and didn't move his arm. They watched Delhi come up to meet them, a floating city, red and white, wonderful.

The touch-down was brisk and gentle and indifferently expert. And at Palam Ernest Felder was waiting for them.

He was fifty years old, but looked younger because of his springy step and dapper carriage. They said he had given Dorette her first chance in films, years ago, and stayed a close friend of hers ever since, though by all accounts at one time he would have liked to be more to her than a friend. He had been the minor celebrity then, and she the raw beginner; now she was the reigning star of the old, wholesome school of sweet family entertainment, and he was still a minor celebrity, perhaps a rung or two lower down the ladder than when they had met, but still a director of mild distinction. Or was it co-director this time? Dorette had mentioned an Indian director who was sharing the responsibility with him on this co-production.

He met them as soon as they crossed the apron of sandbrown earth and entered the airport buildings. A large, muscular hand reached for Dominic's, acknowledging the male as automatically in charge. A shaggy, brindled grey head inclined punctiliously, a weathered, philosophical face, lined with humour and self-indulgence, beamed welcome at them all. A very well-kept body, athletic and lean, made the most of a beautifully-cut grey suit.

'Mr Felse? I'm Felder. Dorrie wired me to look out for you. Miss Barber, you're very welcome to India. I hope you're not too tired after the journey?' He turned to Anjli, and contemplated her long and fondly, while she stared back at him unblinkingly and let her small hand lie limply in his. 'And you must be Dorrie's little girl. Well, well, I haven't seen you since you were knee-high to a kitten.'

Anjli, on her dignity, looked down her nose and said: 'How do you do, Mr Felder!' in her best party tones. But he looked kind and easy-going, and his voice recalled America in this alien land, and she could not help warming to him. 'It's sure nice to have somebody here who belongs,' she said, for once without calculation, and her passive fingers stirred and gripped confidingly.

'Girlie, you're going to have no trouble at all that way, not while my bunch are here just outside town. Film people I bet you know, and film people are the same the world over, even when you've got ten sorts together, the way we have here. I've got 'em all laid on for you, a real party, so Delhi's going to feel like home. I've got the boys outside with the truck, you don't have to do a thing but just hand over to us, and we do everything.'

'It's really very kind of you,' said Tossa, and meant it, 'but I suppose we ought to contact Mr Kumar as soon as possible, oughtn't we?'

'So you ought, my dear, so you ought. But it's coming on evening, and you've all three just been rushed across the world, and it's my belief you need tonight to unwind and put your best moods and faces on ready for the moment of truth.' Bless him, he wasn't going to pretend for a moment

184

that anything about this was easy or normal. He knew his Dorette from long since, and had learned to approach the crises she created with caution and philosophy. 'Now I know she won't have wired him exactly when to expect you, or why would she hand things over to me? Yes, I know she wrote him a warning, three, four weeks ago, but that's the size of it. I know my girl! That cost her plenty. Now before you go to him you've got to have a roof over your heads that you don't owe to him, and friends right there behind you, so you can say simply: "Look, here I am. Am I welcome?" and if not, well, all right, then, that's that, goodbye. Sorry you've been troubled, and no hard feelings. We're not beggars, are we, honey? We've got places of our own to go to, and feet of our own to stand on. Right?'

He was looking at Anjli. There was a bloom of colour flooding the honey of her cheeks, and she looked tall and grave and very independent. 'Right!'

'So I reckon tomorrow morning will be time enough for Mr Kumar. Mornings are the time for starting enterprises. Right?'

'Right! And we can have this evening! We haven't seen *anything* yet. All we did at Bombay was get out of one plane at Santacruz and into another.'

'Miss Lester did say,' agreed Dominic hopefully, 'that she would arrange a hotel for us. We took it for granted that Tossa and I would need one, of course . . .'

'Don't say another word, it's all taken care of. I've booked you all in at Keen's Hotel. It's south of town, off the Lodi Road, but it's cheaper than most and just as good, and I reckoned you might want to stay around town a while, since you *are* here on Dorrie's errand. Shame to waste that air fare, who knows if it may not be once in a lifetime? How's that? Sound OK?'

'Sounds wonderful!' said Tossa with heartfelt gratitude. You didn't find a thoughtful host of this kind every day. 'It's terribly good of you.'

'Come on, then, and let's pick up your luggage, they should have turfed it out by now.' He took Anjli by the hand as naturally as a tried and trusted uncle, and surprisingly she let him. They might all get a little dizzy and confused later, if Mr Felder kept up this pace and all his unit matched up, but at the moment he was certainly a huge relief.

In through the teeming halls of Palam, as loud and busy and stunning as any other international airport, but peacock-hued with glorious saris and bleached white with invading sunlight; and out to the stands where the luggage was deposited, and the porters waited bright-eyed, heads swathed in red cloths, ready to pounce on whatever cases were claimed. Two of them secured the items Dominic indicated, and hoisted them to their padded heads. Dominic would have lifted one case himself, but Felder nudged him good-humouredly aside.

'Don't! It doesn't cost much, even if you over-tip, and these boys have to make a living. This country sure has a lot of people to feed.'

Anjli stood on the steps, and looked at the barren, parched, russet and gold land from which her father had sprung, a waste of reds, dead-rose-petal browns, tawny sand, punctuated with patches of vivid green grass and frail, newly-budding trees. A pallid forecourt, a circle of gardens, a silver-grey road winding away towards the distant white walls of the town. But mostly one level of dust-fine soil, drowned in sunlight so sharp and thin that it seemed there must be frost in the air. In her fine woollen cardigan suit she felt warm enough, and yet there was a clarity that cut like knives when she breathed. And this was Delhi in December.

She didn't remember anything, or at least, not with any part of mind or memory. Only her blood stirred strangely, recapturing some ancestral rapport. Not necessarily in affection; rather with a raising of hackles, aware of compulsions not altogether congenial. It was too bright, too dry, too clear, too open; there was nowhere to hide.

'This way. We're not supposed to park private stuff round here, but what can you do? These foreigners!' Felder led the way briskly round the corner of the buildings to the blinding white concrete where the airport bus was filling up with plump ladies in saris and ponderous gentlemen in white cottons and European overcoats. The truck turned out to be a minibus, from which two unmistakable young Americans leaned to grin at them hospitably and offer large, amiable hands.

'Tom Hoskins is our driver-cum-handyman. There isn't much Tom can't do. And this is Joe Salt, assistant cameraman. We've got it dead easy here, mostly we're playing second-fiddle to the Indians, and believe me, Ganesh Rao knows exactly what he wants, and nine-tenths of the time he's dead right, so ours is a sinecure. Get aboard, ladies, choose your seats, we'll take you round through the city for a ride.'

They climbed aboard willingly, eyes round and attentive at the windows, intent on missing nothing.

'Shouldn't we at least check in at the hotel?' asked Dominic.

'So we will, laddie, so we will, on our way to Mehrauli. Don't want to haul this luggage around, do we? This will be a lightning tour specially for you, because we've got to go right in to the shopping centre at Connaught Circus to pick up one of the gang, and then we're bound due south for the edge of the town, where we're filming. We'll be quite close to Keen's on the way out, and drop your stuff off there. Straight to the town office, Tom, Ashok will be there by now, we're a mite late.'

Tom drove with the verve and aplomb which they were later to associate with Sikh taxi-drivers, and in particular with the devoted virtuosi, also mostly Sikhs and invariably young, who drove the wappish little scooter-rickshaws around the town. Clearly he had been here long enough to know his way around and to have bettered the impetuous elan of the native motorists. They clung to their seats (though Anjli tended rather to cling to Dominic) and stared their fill; and Mr Felder, with wide shoulders braced easily against the panelling and long legs stretched across the gangway, commented spasmodically on the unfolding scene of Delhi.

On either side the steel-grey road the overwhelming brownness of North India, at first a monotone, dissolved, as they penetrated it, into a marvellous spectrum of shades and textures, which yet were all brown. Even the grass was brown, a dry, subtle shade with tints of green breathing through it, to indicate that against first appearances it still lived. Beyond all question the air was alive, the light was alive, the incredibly brilliant sky was alive, radiantly blue and flecked with a few sailing feathers of cloud to emphasize its depth of colour. At first they drove across the barren brown earth as over a dead calm sea, the steely road now growing russet with the reflected glow, its dusty fringes lined with curious crude baskets of rust-coloured iron, like fireless braziers. 'Newly-planted trees,' said Felder, forestalling the question; and then they could glimpse the tender green saplings just peering over their bars. 'You'll see 'em all over the new suburbs. They won't always be eyesores.' Then they were among scattered small houses, dropped almost accidentally about the dun-coloured plain, and abruptly the white buildings congealed into a residential road. On their left rose the heaving brown flank

of the Ridge, on their right, from clustering trees, soared
a phantasmagoria of imposing buildings of every possible
design and style, regularly spaced like huge summer-houses
in a giant's garden. 'The Diplomatic Enclave. They suggested
every country should build its embassy in its own national
style. See those dark-blue domes? Pakistan did that! You
ought to walk through, some time, you won't believe your
eyes. And that huge palace beyond, that's the Ashoka Hotel.
Prestige job. You won't believe that, either . . .'

From Willingdon Crescent they caught glimpses of the
dome of Rashtrapati Bhavan and the twin blocks of the
government secretariat, a brief rear view of the spacious
buildings of the new city; then they were careering up Irwin
Road, head over ears into the pandemonium of modern
Delhi's street life at last, between banks and restaurants
and cinemas plastered with posters tall as towers and vivid
as the rainbow, caught in a whirling current of cars, buses,
bicycles, pedestrians and motorbikes and scooters towing
canopied rickshaws, extravagantly painted with flowers,
birds and garlands, like some wonderful hybrid between
an old-fashioned hansom cab and the cabin of a canal-boat.
This brilliant river brought them suddenly to the whirlpool of
New Delhi's shopping centre, the wheel of radiating streets
they had seen from the air.

'Drive round Connaught Place, Tom, just once, let them
have a look at the nearest thing we've got to Piccadilly.'

It was much more spacious than Piccadilly, a large, regular
circle of park in the centre, ringed with a broad road and a
colonnade of white shops, and eight radial roads lancing away
from the centre like spokes of a wheel. Tom made the circuit
of it at speed, for here there was less traffic and more space,
and the pedestrians had withdrawn to the raised sidewalk that
was sheltered by the colonnade.

'The outer ring is where we're going . . . Connaught
Circus. If you ever want to shop, you could do worse than
start here. OK, Tom, make for the office.'

Tom took the nearest radial road, and turned left into
Connaught Circus, the rim of the wheel. Banks, garages,
restaurants, shops flickered past them in procession, then
invervals of trees and grass, and curious quiet islands of
older buildings cheek by jowl with the new. They halted
before a low green hedge, a narrow strip of garden, and a
tall, plain, Victorian colonial house.

'Temporary headquarters. Down south, near Mehrauli,

we've got a couple of villas for living quarters, but we shall only be there a few days, then we're headed for Benares to do the Deer Park scenes at Sarnath, right where they happened. But this is where we keep our gear and do the office work.'

'What is the film you're making?' Tossa asked curiously.

'Didn't Dorrie tell you? It's an epic about the life of the Buddha. Time was when it would have been called: *World, Farewell*! or some such title. Nowadays we do these things straight, and simply call it *The Buddah*. After all, if you can have a film called *The Bible* you can have one called *The Buddah*, can't you? That's what the producer wants. But Ganesh Rao says the accent is on the man, and it ought really to be called *Siddhartha*. So my guess is, that's what it'll be called in the end.'

'I've *heard* of the Buddha,' Anjli said delicately, not committing herself to total ignorance, 'but I don't really know the story. Could you tell it to me?'

'Ashok is the man you want, he'll tell you everything you need to know. Give him a blast, Tom, he can't have heard us come.'

Tom obliged. The fan-lighted door of the house opened promptly, and a small, slender man in close-fitting trousers and a grey achkan came dancing down the steps with a music-case tucked under his arm. His eyes were black and long-lashed, his smile aloof and courteous, and his colour palest bronze. Surprisingly the rest of his features, full, mobile lips, hooked nose and jutting cheek-bones, were so jagged that he looked like a head by Epstein, and a good one, at that.

He said: 'Welcome to Delhi!' in a soft, shy voice, and clambered nimbly into the minibus, where he dumped his music-case between his feet and clasped fine, broad-jointed hands across his stomach. The first two fingers of his left hand were scored at the tips with deep, stained grooves, many-times-healed and many-times-re-opened wounds, smeared with cream that glistened when the light caught it.

'Meet Ashok Kabir,' said Felder, 'our musical director. You ask him nicely, Anjli, and he'll play you some of his music for *Siddhartha* presently, when we get him warmed up. Ashok, the little lady wants you to tell her about this film of ours.'

Anjli Kumar and Ashok Kabir looked at each other suddenly, attentively, at a range of about one foot, and in their own personal ways fell in love at first sight. Dominic, watching with sharpened senses, thought, good lord, I never dreamed it would be that easy. I needn't have worried, I was just standing in for whoever it was going to be. Anjli saw the native, the initiate, the authority, whose grace was such that he was willing to share what he knew with whoever went to meet him in the right spirit. Ashok, the artist, and himself complete, saw the homing exile unaware of her wishes or her needs, a fragmented child unable to recognise her fractures, much less repair them. They looked at each other with wonder, interest and respect, and had nothing yet to say.

'Now down Janpath, fast as you like,' said Felder contentedly, 'but take it easy where it crosses Rajpath – did I tell you that's the King's Way, you folks? Janpath is the Queen's Way! – so they can get a look right along to the government buildings. You think you've seen something when you've seen the Mall, in London? Wait till you get a load of this! And then go round the back of the Lodi Park to Keen's, and we'll drop the bags off and sign in . . .'

Keen's was an old-fashioned but English-run hotel, in an ancient white Indian house that turned a blank face to the street on all sides, and lived a full life about its internal courtyard and gardens, with a balcony for every room – every suite, if the truth be told – on its first and second floors, where the guests were housed. There was but one way in, masked by a tall green hedge; and inside, there was peace and almost silence, all street noises excluded. Room-boys dressed as rajas made off with the baggage, but they turned out to be one of the trimmings of every hotel, even the most modest, and were amiable enough at very low cost. The new arrivals lingered only long enough to stop feeling stunned, and to extract from their bags the coats which Felder insisted they would need in an hour or so. Then they were borne away to the two villas near Hauz Khas, on the most southerly fringe of the city, where a couple of trucks and a large saloon car had just unloaded the exhausted company from Mehrauli.

The din of voices was deafening but reassuring; who could feel inhibited or a stranger where the general babel made it possible to talk nonsense and not be brought to answer for it? And the array of faces, several of them still in make-up, baffled memory and withdrew names, making it necessary, after a while, to enquire discreetly about the dominant members of the collective; but that was taken for granted, and everyone answered cheerfully for himself. In a large, charming, rather bare room, with tall windows looking out on a neglected garden, they circulated and ate and drank, and in an unexpected fashion were at home. The girls – there seemed to be several girls – kept disappearing, and coming back with something freshly cooked. Everything was improvised, but everything worked. It might not be Indian – how could they judge? – but it was calming and reassuring and just what they needed.

Ashok Kabir sat cross-legged on a cushion, and cradled his sitar in his arms, its long, beautiful, polished body reclined upon his shoulder, the twenty moveable frets gleaming and quivering like nerves along its slender teak neck, the larger sounding gourd at the base of the throat nuzzling his heart. Six main strings, so they said, and nineteen sympathetic ones! And those strings were the reason why the fingers with which he controlled them were gashed deep, and never could be healed. And we think western music is a hard apprenticeship!

'. . . so Prince Siddhartha was born to the Kind Suddhodana and his Queen Maya,' said Ashok in his soft voice, 'and all the auguries were auspicious, though a little puzzling. The wise men told the king that his son would certainly be a very great leader, there was only some doubt as to *what kind*. They said that if ever the prince was allowed to set eyes on an old man, a sick man, a dead man and a holy monk, then he would be the lord of a very great kingdom, but not of this world. And as the king preferred that his son should go on ruling after him in the normal and profitable way of this world, he took good care to bring up Siddhartha in a kind of benevolent imprisonment, surrounded by every kind of pleasant diversion, and excluded from him all sickness and ugliness and pain. And when he grew up they married him successfully to the most beautiful of all the noblewomen of the land . . .'

'Thank you, darling!' said Kamala sweetly, and bowed her acknowledgements with hands prayerfully pressed together and head inclined. She wore a white silk sari embroidered with green and silver thread, and looked rather like the Indian Miss World, only more so. She was, according to Felder, as clever as she was beautiful, and nearly as acquisitive, and it had cost plenty to get her to play the heroine.

' . . . the sweet Yashodhara . . . with whom in any case he was already in love, and she with him . . .'

'Naturally!' murmured Kamala, with a glance at the statuesque figure and consciously spendid countenance of her lord Siddhartha, holding court on the other side of the room with a fresh lime soda in one hand. 'Who could help it?'

They had seen that face on one of the outsize posters in Janpath or Irwin Road, early that evening. There was no mistaking it. Felder had translated the lettering of the name for them; Barindra Mitra, one of the popular demi-gods, for top-flight film stars in India are little less than deities. Barindra Mitra sat cross-legged on his couch as on a throne, all the more devastating in majesty because he was still in costume, swathed in short gold tunic and white silk robe, with one bronze shoulder naked, and on his head a tower-like crown studded with property jewels.

'But the prince grew restive with being cooped up, and soon outgrew all his pleasure-gardens and palaces, and would go out into the city of Kapilavastu. And when he couldn't dissuade him, the king sent out orders through the city that everyone who was sick or ugly or maimed or old should be kept out of the way for the occasion. All the same, when the prince drove through the town with his faithful charioteer Channa, he was suddenly confronted by something he had never seen before in his life, and had never realised existed . . . an aged, senile decrepit, miserable relic of a man at the end of his span. Old Age in person!'

'At your service!' said the jaunty young man who was just handing round a tray of savoury patties. His arms and legs still bore the traces of the old man's artful make-up, and he was still draped in picturesque rags, but he had shed the wig and beard, huddled shaggily at this moment in a corner of the long couch like a sleeping Yorkshire terrier, and his face, but for two painted patches of grained greyness on the cheeks, was in its smooth, high-coloured prime.

'Naturally he asked whatever this creature could be, and if it was really a man at all, and whether it had been born so, or this was a visitation from the gods. And Channa had to tell him at last that what he saw was the common lot of all men at the end, that this poor wreck had once been as young and ardent as the prince himself, and that some day the prince himself would be as was this old man. And Siddhartha drove back to the palace terribly shaken.

Mourning Raga

And that's the scene they've been shooting in Mehrauli this afternoon.'

'Mehrauli being only a village, properly speaking,' said the director Ganesh Rao, in his immaculate and unaccented English, 'but perhaps nearer to Kapilavastu than anything one could fake up in the city. And if you want an excitable but manageable crowd laid on in moments, it's just the place.'

So that was why three of them were still so fresh from the cameras that they had not got rid of make-up and costumes yet. Old Age, Channa the charioteer, and Prince Siddhartha: Govind Das and Subhash Ghose, two professional Bengali character actors, and Barindra Mitra, the star. Anjli sat cross-legged on a cushion on the floor, squarely facing Ashok, and copying his pose to the last finger-curve of the relaxed hand that lay in his lap, the hand with the plectrum strapped to the index finger. She took her dark, disconcering gaze from his face long enough to look round them all, and enjoy the attention she was getting as Dorette Lester's little girl. Felder had been right, the film world is one world over.

'Tomorrow,' said Ganesh Rao, digging thick, strong fingers into his thatch of black hair, 'we're going to finish the other two scenes there, the encounters with disease and death.'

'So he did go again,' Anjli said, and her grave eyes came back to Ashok's face.

'Twice, and he saw what really happens to men. And in the meantime Yashodhara had a son, but it was too late to deflect her husband, however much he loved them both. He saw that age and sickness and death were waiting for them, as well as for him, and that nobody had ever found a way of triumphing over these evils. So he named the child Rahula . . . that means a fetter, because the child bound him like a chain. And the prince rode out one more time, and he met an ascetic monk, who had forsaken the world for solitude, in search of the ultimate peace that no one knows. And after this Siddhartha brooded on the need to find this transcendent peace, this freedom from the wheel of recurring sufferings, not only for himself, not first for himself, but for his dearest, and after them all men. And one night after the pleasures and entertainments of the palace were over, and all the court lay asleep, he got up in the small hours and looked at his sleeping wife and son, and went out from them silently

193

in search of the way. The king had every gate guarded, being afraid of this, but all the guards slept, and all the gates opened of themselves to let Siddartha go free.'

'Play some of the music,' suggested Kamala, leaning over him from behind in a drift of pale silk and perfume. 'Play my song, and then the theme of the departing, let Anjli hear how you can make a folk melody and a classical meditation out of the same notes. Do you know what is a raga, Anjli? They are the basic material for all our classical music, and there are thousands of them, the ragas, each for a special time and season, and a special mood, so that in a few rising and descending notes you have the mind's first statement, the one thought out of which a work of art grows. Tell them, Ashok!'

Ashok explained with his fingers. The teak neck of the sitar leaned confidingly into his shoulder, his scarred fingers pressed the main strings, and with the plectrum he picked out a brief, rising phrase, and brought it sighing down again to dissolve where it had begun. A handful of notes tossed into the air and caught again. He repeated it slowly, to let them follow the sound, and then took it up in tentative chords and began to embroider. Not yet the form in which they had occasionally heard classical ragas, but turning the notes into a simple, folk melody, something even the western ear could accept readily and even memorise. Kamala took up the thread and began to sing wordlessly, in a sweet, forward, wailing voice, the gentle caterwauling of a deserted kitten.

'But that's something even we would find approachable,' said Tossa, astonished. 'I expected it to be much more difficult.'

'It's meant to be approachable, it must reach everybody in this form. If I do not hear it sung in the streets, once the film is shown, I shall be disappointed. And for that it must be grasped on the wing, it will be heard only once. It is the lullaby Yashodhara sings to Rahula after she discovers her lord is gone. And this is how it will be heard at his going.'

This time the theme budded slowly, and began to uncurl in a meditative development. The plangent string tone of the sitar, no longer unfamiliar even in the West, swelled until from a curiously intimate and secret solo instrument it had become a full orchestra. Its sweetness and strangeness had a hypnotic effect, to which the nerves responded, and even though the expected acceleration did not come, or only in a strictly modified form, the usual mounting tension and excitement was present no less, drawing mind and senses taut in almost painful concentration. Some music lulls; this disturbed. And so it should, for it expressed the renunciation of the world and the assumption of the world's burden in one symbolic act. They could almost see the solitary figure steal silently through the apartments of the palace, leaving the sleepers sleeping, and the gates one by one opening before him, until he bestowed his ornaments upon Channa, exchanged his rich garments for the plain yellow robe of a huntsman in the forest, cut off the princely knot of his hair, sent back in sorrow his charioteer and his white horse Kantaka, and walked forward alone into the darkness to do battle with life and death. And at the moment when he vanished the music died away in a shuddering sigh and broke off, unfinished.

Everyone stirred and drew breath, otherwise the silence lasted for a moment; then Anjli asked:

'Do the ragas all have names?'

'Yes, they have names. This is Raga Aheer Bhairab. It is a morning raga.'

'And it had a special purpose? A special mood, Kamala said?'

'It is to be played,' said Ashok, stroking his still faintly vibrating strings, 'in the early hours of the morning, when the guests are departing.'

Felder drove them back to Keen's Hotel about nine o'clock in the evening, a little dazed, a little silent. Anjli was clutching the copy of *The Life of the Buddha* which Ashok had lent her. And again Felder had been quite right, they needed their coats; the air was sharp and very cold, the sky above crackling with stars.

'Where is this place you've got to go? Rabindar Nagar? That's one of the newish suburbs that are spreading out westwards, isn't it? Will you find your way all right?'

'I've got a town plan,' said Dominic. 'We'll find it.'

'I'd come with you, but we want to finish the Mehrauli shots tomorrow, and if we make it we're off by air to Benares the next morning to do the Deer Park scenes. I don't suppose you'll have any trouble. But just in case you do need any help, give me a ring in the evening. You've got the villa number and the office, I'll be one end or the other. Give me a ring anyhow. I'll be glad to know how you get on.'

'We'll do that. And thanks for everything.'

Three

Rabindar Nagar was close to the western fringe of the town, completely cut off from any view of New Delhi itself by the long, undulating brown hump of the Ridge. It was a suburb as yet only half-built, every house in it an individual undertaking and of individual and often surprising taste. This was not where the very rich would build, or the very fashionable; but there was plenty of money here, too, putting up those fanciful white villas and running those substantial cars. Here came the wealthy retired tradesman, the Sikh taxi proprietor who had plenty of transport at his disposal, and didn't mind the long run from town, the small factory owner who couldn't rise to a property in the tree-shaded, fashionable enclaves of the city itself, and the young artist of independent means who preferred detachment, possibly from the distractions of traffic and noise, probably from too autocratic parents. Whimsy could have its fling on a small and fairly economical scale here, and on a limited site. The houses sat cheek by jowl along the neat roadways, and between their rear compounds ran narrow lanes by which the hawkers and salesmen reached the kitchen doors. The rusty iron baskets that shielded new trees bristled everywhere along the roadsides. The sounds, in the early morning, were a curious mixture of domestic and wild, of cars starting up, of the wavering trade calls of the ironing man and the fresh vegetable man along the rear courtyards, bidding for custom, and distant and eerie from the west the wail of jackals prowling the harsh brown land. The ironing man's little cart, with its small charcoal brazier at one end, halted under back windows, women came bustling out with armfuls of laundry to be ironed, and the hot smell of the smoothed cotton and linen was as savoury on the air as bread. Schoolgirls came demurely out of front compound gates in their uniform shalwar and kameez, close-waisted tunic and wide trousers neatly fitted at the ankles, gauze scarf draped over the shoulders with ends floating behind. The bane of all tomboys, those scarves, the first thing to get discarded when they ran out to play hockey on the open patch of ground after school.

Part of this open space was occupied, at the moment, by a cluster of brown tents, in which lived Orissan building workers, employed on two half-finished houses just along the main road. A long chain of them, moving rhythmically, carried away the excavated soil from new foundations, bearing it in baskets on their heads. More than half of them were women. They were the poorest of the poor, but after this hard training in deportment they walked like queens. Their children, in one tattered garment apiece, or none, haunted the open ground and begged vehemently and maliciously from every passer-by.

Two of them converged purposefully upon Dominic, Tossa and Anjli as soon as they stepped out of the taxi. Here were foreigners, their proper prey. A second look at Anjli, as she turned to face them, brought them up standing in considerable doubt; and that was as illuminating for Anjli as for them. And while they were hesitating, a plump lady in a sari came out of the next gate and shooed them indignantly away.

'They are those labourers' children,' she said defensively, in slightly grating English, as though the language had not enough abrasive consonants for her, 'from Orissa. No Punjabi would beg, you please believe me.'

She marched away across the open ground, and the children drew back from her path by a few yards and studied the sky as she went by, to close in again the moment her back was turned, and be shooed away again, good-humouredly enough, by the taxi driver. Dominic paid, and let the car go. He had noticed another taxi stand only a couple of hundred yards away at the corner of the main road.

'N 305' said the tablet on the gatepost simply, and there was a small, beautifully-made wooden mail-box attached beneath the number. The wall of the front garden was white, shoulder-high to a man, and the house lay only a few yards back, also white-painted, two storeys high and flat-roofed, with a perforated balustrade, and in the centre of the roof a sort of light pavilion, glazed in from winds and dust-storms, an ideal summer-house for a sociable man who yet had need of a working solitude at times. The ground in front of the house was paved with squares of a grey stone, with narrow flower-beds and a few shrubs along the walls, and a small, decorative tree in a tub by the door. But the enclosure ran round the detached end of the building, and there degenerated into a utilitarian courtyard of beaten earth, with a line for drying washing, and a low wooden shed built into the corner. Beside the shed, under a bracket roof of sacking stretched on a wooden frame, a small brazier burned with a steady glow, and the faint smell of sandalwood and incense was wafted to them in the thin blue smoke. All the fires of Delhi, sacred and profane, seem to contain the evocative scents of worship. Behind the brazier, cross-legged and motionless, sat a lean, shrunken old man, a loose cotton turban on his head, grey hair and tangled beard obscuring most of his face, a brown blanket hugged round his shoulders. When the three strangers came in through the open gate he raised his head but did not turn in their direction.

At the last moment, with the door before them and the bell-push within reach of a hand, they all hesitated. Felder had talked with blessed bluntness about the moment of truth, about having a roof over Anjli's head that she didn't owe to her father, so that she could meet him on equal terms, and face his acceptance or rejection with unshaken dignity and independence. But when it came to the point, whether she wanted him or not, it was important that he should want her. And there was only one way to find out.

'I'll do it,' said Anjli quickly, and prodded the bell-push with a rose-tipped finger, hard and accurately.

A moment of silence, and then they heard light feet trotting briskly towards the door. Very light feet, naked feet; that characteristic soft slapping of the soles on a stone-paved floor. The door opened, wide to the wall; a revealing gesture, which belongs only to the innocent, open-hearted and generous. A boy of about nineteen, square and sturdy, stood smiling brightly at them across the threshold. He was clean and wide-featured, with close-cropped hair, and wore khaki drill shirt and shorts a size too long for him; handsome muscles bulged the brown arm that held the door open. He bobbed his head repeatedly, and smiled, and said nothing, waiting for them to speak.

'Good morning!' said Dominic, aware of possible non-understanding, but not knowing in the least what to do about it. Names, at any rate, are international currency. 'We are looking fror the house of Shri Satyavan Kumar.'

The smile narrowed and wavered. At least he understood English. 'Yes, this is house of Mr Kumar.' His slight frown,

his lost look, everything about him but his tongue added:
'But . . .!'

'May we speak with Mr Kumar? He will be expecting us.
He has received a letter to tell him that we are coming.'

Nevertheless, Dominic had heard the unspoken 'but', even
if he chose to ignore it. It might mean no more than
'but he isn't in at the moment', which would hardly be
a catastrophe, even if they were keyed up to meet him
immediately, and liable to deflation if kept waiting. Tossa
had heard it, too, she was looking more than naturally wise,
patient and calm. So had Anjli; her face was a demure mask,
no one could tell what went on behind it.

'There is a letter, yes . . .' said the boy slowly. 'But my
master not read letter.' His brown eyes wandered from face
to face apologetically, as if he might be blamed for this
failure of communication. 'The letter is here, I bring it . . .'

'But if we could speak to Mr Kumar,' said Dominic
doggedly, 'we can explain everything ourselves.'

'I am sorry. Mr Kumar not here. No one can take letter
to him, no one know where can find him. More than one
year ago, in the night, Mr Kumar he go away. Never say
one word. Never come back.'

After the moment of blank silence, in which the Orissan
children advanced their toes over the boundary of the
gateway, and the old man behind the brazier shrugged the
blanket back a few inches from his shoulders, and the world in
general incredibly went on about its business as if nothing had
changed, Dominic said in reasonable tones: 'May we come in
for a few minutes? You may be able to help us.'

'Please! Memsahib . . . missee-sahib . . .!' The boy bowed
them in gladly, waved them into a small front room, sparsely
furnished by western standards, but elegant in tapestries,
silks and cushions, and a screen of carved, aromatic wood.
The bare feet turned and pattered to the table, where on
a silver dish lay an air mail letter. Dorette had wasted her
pains.

'Please, here is letter. You take it?'

'No, keep it here,' said Dominic, 'in case Mr Kumar
comes home.' But after more than a year without a word,
why should he reappear now? And yet this was India, and
who knows India's motives and reasons? 'You mean that
Mr Kumar simply went away without telling anyone where
he was going, or when to expect him back? Not even his

mother? His family?' Idiot, there was no other family, of course, he was the only child.

'*Acha*, Sahib. In the night. He did not sleep in his bed, he did not take any luggage, everything left in place. He go. That is all.'

'Like the Lord Buddha,' said Anjli unexpectedly, 'when it was time to depart.' She had a big white canvas handbag on her arm, and Ashok's book inside it; she had been sneaking peeps into the pages even on the taxi ride out here.

'Your father,' Dominic pointed out unwisely, 'was a devout Hindu, by all reports.'

'So was the Lord Buddha,' said Anjli devastatingly. She hadn't been reading to no purpose.

'*Father*?' said Satyavan's house-boy, half-dumb with wonder.

'This is Miss Anjli Kumar, Mr Kumar's daughter.'

He joined his hands respectfully under his chin, his brown head bobbing deeply; he did not question her identity, he believed that people told him the truth, as he told them the truth.

'Missee-sahib, I not know anything, I not here when Shri Satyavan go away. When his servants send word to the big house that he gone, my mistress she send them all away, tell me go keep this place until Shri Satyavan return. Nobody see him go, nobody hear. More than one year now, and he send no word.'

'Your mistress?' said Dominic.

'*Acha*, sahib, Shrimati Purnima Kumar. I her houseboy.'

'And there's nobody here now who was here on that night? When Mr Kumar went away?'

'Sahib, no one. Only Arjun Baba.' He said it with the mixture of reverence and indifference that touches, perhaps, only the dead and the mad, both of them out of reach.

'Who is Arjun Baba?'

'The old man. The beggar. Shri Satyavan took him in, and let him live in the compound. He eats from our table. Now Shri Satyavan is gone, Shrimati Purnima feeds him. It is all he want. This is his home until he die. Arjun Baba very, very old.'

'But he was here then! He may have heard or seen something . . .'

The boy was bowing his head sadly, and sadly smiling. 'Sahib, always he has said he hear nothing, he know nothing. Always, he say this. And, sahib, Arjun Baba is blind.'

It made perfect sense. The old ears pricking, the ancient head turning. But not turning to view. The ear was tuned to them, not the eye. And so old, so very old. And so indebted, in a mutual indebtedness, such as charity hardly knows in the less sophisticated lands of the west. His allegiance belonged only to Satyavan, who if he willed to go must be made free to go. Not all needs are of the flesh.

'Sahib, if you are willing, I think it good you should go to my mistress's house.' He did not say "to my mistress"; and in a moment it was clear why. 'She very ill, ever since Shri Satyavan go from here she fall sick for him . . .'

'But didn't she try . . .? To get in touch, to find him . . .?'

The young shoulders lifted, acknowledging the sovereignty of individual choice. 'If he must go, he must go. My mistress wait. Only now it is bad with her. But there is Shri Vasudev, Shri Satyavan's cousin. He is manager for family business now. Please, you speak with him.'

'Yes,' said Dominic, 'yes, we will. We have Mrs Kumar's address, we'll go there.'

The boy bowed them anxiously towards the door, and out into the warming sunshine, hovering as though uncertain whether to wish them to stay or go, as though it might rest with him to hold fast Satyavan's daughter, and he might be held answerable if she turned and went away as mysteriously as her father. Anjli halted in the doorway and looked at him thoughtfully.

'You are not from Delhi?'

'No, missee-sahib, I come from village near Kangra. Shrimati Purnima came from there, and has house there. My father is her gardener.'

'What is your name?'

'Kishan Singh.' And he pressed his hands together in salute and smiled at her hopefully.

'We shall meet again, Kishan Singh. I am glad you are here to keep my father's house so faithfully and look after Arjun Baba. If you hear any news of him, send it to me at Keen's Hotel. Now we must go to my grandmother.'

Kishan Singh stood at the top of the steps and bowed and smiled her away across the paved garden, in some way reassured; but at the gate she looked back again, and caught Dominic by the arm.

'Wait for me a moment. I want to speak to him . . . the old man. There was nothing wrong with his hearing, I saw that he heard us come.'

'We can try,' Dominic agreed doubtfully. 'But it's long odds he doesn't speak English.'

'Kishan Singh did. But let me try, alone . . .'

Something was changing in Anjli, or perhaps some part of everything in her was changing, her voice, her manner, even her walk. They watched her cross the beaten earth of the yard, and it might almost have been the gliding gait of a woman in a sari, though quite certainly Anjli had never draped a sari round her in her life, and wouldn't know how to set about it even if she had possessed one. She halted before the motionless old man, and though he could not see her, she pressed her hands together in reverence to him, and inclined her head as the boy had done to her.

'Namaste!'

She had no idea how she had known what to say, but when she had said it she knew that it was right. The old head came up, and the sun shone on the sightless face that seemed to gaze at her. A tangle of grey, long hair, beard and brows, out of which jutted a hooked and sinewy nose and two sharp protuberant cheekbones, and great ridge of forehead. All of his flesh that was visible was the same brown as the brown, dry earth under him. A tremendous remote indifference held him apart from her. The sun gleamed on eyes white and opaque with cataract.

Anjli sat down on her heels, facing him across the little brazier, so that her face was on a level with his. Even before she spoke again, the tilt of his head followed her movement. What his eyes owed him, his ears paid.

'Uncle, I am Satyavan's daughter. I am Anjli Kumar. I have come to find my father. Help me!'

Faintly and distantly a convulsion passed through the fixed, unchanging face, like the passing of a breeze over standing water, and again left it motionless.

'Uncle, you were here, no one but you, when my father went away in the night. If there was a secret he wanted kept from all the world, still he would not have kept it from me.' Did she believe that? She had no time to wonder, she was so sure that the old man heard, considered, understood. He was not deaf and he was not mad, and when she mentioned Satyavan's name the stillness of his face became distant and intense, like a listening stone. He believed her, but he did not know her, and he did not take her word against his own experience for what Satyavan would or would not have done. 'Uncle, now I am going to my grandmother, who also wishes to find my father. If you know anything, where he is, how we can find him, I beg you to tell me.'

He had withdrawn a little into his blanket, his head recoiling into cover from the sun. He said nothing at all; she had the impression that he had turned inwards to converse with himself.

'Come away,' said Dominic gently, his hand on her shoulder. 'You won't get anything out of him.'

She started at the touch, and obediently began to rise, but she did not look up. He *had* understood, and there was something he knew, if his slow and profound communion with himself would allow him to confide it; but not yet, she could see that. Impulsively she rummaged in her bag for something, anything, she could leave with him as a token and a gift in one.

'Uncle, think of me. I am Anjli, his daughter. If you have anything to tell me, send someone – send Kishan Singh – to Keen's Hotel to ask for me. You do understand? You will find me at Keen's Hotel. Kishan Singh will know.' She leaned across the brazier, the faint aromatic smoke tingling in her nostrils, and took the old man's hand in hers, and closed the dry, skinny fingers over her good-luck piece, the mounted gold dollar she sometimes wore as a pendant. 'It is for you. Think of me, and send me word! Namaste!'

She drew back from him resolutely, because she knew she was going to get nothing out of him as yet. But before she turned and walked away through the gate she saw the two ancient hands rise, as though quite independently of whatever mind moved – or immobilised – the worn, inscrutable face, and press themselves together momentarily over her token, in acknowledgement and farewell.

'Yes, I've been here,' Anjli said with certainty, as soon as she saw the broad white carriage gates, and the beautifully raked drive curving away between the trees to the distant house that was visible only as a whiteness between the leaves. 'I thought I didn't remember, but now that I see it, I know it's the same. This is where he brought me when I was a little girl.'

'Of course,' said Tossa, 'he wouldn't have the other house then, he was still expecting to stay in America for some years, perhaps even for good. In India this would be his home.'

Anjli passed through the smaller wicket gate with her eyes shut, and walked forward a few steps on the smooth rose-coloured gravel. 'There's a lawn all across the front of the house, and a sort of loggia, with a marble floor. And in the middle of the lawn there's a big fountain.'

There were all these things. There was also a gardener in shorts and drill shirt, dipping water from the fountain basin and watering the flowering shrubs in the scattered round beds, sleeping shrubs only just hinting at budding. Isolated in the emerald green turf, tethered to long, thin snakes of hosing, two sprinklers tirelessly squandered Delhi's precious water supply on preserving the texture and colour and freshness of the Kumar grass.

In a thirsty land privilege can be reckoned in water. Plantation economy, Dominic thought, chilled and daunted, and wondered into what arid byways they had found themselves drawn, aside from the actual life of this painfully real and actual country. It didn't begin with us, he thought, and it hasn't ended with us. We were only an aberration, a contortion of history, suffered almost in its sleep. India twitched a little, and scratched a momentary itch, and that was the coming and the going of the British. But they still have this to reckon with.

'It must be terrible,' said Anjli, suddenly, her fine brows knit in consternation, 'to be so rich!'

As far as they could see, beyond the long, low, pale facade of the house, just coming into view, the artfully spaced trees deployed their varying shapes as decoration, flowers used their colours to punctuate the restful green ground, creamy-white creepers draped the columns of the loggia. Before they reached the curving sweep of the steps that led up to the colonnade and the open double doors within, they had counted five garden boys, watering and tidying and clipping back too assertive leaves, taming and shaping and reducing all things to order. Under the awning of the loggia roof stone urns of flowers were spaced, and out of the open doors a scented smoke filtered. The bell was a looped rope of plaited red silk, but at least there was a bell; they had a means of informing this palace that strangers were on the doorstep, that the outer world did exist.

'I don't want to live here,' Anjli burst out in ill-timed rebellion. In Rabindar Nagar she had looked upon everything, and made no protest, rather advanced a step to look more closely.

'You needn't stay, if you don't want to,' said Dominic,

listening to the receding peal of the bell, eddying back and back into the apparently unpeopled recesses of the house. 'We can always take you back with us. Don't worry about anything. But if your grandmother's ill, at least we must enquire about her. And find out if they do know anything here.'

'Yes,' agreed Anjli, strongly recovering, and dug her heels in faithfully at his side.

Someone was coming, hurried, quiet, obsequious feet sliding over polished floors. A turbaned house-man in white cotton, austere but imposing.

'Shri Vasudev Kumar? said Dominic, evading lingual difficulties.

The man stepped back, and wordlessly waved them inside, into a large hall half-darkened by curtains and palms, and panelled in aromatic dark wood. Far to the rear a staircase spiralled upwards, intricately carved and fretted. The servant bowed himself backwards out of sight through a door to their right, and left them there among the exotics and the impersonal evidences of money and loneliness. Beyond the staircase the room receded to a large window, and beyond that again they caught a glimpse of a half-circle of paved courtyard, and two large cars standing, and occasionally the passage of scurrying figures. Beneath the civilised quietness there was a deep tremor of agitation.

They waited for some minutes, and then a door opened, somewhere out of sight, and let through the murmur of subdued but troubled voices. Then a man came hurrying in by the door through which the servant had disappeared, and confronted the three visitors with patent astonishment. He was not above medium height, but his hard, stringy Punjabi build made him look taller, and his immaculate western suit of dark grey worsted, and the springy black hair crowning his narrow head, accentuated the impression of length. His complexion was smoothly bronze, his features aquiline, and his age somewhere in the middle thirties. He looked every inch the city magnate, director of companies and arbiter of destinies, but with all his machinery temporarily thrown out of gear. His hands were wiping themselves agitatedly on a silk handkerchief, his thin features jerked with tension and his eyes, confronted by three such unexpected and unaccountable people, looked dazed and a little demented.

'You wished to see me? I am Vasudev Kumar. But this is a very inconvenient time . . . . ' His voice was rather high-pitched, and would have been shrill if he had not been so intent on keeping it almost to an undertone.

'Yes, I see it is, and I'm sorry, Mr Kumar.' Dominic went straight ahead because withdrawal without explanations was now, in any case, out of the question. 'I'll try to be brief, and perhaps we can talk at more leisure another day. We have just come from your cousin's house in Rabindar Nagar, Kishan Singh thought it advisable for us to come straight to you. We realise Mrs Kumar is ill, and certainly don't want to increase your anxieties. My name is Felse, and this is Miss Barber. At her mother's request we've brought your cousin's daughter over to India to join her father, but now we find that he is not in Delhi, and has not received the letter which was sent to him. This is Anjli Kumar.'

That was quite a bombshell, he realised, to drop on anyone, especially at a time when he was already beset by family troubles of another kind; but on the whole Vasudev, by the time he had heard this out to the end, looked considerably less distracted, as though one more shock had only to concentrate his faculties. He did not, however, look any more friendly. His black, feverish gaze flickered from face to face, and lingered longest on Anjli. He bowed perfunctorily, with no implication of acceptance.

'My cousin's daughter? But we have received no communication about her, we did not expect . . .'

'No, I realise that. Her mother's letter to Mr Satyavan Kumar is still at his own house, you will find it unopened. I think that will make a better explanation than I can give you. We were expecting simply to bring Anjli over to join her father . . . permanently,' he added, seeing no sense in softening anything. 'Naturally none of us had any idea at all that your cousin had vanished a year or more ago. We heard that only this morning, from Kishan Singh. You'll appreciate that in the circumstance the obvious thing to do was to bring Anjli to her grandmother, as her nearest relative here. In any case, Miss Lester had asked us to do that in case of any difficulty arising. But I'm very sorry that we should happen to turn up at such a distressing time for you.'

Anjli, who had stood woodenly to be inspected, not much resenting the suspicion and hostility of a man she didn't know and had no desire to know, asked now in a wary but determined voice: 'Is my grandmother very ill?'

'She has had two strokes since my cousin went away without a word.' Vasudev's high voice clipped the sentence off resentfully; and indeed he had a grievance, having been forced to step in and shoulder the whole abandoned burden of the family business, while never quite acquiring the status of managing director in the eyes of any of the Kumar employees and hangers-on. And then, into the bargain, the old lady's illness, with its endless demands upon his patience and his nervous resources. 'Yesterday, I am sorry to say, she had a third one. It is very bad. The doctors have been with her all morning. I do not know what I can do for you . . . it is very unfortunate . . .' A momentary gleam of active suspicion flared in his eyes. 'You can give me proof of the young lady's identity, of course?'

'Of course! She has her own passport, and you can check with the American authorities. There is also her mother's letter waiting to be read.'

'Yes . . . yes . . . naturally! Please excuse me, but this is so sudden, I can hardly grasp it. And in the circumstances . . .'

'In the circumstances,' said Dominic, 'having told you the facts, I think we had better leave, and get in touch with you later, when I hope Mrs Kumar will be better. If you have the doctors in the house with her now, we mustn't add to your worries. We are at Keen's Hotel, if you should want to reach us. Otherwise, we'll call you later to enquire about Mrs Kumar.'

Vasudev wrung his hands and twisted the silk handkerchief in a despairing gesture. He did not want them, Dominic thought, upon any terms, but neither was it politic to let them go away like this. There was something more that had to be said, in his own defence, and out it came in a thin, irritated cry: 'It is useless! You have not understood. Mrs Kumar is barely conscious . . . paralysed . . . she cannot speak . . . The doctors say that she is dying!'

There was an instant of silence and shock. Then Anjli said, firmly and finally: 'Then I must see her. Whether I stay here or go back to America, I must see her. While there's time. Surely you can see that. I am her granddaughter, and I have a right to see her, and she has a right to see me.'

There was no doubt that Vasudev was distinctly reluctant to allow any such thing, and they were always in some wonder as to why he gave way. For one thing, he had to cover himself. It would have looked bad if he had let an accredited relative go away without knowing that this might be the last chance of seeing Purnima alive, and it would look equally bad if he denied access to the dying woman now that

207

it was requested. But he could have tried persuasion, and in the event he did no such thing. Perhaps there had been something in Anjli's tone that he recognised and respected, an echo of Purnima, the uncompromising firmness of an Indian matriarch laying down the law, very well aware not only of the limitations of her rights (which are obvious) but also of their full scope (which is not, by any means). At any rate, he gave her a narrow, considering look, and then bowed slightly, and turned towards the inner door.

'Very well! Come this way!'

Tossa, following anxiously, murmured: 'Anjli, do you really think . . .' But Dominic put his hand on her arm, and whispered: 'Leave her alone.'

Anjli walked rapidly after Vasudev, along a panelled corridor hung with brocades the beauty of which would have stopped her in her tracks at any other time. No wonder they needed legions of servants to run about these endless halls. Door after door, glimpse after glimpse, where the doors were open, of silken luxury; and at the end, a final door, that opened on a dimmed room with a small lamp burning in a corner, and a little garish altar on a shelf behind it, an almanack Krishna, blue and sweetly-smiling, a dressing-table covered not with the brocades of Benares but the tinsel embroidery of the bazaars, a picture of Ramakrishna and another of Vivekananda on the walls, the gentle saintly seed and the hurricane wind that scattered it across the world. And in the middle of the room two white-clad servants standing on one side of a low bed, and on the other side an elderly gentleman of almost completely European appearance, sitting with his fingertips on the patient's pulse.

The bed was just a low wooden frame, without headboard or footboard, with laced springs supporting a thin mattress. A dark blue cloth covered with crude, lovely Naga embroideries of butterflies, elephants, cows and chickens, scarcely swelled over the shrunken body beneath it. On the pillow lay a grey head, the still luxuriant hair gathered into a white ribbon; the up-turned face was grey as the hair, one side of the mouth a little twisted, the eyes half-open and fixed. Her hands lay out on the blue coverlet, motionless.

It could have been any Indian woman's room, any but the poorest of the poor. All that wealth and luxury and grace came down at the end into this small, aged figure stretched on a common truckle bed.

Only the eyes were alive. They moved as the strangers

came in, the gleam beneath the lids was not quite quenched. They settled upon Anjli.

Anjli went forward slowly, past Vasudev, past the two women, and stood beside the bed. She joined her hands reverently, and bowed her head over them as she had to Arjun Baba; and this time there was a curious suppleness and rhythm about the movement of head and hands which had not been present before.

'Namaste, Grandmother Purnima!'

The fading brightness watched her; there was no other part of Purnima that could express anything now. Anjli slid to her knees beside the bed, to be nearer, and that movement, too, had a fluid certainty about it.

'Grandmother, I am Anjli, your son's daughter. I have come home.'

For one instant it seemed to Dominic and Tossa, watching, that the ancient, burned-out eyes flared feebly, that they acknowledged the stooping girl and approved her. Anjli pressed her joined hands into the Naga coverlet, and laid her face upon them. A tiny, brief convulsion, so infinitesimal that it might almost have been an illusion, heaved at the powerless fingers of Purnima's right hand, moved them a fraction of an inch towards the glossy black head, then let them fall limp. The blue coverlet hung unmoving, subsided, lay still again, and this time finally. The doctor leaned to touch the old woman's eyelid, to reach for her pulse again. One of the women in white began to wail softly and rock herself. Tossa pushed past Dominic, and took Anjli gently by the arm, raising her and drawing her back from the bed.

'Come away now, leave her to them! Come! We'd better go.'

There was no need to tell her that Purnima was dead. Of all the people in the room Anjli had been the first to know it.

Four

Vasudev overtook them in the loggia, almost running after them with fluttering hands and a dew of sweat on his forehead. The thin line of his black moustache was quivering with agitation.

'Please, one moment! This is terrible . . . I do not know how . . . I am so sorry . . . such a distressing home-coming for my cousin. Let me at least fulfil my responsibilities thus belatedly. You understand, I could hardly believe, so suddenly, with no warning . . . Of course Anjli must come to us, this is her home. Allow me, Anjli, to offer you the freedom of this house, until my aunt's estate is settled and proper provision made for you. My aunt's women will take good care of her, Mr Felse, I do assure you. We have an adequate domestic staff. Really, I insist!'

'I couldn't think,' said Dominic very rapidly and very firmly, 'of intruding on the household at this moment, you must allow us to keep Anjli with us at the hotel for a few days. Until after the funeral. You will have your hands quite full until then, and I think it is better that she should not be involved.'

'I am so upset . . . so inhospitable and unwelcoming, you must forgive me. Perhaps, however, if you really prefer . . .'

'For a few days, until after the funeral, I'm sure it would be better . . .'

He was not really sorry to let them go, though insistent on making the offer with all punctilio. Perhaps he was at as great a loss as they were about what to do next. As for Anjli, she walked down the long drive between her temporary guardians, silent and thoughtful, but completely composed. What she had done had been done naturally and candidly, and now there was no more she could do for her grandmother, unless . . .

'I suppose funerals happen pretty quickly here, don't they?' she asked practically.

'Not necessarily at this time of year,' Dominic said, accepting this down-to-earth vein as the best bet in the

210

circumstances. 'Maybe I ought to have asked him. I expect there'll be a notice in the papers by this evening, at least about her death.'

'Do you think we should go to the funeral? I know I didn't know her at all, but still she was my grandmother. And she understood what I said to her, I'm sure she did. What do you think, ought we to go?'

'I don't know. I don't know exactly what happens. We might only be in the way, not knowing the drill.'

'I guess we might,' she agreed after due consideration, and sensibly refrained from insisting. And the more he thought about her general behaviour, the more he realised that for years she had been standing squarely on her own feet, for want of mother and father as well as grandmother, and for all her compensatory posturing she had never lost her balance yet.

They walked back to the hotel, for Purmina's house was down in the rich and shady residential roads in the south of town, not far from the golf links, no more than ten minutes' pleasant walking from Keen's. Not one of them said: 'What are we going to do now?' though they were all thinking it.

They waited for the evening papers to arrive, and there it was, the announcement of the death of Shrimati Purnima Kumar, the arrangements for her funeral; imposingly large in the type, as was fitting for so prominent a citizen, and such a rich one. And in every paper alike, at least the English-language ones.

So now they had all the facts flat before them; and while Anjli was taking her bath they could look each other squarely in the face and consider what was to be done.

'We can't possibly leave her here with Cousin Vasudev,' Tossa said.

'No, we can't. Of course he may be all right, a thousand to one he is, but with no father here, and no grandmother, and seemingly no wife for Vasudev – I could be wrong, of course, did you get that impression, too?'

'What difference would it make?' said Tossa simply. 'Wife or no wife, we couldn't possibly hand her over to somebody who seems to be next in the running for the family fortune, somebody whose interests, if you look at the thing that way, she definitely threatens. I mean, if Satyavan inherits everything, then even supposing he never turns up, some day they'll have to presume his death, or whatever they do here, and Anjli is next in line. But if there's no Anjli . . .' She let that trail away doubtfully, and kept her voice low. 'But that's being pretty melodramatic about it, wouldn't you say? He doesn't *look* the wicked-uncle type.'

'No, he doesn't. And I don't suppose they're any more common here than in England, anyhow. And yet, with all these millions of people around, it would be awfully easy for one little one, a stranger, to get sunk without trace. The thing is, unless we find her father, then the next move is Dorette's responsibility, not ours, and we've no right to appropriate it to ourselves.'

'Dorette,' said Tossa with awful certainty, 'would dump her on Vasudev and never think twice.'

'Maybe she would, but she isn't going to do it by proxy. Not these proxies, anyhow.'

'Hear, hear! So what *do* we do?'

'I tell you what, I think we'd better ring up Felder and ask his advice. After all, he did offer to help.'

When he got through to the villa near Hauz Khas, it was Ashok Kabir who answered the telephone.

'They're not in yet, they'll probably be late. And they're off to Benares early in the morning. Is it urgent? Why not tell me, and I'll pass the problem on to him and ask him to call you back when he does get in?'

Dominic told him the whole story of Satyavan's defection and Purnima's death, down to the last detail that seemed relevant, and then sat down, a little cheered by Ashok's evident concern and sympathy, to wait for Felder to call him back. Presently Anjli sauntered in from the bathroom of the suite she shared with Tossa. In a flowing cotton dressing-gown, and with her black hair swirling softly round her shoulders, for the first time she looked Indian.

'Watch your step when you go for your bath, Tossa, we've been invaded. Two huge cockroaches – I suppose they come up the plumbing. Put the light on five minutes before you go to run your bath, and I bet they'll take the hint and run for the exit.' She was being, perhaps, deliberately cooler than she felt about these hazards, just as she probably was about her experiences of the morning; but the slight over-statement was merely that, not a falsification. Presented with a burden, she practised the best way of carrying it. Confronted by a problem, she would walk all round it and consider how best to grapple with it. They were beginning to understand their Anjli.

'That's nothing,' said Tossa, 'a gecko fell on me this morning in bed.'

'I know, I heard you squeal. There's another one going to fall on you any minute now.' He was clinging with his tiny, splayed feet to the high ceiling just above Tossa's head, close to the light fixture, lying in wait for flies, a whitish green lizard no more than four inches long, of which more than half was tail. He was so young and small that he was still almost translucent, and only the faint, rapid palpitation of his throat indicated that he was alive, and not a worked fragment of alabaster. 'I'd rather have geckos than cockroaches, any day. Anything with up to four legs,' said Anjli, quite seriously, 'is my brother. Over four, and they're out.'

'What about snakes?'

'Things with no legs are out, too. But not as way out as things with eight. Who was it on the phone? Cousin Vasudev?'

'I called Mr Felder,' said Dominic, 'but he wasn't back from shooting yet. They're going to ask him to call back.' No need to tell her the voice on the phone had belonged to Ashok Kabir; she would have resented being left in ignorance, even in the bath.

It was another hour before Felder's call came through. Anjli was in bed by then, but with her nose buried in *The Life of the Budda*, and at the first ring she was out and streaking for Dominic's sitting-room door. The conversation was brief, and apparently satisfactory.

'Of course!' said Dominic, heaving a vast breath of relief. 'How very simple you make it sound! Thanks a lot, that's what we'll do.'

'And let me know what happens, will you do that? I shall be worrying about that kid from now on until I know, but I'm betting you it will bring results, all right. For the next few days you can get me at Clark's Hotel, Benares – OK?'

'OK, and thanks again. Hope everything will go right with the shooting.'

'Now you're believing in miracles! Never mind, it's gone well today. And you take those girls and have a look at Delhi, don't waste a minute. So long, then, I'll be hearing from you!'

He was gone, energetic and bracing as ever, leaving his effect behind like a potent wine. Dominic hung up, relaxed and grateful.

'What did he say?' They were both at him in a moment, one on either side. '*What*'s so simple?'

'He says, with Mrs Kumar's death notice plastered all over the evening press – and you can bet it will be in the dailies tomorrow, too, – Satyavan will be absolutely certain to see it, wherever he is, and he'll come running to pick up his responsibilities. No son will let anyone else run his mother's funeral. All we've got to do is sit back and wait, to see if your father turns up for the ceremony. And the odds are strongly that he will.'

Nobody said – nobody even thought, in the exhilaration of the moment – '*if he can*!'

For two days they were on equal terms with all the other carefree European tourists in Delhi. They walked about the busy shopping streets round Connaught Place until their feet ached. They proceeded, half-stunned with grandeur, the full length of the King's Way from India Gate to Rashtrapati Bhavan, once the Viceroy's palace, now the residence of the President of India, with its two great flanking blocks of the government secretariat, vast, glowing pink sandstone, one of the better legacies of the Raj, along with the legal system and the indomitable Indian railways. They risked their lives in the hailstorm of bicycles as the clerks of Delhi streamed to work in the morning rush hour, and baked themselves brown in the midday sun in the silent green park among the Lodi tombs, close to their own hotel. Islam weighted India with vast and splendid elegies to death, India herself withdrew elusively, dissolving into ash and essence, leaving life to speak for itself. And so it did, in the children who mobbed the strangers in Purana Quila, the Old Fort, half glorious ruined monument to the past, half refugee village congealed into permanence for want of other quarters; in the magical glimpses of Old Delhi after dark, blanketed figures squatting by stalls half-lit with tiny smokey lanterns, twilight children cross-legged, suddenly mute and inscrutable as gods, and everywhere smokey scents of cowdung and joss and jasmine and sweat and all-pervading aromatic dust, electric on the darkness.

They took a motor-cycle rickshaw out to the Qutb Minar and the enormous ruined city of Tuqhluquabad, south of Delhi, silent and wonderfully peaceful within its broken, giant wall; and from there, having picnicked at ease in the sun, they crossed the road to the tightly-walled enclosure of the domed tomb of Ghias-ud-Din Tuqhluq, compressed as a blockhouse yet beautifully-proportioned, red walls leaning into themselves as solidly as the Egyptian Pyramids, white dome rearing austerely just high enough to peer over the flat brown plain, sprinkled with meagre trees.

They took a taxi to Humanyun's tomb, the resting-place of the second Mogul emperor, delicately attached to the eastern flank of Delhi in an immaculate formal garden. They had no idea that they were looking at something in its own way fully as beautiful as the Taj, which on this visit they could hardly hope to see; nevertheless, their hearts lifted strangely as they looked at the long, level, red terrace, the jut of mellow stonework above, and the poised and tranquil white dome. No floating off, balloon-wise, here, this was a tethered dream, with feet rooted in the ground. At the gate, as they left, a bearded snake-charmer, grinning ingratiatingly, coaxed out of its basket a dull, swaying brown cobra. Everything about it was pathetic, nothing was sinister, except for the single flick of its forked tongue; almost certainly it had no poison-sacs. They wondered if the music enchanted or hurt; there was no way of knowing. They paid their few new pice, and took their taxi back north to the Red Fort to lose count of time wondering among the white marble palaces and the paradisal gardens that overlook the Yamuna river. The complex waterways in the gardens were still dry at this time of year, and the fountains silent, but with a little imagination they could insert a small, lighted lamp into every niche in the lattices of stone where the water-level dropped, and see the silver curve of falling water lit from within and giving off rainbows like the scintillations from a diamond. The Moguls loved water, played with it, decorated their houses with it, built sumptuous pavilions in which to bathe in it, and took it to bed with them in little marble channels and lotus-flower fountains to sing them to sleep.

From this haunted palace in its dignity and quietness the three tourists plunged straight into the broad, teeming, over-peopled clamour of the Chandni Chowk, Old Delhi's grand market-place, screaming with cinema posters and advertisement hoardings, shrill with gossiping citizens and hurrying shoppers. They peered into the deep, narrow, open shops to see the silks and cottons baled and draped in unimaginable quantity, the Kashmiri shawls fine as cobweb, the gold and silver jewellery and the cheap glass

215

bangles, the nuts and seeds and spices, the unknown vegetables, the fantastic sweetmeats. Horse-drawn tongas, scooter-rickshaws, cars, bicycles, stray dogs, pedestrians, all mingled in the roadway in a complicated and hair-raising dance. The noise was deafening. So next, because according to the map they were less than a mile from it and could easily walk there, they went to Rajghat, the spot close to the river bank where Mahatma Gandhi's body was burned after his assassination, and where now a white balustrade encloses a paved space and a flower-covered dais. And there, though there were plenty of people, there was silence.

At the end of the first day they half expected that Cousin Vasudev would telephone or send them a note, either to follow up his tentative recognition of Anjli's identity and admit his own family responsibility for her, or to effect a careful withdrawal and leave the whole thing in abeyance, pending legal consultations. But there was no message.

'I suppose he has got his hands full,' Tossa said dubiously. 'And after all, he is only a cousin, and you could hardly hold him responsible as long as we've got Dorette to go back to, could you?'

'I expect,' said Anjli cynically, 'he's just holding his breath and keeping his eyes shut in the hope that if he doesn't look at us or speak to us we'll go away.'

On the second evening there was still no message. They had spent the afternoon prowling round all the government and state shops in New Delhi, among the leathers and silks and cottons and silverware and copperware and ivory carvings, well away from the banks of the Yamuna where the rites of death are celebrated. Nobody mentioned funerals. Everybody thought privately of the little, shrunken body that had hardly swelled the bedclothes, swathed now in white cotton for the last bath and the last fire. By the time they came back to Keen's Hotel, after a Chinese meal at Nirula's, Purnima was ash and spirit.

And there was no message for them at the desk, and no one had telephoned.

'Maybe he's got a whole party of funeral guests on his hands still,' said Tossa, 'and hasn't had time to think about us yet. I don't know what happens, there may be family customs . . . I know there don't seem to be any more near relatives, but there must be some distant ones around somewhere . . . and then all the business connections, with a family like that . . .'

'We've got to find out,' said Dominic. 'I'd better ring him, if he won't ring us.

He made the call from their own sitting-room upstairs. A high, harassed voice answered in Hindi, and after a wait of some minutes Cousin Vasudev's agitated English flooded Dominic's ear with salutations, apologies and protestations, effusive with goodwill but fretful with weariness and hag-ridden with responsibilities.

'It is unfilial, one cannot understand such behaviour. Everything I have had to do myself, everything. And into the bargain, with these newspapermen giving me no peace . . . It is a decadent time, Mr Felse, in all countries of the world duties are shirked, family ties neglected . . . The old order breaks down, and nothing is sacred any longer. What can we do? It is left for the dutiful to carry other people's burdens as well as their own . . .'

It seemed that Dominic's question had not merely answered itself, somewhere in the flood of words, but also been washed clean away on the tide. Nevertheless, when he could get a word in he asked it.

'Do you mean that Anjli's father has not come home? Not even for the funeral?'

'He has not. Everything is left to me. One cannot understand how a son could . . .'

'And he hasn't written, either? After all, he might be abroad somewhere . . .'

'I assure you, Mr Felse, certain preliminaries are necessary before Indian citizens go abroad. The authorities would know if that was the case, and of course I did, very discreetly, you understand . . . strictly private enquiries . . . My aunt did not wish it, but I felt it to be my duty . . . No, there has been no word from him at all. The position as far as that is concerned is quite unchanged . . .'

Dominic extricated himself from the current, made the best farewells he could, and hung up the receiver. They looked at one another, and for some minutes thought and were silent. Not because they had nothing to say, but because what was uppermost in two minds was not to be expressed in front of Anjli. Why, thought Dominic, blankly, did it never occur to us until now to wonder whether he really did go of his own free will? And whether there might not be a completely final reason why he hasn't come back? And has that really never occurred to Cousin Vasudev, either? In all this time, and with that much money at stake?

'He may not have seen the papers at all,' said Tossa sturdily. 'I know people in England who almost never look at the things.'

'He *can't* have seen them,' amended Anjli with emphasis, 'or he'd be here.'

'But what do we do now? We could hang on for a few days longer, certainly, maybe even a couple of weeks, but if he's as unavailable as all that what difference will two weeks make? And in any case, that would be a gamble, because we can't do that *and* pay for a single ticket back to London for Anjli. So we've got to make up our minds right now.'

Anjli dropped the tiny packet of damp tissue-paper she was just unwrapping, and gaped at him in consternation for a moment; but she was quick to recover her own reticence, which in some unquestioned way had become curiously precious to her here in Delhi.

'You mean you want me to go back to England with you?' she said with composure.

'What else can we possibly do?' said Dominic reasonably. 'We can't deliver you to your father, which was the object of the exercise, or to your grandmother, which would have done as a substitute. The only legal guardian you have is your mother – for the time being, at any rate. I don't see any alternative but to take you back with us . . . do you?'

'We could go and stay at Grandmother Purnima's house for a while, at any rate. He did ask us. That way, we needn't pay hotel bills, and we'd still have enough for my ticket back if it came to that in the end.'

'*We* couldn't. He didn't ask us, he asked *you*. And you said you didn't want to live there. And in any case,' said Dominic, smiling at her ruefully, 'you don't suppose we'd really hand you over to a man we don't know at all, and just fly off and leave you, do you?'

She owned, after a moment's thought, that that was too much to expect of them. 'Well, all right, then, what's the answer?' But she knew, and she knew he was right, by his standards and by hers. Somehow standards seemed irrelevant to this new world; what governed action was something just as valid and moral, but more inward, and not to be discussed or questioned. She picked up the little moist packet, and carefully unwrapped the exquisite bracelet of white jasmine buds Dominic had bought her in Chandni Chowk, strung neatly on green silk cord the colour of the stems. 'Tie it on, would you, please?'

Three days ago Dominic would have suspected that
confiding gesture of her wrist towards him, and the way
she inclined her head over the dewy trifle as he tied the
green cord. Now she seemed three years older than her age,
and every touch and sound and look of hers he accepted as
genuine. She turned her wrist, leaning back to admire. 'They
wear them in their hair, don't they? I could do that, too, if I
put mine up, there's plenty of it. A big knot on the back of
my neck, like this, and the bracelet tied round the knot . . .
Imagine all those gorgeous flowers, in winter! Did you ever
see such gardens?'

'The answer,' Tossa said, watching the two of them with
a faintly ironic smile, 'is that we all go back to London.
There's nothing else we can do. We'll have to see about your
ticket and flight in the morning.'

'You're the boss,' said Anjli. 'All right, if you say so,
that's what we do. Now, if you folks don't mind, I'm going
to put our bathroom light on and alert the enemy to get right
out of there, and in about five minutes I'm going to have my
bath.'

She had to go out into the corridor to go to the suite she
shared with Tossa, next door; and in the corridor she met
her least favourite room-boy, on a pretentious inlaid tray a
very grubby folded scrap of paper. His grin – it was a curious
side-long grin, the antithesis of Kishan Singh's radiant beam,
and his eyes never met hers for more than a fraction of
a second, but slid away like quicksilver – convulsed his
thin dark face at sight of her, and he bowed himself the
remaining four yards towards her, and proffered the tray.

'Missee-sahib, messenger he bring this for you. Say, please,
give privately. Your room dark, I think perhaps better
wait . . .'

He had a confiding, you-and-I-understand-each-other voice
and manner. She hadn't been a film star's daughter all her
life without meeting his like in many different places. She
dropped a quarter-rupee on the tray and picked up the dirty
little note with more curiosity than she showed.

'Thank you! That's all!'

He withdrew backwards, not out of extreme humility, but
to watch her face and bearing as she opened and read the
note; which got him nothing, for she didn't open and read
it until she had stared him into turning and slithering away
towards the stairs. Then she had it open in an instant, and

held under the light in the corridor. She could see there was
no more than one line to read; a glance, and she had it
memorised.

English characters sprawled shapelessly and shakily across
the paper, the pencil now pressing, now feebly touching, an
old man's hand:

'Daughter, come morning before light alone.'

She had unfolded it so hurriedly that something small had
fallen from it at her feet. She picked it up, and her fingers
knew it before ever she got it raised to the light. It was her
gold dollar, the token she had given to Arjun Baba in the
courtyard of her father's house in Rabindar Nagar.

The room-boy was on the stairs when she caught up with
him. There was no time to be diplomatic; instinct told her,
instead, to be autocratic. And, given co-operation, generous.

'Boy!' He turned, responsive to the tone, with more
alacrity than usual. 'Who brought this note?'

'A messenger, missee-sahib!' The obsequious shoulders
lifted eloquently. 'Perhaps a porter? Or he could be
somebody's office peon. In a red head-cloth, like a porter.'

'And he left no other message? Just brought the note?
How long ago?'

'Missee-sahib, only this minute. I come upstairs, your
room in darkness, when I see you come . . . That peon
maybe still only in courtyard there . . .'

Of course, there was no other way out. To enter Keen's
you must thread a narrow archway in from the street,
walk round a high hedge and so come into the interior
court; and if driving a car, you must drive from a double
gate higher up the street, right round one wing to the
same paved patio. Anjli dropped half a rupee on to her
least favourite room-boy's tray, and turned and ran from
him without concealment, straight to the landing window
that gave on to the courtyard gallery. Creepers wreathed
the outline of the night in feathery leaves. Down below,
lights shone upon the white paving and the scattered shrubs
in their huge ceramic pots. Away across the expanse of
silver-washed whiteness, towards the enclosing dark of the
high box hedge, a foreshortened figure strolled at leisure, but
still briskly, for the night air was sharp to the edge of frost.
Under the last of the lights she saw the extravagantly-tied,
wide-bowed headcloth, faded red. Like an office peon! She
did not know the term, but she understood what it meant.
The more menial the function, the more compensatory the

uniform. On the whole not a bad principle. But Arjun Baba had no office peon to run his errands, and this was not Kishan Singh. Perhaps a kind neighbour with a job in the city. Perhaps a public porter earning a few extra pice and acquiring merit.

The man below her – he was rounding the corner of the box hedge now – was whistling. The notes came up to her clearly in the almost frosty air and the nocturnal stillness. She followed them subconsciously, plaintive notes rising, turning, falling, simple and poignant, like a folk-tune. She caught herself picking up the cadence accurately before she realised what she was hearing.

But it was impossible! No, that was nonsense, she knew what she was hearing, once the memory fell into place. But how was it possible then? 'Siddhartha' wasn't anything like finished yet, not even the shooting. The music had certainly not yet been recorded. How could a street porter or an office messenger know the entire air of Yashodhara's bereaved lullaby, the simplified theme of the Buddha's morning raga?

Leaning over the rail of his balcony, Dominic pricked up his ears abruptly, listening.

'Hey, did you hear that? Listen!'

'Somebody whistling,' said Tossa, unimpressed, 'that's all. They do it even here. You remember, Ashok said . . .'

'Hush!'

She hushed obediently; he was very serious about it. She held her breath, following the tiny, silvery trail of notes up and down, a curiously rueful air. It receded, suddenly muted by the high hedge, but still heard, growing clearer again for a while as the angle changed, then cut off finally by the bulk of the wing. Now he must be in the street, lost among the trees. Theirs was a select residential road, silent at night. Indian cities have their preserves of silence, even close to the hub and the heart.

'Did you hear it? Did you get it?'

'I heard him whistling,' she said wonderingly. 'What about it?'

'You didn't get what it was he was whistling?' And Dominic picked up the air himself, and whistled it softly in his turn; he had an ear for a tune even at first hearing. 'You don't recognise it? But was it the same? The same as his?'

'I think so. It sounds the same. Why? How did you know it?'

'I heard it the other day, and so did you. It's the song from Ashok's music to the film, don't you remember? The simple one, the one Kamala sings. He *said* he'd be disappointed if they weren't whistling it in the streets before long. But not before the film's released! What on earth's going on?'

'But are you sure?' she asked doubtfully. 'After all, the ragas are everybody's property, you just take them and improvise on them, don't you? Somebody could accidentally produce a tune that recalled Ashok's, couldn't he? I mean, the unit is in Sarnath – or back in Clark's Hotel at Benares, probably, at this hour. Not in Delhi, anyhow.'

'I know. I must be imagining things,' agreed Dominic, shivering, and turned back from the staring stars into the warmth of the room.

Five

Anjli arose in the early hours of the morning, and stood beside her bed for a little while, listening to the silence, which was absolute. Not even a stirring of wind in the trees outside the open window. The air was clear, still and piercing, like dry wine.

She was just getting used to the size of the room, which held two beds, and could have accommodated ten. The distance between her single bed and Tossa's made movement easy and safe. She dressed with care and deliberation, because she had the deep conviction within her that she was not coming back, that she had better get everything right the first time, for there was not going to be any chance of revising measures once taken. Delhi would be as cool as an English spring for some weeks yet, the nights cold, midday perhaps reaching summer warmth in the sun. Better be prepared for all temperatures. She put on the lambswool and angora suit in muted strawberry pink, took a scarf and her light wool coat, and slipped her feet into supple walking shoes. Then she carefully tucked into her large handbag a cotton dress, sandals, toilet necessaries and a towel. That was all. The Lord Buddha, when he passed through the palace gardens among the oblivious sleepers, carried nothing but what he wore, and even that he gave away when he entered the outer world and sent Channa back with the weeping white horse Kantaka.

She had some money of her own, changed into rupees for shopping, and some travellers' cheques. Her passport, her own personal papers – it seemed wrong to possess any of these. But she was living in this present world, and its customs were not those of Kapilavastu, and a certain respect was due to the laws of the land. So she allowed herself the money and the credentials. And at the last moment she turned back to her dressing-table, and painstakingly tied round her left wrist the slightly wilted bracelet of jasmine buds. Dominic was, after all, rather sweet, and it wasn't like allowing oneself real jewels. The Lord Buddha had divested himself of all his jewels before he exchanged his rich silk robes for a huntsman's homespun tunic in the woods. Maybe she could exchange her expensive cardigan suit for shalwar and kameez and a floating, infuriating gauze scarf such as the schoolgirls wore. She peered into the dark mirror, where a faint cadence of movement indicated the ghost of Anjli peering back at her, and imagined the transformation.

In the other bed Tossa slept peacefully. She never stirred when the door of the room was gently opened. Anjli looked back, and was reassured, and at the same time curiously touched. She hadn't expected much from Tossa, to tell the truth; anyone her mother deputed to do her dirty work for her was automatically suspect. But Tossa had been a surprise; so quiet, and so reasonable, and so aware, as if she knew just what was going on. Which was nonsense, because there couldn't really be two Dorettes, could there? And how else would she know? Not stupid, either, she could put her foot down gently but finally when she liked. Anjli hoped they would not feel too responsible, and that she would soon be able to get in touch with them and put their minds at rest. Also that they would spend the last dollar of Dorette's money on seeing India before they sent back to England.

The corridor was lit only by a small lamp at the end. No one was moving. She listened, and the whole house seemed to be one silence. Anjli closed the door of the room softly behind her, and tiptoed along the darker wall towards the landing window that led to the balconies. There was a stairway to the courtyard there; and there were no gates or doors closing the archway that opened into the street. She knew the lie of the land by now; by the carriage gates farther along there were always a few rickshaws and taxis hopefully waiting, even at night.

She was not going back to Dorette's synthetic world. Not now, nor ever. There were plenty of things in India that she didn't want, the cockroaches, the flies, the dirt, the lean, mad-looking tonga horses, half-demented with overwork and rough usage, the maimed animals no one was profane enough to kill but no one was vulnerable enough to pity, the hunger, the disease, the monumental indifference. Nevertheless, India was all she wanted, India and the links that bound her to it, notably her father, the indispensable link.

There was a room-boy curled up asleep in the service box at the end of the corridor. She passed him by silently, and he slept on. Down the stairs into the courtyard she went, and from shadow to shadow of the spaced trees across to the end of the box hedge – perhaps it wasn't box, but it looked like it, and that was how she thought of it – and round it into comparative security. Now there was only the porter's box by the archway. They were asleep there, too. She stole past them like a ghost, and never troubled their dreams. She was in the street, melting into the shelter of the trees, alone in the faintly lambent darkness.

She thought of the receding red turban, and the fine thread of melody whistled across the evening air to her, like an omen; it no longer troubled her, it was inevitably right now, at this hour. The early morning, and the guests – the guest! – departing . . .

At the last moment she thought better of taking a rickshaw from the end of the carriage drive, though there were two standing there. She crossed the road, instead, and circled round them, keeping in the shelter of the trees; for when enquiries began to be made about her departure, these would surely be the first people to be questioned. Close to the southern end of Janpath was Claridge's Hotel, and there would just as surely be a taxi or two waiting there.

There was one car, the Sikh driver asleep behind the wheel, and one cycle-rickshaw, with a lean brown boy curled up in a blanket inside the high, shell-shaped carriage. Anjli chose the rickshaw. It would take longer to get her out to the edge of town, but it would pass silently everywhere, and not be noticed. It would be cheaper, too, and she might yet need her money. Who knew how far she would have to travel to find her father, even if Arjun Baba could tell her the way?

The boy awoke in a flash, uncurling long, thin limbs like a startled spider, and baring white teeth in a nervous grin.

'Will you take me,' said Anjli, low-voiced, 'to the new school in Rabindar Nagar?' She could have given the number of the house and been dropped at the door, but the hunt for her, if pursued devotedly enough, might even turn up this boy; and besides, if her father's secret was so urgent, she did not want any witnesses.

The boy bowed and nodded her into the carriage, and pushed his cycle off silently into the roadway. It was a long drive, she knew, perhaps a little over two miles, but she was a lightweight, and the bicycle was new and well-kept; it would still be practically dark when they arrived. The shapes of New Delhi flowed past her mutely in the dimness, trees and buildings, occasionally a glimpse of a man stumbling to work, still half-sleeping, sometimes the smokey glimmer of little lanterns attached to the shacks where vegetable-sellers slept beside their stalls, waiting to unload the goods brought in at dawn. The stars were still visible, silver sewn into velvet. Now they were out of the city and cruising along the airy terrace of the Ridge for a while, where the air was sharp and bitterly cold, dry and penetrating as the sands from which it blew. And now the first small white villas, making pale patterns against the smoke-coloured earth that would be tawny by day.

The boy halted obediently at the shiny new gates of the school, and asked no questions. Probably he had no English, for he said not a word throughout the transaction, though he must have understood enough to bring her where she wished to be. When she opened her bag they needed no words. He had already summed up her appearance, her clothing and her innocence, perhaps even over-estimating the innocence. He smiled at her beguilingly, and deprecatingly raised two fingers. He thought she didn't know exactly how many new pice per mile he was supposed to charge; but her mind was on other things, and in any case her mood was that of one turning back upon the world's goods. She gave him his two rupees, and it was a good investment, for he promptly mounted his cycle and rode away before she could change her mind. So he never saw which way she turned from the school.

Only a hundred yards to go now. It was still almost fully dark, only the faintest of pallors showed along the horizon, transforming the sky into an inverted bowl of black rice-grain porcelain with a thin gold rim. She saw the shape of Satyavan's house rise along the sky-line ahead, the only one with that little princely pavilion on the roof; she wondered for a moment if he had a garden up there, or at least small decorative trees in tubs, like the one beside the front door below. All the whites of the white walls were a shadowy, lambent grey, for as yet there were no colours, only cardboard forms, not solids but merely planes. She came to the gate of filigree iron, and for a moment wondered what she would to if it turned out to be locked or chained; but the latch gave to her hand soundlessly. At the end of the garden wall, drawn aside from the roadway, a small van sat parked in the worn, straw-pale grass. Did that mean that someone had come home? Or was it merely the property of the man next door, the plump lady's husband, who was probably a travelling salesman, or a veterinary surgeon, or something else modestly professional with need of transport?

She let herself into the compound. The house was dark and quiet, and Kishan Singh, with no need to rise early, was surely still fast asleep. But in the distant corner of the earth yard a small gleam of light shone, and the now familiar scent of dust and humanity and incense, funereal, vital and holy, stung her nostrils as she tiptoed across the front garden.

In front of his corner kennel, under his lean-to roof, Arjun Baba sat just as she had seen him three days ago, huddled in his brown blanket against the night's cold, peering down sightlessly into the minute flame of his brazier. A glossy red reflection picked out the jut of cheek-bones and brow from the tangle of grey hair and beard that hid his face. When he heard her step he raised his head, but did not turn towards her. She had a feeling that three days had been lost, and all that had passed in them was a fantasy, not a reality; or perhaps that those three days had been demanded of her as a probation for what was still to come. Perhaps he had not even expected her. Yet she was here.

She crossed the few yards of bare, beaten earth with the soft, gliding walk of a woman in a sari, and sank to her heels, squatting to face him across the brazier.

'Namaste! Uncle, I am Anjli Kumar. You called me, I have come.'

The old man shifted slowly in his blanket, and linked his hands beneath his chin in greeting. A creaking voice blew through the tangle of grey hair and said hoarsely: 'Namaste!'

'Uncle, you have something to tell me?'

The ancient head wagged in the ambiguous manner she had learned to interpret as: Yes. Slowly he shrugged back the blanket from his shoulders, and lifted his eyes to her face.

It was the gleam of the brazier that warned her. She had braced herself unconsciously to contemplate once again the opaque white membrane of cataract filming over the sightless eyes, and instead there was a bright darkness with a hard golden high-light, the sharp pheasant-stare of eyes that saw her very clearly. For an instant she stared back transfixed and motionless; then without a sound she recoiled from him and sprang to her feet, whirling on one heel to run like a deer.

A hand reached out across the brazier and caught her by

227

the long black braid of hair, dragging her back. She opened
her lips to cry out, but the blanket was flung over her head,
and hard fingers clamped the dusty folds tightly over her
mouth and nostrils, ramming the cloth between her teeth.
a long arm gripped her round the waist and swung her off
her feet, and in a moment she felt something drawn tightly
round her arms above the elbow, pinning them fast. She
tried to kick, and the voluminous folds of the blanket were
drawn close and tied, muffling every movement. A hand felt
for her mouth, thrust the woollen stuff in deep, and twisted
a strip of cloth round her head to fasten the gagging folds in
place.

The hair-line of gold along the horizon had thickened into
a pale-rose-coloured cord. Just before the first backdoor
tradesman pushed his hand-cart into the alley between the
houses, the little van parked on the grass started up, and
was driven decorously away towards the main road.

Six

Dominic awakened to an insistent tapping at his door about eight o'clock, to find the room flooded with sunlight. He rolled out of bed and reached for his dressing-gown so abruptly that one gecko, until then apparently petrified in a corner of the ceiling, whisked out of sight under the rickety wiring, and another, prowling within inches of Dominic's heel as he hit the floor, shot away in a fright, leaving behind on the boards a two-and-a-half inch tail that continued to twitch for ten minutes after its owner had departed.

'Dominic, are you awake? It's me, Tossa. Open the door!' She fell into the room in a cloud of nylon ruffles. 'You haven't seen anything of Anjli, have you?' A silly question, she realised, his eyes were barely open yet. 'She's gone! I woke up a little while ago, and she isn't anywhere to be seen, and her bed's cold. I thought at first she was in the bathroom, but she isn't. Her pyjamas are there folded on the pillow. But *she's gone*!'

Her glance fell upon the wriggling tail at that moment, and her eyes opened wide in incredulous horror, for she had read about, but never yet encountered, the more unnerving habits of the smaller lizards. But she was too preoccupied to spare a word for the phenomenon Dominic plainly had not even noticed.

'It's a fine morning,' he said reasonably, 'she'll have gone off for a walk. I don't suppose she's any farther away than the garden.'

Tossa shook her head emphatically. 'She's taken that outsize handbag of hers. I checked as soon as I realised . . . It's got all her money in it, and her passport. Her coat's gone from the wardrobe, and a cotton dress . . . and her washing things have vanished out of the bathroom. No, she's up to something on her own. Whatever it is, she planned it herself. You know what I think? I'd have sworn even at the time she was being too quiet and reasonable. When it came to the point, she simply didn't want to go back home.'

'But she surely wouldn't run off on her own, just to give

229

us the slip? She's got nobody here to turn to, after all, even if she does hate the thought of going back to England.'

'She's got a cousin,' Tossa reminded him dubiously.

'She didn't show much sign of taking to him.'

'I know. But he's the only relative she has got left over here, as far as we know. We'd better try there first, hadn't we?' Her eyes remained fixed on the abandoned tail, now twitching solemnly and regularly as a metronome. Her toes curled with horror. 'Don't step back!' she warned; his bare foot was just an inch from the pale-green tip.

Dominic looked down, uttered a startled yelp, and removed himself several feet from the improbable thing in one leap. 'Good lord, what on earth . . .! *I* haven't done that, surely? I swear I never touched . . .'

'They say they do it when they're scared,' said Tossa, and wondered if she had not shed an appendage herself this morning, a taken-for-granted tail of European self-confidence and security. 'I think they grow another. She can't really have gone off and left us permanently, can she? Surely, she'd be afraid!'

'Go and get dressed, and we'll see if she comes to breakfast. If not, maybe some of the hotel staff will have seen her go out.'

That was good sense, and Tossa seized on it gratefully; Anjli had a healthy appetite, and was always on time for meals. But this time the magic did not work. The two of them met at their table in the ground-floor dining room, the garden bright and empty outside the long windows; the tea arrived, strong and dark as always, the toast, the eggs; but no Anjli.

They went in search of the room-boy. Last night's attendant was off-duty for the day, and the shy southerner who had just tidied away the gecko's tail, finally limp and still, had seen nothing of Miss Kumar. Nor had the sweeper in the courtyard, nor the porters at the gates. All this time Dominic had had one eye cocked for the truant's return, fully expecting her to saunter in from a walk at any moment; but time ticked by and the possible sources of information dried up one by one, and still no Anjli. By a process of elimination they arrived at the reception clerk, who was hardly a promising prospect, since he had come on duty only at eight o'clock this morning, when Anjli's absence had already been discovered. However, they tried.

'Miss Kumar? No, I have not seen her this morning, I

am sorry.' The clerk was a dapper young man, friendly and willing to please. He looked from one anxious face to the other, and grasped that this was serious; and it was in pure kindness of heart that he felt impelled to add something more, even if it was of no practical help. 'I have seen nothing of her since she came in with you yesterday evening. To be sure, I remember there was a note delivered here for her later . . .'

'Note?' said Dominic, pricking up his ears. He looked at Tossa, and she shook her head; not a word had been said about any note. 'Did she get it?'

'Of course, sir, I sent it up to her as soon as it came, by the room-boy.'

'You don't know who it was from? Who brought it? Certainly not the postman, at that hour.'

'No, sir, I cannot say from whom it came. It was a common peon who brought it, some shop porter, perhaps. Though I do recall that the note was not in an envelope, but just a sheet of paper folded together – a little soiled, even . . .'

It did not sound at all like the immaculate Vasudev. And who else was there in Delhi to be sending notes to Anjli? The film unit was away in Benares, and no one else knew her.

'About what time was this?'

'I cannot say precisely, sir, but a little after nine, probably.'

Anjli had announced her intention of going for her bath at about that hour. And only a few minutes later, that floating wisp of melody had drifted in at the window that overlooked the courtyard . . . No, he was imagining connections where there were none. Tossa was right, the ragas were there for everyone to use and enjoy. It was placing too much reliance on his unpractised ear to insist that what he had heard was not merely Raga Aheer Bhairab, but Ashok's unique folksong variation of it, and no other.

So they were back to the necessity of beginning the hunt for Anjli somewhere; and the obvious place was Purnima's house. Where, of course, they told each other bracingly in the taxi, Anjli would certainly be.

'Note?' Vasudev's thin black moustache quivered with consternation. 'No, indeed I assure you I sent my little cousin no note. I would not dream of addressing her except through you, when you have been placed in charge of her by her mother. I have been considering, indeed – I intended to

231

telephone you today and ask you to call . . . Some proper provision must be made, of course. But I did not . . . This is terrible! You do not think that someone has lured her away . . .? But who knew of her presence here? Your friends of the film unit, you tell me, are in Benares. Otherwise who could know you – and Anjli – here in Delhi, and know where to find you?'

'We've been in contact with a lot of people in the town, of course,' admitted Tossa, 'but only casually, the sort of tourist contact one has with shops, and restaurants, and guides . . . and what could be more anonymous? The only place where we're *known*, so to speak, apart from here and the hotel, is the house in Rabindar Nagar – your cousin Satyavan's house . . .'

'Of course!' Dominic snapped his fingers joyfully. 'Why didn't I think of it! Kishan Singh! A slightly grubby little note brought by a paid messenger . . . It could be! Kishan Singh may have had some news of Anjli's father. Perhaps he's home!'

Vasudev looked first dubious, and then hopeful; and after a few seconds of thought, both excited and resolute. He came out of his western chair in a nervous leap. 'Come, we shall take the car and I will drive you over there to Rabindar Nagar. We must see if this is the case. Indeed, one hopes! That would resolve all our problems most fortunately.'

He ran to the rear door of the palatial hall, and clapped his hands, and in a few moments they heard him issuing clipped, high-pitched orders. Presently the car rolled majestically round on to the rosy gravel, with a magnificently turbaned Sikh at the wheel. A glossy new Mercedes in the most conservative of dark greys, and its chauffeur's pride and joy, that was clear by the condescending forbearance with which he opened the door to allow them to enter its sacred confines. But that morning he was not to be allowed to drive it; Vasudev did that himself, and did it with a ferocity and fire they had not expected from him. Their taxi driver, on the first occasion, had taken half as long again to get them to Rabindar Nagar.

At the first turning into the new suburb from the main road Vasudev braked, hesitating. 'It is long since I was here, I have forgotten. Is it this turn?'

'The second one. N block, it's only a couple of hundred yards farther on. Yes, here.'

At the half-finished houses the bold, gypsyish, stately

women of Orissa walked the scaffolding with shallow baskets of bricks on their heads, and made a highly-coloured frieze against the pale blue sky, their fluted skirts swaying as though to music. At sight of the opulent car the half-naked children padded barefoot across the open from their low, dark tents, running beside it with pinkish-brown palms upturned and small, husky voices grating their endless complaint against possessing nothing among so many and such solid possessions. There was no obsequious tone in this begging, it accused, demanded and mocked, expecting nothing, and ready to throw stones if nothing was given. But this time the plump lady from next door did not chase them away. She was there, she and a dozen others, clustered round the open iron gate of N 305, all shrilling and shrugging in excited Hindi, a soprano descant to a louder, angrier more violent clamour of male voices eddying from within the compound. No one had time now for errant children; the centre of all the attention was there within the wall, out of sight. And even the Orissan infants, having come to beg, sensed that there was more to be had here than new pice, and winding the excitement, wormed their way in under elbows, between legs, through the folds of saris, to see whatever was there to be seen.

'Oh, God, no!' prayed Tossa silently in the back seat, tugging at the handle of the door. Little girls vanished, little girls reappeared, horribly changed. Everybody knew it happened. But not here! With all its violence and despair and hunger, somehow India had felt morally clean and safe to her, she would have walked through Old Delhi at night, alone, and never felt a qualm, something she couldn't have said for Paddington. Yet unmistakably this had the look of a crowd round the police van, the ambulance, the sorry panoply of murder or rape.

They clambered out of the car, clumsy with haste.

'Oh, dear! Oh, dear!' Vasudev keened, his voice soaring with agitation. 'Something has happened! Something is wrong here! Miss Barber, you should please stay in the car . . .'

But she was already ahead of them, boring into the small butterfly crowd about the gate, and thrusting her way through without ceremony. They followed her perforce, clinging to her arm, urging her to go back. Tossa hardly noticed. It was bad enough for them, but it was she who had taken on the job, so lightly, so selfishly, coveting India

233

and hardly thinking, at first, about the child who was being posted about the world like a parcel . . .

She extricated herself frantically from the gold-embroidered end of a lilac and white sari, and fell out into the open space of the compound, and Dominic flung his arm round her and held her upright. The door of Satyavan's house stood wide open, and on the white paving before it Kishan Singh, his guileless eyes round and golden with fright, sobbed and protested and argued in loud Hindi, alternately buffeted and shaken between two vociferous Punjabis in khaki shorts and tunics. Another man in khaki, obviously their superior, stood straddle-legged before the trio, barking abrupt questions at the terrified boy, and swinging a short rattan cane of office in one hand. He was a handsome turbaned Sikh, his beard cradled in a fine black net, his moustache waxed fiercely erect at the ends. Whatever had happened, the Delhi police were in possession here.

Kishan Singh, turning his bullet head wildly from one persecutor to the other, caught a fleeting glimpse of the new arrivals, and uttered a shrill cry of relief and joy. Crises in India are chaotic, voluble and exceedingly noisy, and he had been adding his share to this one, but only out of panic. With someone to speak for him, he regained his sturdy mountain calm.

'Sahib, memsahib, please, there is a very bad thing happened. You tell these men, I am honest, I have done nothing wrong . . . Why should I call police here, if I did this thing?'

Dominic looked squarely at the Sikh officer, who was plainly the man to be reckoned with here. 'Kishan Singh is the caretaker of this house, and has been a good servant to Shrimati Purnima Kumar and to her son. If Shrimati Purnima were still alive, I know she would speak for her boy, and I feel sure Mr Kumar here, her nephew, will tell you the same. I don't know what has happened here, but I know that Kishan Singh is to be trusted.' Did he really know that, after one short encounter? Yes, he did, and he wasn't going to apologise for the brevity of the acquaintance to this man or to anyone. With some people, you know where you stand, with some you don't. Kishan Singh belonged among the former group. There is an innocence which is absolute, and there's no mistaking it when you do meet it.

'I understand,' said the Sikh officer, eyeing them narrowly, 'that this boy is the only resident here. Is that the case?' His

English was all the better because his voice was a sombre bass-baritone.

'Yes, I understand that is true. Apart from the old man who lives in the compound here, as a kind of pensioner of the family.'

'Ah . . . yes,' said the police officer gently. 'That is the point. We are, unfortunately, debarred from referring to this elderly gentleman as a witness.'

'I know he is blind. You mean there has been a crime on these premises?'

'A very serious crime.' He made a brief gesture with the cane in his hand, and deflected all attention into the distant corner of the compound, partially cut off from view by the jut of the house wall. Tossa wanted to close her eyes, but did not; what right had she to refrain from seeing what was there to be seen? The poor little girl, shuttlecock to this marital pair who didn't care a toss about her, and now fallen victim to some incomprehensible perversion that was an offence against India as well as against youth and girlhood . . .

'Come, you should look more closely,' said the Sikh, and led the way, turning once to say with authority: 'The lady must stay here.'

The lady stayed; she could not very well do anything else. But her eyes, which had excellent vision, followed them remorselessly across the sparkling white paving, across the beaten, rust-coloured earth, under the lightly-dancing clothes-line, to the shed and the lean-to roof in the corner, where Anjli . . .

No! There was no honeyed rose of Anjli's skin there, and no midnight-black of her hair, and no midnight-black of her hair, and no silvery angora pink of her best jersey suit. There were two policemen and one dried-up little medical civilian sitting on their heels around something on the ground; and when the Sikh brought his accidental witnesses over to view the find, these three rose and drew apart, leaving the focus of all attention full in view.

He could not have been found there, any chance passer-by in the side street might have looked over the wall and seen him; they must have brought him out into the light after measuring and recording his position on discovery, somewhere there in the corner shed, fast hidden from sight.

The dull brown blanket was gone. Only a thin, skinny little shape, hardly larger than a monkey, lay contorted on the darker brown earth of Satyavan's yard, bony arms

curled together as if holding a secret, bony legs drawn up
to his chin, streaky grey hair spread abroad like scattered
ash. There was so little blood in him that his face was
scarcely congested at all; but there were swollen bruises on
the long, skinny, misshapen throat to show that he had died
by strangulation.

The eyes were open; blank, rounded and white as pearls.

Arjun Baba, that very, very old man, had quitted the
world in the night, and left no message behind him.

Kishan Singh padded across the yard at the policeman's
heels, protesting: 'I did not touch the old man, I swear it.
Sahib, why should I touch him? All this year I have given
him food, and brought him his *pan*, and been as his servant,
as my mistress told me. Always when I rose in the morning
he was sitting by his brazier . . . Today he was not there. I
called him, and he did not answer, and therefore I looked
within . . . Sahib, he was lying there in the dark, as you see
him, so he was. I saw that he was dead . . . Also I saw how
he had died, and therefore I ran for the police. Should I do
that if I had killed him?'

'It would be the best way of appearing blameless,' said the
Sikh officer drily, 'if you had the wit.'

'But why should I wish to harm him, I? What gain for me?
You think such a person had money to be stolen?'

'You may have grudged the effort of feeding him. Perhaps
he was in your way. It would be easy to make away with
some of the furnishings of this house, without a witness
always in the compound . . .'

'The old man was blind . . .'

'But very quick of hearing,' called the plump lady from
next door, bright with excitement at the gate; and all the
neighbours joined in in shrill Hindi, shouting one another
down. 'Everything he heard! I had only to set foot on my
roof, and he would call up to me. He knew by my walk when
I had my washing basket on my arm.'

'This boy has been always a very trustworthy servant,'
Vasudev urged in agitation. 'I cannot believe he would hurt
the old man.'

'You do not know what he might do, being master here as
well as servant. Young people have no time now to care for
the old . . . Arjun Baba was a trouble to him, that is how it
was! Who else was here to do this thing, tell us that? In the
night we are not minding our neighbours' business here, we

are good people. Very easy to make away with the old man in the night, and then find him – oh, yes, all innocently! – in the morning and run to the police.'

Other voices rose as vociferously, arguing against her. The two policemen, affronted by the steady surge of curious people across the threshold into the front garden, began to push them back outside the gate, were shrilled at indignantly in consequence, and shouted back no less angrily. The noise soared into a crescendo that was like physical pain. And all the while Dominic and Tossa gazed at the shrunken, indifferent corpse of Arjun Baba, old age torn and savaged and discarded where they had dreaded to see Anjli's youth and grace. It is a terrible thing to feel only relief when you are brought face to face with a murdered man. They felt themselves, in some obscure way, responsible, if not for his death, yet for the absence of all mourning; if the world had not owed him a living, yet surely it owed him at least justice and regret now that he was dead.

'If you did not do it, then who did? Who else would want to kill such an old man? Who were Arjun Baba's enemies?'

'He had no enemies . . . No friends now except me . . . and no enemies . . . I do not know who would do such a thing. But I did not . . . I did not . . .'

In the fine drift of dust along the lee of the old man's hut a tiny gleam of whiteness showed. Dominic stepped carefully past the stringy brown feet, and stooped to pick up the small alien thing no one else had yet noticed. It lay coiled in his palm light as a feather, seven inches or so of fine green cord stringing a bracelet of white jasmine buds, threaded pointing alternately this way and that. After sixteen hours they were a little soiled and faded, one or two torn away from their places, but they were still fragrant. He saw that the green cord was not untied, but broken; and silk is very strong.

Anjli had been here!

He began to see, vaguely, the shape of disturbing things. Anjli had been here, and the flowers she had worn had been ripped from her wrist with some violence, perhaps in a struggle. And the old man, the only one remaining who had been here when Satyavan vanished in the night, was dead. Anjli had given him a token, and coaxed him to tell her whatever he knew. And last night Anjli had received a grubby note brought by a common messenger, a note which had sent her out secretly before dawn. To this place. For so the jasmine flowers said clearly.

He turned to the Sikh police officer, shouting to make himself heard. 'Have your men examined all Arjun Baba's belongings? May I know what you found?'

'Belongings? Sahib, such a man has nothing . . . a brazier, a headcloth, a loincloth, a blanket . . .'

'But you see he *hasn't* got a blanket! And it was a cold night!'

It was true. The policeman cast one swift glance into the hut, and frowned, and looked again at Dominic, who was becoming interesting. With more respect he enumerated one by one the few poor items of Arjun Baba's housekeeping.

'Nothing more? Not even a tiny thing like a gold coin?'

A shrug and an indulgent smile. 'Where should such a man get gold?'

Had the token been sent back, then, as bait to bring Anjli? And if so, by whom? By Arjun Baba in good faith? Or by his killer? A missing gold dollar to lure her to the meeting in the dark, a missing blanket to muffle her cries and smother her struggles . . .

'I'll tell you,' he said, 'where he got gold. From a young girl who came here with us a few days ago, and gave him the dollar she wears on a chain for luck. We came here looking for her, and I really think we'd better tell you the whole story, because it looks as if she has been here in the night, and whoever killed Arjun Baba has also taken Anjli away. Can't we go into the house, where it will be quieter? This may take some time.'

It would have taken less time than it did if someone could have restrained Vasudev's slightly hysterical commentary of pious horror and masochistic self-reproach. Wasn't he, perhaps, protesting even a shade too much? Tossa's thumbs were pricking painfully before the whole story was told. True, Vasudev had willingly brought them here, and in a hurry, too, but might not that be part of a carefully-laid plan? The anxious relative, conscience-stricken over his own shortcomings towards his young cousin . . . who was going to look there for a murderer and kidnapper? There was a lot of Kumar money, and this dutiful managing director of all that wealth had got into the habit of thinking in millions by now. Who could wonder if . . .? Some people would even have difficulty in blaming him!

'It would seem,' said the Sikh policeman, summing up with a good deal of shrewdness, 'that this young lady is the child not merely of one very wealthy person, but of two almost equally subject to envy. If, as you say, she has indeed been kidnapped, the motive must be gain. There is almost no other known motive for kidnapping, unless the object is matrimony. For love, of course! One understands that gain may also be involved in matrimony, but that is by the way. Then the first question that arises is: how many people, here in India, knew that Miss Kumar is worth much money as ransom? All of the members of this film company, that is certain. Most are Indians, they would know that the Kumar family are millionaires. The others, the Americans, even if they were not so well informed about the Kumars, would know that the mother is famous and rich.'

'They'd know more than that,' said Dominic bluntly. 'American film actresses don't usually marry poor Indians.'

'That is well observed. Money, Mr Felse, is inclined always to money, there is an affinity. So we have all the film company. And who besides? Your household, Mr Kumar, I think could hardly be ignorant of the young lady's value, after her visit to Mrs Kumar's death-bed. News is very quick to travel among servants, and you have many servants. Then also, let us not forget, this house-boy here, Kishan Singh, is not an idiot, and Miss Kumar had expressly revealed her identity to him . . .'

'After I had already done so,' said Dominic stoutly. Whatever happened, he could not imagine circumstances in which he would suspect Kishan Singh.

'Very naturally. The fact remains, he was, by your account, the first after the film company to know of Miss Kumar's value. But when we have said that, let us not be misled, we have not closed the number of our suspects. Film stars are news. For all we know there may have been paragraphs in the papers about Miss Kumar's arrival in India. It would need only one observant person on the same flight. And once here, interested eyes may have observed your visit to Mrs Kumar's villa. Also here.'

'That lets nearly everybody in,' admitted Dominic glumly.

'Nevertheless, those with close personal knowledge – priority knowledge, one could say – must take precedence. Leave it to us, we shall investigate every person concerned. There remains the possibility that Miss Kumar is at liberty, and for her own reasons in hiding. This we can surely confide to you, Mr Kumar. Miss Kumar, I understand, is not familiar with Hindi. But a personal advertisement in the

English-language press would be, I suggest, a good idea! She
may very well read the papers! She will be unable to resist
looking to see what they say about her!'

Vasudev seized on it as on a lifeline in a very rough sea.
Practicalities were his line. He was out of his chair in an
ecstasy of enthusiasm, looking at his watch.

'I shall see to it at once. There is the evening press . . . if
you will pardon me, it would not be too late . . . But my
guests . . . is it possible to arrange transport wherever they
may wish . . .? Or perhaps I could return a little later . . .?'

'It's quite all right, thank you very much,' said Tossa.
'There's a taxi rank just on the main road.'

'Then if you will excuse me . . .! Please do get in touch if
you should have any news, and naturally I will do the same.
Your servant, Miss Barber!'

He had a small leather-bound notebook in his left hand
as he galloped out of the room, and a ball-pen in his
right, so anxious was he to get his come-home-all-is-forgiven
advertisement framed for the evening papers. And it might
be genuine, and it might not, and who could hope to tell
the difference? The Sikh officer, perhaps. He stood at the
window, frowning down towards the dusty frontage, until
the Mercedes had started up and rushed away with aplomb
in the direction of the main Delhi road. But by the sombre
look on his face as he turned back into the room, he had
come to no very definite conclusion about Vasudev. Nor,
perhaps, about them? After all, if Anjli was a prize, who
knew her worth better than they did, and who had been in
a better position to manipulate her movements?

'Now, Mr Felse, a few more questions.' They turned out
to be more than a few. Had he, had Tossa, ever previously
been in contact with any of the Kumar family? What did
they know of them? It was very clear why Vasudev had been
sidetracked out of the picture for the moment. Patiently they
went over and over their very brief acquaintance with the
Kumars, witholding nothing.

Had they had any undisclosed communication with Kishan
Singh? They did realise that even if some other person with
more sophisticated ideas conceived the plan of kidnapping
Anjli and holding her to ransom, yet Kishan Singh was the
obvious tool to use?

'He's the last tool *I* should use,' said Dominic with
conviction, 'for anything dirty.'

'An innocent face may be a gift from God even to the

unworthy. But we were not – or did I not make that too clear? – speaking necessarily of *you*. Kishan Singh may even have conceived the plan himself after witnessing – you *did* say he witnessed it? – the scene between the young lady and the old man. How easy to send her the symbol and ask her to come here! About that I am sure you are right. She may, as it were, have originated the whole plot herself in that impulsive act.'

And had they anything to add to their account? Any forgotten detail? Dominic, by this time, had remembered that he had not mentioned hearing, or thinking he heard, Ashok's morning raga whistled the previous night in the courtyard of Keen's Hotel, at the very time when the note was being delivered to Anjli; but he had seen enough of the way the land lay to keep that item to himself now. The issue was confused enough already, why introduce into it what he might well have imagined, and what would certainly smell like a red herring to this suspicious person interrogating him?

'Very well, let us leave it at that for the moment. You will be available, please, at Keen's Hotel, you will not move from Delhi at present.'

'We are not going anywhere,' said Dominic steadily, 'until Anjli is found. And I hope you are not thinking of detaining Kishan Singh, because he, too, will be available whenever you need him. He won't leave here unless the Kumar family tell him to, and a word from you will take care of that.'

'You are very concerned for the house-boy, Mr Felse. It is generous on your part – and interesting.'

'I am concerned because he is young, alone here – his mistress, as you must know, is recently dead, and his family in the hills – and quite certainly totally innocent. You have only to look at him. He has never in his life entertained a malicious thought, much less deliberately hurt anyone. Arjun Baba was as sacred to him as the sparrows that fly in and out of the house. The boy was responsible for him to Mrs Kumar, whom he revered absolutely . . .'

'And who, as you have pointed out, is dead. One person's death may bring about a total disintegration for her dependants . . .'

They were raising their voices, both of them, and that made Tossa aware, quite suddenly, in what low tones they had been conversing for several minutes past. She pricked up her ears, and leaned upon a wall of noise that was not there, and fell through it into full consciousness. The din from the yard, that flat, clattering chaos of voices one gets used to in India, aggravated here by excitement to a sustained pandemonium, had almost completely ceased. When, she had no idea. Simply, it was gone. She reared her head, straining after it, and recaptured only a gentle, single murmur, unbelievably placid and reassuring.

'Listen!' she said peremptorily; and in sheer surprise they fell silent, too. 'It's gone quiet. What's happened?'

The wonderful hush fell on them and charmed them into stillness. And stillness and silence, in Delhi, represent a new and more menacing crisis. The Sikh officer wheeled and strode to the window, with Dominic and Tossa pressing discreetly on his heels. They stared down into the yard together, forgetting all disagreements; for in their own way they were all the forces of law, and law had not sufficed to bring about silence and stillness in the confines of N 305, Rabindar Nagar, in the teeth of suspicion and disorder.

Drawn up in front of the gate stood an extraordinary car. Only a Rolls-Royce, perhaps, could have driven up so quietly as to be unnoticed. It was certainly an extremely antique Rolls-Royce, not at all well-maintained as far as its noble chassis was concerned, though apparently mechanically in first-class condition. Orissan children swarmed about it with absorption and delight, and were fended off good-humouredly, when necessary, by a long, slender, crop-haired driver in khaki shorts and bush jacket, who lounged at ease on the running-board. The women at the gate had stopped yelling, and stood decorously in a staged group, expressive of grief and modesty and respect, all facing inwards towards where Arjun Baba's little wasted corpse lay uncomplainingly exposed. Beside the body stood a personage as remarkable, in his unassuming way, as his car, and for all his venerable appearance no more than half as old again. Put the man down as rising sixty, the car as around forty, and you wouldn't be far out. Neither showed its age except in non-essentials. It was perhaps incipient baldness which had induced the man to shave his subtle and exquisitely-shaped crown, and climatic, seasonal rust which had suggested the removal of the world-famous radiator cap, and the substitution of a small brass knob from a bedstead; but both were spry, agile, in full working order, and would take some catching when in the mood.

The man was not even tall; he didn't have to stoop to lay an arm about Kishan Singh's shoulders, and Kishan Singh was squat and square. Nevertheless, the impression of lofty height was there, dominating everyone within sight. It may have been the erect and aloof carriage, it may have been the slight withdrawal of the naked, golden, ascetic head on its slender neck, the poised effect of a stylised bronze which withdrew him into the field of art. It certainly was not innocent, but equally certainly it was not posed. He knew what he was, and employed it fully for his own inscrutable ends; and what mattered was what dictated the ends. He had a gentle bronze face, thin of feature and disarming of expression, live dark eyes moving modestly within the sculptured head, fleshless bones as serene as weathered mountains, and a benevolent smile like the antique stone smile of Angkor, at once calming and shattering. He wore a robe of saffron cloth that fell in chiselled folds to his ankles, and over it a knitted shawl draping his shoulders. His feet looked like bronze skeleton feet in the worn leather sandals. He had his arm round Kishan Singh's shoulders; the aura of his protection encompassed the boy in an almost visible glory. The two policemen hovering in the fringes of his influence looked now like attendant figures in a religious picture.

What was most humbling of all, the dominant figure sensed the presence of the watchers at the window above, within a minute of their gathering there, and with a gesture of his hand most courteously invited them to descend and rejoin the tableau.

Which, for want of a more appropriate response, they forthwith did.

Seven

'You must forgive us,' said the newcomer, 'for so inopportune an arrival. We had no idea that we should be intruding upon a problem and a tragedy. My name is Premanathanand. I am one of the members of the Native Indian Agricultural Missions, and I came here today to visit the home of my old friend Satyavan Kumar. I have been away on field studies among our settlements until recently, and for some time have had no opportunity of seeing him, and it is a friendship I value. But these ladies tell me – and the house-boy here – a good boy, I knew him in Mrs Kumar's household in Kangra – that Mr Kumar is not here at present. Also that there is a matter of the young girl, his daughter, who has vanished from the care of her guardians.' That, of course, must have come from Kishan Singh, who had been the only one of these people close enough to overhear what had passed between Dominic and the police officer before they went into the house, and who would tell everything without reserve to a man he trusted. In which case, Dominic thought, he would also have told him that Satyavan had been gone more than a year, and no one, not even his own mother, had known where he was, and no one knew now. That made this already interesting person even more interesting, since he had glided so gently over Satyavan's absence, as though he had merely gone away for the weekend.

And it was, now that he came to study it at close quarters and somewhat below the level of his own, an extraordinarily ambiguous face, at once candid and withdrawn, giving and reserving, just as his smile both comforted and disquieted. Every detail you looked at was as ordinary as the dusty soil of Delhi; the saffron robe, if you observed it closely, was worn, a little faded, and frayed at the hem, the brown knitted shawl round his shoulders had a stitch worn through here and there; his hands were sinewy and broad-jointed and used to hard work; the spectacles on his thin, straight nose were steel-rimmed and had battered wire ear-pieces, and one lens was thicker than the other, so that they tended to sit askew, and the eye seen through the thick lens was startlingly magnified. Yet the sum of the parts was so much more than the whole that accurate observation was disarmed. His voice, mild, clear and low, held the same ambivalence as his appearance; its serenity had a calming effect, but it left disturbing echoes behind in the mind, like the still, small voice of conscience.

'It is not for me,' he said courteously, smiling at the police officer, 'to ask questions in what must seem no affair of mine. Though as a friend of the child's father, I cannot but be concerned for her safety.'

And, perhaps it was not for him to ask, but he had made it clear that he would like to be told, and the Sikh officer told him. The large-lidded, intelligent brown eyes proceeded from one face to another, acknowledging the characters in the drama, smiling benignly upon Tossa and Dominic, brooding impassively over the small dead body now covered with a white sheet from the sun and the stares.

'It would seem,' he said at length, 'that someone who knew of Miss Kumar's gift and request to Arjun Baba conceived the idea of making use of that incident to lure her here, so that she might be abducted. It was necessary to the scheme that Arjun Baba should be removed both to get possession of the token, and also so that someone else could take his place, and wait here for the girl. It seems, therefore – do you not agree? – that though we have here two crimes, we have but one criminal.'

'That is my conclusion also, Swami,' said the Sikh respectfully.

'It would therefore be well, would it not, to concentrate on solving the crime which affords the best possibility, first, of salvaging something from the harm intended, and, second, of affording a sporting chance of arresting the criminal.' His varied and surprising vocabulary he used with the lingual dexterity of a publicist, but with the absent serenity of one conversing with himself. 'Arjun Baba here is dead and cannot be saved. But the girl is alive and must be kept alive to be worth money, and therefore she can be saved if we are circumspect. And upon the second count – he who killed Arjun Baba has now no interest but to remove himself from here and hide himself utterly. But he who has taken the child *must make overtures*, in order to gain by his act, which was his whole object in taking her. Therefore he must make the first approach, and in making it may reveal himself.'

'Exactly, Swami. And therefore it is clear that we must concentrate on the kidnapping of the girl, and we shall thereby also find our murderer.'

'You are excellently lucid, Inspector,' said the Swami with admiration and relief. 'You make everything clear to me. You would conclude also, if I follow you correctly, that since the father is not here and knows nothing of this crime, there are not two posssibilities: either the criminal knows where to find him, and will approach him directly; or he does not know, and will therefore approach the equally plutocratic mother. Or, of course, her representatives.' His benign but unequal gaze dwelt upon Tossa and Dominic, and returned guilelessly to the Sikh Inspector of Police. 'I am glad that so serious a case has fallen into the hands of such an intelligent officer. If there should be any way in which I can help, call upon me. You know where our Delhi office is situated?'

'I know, Swami. Everyone knows.'

'Good! Whatever I can do for Satyavan and his daughter I will do. And this boy may be left in charge of this house? It would be well, and I will vouch for him, that he will be here whenever you wish to question him . . .'

'I had no thought of removing him from his trust, Swami.' And that might be true, or might be a gesture of compliance towards this respected and remarkable man; but Kishan Singh would welcome it, whatever its motive.

'Then I shall leave you to your labours. Ah, yes, there is one thing more. Arjun Baba has neither wife nor sons. When you release his body for the funeral rites, I beg you will give it into my charge.'

'Swami, it shall be done as you wish.'

The Swami's mild brown eyes lingered thoughtfully upon Tossa and Dominic. 'I am sorry,' he said civilly, 'that you have suffered such a troubled introduction to this country of ours. If you are now returning to Delhi, may I offer you transport? There is plenty of room, if you do not mind sharing the back of the car with some grain samples we are carrying. And I should like, if you have time, to offer you coffee at the mission.'

'Thank you,' said Dominic, stunned into compliance like everyone else in sight, 'we should be very grateful.'

The policemen, the women at the gate, even the Orissan bandit babes, fell into a sort of hypnotised guard of honour as the Swami Premanathanand walked mildly out of the compound of N 305, Rabindar Nagar, with the two English strangers at his heels. The long, languid driver rolled himself up nimbly from the running-board and opened the rear door for the guests, but no one was looking either at him or at them, all eyes were on the Swami. He had, perhaps, the gift of attracting attention when he chose, and diverting it when he chose. At the moment it suited him to be seen; perhaps in order that other things should pass unseen. He took his seat beside the impassive driver. The small grain sacks in the back were piled on the floor, and hardly embarrassed even the feet of the passengers. The Rolls, especially in its ancient forms, is made for living in. With pomp and circumstance they drove away, almost noiselessly, from the scene – they all thought of it now first and foremost as that – of Arjun Baba's death.

Anjli Kumar, quite certainly, was still alive to be salvaged.

The Delhi headquarters of the Native Indian Agricultural Mission lay in Old Delhi, not far from the crowded precincts of the Sadar Bazaar. They had half-expected a gracious three-acre enclosure somewhere in a quiet part, with green lawns and shady buildings; instead, the car wound and butted its way between the goats and tongas and bicycles and children of the thronging back streets, and into a small, crowded yard surrounded by crude but solid wooden huts. In a minute, bare office two young men conferred over a table covered with papers, and at the other end of the table a girl in shalwar and kameez typed furiously on an ancient, spidery machine that stood a foot high from the board. All three looked up briefly and smiled, and then went on passionately with what they were doing. In an inner room, creamy-white, a brass coffee-table and folding canvas chairs provided accommodation for guests, and a cushioned bench against the wall offered room for the hosts to sit cross-legged. A litter of pamphlets and newspapers lay on the table, and all the rest of the walls were hidden behind bookshelves overflowing with books.

The girl from the typewriter brought coffee when she had finished her page, and the Swami sat, European-style, round the table with them. And presently the driver came in silently and seated himself Indian-fashion at the end of the bench, respectfully withdrawn but completely at his ease, drinking his coffee from a clean but cracked mug, and watching the group round the table with intelligent black eyes and restrained but unconcealed curiosity. He had shed his sandals on the threshold; his slim brown feet tucked themselves under him supply, and the hands upturned in his lap, nursing the mug of coffee, were large and sensitive and strong. The Swami did not hesitate to refer to him when he wanted another opinion, or confirmation of a recollection.

'Girish will recall when last Satyavan visited me here. It is surely more than a year.'

'It was in September of last year,' Girish confirmed. His voice was quiet and low-pitched, and his English clear as his master's. Unsmilingly he watched the Swami's face.

'I do not wish, of course, to take your responsibility from you. It was to you that the child was confided, and you best know her mother's mind. You have told the police all that you can, and now you will consider, I know, what more you must do. But if you have anything to ask of me, at any time, I am here. We have a telephone, write down the number, and call me whenever you will.'

By that time he knew where they were to be found in Delhi, and all about them, even to the one thing they had not told the police. He sat mildly smiling, or even more mildly grave, and they told him things they had hardly realised they were thinking.

'But that's too fanciful,' Tossa said doubtfully. 'Dominic is musical, but I can't believe he could simply recognise Raga Aheer Bhairab when he heard it . . . not after a single hearing.'

'But that's the whole point,' Dominic objected warmly. 'I never claimed I recognised Raga Aheer Bhairab, what I recognised was a straightforward folktune, a song Ashok himself said had to reach everybody at first hearing. And the more I think about it, the more I'm sure that's just what it did. I bet somebody who had heard the Brahms Wiegenlied only once would know it again the next time.'

'However, as you tell me, this film unit is now in Benares. And this man, the director . . .?'

'Mr Felder,' said Dominic.

'He is, you say, an old friend of the girl's mother, the friend to whom she turned when she wished someone to meet you on arrival. You would say that he has her confidence?'

'Yes, I'm sure he has.'

'In the absence of both parents, he might, perhaps, be the best adviser? But you will consider what you ought to do, and do it, and it is not for me to meddle. If I can provide any helpful information, I shall get in touch with you. And if you receive news of the child, I beg you will let me hear it, too.'

They thanked him and promised.

'Girish will drive you back to your hotel.'

Dominic sat beside the taciturn chauffeur on the journey back to Keen's, and studied the profile beside him curiously out of the corner of his eye. A hawk-like Punjabi profile, high-nosed, clear of line, with a proud, full, imperious mouth, and cheeks hollow beneath bold, jutting bones. When he smiled all his features flashed into brightness; but he smiled only once, when Tossa asked diffidently exactly what the Swami was, monk, priest,Brahmin or what.

'The Swami is himself, what else can one say? He does not conform to any prescribed order, and he does not recognise caste. He does not do what is expected of him, or even what is required of him – he is too busy doing what he wants to do and what has to be done. I doubt if any group would dare to claim him – or care to own him,' he added, more surprisingly.

'And what does this Agricultural Mission of his do?'

'Whatever it can to improve stock – but *that*'s an uphill struggle! – or bring in better methods of farming and cultivating. Through village co-operatives, small voluntary irrigation works, improved seed, local dairying schemes, new cropping methods – anything, wherever we can find the right material for the work. We try to make such village co-operatives self-supporting, and even self-reproducing. To be clear of debt is to attract envy. To show a profit is to stimulate imitation. We have some foundling farms, too, where the children who are left to fend for themselves by begging can do a small share of the work and get a fair share of the food. Even a seven-year-old is useful for some jobs.'

'Seven . . .!' Tossa drew breath incredulously. 'But surely such young children . . . You mean you *get* them as young as that? Just drifting in, *on their own*?'

'On their own,' he agreed. The ancient Rolls turned majestically into the drive of Keen's Hotel. 'In our country, too,' said Girish levelly, staring ahead between the high hedges, 'there are neglected and forsaken children.'

They argued it out between them over a lunch for which neither of them had any appetite, and came to a decision.

Even if they had not been gently prompted by the Swami they would probably have come to the same conclusion.

'Even with the police in on it,' said Dominic, summing up, 'we've still got to face our own responsibility. We simply have to let someone know what's happened. Kumar's out of reach, and Dorette – let's face it, what good would it be telephoning Dorette? All we'd get – all Anjli would get – would be hysterics. Dorette wouldn't come out here to take charge herself, not with a film half-finished, and that's the sober truth. And even if she did, she'd be no use at all. But there's Felder. *She* turned to him when she needed somebody here, in a way he's sort of representative of Dorette. And he's sensible, and knows his way about here. If he says we must call Dorette, then we'll do it. But let's at least consult him first.'

So he telephoned Clark's hotel at Benares, and by luck the unit happened to be in for lunch. The sound of Felder's vigorous voice over the line was cheering, and the promptness of his decisions bracing.

'Now look, you hold it right there, and I'll be with you as soon as I can. We haven't finished shooting, but this is an emergency, and they'll just have to get along without me. There's an afternoon flight, if I can get a seat on it. Don't worry, the airlines office is right here in the hotel. You stay close to home, in case there are any messages, and I'll come straight to you there.'

'Messages?' Dominic repeated, thinking hopefully of the police calling to tell him Anjli was already traced, and as good as found.

'Well, they can't get at *him*, if no one knows where he is, can they? And you're the nearest available channel to Dorrie, aren't you?'

Air travel comes into its own in India, where you can transport yourself at very reasonable cost from Calcutta to Gauhati, or Trivandrum to Madras, or even from Delhi to Srinagar across a minor range of the Himalayas, in roughly the time it takes to go from Birmingham to London by train. Thus it happened that Ernest Felder, having bluffed and persuaded his way into the last available seat on the afternoon plane from Benares, was in Keen's Hotel by seven in the evening, his grey hair on end, his lined, easygoing face for once desperately grave. Over dinner, which by that time they all needed, he got them to tell him the whole story all over again, in detail, and with as much detachment as was possible in the circumstances. He didn't exclaim, he didn't swear, he simply listened with every nerve, helped out with a question here and there, and soothed them by the very fact of his large, zestful, intent presence and the degree of his concentration. If sheer compact energy could recover Anjli, she was as good as saved.

'Now, let's not get tangled with non-essentials. The facts are, someone went to a lot of trouble to get Dorrie's girl. And there's no reason on earth why such an elaborate plot should be laid to get her into the right place, except just plain money. Somebody knows her value. There's a rupee millionaire of a father, and a film star mother. There's money, and plenty of it. Right?'

They could not but agree.

'So they now have to get in touch with all that money, in order to tap off as much of it as the traffic will stand. Right? And as we've said, the father is out of the picture . . . *unless* the kidnappers know more than we do. If they know how to get in touch with him, so much the better, that will bring him into the open, and we can all join forces. But if they don't they're going to be after Dorrie. But my guess would be, not directly. There are complications once you start sending messages of that kind across frontiers, from here to Europe – even if they know where to find her, and my guess is they may not, though pretty obviously they must know who and what she is. No, they'll make their play in the safest and nearest direction. And that's *you*! You represent Dorrie here, you're Anjli's temporary guardians. My bet is that you can expect instructions from whoever's got Anjli, and pretty soon.'

'Supposing there's any choice,' said Dominic firmly, 'we can't risk Anjli.'

'No, I agree. Any instruction they give must be obeyed absolutely. We can't take any chances with Dorrie's kid. I wouldn't with anybody's kid, for that matter. What about this Cousin Vasudev you were talking about? You reckon they're likely to contact him? . . . as kind of a tap for the family money? Family is a great thing here, they might well figure he'd pay out for her, supposing he has legal access now to the funds. Company or family. I don't know how they're fixed.'

Tossa and Dominic didn't know, either. Their voices took on a certain reserve when they spoke of Cousin Vasudev.

'Sure, I know! He stands to gain. But he could be on the level, too. And if he isn't, it won't do any harm to shake him up now and again, he might give something away. But whoever took the little girl knew all about that gold dollar, that's what gets me. And this cousin of hers didn't – or at least not from you, not until today . . .'

'But he could have from Kishan Singh,' Tossa pointed out. 'We told him we'd come straight from there, he might very well question the house-boy afterwards, and Kishan Singh would tell a Kumar everything. From his point of view, why not?'

'That's true, that's very true. Maybe a neighbour, even, could have overheard when she gave it to the old man. I don't know, I just don't know! All our bunch may have known all about it, from that time you telephoned for me and got Ashok, and gave him the whole story to hand on to me . . . but then, most of the bunch are away in Sarnath still, and have been since early the morning after you called, before Anjli was snatched.'

Dominic had laid down his fork with careful quietness. '*Most*?' He met the blank, enquiring stare, and elaborated uneasily: 'I thought you *all* were.'

'Well, all the working unit, yes, and nearly all the players. Not Kamala, of course – Yashodhara doesn't appear in the Deer Park scenes. This is where the sacred brotherhood line begins. No women on the scene for a while.'

'I see.' Dominic reflected that he should have taken time off, like Anjli, to read the book, and he might have been somewhat wiser in his assumptions. All the women left behind in Delhi! He thought for a moment, and asked without undue emphasis: 'And Ashok?'

'Ashok? In India you don't ask an artist of that calibre to run around after you, *you* run after *him*. We show the rushes for Ashok, right here in Delhi, and he broods over them three or four times, and comes up with the music for the sound-track when he's good and ready. Oh, yes, he likes to spend a good deal of time with us down at Hauz Khas, but that's a bonus. He enjoys us. But not enough to go blundering about in Sarnath with us on the day's grind.'

'I see,' said Dominic again, making more readjustments. But this picture of Ashok, on the face of it, removed him still farther from any possibility of participation in a sordid crime for gain. 'I suppose he must be in the film star class himself, then?'

'Just about. I know what you're thinking of – this tune you heard the chap in the garden here whistling – but you don't even know that it was the chap who brought the note, do you? And for goodness sake, some of the sweepers and drivers around the villas and the office could have heard Ashok playing that theme and picked it up. He meant it to be catchy. And believe me, he isn't satisfied with one run through when he's recording, not to mention all the practising beforehand. I shouldn't worry too much about that. Even if you're right about it!' And plainly he was by no means convinced about that, and on the whole Dominic could hardly blame him. Nobody else had been convinced, either, not even Tossa.

'Mind if I hang around with you this evening? Just in case anything happens?'

'I wish you would!'

'I shouldn't have any peace if I left you to it,' said Felder almost apologetically.

They adjourned to Dominic's sitting-room, and waited the evening through; and no one got much rest, when it came to the point. The strain of waiting for something to happen is not conducive to conversation, and presently even monosyllables faded out. Eight o'clock passed, and nothing broke the tension. Nine o'clock, and still nothing. Half-past nine . . .

Felder shook his solid shoulders and sighed. 'Nothing's going to happen tonight, it seems. I wonder if they went for Vasudev and family loyalty, after all?'

And it was then that the telephone rang.

All three of them started wildly, as if a gun had been fired; all three of them came to their feet, staring at the instrument, even reaching out for it, half afraid to take the plunge. Dominic looked up over the white handset at Felder.

'Yes,' said Felder rapidly, 'you take it. Hold it till I open the door, then answer it, and if it *is* – give me the sign, and I'll slip down to the switchboard and see if it can be traced. And – *listen*! – if it is, talk back, hold him as long as you can, give us a chance. *And don't miss a word he says*!'

He took a couple of quick strides backwards and opened the door of the room. Dominic lifted the receiver.

'Hullo . . . Dominic Felse here.'

'You are the gentleman who has lost some valuables,' said

a high, strident, clacking voice in his ear. 'I have them, they can be recovered.'

Dominic's mouth was suddenly so dry that for a minute he could not make any answer. He nodded strenuously at Felder across the room, and the big man slid noiselessly through the door he was holding open, and drew it to after him, releasing the latch slowly so that it made not a sound. In the telephone the voice crackled impatiently: 'I know you hear me. You want your lost property back. I can provide. Of course at a proper price.' An old voice, he thought, or at least elderly; its tone cracked when it was raised, it had no body in it, and no juice. On first hearing, either male or female; but he thought, male. He moistened his lips feverishly, and instinctively began to waste time.

'Who is that? Are you sure you're on the right number? This is Felse speaking, you wanted me?'

'It is you who want me, my friend,' said the voice, and cackled painfully in his eardrum. 'If you want Miss Kumar, that is.'

'How do I know you really have any information about Miss Kumar? Where are you speaking from? Who are you? How do you know anything about it?'

'That is very well put, how do I know! How could I know, except that *I have her*? Oh, she is safe, quite safe. You want proof? Miss Kumar has American passport . . .' Horrifyingly the old voice rattled off its number, the place of its issuing, the personal details of her description, and giggled unnervingly at the blank silence that ensued. 'You can have this lady back for two hundred thousand rupees – cash.'

'But that's impossible . . . you must allow us time, at least, how can we command cash at short notice . . .?' Dominic protested, feeling round the apparently empty recesses of his mind for any prevarication he could find, anything to keep the man talking; while at the same time he struggled to record every word that was said. 'I don't believe you have her. You could have found her handbag, or stolen it, and got hold of the passport that way. If she's there, let her speak to me, and I'll believe . . .'

The voice cut him off sharply. 'Listen, if you want her! You get that two hundred thousand rupees, you get it in mixed notes and put it into a cheap black school bag. And on Sunday afternoon at two o'clock . . .'

'Sunday?' gasped Dominic in utter dismay. 'But that's only two days! How can we . . .'

' . . . on Sunday, I say, you go, you and the woman also, to the Birla Temple. You leave your shoes with the lame boy who sits at the foot of the steps, on the right, and with your shoes the case with the money. Then you go into the temple and stay within for half an hour, not one minute less. Do not try to keep watch on your shoes, do not say one word to the police, or anyone else, if you want to see the girl again. Put on your shoes and go back to your hotel. On Sunday evening I call you again and we arrange about the child. *If* you have done as you are told.'

'But, listen, we want to co-operate, but it's a question of time, damn it! – You must give us longer than that . . .'

'Sunday. If you want her.' The line echoed one quavering ring, and was dead. Dominic held the receiver numbly for a moment, and then very gently cradled it. His knees gave under him, and he sat down abruptly. 'My God, it's impossible, we *can't*! I don't believe it can be done, not by cable, not even by telephone.'

'Why?' Tossa urged, pale and quiet. 'What did he say? What is it he wants?'

'Two hundred thousand rupees by Sunday. *Sunday*! Now we've *got* to call Dorette Lester, we've got no choice. But I doubt if we can get the money through by then, whatever we do . . . whatever *she* does!'

'We *have* to. There has to be a way. I don't even know,' she said helplessly, 'how much two hundred thousand rupees is. It sounds a fortune.'

They were still gazing at each other, stunned into silence, when the door opened, and Felder came into the room. Both tense faces turned upon him, though without much hope. He shook his head glumly.

'A call box, somewhere central, that's all we had time to get. Probably on Connaught Circus. One step out of the box, and he'd be a drop in the ocean. Not a chance of getting anything on him. What did he have to say?'

Dominic cleared his dry throat and told them, practically word for word. It wasn't the sort of message he was in any danger of forgetting.

'He didn't give anything away . . . about himself? What did he sound like? I suppose,' he added, struck by a sudden doubt, 'it *was* a he?'

'I think so. Yes, I'm sure. But at first I did wonder . . .

a high-pitched, thin voice . . . old . . . No, he didn't give a
thing away. And now,' said Dominic, 'there's nothing for it
but to tell Miss Lester, and hope she can cable the money in
time . . . But, damn it, *Sunday*! It won't be a banking day
here. We've only got tomorrow.'

'There's Vasudev,' ventured Tossa dubiously. After all,
they had harboured doubts about Vasudev's cousinly
solicitude. All that money, old Mrs Kumar newly dead,
Satyavan, by his own design or another's, utterly vanished,
and only this little girl between Vasudev, the dutiful manager
and nephew, and all those millions of rupees and that
commercial empire. Even if he hadn't got her out of the
way himself, what a temptation this might be to want her
kept out of the way now, to hinder, not help, any attempt
to pay the ransom and recover her alive.

'And besides,' said Dominic flatly, as if he had followed
her unspoken thoughts thus far, 'we've been warned, not a
word to any outsider. Maybe they haven't realised that we've
got Mr Felder in on the job already, but I bet they wouldn't
miss it if we went near Vasudev between now and Sunday
afternoon. And we daren't take any risks with Anjli.'

'It won't be necessary, anyhow,' said Felder slowly. He
sat down heavily, and his big shoulders in their immaculate
tailoring sagged back into the chair as if he had suddenly
grown very tired. 'It won't be necessary to frighten Dorrie
yet, either . . . if all goes well, it need never be necessary,
only in retrospect. We'll put up the money, and we'll make
sure of being on time with it. As you say, we can't take any
risks with Anjli.'

They were watching him with wonder, and as yet carefully
suppressing the hope that he knew how to work miracles,
and could make his word good now.

'No, *I* haven't got that sort of money here, don't look at
me like that. *I* haven't, but the company has. We've got
a big credit in the bank here to cover this Buddha film.
And it so happens that it will run to two hundred thousand
without being sucked dry, and when necessary my signature
is enough to draw on it. If I left anything undone that I
could do for Anjli, I'd never be able to look Dorrie in the eye
again. And she'll replace the loan as soon as she knows the
facts. Tomorrow I must draw the money out of our bank,
and you can buy a cheap school briefcase, just as he said,
and we make the payment. *You* make the payment, rather
– and *I* stay out of sight and keep an eye on your shoes.'

The wild flush of relief came back to Tossa's face, and the brightness to her eyes. Dominic let out a long, grateful breath.

'Oh, *lord*, if we *could*! Is it really all right for us to borrow it? But you wouldn't try anything then, would you? I mean, we agreed we had to obey instructions, for Anjli's sake.'

'I would not! But I'd have a shot at trailing whoever takes the briefcase, that's for certain. Once we get Anjli back, I'm all for putting the police on to her kidnappers.'

'But is it going to be possible to hang around and watch the place, like that? Won't you be too noticeable?'

'You haven't seen the Lakshminarayan temple on a Sunday afternoon! It's like a fun-fair. Cover galore and thousands of people. Might make it hard for me to keep an eye on him, but it will certainly reduce his chances of spotting me. It's worth a try, at any rate.'

'The Birla temple, he said,' Dominic pointed out.

'Same thing, laddie. Lakshminarayan is its dedication, and the Birla family built it. They had to do something with some of the money, it was getting to be a bore.' There was a faint snap of bitterness in this lighter tone; no wonder, when they had need of a comparatively modest sum at this moment for so urgent a reason, and were put to such shifts to acquire it.

'I can't tell you,' Dominic said fervently, 'how grateful we are for your help.'

'Not a word, my boy! I've known Dorrie for years, and didn't she ask me to keep a fatherly eye on you over here? But I tell you what, I'd better get out of here by the garden way tonight, hadn't I, and keep away from you except where we can be strictly private?'

He rose and stretched wearily. There were times when he looked an elderly man, but always withindoors and in presence of few if any observers.

'Is there nothing I can be doing?' Dominic asked anxiously, aware of having ceded his responsibilities to a degree he found at once galling and reassuring.

'Sure there is. You can go out in the morning – maybe alone would be best, if Miss Barber doesn't mind? – and buy a cheap, black, child's briefcase. Somewhere round Connaught Place there are sure to be plenty of them. And about half past ten you could oblige me by being inside the State Bank of India, the one in Parliament Street. If you're seen going in there, that can only be a good sign. And I'll come separately, they won't know me. And we'll take out

that two hundred thousand rupees – that's something over
eleven thousand pounds, I'd say offhand. You know, that's
not so exorbitant, when you come to think about it! – and
see it packed up all ready for the pay-off, and packed into
that briefcase. And in a couple of days we'll have Anjli out
of bondage.'

Eight

On Saturday morning they drew out the money from the film company's account in the State Bank of India in Parliament Street. Dominic was there waiting with his plastic school briefcase in his hand before Felder arrived; in good time to admire the imposing appearance his colleague made after a night's rest and careful toilet, immaculate in dark grey worsted. The clerk treated the whole transaction as superbly normal, and was deferential to the point of obsequiousness, perhaps because of the size of the withdrawal. Felder was carrying a much more presentable briefcase in pale chrome leather; Dominic had never seen him look the complete city sophisticate before. Even his tone as he asked for the money to be made up in mixed notes was so casual and abstracted that any other course would have seemed eccentric.

So that was that. They were moving at leisure away from the counter, with two hundred thousand rupees in assorted denominations in a large, sealed bank envelope, linen-grained, biscuit-coloured and very official-looking. It seemed like having a hold on Anjli again. Suddenly it seemed an age since Dominic had seen her face or heard her voice, and he remembered the jasmine flowers, with the strange ache of an old association fallen just short of love.

'Put it in the case now,' suggested Felder in a low voice, proffering the crisp new parcel before they were in view from the doorway. 'Or would you rather I locked it in the office safe until the time comes?'

'Yes, you keep it. Drop it off at the desk for us tomorrow, there'll be plenty of people in and out. Supposing there is someone watching me now, he may think it a good idea to knock off this lot before I can get it back to the hotel, and then ask for more. How can I be sure?'

'All right, as you like.' Felder shrugged his shoulders ruefully. 'I suppose it is my responsibility.' The envelope disappeared into the chrome leather case, swallowed from sight with a magnificent casualness. Briefcases of that quality went in and out of here by the score, black plastic scholastic ones were much rarer in this temple of commerce. Dominic felt grateful that he had bought Everyman copies of the Hindu scriptures and the Ramayana and Mahabharata, to give a semblance of gravity to his own flimsy burden. They could easily have been mistaken for money, viewed from the outside.

'In the morning, then, about ten, I'll bring it to the desk. Better be somewhere close, in case. And when you leave the temple in the afternoon, come in to Nirula's for tea. I'll be there.'

'We will,' said Dominic.

'Go ahead first, then, I'll give you ten minutes or so.'

Dominic walked briskly out of the imposing doors of the State Bank of India, and away down Parliament Street, with his tawdry briefcase filled and fulfilled with the wisdom of thirty centuries of Indian thought and feeling. Worth a good deal more, in the final issue, than two hundred thousand rupees, even taking into consideration the relative impossibility of adequate translation.

It was the longest Saturday they ever remembered, and the only good things left about it were that they had at least a hope of recovering Anjli, and that they were spending the agonising time of waiting together. Felder kept away from them, and that was surely the right thing to do. And they made contact with no one, so that if they were watched the watchers might be quite certain that they had not infringed their orders. They went no farther from their hotel than the Lodi park, where they sat in the sunshine among the fawn-coloured grass and the flowers, the amazing, exuberant, proliferating flowers of the season, and looked at the towering rose-coloured tombs with which the Lodi dynasty had burdened the Delhi earth, and thought about Purnima's modest pyre by the Yamuna, and her little heap of ashes going back to the elements, and nothing left of weight or self-importance or regret. And it seemed to them the most modest of all ways of leaving this world, and the most in keeping with the spirit's certainty of return; until, of course, the cycles close in the last perfect circle, and you are free from any more rebirths.

But they did not stay away long, because they were afraid of being out of reach, even by ten minutes' walk, in case there was some new message. They had very little sleep that night. Felder, in the smaller villa at Hauz Khas, fared no better. All of them were up with the first light, and aching for the afternoon to come.

To reach the Shri Lakshminarayan temple, if you happen to be in the shopping centre of Delhi, Connaught Place, you strike out due west along Lady Hardinge Road, and it will bring you, after a walk of about a mile, straight to that amazing frontage. Don't expect anything historic; the temple was built towards the end of British rule, as a gesture towards the wholeness of all the Indian religions, which are still one religion, so that it belongs to orthodox Brahmans, Sikhs, Jains, Buddhists, and anyone else, in fact, who comes with sympathy and an open mind. It is dedicated to Narayan and Lakshmi, his spouse, but it also houses images of others of the Hindu pantheon. Which pantheon is itself an illusion, a convenient veil drawn over the face of the single and universal unity; convenient, because its multifarious aspects provide an approachable deity for everyone who comes, from the simplest to the most subtle, and from the most extrovert to the most introvert, and all routes that lead to the universal essence are right routes.

What Dominic and Tossa saw, as they turned into the final straight stretch of the road and emerged into the broad open space of Mandir Marg, facing the forecourt of the temple, was a huge, gay, sparkling construction in several horizontal terraces, above a sweeping flight of steps, and crowned above by a triple shikhara, three tall, fluted, tapering towers, shirred in a pattern imitative of reed thatching, each capped at its sealed crest by a yellow cupola and a tiny gilded spire. The towers were mainly white, picked out with yellow, the levels below them were white and russet red and yellow, lined out here and there with green, arcades of mannered arches and perforated balustrades. All the textures, all the colours, were matt and gauche and new; and with their usual assured recognition of realities, the modern inhabitants of Delhi had taken the place for their own. Felder had not exaggerated. It was a fairground; a happy, holiday, Sunday-afternoon crowd possessed it inside and out.

Mandir Marg was teeming with people and traffic. They crossed it warily, Dominic hugging the cheap little briefcase that contained the bank's envelope full of money, which Felder had left at the desk at Keen's that morning.

There was plenty of space for all who came, about the front of the temple. But approximately half of that space was cordoned off behind frayed white ropes, sealing off the actual front of the temple wall beside the staircase. Within this enclosure stood and sat half a dozen or more vociferous Hindus, jealously guarding serried rows of footgear discarded here by the faithful, and waiting patiently for their return. Just to the right of the steps sat a diminutive brown boy, slender and large-eyed, one thin leg tucked under him, one, clearly helpless and distorted at the ankle, stretched out like a purposeless encumbrance at an improbable angle. A home-carved crutch lay beside him. He had more than his fair share of sandals and shoes to mind.

Tossa and Dominic shook off their sensible slip-ons, and proffered them tentatively across the cords. There is always the problem of tipping now or when you recover your property. The uninitiated prefer to play safe by doing both, even if this involves over-paying. Dominic gave the boy a quarter-rupee, reserving the other quarter for when they emerged, and held out the briefcase to be placed with their shoes. The child – how old could he possibly be? Thirteen? – seemed to be content. Even conscientious, for he lined up the two pairs of shoes with careful accuracy, and stood the briefcase upright between them. And yet he must be in on this thing . . . Or was that necessarily so? There could be somebody he knew and trusted, a credible story, a planned diversion . . . No, better withhold judgement.

They climbed the steps. Delhi receded and declined behind them. Through the arcaded doorways sweet, heady scents wafted over them, sandalwood, incense and flowers, an overwhelming, dewy splendour of flowers. This is the season of flowers in Delhi; the marvellous shrubs and trees blossom a little later. But the sense of approaching a fairground remained. Why not? Fairs are essentially religious in origin, and if they are joyful occasions, so should religion be.

They stepped into spacious halls faced everywhere in parti-coloured stone and polished marbles, brightly lighted, swarming with curious, reverent, talkative people, notably hordes of alert, lively, fascinated children. Formalised gods sat brooding immovably under mini-mountains of flowers, little bells chimed ingratiatingly, reminding the remote dreamers that small, insistent worshippers were here requesting attention. Everything was fresh, naive, festive and confident; religion and everyday life knew of no possible barrier or even distinction between them. The fragrance was hypnotic; there was a kind of radiant dew upon the air. And yet if you cared to be hypercritical you could fault everything in sight as garish, crude and phoney; you would be mistaken, but in that mood you would never recognise the fact.

The pale, sharp sunshine fell away behind them, and the delicate blue fingers of perfumed smoke brushed their faces. They had been told not to watch their shoes, and not to emerge again for half an hour exactly. They obeyed instructions to the letter.

Felder stood on the opposite pavement, watching the ceaseless flow of people about the steps of the temple, the play of coloured saris and the flutter of gauze scarves. A man alone could stroll this length of street on a Sunday afternoon for as long as he would, and it was highly improbable that anyone would notice him among so many. From time to time he moved along to a new position, drew back into the shade of the frontages for a while, crossed the street to mingle with the crowd over there in the sun, and even climbed the steps and wandered along the open terrace; but seldom, and only for seconds, did he take his eyes from the little black case propped upright between the two pairs of shoes. At the far end he descended again to the street and made his way back along the edge of the roped enclosure, among the darting children and the idling parents, and the hawkers selling glass bracelets, spices coloured like jewels, bizarre sweetmeats and heady garlands. Half an hour can seem an eternity.

No one had approached the lame boy's corner, except to hand over more shoes to be guarded. The briefcase lay close to the rope, within reach of a hand, and the boy was busy; it would not be impossible to snatch the thing and vanish with it among the crowd. But there it stood, demurely leaning against Dominic's shoe, a small black punctuation mark in a pyrotechnical paragraph.

A quarter of an hour gone, and nothing whatever happening. He turned to retrace his steps once again, and cannoned into a wiry fellow in khaki drill trousers and shirt and a hand-knitted brown pullover in coarse wool. The man was bare-headed and clean-shaven, his complexion the deep bronze of an outdoor worker; and by the way he recoiled hastily and obsequiously from the slight collision, with apologetic bobbings of his head, Felder judged that he was not a native of Delhi. When Felder, for some reason he could not explain, turned his head again to take another look at him, the fellow was still standing hesitant on the edge of the pavement, looking after the man he had brushed. He looked slightly lost among this confident crowd, and slightly puzzled, as if he had somehow come to the wrong place.

Felder put the man out of his mind, and concentrated again upon the black briefcase. But eight minutes later, when he came back that way, the man was still there, and this time the thin face with its strongly marked features and large dark eyes turned towards him with clear intent.

'Sahib, I beg pardon,' he said low and hesitantly in English. 'Can you please help me? I am stranger here. I am not from Delhi, I come from the hills. Please, this is Birla Temple?'

'Yes, that's right.' He had no wish to stop and talk, but it would be difficult to withdraw from this unsought encounter too ruthlessly, for supposing there was more in it than met the eye? Supposing someone had become suspicious, and was keeping him under observation, as he was keeping watch on the briefcase?

'And, sahib, is here also Birla House? I wish to see Birla House.' In the gardens of that princely residence the Mahatma was shot and killed; but it lies a matter of two miles away from the Lakshminarayan temple. Felder supposed it was possible that a simple hillman sightseeing in Delhi might expect to find the two in close proximity.

'No, that's quite some way from here. You could get a bus, I expect, it's well south, close to Claridge's Hotel.' Absurd, he thought the moment he had said it, as if this chap from out of town would be likely to know Claridge's.

'Sahib, I have no money for bus.' Clearly he was not asking for any, either, it was a perfectly simple statement. 'I will walk, if you can show way.'

Felder had to turn his back on the temple for that, and point his pupil first directly away from it, down Lady Hardinge Road towards Connaught Place. 'Take the third turning on the right into Market Street, and go straight on down to the parliament building. You've seen it?'

'*Acha*, sahib, that I have seen.'

'Then you cross directly over the Rajpath, and keep straight ahead down Hastings Road, and at the end of Hastings Road you'll find Birla House occupying the corner of the block facing you.' Accustomed to the visual imagination, Felder demonstrated the direction of the roads in the air, an invisible sketch-map. The dark eyes followed it solemnly, and apparently with understanding.

'Sahib, you are most kind. I am grateful.' Large, lean, handsome hands touched gravely beneath the hillman's chin. He bowed himself backwards towards Lady Hardinge Road, and then turned and walked purposefully away.

Felder heaved a breath of relief, watching him go. It was all right, after all, the man was genuine, and had had no interest in him but as a source of information. He turned quickly, and his eyes sought at once for the small black speck close to the lame boy's side, sharp and sinister against the pale tawny ground. The interlude had not caused him to miss anything, it seemed.

The half-hour was over, and Dominic and Tossa were just emerging into the blinding sunlight from the fragrant dimness of the temple. And the black briefcase was still there.

In the quietest corner of Nirula's they gathered over the tea Felder had already ordered before the other two arrived. They had no heart for it, but he poured it, just the same. They were going to need every comfort, even the simplest.

'But what went wrong?' Tossa was asking, of herself no less than of them, and with tears in her eyes. 'We did everything he said, we didn't tell anyone else – they *can't* have known about *you*! – and we didn't say a word to the police – and you don't know how unlikely that is, until you know Dominic, his father's a police inspector, and all his instincts bend him their way, they really do! And yet we *did* play it the way we were told, and we were in good faith, though it's horrible to submit to an injustice like that . . . And yet at the end of it all, here it still is, not touched, and we're no nearer getting Anjli back!'

The briefcase lay on the cushioned bench-seat between them, plump and weighty as when they had surrendered it to the lame boy.

'We just couldn't believe it, Mr Felder! What are we going to do now? And what made them hold off? They can't have known about you, *can they*? Could they possibly have spotted you hanging around, and called the whole thing off?' She was ashamed of the suggestion as soon as she had made it, after all he had done for them. 'No . . . I'm sorry, don't listen to me!'

'I don't believe anyone did notice me,' Felder assured her gently. 'All the more because I did once wonder . . . but it turned out quite innocently. No, I just don't believe it.' His eyes lingered speculatively on the briefcase, smugly filled and flaunting its roundness. He frowned suddenly, regarding it. In quite a different tone, carefully muted so as to arouse no extravagant hopes, he said: 'Open it! Go ahead, let's be sure. Open it.'

Dominic stared and bridled, and then as abruptly flushed and obeyed. They were jumping to conclusions; they hadn't even looked. He pushed a thumbnail fiercely under the press fastener that held the case closed – how flimsy, and how quickly sprung! – and drew out the identical biscuit-coloured bank envelope they had placed there, still sealed as it came from the bank, nearly four hours ago. He stared at it with chagrin; so did they all. Then abruptly Felder uttered a small, smothered sound of protest, and took up the packet, turning it in his hands. He ran his fingers under the transparent tape that sealed the flap, and wrenched it open. Out into his lap slid a tightly-packed wad of sliced news-print. He ran the edges through his fingers, and the soft, close-grained, heavy segments mocked them all. There was not a banknote in the whole package, nothing but shredded newspaper.

'My *God*!' said Felder in a whisper. 'After all! Then he *must* have been planted . . . No, I can't believe it, they never had time!'

'It wouldn't,' said Dominic slowly, 'take very long. A fastener like that is a gift. But only if you had another packet ready to substitute. If they watched me go into the bank yesterday . . . But could you possibly guess at the bulk of it so closely? I suppose the bank envelope wouldn't be any difficulty. But *could you*? And was there any time when it could possibly have happened?'

'You could,' said Felder, with soft, intense bitterness, 'if there was enough at stake, I suppose. And yes . . . there was maybe two and a half to three minutes. I'd swear it wasn't longer. There was this countryman from somewhere in the hills . . . I had the feeling he might have been planted on me, but when he went away so promptly . . .' He told them, baldly and briefly. 'It couldn't have been more than three minutes in all, that I'll swear. As soon as I told him, he went. He never even looked back. I'd know him again, that's for sure! But God knows where he is now! And yet he sounded genuine, and when I told him his way he was off like a hare.'

'Does it matter?' said Tossa suddenly. Her eyes were bright and hopeful. 'Maybe we didn't pin him down, whoever he is, but does it matter so much, after all? The money's been collected. It wouldn't take much ingenuity to get hold of a large bank envelope, would it, once they'd seen Dominic go in there yesterday morning? But what matters is, the ransom's been collected, after all. They've got what they asked for. They promised us a call this evening, if we played by their rules. They promised us a call "to arrange about the child". They've got what they wanted, why shouldn't they let us have her back now? They're safer that way, and they've scored a success, haven't they?'

She was right there was no doubt of that. Maybe they had failed on one count, but it was a failure that might very well net them a total success on the main issue.

And the main issue was, and always would be, Anjli.

They waited all the evening in Dominic's sitting-room at Keen's, whither Felder had repaired via the garden staircase and the balcony. Eight o'clock went by, nine o'clock, half past nine . . . The telephone remained obstinately silent.

But at a quarter to ten there was a sudden insinuating rapping on the door. Dominic sprang to open it, even though it was not at all what they had expected.

Into the room, serenely calm as ever, and beatifically smiling, walked the Swami Premanathanand. Down below in the courtyard the ancient Rolls stood with folded wings and reposeful outline, like a grounded dove.

Nine

'I trust you will forgive,' said the Swami courteously, 'so late and unceremonious a call.' He looked from Dominic to Felder, whom he had never seen before, and his wise brown eyes, behind the unequal lenses, refuged deep in the shadow of large ivory eyelids and kept their own counsel. He even seemed able to suppress the unnerving magnifying power of the strong lens when he chose. 'I am afraid that I have interrupted a private conference. But you will understand that I am exercised in my mind about Mr Kumar's daughter. I may speak freely?'

'Yes, certainly,' said Dominic, torn several ways at once and quite incapable of resolving the struggle. 'This is Mr Felder, who is an old and valued friend of Anjli's mother. Mr Felder is directing a film here in India, and he has been very kind to us since we came. And this is the Swami Premanathanand, of the Native Indian Agricultural Missions, who is an old friend of Mr Kumar.'

'Delighted!' said Felder feelingly. 'We can certainly use another friend here . . . and another good sound head, too. If I'm right in taking it that the Swami knows what's going on?'

'I have that honour,' said the Swami shyly, and modestly accepting the chair Dominic offered. Tonight he wore an old European trench coat, minus the belt, over his saffron robe, and when he stripped it off in the warmed room his one shoulder emerged naked and polished and adamant as bronze, bone and sinew without the more dispensable elements of flesh.

'You have received no trustworthy news about Anjli's whereabouts?'

'No,' said Tossa miserably. 'But we *have* had a telephone call to say she's being held to ransom.' She could see no reason at all for concealing anything that had happened; passionately she recounted the events of the afternoon. 'And we're no farther forward at all, and they're not going to keep their bargain. We've been waiting here all the evening for a

268

telephone call, and *nothing*! They've cheated us. And now we haven't any way at all of getting in touch with them, it was a one-way traffic. We've just poured that money down the drain, and it wasn't even ours, it has to be replaced. And I can't bear to think . . .'

'If money has been demanded and taken,' said the Swami, smoothly interrupting the downward cadence of her grief and self-blame, 'then clearly money is the means to further negotiation. This first sum was very easily come by, there is a strong temptation to repeat the success. Do you not agree, Mr Felder? You are a man of the world, where money counts for more, perhaps, than we realise who want it only to invest in crops and food and development. The actual notes we scarcely even see. Nevertheless, they exist, and there are those who know how to value them. And there are those who have them, and know how to devalue them when there is something of great worth to be bought.'

'I'd give whatever I could raise,' said Felder warmly, 'to get Anjli back. But I've shot not only my own bolt, but the company's too. Right now I'm bankrupt. If Dorrie stands by me, I'll pull out of it. If she doesn't, I'm sunk. And what did I buy for her? Not a thing!'

'You have done what you could. It is now for others, perhaps with greater responsibility, to do as much as you have done. Also it is for them to appreciate at its true worth the thing which you have done.' Benevolently the great eye, like a rare and awe-inspiring omen, beamed through the pebble-thick lens, and again was veiled as his head turned. Like the lance of light from a light-house its brief, comprehensive flash encompassed them all, and withdrew itself into dimness. He raised a lean, long-fingered hand, and took off his glasses. Mild, short-sighted eyes, one brighter than the other, blinked kindly at Dominic. 'Since I saw you I have been active ceaselessly upon one problem, that of where Satyavan Kumar might be found. I have sat beside the telephone and pondered the possibilities, testing all I considered valid. There are universities where he has studied, colleges where he has lectured, laboratories where he has taken part in research. There are the ordinary places where he directed, not always willingly, the business of his family's interests. But there are also places to which he withdrew sometimes for refreshment of the spirit, ashrams, solitudes, hermitages . . . And some of these I have, in the past, shared with him.' He looked up obliquely, smiling with the delicate pleasure of a child bringing gifts, but a child acquainted, in some obscure amalgam of innocence and experience, with maturity and age. 'I have run up,' he said, with the sprightly nonchalance that emerged so surprisingly from his normally measured and precise vocabulary, 'the very devil of a telephone bill. But *I have located Satyavan.*'

'You *have*?' Dominic shot out of his chair joyfully. This couldn't be the whole answer, it couldn't solve everything, and above all it couldn't absolve Tossa and himself, but the surge of relief and release he felt was wonderful. The father should have been there from the beginning, he should never have let go, at any cost, of that fragile essence of himself that survived in Anjli. He shouldn't have given up what was his; and he must know it, in this extreme, better than anyone. If he was found, they had an elemental force on their side, a tornado that would sweep away obstacles like a breeze winnowing chaff. 'Where *was* he, all this time? What's he been *doing*?

'Is he coming?' demanded Tossa, slicing straight through to essentials.

'Where he has been I cannot tell you, surely in many places. Where I found him was in a place of the spirit where we have sometimes rested together when there was need. One does not ask too many questions of those one meets there, for only the answer to one question is of any importance, and that is; from here, wither? And yes, he is coming. There will be a plane from Madras arriving tomorrow a little after noon'

'Then he didn't know,' said Tossa, quivering, 'that his mother was dead? He didn't see the newspapers?'

'He did not know until it was too late . . . no. One does not always read newspapers. There is a time *not* to read them, if you wish to remain upright.'

'Then you had to tell him?' she said, her eyes, dark and luminous with sympathy, fixed on the austere old face that confronted her with such serenity. 'That must have been very hard for you both. And then, his child . . .'

'It is never easy,' said the Swami apocryphally, 'to return to the world. Until you have left it, you cannot know how hard. But there is no other way forward and none back. Yes, I told him all that it was necessary to tell. And tomorrow in the afternoon he will be here.'

'But what can he do?' demanded Felder. 'God knows I shall be glad to have him emerge into the light again, and get hold of his responsibilities. He's taken his time about it! But it's the kid we're concerned about, and how is he better placed than we are to get her back? Damn it, we did what they told us to do, we paid what they asked for, and they're ratting on the deal. What more has he to offer, when it comes to the point?'

'About twelve million rupees more,' said the Swami Premanathanand with all the aplomb and all the cold blood of a banker or a saint. And he added patiently, as to unrealistic children: 'Do not forget we are concerned with people whose requirement is essentially simple . . . money. That puts us in a very strong position, because Satyavan is in command of a very great deal of money – now, as you know, in almost complete command of it – and to him it means very little. It sweats from his finger-ends, money. Daughters are infinitely harder to come by. He will pay whatever is necessary to recover Anjli. He has told me so with his own lips. To the limit of what he has, he will pay for her.'

'But how,' wondered Tossa distractedly, 'do we get in touch with them? They can reach us, but we don't know how to reach them.'

'That probably won't be a problem,' Dominic said bitterly, 'as soon as her father emerges. After all, they must be watching absolutely any developments in connection with the family, they wouldn't miss a thing like that.'

'You may well be right. But in fact Satyavan has left as little as possible to chance. I have here the text of a personal advertisement which I have composed at his dictation.' He felt in the deep pocket of the trench coat, which was draped like a cloak of office over the back of his chair, and produced a folded sheet of paper. 'It is his wish that this shall appear in tomorrow's newspapers . . . all the main ones – in the personal column. It is too late to get it into the morning press, but we are in time for the evening papers. If we are not successful with this approach, then of course it may be necessary to let the newsmen have some item to use concerning the return of Mr Kumar, but for the moment he judged it better to come home as quietly as possible and attempt a private contact.' He unfolded the sheet of paper, and perched his spectacles back upon his long, narrow, beautiful nose. 'This is how it reads: "Anjli: Am interested in your merchandise. High price if delivered in good condition. Full guarantees." Then I had intended to give Mr Kumar's home number and request a call at a

271

fixed hour any evening – hoping, of course, that it will come tomorrow evening if the advertisement has been seen. But if you would permit, I think it would be better now to say only: "Call usual number, eight p.m. Kumar." If you will allow this telephone to be used as before, I think it might avoid alarming the vendors.'

Felder uttered a soft whistle of admiration. 'You think of everything!'

'If one must do such things at all, it is necessary to think of everything. And therefore I cannot any longer avoid,' said the Swami mildly, 'pointing out to you the one remaining possibility with which, unfortunately, we also have to count. Though it may well be that you have thought of it for yourselves, even if you have refrained from expressing it. Anjli may already have been killed.'

Tossa nodded wretchedly, Dominic stood frozen eye to eye with the fear he had hoped she need not share, and Felder protested aloud, all in the same instant.

'Good God, no! They surely wouldn't hurt the child. I'm sure she must be alive and safe somewhere.'

'It is common practice in cases of kidnapping. Such people tend to make certain that they can never be identified, and the obvious witness is the victim.'

It was doubly terrible to hear this said in that tranquil, matter-of-fact voice. Felder looked grey with shock and a little sick; but still he shook his head vigorously, resisting the foreboding. 'No, it's impossible. I'm certain she's alive and well.'

'Let us hope so. But the criminals have not kept their bargain with you. There must be a reason why you have not received the expected call. Either it is a further gesture of greed to hold on to her for still more money, since the first demand was so encouragingly successful. Or else they cannot produce her, and you will hear nothing more. Her father's arrival will resolve that problem. For I must tell you that he will insist on seeing with his own eyes that his daughter is unharmed, before he even enters into negotiations. What is more, on my advice he insisted that you, who may now know her more certainly than he himself would, shall also see her and verify that it is indeed Anjli. He has not set eyes on her for six years, a substitute might be passed off on him if you were not present to confirm her identity.'

'But how,' asked Dominic with patent dismay, 'can we hope to make them agree to taking a risk like that?'

'That is for them to arrange as best they can. Satyavan will agree to any safeguards they suggest, provided he can satisfy himself that there still exists something to be bought. If they want their money – and it will be worth their while – they will go to some trouble to arrange it.' He added: 'I also have promised that the police will not be drawn into the affair by me, though of course, as you know, they are already informed about the crime itself. A quick settlement is therefore much to the criminal's advantage.'

'I hate,' said Dominic with sudden and uncharacteristic passion, 'to think of them getting away with it.' And it came out as a plain protest against the Swami's apparent acceptance of the possibility. True enough, the main thing was to recover Anjli alive and well, and restore her to her rediscovered father. But even so, the ugliest and meanest of crimes . . . not to speak of Arjun Baba's thin but tenacious thread of life, snapped almost by the way . . .

The Swami rose, faintly smiling, and put on his trench coat. 'I am more fortunate than you in this respect, that my beliefs assure me that no one ever *gets away* with anything. There is a constant account which must balance. In what form of life these people will return to earth it is useless to conjecture.'

'Cockroaches, probably,' said Tossa with detestation, and saw Felder wince perceptibly. In India cockroaches are the nightmare of the uninitiated.

'Ah, cockroaches are sagacious and relatively harmless creatures! Do not attribute human malice to them. And now I shall leave you,' said the Swami, 'until tomorrow evening. If you agree that I may bring my friend here to hope for his daughter's return?'

'Yes, please do! None of us can rest until we get her back.'

Only after he had withdrawn did it occur to Tossa, to her amazement and shame, that they had not offered him any refreshment in return for his typist's excellent coffee. The magnetism of his presence was such that one sat at his feet while he was in the room. And yet, when it came to the point, what did they really know about him?

Felder went out on to the balcony outside the window, and looked down into the courtyard, curious about the ancient Rolls with its tattered body and indestructible heart. The driver had just observed the Swami approaching from the garden entrance of the hotel, and slid nimbly out from behind the wheel to open the door for his master.

'Wouldn't you know he'd have that sort of car? I bet everything he does and everything that belongs to him measures up. Say what you like about this country, at least it has a sense of *style*.'

Tossa and Dominic came to his side and stood looking down with him as the Swami clambered majestically but athletically into the lofty front passenger seat, which had something of the throne about it. As Girish closed the door a large taxi came prowling into the patio from the drive, and its headlights focussed directly upon the Rolls. Girish moved at leisure round to the driving seat, head raised to free his vision from the momentary glare. Felder uttered a sudden sharp moan of astonishment, and leaned out far over the balustrade.

'Oh, *no*! It can't be . . .!'

'Can't be what? What's the matter?' Dominic asked in alarm.

'That fellow . . . Look! The driver . . .' At that moment the headlights swerved from Girish, and left him to climb into the Rolls in shadowy obscurity, and so start up his noble vehicle and drive it away.

'Girish? What about him? He's the Swami's regular one . . . at least, he's the same man who was driving him when we first met him.'

'He's the hillman who stopped me outside the temple this afternoon,' Felder said with certainty, 'and asked me the way to Birla House. That's who he is! The guy who took my attention off the pay-off briefcase just long enough to get the contents swopped over.'

'*Girish*? But he . . . damn it, he drove us home . . . Are you *sure*?'

'I'm sure! I'd know that face again anywhere. Now you tell me,' said Felder savagely, 'why a man who can drive his boss about Delhi smartly enough to be worth his pay should have to ask his way to Birla House? Go ahead, tell me! I'm listening.'

After which, it was hardly surprising that a conveniently anonymous taxi, with three people aboard besides the driver, should sit waiting for the arrival of a plane from Madras, at something after noon the next day at Safdarjung Airport. The passengers didn't care to venture out on to the tarmac, because the ancient Rolls was there in all its glory, with Girish lounging at the wheel, and the Swami Premanathanand had gone briskly through the airport buildings to the landing frontage, to wait for the emerging travellers. Instead, the taxi parked in a convenient position to watch the new arrivals proceeding towards their town transport. The Sikh driver, efficient, intelligent and uninterested in his freight, had taken out the newspaper he had bought half an hour previously, and was reading the news pages. He skipped the agony column; which was a pity, because one of its small ads. began: 'Anjli: Am interested in your merchandise. High price if delivered in good condition . . .' Felder had bought a paper too; so they knew exactly what the advertisement said. But the dignified and faintly disdainful Sikh didn't look at all like a probable kidnapper.

The passengers from the Madras flight were coming through. A bustling lady in a sari and a woollen coat, with a child in one hand, and transistor in the other, a bandy-legged little husband in a Nehru cap and European suit following with two suitcases; a blasee girl, either English or American, worn-out with sight-seeing and pursued by two porters; a quiet, sensible couple, probably Australian – there must really be something in that legend of easy-going democracy – talking placidly to their one porter as if he lived next door back home, and giving the pleasant impression of effortless enjoyment; and then the flood of southern Indians, small-featured, delicately-built, golden-skinned, alert and aloof, good-humoured people balancing curiosity and self-sufficiency like acrobats. And finally, the Swami Premanathanand, pacing at leisure beside a tall, erect, haughty Punjabi – no mistaking those lofty hawkish lineaments – in the most expensive and yet unobtrusive of tailorings in a neutral tan. They came out through the glass doors talking earnestly, totally absorbed. The stranger was thicker-set than many of the Punjabis Dominic and Tossa had seen, with something of the suavity and goldenness of the Bengali about him, but the jutting nose and flaring nostrils were there, and the fastidious, full-lipped mouth, and the hooded eyes. Bengali eyes have a liquid softness, they suggest reserve but not reticence. These eyes were proud and distant, even, at first encounter, hostile. He had beautifully-cut black hair, crisp and gently wavy, and the sophistication of his movements was what they had expected. The manner of his conversation, urgent, quiet and restrained, tended to bear out everything they had heard or thought of him. He was so well-bred that he might as well have been English.

'That's it!' said Dominic flatly. 'Not much doubt. *He*'s genuine!'

The new arrival was brought up standing at sight of the Rolls. It would not have been surprising to see him insert a monocle into his eye to survey it more closely, but he did not. Delicately he stepped up into the back seat, presumably not merely cleared of grain samples for this occasion, but dusted as well; and the Swami mounted beside him as nimbly as ever, twitching the skirt of his robe clear with an expert kick of one heel.

The Rolls turned ponderously, and swept superbly away towards the centre of Delhi.

'All right, driver,' Felder said, at once resigned, puzzled and uneasy. 'Back to Keen's Hotel.' And when they were in motion, not too close to the resplendent veteran sailing ahead: 'Back to square one! It looks like him, and it must be him. Anybody could check the passenger list, after all. So where do we stand now? Don't tell me that driver of his is on the level!'

They didn't tell him anything, one way or the other; it remained an open question all the way back into town.

The Swami brought his friend to Keen's Hotel punctually at half past seven in the evening, apparently deeming it necessary to allow them half an hour for the social niceties before the stroke of eight, when they would all, almost certainly, freeze into strained silence, waiting for the still hypothetical telephone call. Felder, in fact, was the last of the party to arrive, and came in a great hurry from the Connaught Circus office, with a much-handled script under his arm.

'Not that I'm thinking of leaving,' he assured them all, with a tired and rueful smile, 'not until this business of Anjli is cleared up. But I must do a little work sometimes. I hope and pray I'm going to be able to fly back to Benares soon with a clear conscience.' It was easy to see that in spite of his poise the strain was telling on him. He turned to the stranger and held out his hand, not waiting to be formally introduced. 'Mr Kumar, I'm Felder. I expect you know the score about all of us already from the Swami here. I needn't tell you that you have the sympathy of every one of us, and we'll do absolutely everything we can to help you and Anjli out of this mess.'

'I understand from my friend,' said Kumar quietly, 'that

you have already done all and more than I could possibly
have asked of you. I'm very grateful, believe me. We must
set that account straight as soon as possible. But you'll
forgive me if my mind can accommodate only one thought
at this moment.'

He stood in the middle of Dominic's extravagant hotel
sitting-room, immaculate in his plutocratic tailoring, a
curiously clear-cut and solitary figure, as if spot-lighted by
his deprivation and loneliness on a stage where everyone else
was a supernumerary. He was not so tall as they had thought
him to be, but his withdrawn and erect bearing accounted for
the discrepancy. The patina of wealth was on his complexion,
his clothes, his speech, his manner; but that was neither his
virtue nor his fault, it was something that had happened to
him from birth, and if it had one positive effect, it was to
add to his isolation. He was a very handsome man, no doubt
of that; the gold of his skin, smoother than silk, devalued
whiteness beyond belief. Maybe some day they would get
used to that re-estimation of colour, and realise how crude
the normal English pink can be.

The Swami, a benevolent stage-manager, set them all an
example by seating himself calmly, and composing himself
for as long as need be of nerveless waiting. 'We are all of
one mind, and all informed about what we have to expect.
We have taken all possible steps to deserve success, let us
then wait decorously and expect it. We are contemplating an
exchange which will be to the advantage and convenience of
both parties, there is therefore no need to anticipate double-
dealing. It would be worth no one's while.' His practicality
sounded, as always, unanswerable; but Kumar, even when he
consented to follow his friend's example and sit with folded
hands, was tense from crown to heels.

'If the call does come,' ventured Dominic, 'should I
answer? And hand it over to you, sir, if it's the same
man?'

The Swami approved. 'The number is your number. And
there could, of course, be some quite innocent call. Yes,
please answer in the first instance.'

It was barely twenty minutes to eight, and the scene was
set already. There was nothing now to look forward to but
the gradually mounting tension that was going to stretch
them all on the same rack until the bell finally rang. Except
that they had barely set their teeth to endure the waiting
when they were all set jangling like broken puppets, as the

innocent white handset emitted its first strident peal of the evening. Never, thought Tossa, huddled in her corner, never, never will I live with a telephone again. Better the telegraph boy at the door every time.

Dominic picked up the receiver. There was sweat trickling down into his eyebrows, prickly as thistles. A voice he hardly knew said distantly: 'Hullo, Dominic Felse here!'

He should have known it was too early, he should have known the damned instrument was going to play with them for the rest of the night. A gentle, courteous, low-pitched voice said in his ear: 'Good, I was afraid you might all be out on the town. I looked in the dining-room, but not a sign of you there. This is Ashok Kabir, I'm down in the foyer. May I come up? I brought a little present for Anjli.'

Distantly Dominic heard himself saying, like an actor reading from a script: 'I wondered why we hadn't heard anything from you. Have you been out of Delhi?'

'Ever since the unit left for Benares. I had three concerts in Trivandrum and Cochin. I'm only just back. Am I inconvenient just now? Maybe you were getting ready to go out. I should have called you from Safdarjung.'

'Anjli . . .' Dominic swallowed whatever he might have said, looking round all the intent faces that willed him to discretion, and unhappily giving way to their influence. There was only one thing to be done. 'Wait just a moment for me,' he said, 'And I'll come down to you.'

He hung up the telephone, and they could all breathe again. 'It's Ashok,' he said flatly. 'He's just back in town after a concert tour in the south, and it looks as if he doesn't know anything about Anjli being missing. He's brought a present for her, he's expecting to see her. I said I'd go down to him. Now what do I do? Tell him the truth and bring him up here to join us?'

Very placidly, very gently, very smoothly, but with absolute and instant decision, the Swami Premanathanand said: 'No!' It was impossible to imagine him ever speaking in haste, and yet he had got that 'No!' out before anyone else could even draw breath.

'We have five people here already,' he pointed out regretfully, as all eyes turned upon him, 'who know the facts. Five people with whom the vendors have to reckon. I think to let in even one more is to jeopardise our chances of success.'

'I am absolutely sure,' said Tossa, 'that Ashok is to be trusted. He is very fond of Anjli. I know!'

'And I feel sure you are right, but unfortunately that is not
the point. He could be the most trustworthy person in the
world, and still be enough to frighten off the criminals from
dealing with us.'

'He is right,' said Kumar heavily. 'We are already too
many, but that cannot be helped. We *can* help adding to
the number and increasing the risk.'

Anjli was his daughter, and he was proposing to pay out
for her whatever might be needed to bring her back to him
safely. There was nothing to be done but respect his wishes.

'Then what do I do? Go down and get rid of Ashok? Tell
him Anjli's out? Supposing he's already questioned the clerk
on the desk?'

'He would not,' said the Swami absently but with certainty.
'He would question only you, who had the child in charge.
Yes, go and talk to him. Tell him Anjli is not here this
evening.' He adjusted his glasses, and the great eye from
behind the thick lens beamed dauntingly upon the unhappy
young face before him. 'Listen,' he said, 'and I will tell you
what you shall say to him, if you require from me an act of
faith. Put him off for tonight, but invite him to come for
coffee tomorrow evening, after dinner . . . with you, and
Miss Barber here, and Anjli.'

Dominic stared at him steadily for a long moment,
considering how deeply he meant it, and realising slowly
that the Swami never said anything without deliberate intent.
It might not, of course, be the obvious intent, but serious,
final and responsible it would certainly be. The only way to
find out what lay behind was to go along with him and take
the risk.

'All right!' he said. 'That's what I'll tell him.' And he
turned and walked out of the room and down the stairs to
the foyer where Ashok waited.

It was then just twelve minutes to eight.

Ashok unwrapped the little ivory figure from the piece of
grey raw silk in which the carver had swathed it, and set it
upright in Dominic's palm. She stood perhaps four inches
high, a slender, graceful woman latticed about with lotus
shoots and airy curves of drapery, her naked feet in a lotus
flower, and a stringed instrument held lovingly in two of
her four beautiful arms. Ashok's expressive, long-lashed eyes
and deeply-lined gargoyle face brooded over her tenderly.

'It is a veena, not a sitar, but Anjli will not mind. This is

Saraswati, the mother of the vedas, the goddess of the word, of learning, of all the arts. Perhaps a good person for her to consult, when she finally faces her problem. I found her in a little shop I know in Trivandrum, and I thought Anjli would like her. I am sorry to have missed her, but of course I gave you no notice.'

'I'm sorry about that, too. But if you're free, could you join us here tomorrow night for coffee? About eight o'clock or soon after? We shall all three be very happy to see you then,' he said, setting light to his boats with a flourish; and he did not know whether he was uttering a heartless lie which must find him out in one more day, or committing himself to an act of faith to which he was now bound for life or death. At that moment he did not know whom he trusted or whom he distrusted, he was blind and in the dark, in a landscape totally unfamiliar to him, in which he could find no landmarks. Yet there must, for want of any other beacon, be a certain value in setting a course and holding by it, right or wrong; thus at least you may, by luck rather than judgement, set foot on firm ground at last and find something to hold by.

'Gladly,' said Ashok, 'I shall look forward to it.' He had asked no questions, and even now he asked only one: 'Her father has not yet come to take charge of her?'

'We've heard from him, indirectly,' said Dominic, picking his way among thorns. 'I hope he'll be with her very soon.'

'Good, so it was worth waiting a little.' Ashok nodded his splended Epstein head in contentment, and picked up his light overcoat, draping it over one shoulder of his grey achkan like a hussar cloak. 'Until tomorrow, then! And my reverences to Miss Barber and Anjli.'

He had a taxi waiting for him in the courtyard, one of the biggest Dominic had ever seen; and at the first step he took into the open air the car came smoothly alongside, placing its rear door-handle confidingly in his hand. That was the kind of service Ashok, for all his reticence and modesty, commanded in Delhi, and probably throughout India, for that matter.

The Swami's Rolls stood in tattered majesty at the end of the ground-floor arcade. The taxi driver gave it a long, respectful look as he turned his own car to drive away, and Ashok, from the rear seat, eyed it even more thoughtfully. Dominic noted, before he turned to go back upstairs in haste, that for once Girish was nowhere in evidence.

The second telephone call came on the stroke of eight, and thereby held up the one for which they were waiting. But the voice that demanded briskly and cheerfully: 'Have you got my co-director there?' was merely that of Ganesh Rao, back from Sarnath a couple of days ahead of schedule with the Deer Park scenes in the can, and anxious to get some early co-operation over the rushes.

'Let me talk to him!' Felder took over the receiver. 'Yes, Felder here! Sure, I'll be out at Hauz Khas in an hour or two, if all goes well. Have you got the whole bunch back safely at the villas? You must have made good time.' In the background he could hear the usual exuberant babel of voices, the girls shrilling and laughing, Channa the charioteer fluting mellifluously, the young American technicians deploying their large, easy drawls, the clinking of glasses, the usual party atmosphere. When he hung up his face was grey with strain; and as soon as the receiver hung in the cradle it pealed again, viciously.

Dominic snatched it from under Felder's hand. This time it must be, this time it had to be, no one could stand much more of this.

'I am calling,' said the unpleasant, clacking old voice, rattling consonants like bones, 'in answer to your advertisement.'

Without a word Dominic held out the receiver to Kumar, who was already stretching out his hand for it. For a moment they could clearly hear the juiceless tones continuing, then Kumar cut them off sharply.

'Listen to me, and let us be clear. I am Kumar. You have what I want, and I am prepared to pay for it. But there will be no deal, there will be no discussion, even, until I have seen for myself that my daughter still lives. Not one rupee until then. No, I will not even speak of money until I am satisfied. You have my word that I have taken no steps to try and trace this call, or to find you, nor shall I do so. If you restore me what I want, neither I nor any of the people here with me will take any action against you. It is my word, it will have to be enough for you. If you cannot trust me far, you must know I cannot trust you at all. You will show my daughter to me, and to these friends of mine who have seen her more recently than I have. You will show her to us in good condition, or you will get nothing. I am a business man, I do not buy pigs in pokes. Then we will talk terms, and arrange an exchange which will protect both of us. You understand me?'

The old voice hectored, rising, growing angry.

'You hold just one saleable article, my friend,' snapped Kumar, 'and I am offering to buy it . . . when I have satisfied myself that it is exactly what you are representing it to be. I have promised you we will do no more than that. I have promised you a high price. If you do not want to deal on those terms, where do you think you will find a higher bidder? The circumstances are your problem, not mine. Make up your mind.'

There were brief, acrimonious questions, a note of something like anxiety now in the tone.

'Certainly. If you make it possible, the exchange can take place tomorrow. First let us see her. Then call me here, and I shall make no more difficulties than I must to ensure that she *remains* as we have seen her. There is no question of trust. Each of us must formulate his own safeguards. But do you question that my word is worth more than yours? Make your dispositions, then, we are waiting.'

After that he sat quite silent, listening with admirable concentration and patience for some minutes, the clapper vibrating viciously in his ear. He heaved a long, careful sigh. 'Very well! On behalf of all of us here, I agree.'

Very slowly, as if the smoothness and silence of the action mattered vitally, he cradled the receiver, and sat back in his chair with a shivering gasp, wiping his moist hands frenziedly on a vast silk handkerchief.

'Well, it's arranged! Tomorrow, at twelve o'clock, all five of us – oh, yes, whoever he is, he knows how many of us there are! – are to meet for lunch in the first-floor restaurant at Sawyers', on Connaught Circus, near Radial Road Number Five. A window table will be booked for us in advance – in my name! There is a sweet shop just opposite. Promptly at a quarter past twelve Anjli will be brought by taxi to that shop to buy sweets. He says we shall see her clearly. But if any one of us attempts to leave the table and interefere with her, we shall never see her again. And *if* we all obey orders, and finish our lunch and go home, then he will call us again to talk terms and make arrangements for the exchange.'

'And do you believe,' asked Tossa in a whisper, 'that he'll keep his word?'

'I think,' said the Swami Premanathanand, very gently but with complete detachment, 'that he will greatly prefer money and no trouble rather than no money, a dead Anjli and a great deal of trouble. Do you not agree, Mr Felder?'

Felder made a small, protesting sound of revulsion and distaste. Of the impersonal mental processes of India he had had more than enough. 'I think he took her for money, and he'll twist circumstances all the ways he has to, to get money for her. So far he hasn't committed any capital crime, why should he take such a risk now?'

'No capital crime. Well, of course,' said the Swami deprecatingly, 'there is only the little matter of Arjun Baba.'

'Who,' asked Felder simply, 'is Arjun Baba?'

It came as a shock, if a minor shock, to realise that he was in perfectly good faith. They had rushed to confide in him about Anjli, ready to take advantage of sympathy and help wherever it offered, they had mentioned the old man who had been used as a lure for her, but this was the first time Felder had ever actually heard the name of Arjun Baba. Names are powerful magic. That anonymous wisp of India, a puff of grey dust blown away almost unwittingly by the wind of somebody's greed, suddenly put on a man's identity and was illuminated by a man's soul; and suddenly, for the first time, Felder was gazing with horror at the reality of murder.

The Rolls, starting up with somnolent dignity, drove away out of the courtyard with the Swami erect and impassive in the front passenger seat. Kumar, though he had left in the company of his friend, was apparently not dependent on him for transport.

'I don't like it!' said Felder, watching the old car round the tall hedge and vanish from view. 'I can't help it, there's something going on that I don't like and don't trust, and there goes the man who's stage-managing the lot of us. It was that driver of his who distracted my attention from the money, just long enough for the parcels to be swopped over. And now tonight, why didn't he want us to let Ashok in on the truth? Why? You saw as well as I did how he jumped in to put his foot on that instantly. Oh, sure it made sense – sense enough for Kumar to echo what he said. And yet – you've seen him at work, he sits there like a god, and nods, and we all do what he says. And now we're all committed to this lunch tomorrow. And *he*'s the one who's pulling the strings!'

'As long as he pulls the one that produces Anjli alive,' said Dominic, shaken but helpless, 'does it matter?'

'No . . . if he does that, no, nothing else matters. Not until afterwards, anyhow. No, that's right, we haven't got much choice, have we? She's what matters. Once we've got her back, we can afford to get inquisitive.' His tone said that 'inquisitive' was an under-statement.

'You don't really believe,' whispered Tossa, appalled, 'that the Swami can be behind Anjli's kidnapping? But he's her father's friend. You can see it's true. They've known each other for years.'

'That's right! And who knows better than the Swami how much money his friend's good for, and how little he'll miss it? And who can get him to dance to his tune better?'

'But it's crazy! He doesn't care about money. It means nothing to him . . .' she protested, shaking.

'No, not in dollars, or rupees, or pounds sterling, not one damn' thing. Only in grain seed, and pedigree stock, and agricultural plant, and expert advice . . . An opportunity's an opportunity, whatever you want the cash for, it doesn't have to be for yourself. *Why didn't he want Ashok to know*? Why was his driver watching me on Sunday, why did he pretend to be an innocent in Delhi, when he knows it like the palm of his hand?'

They laboured to find answers for him, and discovered that they had none for themselves. The thin fingers of the Swami Premanathanand were indeed unobtrusively present in the plot wherever they looked, gently stirring, bringing the mixture to the boil.

'Our hands are tied, anyhow,' said Dominic flatly. 'If he really is behind the whole affair, then he genuinely intends to hand over Anjli tomorrow. And there's nothing we can do except go along with him until she's safe.'

On which exceedingly chilly comfort they separated for the night, Felder to the villa at Hauz Khas where Ganesh Rao was waiting with the rushes from Sarnath, and Tossa and Dominic to a belated sandwich and a lime soda in the bar, and then a solitary walk round the quiet streets near the Lodi Park. It was the walk that completed their sense of disorientation and confusion; for they returned by way of Aurangzeb Road, and passing by the drive of Claridge's, were just in time to see one of the handsome, well-groomed,

well-heeled couples of Delhi strolling arm-in-arm from the
hotel to the taxi rank. A good-looking, austere, proud, pale
Punjabi in a European suit, and a very lovely woman in a
white and gold sari on his arm, her towering beehive of
lustrous black hair defying fashion, which one so beautiful
could well afford to ignore. There was nothing indecorous
about them, they were talking together gravely and quietly,
their faces intent. There was nothing about them, indeed, to
excite any feelings but those of pleasure and admiration –
except that the man was Satyavan Kumar, and the woman
– once seen, never forgotten – was Kamala, whom they
knew best as Yashodhara, the bride of Prince Siddhartha,
the Buddha.

Ten

Anjli sat on a string bed in a tiny room about eight feet square, lit by one little smokey window far above her head. It was the fourth day she had spent in this place, and she knew every article in the room, every fine crinkle of cracks in the dun-coloured plaster of the walls, every crease in the garish almanack pinned above the rickety wooden chest. The ceiling was disproportionately high, the floor of rough concrete with one threadbare cotton rug. On the bed was a thin flock mattress, and a grey blanket. The chest of drawers was of thickly varnished and heavily scratched wood, dark red, with an artificial silk cover in several violent colours spread over it, and above it the smooth, effeminate blue Krishna smiling over his flute with those kind, mischievous, amoral, dangerous eyes of his, the eyes of a fairy rather than a god. Propped on the gay cover were one faded family photograph, so faint now that it had nothing to say to her, not even whether the persons in it were male or female, and one picture of Sri Ramakrishna, cut from a newspaper and stuck askew in a carved wooden frame.

There was nothing else in the room. And all three of them slept there at night, the two little girls on the string bed, the woman on a rug spread on the floor beside them.

This was not the whole of Anjli's present world, however. She could pass at will through the single door of the room, or most of the time she could do so; but that would merely bring her into a short clay-coloured passage, locked against her at the nearer end, and at the other leading only to two even tinier rooms, the first an Indian bathroom, a concrete box just big enough to stand up in, with a cold water tap on the wall and a drain in the centre of the gently sloping floor, the second a flush lavatory, eastern style, with a porcelain basin sunk in the floor and two raised platforms for the feet. There the passage ended in another locked door. But she thought that wherever she might be, she was on the ground floor, for at the minute window of the lavatory leaves leaned down to her at an angle which suggested the lowest branches of a tree.

This was all she knew, and after four days she knew it like the palm of her hand; but she could not deduce from it anything that might be useful to her.

There was nothing the matter with Anjli's mind or memory, she was not too much afraid to sift detail from detail and build them laboriously into a picture of her days, but the picture could never be complete, for this place of her confinement was a bubble, without a material location at all. She remembered perfectly the gleam of the old man's eyes across the brazier, the instant flash of intelligence that warned her this was not Arjun Baba, and spurred her into flight. She remembered the sickening half-suffocation under the folds of the blanket, the struggles that wasted themselves feebly, and soon ceased when she realised that she was in a van in motion. She had not lost consciousness at all, but face-down in her odorous wrappings on the floor of the van, with no light, and the vehicle turning and circling and dodging to complete her confusion, she had lost all sense not only of direction but of distance. Towards the end she had lapsed into something close to a faint, starved for air. Now she did not know even whether she was still in Delhi, much less in which part of it.

Two people between them had carried her in from the van, she thought by the locked door beyond the lavatory, but even of that she could not be sure. All she could be certain of was that they had released her from her wrappings in this room, the old man and the woman between them, and here she had been ever since, watched and guarded.

The old man she saw seldom, he came only now and again to make sure that his catch was still safe. During his few visits she had studied him closely, because she had now no resources but her own ingenuity, and the only food she had for that was observation. The more she recorded, the more chance that some day she might find a weak place in the fortress and its garrison. But she felt from the beginning that it would not be in the old man. Now that she came to study him at close quarters she saw that he was not at all like Arjun Baba, and certainly not nearly so old and frail. This one, grizzled and bent though he might be, and tangled in a wealth of beard, would have made two of Satyavan's pensioner. He was broad-shouldered, sturdy and muscular, and she had already experienced the strength of his arms and hands. He had a harsh, querulous, irascible old voice that grated unpleasantly on the air and even more unpleasantly on the mind, suggesting as it did a short temper, and a nature subject to malice and panic. He spoke to her not at all, not even one word. It was to the woman he talked, hectoring, bullying and demanding, in Hindi. And the woman did everything he ordered, in cringing haste and for the best of reasons, because she was afraid of him.

It seemed to be the woman who lived here. She was much younger than the man. She looked, perhaps, fifty, but there were factors which caused Anjli to reason that in reality she must be considerably younger still; notably there was the girl, who seemed to be about Anjli's own age, give or take a year, and yet was almost certainly this woman's daughter. So it wasn't time, it was circumstances that had aged the mother. She was painfully thin and worn, her features blurred by timidity and hopelessness, the only rich thing about her her great coil of dark brown hair. She wore blouses and saris of plain cotton dyed in single colours, and so faded with washing that the once brilliant red had ebbed to a streaked and withered rose. When the old man was there she was a quivering, wary creature obsequious to his every gesture and word, and yet in some insinuating way she seemed to place herself between his possible animosity and Anjli. And when he was not there she was timid and gentle, she offered food with consideration, she left the bed to the children; but she was too cowed ever to be an ally, and too much afraid of the old man ever to forget to lock a door.

Her cooking was done somewhere outside. Anjli pictured a lean-to shed in a corner of a small compound, with pots hissing gently over the inevitable charcoal braziers, such as she had seen in the modest residential areas of Rabindar Nagar. Altogether, there was something about this woman's living quarters which did not suggest the most primitive poverty, by any means, poor though she undoubtedly was. A certain respectability and security existed here. Somebody's housekeeper, perhaps? The old man's? But no, he did not live here, she was almost certain of that. And what sort of place was it, in any case? These rooms were so enclosed that traffic noises did not penetrate. She could not even guess at the kind of road or street that lay outside her prison.

And then there was the girl. Late in the afternoon of the first day she had manifested herself, first as a young, curious voice plying the woman with questions, somewhere beyond the locked door. And surely there had been a low, continuous hum as background to their exchanges, a sound which made itself known in retrospect as the purr of a vacuum cleaner? Anjli could never be quite sure about that, but perhaps only because the idea seemed to her so fantastic. She forgot about it, in any case, when the woman unlocked the door and the girl came sliding through it, and stood staring, mute with shyness, at her mysterious contemporary.

Her name was Shantila, for Anjli had heard her mother call her so. She was learning English at school; but as yet she spoke it very haltingly, and indeed for the most part, even in her own language, was a very taciturn child. Life had not encouraged her to be voluble. She was a couple of inches shorter than Anjli, but otherwise they were well-matched in size, as was soon demonstrated; for on his next visit the old man had issued his orders, and Anjli had forthwith been given some of Shantila's school clothes to wear instead of her own jersey suit. White shalwar and deep blue kameez, and the inevitable gauze scarf in white. Would a country school make use of such a uniform, or could she rely on it that she was still in Delhi? No use asking Shantila, she had all too clearly been told to avoid such subjects. Probably she had even been told to keep away from the prisoner. She vanished whenever the old man was there. But in his absence the attraction was too great. Shantila was free to pass through the locked doors if she wished; but after a day Anjli began to understand how barren a freedom this was to her. The most fascinating and wonderful thing in her world drew her inward into Anjli's captivity.

At first she simply sat and stared, devouring with her eyes every facet of the strange girl's strangeness, the supple leather shoes in their antique leather shades melting from deep red to mouse-brown, the delicate silvery-pink colouring of the woollen jacket and skirt, the finger-nails shaped and tinted like rose petals, all the exotic accoutrements of Anjli's westernness. On the second day, approaching with daring shyness, she began to touch, to stroke the kitten-softness of the angora and lambswool jersey, and even the smooth texture of Anjli's lacquered nails.

They arrived at a kind of understanding almost without words. Shantila shook her head nervously when she was questioned, so why question her? What she let fall unwittingly might be worth much more. Moreover, Anjli found that she could not pursue a creature so wary, and with such evident reasons for her fears. This was not and never could be an enemy, and there are measures which are inadmissible except with enemies. Even her own desperate need to act in her own defence did not alter that.

She knew, of course, what must be the reason for her abduction. There could be only one. She was the child of money, and someone intended to get money in exchange for her. The trouble was that she was too sophisticated to conclude that that in any way guaranteed her safety; she knew of too many cases to the contary. But so far, at least, she was hoarded like treasure, and with luck she might yet have time to find a means to help herself. But preferably not at Shantila's expense.

They slept together on the sagging bed at night, and drew delicately apart when they inadvertently touched, with a kind of mutual respect that could have arisen in no other circumstances; and then, when they touched of intent, in search of a mysterious measure of comfort, they did not withdraw.

And this was the fourth morning. The sun was already high, for the leaves that whirled and span just within view from the lavatory window were gilded through. Shantila had come home from school, and had no more classes that day. They ate their mid-day food together, and Shantila sat content as on the first day to watch and wonder. For her Anjli was inexhaustible. Even now that the fabulous clothes were gone, the glamour had not departed. And there was still her necklace and polished round beads, in a dozen melting shades of brown and grey and green. Shantila had no jewellery; even her mother had only two or three thin glass bangles to her name.

Anjli saw how the huge, hungry brown eyes dwelt on her necklace, not coveting, only marvelling, satisfied with contemplation because there was no further possibility. Dorette had brought the beads back for her once from Scotland, they were only the subtle semi-precious pebbles of the Scottish hills, rounded and polished and strung into a neat little choker, eminently suitable for a young girl. What they were to Shantila, she saw suddenly in a wonderful, inverted vision, were the jewels from the ends of the earth. They had no value until you realised they had a transferable value, and then they were beyond price. How stupid, then, that they should stay where they were worthless, when they could so easily go where they were treasure.

Anjli put up her hands to the back of her neck, and undid the silver clasp.

'Turn round, let me put it on for you.'

She lowered the chain of stones to Shantila's neck, and Shantila drew back from it instinctively, shaking her head in fright and putting up a hand to fend off the gift.

'No . . . no . . . they are yours . . .'

'No, they are for you. I want to give them to you. If you like them? You *do* like them?' She said simply: 'I have others.' And she thought: 'I *had* others!' and wondered when, if ever, she would see them again.

Shantila's eyes, still dubious but unable to lie, shone huge as moons with pleasure. Anjli fastened the clasp, and stood back to look at the effect, and Shantila's awed fingertips explored the cold round smoothness of bead after bead in astonishment and delight. The two girls looked at each other long and steadily, in recognition and wonder and satisfaction over the exchange of something undefined, the completion of some bargain in which both of them had gained.

They were so engrossed in their own mutual discoveries that they had not remarked the voices raised outside in the passage. The sudden opening of the door, the apparition of the old man on the threshold, massive head sunk into the brown shawl he wore round his shoulders, shook them apart with a disagreeable shock, as though they had only now realised his possible significance to them both.

'Come, Anjli,' said the ancient, gravelly voice, with a horrid note of ingratiation that matched the fond, false smile on the bearded face. 'You are going shopping with us.'

He took her by one wrist before she could even reason whether there was any sense in resisting, or indeed anything to be feared in complying. The woman, shrinking at his shoulder, obediently took her other arm. Shantila ventured to follow them uneasily along the passage to the rear door, but then the old man turned his head and scowled her back, and she stood motionless where they had left her, watching them go.

It was the first time Anjli had even seen this narrow wooden door opened. It brought them out into dazzling sunshine in a small, high-walled yard, the sparkling leaves of one tree leaning over the wall. There were two or three sheds, as she had expected; there was a car of unobtrusive age and make standing in the shade; and just outside the open yard gates, in a narrow lane, there was an unmistakable Delhi taxi waiting for them.

They put her into the middle of the back seat between them, the woman holding her left arm, the man her right; and as the taxi began to move, the man twitched her scarf dexterously round her eyes, and blinded her until they were well away from the house and yard. She did not resist; and in a moment he let her emerge, for though there was no disguising Delhi, one Delhi street is like enough to another to confuse all those who do not know it well.

So they were still in the city, that was something gained. Anjli sat silent but tense between them, watching and thinking. What was to happen now? Had she already been ransomed, and was she now to be set at liberty? She could not trust too easily in any such optimistic assessment of her position. Then why? Had her hiding-place become unsafe, and was she to be transferred to another? Then she had better be ready to seize even the last chance that might offer, here in the streets. Anything could be true, except, of course, that they were simply going shopping.

They drove for some while in the spacious streets of the new town, but never could she find a firm landmark; and when at length the driver brought them to the sweet shop opposite Sawyers' Restaurant, he did so by the nearest of the radial roads, so that the long, smooth, crescent curve of Connaught Circus should not be obvious.

The car drew up closely to the curb.

'Come,' beamed the old man, 'we are going here. To buy some sweets for you and for Shantila. You will be very quiet and sensible, will you not, Anjli? For your father's sake, remember that!'

She could have outrun them both, but they never let go of her wrists. And there was no one close, to whom she could call, no traffic policeman, no passing English tourist. She stood for a moment hanging back between them on the broad pavement, and looked all round her with one rapid glance at the shining day that offered her no help; a Delhi schoolgirl of fourteen in shalwar and kameez, out shopping with her mother and grandfather. Who was going to give her a second look? She yielded to the pull of their hands, and went with them into the shop.

'Yes,' said Dominic, leaning over Tossa's chair to strain his eyes after the slight figure vanishing under the shop awning, 'that's Anjli!'

'You are quite sure? It's so long,' said Kumar defensively, 'since I saw her.'

'Quite sure,' said Tossa.

'It's Anjli, all right,' Felder confirmed, and his voice shook with tension. 'Now, for God's sake, what do we do?'

'Exactly what we promised,' said the Swami Premana-thanand gently, not even leaning forward in his chair. 'We remain here, making no move to alarm her captors. We wait for further word. So far, you will agree, they have kept their part of the bargain.'

'But, damn it, she's there, right under our eyes, and only those two decrepit people to keep her from us . . . if we went straight down now, and into the shop after them . . .' Felder mopped sweat from his seamed forehead, and breathed heavily.

'We were also warned that if we made any such move we might never see her again,' the Swami pointed out gently, and sipped his soup. 'We cannot take such a risk. We must abide by our side of the bargain, too. For her sake.'

'I suppose you're right.' Felder subsided with a vast and bitterly reluctant sigh.

'They're coming out,' whispered Tossa.

All three linked, as before, both Anjli's arms prisoned. The box of sweets they had bought was carried under the old man's arm. Helplessly the five in the first-floor window of Sawyers' watched the trio move unhurriedly to the edge of the pavement, and saw the Sikh taxi-driver lean to open the rear door for them. First the woman vanished within, then the child, then the old man. The door closed on them with a brisk bang.

'We *can't* . . .' breathed Felder. But none of them moved. The Swami sat erect, a small, rueful smile curving his lips. The noon traffic round Connaught Circus swirled placidly, thinning for the siesta. Into the scattered stream the taxi moved gracefully, like a floating leaf, caught the full current and was away. A garishly-decorated scooter-taxi brushed by it in the opposite direction, and another as gay let it pass at a side-street before turning off. A few cars swung here and there in a dance. Out of a garage yard a more powerful motorbike-taxi sailed with a roar, dark green awning flapping, and rocketed away in the same direction Anjli and her escort had taken.

The Swami appeared to be watching nothing, and to see nothing, but he had in his mind a complete map of all these complex traffic movements. Everyone else was staring frantically, but none of them observed the one significant thing which had happened. For the driver of the motorbike rickshaw, had not been as invisible to them as all the other casual service personnel of Delhi, the postmen, the peons, the porters, would have been recognised at once as Girish, his master's monumental Rolls for once abandoned. Girish had made no promises, and taken part in no bargain. Girish was a free agent.

The taxi proceeded without haste round the curve of Connaught Circus, the motorcycle-rickshaw followed at a nicely-judged distance. There could hardly be a better instrument for pursuit in Delhi, where in any street of the new town at any time of the day you may see at least three or four of them, all looking much alike. Nobody pays any attention to them, unless he wishes to hire one, and even then it is not unusual to watch them sail disdainfully by, for in the deep shade of their awnings it is difficult to be sure whether they are occupied or not. Nor does anyone turn a hair at seeing them driven at crazy speeds, so that even an alerted quarry might have great trouble in getting away from them. Girish, however, had no intention of betraying himself. His object was to trail them to their destination, not to overhaul them. He hung back by fifteen yards or so, driving obliquely behind the taxi so that he should not become obtrusive in the driving mirror, allowing other vehicles to intervene now and then, varying the pattern of his pursuit, the big machine idling happily under him. He foresaw no trouble. All he needed to know was where they were holding her, and then the rest was up to him. In the meantime he did not mean to make any mistake.

Nor was what happened next due to any error on his part. It was something against which he could not possibly have taken precautions.

In the back of the taxi Anjli sat between her guards, quivering with tension and aware that time was running out. They were on their way back to the tiny, obscure dwelling in the quiet yard, and once they reached it she would have lost her only opportunity. This inexplicable trip back into the world, on the face of it completely senseless, must mean something, if only she could grasp what. Had she merely been removed from the place for a brief while because someone dangerous was expected there? Had she been put back into apparent circulation simply to show her to someone, to disarm suspicions of who or what she was? It had to mean something that could help her to know how to act, and here were the minutes and seconds dwindling through her fingers, and nothing gained. Uneasily she craned on all sides, searching the pavements that unrolled beside her. The old man had loosed his hold on her. She turned and swept her hand across the dusty rear window, peering back along their track. She saw the motorcycle-rickshaw that should have meant nothing to her, the long, slim, lightly-balanced body of its driver; she saw, and studied for one broken moment with astonished passion, the lean, aquiline face with its bold bones and intent, proud eyes fixed unmistakably on the car that carried her.

She uttered a shriek of exultation, and whirled to pound with both fists upon the Sikh driver's shoulder. 'Stop!' she cried, in a voice of such authority that his foot instinctively went down on the brake. 'Stop, at once!'

The old man had her by the arm again by then, though it took him all his time to hold her. She had not lost her instinct for the last chance; when the driver braked they were all three flung forward in the seat, and she reached across the frightened woman and tore at the handle of the door, willing to push the woman out before her and jump for it if only they gave her time.

She was just too late. 'Drive on, drive on, quickly!' bellowed the man beside her, and all the cracked tones of age had fallen away from his voice in this crisis. 'Don't listen to her. You see she is ill . . . she is mad . . . we must get her home . . .' The car lurched forward again powerfully and gathered speed, and Anjli was flung back helplessly into the cushions. The woman was sobbing with excitement and dread. The man cursed her savagely, cursed Anjli with even more heartfelt passion, and crouched scowling through the back window. He knew now that they were followed. She had done the one thing she should not have done.

'Faster, faster! There is a motorcycle-rickshaw following us. You must lose him . . . you must! I promise you double your fare if you get us back safely.'

They were threading traffic at speed now, taking flagrant

risks to put other vehicles between them, whirling dangerously out of the main stream, plunging through side-streets, Anjli was lost again, the city went round her like a kaleidoscope. She tried to pull herself up to the window, and the old man took her by her braid of hair and thrust her down again. She struck at him with all her strength, clenched her fingers in his beard and tugged. Spitting curses, he took her by the wrists and unlaced her fingers by force, one by one.

'Faster, faster . . . this bullock-cart . . . Quickly, pass it, and it will block the way for him! Yes, *now*! No, no, not to the back, drop us at the front here, there is not time . . .'

The taxi hurtled to a halt, groaning, the doors were flung open, and Anjli dragged out, dishevelled and panting, and hustled across a narrow garden and in at a fan-lighted door. She heard money change hands hurriedly, enough money to close the taxi-driver's mouth. She heard the car accelerate in haste and dash away. The outer door slammed again upon the old man. He came into the cool, bare white office in which she stood with the shivering woman, a bristling caricature of fury and terror, dripping words like acid, holding his head as if it ached beyond bearing.

So now, too late, she knew. She knew where she was, where she had been all these four days. That tall, Victorian-colonial facade she was not likely to forget, nor the little garden and the low hedge before it. If they had not been forced for lack of time to come in by the front way she might never have recognised the place. Outside that door she had waited with her friends for Ashok Kabir, on the first evening in Delhi. All this time she had been held prisoner in the caretaker's quarters of the film company's Delhi office and store, on Connaught Circus.

And now that she had begun to make discoveries, it seemed there was no end to the things she knew. She knew that the old, cracked voice, when shaken out of its careful impersonation by a crisis, grew full and resonant and loud. She knew that when she had clenched her fingers in his beard what he had felt had not been pain, but only alarm; why else should he have disengaged her hold so carefully, instead of hitting out at her with all his force?

She let him come close to her, the awful, bitter, incomprehensible words nothing to her now. She stood like a broken-spirited child until he was within her reach, and then she lunged with both hands, not at his beard this time, but at the thick bush of grey hair, bearing down with all her weight, ripping it from his head. Wig and beard came away together in her clutch, tearing red, grazed lines across his cheeks and brows where they had been secured. Nothing remained of the senile elder but two round, grained grey patches of make-up on his cheeks, the carefully-painted furrows on his forehead, and the tangle of hair that Anjli let fall at his feet, curled on the floor like a sleeping Yorkshire terrier. What was left was a sturdy man in his thirties, high-complexioned, smooth-featured, with close-cropped black hair.

'Now I know you,' she said, without triumph, for she knew that she had made an enemy in a sense in which she had never had an enemy before. 'You are not just an old man, you are *Old Age. Old Age and Death*. I even remember your name. Your name is Govind Das.' And suddenly and peremptorily she demanded, as if it emerged now as the most important thing in the world, and the most crucial issue between them: '*What have you done with Arjun Baba*?'

Govind Das took two lurching steps towards her, and beneath his red-brown skin the blood ebbed, leaving him dull and grey as clay. The woman, shivering and pleading, edged a timid shoulder between the two, and he took her by her sari with a clumsy, violent gesture, and flung her out of his way. He gripped Anjli's arm, and dragged her away out of the empty office, back to the locked door beside the little living-room, the woman following all the way, her eyes great with terror, her tongue stumbling through agonised protests. It seemed she might even raise the courage to defy him, but Anjli knew she never would, she had been under his thumb too long.

The key was in the living-room door, he turned it and pushed Anjli blindly within, so awkwardly that she fell against the edge of the bed. For one moment she had caught a glimpse of the lavatory door being drawn gently but rapidly to, as Shantila hid herself within. Shantila knew about anger, and had learned to withdraw herself out of its reach; and this by its very quietness was no ordinary storm.

The key turned in the lock again. She had gained nothing, she was back in the old prison. Another key grated; the door at the end of the passage, the door through which she had just been dragged from the offices, was secured against her. And somewhere beyond it broke out the most horrifying dialogue of rage and pleading and despair she had ever heard. She understood not one word, and yet she understood everything that mattered; she knew that this was crucial, and that her own fate now depended on the outcome. The man raved and threatened, and even more shatteringly burst into desperate tears; the woman urged, coaxed, wept, argued, even protested. Sometimes, Anjli thought, listening with her cheek against the door, Govind Das struck her, but still she did not give up.

Crouching thus to the keyhole, she heard a soft step in the corridor, and the steadying touch of a light hand against the wall. Shantila, too, was listening there, and Shantila understood what they were saying. Anjli drew a deep, steadying breath, and waited. She dared not speak. Probably these two would hear nothing until they had fought out to the end this tremendous battle over her, but she dared not take the risk.

Very softly and cautiously the key began to turn in the lock, and inch by inch the door swung open. In the doorway Shantila beckoned, the fingers of one hand pressed to her lips.

'Quickly!' It was only the hurried ghost of a whisper, urging her. 'You must go . . . my uncle is afraid now . . . you've seen him now, you know him, you can tell about him . . .'

Anjli crept to her side. They stood for an instant almost cheek to cheek, listening.

'He wants to kill you,' Shantila's lips shaped soundlessly, 'so that you cannot tell. They told him, keep you safe, not hurt you . . . but now he's afraid . . .'

The careful disguise of Old Age, and all his expertise in the part, had been no protection to him in the end.

They edged their way silently into the corridor, and carefully Shantila re-locked the door. With held breath they tiptoed past the bathroom and the lavatory, and gingerly turned the last key that let them out into the sunshine of the compound.

The heavy wooden doors were locked, but the thick crossbars and the iron stanchion that held them in place made good aids for climbing, and they were both light-weights and agile. Anjli hauled herself up to the top of the gate and straddled it, leaning down to offer a hand to Shantila scrambling after her. Through the leaves of the single tree the noonday sunlight sprinkled the film company's old utility with gold. And somewhere within the rear premises of the old house a man's voice uttered a great, mangled howl of terror and dismay.

'Quick, give me your hand!' Anjli hauled strongly, and in a moment they lay gasping together over the crest of the gate. The rickety wooden door they had locked behind them shook and groaned to the impact of a heavy body, reverberated again and again, but held fast. The two girls scrambled over the gate and lowered themselves to hang by their hands. Shantila fell neatly on her feet, Anjli grazed her elbow against the rough wood and left a smear of blood on her sleeve. Behind them a window on the first floor opened, a deep sash-window that gave on the flat roof of the bathroom, and Govind Das came leaping through it with a convulsed face, and eyes half-mad with fear and hate, and let himself down in a scrambling fall to the compound. He saw, and they knew he had seen, the small, clenched fingers loose their hold on the crest of the gate. He heard, and they knew he heard, their light feet running like hares away down the crooked lane, and out into the street.

It was not for comfort they took hands and matched their steps; it was so that neither of them should be the fleeter, for now they were one creature in one danger, and there could not possibly be any half salvation.

The iron strut of the compound gates rattled against the wall, the unlocked gates hurtled wide and shuddered to the impact. In a moment the engine of the film company's utility started into life, and Govind Das drove it out into the lane, and away at high speed towards Connaught Circus, where Anjli and Shantila fled from him hand in hand.

Round the corner in Parliament Street, where the spacious side-walks and the green shade trees began, traffic was indulging in its midday siesta, only an occasional car rolling at leisure down the wide, straight road. Screened by a little grove of bushes, a telephone kiosk sat in the green border between road and pathway. A large motorcycle-rickshaw with a deep green awning was parked beside it, and within the box Girish had just dialled the number of Sawyers' restaurant, and was talking to the Swami Premanathanand.

'I lost them. Bad luck with a bullock wagon. But I overtook the same taxi only a minute later, going round the Circus from here towards Irwin Road, empty. They're somewhere in this block, right on the Circus, between Janpath and Parliament Street. Yes, I'm certain. I know his number. I'll get the police to pick up the driver, and when he finds out what he's up against he'll surely talk, for his own sake.'

He was listening to the Swami's brisk reply, and gazing out through the glass panels of his kiosk when everything happened at once. Past him down Parliament Street from the Circus came two young girls in identical white shalwar and blue kameez, gauze scarves flying. They held hands, and ran like athletes, with set faces and floating plaits, ran as if for their lives. Unwisely but understandably, they had chosen to run in the roadway, because there was almost no traffic, and the few saunterers on the paths would have held them up to some extent. But even one car is enough to be dangerous,

especially one driven as crazily as this black veteran coming
hurtling down behind them from the circus. You'd have
thought he was actually trying to run the children down . . .

Girish made never a sound. The telephone receiver dropped
from his hand and swung for a moment, distilling the Swami's
dulcet tones into empty air. The door of the kiosk hurtled
open and slammed shut with a force that broke one pane
of glass, and before the pieces had finished tinkling to the
floor, Girish was astride his motorcycle and had kicked it
into life and motion. He sailed diagonally across Parliament
Street, straight into the path of the oncoming car. The girls
were hardly ten yards ahead when the impact came, and they
leaped tormentedly forward like hares pursued, and never
looked behind.

Govind Das saw from the corner of his eye the heavy
rickshaw surge forward, bent on ramming him. He had
just enough sanity and just enough driving instinct left to
take the only avoiding action possible. He swung the wheel
to the left, to minimise the crash, and the motor cycle took
him obliquely in the right front wing and swept the car
onward into the grass belt between roadway and path. In
an inextricable mass of metal the two vehicles lurched to a
stop, and subsided in a dissolution of plates and parts, the
horrid noise eddying away in diminishing echoes between the
trees. In the stunned moments before anyone came running,
Govind Das dragged himself dizzy but uninjured out of the
driving seat, and slid away hastily from the scene. A car
stolen from the film company's premises . . . a reckless
driver . . . a crash . . . what was there new in that. All he
had to do was take care of the girl, and then get back and
report the car missing.

He could still see the two little figures in blue and white,
well ahead now. They had made a mistake, they were heading
for the great iron gates of the Jantar Mantar Park, down there
on the left of the road. He needn't even hurry.

He looked back once, and the driver of the motorcycle
- was he crazy, or something? Govind Das didn't even know
him, had never set eyes on him before! - still lay in the road,
huddled beside the wreckage. Dead or alive, did it matter?
No doubt an ambulance would be along for him in a matter
of minutes, as soon as someone grasped what had happened
here. Govind Das turned contentedly, and loped gently after
Anjli Kumar, towards the park gates from which there was
no escape. This wall would be too high for them to climb.

Girish had swung his legs clear of the machine and jumped just before the moment of impact, but the impetus of his rush had carried him into the wing of the car just the same, though with less violence. He hit the road hard and flatly, knocking the breath out of his body, and his head struck the metal of the car body with enough force to stun him for some seconds. He opened his eyes upon the gravelly surface of the road, one cheek skinned, the grains of dust like boulders against his lips; but the first painful movements assured him he was alive, and had no breakages. Dazedly he drew up his knees under him, and raised himself from the road.

There had been no one very close to the scene of the crash, but from both directions now people were coming on the run. Hastily Girish withdrew himself behind the crumpled bulk of the two vehicles, and melted backwards into the shelter of the trees. Easy to vanish here, and he had no time to answer police questions, not yet, not until those children were recovered alive. They had disappeared utterly from view now. He removed himself far enough from the wreck to escape notice, and then moved out into the roadway and stared ahead down the long, straight vista of Parliament Street. They were nowhere in sight, yet he could not believe that they had run so far ahead in the time. There were two possible turns off, somewhat ahead but still possible, Jai Singh Road on the right, and the lane opposite to it. And before that, of course, there was the gate into the park.

That made him look to the left, where the iron filigree of the gates stood open in their high wall. He was just in time to see Govind Das turn in towards the gravelled paths of the gardens, limping slightly, in no haste. Until ten minutes ago he had never seen that man in his life, but he could not see him now, even at this distance, without knowing him again.

Girish wiped the smears of blood from his face with a crumpled handkerchief, and set off at an unsteady trot after his quarry.

The Jantar Mantar is the oddest monument of Delhi, and one of the most charming, though without guide-book or guide you might wander round it for days and be no nearer guessing at its purpose. It looks as if some highly original modern sculptor-architect, in love with the space-age, had set to work to decorate this garden with the shapes of things to come. In reality the buildings are nearly two hundred and fifty years old, but it is no illusion that their creator was in love with space. For this is just one of the five giant observatories built around India by the Maharajah Jai Singh the Second, of Jaipur, town-planner and astronomer extraordinary, in the early eighteenth century. Six immense masonry instruments, nobly spaced through the fine gardens with which the Indians inevitably surround every antiquity, tower even above the royal palms. Their shapes are as beautiful as they are functional – or as they were functional in their heyday – and their colour is a deep, soft rose, picked out here and there with white, so that their cleanness and radiance adds to the fantasy of their forms. A pair of great, roofless, rose-coloured towers, each with a stone column in the centre, each with its walls regularly perforated by empty window-niches, once recorded the ascension and declension of the stars. A structure like half a giant rosy fruit lies obliquely tilted, white seeds of staircases glistening within its rind. Two lidless concrete inkwells open their dark interiors to the sun, and several short staircases invite visitors to mount and walk round their rims. There are stairs everywhere, even some shut within enclosing walls and apparently inaccessible from any point. There are doors hanging halfway up sheer old-rose walls, with no visible way to them. There are open rectangles of snowy concrete like dancing-floors, and curved projections of stone like hands cupping and measuring shadow. And all around these giants lie watered lawns punctuated with flowering shrubs, long herbaceous borders flanking the red gravel paths, and tall royal palms, their smooth trunks swathed in silver-grey silk.

Into this superb fantasy the two girls darted, still blown on the winds of terror and resolution, but running out of breath. A few people strolled ponderously along the gravel paths, a few clambered about the many staircases, one or two sat on retired benches in the shade, placidly eating sandwiches. But they seemed so few, and so unreal, as though someone had put them in, carefully arranged, to complete the dream. It seemed impossible that one could approach and speak to them, and actually be heard and answered. Anjli's stunned senses recorded but could not believe in the wonders she saw. She knew nothing about primitive instruments of astronomy, and had had no notion of what awaited her within the wall. She had a stitch in her side, and her chest was labouring, she had to stop. Here among the trees, and under the gigantic shadows, surely they could elude one man, even if he followed them here. And if he passed by, all they had to do was wait, and venture out when it seemed safe, and take a scooter-taxi to Keen's Hotel. She had no money, her bag had been taken from her along with her own clothes, but the driver would not ask for payment until he brought them to their destination.

'I've got to rest,' she said, gulping air, 'I can't run any more.'

'Come farther,' urged Shantila, quaking, 'come to the trees. There he won't see us.'

They took the left-hand path, which stretched straight ahead from the gate, because it led to groves where they could lurk in cover and still watch the gateway. They walked now, though in haste and with many glances behind, stumbling a little from pure weariness of spirit rather than of body. They passed the rosy, petrified fruit the giant's child had dropped, a pomegranate full of white steps for seeds. The most awe-inspiring of all Jai Singh's immense conceptions hung over them. They saw it from this angle as a lofty needle of stone, sailing sheer out of the ground for nearly sixty feet, with a round drum of stone on the top. It looked like a monolith, but as they hurried forward they drew alongside it, and saw that this sheer face was actually the shortest side of a right-angled triangle laid on its edge. Upwards by the hypotenuse, breathtakingly steep, a lady in a sari was proceeding towards the summit, plodding stolidly, a flutter of blue and white silk. One more staircase for all game tourists to climb, the most daunting of them all. The containing walls that protected her scarcely reached her knees. At the top there was no handrail at all round the sheer drop of nearly sixty feet, and perhaps two feet of clearance all round the stone drum.

Anjli stumbled towards the bushes and sanctuary, suddenly terribly tired, oppressed even more by these unforeseen and incomprehensible marvels than by her own half-digested experiences. She had not the least idea that she was staring at the monumental gnomon of one of the biggest sundials in the world, Jai Singh's 'Prince of Dials'. If someone had tried to explain it to her then, she would not have understood. She was very close to the limit of her forces, and only too deeply aware that Shantila, loyal and loving as she might be, could not help her any more. They had reverted to their basic simplicity. It was a long time since Anjli had felt herself a child.

In the green coolness and dimness under the trees, themselves hidden, they found a seat where they could watch the gate. A few people came and went, but several of them were gardeners. Always, in Indian gardens, there are almost more gardeners than visitors. Anjli sat forward and cradled her head in her arms until her breath came more easily; and a terrible drowsiness laid hold of her and smoothed her eyelids closed.

Shantila's sharp little elbow stabbed her side. She heard the first indrawn breath of panic. 'He has come! He knows we are here!'

Anjli jerked up her head and rose to peer tensely through the leaves. There was no mistake. The incongruous head, short black hair still ruffled from under the wig of Old Age, cheeks marked by round grey patches of make-up and forehead seamed with false wrinkles, leaned forward like a hound on a scent, probing down this very path which they had chosen as a way to safety.

They clung together, hesitating far too long. If they had run at once, clean across between the instruments to the other side of the garden, they could have got back to the gate unobserved. Even if they had withdrawn a few yards farther into cover, hiding among the gardeners' delicately concealed tools and compost, they might have escaped his notice. But they were at the end of their resources, and having waited too long, they took hands and ran, across the gigantic approach to the gnomon, there to hesitate again in the shelter of the stone walls, waiting to see him pass them on the path he had chosen. He did not pass. He had seen them flash across the open in their unmistakable blue and white, and had lingered slyly under the sheer face of the tower, edging his way round to the other side, from which they would not be expecting him.

Aware of their nakedness, they had stopped to creep into the first steps of the great staircase, hoping to be hidden from either side. It was the worst thing they could have done. Suddenly he was there, not ten yards away from them, poised to intercept them whichever way they ran; and in order to run at all they had first to break free from the low, containing walls, for they were crouching some few steps from the ground.

Reason no longer had any part in what they did. There was only one way they could retreat from him and remain out of reach, and there was no power left in either of them to reckon for how long. Every moment free of his grasp counted. They bargained only for that, seconds of freedom; beyond there was nothing certain. As he lurched towards the foot of the staircase they scrambled to their feet and ran from him, frantically, frenziedly, up the steps with all the breath and all the muscular force they had, utterly reckless of things which in any other circumstances would have halted them with horror. There was just room for two people to pass on those steps. The walls at the sides scarcely reached their knees. The gradient, though of this they had no idea, was approximately one in two. Below, there was nothing but hot white concrete waiting to receive them. They looked up, and nowhere else. Nothing else was possible. There was not a single person moving, up or down, on all those white steps, except themselves. There was no one warily circling the stone drum on the summit. There was no one left in the world but themselves, and the man who had begun, with hideous leisureliness, to follow them up the gnomon.

There was no railing, there on the top. Thousands of unsuspecting children climbed these stairs every year, how many played too confidingly around the stone drum on the top? It was nearly as tall as a man, taller than these two girls. Parents might lose sight of their daring offspring, it needed only a little scuffle – children have no idea of danger. How thoughtful of them, how thoughtful, to provide this way out! One of them or both, what did it matter? If the vital one went, the other would be too terrified to cause any further trouble. She was, after all, his elder brother's posthumous daughter. And she had no money, no allies, no power . . . not like the other one. No, let Amrita keep her if it worked out that way. Why not? Neither of them would ever dare to point a finger at him. As for him, that other, how easy to give orders and sit back and stay immune! Let him do what he liked, he had no weapons that would not turn against himself. Next time let him do his own dirty work, and find his way out of his own traps. This was the last time Govind Das meant to carry another man's burden!

And no one following up here. No one. Perfect!

He might have to carry Shantila down the steps. No matter, she would not be any trouble, once the other was gone. That one, with her fine clothes, and her confidence, and her way of looking that was not Indian, not Western, but something between, something unique, a manner all her own, native and strange – everywhere native, everywhere strange. He wondered about that parentage of hers. He had never seen her sire. That had been a weakness, for surely she was her father's daughter.

They were slowing now, blown and aching from the long, steep climb. Take it easily now, there must be no violent action to be seen on the skyline here, nothing but gentleness, nothing but family affection suddenly ruptured by tragedy. He could not look down now, he was too high. Fifty feet can seem so much more, without a handrail, with only two feet of level ground between you and space. Slowly, step by step, there was no haste, since there was no way out.

On the last few stairs they were reeling and fumbling with exhaustion, and the man was only a few steps behind. Anjli groped her way ahead, one hand reaching back for Shantila's hand, but often missing it, sweat running down into her eyebrows and lashes, stinging her lips, sickening her. Only to put that stone cone between herself and her enemy, even if there was nothing to hold by, and no way of evading him in the end. Her cleanness, her personality, depended on eluding his touch. There were no other ambitions left to her.

She saw as in a dream the marvellous panorama of Jai Singh's vision from this altitude, and the quiet stretch of Parliament Street outside the wall, beyond the silvery palms. She saw the ripe, rosy fruit at her feet, hemmed with flowers, and the mysterious castle towers behind, spinning on their white central columns, dovecotes for stars. Then, only just behind her, she heard Shantila stumble and fall, clinging to the edge of the step, sobbing with frustration. She turned, reaching to help her up; and past the little heaving body her enemy stepped triumphantly, a hand already reaching out for her.

Shantila saw in the corner of her eye the deliberate foot climbing past her, saw it poised to touch the step above, saw the confident, greedy hand extended. With all the strength she had left she clenched both her hands in the string of her necklace, and tugged the cord apart. A sharp stab of pain seared her throat, beads of blood sprang along the wound and spilled among the Scottish beads. The pebbles from the Cairngorms spurted and danced across the white steps, bouncing, twirling, hard and round and adamant, merry as marbles in a game and double as dangerous. She heard them ring tiny, hard, gay notes of music, cannoning off one another, diverting one another, filling the whole width of the staircase with the irresponsible gaiety of murder. She actually saw Govind Das set his foot squarely upon no less than three of them. But it was the easy leaning forward, the disarrangement of his weight, which actually disposed of him.

The beads rolled, seeking a way downwards, safe enough in any fall. They spilled him forward on his face; his feet went out from under him, and the hand reaching confidently for Anjli's arm missed by inches, and groped helplessly upon the air, baulked of any resting place. He tried to swing his weight and recover his balance, and the only effect was to turn him towards the abyss from which he had climbed, and fling him face-forwards into it. He hurtled past Shantila on the downward road, and she saw his face intent, puzzled, hopeful, still wrestling for balance and incontinent after life, a young man's face incredulous of disaster, certain of salvation. But afraid, afraid, inhumanly afraid! Shantila was fortunate, for she had no terms in which to describe what she had seen, and no one was ever going to demand of her that she should find words for it. It is possible to forget what you have never formulated.

As for Anjli, she never saw it. All she saw was the beads rolling, the foot betrayed, the balance lost, and all this in a moment of time. She stood frozen, unable to withdraw from the hand which nevertheless failed utterly to touch her. From stair to stair, derisively, the Cairngorm pebbles rolled inviolable, skittishly evading every attempt Govind Das made to recover his equilibrium. From stair to stair they bounced happily, like water seeking their own level, oblivious of the plunging, lurching feet that fought in vain for a firm foothold. And after a moment he outran his destroyers, lunging, falling, leaping endlessly downwards, first running, then rolling, then bouncing like a thrown ball, then tossed like a rag-doll, arms and legs flying, bones cracking, an inarticulate thing coursed interminably down the hundred feet of one-in-two slope towards the concrete ground which was the home level, the final goal.

Far down the long white slide the fore-shortened figure of a man had begun to climb after them. They saw him only now, and cried out together in alarm and despair, for how could he possibly evade the grotesque projectile that was hurtling down upon him? He had come too far up the steps to be able to retreat and leap out of the way. He threw himself down, flattened along the stairs with braced feet under the one bordering wall, an arm flung over the rim to anchor him. Nothing could now have arrested the flight of Govind Das. His flailing body struck the tensed bow of Girish's shoulders, and rebounded on the crest of the opposite wall, sliding helplessly down it for several feet before the uncontrolled weight dragged it over the edge, to fall with a dull half-liquid sound on the bone-white concrete below.

Girish took his head out of his arms, and levered himself up from the steps. There was no more sound from below, and no more movement.

'Be careful!' called Anjli's anxious voice from above him. 'The beads . . . on the stairs . . .'

Then he saw them, one by one gently trickling down towards their own level, unbruised, adamant, the coloured pebbles from the mountains at the other end of the world. He met and passed them on his way upwards, and gathered the ones that came most easily to hand, so that no one else should mount here and accidentally follow Govind Das to his death. But many eluded him, for all the real passion of his senses and his heart was fixed on the children. Slowly they crept down to meet him, Anjli in front, one hand stretched back to clasp the hand of her friend. She felt her way from step to step with the methodical movements of exhaustion, when you cannot afford a first mistake because it may well be your last. Her face was pale and clear, almost empty as yet because fear had so recently quitted it and left it virgin. Her eyes, immense, so bruised with experience that they might have been darkened with kohl in the native way, clung unwaveringly to his face.

They were above the midway mark when they met. Anjli took her hand gently from Shantila's hand, so that she could join her palms on her breast in the proper reverence.

'Namaste!'

He held out his arms, and she walked almost shyly into them, and he kissed her forehead. They came down the steps together all linked in a chain of three, Girish in front for a barrier against any fear they might still feel of lesser things, now that the great fear was gone, Anjli's right hand in his and her left hand in Shantila's. They came slowly, because none of them was in haste now, and none of them was free of the great, clouding lassitude of achievement that hung upon this denouement. They must have heard the voices below, they must have seen the curious gathering at last, too late to be helpful, in time to be in the way. From nowhere someone had conjured two police officers. Through the gates an ambulance was driving. It had failed to find a victim upon the scene of the road accident in Parliament Street, but it would not go back empty-handed from here.

And there were other faces, faces Anjli knew well and some she did not know, but clearly all united in this moment, gathering there at the foot of the steps to welcome her back among them. Dominic, and Tossa, and Mr Felder, all radiant with relief, and an elderly, ascetic gentleman with a saffron robe and a shaven skull and lop-sided spectacles, gently beaming in the background, and an immaculate person in exclusive tailoring, who by his contented smile was clearly also a member of the alliance. She had never realised she had so many friends here. Find one, and you have the key to many more.

Anjli stepped upon solid ground, and her knees trembled under her. The ambulance men were just picking up and screening from sight all that was left of Govind Das.

Twelve

There were nine of them present in Dominic's hotel sitting-room over coffee that night. The promise made to Ashok had been no vain one, after all; he came straight from a recording session, his head still full of music, to find Anjli, in her own western clothes and with her normal poise rather enhanced than impaired, seated dutifully between Dominic and Tossa, and apparently totally engrossed in pouring coffee for their guests. The Swami Premanathanand sat cross-legged and serene at one end of the cushioned settee, with his driver Girish balancing him at the other end, a silent man with a faint smile and a grazed face, one profile beautiful in a falcon's fashion, the other marred. Felder lay relaxed in a reclining chair, after days of tension. And the last-comers, or so it appeared, surprised everyone, except the Swami, who was not subject to surprise. For Satyavan Kumar did not come alone, but brought with him Kamala, fresh from the expensive salon of Roy and James with her glossy pyramid of black hair heady as a bush of jasmine, and her superb body swathed in a new sari of a miraculous muted shade between lilac and rose and peach. She kissed Anjli, with so serene an implication of divine right that Anjli took no offence, fluttered her fingers at Ashok, and said: 'Darling!' The simplest chair in the room became a throne when she sat in it. 'I should be apologising,' she said, smiling at Dominic, 'I wasn't specifically invited. But I wanted to celebrate, too. I hope you don't mind?'

'I am afraid,' said the Swami, looking modestly down his nose, 'that some of us here are not as well informed about the nature of this - celebration - as the rest. Perhaps first I should explain exactly what has been happening during the last few days.' And he did so, with such admirable brevity that he was done before anyone had breath to comment or question. 'The only apology, perhaps, is due to you, Mr Kabir. You must forgive your young friend here, it was at my suggestion that he refrained from telling you the truth yesterday. We have not met before, but by sight and by reputation, of course, I know you well, and I assure you it was not from any doubts about you that I excluded you from our counsels. I had a respectable reason, which perhaps will appear later. The invitation to you to join us here tonight was a promise, which you see we have managed to fulfil. I hope it may be taken also as an apology in advance.'

'No one owes me any,' said Ashok. He looked at Anjli, and his sensitive, mobile face pondered in silence the changes in her. 'If this thing had happened, all of us who knew of Anjli's background were suspect. How could I be exempt? You say that Dominic heard and recognised my music . . . Kamala's lullaby. Where else should you look, then, but among those of us who knew that music? And we were not so many.'

'Not so many,' agreed the Swami. 'And most of them like Mr Felder here, were in Sarnath at the time of the kidnapping, as you were in Trivandrum, though we did not then know that.'

'*I* was in Delhi,' Kamala said helpfully. 'Yashodhara doesn't appear in the Deer Park scenes. None of the women do. And Subhash Ghose was here, too, and . . .'

'And Govind Das,' concluded Felder ruefully.

There was a small, flat silence. 'We hadn't realised,' said Dominic then, 'how many might be left in town. We thought the whole company had moved to Benares. Of course we thought first of the company, but filming in Sarnath seemed to put you all out of the picture. And yet I was always quite certain about Ashok's morning raga. I knew what I'd heard. I'll admit there were times when we didn't know whom we could trust, or even whether we could trust anybody . . . even the Swami here. Even you . . .' He looked up across the room at the two handsome, smiling people sitting comfortably side by side there, with an almost domestic ease and felicity. 'Last night, Mr Kumar, after you left, Tossa and I were walking round by Claridge's. We saw you leaving together by taxi . . .'

Ashok's eyebrows had soared into his hair. '*Kumar*?' he said half-aloud, astonished and mystified.

Kamala laughed gently. 'Yes, I see that we made difficulties for you. After all these years we still prefer to dine together when we can. Krishan is a serious character actor, I am, let's face it, a fashionable star. Never in our whole married life have we been able to play together in the same film. We are both contrasuggestible. The whole pressure of our work drives us apart. That is why we spend all the time left to us together.'

'Krishan?' Dominic said, confounded.

'*Married* life?' repeated Felder, slowly sitting upright in his chair. 'I didn't even know you *were* married . . .'

'No, darling, of course you didn't. We have a theory. The least publicised marriages are the most durable ones, and we happen to like being married to each other. And after all, you've known me only a little while, and only as one of a company at work.'

'But to *Kumar* here . . .?'

'Oh, no darling, not *Kumar*. How confused you are, I'm so sorry I'm not making myself clear. No, my husband is Krishan Malenkar, and if I may say so, a very good actor indeed. If you should ever be casting a film with an Indian business background, the Swami tells me he made a most appealing, as well as convincing tycoon.'

'But if *he*'s not Kumar,' persisted Felder feverishly, 'then *who is*?'

Anjli looked all round the ring of astonished faces, and suddenly rose from her place, unable any longer to subdue the blaze of joy and achievement that shone out of her. She crossed the room to where Girish sat, and put a hand possessively on his shoulder, and he smiled and drew her down beside him.

'*This* is my father,' she said proudly, as if she found it incomprehensible that they could ever have been in doubt. 'I knew him as soon as I saw him driving after us. I knew he would come for me.'

All eyes had turned upon the Swami. 'But *why*?' demanded Felder on behalf of them all. 'Why was it necessary to conceal the fact that her father was right here with you? I don't understand what sense it makes.'

'Oh, come!' protested the Swami mildly. 'You do yourself less than justice, Mr Felder, I'm sure. It cannot be so difficult to see a good reason for suppressing Satyavan's identity, since circumstances made it possible. I did not then know which of you, if any, could be trusted. Satyavan, since he left home, had indeed been a law unto himself, and like everyone else, I have seldom known for long where he could be found; but at various times he has been working in several of the Mission's projects, and from time to time I have been in touch with him. At the time of his mother's death I had

313

no idea where to find him, and he did not read the papers regularly, and only learned of her death too late to be present at her funeral rites. As soon as he did hear, he came. To me! We drove together to his house, it was his intention to begin at once to set his affairs in order. You,' he said, turning his mild, bright eyes upon Dominic and Tossa, 'know what we heard and saw when we came to Rabindar Nagar. Should I then have produced him and named him to you, whom we did not know, you, who had been in charge of the child and might be involved in her abduction? No! It was the strength of Satyavan's position that he had not been seen in Rabindar Nagar for more than a year, that many of his neighbours were new, that he returned now straight from the field, not a Delhi businessman but weather-beaten and dressed for work, and driving the Mission car . . . He wished to remain in the background, unknown and free to move as he would, for it was *his* daughter who was at risk. From that moment, therefore, we watched you in everything you did, and equally all those who had contact with you. It seemed that any demands for ransom must come through you, and so it turned out. And after the first payment failed to produce Anjli, I judged it necessary to provide another father, a convincing father of the right type, and to have him emerge into the limelight and take charge.'

'But why?' insisted Felder. 'I still don't see the purpose of it.'

'Oh, a very specific purpose. His job was to insist on seeing Anjli alive before more money was paid. For, you see, until then we had no means whatever of being sure that she had not been killed. Yes, yes, Mr Felder, you were horrified at the suggestion, I know, nevertheless it is common form in these cases. But when my good friend Malenkar played his scene, insisted on seeing with his own eyes – and incidentally with ours, too! – that she still lived, *and when there was no demur*, then we had a certain degree of security. A fairly substantial degree, in fact. Enough to make plans. For Satyavan, apparently a servant, and therefore virtually invisible, was free to observe and to act. On his behalf no one ever made any bargains. These are my reasons for acting as I did. Was it well done?'

'*Yes*!' said Dominic and Tossa together fervently. '*Very* well done!'

'And that is why I could not let Mr Kabir come upstairs and join us here last night. I cannot say whether he actually knows Satyavan by sight, though I thought it a possibility. But I *did* know that he is very well acquainted with Malenkar, and would most probably have given the show away on the spot.'

'*To which one of us*?' Dominic asked very gently.

The Swami's mild eyes sharpened upon him almost alarmingly, if there had not been in the brief, brilliant glance a suggestion of distinct approval.

'Ah, I did not then know of the activities of Govind Das. I was still acting on the assumption that the director of the affair might be any one of you. It seems now that the whole thing was planned and carried out by this one man.'

'A bad business,' said Felder soberly.

'As you say, a bad business. It turned out so for him.'

'Small part actors don't make much money. Probably here they don't get to many parts, either. Or anywhere, for that matter, these days. I suppose seeing temptation trailed in front of his nose like that was too much for him – the daughter of a millionaire and a film star, and only two students new to India taking care of her. It must have looked easy! Well, thank goodness it's over! The poor wretch who planned and did it is dead. He's paid. That's the end of it.'

A long, communicated sigh went round the room, and subsided into a deep and thoughtful silence.

'Except,' said Anjli suddenly, erect and sombre by her father's side, '*if* he did it all alone, why did Shantila say *they'd told him* not to hurt me? That's what she said. Tomorrow you can ask her.'

A curious flutter of uneasiness stirred the air.

'And *if* he did it all alone,' Dominic said slowly, 'then he must be a genius, to be able to come up with that scheme about lunch at Sawyers' and a taxi to the sweet shop opposite, the very minute he was faced with having to arrange a way of letting us see Anjli. Now if he'd already been primed by somebody who *knew* what was going to happen . . .'

'And what,' wondered Tossa, 'if he *did* do it all alone, what has he done with the money from the first payment we made at the Birla temple? Because you know what the police said – they haven't found a trace of it at his house or in his sister-in-law's quarters at the office.'

'And if it wasn't he who took the money from the briefcase,' supplemented the Swami, warming to the theme, 'then who was it? And where is it now? It would be so much more satisfactory, would it not, to recover it? Even film stars who *do* make a great deal of money should not be made the victims of extortion.'

'They certainly shouldn't,' agreed Felder warmly. 'I've still got to justify that to Dorrie, but at least she still has a daughter, thank God. It does seem a pity, but it hardly looks as if we'll ever see that money again.'

'Oh, do not lose heart,' the Swami encouraged him benignly. 'Perhaps, after all, there is still hope that the police may discover it somewhere.'

'Well, if they do, presumably there may be some hope of deducing how it got there. Until then I'm afraid we haven't much chance.'

And indeed it seemed that it was over, and that there was no longer anything to hold them all here together; yet no one made any move to go. It was almost as if they were waiting for something to happen which would release them and let them fly apart again into their proper orbits, Dominic and Tossa, tired, relieved and infinitely grateful, back to England, the Swami to the minute office from which he pulled so many valiant and unexpected strings in the life of unprivileged India, Krishan Malenkar and his Kamala to their well-guarded private life, Anjli wherever her new father led her, deeper and deeper into the complex soul of this sub-continent, Ashok back to the cosmic solitude where the great artists create their own companions, like self-generating gods; and Felder . . .

Someone rapped at the door, briskly, quietly and with absolute authority.

'Come in!' called Dominic.

Inspector Kulbir Singh came in with aplomb. His black beard was tucked snugly into its retaining net, his moustache was immaculately waxed at the ends, which turned up in military fashion to touch his bold cheek-bones. In his hands – gloved hands – he held a large, fat bank envelope, linen-grained, biscuit-coloured. Every eye in the room fastened on it, and for an instant everyone held his breath.

'Ladies . . .Swami . . . gentleman, forgive this intrusion. There is a small matter of identification with which you can help me, if you will.' He came forward with assurance, and laid the envelope upon the coffee table, drawing out delicately wad after wad of notes. 'No, no, please do not touch. There is the question of finger prints. I would ask you only to look at this packet . . . you, Mr Felder, Mr Felse and

Miss Barber. The total amount, you may take my word, is two hundred thousand rupees, as you see in notes of various values. It is contained in an envelope of the State Bank of India, issued at the branch here in Parliament Street. Their stamp bears last Saturday's date. I must ask you if you can identify this package.'

They stood staring all three, alike stricken into silence. Dominic was the first to clear his throat. 'It looks very like the money Mr Felder drew from the bank, in my presence, on Saturday morning. The amount is right.'

'Miss Barber?'

'I wasn't at the bank. I saw the package the next day, when Mr Felder left it at the desk, downstairs. This one looks the same. I feel sure it is. There was a linen thread half an inch too long, projecting out of that left corner of the flap, just like that one. My prints should be on the envelope, if it's the same one. I collected it from the desk, and Dominic put it into the briefcase.'

'Thank you, that is very helpful. Mr Felder? Does it appear the same to you?'

'I can't be sure. One bank envelope is very like another. It could be the same.'

'Even to the amount inside it, Mr Felder?'

'I've said, it could be the same.'

'In that case your prints should also be on the envelope, I take it, since you handled it.'

'Yes, certainly I did. I kept it safe until I delivered it to this hotel on Sunday morning.'

'But you would not expect your prints also to be on the notes?'

'Of course not, why should they be? I took the package from the bank teller intact, and as you know, it was paid over to Miss Kumar's kidnapper at the Birla temple on Sunday afternoon.' He raised his head, and stared Inspector Singh stonily in the eyes. 'Where did you find it?'

'In a locked suitcase in a room in the Villa Lakshmi at Hauz Khas, Mr Felder – the bedroom occupied by you.'

Felder drew back from him a long pace; all the deep, easy-going lines of his face had sagged into grey pallor.

'You know what this is, don't you? A plant to leave me holding the baby. Yes, I drew the money, yes, I handled the parcel, that you know already from all of us, what have I got to deny? We paid that money over at the temple, as we were told to do. There was a parcel of sliced-up newsprint left in its place, and that we've told you, too, it isn't any secret. But if you think I made that exchange, think again. Kumar here was watching me all that afternoon. He knows I never went near the place where the briefcase was.' He swung on Satyavan, who sat unmoved, his arm round his daughter, his grazed cheek seamed with darkening scars beneath the levelled black eye. 'Tell him! You were watching me as I was watching the briefcase. You came and started talking to me, and that cost us – how many minutes? Three? Enough for the exchange to be made. I wasn't watching during those few minutes, and neither were you.'

'That is true, Inspector,' said Satyavan. 'I spoke to him. For perhaps as long as three minutes he was not watching the case, and neither was I.'

'*But I was,*' said the Swami's voice, with infinite gentleness and absolute certainty.

Everyone turned, almost cautiously, as though he might vanish if they were too abrupt. He sat relaxed and tranquil, his face fixed in a slight and rueful smile, and all the reflected light in the room had gathered in a highlight on his golden shoulder, like a lantern set in the protruding bone.

'Yes, I, too, was present. Satyavan and I had been following your movements and those of these young people ever since the murder and the abduction of the child. Satyavan came and spoke to you because he believed you had noticed him, and suspected his interest in you. But as it appeared, his approach was welcome and useful to you. Yes! But all that time I was sitting in meditation on the terrace of the temple. No one finds it strange that such as I should sit and meditate, even for long periods, even upon something so mundane as a briefcase and two pairs of shoes. No, it is perfectly true, you did not go near them in all that time. That I confirm. *But neither did anyone else!*'

The silence waited and grew, allowing them time to grasp that and understand what it meant.

'From the moment when this boy placed it there to the moment when he took it up again, no one touched it. Therefore it was, when placed, exactly as it was when removed, filled only with newsprint. The ransom – the first ransom – had been collected in advance. By you! Miss Lester would have repaid it to the company without a qualm, would she not, since it was employed in her daughter's interest?'

Felder opened his dry lips, and tried to speak, but made no sound.

'Even film directors, Mr Felder, do not always make enough money for their needs, and cannot resist temptation when it walks across their path. It is a question rather of the moderation and control of one's needs. Of the conquest of desire. But your desires were clearly immoderate. Therefore, when you could not resist retaining Anjli in the hope of further easy gain, we placed before you the bait of a second and greater ransom, to discover whether she was still safe, and to ensure that you would keep her so.'

'What do you take me for?' Felder had found his voice now, it burst out full and strong with genuine indignation. 'I wouldn't have hurt a hair of her head. I always meant to give her back safe and sound. What do you think I am? I may have needed money, I may have taken short cuts, but Dorrie's girl wasn't expendable.

'No,' agreed the Swami, with deep sadness. 'No, the half-American child, *your friend's* child, was not expendable to you. You gave your accomplice his orders to keep her safe, not to hurt her . . .of course, you are a humane man, you did not kidnap or kill – *not in the first person, only by proxy*. When you hired him, did you ask him how he meant to carry out his coup? Did you tell him, no violence to anyone? No, you shut your ears and left it to him. He was paid, was he not? A wisp of Indian dust, an old, decrepit creature, a beggar, hardly a man at all to you – *Arjun Baba was expendable*!

'Let us, however, be realistic,' observed the Swami, breaking the long silence which had descended on the room after Ernest Felder had been taken away. 'He cannot be charged with the murder of Arjun Baba. Quite certainly he did not commit that crime himself, and with Govind Das dead it will be almost impossible to prove that it arose as a direct result of the conspiracy Felder inspired. Indeed, I doubt if they will ever be able to charge him with the abduction, unless he is foolish enough to repeat the virtual confession we have just heard. Govind Das cannot convict him, and I doubt if Mrs Das ever so much as heard his name mentioned. Probably the only charge they can hope to bring home is of the misappropriation of that company money.'

'There is also something to be said,' Satyavan said softly, 'even for Felder.' Anjli's eyes were drooping into sleep, and her head was heavy on his shoulder. 'My wife was indebted to him for all her early chances in films. He is not the only one of whom she has made use when it suited her, and forgotten for years in between, but perhaps he was the most complaisant. If she wanted to send Anjli here to me, it would be quite natural to her to look round and see who might be useful to her in the matter. Ernest is filming in Delhi? How convenient! Of course, get him to meet the party and do whatever is necessary. He always had complied, why should he let her down now? She is now much more successful, much more wealthy than he, but she still asks, and he still complies. She put the opportunity into his hands, perhaps even the temptation into his mind. It may well have seemed to him that she owed him far more than he meant to extort from her. And am I not partially guilty? I do not believe he decided to act until I failed to come to the aid of both my mother and my child, and left her an easy prey. It's too deep for me. Maybe justice will have to find its own way to every one of us in its own time. I have no doubt it will arrive in the end.'

'It has caught up already,' said Ashok gently, 'with you.' And he caught the drowsy eye Anjli had just re-opened, and made a faun's face at her. 'Have you forgotten? When Yashodhara bore a child, the Lord Buddha cried: "It must be named Rahula. For a fetter is fastened upon me this day!" '

'I shall call you Rahula,' said Satyavan, tightening his arm about his daughter, 'when you most tyrannise over me.'

Anjli smoothed her cheek against his shoulder like a kitten, and smiled. 'Rahula was a boy. Girls are different. The Lord Buddha should have had a girl.' She looked up at him, suddenly grave and momentarily wide-awake. 'What will happen to Shantila's mother? She was good to me. As good as she dared be.'

'Be easy, my Rahula! No charge will ever be made against Mrs Das with my support. If she had not had a daughter, I should now have been searching in vain for mine.'

'And Shantila?'

'Shantila is your sister, and therefore my child. We must find a safe job for the mother, and she shall be always with you, if you want her.'

'Yes, please, I do want her. We ought to buy her another necklace,' she said indistinctly, 'in place of the one she broke.'

'That is very true,' he said, drawing her more securely into his arm, for she was half asleep. 'Remind me!' He looked up over her head at Dominic and Tossa, and said in a glowing whisper: 'It is late, I shall take her away with me. But tomorrow, wait for us, we shall come to fetch you to Rabindar Nagar.'

They protested dutifully that their job was done now, that they must make their preparations for going home.

'Not yet, not until you must. You will be her guests, she will be happy harrying Kishan Singh to make everything ready for you. Do you not see that my mother Purnima left a true Indian matriarch to be her heiress? I have resigned my life to this creature.' By then she was fast asleep in his arms. 'Ashok, I must warn you, for I see that she may well demand that I propose a match with you – she will have no dowry, she has been urging me to give away everything I have.'

It was past midnight, and they had hardly marked the hours slipping by. When they went out by the balcony to the garden stairs, the stars were lacquered in thick coruscations over the velvet Delhi sky, and there was the shimmer and purity of frost in the air. One by one, a procession massed reverently about Anjli asleep on her father's shoulder, they went down the white steps, and issued with shadows for sails upon the white, paved ocean of the patio.

'At this same hour, I think,' said Satyavan, whispering over his daughter's head, 'I got up in Rabindar Nagar, and found, like the Lord Buddha himself, that the gods had filled the universe with the thought that it was time to go forth.'

'Where?' asked Dominic, hypnotised.

'That is of secondary importance. What matters is to leave what has always been, and look for what has never been yet. I had had riches and marriage and a child, and I had nothing. Nothing is not enough for any man. The only answer is to abandon that nothing, and go in search of something. A different kind of treasure, perhaps. A different kind of salvation. Perhaps not salvation at all, only the loss of oneself.'

'What will you do now?'

'My cousin – you hardly know him – he is a good fellow, he will enjoy living in my mother's house and managing my mother's companies. He will make money, but not want to keep it. As for me, in the past year I have become half a soil scientist and half a stock-breeder. What this Rahula of mine will become I cannot yet guess. I told you, she is encouraging me to put everything I have into the missions.

Nobody knows yet what *she* has to put into them. I am
afraid it may be more than I can command. We have a
whole sub-continent to grow into, she and I. Tomorrow,'
he said, with deep content, 'you will come and join us.'

'No – you've only just discovered each other—'

'We have a lifetime,' said Satyavan, breathing in the night,
'and you have return tickets valid for weeks yet. When does
your new term begin?'

'Come,' said the Swami, waiting by the door of the Rolls,
'would you like me to drive you?'

Just now the stars must be nesting in the niches of the
magic towers at the Jantar Mantar, like doves coming home
to their cotes.

'Good night!' whispered Malenkar, holding the door of
their car for his wife.

'Good bye!' breathed Kamala. 'Ashok, can we give you a
lift?'

'I'll send you a recording of the music,' promised Ashok,
and touched the butterfly ribbon of Anjli's plait as her father
lifted her gently into the Rolls, among the grain-sacks and
the experimental feed. She had everything in the world she
wanted, and she was never going to look back.

'Tomorrow . . .ten o'clock!' whispered Satyavan.

The Malenkar Mercedes drew away first, the lofty Rolls
proceeding majestically after. The two of them were left alone
in the silence bone-white with moonlight. The unuttered notes
floated silently across the pale space and nested in the tall
hedge behind which the cars had vanished.

'Raga Aheer Bhairab,' said Tossa in the softest of
undertones. 'To be played in the early hours of the
morning . . .'

' . . .when the guests are departing . . .'

Death
to the Landlords!

Prologue

On the Road to Thekady: Saturday Evening

The sadhu sat just within the shadow of the trees at the left-hand bend of the road, not fifty yards from the mottled and overgrown wall of the forestry bungalow's green enclosure. The road from the plains up to the lake coiled through the belt of forest towards the crest of the hills in great, smooth serpentines, a polished steel-blue ribbon shading off to ash-grey at the edges, then to ochre, before it faded into the bleached grass on either side. At each sweeping curve the trees withdrew to leave ample space for the turns, and at every such stage there was some feature apparently carefully positioned to take advantage of the site thus provided. At the turn below, a fruit-stall glowing with oranges and jack-fruit and bananas. At the turn above, the gates of the drive that led to the forestry bungalow. At this left-hand turn between them, half-veiled by the long grass and the overhanging darkness of the branches, a six-foot column of rough stone, so old and worn that its carving had almost eroded away, leaving only the elusive shapes of arms and hands that seemed to appear and disappear as oblique shadows gave them form, and to vanish completely in too direct a light. There had been a face, flattened away now into a featureless oval, and the scratched indications of turbulent hair. From the hips down – there was the negligent thrust of a hip still to be seen in certain lights – he was coated with an accumulation of dust from the roadside, clinging fast to his old and infrequent baptisms of reverential oil. His feet – he stood firmly upon massive and unmistakable feet – still glistened, protected by the long grass, and a sprinkling of coloured dye, red and orange, spattered his insteps. There was even a handful of marigolds, a day old and withered, nestling at the foot of the stele. He might have been any one of the pantheon, except that the blunt, truncated shaft of stone a yard or two away, oiled and garlanded even here in this remote place, was recognisably the lingram of Siva.

There had been more masonry here at some time, perhaps a small shrine, but only the dressed stone platform of its floor remained, affording a small dais in the shade, on which the sadhu sat. He was lean and muscular, long in the torso, and he sat cross-legged, the dusty, pale soles of his feet upturned, the pinkish palms of his long hands cupped in his lap. A length of cotton cloth in the familiar ochreous peach colour was draped over his left shoulder and swathed about his hips, and several strings of carved wooden beads and coloured cords hung round his neck. Tangled, oily curls of hair hung over his temples and shadowed his face, and on the ash-smeared forehead between the snaky tresses were drawn three horizontal lines, a vertical oval seal of red colouring uniting the three in the centre; one of many sect marks worn by the devotees of Siva. He was the colour of bronze, and as motionless as bronze, and the ceaseless faint quivering of the thick leafage that shaded him cast greenish lights over his oiled skin, and made him look like metal rather than flesh. His eyes, lowered beneath ash-bleached lids and thick black brows, gazed somewhere deep into the earth at the edge of the road, and his face never moved. In front of him in the grass his wooden bowl rested, empty.

The Periyar Lake lies about two thousand five hundred feet up in the Western Ghats, and about a hundred and twenty miles from the toe of India, but the road up from Madurai crosses higher ground on the way to it, and the altitude somewhat delays the hawk-like swoop of the night that drops abruptly, with only the briefest of twilights. It was during the curious, hushed pause before the transformation from daylight to dark that the Land-Rover came humming briskly up the serpentines from the plain, rounded the bend beside which Siva and the sadhu kept watch, and turned in at the gates of the forestry bungalow. The sadhu moved never a muscle, and gave no indication of having seen or heard its passing, as deep in meditation as the forest behind him in silence.

A few minutes later two girls came walking up the road from the fruit-stall at the turn below, with their arms full of bananas and small, rough-skinned green oranges, the kind that are still green when they are fully ripe and sweet as honey. One of the pair was Indian, in a plain green and white sari and a white cotton blouse, with her black hair plaited and coiled in a great sheaf on her neck. The other, slim and small-boned and blonde, was English even at first glance, and had sensibly not tried to conceal the fact inside a sari. Nothing could have disguised that fair complexion, or the pale, straight hair that hung limply to her shoulders, framing an oval face. Instead, she had compromised by adopting plain black trousers, worn with a short-sleeved shirt-dress. They were hurrying, because they wanted to get back to the bungalow before the darkness fell completely, for here between the thick swathes of forest the night would be velvet-black, almost palpable.

They drew near to the sadhu, and he was as oblivious of them as of the Land-Rover a few moments ago. The fair girl, who had noticed and remarked on him as they walked down to the fruit-stall, peered curiously into the shadows as they passed, and caught the faint gleam of oil and bronze, motionless under the branches.

'He's still there. Do you suppose he stays there all night, too?'

'I doubt it. It will be cold in the small hours, up here. They come and go as they please, there are almost no rules.'

Priya had the detached tone and ambivalent attitude of the Indian towards self-styled holy men. The basic equipment needed for the profession is simple and inexpensive; only one item, the holiness, need cost a man very much, and though some undoubtedly insist on and achieve it, many more, perhaps the majority, manage to make do without it. There is no immediate way of distinguishing the one kind from the other.

Patti hesitated, looking back over her shoulder. 'Is the bowl there for money?'

'For any sort of alms,' said Priya, 'but preferably money.'

'A chance to acquire merit,' said Patti, a little sadly, a little cynically, making fun of herself but still looking over her shoulder. Suddenly she stopped. 'Wait for me a minute, will you? Here, hold these!' She dumped her load of fruit into Priya's arms and turned impetuously to dart back towards the shrine, groping as she went in the depths of the big shoulder-bag she carried. The jingle of small coins came back to Priya's ears, and the darkness lurched a little lower, sagging towards them from the tree-tops.

Patti stepped delicately into the dry, bleached grass, and the rustle of her footsteps should have reached the sadhu's ears even in a trance, but he gave no sign. She stooped towards his wooden bowl, and he did not raise his eyes or rear his head. She stared intently, but all she could distinguish now was the faintly luminous shadow of a man encased in deeper shadow, as motionless and impervious as the Siva beside him.

'*Namaste!*' she said, touching her hands momentarily together over her offering; and she laid it in his bowl, and drew back. She thought the head moved a little, in distant acknowledgement, but that was all. She turned away with a sense of disappointment, and ran to rejoin Priya and relieve her of her load.

'Not exactly effusive, are they? Still – just for luck! Who knows! He may remember me in his prayers at the right moment.'

They walked on together quickly, and the next curve of the road carried them away out of the sadhu's sight, and cut off the fresh, intrusive voices that rippled the silence.

He still had not moved or uttered a sound.

The night came down like curtains of black silk, filling the trough of the roadway between the trees with fold on fold of darkness.

One

Thekady: Saturday Evening

There were two cars already parked in front of the long, low, ochre-yellow bungalow when the Land-Rover wheeled into line beside the porch; and at sight of the first of them, the ancient, sky-blue Ford with the grazed door and the retouched wing, they all three uttered a hoot of recognition, at once derisive and appreciative.

'Here we go again!' said Larry Preisinger, switching off the engine. 'Didn't I say we would be running into the whole circus again before we reached the Cape? It's always the same. I drove this thing round Gujarat State, and the same folks I saw at the first halt haunted me all the way. Might skip an overnight stop here and there, hut give 'em a few days and they'd show up again. An Indian couple from South Africa with three kids, visiting the home country, a middle-aged pair from New Zealand doing the world by easy stages and two young Czechs draped with about four cameras each. Now we've got the French for a change.'

'We might do worse,' said Dominic Felse thoughtfully.

'Yeah, we might, at that!' On the whole, in a wary fashion, they had approved of the Bessancourts. He looked doubtfully at the second car, a big black saloon, battered but imposing, but it told him nothing about its incumbents. A tourist car, probably, hired out for the weekend with driver, from Madurai. 'Looks like we'll be camping tonight. With two car-loads they *must* be full up inside.' Not that he minded; they were well equipped, with light sleeping bags, and a mosquito net that rolled up into the roof when not in use. Three can manage without too much discomfort in a Land-Rover, given a little ingenuity, and he had provided the ingenuity before he ever set out on this marathon drive round India, picking up co-drivers for sections of the route wherever he could, for company and to share the expenses. Dominic, acquired in Madras and on leave from some farming job, was one of the luckiest breaks he'd had so far, around his own age, a congenial enough companion, a good driver, and prepared to stick with him as far as Cape Comorin, and probably all the way back to Madras, too.

Lakshman unfolded his slender length from among the baggage, and slid out of the Land-Rover. 'I will go and talk to the *khansama*.' He paused to look back and inquire, in his gentle, dutiful voice that balanced always so delicately between the intonations of friend and servant: 'If there are no beds, you would like at least food? It would be a change from my cooking.'

'It might be a change for the worse, but sure, let's risk it.'

Larry had been travelling with Lakshman Ray for nearly six weeks now, and had given up trying to get on to closer terms with him. Lakshman, whether he knew his place or not, certainly knew his employer's place, and firmly kept him there. With the greatest of deference, amiability and consideration, but implacably. He had done this sort of courier-interpreter job before, with other lone tourists, and had encountered, or so Larry judged, patrons with very different views on this relationship from those Larry himself held. Give him time, and he'd make any necessary adjustments himself; no sense in trying to rush him. Lakshman was the youngest of the three of them, barely twenty and still a student, until want of funds had driven him out to earn money for further study by such journeys as this. He had to get everything right, and he was taking no risks. Perhaps he didn't even want to slide unsuspectingly into a friendship for which he hadn't bargained. A cool young person, shy, soft-voiced, self-possessed and efficient, he spoke both Tamil and Malayalam in addition to his own Hindi, so he was equally effective in the north or the south. Sometimes, Larry suspected, Lakshman had difficulty in remembering to keep Dominic at the same distance as Larry himself; Dominic wasn't paying his wages.

The bungalow, seen by the glow from its own windows and the Land-Rover's side-lights, was a pleasant, solid building of brick and plaster, with a deep, arcaded porch, and looked big enough to house quite a number of travellers, if the usual tourist bedroom-cum-livingroom in India had not been about as big as a barn, and with its own bathroom or shower attached. Three such suites, say, plus the kitchen quarters, and there would be no room left. No matter, the Land-Rover was good enough.

Lakshman came back gesturing mildly from a distance, and shaking his head; and behind his back the *khansama* stuck out a bearded head in a loose cotton turban from the kitchen door to take a look at his latest guests.

'The place is quite full, but he will feed us. And there is a *chowkidar*.' The security of the bungalow's grounds and the protection of its watchman were not to be despised.

'Good, then how about borrowing a shower, before the proper tenants get to that stage?'

'It can be arranged.' He was looking from them to the anonymous black car, and his smile was less demure than usual. 'Do you know who is also here?'

His look and his tone said that they were hardly likely to thank him for the information, though it might enliven their stay in its own fashion. It was not often that Lakshman looked mischievous, and even now he had his features well in hand.

'Sure we know,' said Larry obtusely, his mind on his shower, '*madame la patronne* and her *mari*.'

Prompt on the close of his sentence, as if responding to a clue, a high, clacking voice screeched: 'Sushil Dastur! *Sushil Dastur*!' from an open window, in a rising shriek that could have been heard a mile into the forest; and light, obsequious footsteps slapped hurriedly along the hallway inside the open door to answer the summons.

'Oh, *no*!' groaned Larry. 'Not the Manis! So *that*'s the chauffeur-driven party, is it? We might have known! What did I tell you? Start touring anywhere you like, and within a hundred miles radius you keep seeing the same faces.'

'And hearing the same voices,' Dominic remarked ruefully. 'Poor little Sushil, he certainly hears plenty of that one. I wonder he stands it. And Bengali women *don't* usually squawk – they have soft, pleasant voices.'

'Not this one!' It was scolding volubly now in Bengali, somewhere within the house, punctuated by placating monosyllables from a man's voice, anxious, inured and resigned. 'Maybe he doesn't even listen, really, just makes the right sounds and shuts up his mind. Otherwise he'd go up the wall. And his boss is worse, if anything, even if he doesn't split the eardrums quite like his missus. Jobs must be hard to come by, or Sushil would have quit long ago.'

'I get the impression he is a relative,' Lakshman said with sympathy. 'Of the lady, perhaps – a poor cousin. And you are quite right, for a clerk with no paper qualification it is not at all easy to find a good post. And perhaps he is more comfortable with this one than we suppose. It is security of a kind.'

They had run into the Manis twice since leaving Madras, once briefly at Kancheepuram, plodding doggedly round that fantastic city's many temples, and once at an overnight stop at Tiruchirapalli, where Mr Mani had constituted himself chairman of the evening gathering of guests at the travellers' bungalow, and unfolded his and his wife's life story in impressive detail. They were from Calcutta, where they had several textile shops, and they had come south to Madras for the first time to visit their married daughter, whose husband ran a highly successful travel agency. Thus they had the best possible help and advice in planning an extended tour of the south of India. Ganesh had made all the arrangements, Ganesh had ensured that they should not miss one famous sight while they were here. They had certainly missed none in Tiruchi. They had been observed in the early morning, before the stone steps were too hot for comfort, toiling dauntlessly all up the exposed face of the rock, Mrs Mani with her elaborate sari kilted in both hands, and Sushil Dastur scurrying behind with her handbag, her husband's camera and the scarf she had dispensed with after the first morning chill passed; and again later taking pictures of the budding lotus in the temple tank below. And in the afternoon they had taken a taxi out to Srirangam, and toiled relentlessly round every inch of that tremendous temple, with very little in their faces to indicate what they thought of its stunning sculptures, or indeed whether they thought at all.

Mr Mani's name was Gopal Krishna, and he was a firm, thickset, compact person of perhaps fifty, smoothly golden-brown of face, with crisp greying hair and large, imperious eyes that fixed the listener like bolts shackling him to his chair. He was so clean-shaven that it was difficult to believe he ever grew any whiskers to shave, and so immaculate, whether in spotless cream silk suit or loose white cotton shirt and trousers, or even, occasionally, a dhoti, that he made everyone else around feel crumpled, angular and grubby. He walked ponderously and impressively; one thought of a small, lightweight but inordinately pompous elephant. His voice was mellifluous but pedantic; it acquired an edge only when it addressed Sishil Dastur.

Sudha Mani was softer, rounder and plumper than her husband, and some years younger, and to do her justice, she was a pretty woman, with her pale gold cheeks and huge, limpid eyes, and curled, crisp rosebud of a mouth. But the eyes stared almost aggressively, and the tightness of the rosebud never moved a degree nearer blooming; and when the petals did part, she squawked like a parrot. She wore beautiful, expensive saris and rather too much jewellery, all of it genuine; but everyone here put capital into gold and silver ornaments. And she wore flowers in the huge knot of black hair coiled on her neck, but the flowers never seemed to survive long.

From here they had heard all about her first grandchild, and her troubles with servants, and the extreme sensitivity of her temperament. And from Gopal Krishna all about the state of the textile business, and his own commercial astuteness and consequent wealth.

Only almost accidentally had they ever discovered more than his name about Sushil Dastur, who fetched and carried, ran errands, took dictation, conferred long-distance with the management of the Calcutta shops and generally did everything that needed doing and many things that didn't around the Mani menage. His name they couldn't help discovering within half an hour. 'Sushil Dastur!' echoed and re-echoed at ten minute intervals, and in varying tones of command, displeasure, reproach and menace, wherever the Manis pitched camp. Private secretary, clerk, general factotum, travelling servant, he was everything in one undersized, anxious body.

In reality Sushil Dastur was not by any means so fragile as at first he appeared, but he was short, and seemed shorter because he was always hurrying somewhere, head-down, on his master's business; and the amount of prominent bone that showed in his jutting brow and slightly hooked nose contrasted strongly with the plump smoothness of the Manis, making him look almost emaciated. His brow was usually knotted in a worried frown above his large, apprehensive dark eyes, and his manner was chronically apologetic. Curly dark hair grew low on his forehead. Subservience had so far declassed and denatured him that it seemed appropriate he should always wear nondescript European jackets and trousers of no special cut, in a self-effacing beige colour. On the rare occasions when he appeared in an *achkan* he looked a different person.

'Looks like being old home week, all right,' Larry remarked glumly. For nothing was more certain than that all these people would be heading for the Periyar Lake in time for the early watering the next morning. There was nowhere else for them to be going in these parts. From the coast as from Madurai, from the west as from the east, the roads merely led here and crossed here; and few people passed by without halting at the lake to go out by boat and watch elephants. Other game, too, with luck, sambur, deer, wild boar, occasionally even leopard and tiger, though these last two rarely appeared; but above all, elephants, which never failed to appear, and in considerable numbers. 'You know, without wanting to seem intolerant, I'd enjoy my cruise more without the Mani commentary.'

'We could have a small private boat, if you wish,' said Lakshman tentatively. 'But it would cost more, of course.'

'Could we?' Larry perceptibly brightened. 'They have small launches there, too?' He looked at Dominic. 'How about it? We've stuck to our shoe-string arrangements so far, what about plunging for once?'

'I'm willing. Why not?'

'I'll go and telephone, if you really wish it,' offered Lakshman. 'It would be better to make sure.'

'Yes, do that! Let's indulge ourselves.'

The advantage, perhaps, of being a shoe-string traveller, is that you can, on occasion, break out of the pattern where it best pleases you, and do something unusually extravagant. The thought of having a boat to themselves, and all the huge complex of bays and inlets of the lake in which to lose the other launches, was curiously pleasing. Even on a popular Sunday they might be able to convince themselves that they were the only game-spotters in the whole sanctuary. Dominic was whistling as he reached into the back of the Land-Rover for his towels and washing tackle.

It was at that moment that the two clear, female voices began to approach through the darkness from the direction of the gate, and there emerged into the light from the windows two girls, one Indian and dark, one English and pallidly fair, carrying nets of green oranges and bunches of rose-coloured bananas in their arms.

Two pairs of eyes, one pair purple-black, one zircon blue, took in the Land-Rover and its attendant figures in a long, bright, intelligent stare.

'Well, hullo!' said the fair girl, in the bracing social tone of one privately totting up the odds. 'You must be the outfit that passed us just down the road, when we were haggling for this lot. Staying over? I thought they were full up.'

'They are,' said Dominic. By this time he was well aware that Larry never responded to any overtures, especially from females, until he had had the time to adjust, and to review his defences. Some girl must once have done something pretty mean to him, and all others had better step delicately. 'We sleep out in the moke. But yes, we're staying.'

'We came up by the bus. No use going on to the hotel, until tomorrow, anyhow,' she said simply. 'We couldn't afford to stay here, and it was too late for this afternoon's cruise when we got here. I suppose you'll be heading for the lake tomorrow morning?' Her eyes flickered thoughtfully towards the Land-Rover again; he didn't blame her for taking thought for the morrow, public transport was liable to be both unreliable and, on a Sunday, overcrowded. But she didn't ask, not yet. It was too early, and she wasn't going to be as crude as all that. As for the Indian girl, she stood a little apart, cool and still, watching them with a thoughtful and unsmiling face.

'So will everyone around, I imagine,' Larry said cautiously.

'You're American, aren't you?' she said, interested.

'That's right. My name's Preisinger, and this is Dominic Felse – he's English. As I think you must be.'

'Not much good trying to hide it, is it?' She shook her pale locks and laughed. 'I'm Patti Galloway, and this is my friend Priya Madhavan. If I had the colouring I'd like to sink myself into the background, and all that, but I decided long ago that it was no good. Priya's from Nagarcoil, we're making our way there gradually, and taking in the sights on the way. Where are you heading?'

'Oh, south. Down to the Cape, and then by Trivandrum and Cochin back to Madras. Dominic drops off at Madras. After that I don't know yet.'

Her eyes had opened wide. 'You must have a lot of time to spare. What do you do? Have you been working here? Or do you live here all the time?' She was restlessly full of questions, but there was something artless and disarming about her directness; and if it was disconcerting that she waited for no answers, at least that gave Larry time to make up his mind. Why not, after all? Lakshman was just coming out from the arcaded porch with a slight, contented smile that said he had been successful, and there would be a private boat for them tomorrow. And the girls had their own plans, which apparently involved the family of one partner, and therefore were hardly likely to be changed as the result of a chance meeting like this. He could afford to be generous without any risk of getting in too deeply.

'We were just going to sneak in and cadge a shower, as a matter of fact, before eating. If you two are on your own, and would care to join us, we should have a boat of our own for tomorrow morning. Why don't we eat together and fix everything up over the meal?'

The furniture of the bungalow's public room was of the simplest, but there were two tables, chairs enough and electric lighting that flickered alarmingly at times, but survived; and the *khansama*'s omelettes were good, and the fruit from the stall fresh and excellent. Since the tables were of the same size, it was natural to break up the guests into two equal parties of five; and that made it easy for the first on the scene – and inevitably that was Lakshman – to appropriate one of them for his employer's party and his employer's guests. Whether he approved of the addition of the girls to their number there was no way of knowing; his manners, as always, were graceful and correct.

Patti watched the other parties assemble with wide-eyed curiosity. Sudha Mani swept in wreathed in a nylon sari ('Not at all practical,' Priya said critically, 'synthetics slip terribly, and don't drape like live fabrics.') and a great many rather fine bracelets, forgot her handbag, and sent Sushil Dastur scurrying off to fetch it. Her husband was to be heard deploring in English, presumably for the benefit of the foreigners, the economic policies of the Indian government, and the burdens under which business suffered, but he ended, as usual, with the shortcomings of labour. And even this subject came down, inevitably, from the general to the particular, for it seemed there was a letter which Sushil Dastur should have written and dispatched, and had not, and a valuable order might be jeopardised as a result.

'If I do not supervise everything myself, nothing is ever done properly. Employees nowadays do not concentrate, they have no wish to work, only to pass the day and be paid. I was trained in the old school, hard I had to work, and by hard work I built up the business I have now.'

The Bessancourts spoke English reasonably well, a virtual necessity for other European tourists in India; and to judge by the conversation, they too had encountered the Manis previously in their travels, for the note of greeting was personal, even cordial. A familiar face in a strange land is a familiar face, and welcome, at least until you find yourself seeing altogether too much of it. Dominic could not imagine the Bessancourts and the Manis having much in common, or choosing to spend too much time together, but to have company over a meal is pleasant enough.

Madame Bessancourt was middle-aged, thick in the bust, and thick in the hips, with a heavy, shrewd, sallow face and black hair, barely beginning to turn grey. She had achieved something remarkable in her solution of suitable dress for this trek. She had taken to the *shalwar* and *kameez* of the Punjabi women, in dark colours and amply cut for comfort, and astonishingly she looked completely at home in them, and almost Indian. The yellowish tint of her cheeks, her black eyes and black hair, the heavy body that belonged by rights in the unrelieved, noncommittal black of the *patronne* of some small hotel in Artois, nevertheless put on this alien dress with complete authority. Maybe there wasn't really much difference between the French matron and the Indian matron, both masterful, practical and not to be taken lightly.

Her husband, on the other hand, had made no concessions. He was square and solid, with a balding head so uncompromisingly Alpine and a moustache so obviously French that any effort to conceal their origin must have failed from the start. So he wore suits exactly like those he would have worn at home, but made in lightweight cloths, and allowed himself an old Panama hat against the sun, and that was the extent of his special preparations.

'What do you suppose they *do*?' Patti wondered, watching them in fascination. 'At home, I mean? You just haven't a chance of guessing, have you? I suppose they could be retired, but they're not so old, really.'

'Heaven knows! Maybe a small factory somewhere – family business – and a son's taken over,' suggested Dominic, more or less seriously. Speculation is irresistible, and he had been wondering ever since they first set eyes on them. 'They bought that car in Bombay as soon as they landed, and God knows where they haven't taken it by this time. They both drive – well too. They stay in dak bungalows or railway retiring rooms, and do everything as cheaply as they can – though that may be French parsimony rather than lack of funds – but they don't miss a thing. What they do, they do, a hundred and five per cent.'

'Perhaps,' Lakshman suggested, 'they won some big lottery

prize, and this was a dream – and now they take possession of their dream.'

'Yes, but even so,' persisted Patti, still enchanted by Madame Bessancourt's ambivalent, Indian-French solidity, self-possession and repose, 'why *India*?'

'Yes,' agreed Larry pointedly, watching her sombrely across the table, '*why* India? Why in your case, for instance?'

'Me? Oh, I finished school two years ago, and didn't want to go on to a university – not yet, and anyhow, I'm not clever, I might have had trouble getting a place – and I was stuck full of youthful idealism and all the current jazz, and I thought India was just the groovy place, the place that had the answers. You know how it was! Maybe it isn't any more, I've been here two years.' She bit into the dimpled green skin of an orange, and began to peel it, frowning down at her fingers, which were thin, blunt-nailed and not particularly well-kept; even gnawed a little, Dominic noticed, alongside the nail on both forefingers. She had a nervous trick with her eyelids, too, a rapid, fluttering blink, but perhaps that was simply out of embarrassment, because all attention was now centred upon her. 'So I thought I'd volunteer to come out here and teach for a couple of years before I went to college, and though I'd missed the regular Voluntary Service Overseas draft – and anyhow, they might not have considered me the right type – I got this job in Bengal through one of Dad's business friends who had connections over here. Just an ordinary school that used to be a mission school, and there was teaching in English as well as Bengali, and I had to help all the classes with their English.'

'Did you learn any Bengali?' Dominic asked with interest.

She looked up at him quickly. Her eyes were really an extraordinary colour, pale yet very bright, like a slightly troubled sea over sunlit sand. 'Some. I can get by, but I couldn't conduct a real conversation. Oh, it's been fine in its way, I'm not complaining. Only I came here thinking this was where the low living and high thinking was, and the way to understanding, and India was going to show me what was wrong with all the rest of us. And what do you know? – here they are, almost the most quarrelsome race I've ever struck, almost the most corrupt, and all the high thinking is just talk, talk, talk, and the government is as mixed-up and inhibited and old and tired as any of ours, and I can't see any end to it – or even any beginning of getting out of the mess. But maybe it's me,' she said disarmingly, and smiled up suddenly at Priya, and at Lakshman. 'Don't get me wrong! The best here are *the best* – the best you're going to find anywhere on earth. But as for the system – did we really ever expect so much of it?' She tilted her head, looking from Larry to Dominic, for plainly they were in this, too. 'I'm on my finishing leave now, I get two months paid, and I'm still travelling hopefully. But where to, God knows! How have *you* managed?'

Dominic waited for Larry to speak, and he didn't; for some reason Patti had shaken him, and his brooding face was the only thing about him that was going to be eloquent just yet. So Dominic filled the gap.

'I was lucky. Every time I hear anyone else talk about India I realise it. I got pitched in here on a special job, without any time to have preconceived ideas, and everything about the job came unstuck, and I was left living off the country. When there's a real crisis you find out who amounts to anything, and who doesn't. That's when I met the man I'm working for now – the Swami Premanathanand. You couldn't very well be any luckier than that, whatever the hole you're in. No, India didn't let me down. That's why I came back. But to work, not to meditate.' He was aware that that might sound a trifle superior, but that was something he couldn't help. 'That's the way it hit me, and I got hooked accordingly. And I've said I was lucky.'

'But where are they *going*?' persisted Patti fretfully. 'I can't see any future.'

'I haven't looked, I've been too busy with the present.'

'But what do you actually *do*, then?' she asked doubtfully.

'I work for the Swami's foundation, the Native Indian Agricultural Mission, on one of their farms near Tiruvallur. Doing anything – driving, messenger-boy, vet's assistant, whatever's needed. But mostly I seem to have become the district tractor-mechanic.'

'But isn't that sort of set-up just another way of being a big land-owner?' Pattie objected warmly.

'Hardly! Everything we run is run on a co-operative basis. Each village is its own board of directors, and everything above a bare living for the central staff is ploughed back into the business.' But he was not particularly disposed to talk about it; he was on leave, and she already knew everything she needed to know about him.

'Do you think all that's really going to *change* anything?' she wondered wistfully.

'It already has. Since we set up this particular grouping we've nearly doubled our rice yield annually – partly by increasing acreage, and partly with better double-cropping. Did you know that Tamil Nadu is going to be a surplus state any minute now? Not just through us, of course, we're a very minor force, but we do work in with the government's intensive district programme, and that's far from minor.'

She looked reluctantly impressed, and at once sadly incredulous and warily hopeful. 'I suppose your people farm back home? I didn't have anything as practical as that in my background. My dad's a retired army officer. I was born into the establishment.'

'So was I,' said Dominic with a fleeting grin, 'only a different branch. Mine's a policeman. Well, no uniform now, actually, he's deputy head of the county CID. I haven't got anything more practical to offer than an arts degree, either, and that doesn't dig any wells here. Or at home, for that matter. Everybody thinks it entitles him to be a teller, when we've already got too many tellers and not enough doers. So I thought I'd come over here and see how the doers live.'

'Awful waste of a degree, though,' protested Patti, rather surprisingly reverting to type.

'Not a bit! It won't rot.'

She considered him thoughtfully for a moment, background, parentage, eccentricities and all, and looked more than half convinced. 'Well, maybe you've found something that'll stand by you,' she said handsomely. 'I wasn't that lucky. I never felt I was doing anything much, or getting anywhere. It seemed as if you'd have to smash the whole thing and start afresh before you'd see any results.'

'And what will you do now?' asked Larry, watching her soberly over the bowl of fruit. 'When your paid leave's over, I mean? Go home?'

'I suppose so. I've got some of my A levels to repeat if I want to teach seriously, but I haven't made up my mind yet. Yes, I guess I shall go home. Maybe try somewhere else. There's supposed to be a second country somewhere for everybody, so they say. Maybe the stars have to be right. How about you?'

'Me? Oh, I suppose I came here looking for the pure wisdom, like you. Though I ought to have known better. I'm an anthropologist by inclination, but a civil engineer by profession. I've been working on the plans for a small

340

irrigation project up in Gujarat, but it looks as if various committees are now going to sit on the idea for years, and if they don't squash it altogether they'll probably alter it around until it's useless. I thought I might as well have a look around the country while they're considering the matter, so I bought the Land-Rover in Bombay, and set off more or less at random southwards. And Lakshman here comes along to take care of me.'

Lakshman gazed back at him serenely and amiably, but did not return his smile. Indian people, except those of the hills, do not find it necessary to smile whenever they catch your eye, but will gaze back at you directly with faces unyieldingly grave and thoughtful. In the hills they smile because they obviously enjoy smiling. And Indian people, Dominic thought critically, studying the two golden amber faces beside him, who can be the noisiest people on earth, also know how to be securely silent and to withhold even an eloquent gesture. Priya's delicate face, silken-skinned and serene, betrayed nothing at all beyond a general, detached benevolence. Suddenly he felt more curiosity about her than about her companion.

'Now we've all declared ourselves, except you, Miss Madhavan.'

'I am not at all novel or interesting,' she said in her quiet, lilting voice; and now she did smile, her chiselled lips curving and unfolding as smoothly as rose-petals. 'I am a nurse at the General Hospital in Madras. I have a large family of brothers and sisters, and my eldest sister happens to be a teacher in Bengal, and a colleague of Patti's. So now that I have my long leave, and Patti is free to visit the south, I invited her to meet me in Madras and come home with me for a visit. That is all about me.'

It was very far from all about her; there were reserves behind that demure face and those cool, thoughtful, purple-black eyes that would take half a lifetime to explore.

'So you've actually known each other, apart from letters, only a matter of days? We're all starting more or less equal,' said Larry. 'I picked up Dominic in Madras only five days back. We'd corresponded, just fixing things up for the trip, but we'd never seen each other until then.' He took a banana from Patti's hospitably offered bowl, a bulbous bow in an incredible colour between peach and orange and old rose. 'This at least I'll never forget about India, the fruit. Did you ever see such a shade as that in a banana before?'

'Never!' she agreed vehemently. 'And I've seen them all kinds and sizes, from the three-inch curvy ones like a baby's fingers, to hedge-stakes a foot long and pale, greenish lemon. I saw these when we passed the stall in the bus, and we simply had to walk back and get some.'

'Where was that?' Larry asked. 'I never noticed any stall as we drove up.'

'It was getting dusk then, and he hadn't lighted his little lamp, you wouldn't notice us. But we saw you go by. Two turns down the road – I expect he's packed up long ago, probably just after we were there, there wouldn't be much traffic up here after dark. One turn down the road there's what's left of a shrine of Siva. It looks pretty old, too, the carving's nearly worn away, but they still bring oil and marigolds.'

'No, really? As close as that? I might take a flashlight down and have a look at that presently.'

'Wouldn't tomorrow morning do?'

'Not a hope! We've got to be afloat before six, or we shall miss the best of the show. They might not hold the boat for us, either – don't forget it's Sunday. The best times, the two periods in the day when the animals come down to water, are from six in the morning, and about half past three in the afternoon until dusk. And it takes a little while to get out to the best vantage-points – there's a whole lot of lake up there.'

The Bessancourts were withdrawing, with polite good nights to the Manis. They passed by Larry's table on their way to the door, and bowed comprehensively to the company, uttering in assured, incongruous duet: '*Au 'voir, m'sieurs, m'dames*!' Everyone turned to smile startled acknowledgement, for once united: 'Good night, *m'sieur, madame*!'

'The French,' said Patti with conviction, as soon as they were out of the room, 'are *formidable*!' It was a good word for the Bessancourts. 'What can they want here?' she demanded in a feverish whisper. 'What brought them here? I don't understand!'

Dominic, still charmed and touched by that courteous departure, so reminiscent of a respectable couple quitting a small restaurant in St Dié or Chaumont, wondered if it was so vital to understand. Wasn't it their business? Why not just be glad about that impressive, three-dimensional reality of theirs? But Patti wanted to recognise, to docket, to know all her landmarks.

'Where did you first see them?'

'At Mahabalipuram, among all that fabulous free sculpture. In the Mahishasura-Mardini cave, actually, standing like another rock, staring at the sleeping Vishnu. She looked exactly as if she was studying the joints in a butcher's window before buying, but I'll swear for ten minutes and more she never moved. Her old man stands just as still and gazes just as attentively, but in a different way. As though he were standing respectfully but impregnably in a church that wasn't his own, but still he saw the point for those who belonged there.'

'You like them,' said Priya suddenly, in her soft, detached voice, and smiled at him with her eyes as well as her lips.

'Yes, I like them.' Heaven knew he wouldn't have the art ever in this world to achieve communication with them, short of a miracle, but he believed confidently there was everything there to like.

The Manis were leaving, too, in a series of short, abortive starts and stops. 'Sushil Dastur, my bag – you have left it behind!' 'Sushil Dastur, please arrange about the breakfast and early tea . . .' 'Sushil Dastur, don't forget you must see to that letter, there will be a post from the hotel . . . And the alarm at five, remember!'

('That goes for us, too, don't forget!' Larry warned in an undertone.)

They passed in procession, pausing momentarily to exchange valedictory compliments.

'You'll be making the morning run?' asked Larry politely.

'Ah, but not with the public launch!' Mr Mani wagged a triumphant finger and beamed his superiority. 'We have an introduction to an influential resident here. He has a villa on the lake, and the hotel places a boat at his disposal. He has invited us to be his guests tomorrow. It is a great honour.'

'A privilege!' sighed Mrs Mani, adjusting her green and silver sari over her plump and tightly-bloused shoulder. 'He is a most distinguished man – and wealthy!'

'A business associate of Ganesh, our son-in-law. Ganesh has very important connections . . .'

They departed in a cloud of self-congratulation, and Sushil Dastur, trotting behind, turned his lustrous eyes in a timid smile and said: 'Good night, ladies – gentlemen!' with almost furtive goodwill, as if he feared he might be doing the wrong thing.

And with that the evening ended, since the next day was to begin at five. Except that Larry had sufficient energy left to light himself down the two coils of road between the black, perfumed walls of the forest, to examine the Siva stele. Lakshman felt it to be his duty to go with him, and even to repeat, very seriously, his warnings about never going out in the dark in open country without a strong torch, for fear of snakes.

When they came back, Dominic and the girls were still standing beside the Land-Rover, looking up at the immensely lofty black velvet sky coruscating with stars, and festooned here and there, as in India only the hill-skies and the shore-skies normally are, with coiling plumes of cloud.

'That's a find you made down there, Patti,' Larry said approvingly. 'I want to stop off before we go down again to Madurai, and get some slides. I'd need to consult somebody who knows more about style than I do, but my guess is that figure wasn't carved any later than about the seventh century. It could even link up with some of the stuff at Mahabalipuram, to my mind, only it's had a rougher passage.'

'I suppose the sadhu isn't still sitting there?' said Patti idly, withdrawing her zircon-blue eyes from the heavens.

'Sadhu?' said Larry in vague surprise, dropping his torch into the front seat of the Land-Rover. 'What sadhu?'

Two

Thekady: Sunday

The hotel stood on slightly rising ground, the length of a dark, moist drive from the road, and resembled nothing so much as an over-sized and under-maintained mid-Victorian rectory, complete with untrimmed shrubberies and too tall trees growing too close to the windows. Even the hard earth drive and the few slightly ragged flower-beds fitted into the image. And though they had climbed over the crest of the ridge and begun to descend again, there was still no sign of the lake; nothing but forest, sometimes thick as a creeper-draped stone wall on either side of the road, sometimes opening into what was almost park-land, with lush turf in which the trees stood gracefully spaced, waist-deep in grass.

Larry was a fanatical time-keeper, having learned the necessity the hard way. They had been the first party away from the bungalow and would probably be the earliest afloat here. The few people moving around at parked cars in the hotel grounds, or in and out of the open door, were almost all staff.

'If you will wait five minutes for me,' Lakshman said, scrambling out from among the gear stowed in the back of the Land-Rover, 'I must check in with the hotel desk, and find our boatman.'

By the time he emerged again they had secured the Land-Rover's steering with an ingenious padlocking device of Larry's own invention, briefly examined the palm-decked amenities within the hotel, still dim and almost unpeopled in the dawn, and moved round to the small terrace at the rear of the building.

And there at last was the Periyar Lake, or at least the first glistening reach of it, curving in to lip the soft green swell of turf some forty feet or so below the level of the terrace, and winding away in the distance to lose itself among folded green slopes of grass and trees. The far-off ranges modulated from green to blue, smoke-grey, and dissolved into the pearly light of a morning as yet sunless. A flight of steps led down from the terrace to the grass, and thence a long, curving causeway swept away righthanded into the water, like a Devonshire hard, its coral-coloured surface breaking gradually through the green of the grass only to lose itself again beneath the quivering dove-grey of the shallow water. On the right flank of the hard, within its protecting curve, three or four white launches were moored; and from there a belt of stiller water, broad and pewter-grey, launched itself out across the lake-surface. To the left, where the bay rounded in a sickle of shore and curved away again, they saw the first ghostly gathering of dead trees, skeletons standing six feet or more out of the water, quite black, all their lesser branches long since rotted away. From the water's edge rose a band of about a hundred yards or more where the grass was pale, thin and low; then at highwater-mark the lush, man-high growth began, and the living trees, not jungle here, but fairly open woodland, through which the first rays of the sun filtered and found the mirror-surface, to splinter in slivers of blinding light when the fitful dawn-wind troubled the lake. There were clouds, soft, light and lofty, above the receding folds of the forest.

'No wonder the English felt more at home in the hills,' Dominic said, as they stood gazing in sharp, nostalgic pleasure. 'It wasn't only the temperature, it was the whole look of the place. You've only got to get high enough, and you've got English trees, English gorse and heather, even an English sky. You never realise how you've missed the variety of cloud until you see it again after months of staring at absolutely naked blueness.'

'Then perhaps they felt really at home,' murmured Priya, with the first spark of mischief he had observed in her, 'when the monsoon rains began.'

'Personally,' Patti said sceptically, 'I can do with quite a lot of naked blueness before I start complaining. That's one of the things I *do* like about India, and one of the things I'm going to miss if I do go home.'

'You haven't made up your mind, then?' Larry turned to look at her with more interest than he had yet shown. She was duplicating, Dominic thought, a dilemma of Larry's own. Both of them were drawn, and both of them repelled; and both of them, each in a different fashion, held it against India that they did not know what to do.

'Oh, I don't know! – It's the parents, you know – I'm the only one, and they gave me the works, private schools, music lessons, riding lessons, the lot! I keep feeling I've got to give them sort sort of return for their money. But then, even if I do go back and work at it, I sure as hell know the end product isn't going to be what they were bidding for. Maybe they'd be safer if I stayed here – I mean, you can do quite a bit of romancing about a daughter several thousand miles away, but it's no good if she keeps blowing in and smashing the image. And I do love this country – hate it, too!' she added honestly. 'Some of the components are marvellous, if only you could break the whole lot apart, and put them together again in some form that would actually *work*.'

'And couldn't you say that just as accurately about any country under the sun?'

'I suppose you could. I *know* you could. So why go home? Why go anywhere? Start from where you are.'

'I did,' he said grimly, focusing his Werra on the dead trees that spread their arms rigidly now over quivering silver water. 'I started practising shattering it to bits and rebuilding it nearer to the heart's desire right where I was, on a New England campus. I've had the New Left and the activists – from mid— to extreme— to off-the-map and up-the-wall. They never changed a thing except themselves, and so far as I could see, that was no change for the better. And all they shattered were people – usually innocent people – as even policemen can be,' he added sourly, and turned his back on her abruptly, and the shutter clicked.

'Then where *do* you go after that?' she said, and she had been so startled by this burst of confidence from him that it was almost a cry of appeal.

'If I knew that, I should be on my way.' That was the most Dominic had ever yet heard from him about his own intolerable situation, and perhaps the most anyone was going to hear until he resolved it one way or another. 'Good, here's Lakshman, we can get off now.'

Lakshman came round the corner of the hotel in conversation with a young fellow of his own slender build, but taller and more muscular. He was dark-skinned and clean shaven, with a prominent nose and strong brows, above narrowed dark eyes that had the seaman's look of focusing upon distance. He salaamed briefly and cheerfully, and favoured them all with a broad and gleaming smile.

'Sir, I am Romesh, your boat-boy. Ladies, you please come this way.'

He pattered before them down the steps in his worn

leather sandals, and led them down the tongue of grass and the curving causeway to the boats. His working wear consisted of khaki shorts and a tunic of white cotton, with a red sash round his waist, and a loose white cotton turban, with a short cockade of pleats over his forehead and a balancing fan of pleated folds on his neck.

Patti danced down the steps after him, Priya following more sedately. 'Romesh, you speak good English. That's lucky!'

'I speak a little, memsahib. Not good !' He turned upon her a flashing smile, half-bold and half-shy; she saw that he was quite young, probably only a few years older than herself. 'But I try to show you all game, very good. It will be fine morning, many elephants come.'

He loosed the rope that moored the smallest of the white boats; the canvas canopy slapped gently in the breeze, and then was still. The vast, bright body of the sun glowed through the trees, and the clouds, unbelievably high in a pale sky, began to sail slowly like boats on a reflected lake. Romesh drew in the line and steadied the boat, holding out a hand to help the girls aboard. There was comfortable room for them all, and seats to spare. The largest boat, rocking languidly to the motion they created, must hold as many as fifteen passengers without crowding.

Romesh kicked off his sandals and sat down to the motor, and in a moment teased it into life. They slid out into the deep channel, clear of the skeleton trees, and headed across the first bight of the lake. On either shore the bare, peeled area of grass rose, steeply or gradually, to the contour of the high-water-mark, and there the grass and bushes soared to a man's height, and the trees crowded close.

'The water is rather low,' said Lakshman, 'but that is good, because then the animals must come well clear of cover to reach the water, and we shall have a good view. Sometimes it is much lower even than this, and then it is more difficult for the boats, because there is so much dead forest.'

Close to the shore, wherever they turned, there was always at least one spectral tree to be seen. In the deeper passages whatever remained of the drowned giants – if anything remained – was far below the draught of motor launches. They looked back, and the hotel and the landing stage were already out of sight. The note of the boat's engine was low, leisurely and quiet. Romesh scanned the shores as they moved, watching for anything living that might emerge from the rim of the trees.

'He is trained to catch any movement. If he sees something he will not make any sound, but point. Then he'll try to bring the boat in more closely and switch off the engine, so that we can watch without disturbing them.'

They had, as it seemed, an immense world to themselves. It was difficult to grasp the scale of these hills and these remarkably English-looking trees, until Romesh stiffened and pointed, and found them their first elephants. In a sheltered bay on their left hand, a whole ponderous herd winding its way down through the trees, across the open belt of spongy grass, and into the silvery shallows. Beside the boles of those trees the two big tuskers shrank to the dimensions of toy animals. There were seven or eight cows, and four calves, varying from a half-grown youngster to a small, skittish baby. They played and splashed and squealed like puppies in the shallows, sending up fountains of spray, while the elders wallowed blissfully, and heaved themselves ashore to graze afterwards streaming water like granite cliffs deluged by a flowing tide. Romesh, flashing white teeth in a delighted, proprietorial grin, shut off the engine and let the boat slide slowly inshore between the drowned trees, and they watched for a long time, until the herd moved off at leisure into the forest.

After that it was elephants all the way; they saw them pacing in line, far up on a half-cleared hillside, moving methodically down towards the lake. They saw them bathing in half a dozen sheltered coves, and paused each time to draw inshore and take pictures. Several times they saw deer, and once, where the shores opened out in grassland and they emerged into the widest part of the lake, a large sambur grazing, bulky as a bison. The sun rose higher, and the clear heat of the day came on, but the fresh currents of air across the water were cool and fragrant. Silver-blue before them, under a deepening blue sky only delicately dusted with cloud, the lake expanded broad and calm, and here the light was dazzling. They could see the long barrage of the Periyar dam far in the distance. After the enclosed, steep-shored bays the elephants preferred, this was a minor sea.

'It's time to turn back,' Lakshman said reluctantly, 'if we are to get the boat back on time.'

'What a pity!' Patti sighed. 'This is glorious. How long ago was the dam built, Lakshman?'

'Last century, it's an old one. I think about 1890. It turns the Periyar river through a long tunnel, and makes it flow east down into the Madurai plains. It used to go west to the Malabar coast.'

'And the wild life sanctuary, is that old, too?'

'Quite old, it was made while this was still Travancore State territory. It's been established so long that it has many, many herds of elephants.'

'You like to keep boat?' Romesh suggested hopefully. 'Come again in afternoon? Sometimes is better in afternoon. Maybe even see tiger.' He had brought the boat about, and they were heading gently back for the narrows.

'Oh, could we?' She looked hopefully at Larry. 'Is it very expensive? Couldn't you be our guests this time? If you don't have to rush away?'

They looked at one another, and apart from the question of who paid, which could be left in abeyance for the time being, there was no need for much persuasion. The beauty of the place and the fascination of the animals made departure seem a deprivation; at least they could have one more trip, for the late afternoon watering.

'All right, why not? If the boat isn't already booked for the rest of the day? After all, it is Sunday, there are sure to be a few trippers.'

'I take you,' promised Romesh heartily. 'I fix it for boat.'

'Good for you!' Patti was delighted. 'Romesh, you're a treasure. What's the rest of your name, may we know?'

He flashed his magnificent teeth at her in a pleased grin. 'It is Romesh Iyar, memsahib.'

'A good Keralese name.'

'Yes, memsahib, from Quilon.'

They were between the steep banks again now. Once or twice they caught sight of buildings close to the water, one, as Romesh told them, formerly a palace. They were encountering, too, the boats which had set off later than theirs, and had just reached this stage in the pilgrimage. The big launch, packed with the Sunday whites of husbands and the fluttering saris of wives and flower-tinted dresses of children, ploughed steadily ahead into open water, passing them closely.

'I see the Bessancourts made it,' Larry said.

There they sat among the butterfly passengers, he in his sober grey suit and Panama hat, she in her black *shalwar* and grey and white *kameez*, with a white muslin scarf over her pile of black hair. They looked about them at the strange and beautiful world of the Periyar Lake with wide, attentive, appraising eyes; and when they saw their young acquaintances in the small launch they did not wave, but inclined their heads with the tightest of French smiles, as on an after-church promenade in Combeaufontaine or Oulchy-le-Chateau.

They were drawing near to the final inlet that would bring them back within sight of the hotel, when they met the smart white launch, as small as their own, but newer. Mr and Mrs Mani sat installed among its cushions in jubilant state, beaming like gratified children; and Mrs Mani, though somewhat taken aback at recognising her acquaintances in a private boat when she had certainly taken it for granted they were passengers among the rest in the communal launch, nevertheless fluttered a silk handkerchief at them graciously, and achieved a very accomplished smile for their benefit. Sushil Dastur sat in the stern of the boat, very neatly and nervously, his knees drawn up, hugging the inevitable briefcase that went with him everywhere. And opposite the Manis, lounging along the whole of one seat with a cushion at his back, sat a tall, bulky man in a tussore suit and a snow-white shirt, grey hair curled in tufts over his ears, and the sunlight glinting blindly from the lenses of his gold-rimmed glasses. They saw him briefly in passing as a sculptured mask in bronze, without eyes, with a heavy mouth and jaw and a thick, pale throat.

Romesh exchanged the smallest flick of a hand with the other boatman, and grinned to himself. When he laughed he looked even younger, and childishly mischievous.

'So that's the wealthy and distinguished business contact,' Dominic remarked, when the other boat was out of earshot. Romesh looked up brightly from the wheel. 'You know him, sahib?'

'Never saw him before. Never heard of him until last night. His guests told us they would be sharing his boat today, that's all. Do *you* know him?' He added with interest: 'He has a house somewhere here on the lake, hasn't he?'

'Quite close, sahib, over there, not far from the road.' He was shaking gently with suppressed mirth. 'I am laughing because Ajit Ghose, that boat-boy, he is new here one month only, he does not know! *I* was on list to take that boat today, and this Ajit, he thinks to himself, this client is very rich man! So he gets list changed, to have that boat for himself. I saw what he want, but I let him do it. Me, I know this Mr Mahendralal Bakhle. He is rich, but he is not generous. It will not be so fat a tip as Ajit thinks.'

'*What* did you say the man's name was?' Patti asked sharply, turning to stare after the diminishing boat with abruptly quickened interest.

'Mahandralal Bakhle. You know that name, memsahib?'

'Not exactly – it just sounds familiar, somehow. I think I've read it somewhere,' she said. 'Wasn't there something about him in the papers – about trouble on his farms, and some labourers who were killed? I'm nearly sure that was the name.'

'It is possible. He is a big landlord, own much land down in plains, near Sattur.'

'But surely,' Dominic objected, 'there's a limit to the amount of land any one person can own now – twenty-five acres, or something quite modest like that.'

'Oh, yes, sahib, that is true, but there are ways. Some landlords say that they part with their land, give it to their womenfolk, but often it is not true. Mr Bakhle, he still controls everything, all that land.' Romesh's English failed him, and he waved a frustrated hand, and addressed himself to Lakshman in Malayalam.

'He says,' Lakshman reported, 'that Bakhle was mixed up not long ago in some very nasty trouble with his Harijan labourers. That must be what Miss Galloway is thinking about. They wanted a rise in pay, and then there was an armed raid on their village, and several people were killed. Everyone seems sure that Bakhle had hired the strong-arm men to do the job for him.' He lifted his shoulders in helpless distaste. 'It could happen. Such things have been known.'

Priya, who was so silent and self-contained, and yet missed nothing, said simply: 'I have known such casualties come into our wards. There is very strong feeling among the Harijan labourers, and there is also great pressure being used against them.'

'Not, in fact, a very popular man, this Bakhle,' Larry deduced.

'With reason, it seems,' said Patti, casting a last long, dark look after his boat before she turned her back on it.

'Very much disliked, so Romesh says,' agreed Lakshman.

'But also very much envied and courted. Money is money, it talks loudly everywhere.'

'Prefer present company,' said Romesh boldly, and showed his teeth again in a bountiful smile.

'Well, thanks,' said Larry drily. 'Even if this doesn't turn out to be a very generous tip, either?'

'Even if there is *no* tip,' Romesh asserted firmly, and brought the boat gently to rest, with a tiny hiss of compressed ripples, against the shoulder of the hard.

The Manis must have been invited to lunch at the villa, for they did not reappear at the hotel until nearly three-thirty, when it was time to embark again for the afternoon watering. Sunday whites and Sunday saris were assembling again in the party launch, and among them the sombre Bessancourts sat like monuments to France. And in from the gardens came Sudha Mani, the folds of her rose-coloured sari fluting round her plump ankles, her bracelets jingling with triumph, Gopal Krishna treading ponderously at her back, and Sushil Dastur at heel like a tired little dog.

'Sushil Dastur, go and order tea.' She sank into a cane chair among the palms and fanned herself gracefully. 'And see what kinds of sweets they have, and choose me some of those I like. Be quick! No, give me the flowers, you are dropping them.' She installed her booty on a spare chair, and beamed at Patti and Priya, who were just going out to the landing-stage. 'From Mr Bakhle's garden! So beautiful, aren't they? He has such a fine garden. Was it not wonderful this morning?'

'Wonderful!' they agreed truthfully.

The afternoon cruise was curiously different from the morning one; a completely changed light draped the hills, clear, yellowish, very still. The sky was washed nearly clean of cloud, and of a wonderfully pale, bright and remote blue. They remembered that dusk would come early here, and deceptively; there would still be full daylight in the open water when the many deep inlets were already drenched in darkness. But as yet it was bright sunlight, only just slanting towards the west.

'Look, Bakhle's out again!' Larry pointed a finger into one of the still, green aisles of the lake as they passed; and there was the immaculate white launch idling gently offshore, with the silk-clad figure of Mahendralal Bakhle lolling at ease on his cushions, perhaps asleep, or near it.

He had no voluble guests to entertain now, and the boat-boy was ready to respond to his every inclination, mindful of that fat tip he expected at the end of the day from a man so rich. The thought made Romesh chuckle happily and wickedly to himself as he observed them.

'That Ajit Ghose, he is so clever! Those people from Bengal, they think everyone in the south is stupid.'

'Their mistake,' said Patti drily. 'He's from Bengal, is he?'

'Yes, memsahib. He is not bad fellow, only he does not talk with us much, not friendly. Maybe only he is a long way from home.'

'And you don't know why he came south to work? I'd have thought the south had its own unemployment problem.'

Romesh shrugged and let that go, having nothing to say on the subject. 'See – elephant!' His pointing finger indicated them with precision, high on the steep hillside where the sun filtered through the trees and turned animals and earth to moving gold and static gold. In orderly file they paced after their tusker leader, the cows and calves following confidently; and though they seemed to move with the deliberation of doomsday, they covered the ground at an amazing pace, bearing obliquely downhill to the water. And now they were more playful and more relaxed than in the morning, scratching themselves meditatively on the ghostly trees, surging through the breast-deep water with a bow-wave breaking in phosphorescence before them, the little ones bouncing and frolicking in abandoned joy, the elders curling their trunks over them protectively.

Patti said: 'I love elephants!' And after a moment of silent watching she said sadly: 'Why can't we have a community like that, as placid and as natural and as perfect!' And indeed there was a conviction of untroubled happiness and kindliness here which at this moment seemed to justify her.

'Some worlds,' Larry said dourly, 'are simpler than others. You take what's dished out to you, and pay for it. Not like the Spanish proverb!'

'Look!' whispered Lakshman. The boat lay motionless now, and under the slope of trees it was premature dusk. 'They're going to cross!'

What moved them to it no one could guess, but the tusker and his younger fellow had waded far out into the water, and the cows were moving without haste after them, and marshalling the little ones with them. The whole herd was surging steadily into the lake, and setting course unmistakably for the other shore. Forward they lurched until tusks and trunks and massive shoulders and twitching ears had all vanished under the water, like ships sinking at their launching; but when only the domed, glistening tops of their heads remained visible, the lurching gait changed, and they swam. Like animated black stepping-stones, the herd sailed across the narrow arm of the lake with hardly a ripple, unhurried, majestic, oblivious of the boat that lay off in entranced silence, watching their passing from some thirty yards away. Occasionally a trunk came up for air, waved gently for a moment, and was again withdrawn, or the tip of an ear ruffled the surface. The watchers hardly drew breath until the cluster of rounded stones drew near to the steep shore opposite, and the leaders heaved their huge shoulders clear of the lake, streaming water and phosphorescence, and thumped imperturbably up the slope and into the tall grass, to disappear among the trees. The cows thrust up their heads one by one and followed, nuzzled by their calves, and all the glistening herd passed out of sight with hardly a sound.

Patti drew a long, awed breath. 'My God, and I never even knew they could!'

They looked at one another like people awakening from a dream. After that, anything was going to be an anti-climax. Why look for more elephants? They had been so close that they could almost have leaned over and patted the littlest calf on its bobbing pewter head as it sailed by. And while they had been spellbound here, the day had lurched a long step towards its ending, at least here between the shrouding forested hills. In the opener water it would still be bright

'Have we still got time to go on to the wider part?' Larry asked. 'It must look marvellous in this light.'

Lakshman conferred with Romesh, and Romesh in his obliging fashion hoisted a shoulder, and flashed his grin, and said that they need not worry about staying out beyond their time, they had plenty of fuel, and there would be no more cruises after this one. So they headed for the open water, silvery and placid mile on mile to the dam; and the day changed its mind and came back to full sunlight as soon as they were out from between the enfolding arms of the forest. Several times they saw elephants again, and several times deer, and the sky over them became the clear, pre-sunset sky of a summer day at home, shading down from deepest blue at the zenith to jade green at the rim of the world. The

355

few feathers of cloud were coloured like roses, in variations of pink and gold.

They turned back at last. Romesh was just bringing the boat about in a long, sweeping curve, the water hissing along its side, when they all heard a distant, muffled report, not at all loud, but borne across the mirror of lake as though it came from everywhere at once, or from nowhere.

'What was that?' Larry demanded. 'I thought there was no shooting here. It isn't a hunting reserve, it's a wild life sanctuary.'

'That is right, sahib,' Romesh confirmed. 'But sometimes wardens must shoot injured animal, or rogue animal.'

'But it didn't sound like a gun to me,' Dominic said. 'More like what you hear at a good distance when they're blasting in a quarry. But I don't suppose there's such a thing for a hundred miles around here.'

They listened, straining their ears, but the sound was not repeated. They had the broadest expanse of the lake to themselves, and the silvery hush of the hour was like a glass bell enclosing them.

'Ah, we're dreaming!'

But they had not been dreaming. Looking ahead as they sped towards the narrows, they saw a tiny puff of iridescent cloud rise and assemble in the sky far before them, and there hang shimmering like gilded dust for some four or five minutes before it disintegrated. In a countryside almost without aerial pollution, even a shot in a quarry would have produced little more than that. And before the arms of forest rose on either side to shut them in, it was gone.

The successive bends of lake became surfaces of steel mirror, reflecting pastel channels of sky, and shut in by black walls of forest. But wherever a wider bay opened the light took heart and returned. It was well after six o'clock when they came back to the place where they had seen the elephants cross, and instinctively looked again at the shore from which they had set out, where a few dead trees provided scratching posts in the shallows, and man-tall reeds grew, a paler patch in the dusk.

'What's that?' Larry asked, pointing. 'There in the reeds, look – something white . . .' Reddish elephants they had seen, but a white elephant would be too much to ask. Deer, perhaps? Anything pale would look white at this hour.

They peered, and caught the gleam he had been the first to see. Too white for deer, and too motionless; something low in the water, half obscured by the vertical stems of the reeds. 'Wait!' said Dominic sharply. 'Ease up, Romesh, there's something queer there— Take us in towards it a bit.'

Romesh slowed down, and obediently turned the boat's nose into the bay. They drew nearer to the pale patch, and it took on shape, veiled as it was, the curve of a white hull, a tatter of canvas trailing overside into the water.

'It's a boat – but it's foundered – it's filling!—' Dominic leaned over the side, and caught the quicksilver gleam of water inside the settling hull, and something else, pale wisps and bulges of cloth, awash among the bilge and hanging limply over the distant side. 'Something's happened— Closer, Romesh, get us alongside. My God, there's someone in her!'

They were all braced intently at his back as he kneeled on the seat and leaned far over to get a hand on the gunwale of the other boat. Patti's voice said, in tones of stunned and frozen unbelief: 'There can't be! It's only old rags – it's an old boat, it must have been abandoned here long ago . . .'

'Impossible, we couldn't have missed seeing it.'

The reeds rustled, brushing their hair and sleeves. Dominic got a hand on the rail and steadied them along-side; and now they could all see down into the unmistakable shell of Mahendralal Bakhle's smart white launch, awash from end to end with sluggish water.

All its seating nearest the engine was torn and splintered, and the motor itself hung drunkenly forward into the wash, a mass of twisted and fused metal. Every seam had been started, and oozed water and slime. The boat boy lay with one arm trailing over the side, gashed by flying splinters and raked raw by blast, a few rags of his clothing dangling. And in the bottom, the water whispering from side to side over his shattered face as the boat swayed, lay what was left of Mahendralal Bakhle, in the muddy shreds of his tussore suiting. His chest was pitted with shrapnel wounds, and his gold-rimmed glasses, disintegrated into lethal slivers of metal and glass, had obliterated his eyes more thoroughly than the reflected light of the sun had hidden them at noon, and penetrated beyond into his brain. No bubbles arose through the water that covered his mouth and nostrils. The arms that lolled on either side his body terminated in the mangled shreds of hands.

Suddenly Patti uttered the most frightful sound Dominic

had ever heard, a long, rending, horrified scream that rasped her throat amd scarred their ears. And having once begun, she screamed and screamed, and could not stop.

Three

Thekady: Sunday Evening

They reacted after their kind. Lakshman caught the hysterical girl in his arms, turned her forcibly away from the horror and shook her until her broken cries gave place to blessedly subdued weeping. Priya, the nurse, kilted her sari to the knees, and was over the side as nimbly as a cat, standing on the broken stern seat of the other boat, with the water lapping her ankles. She leaned down to the lolling boatman, slid her arm under his shoulders, and turned up his head and face to what was left of the light. He was clear of the water, at least he had not drowned. But one arm was raw meat from the elbow, and he was bleeding fast into the debris of the boat.

'He is not dead – yet . . .'

Dominic climbed over into the hull to help her, knee-deep, and straddling Bakhle's body with one foot braced on either side.

'If we can get him into our boat, I might be able to stop the bleeding.'

Dominic got his arms round the man's thighs, and Larry came out of his daze with a shudder and a lurch, and leaned over to take from Priya the burden of the head and shoulders. It was astonishing what a weight this fragile-looking girl could lift, with one arm hooked expertly into the victim's surviving arm, the other hand steadying his rolling head. The white turban was a trailing rag, dirty and stained, but she did not discard it; it would serve as a tourniquet. They got the limp burden over the side and stretched out on a seat. She looked down briefly at Bakhle's body, and the green water lay motionless over the ruined face.

She looked up into Dominic's eyes. All the delicate lines of her features had sharpened and paled; she was a different girl. 'We can't do anything for him – he's dead.' And she turned to the one who was not dead – yet. On her knees beside him, blood and slime fouling the skirts of her sari, she rolled up the wet turban into a tight ball, and wedged it under the injured man's armpit; and the rags of his forearm smeared her breast as she did it, and she did not even notice. 'Romesh, give me your turban – quickly!'

He stripped it off with trembling hands, the whites of his eyes shining in the dusk, and long curls of black hair fell about his ears. She took it without so much as looking at him and bound her pad into place, securing the upper arm tightly over it. She knew how to handle a weight greater than her own, and what she was doing she did with all the concentration and passion that was in her.

Crouched in the stern of the boat, as far as possible from the horror overside, Patti sat limp and shivering with cold, her fist jammed against her mouth, her eyes immense with shock. And after a long, mute moment she turned and leaned over the side, and was direly sick. Lakshman hovered, alert and anxious, one eye on her and one on the boatman's limp body.

'We ought to take *him* in, too,' Dominic said, staring down into the bilge, 'if we can.'

'Waste of time, nobody's going to be able to do anything for him.'

'We could take boat in tow,' suggested Romesh, through chattering teeth.

'We'd lose it as soon as we got it off the mud. Pure chance it happened close inshore. Once in deep water she'd go down like a stone.'

'What *did* happen?' Larry asked feverishly. 'Could the engine have blown up? Is it possible?'

'Give me a hand, we'll try to get him aboard.'

But they were spared that, for as soon as Larry's weight was added to Dominic's the boat began to slip away from shore and settle deeper. It was clear that without proper tackle they might only dislodge it and send it off again into deeper water, where it would certainly sink. Hastily they secured the broken hull to the nearest tree, and clambered thankfully back aboard their own boat.

'Get her going, Romesh, back to the hotel as fast as you can. We've got to get hold of a doctor, quickly.'

Romesh sat crouched over his motor, shivering but controlled, and set the boat moving at its best speed out of the bay and back towards the hotel landing-stage. On her knees beside the patient, Priya tightened her tourniquet, and watched the creeping streams of blood thin out and almost cease. But so much had been lost already. Dominic knew by her face that she had not much hope.

'He is so cold! If only we had turned back earlier, we might have saved him. Romesh, is there anything in the boat, a rug, anything to cover him?'

There was a thin blanket folded on one of the seats. They tucked that over him, and waited, silently, for the boat to round the last green spur and thread the last belt of dead forest to the hard. Patti, stunned and mute, sat with a handkerchief pressed to her lips, and made not a sound. Nobody had any longer anything to say. Not until they touched, and Romesh jumped ashore and made the boat fast. Then Dominic ordered:

'Run, go straight to the manager and tell him. Send for a doctor first, and send someone down with a stretcher or a door to carry him up. And blankets! After that, tell him to call the police.'

'The police?' said Larry, shaken. 'Yeah, I suppose they'll have to come into it, even it was an accident—'

'It wasn't an accident,' said Dominic briefly, and stooped to lift the unconscious man's head and shoulders. 'Unless I miss my guess, it was a bomb. And we heard it go off – remember?'

They remembered; and now they understood. A distant, muffled report, like a shot in a quarry, and a puff of luminous dust hanging in the sky, a tiny cloud no bigger than a man's hand.

Exactly where the police came from they never discovered, but they were there within the hour. An inspector, his sergeant, and two uniformed men appeared in two cars; an ambulance was already there before them.

Most of the day-trippers had departed with the bus, but there were still a number of people around the hotel, and now no one could be allowed to leave until he had been interviewed and received police permission to proceed. The entire household was gathered withindoors under the supervision of a watchful and slightly officious Tamil constable, while the hotel's boatmen and the police officers salvaged the remains of Mahendralal Bakhle and his launch. Patti was clearly in no state to be of any assistance to anyone, she sat silent and cold with shock, staring before her; and since they had been six people in the boat, and five could give just as clear an account without her, the inspector, of his own volition, sent the doctor to give her a sedative, and bespoke from the hotel a room where she could be rolled up in blankets and left to sleep. By that time it was clear that they would not get away from Thekady that night.

'But this is terrible!' lamented Mrs Mani, dropping tears of alarm and indignation into her scented handkerchief. 'It is a dreadful thing! Poor Mr Bakhle! Such a tragedy – such a distinguished man!'

'A frightful accident!' her husband echoed, and there was no pretence about his agitation. Had they not been in that very boat all the morning? Suppose it had happened then? 'To think that only a few hours ago we were speaking with him! He showed us his garden . . . And what do we know? Why must we be kept here? Now we have to pay for our car an extra day, with the driver, and we had intended to be back in Madurai tonight . . .'

A frightful accident. That was what they were all thinking, no doubt, and that was bad enough.

The Bessancourts sat patiently among the palms, rock-steady, waiting to be interviewed when their turn came. Their programme was not so rigid that a day's delay could upset it. They had nothing with which to reproach themselves, and nothing to fear; they would tell what they knew, which was merely their own movements during the day, and that would be that. And since they were not players in the drama, but merely caught up accidentally in its fringes, they did not expect the police to give them a high priority in their list, and were resigned to a long wait, but a dignified one. Madame Bessancourt, from some survival kit of her own, had produced a large, half-finished sweater, and was doggedly getting on with her knitting.

They were kept waiting more than another hour before Inspector Raju came into the main lounge, where the guests were assembled.

'I should like first to see Mr Preisinger and Mr Felse and their party, who found the damaged boat. Also their boat-boy. If you will come this way.'

A small office had been placed at his disposal; with chairs enough to accommodate them all, the room was full, for one corner was already occupied by Sergeant Gokhale and his notebook. The sergeant was young, alert, and spruce to the point of being dandified, and apparently quite prepared to take down statements given in English. Like his superior officer, he was in plain clothes; evidently they were dealing with the detective branch. Romesh came in last, summoned from somewhere behind the scenes, his face wary and tired, and a little frightened.

Inspector Raju was tall and lean and greying, a man perhaps in his early fifties. He had a thin, lined face and intelligent eyes that missed nothing, from the stains on the sari Priya had as yet had no opportunity to change, to Romesh's shrinking uneasiness; and his complexion was no darker than a sallow European tan at the end of an average summer.

'Now – I had, of course, a brief verbal statement from Mr Felse on my arrival. It was laudably concise and accurate, everything I needed at that time. But now I want you all to think back and give me a full account of your day, in detail. There is time. And what one omits, another may remember. Perhaps Miss Madhavan could give her account first, then she may go to join her friend. There is no need for me to see Miss Galloway tonight; by morning she may be more herself. It was, I know, an ugly experience.' His eyes flicked one appraising and appreciative glance at Priya, who had also suffered the same experience, but sat here composed and calm. 'You do understand that you will have to pass the night here? I have asked that arrangements shall be made for you.' Another thought struck him. 'But perhaps you have not your luggage with you, since you were not expecting to stay?'

'We have everything in the Land-Rover,' said Larry. 'We'd intended driving back to Madurai this evening, so we settled our account at the forestry bungalow.'

'Good, then we shall not be putting you to any great discomfort, thought I am sorry for the delay. Yes – very well, Miss Madhavan?'

Priya accounted for her day briefly and thoroughly, taking time for thought. When she had finished she said punctiliously: 'I am trained, of course, to be able to deal with casualties. It is an acquired skill, not a virtue. I think Miss Galloway has really lived a very sheltered life, though I am sure she would not think so herself. Could I ask you, Inspector, if my patient – if he is still alive?'

If he hesitated, it was only momentarily. 'So far, he is, and that is thanks to you. But I would not hold out too much hope for him. It was necessary to risk rushing him down to hospital, he needs surgery at once, and of course they are already giving him blood, but— Well, we shall see! Thank you, Miss Madhavan! You can go to your friend now.'

Priya went; and one by one the others added what they could to the picture of the day. Raju called on Dominic last of all.

'And what was it that made you think this might not be an accident, Mr Felse?'

'I didn't see how it could be. I could imagine a minor blow-out from an engine, but nothing of this kind. This had wrecked the whole boat, every seam had started. And the violence of injuries . . . it looked more like some kind of explosive gadget, deliberately planted. And that made me think of the sound we'd heard, and the cloud we'd seen. It would have been somewhere over those stretches of lake.'

'And the timing? You did not notice the exact time of the report?'

'By pure chance, yes, I did. Not because of the explosion, but because we'd just decided we ought to start back, and Romesh was actually turning the boat then. I did a sort of mental check on how long it would take us to get back. It was then ten minutes to five.'

'Thank you, that is useful. Very well, now you may all go. But you will not leave the hotel until given permission.'

But as they were filing out at the door he suddenly called: 'Mr Felse!' And when Dominic obediently turned back he added in a lower tone: 'Come back for a moment, Mr Felse, and close the door. Sit down again.' He sat back in his chair and sighed, and then smiled at Dominic very persuasively: 'May I say that you have been most useful to us in this case? But for you I doubt if we should have been called in so quickly, and but for your party, and especially that admirable young woman, we should not have stood even the slim chance we stand now of ever getting a statement from the boat-boy Ghose. I don't rate it high, but at least it exists. I think I owe you a little information in my turn. You may like to know that you were perfectly right. We have been going over the boat very carefully – that is why we delayed so long before seeing you. There was indeed an explosive device planted in it. As far as we can judge up to now, it was taped under the engine. From the position of the bodies it would appear that Mr Bakhle was at the wheel himself when the explosion occurred, and Ghose was behind him, in the stern. The firing mechanism was a small clock, and we have found the dial and parts of the bomb. It would seem that it was timed for five o'clock.'

'Then it fired in advance of the time,' said Dominic.

'So it seems. A faulty device, but it was effective, all the same. You see the force of the timing. If the boat was taken out during the afternoon watering period, it was likely to be wrecked somewhere at the extreme of its range, well away from any inhabited place, and therefore, in all probability, from all help. It was an entirely professional job, Mr Felse – well put together, and no bigger than a medium-sized torch. And an important land owner – and let me be frank, one much disliked locally – has been wiped out.'

'It seems,' said Dominic carefully, 'that Mr Bakhle preferred to stay somewhat nearer home than usual this afternoon. He had guests this morning, and perhaps he was tired, and didn't feel like going far. If the boat had really been at the limit of its range for the usual time allotted, it would have been where we were, out in open water. And it would have sunk totally, probably without trace.'

'That is indeed the probability. Though with explosives there is always an element of chance. In our country, as in yours, Mr Felse, there are certain categories of people, distinct even among terrorists, whose favourite tools are the gun and the bomb. I am interested in your attitude to this affair, and I feel it only right to suggest to you that you and your friends, merely by virtue of being the first arrivals on the scene, and close and intelligent witnesses at that, may be at some risk yourselves. The evidence, as you have said, was most probably meant to disappear into deep water. But it did not, and you have become closely involved with it. I don't say there was much for you to deduce – I do say that the Naxalites would have preferred not to run that risk.'

'Naxalites?' Dominic looked up at him sharply. 'You really think they could be in it? Here?'

'Here and anywhere. They may have originated in Bengal, they certainly have not stayed there, though they are less organised elsewhere. One of their weaknesses, indeed, is that the strings have almost always to be pulled from Bengal. But they extend everywhere, from Darjeeling to the Cape. "Death to the landlords!" is as valid a rallying cry in the south as in the north.'

There was more than that; Dominic could tell by something withdrawn and watchful in the deep-set grey eyes. They had recovered part of the mechanism – the strings were almost always being pulled from Bengal – there could be ways of identifying where that bomb had been manufactured, perhaps even by whom.

'Then the probability,' he said slowly, 'is that we have an agent from the north working here – not necessarily a Bengali, but sent from there. And you, I think, were already looking for him before this happened.'

The inspector smiled. 'Mr Felse, you will do well not to enlist in our police, and not to learn any more.'

Dominic smiled, too. 'I'm halfway there, as luck will have it. My father is a detective-inspector in England, I grew up in the tradition, even if I didn't join the force. I grudge it that the lunatic Left, in any country, should discredit the legitimate Left by trying to turn killing into an approved weapon, and I hate it when their phoney grievances alienate sympathy from the genuine grievances that are there all the time, and need to be noticed and taken seriously. I don't say even Bakhle was expendable – but surely Ajit Ghose wasn't. One more life, a perfectly innocent one, is all in the day's work, it seems.'

'One or a hundred, I assure you. It's all right – in this room we are quite private, I have seen to that, and Sergeant Gokhale here, though an impudent and insubordinate young man, is perfectly discreet.' Sergeant Gokhale cocked one dark eye at his superior and smiled faintly, undisturbed at being discussed in this manner; they had evidently worked together amicably for some time. 'But I should not theorise outside this room, not even among your friends. Here you may.'

'I was thinking of the bomb,' Dominic said. 'If it was set to go off at five, then it was planted – or at least activated – since five this morning. I don't know if the boat was used yesterday . . .'

'It was, both morning and evening. And in the evening it was refuelled and serviced by the head boat-boy here, who is absolutely reliable – a local man who has worked here for many years. No, I think we can ignore the possibility that someone affixed that device at one visit, and then came back to set it. We can concentrate on the time since five this morning . . .'

'Then who had access? Judging by the time when we met Bakhle's boat this morning, it was rather late in leaving . . .'

'You are right, it did not leave until well after seven, and it came back about eleven. So from five until seven-twenty-five it was at the landing stage, and again from eleven until three-fifteen. During the first period access would be very easy for anyone connected with the boat service or the hotel.

Possibly even for outsiders. During the second there would be quite a number of people around, and though access would be easily possibly, it would also be risky, since anyone unauthorised might very well be challenged if he approached the boat, and would in any case run the risk of being noticed, remembered and identified afterwards. One would choose the early morning in preference, I think. And then there were the morning guests, Mr and Mrs Mani and their servant. I shall be seeing them, of course. They are from Bengal . . .'

He let that tail away gently into silence, one eye on Dominic. He didn't believe in it very seriously, but he had an open mind.

'They were very flattered and excited about having an introduction to Mr Bakhle,' Dominic said. 'But I suppose that would be the line to take if they wanted the introduction and the invitation for a special purpose. Not very likely Naxalites, on the face of it, they have a lot to lose, and nothing to gain, which is usually the determining factor. Though not always, I suppose. But more important, all the letters of introduction in the world couldn't have *guaranteed* them an invitation to share his boat.'

'That is true. Also terrorist agents do not commonly proceed in threes, and for one to be such an agent without the risk of being suspected by the others might be difficult. Still, there could be vital secrets even between husband and wife, much more between master and servant. And as for possessions – have you noticed that the tenets of a creed are sometimes religiously observed by the rank-and-file adherent, but do not seem to be binding on the leaders of the cult? There are Naxalite bosses who are themselves greedy and tenacious landlords. Well – and you cannot think of anyone else who had ample opportunity, and was also from Bengal?'

'Yes,' said Dominic, after a long pause during which they looked each other measuringly in the eye, with a degree of wonder and curiosity. 'Only it makes no sense. Yes. I didn't miss the connection. Nobody had more opportunity than Ajit Ghose, nobody could hop in and out of that boat with as obvious a right as he could. For him it would have been easy, he was taking out that boat today, nobody would think of questioning him. And he comes from Bengal, and he's been here only a short time. Romesh told us. And he told us more – that originally *he* was down as Bakhle's boat-boy for today, and Ghose contrived to have the duties changed, so that the job went to him instead. I haven't forgotten. But it would be crazy! He stood to blow himself up, too. *If* he did it, he *did* blow himself up.'

'He may not have intended any such development. Terrorists have died by their own bombs before now.'

'Not with that much room to manoeuvre. He could have fixed it to go off when he wasn't aboard—'

'How? You think a man like Bakhle would ever go aboard first and wait for his boatman? At the landing stage, whatever pretext he might have made to absent himself, it would not have been a practical proposition. He would have been under suspicion immediately. No, if it was to happen in the boat, it had to be well out in the water, and therefore he had to be there. But don't forget the circumstances. They were close to shore, and it would appear that Bakhle himself was at the wheel at the time, apparently quite a frequent habit of his, and perhaps not difficult to contrive more or less at will. Thus Ghose would be behind him, while Bakhle's attention would be focused ahead. I have already confirmed that Ghose is a strong swimmer. May he not have intended to slip overboard shortly before the hour, and swim ashore? The boat was to founder. What would the boatman be then but a lucky survivor who happened to be blown overboard, and had no chance to help his passenger? If he wished to continue here and behave as an innocent victim, I think his chance of success would be pretty good. If he wished to disappear, having accomplished his immediate mission, that, too, would be easy. *But . . .*'

'But,' said Dominic flatly, 'the timing mechanism was faulty, and the bomb went off ten minutes early.'

'It is possible. I don't say more. We shall be examining his belongings, and tracing his antecedents. As we shall in the case of everyone else concerned.' He rose to indicate that the interview was over. 'Meantime, remember only that your position, and that of your friends, just *may* be a slightly exposed one, if someone fears that you may have noticed too much and too accurately.' And he added: 'A last point – your really devoted Naxalite might well contemplate the sacrifice of his own life with equanimity, if it was a necessary risk in the cause of taking Bakhle's. I don't say he would surrender it gladly, or refrain from all possible precautions; but he would not let that consideration stop him. As usual, it is only among the top ranks of the hierarchy that total cynicism prevails. The rank-and-file can be truly dedicated.'

Dominic was halfway to the door when he halted and looked back. 'But if you're right, then the terrorist is already *hors de combat* – even if he's still alive.'

'So?'

'So there seems no continuing threat to any of us.'

Inspector Raju said gently: 'It is not yet certain that the solution I have outlined is the correct one. But even if it is . . . Mr Felse, Ajit Ghose, though literate, is almost without education. He may have planted the bomb – he certainly did not make it. Someone supplied him with it, and taught him all he needed to know to make it effective. Someone, somewhere, will be busy observing the results.'

Four

Thekady: Monday Morning

Patti came out of her sedated sleep reluctantly and sluggishly, to sense the white of day outside her eyelids; and for a while she lay without opening them, unwilling to face the world. But even inside her own closed mind she could still see the obscene horror of abrupt death, the mangled body stirring rhythmically and helplessly in the water, the upturned face with blood and mud for eyes. A man who, according to Romesh, had hired thugs to attack and kill, simply to suppress a demand for better pay. Remember that, too . . . This is a dirty world, and nothing is ever simple. But to kill that way, from a safe distance, and not caring in the least about the wretched, innocent boat-boy, who had never hired thugs to kill anyone, and owned no land. There are things which can never be justified . . .

She knew she would have to open her eyes at last, and get up and dress, but she waited until she heard the soft rustle of Priya's cotton sari, and knew that her friend was already up and busy, and maintaining this considerate silence only on her account. Then she lifted her lids resolutely, and sat up in bed. Priya was standing in front of the mirror, braiding her long black hair. She had on a low-necked white blouse and an amber-and-gold sari this morning; and the soiled sari she must have washed last night, and draped in the shower room to dry. She turned quickly at the slight sound, and smiled at her room mate composedly, if a little anxiously.

'Good morning! How do you feel today?'

'Doped,' said Patti truthfully. But not, she thought, heavily enough; I can still see him. 'And stupid. And ashamed. I'm sorry I was such a dead liability yesterday. But I'd never seen – never imagined – anything like that. Even if you tried to describe it, to someone who'd never actually seen such a thing, it wouldn't mean anything. But when you run your nose right into it . . .'

'I know,' said Priya warmly. 'It was not your fault at all. Don't think about it any more – at least *try* not to think about it.'

'It'll be a long time before I stop,' Patti said wryly. 'Priya – how do you ever manage? I mean, in a casualty department, when these things are brought in – hit-and-run victims, gang killings, knifings in fights – all that . . . How do you set about keeping your cool? Or do you just get used to it in time?'

'No, you do not get used to it,' Priya said almost with asperity. 'Or rather, perhaps you do and you don't, because if you don't – in one way – you can't bear to go on being a nurse, and if you do – in the other way – you had much better stop, because you're not fit to be a nurse. Your mind gets used to it, and then you can use your faculties to try and combat it. But your heart never gets used to it, and you never stop being hurt.' She added deprecatingly, suddenly aware of her own warmth: 'It is not for everyone, of course, why should it be?'

'Not for me,' said Patti with decision. She swung her feet to the floor, and sat on the edge of her bed. In the corner of the ceiling a tiny jade green gecko clung upside-down, motionless but for the slow lift and fall of transparent eyelids, and the pulse in his throat, which vibrated almost too rapidly to be seen. Harmless, mysterious, jewel-like little things. The more I see of men, the more I like animals! But we're all caught, aren't we? You can't resign, once you're born.

'He seems to have been guilty of some deaths himself,' Priya said, attempting comfort that seemed to her quite irrelevant, but might make a difference for Patti. 'It is not only Romesh, I have been asking. Everyone knows the story, and most people believe it was he who was responsible for that attack. And it was a very bad case – one family was burned in its hut. But the raiders got away, and no one can prove anything.'

'No,' Patti agreed, reviving, 'I gathered he wasn't a very nice man.' She got up and pattered across barefoot to the shower room, suddenly brisk and resolute, as if she had made up her mind about facing both today and yesterday, and had to take the plunge now, and violently, or lose the initiative altogether. 'Do you suppose Inspector Raju's still here? I've got to see him . . .'

'Just a minute,' Priya called back from the bedroom. 'There's someone at the door.' And she went to open it, to find herself confronting a sleepy but still debonair Sergeant Gokhale. Even after a sleepless night he was not so tired that he could not take pleasure in the sight of a good looking girl fresh and spruce from her morning toilet, and not so devoted to duty that he could not make use of his eyes and his smile to convey his pleasure.

'I hope I'm not disturbing you too soon, Miss Madhavan. Inspector Raju would like to speak to you in his office – the room he was using last night. But at your convenience, there is no hurry.'

'Thank you, it's quite convenient now. I will come.' And she called towards the shower room: 'The inspector wants to see me. I won't be long. Do take down that sari, if it's in your way.'

'I already have. All right,' said Patti's voice, half resigned and half relieved, 'after you!'

She was dressing when Priya came back. She came in very softly and quietly, as was her way, and began to collect up her night things without a word, her hands competent and quick as ever; and it took Patti several minutes to realise that there was a different quality about this silence, a private tension, not at all out of hand – she had never seen any emotion get out of hand in Priya so far – but nevertheless troublous and dismaying. Then, looking up with carefully screened attention through the drift of her fair hair as she brushed it, she saw tears overflow slowly from the dark eyes. She dropped her brush and was across the room in an instant.

'Priya, what is it, what's the matter? What did he want with you?' She flung an arm round the slender, straight shoulders, and then, in terror that her touch was too familiar and would be unwelcome even in these circumstances, snatched it away again. And Priya smiled faintly but genuinely, and smudged the tears away again. No new ones followed them.

'It's all right – that is, it isn't anything unexpected. I didn't look for anything else. But I told you, it never gets any more bearable when you lose one . . .'

'But what's that inspector been doing to you?'

'He is very kind, and it was nice of him to think of telling me. Of course he knew it was what I really expected, but how did he know, then, that it still mattered so much?'

'But what did he *say* to you?' Patti persisted furiously.

'He sent for me to tell me that Ajit Ghose is dead.'

'Oh, *no!*' Patti whispered.

'But of course! It was foolish to consider any other possibility, because practically speaking there *was* no other possibility. But still one tries. He died on the operating table. They got him so far alive.'

'Then he never spoke? He never had the chance to tell them anything?'

'He never recovered consciousness at all.' She went on assembling her belongings in a neat pile, and looked round the room to make sure nothing had been forgotten. 'After breakfast I think he means to let us all leave. I mean the inspector, of course. He was most kind. He tried to comfort me by telling me something more – that is perhaps as well that Ajit Ghose died. He said I could also tell you, if I thought it would help to compose your mind.'

'I shall be seeing him,' Patti said, staring sombrely into her own thoughts.

'He says it isn't necessary, unless you wish it. Besides, it really does seem unnecessary now. He told me that Ajit Ghose came from Bengal only a month or so ago, just as Romesh told us, and it was true that he asked for the duties to be changed so that he could go with Mr Bakhle's boat. Romesh thought it was for the sake of a big tip, but now it seems he may have had other reasons.'

Patti's eyes changed their focus, stared at the incredible idea, and turned then to stare at Priya. 'You mean that *he* planted . . .? The boat-boy himself? Of course I see he was the only one who could do it without any difficulty or risk at all, but then . . . *No risk*! My God, I'm crazy! Why, it would be suicide!'

'Well, not quite, as they see it. Though if they're right he must have been willing to accept the risk of suicide. They say he was a fine swimmer, he may have intended to slip overboard and swim clear before the explosion, but he would need to leave it until the last few minutes, you see. And as it turns out, the bomb was a little faulty. It went off ten minutes before time.'

Patti pondered, wide-eyed, wringing her hands restlessly in the lap of her demure shirt-dress. Her face was quite blank, her pale pupils fixed. 'But they must have more than that, to be so sure. There must be something else they know.'

'Yes, there is. They've been going through his things. People like Ajit don't have much – a few clothes, a blanket, a bed-roll, maybe a pot or two, a few books if they're literate. He was – barely, but he had one or two books. One was "Shakuntala" – you know it? In among the pages they found several Naxalite leaflets and some Maoist literature. It is what they expected. What they were looking for.'

Patti sat quite still and silent, gazing before her. 'And you think,' she said, 'that it's really true? They're sure of it? He threw his own life away to make sure of taking Bakhle's life? Then he wasn't just the pathetic, innocent victim I thought he was? My God!' she said, more to herself than to Priya, 'It's terrifying!'

'He thought it would put my mind at rest,' Priya said with a rueful smile. 'The inspector, I mean. So that I should know that, too – that he wasn't just an innocent victim, that he died as the result of his own act. He thought it would make a difference!'

'Doesn't it?' demanded Patti, astonished. 'It does to me.'

'It doesn't to me, not very much. I told you, you never get used to losing one. What he may have done doesn't make much difference. Except that he might have lived to die a worse way. Shouldn't we go and see if the men are up? They were going to sleep in the Land-Rover – there weren't enough rooms.'

Patti rose slowly, like one still in a dream. 'You are incredible! I'm frightened of you, and I envy you, you know that? I can believe in *you* dying for a cause – without any heroics, either, just in cold blood – like Ajit Ghose!' A sudden thought struck her, and she halted with her hand on the handle of the door. 'He was telling you quite a lot, wasn't he, this inspector! Do you think he's going to let everybody know? That his case is successfully closed already?'

'I think,' said Priya, considering, 'that he may. Perhaps for a reason of his own.'

'Oh? What do you mean by that?'

'I think,' she said carefully, 'that Inspector Raju has his reservations. Yes, he surely believes that this is the truth about Mr Bakhle's assassination. There seems no doubt about that. But not the whole truth. You see, this was only a half-educated man, however intelligent he may have been . . .'

'And however fanatically devoted. Yes, I see that. It takes specialist knowledge to make bombs.'

'Yes. Could Ajit Ghose have done all this quite alone? So by letting it be known that the case is closed, I think Inspector Raju is setting out to put someone else at his ease, too – and off his guard.'

* * *

At breakfast in the hotel dining room, when most of the delayed travellers were already present, Inspector Raju made his announcement. First in Tamil, then in English, for the benefit of the foreign element, which even included a couple of innocent Germans, late arrivals and pathetically ignorant of all that was going on. In halting German Larry translated for the hapless engineers from some northern hydro-electric undertaking:

'Everyone present is now at liberty to proceed, subject to leaving with the police particulars of exactly where he can be contacted in the next few days, if it should be necessary. The case is now satisfactorily concluded, but we may need to get in touch with certain witnesses in connection with the detailed documentation of the events of yesterday. Will everyone who is ready to leave please report first to the police office on the premises. Thank you!'

Madame Bessancourt, without a word, rolled up her knitting and put it away in the capacious black bag that never left her side. Monsieur Bessancourt, with the same deliberation, picked up his Panama hat in one hand and their overnight portmanteau in the other, and they were ready. The first to be ready, as they had been the most patient and imperturbable during the delay. Police matters were to be accepted and respected in every country, but no need to waste time once the release was given. They passed by the table where Larry's party sat at breakfast, and performed their ritual bow as gravely as always.

'Are you heading back towards Madurai?' Larry asked, by way of making conversation in passing.

'No, we are going on to Kottayam, and then down the coast to Quilon and Trivandrum.' Monsieur Bessancourt glanced down at the folded map in his breast pocket as if for confirmation. 'And on to the Cape afterwards. And you?'

'The other way. We go back on our tracks nearly to Madurai, then south towards Tirunelveli. Later we shall be going on to the Cape, too.'

'Then perhaps we may meet there,' said Madame graciously. Inevitably, Dominic thought. Nobody is going to be touring this near to Cape Comorin, and not go the rest of the way, and by any route the distance is much the same. The odds are we shall all meet there.

Ellis Peters

'We must go and tell our plans to the inspector. It is tragic that this beautiful place had to be spoiled by such an act. And for your so terrible experience I am sorry. I hope you can forget what you could not help. *Au 'voir, messieurs – mesdames!*'

They all murmured their thanks and appreciation, and wished the departing travellers: '*Bon voyage!*' And the indomitable pair disappeared duly into the little office, recorded their timetable, walked out to their battered blue Ford and drove away.

The Manis had come in too late to hear the announcement; only Sushil Dastur, fussing anxiously about their table and exerting himself to make sure the tea and eggs should be just as they preferred them, listened with patent relief and gratitude, glad to have good news to relay to his employers as soon as they appeared. Theirs, after all, had been the worst situation; had they not spent the entire morning in the boat in which the bomb had been planted? Naturally they had all protested their horrified innocence, and exonerated one another, but all the same they must have spent an acutely uneasy night.

'Even we,' Larry remarked, 'should have been feeling pretty queasy, if all five of us hadn't spent the entire day together – barring the odd private moment, of course. An example of safety in numbers.'

Sudha Mani fluttered into the dining room at last looking the worse for a restless night, her pretty face rather puffy and pale, her husband treading heavily after her, as though unusually deflated and tired. If he had not had good news to relay, Sushil Dastur would probably have been suffering for their discomforts. As it was, the watchers could see from across the room the sudden glow of relaxation and ease as Mr and Mrs Mani heard that they were free to leave; and in a very few moments the old assurance and self-esteem began visibly to re-inflate their sagging curves. Sudha reached for the teapot, and with recovered appetite they attacked the eggs that were set before them. To judge from their distant exchanges, seen but not overheard, they even had heart to reproach Sushil Dastur for the cook's shortcomings before they dispatched him, fairly obviously, to see their luggage portered back to the hired car, their bill paid, and the Tamil driver aroused from his semi-permanent repose in the back seat. They meant to lose no time in getting away from this place which had promised so radiantly and performed so

376

viciously. No doubt they regretted ever hearing the name of the distinguished Mahendralal Bakhle, let alone bringing a letter of introduction to him.

'I suppose we'd better pack up and get out of here, too,' Larry said.

'I'll go and settle the bills,' said Lakshman, rising.

The girls, in slightly embarrassed haste, began a duet of insistence on paying their share, but Larry quashed that at once, or at least postponed all consideration of it. 'Later – don't bother now. Lakshman will pay everything, and we can think about it later. After all, there's no hurry, you're coming down with us as far as the railway. Go ahead, Lakshman, and we'll go and check out with the inspector.'

They had to pass close by the Manis' table on their way across the dining room, and Sudha, just recovering her volubility in full, halted them with an appealing hand.

'Can you imagine what people are saying! – Think how terrible for us! It was that boatman! – Yes, right in the boat with us all the time, and looking like any other boat-boy, so quiet and willing. And we could have been blamed – such a dreadful position we were in.'

'I'm sure the inspector didn't suspect you,' Dominic said soothingly. 'Naturally he had to question all of us.'

'Yes, but even now we must tell him where we are going, where we can be found . . . Why should that be, if it was that boat-boy?'

'That is mere routine,' said Gopal Krishna comfortably. 'Even if there is no arrest and no trial, because the man is dead, still they must file the records of the case. And suppose they should want to confirm some detail of the time with us? Or with Mr Preisinger here? It is the same for all.'

'That's it exactly,' Larry confirmed soothingly.

'You are going on towards the coast?' asked Mani.

'No, back towards Madurai.'

'We, too, of course, the car we have hired there, we must return it. Then we think of going out by train to Rameshwaram for one or two nights, before going on south.'

'I am so thankful,' Sudha said fervently, 'that they found out so quickly it was that boat-boy. Imagine, he had Naxalite propaganda hidden away in his belongings. I ask you, did that man look like a terrorist? You cannot any longer trust anyone or anything.'

'Hush, my dear, don't distress yourself,' murmured Gopal

Krishna, patting her plump amber hand. 'It is all over now. You must forget about it.'

'That is so easy to say,' she protested fretfully, 'but it is not so easy to forget one has sat in the same boat with a murderer.'

'Two murderers,' Larry corrected cynically, but only in a whisper, and not until they had moved on from the table and could not possibly be overheard. 'One with money, one with none. One who hired thugs to do the job for him, the other who did it himself, and felt so strongly about it that he made sure by killing himself as well. But you know which of the two *she*'d retain some respect for, don't you?'

'Ah, so you're off already,' said Inspector Raju, looking up at them over a table strewn with papers, the debris of a hasty breakfast, and the cigarette butts of a sleepless night overflowing from two glass ashtrays. He had discarded his tie and his jacket, and his lank, greying hair stood on end in all directions from the activities of his long, thin fingers. Even Sergeant Gokhale looked less immaculate than on the previous evening. 'No doubt you have heard by now how this affair has come out? Now it only remains for me to wish you a good journey wherever you are going, and happier arrivals than this one has been.' He did not look at Dominic with any more pointed significance than at the rest of them; the conversation of yesterday might as well never have taken place.

'Is it quite certain that this man Ghose was responsible?' Larry asked curiously.

'Miss Madhavan did not confide in you all?' The inspector looked at Priya with a small, glimmering smile. 'What admirable discretion! But yes, it is generally known by this time. Why not? We have found ample evidence in the dead man's possessions that he was deeply involved with the Naxalite terrorists, and the head boatman confirms that it was at Ghose's request that he changed round the duties for yesterday. There is not much room for doubt.'

All very decisive and satisfactory, Dominic thought, meeting the placid grey eyes. A case quickly and tidily solved, and a nice clear field ahead for that other person, the one who supplied the bullets but did not fire them, to lower his guard and emerge from cover, like the animals crossing that treeless belt of scrub grass to reach the water. Where, if he happens to be anyone present here, someone who has appeared only as an innocent bystander in this lake atrocity, he will not only afford the police a good view of him, but will also be on a long lead and ready to be hauled in at will. Because they're going to know where every one of us is – or says he's going to be – for the next few days, longer if they feel like continuing the supervision; and they're going to be checking that we really are where we say we are.

'I think,' said Priya, looking hesitantly at Patti, 'that Miss Galloway wanted to speak with you, Inspector.'

'At your service, Miss Galloway. I hope you are feeling better this morning?'

For once Patti looked disconcerted, even stammered a little. 'Thank you, I'm quite all right. It was only that I rather thought *you* would want to talk to *me*, since I made such a fool of myself keeling over like that last night. I don't suppose I can add much to what the others told you, but I thought you'd probably want to see me, anyhow.'

'That was very correct of you. But I think there is no need to trouble you any more. Now if you will give us particulars of your future movements, Sergeant Gokhale will note them down.' He pushed back his chair from the table, and stretched out his long legs with a tired but well satisfied sigh. 'You are all going on together for the time being?'

'From here, yes,' Priya said, after a pause to allow Patti to take the initiative if she chose, and a quick, shy glance at Larry. 'Mr Preisinger has been kind enough to offer us a lift down to the railway line at Tirumangalam, and from there we are going to take the train to Tenkasi Junction. By this evening we shall be in Kuttalam – Patti wanted to see the resort there, and the Chittar Falls. But we don't yet know where we shall be staying. If there is room at the travellers' bungalow we shall stay there overnight, perhaps tomorrow night, too. We could report there to the police, if that will do, and say where we are living. Then the next day we shall go by train to Tirunelveli, and by the bus to Nagarcoil, and there we shall be staying with my parents. I will give you the address.' She recited it gravely, and Sergeant Gokhale wrote it down.

'Thank you, that is quite sufficient. And Mr Preisinger and Mr Felse?'

'After we drop the girls,' Larry said, 'we're going on by the Tirunelveli road to a spot near Koilpatti. It's a village you reach by a minor road, slightly higher up in the foothills. What's the name of it, Dom?'

379

'Malaikuppam. It's on my account that we're making this detour. I have to visit somebody there, and we're invited to stay a couple of nights. We ought to reach the place early this evening, with any luck, so we shall be there tonight and tomorrow night. I don't know what he calls his house, but it's the main house of the village. Our host's name is Purushottam Narayanan.'

'I see. And you will be there two nights. And then?'

'Then,' said Larry, 'we go on to Nagarcoil and the Cape. Probably in one day, it's no distance, not more than a hundred and twenty miles. We shall stay at the Cape hotel at least one night, maybe two. If you could give us a telephone number, we can report any changes direct, or go to the local police as you wish.'

'No need to do either until you leave the Cape, but in any case I will give you the telephone number of my own office, in case *you* need *me*.' He smiled as he quoted it for them to take down; a slightly oblique and unamused smile. 'Thank you, that is all. I wish you all good travelling and safe arrival.'

'Just a minute! Please . . .!' Patti broke in quickly and eagerly. 'Could I . . . If Priya doesn't mind, I should like to change our plans. But it depends on Mr Preisinger, really.' She turned to look appealingly at Larry. 'Could you bear it if we asked to travel on with you, instead of going by train? I know I did say I wanted to see the Chittar Falls, and this Kuttalam place in the hills, but after what's happened here, honest to God, I'd be so much happier with a safe escort. And you see, I didn't realise until now that you were actually going through Nagarcoil. If you can possibly put up with us for a couple of days more, and take us all the way to Priya's folks, I'd gladly do without the Chittar Falls.'

'But, Patti, they are going to stay with a friend,' Priya objected, mildly shocked at this bold asking.

'I know, but surely there'd be a dak bungalow or a rest house somewhere near, where we could bed down. We wouldn't be in the way, honestly.'

There was no way of knowing whether Larry objected bitterly or welcomed the suggestion, for his face was never particularly expressive, and at this moment he was caught at a disadvantage. They had, after all, joined forces more or less by chance in the first place, and none of them had expected the alliance to continue. More embarrassing still was the fact that Priya had entered her protest so promptly, and deprived him of the opportunity of appearing genuinely warm about the prospect; he should have spoken up immediately or not at all. Not that it made any real difference, except to his self-assurance, for there was still only one thing he could do, and he did it with the best grace he could achieve.

'Of course, we'll be delighted to take you. No difficulty whatever about the transport end of it. And if accommodation is short, we can always camp again. How about it, Dom? Do you think this friend of yours would be very much put out if five of us descended on him instead of three? He never turned a hair at taking on Lakshman and me.'

'He isn't exactly a friend of mine,' Dominic said scrupulously, 'not yet, anyhow. I've never set eyes on him. But his father was a friend of my boss, and the son's asking for our help and advice with his land, not being in the least prepared for the job. His father was only in the late forties, he didn't expect to have to give his mind to running the estates for years and years yet. From all I can gather, a dozen people could descend on the place and hardly be noticed, but perhaps I'd better call him up and explain the situation first.'

'Oh, no,' protested Priya, colouring to a warm peach colour which was her version of a blush. 'Please, you must not ask him for hospitality for us, that is too much.'

'I won't ask. Except, perhaps, whether there's a travellers bungalow or a small Indian hotel anywhere within reach. But you mustn't grudge him the possibility of offering,' he said, half teasing her, something he wouldn't have ventured to do yesterday. And she smiled briefly but brightly, instead of remaining grave and slightly distressed; another thing which would not have happened yesterday. They had travelled a long and by no means obvious way in twenty-four hours.

'Settle it with Mr Narayanan,' said Inspector Raju tolerantly, 'and let me know.'

Dominic was back from the telephone a few minutes later with the answer he had confidently expected.

'We are all invited most warmly.' Purushottam's words, not his own, delivered with both constraint and ceremony in the purest of pure English, straight from Cambridge but rooted deep, deep in the soil and rock of India. He had heard the voice once before, but as yet had never seen the face and form that went with it, and he wondered often and curiously what he was going to find in the flesh. All

381

he knew was that Purushottam Narayanan was a year or so his junior, and had been studying in England until his father died, and tipped him headlong into the vexed affairs of a large, wealthy, but recently somewhat neglected estate. To judge by his telephone manner, classical English was something he lived with intimately, awake and asleep, but colloquial English had made no mark on him so far. 'Don't worry about anything, Priya, he means it and he'll enjoy it. Don't forget he's just been bereaved, newly home after several years in England and he must feel like a maladjusted alien. A little company will do him good.'

'It is most kind of him,' said Priya, not altogether happily, but with a reconciled smile. And her peach-bloom blush deepened to a dark rose colour. 'He must have much on his mind. We shall try not to disturb him more than we need.'

'Good, then that is settled,' said Inspector Raju briskly, 'and we can contact you all at Malaikuppam.' Sergeant Gokhale amended his notes accordingly. 'A good journey! I hope you may also have an uneventful one from now on. One such experience is more than enough.'

They went out to the freshness and radiance of a fine morning, and the Land-Rover standing waiting with a bonnet starred and sticky with honeyed droppings from the flowering trees.

Dominic came round from the kitchens with a box full of prepared food and fruit he had taken thought to order on rising, in case they should find it more convenient to picnic on the way. There were little three-cornered pastry cases stuffed with vegetables, and crisp pancakes sprinkled with paprika, the dough-cake type of bread called *nan*, and joints of chicken fried in golden batter. And fruits of all kinds, and a bottle of boiled water. No need now to go in to the railway junction at Tirumangalam; they would save a little time, and eat better with these provisions than at any restaurant they were likely to encounter on the way, not to mention being able to choose the place, the shade and the view.

Outside the back door Romesh Iyar squatted on his heels, strapping up a meagre bed-roll which presumably contained all his portable goods. Today he was not in his white tunic and turban, but wore khaki shorts and a bush shirt, and his curly hair fell in black ringlets over his intent forehead. As Dominic's shadow fell upon him he looked up, and showed a resolute but thoughtful and wary face, which mellowed into an ingratiating smile of recognition.

'*Namaste*, Felse sahib! You go Madurai now?' He had been well tipped, and was well disposed, but he did not look particularly happy. 'I go away, too. I go by the bus soon.'

'You're leaving here? Leaving your job?'

Romesh rotated his head fervently from side to side in violent figure-eights of affirmation, and showed the whites of his large eyes. 'I not stay here now, this is bad place. I not stay here where the boat-boy gets killed. I tell inspector sahib, tell boss, too. This place no good for me any more, so I go.'

'But it's over now. It's all over, nothing more will happen. It was a good job, wasn't it? I shouldn't quit just for that.'

Romesh hoisted his wide, lean shoulders under the baggy bush-jacket and set his jaw. 'No good here for me now. I not stay here, not like it here. Must go.'

'And Inspector Raju knows you're leaving?'

'Oh, yes, sahib, I tell him, and he say OK. I report to policeman night and morning, then everything OK. I tell him where I go, and he say all right.'

'And where will you go? What will you do?' Dominic fished out the small coins from his pocket. 'You're going to need bus fare. Here, put this away!'

Romesh pocketed the coins in his turn with a slightly brighter smile and a bob of thanks. 'I go see my brother in Tenkasi, maybe they got job for me on railway. If that no good, I try in Quilon or Trivandrum. Every day I tell police where I stay, do everything they say. Only I not stay here.'

He had made up his mind, and nothing would change it. He squatted patiently and doggedly beside his bundle, and settled down to wait for the daily bus, his back already turned on Thekady and Periyar Lake.

'Well, good luck!' said Dominic, and went on to join his companions.

On the way down the forest serpentines on the eastern side of the range they made a brief halt below the forestry bungalow, so that Larry could get his slides of the Siva stele among the trees. The light was clear and brilliant, the conditions perfect; and now that they were clear of the lingering shadow of the tragedy at Thekady they were all recovering their spirits and beginning to look forward again instead of back. Only Patti was rather quiet; still slightly dopey after her sedatives, she admitted, and perhaps also anxious to make it clear, since she had more or less extorted this invitation, that she intended to be as unobtrusive and as little trouble as possible.

The fruit stall was there in its usual place below, lavish as a harvest festival. Only the sadhu was missing; there was no one sitting beside the lingam in the shade of the trees, and not even a flattened patch in the grass to show he had ever been there.

Five

Malaikuppam: Monday Evening: Tuesday

They halted for lunch on a strip of sand beside a stream, just
off the road, where they had a patch of shade from a clump
of young coconut palms, and a wonderful view of the distant,
convoluted blue heights of the Western Ghats, out of which
they had come, and which, under a variety of local names
and shapes, accompany the southbound road almost to the
Cape. And in the afternoon they passed through Sattur, and
remembered Mahendralal Bakhle, whose disputed lands lay
somewhere in the neighbourhood. From Koilpatti they soon
turned right, at Dominic's somewhat hesitant direction, into
a minor road, white as flour, climbing gently between paddy
fields greener than emeralds, and tall palmyra palms, with the
half-veiled blue complexities of the hills endlessly changing
shape before them. And by the first downward swoop of
evening they reached Malaikuppam.

It lay on a gentle slope, facing south-east, and the rice
here had become a different strain, a hill-rice, the upland
crop almost golden in colour, and in one field being cut.
Groves of trees framed the village as they approached it.
There was a pond on one side, and two boys were splashing
along its edges, minding the water buffaloes that wallowed
in its coolness with their blue-black hides gleaming and their
patient, placid faces as near expressing happiness as they
would ever be. In one place they saw tobacco growing, its
huge leaves shading from pale green to yellow, its stems
five feet tall. It did not look rich country, but neither
did it appear depressed or poverty stricken; and yet life
in rural India is commonly lived on a knife-edge of debt
and destitution, and they all knew it.

There were women just gathered at their evening chore of
drawing water from a big, stone-rimmed well on the dusty
village square. One of the girls stood aloft on the four-foot-
high rim, outlined against a sky turning to orange and gold,
and the others handed up their brass pots to her to fill. Poised
with thin brown toes gripping the stone, she dipped and raised
the brimming pots, her anklets and bangles gleaming, and all

her gestures were pure and graceful and economical, a lesson in movement. Larry halted the Land-Rover, and all the dark female faces turned to stare at them in candid curiosity, and laugh aloud in frank appreciation of their oddness and incongruity. It was a disconcerting experience which all the foreigners among them had suffered several times before. But when Lakshman leaned out and asked for guidance in fluent Tamil, the nearest woman approached willingly and cheerfully, and pointed them the way. Higher than the village. A little way uphill, and they would see the gates.

They saw the wall first, lofty and white, capped with crude red tiles, and it went on almost as far as they could see. Then they came to the gates, wrought iron gates that stood wide on a short, dusty drive and a broad central court, round which the various buildings of the household were grouped somewhat haphazardly, many of them having been added at different times. Everything was low, one-storeyed and white, and shaded with overhanging eaves; and the first buildings they passed were clearly the dwellings of farm servants and household retainers, of whom there seemed to be a great many. Then there were buildings that appeared to be barns and store rooms, all space around the broad open area of trodden earth that gave place, a little higher, to a paved court. The end of the vista was filled in by a wide terrace, with steps leading up to it, and crowned by a long, low, single storey house, white-walled and red-tiled, a little like a ranch house but for the strong batter of the walls and the shaping of the roofs. Over the tiles the ornamental bushes and fruit trees of a garden peered, and beyond was a grove of forest trees looking over the boundary wall.

'Riches without ostentation,' Patti said critically. 'I sort of knew it would be like this. At least it doesn't look English. Have you ever been in the Nilgiris, and seen all those dreadfully unsuitable houses that look like something left over from Queen Victoria's jubilee, and are all called "Waverley" or "Rosemount" or "The Cedars"? You wonder whether you've slipped through a crack in space and time, and ended up somewhere quite different. At least this *is* rural India, not suburban Cheltenham.'

'I was once invited to a Women's Institute meeting,' Priya said unexpectedly, 'in Bangalore.' Everyone turned, even at this vital and anxious moment of arrival, to gape at her in astonishment, the statement came so startlingly, not in itself, but from her. 'I didn't go,' she said demurely, 'I had an extra duty. I was nursing there then. But I would have gone, if I'd been free.'

'Isn't it marvellous?' Patti said gratified. 'You know when the real imperial rot set in? When the British memsahibs arrived! The men were quite willing to learn the ropes and go quietly and discreetly native, and no one would have been any worse for it. But once the wives were let in, and the families, and the damned establishment, it was all over. Everything had to conform to the home life of our dear queen, and everybody stopped learning anything about the home life of the native Indian, and profiting by it. It didn't matter any more, it was just something to be brought into line. Which of course it never was. Thank God! You can't just run around the world trying to teach other people respectability, when what that really means is respect for an Anglican doll in a crinoline!' She caught Dominic's eye, dwelling upon her consideringly as Larry brought the Land-Rover to a halt close to the terrace steps. 'Yes, you're right, I'm talking too much because I'm nervous. I invited myself here. I know it.'

'You talked a blue streak of truth there,' Dominic said honestly. 'I wouldn't worry about your rights and titles. This sort of caravansarai absorbs visitors wholesale. Come on, let's go and find the host.'

They clambered out, shaking the dust out of their clothes self-consciously. Lakshman withdrew into the background here; this was no duty of his. It was Dominic who led the way up the staircase to the terrace, and crossed to the open door under the wide eaves.

And suddenly, none of them ever quite knew how, there was a young man standing under the lintel, waiting formally to welcome them. They had heard nothing; he moved gently and fastidiously, after the manner of his race and the code of his aristocratic line. But he had heard the Land-Rover arrive, and needed no other summons, being the punctilious host he was. Probably he had been listening for their engine for an hour and more, whatever he had been doing in the meantime. He stood quite still in the doorway of his house to welcome his guests, the least pretentious figure in the world, and the gravest, a slim, neatly moulded young man in thin grey flannels and an open-necked white shirt, with short-cropped black hair that waved slightly on his temples, and a spark of something intimately connected with England and the English, in his large, proud, aloof and lonely dark eyes.

'I'm Purushottam Narayanan,' he said, in a clear, courteous, almost didactic voice. 'Everything's ready for you. Do come in!'

The hospitality of the Narayanan household was absolute but not elaborate, the furnishings of the rooms comfortable but simple, and Indian style, like the dinner they presently ate in a large and rather bare room overlooking the terrace and the small, glimmering fires and lamps of the village below. Cutlery and some nine or ten dishes of various vegetables and curries were set out on a large table, and everyone on entering was handed a warmed plate and turned loose to charge it as he felt inclined. The host, attentive, grave and reserved as yet, told them what each dish contained, and added punctilious warnings where he felt the contents might be rather highly spiced for their tastes. Then they all sat down with their selections at a smaller table set in the window, and two servants hovered in the background, ready to offer replenishments at a nod from their master.

Afterwards the servants brought bowls of a creamy sweet made with rice, its surface covered with tissue thin sheets of silver foil, which were also meant to be eaten; and fruit, in a bowl of water, and rich, strong coffee.

By this time they had exchanged all the courtesies, the host expressing his gratitude for their company and his pleasure in it, the guests their thanks for his kindness and their appreciation of all the thought he had given to their comfort; and still they were no nearer knowing whether his pleasure was personal or formal, his gratitude heartfelt, even desperate, or merely an acceptable phrase. He sat among them, cross-legged at one end of the long seat built into the window, talking intelligently about merely current things, such as the Indian scene, and their journey, and their intended onward journey, his large, unwavering dark eyes moving intently from face to face, and no gesture missing and nothing undone that could contribute to their wellbeing; but some inward part of him might as well have been, and probably was, a million miles away from them.

He was by no means a small man, being fully as tall as Dominic, though still a couple of inches short of Larry's gangling height; but he was built in the slender South Indian style, with light bones and smooth, athletic flesh, and in repose he looked almost fragile; an impression reinforced by the refinement and tension of his face, which was clearly but suavely cut, without any of the hawk-likeness of Lakshman's Punjabi features. The moulding of his lips was fastidious and reticent, the poise of his head very erect, even drawn a little back, as though in insurmountable reserve. And out of this austere countenance the melting southern eyes gazed doubtfully, withholding communication, even while he discoursed politely and plied them with favours.

But there was nothing indecisive about the face, and nothing to suggest that the part of him he kept private was not engaged at this very moment in furious and resolute activity of its own.

'I must apologise,' he said, when even the coffee had been cleared away, 'for being such a poor host. I have been too preoccupied with this responsibility here, to which I'm not accustomed at all. Give me a few months, and when I have all this moving as I want it to move, then you must come again, and let me have more time to show you the countryside.' Not a word of his father's death and his own recall to take over the household; such family concerns must not be inflicted upon girl guests. 'I realise that you have made your own plans, too, of course. But you will at least have tomorrow? You need not leave until the next day?'

'No, Wednesday morning we'd planned on moving,' Larry agreed.

'And at what hour ought you to set out?' For the first time he smiled, a little self-consciously. 'I'm sorry, that sounds terrible. I would be happy if you need not leave at all that day, but you see, my father's lawyer is coming that morning to help me clear up all the affairs my father left in confusion. He was ill for some time before he died, though we never realised how ill, and things were a little neglected, not to mention a law-suit he had with a cousin over a plot of land lower down in the plain. That's why I have been locking myself in his office all day and every day, trying to get everything sorted out for when the solicitor comes. I would like to arrange my meeting with him for an hour that won't inconvenience you at all.'

'We ought to make an early start,' said Larry. 'We have to drop the girls in Nagarcoil, and then go on to Cape Comorin. I think we should say seven in the morning.'

'Then I shall arrange for Mr Das Gupta to come at eight. I shall send my car down to Koilpatti to fetch him, after you have left. He drives, but badly, and our road up here is not good, he will be glad to have transport. Now we need not think any more about departures. You have tomorrow, and we can do quite a lot with that.' He looked across at Dominic. 'You will come out with me and have a look at the set-up here? I should be grateful. I have some ideas, but you will know better than I if they are practicable.'

'I'm only a herald for the Swami,' Dominic said, 'he's coming down himself as soon as he can. But naturally I was hoping to get a look at things while I'm here, and let him have an outline of what you have in mind. There'll be a good deal of ground to cover?'

'We can put in all day on it, easily. Perhaps we could borrow the Land-Rover for the day?' He turned to flash a sudden engaging smile at Larry. 'And Dominic tells me – he mentioned it on the telephone – that you are a civil engineer, and have been working on an irrigation scheme up north. Is that right?'

Larry admitted it, without bothering to add that he feared for his plan's survival.

'Then you're just the man we want! Please come out with us. You see, further up here towards the hills we have a small river which is a tributary of the Vaipar, and centuries ago there was a whole system of tanks built down its course, with earth dams. They've been out of use and overgrown – oh, three hundred years, I'd guess – but I believe it wouldn't be impossible to reconstruct the whole system. With earth dams they were a poor risk in the rains – if the top bund went, the whole lot went, that's why they were abandoned. But it wouldn't be so difficult, with a little capital, to put in a more durable system now on the same line. Come with us, and see!'

'Sure I'll come, glad to!' And Larry would have been willing and ready to launch into a whole technical discussion of the water situation in Tamil Nadu, and the possibility of harnessing more of the rivers of Kerala, on the narrower, better watered west of the Ghats, to irrigate the drier plains on the east; but Purushottam diverted the flow. It was necessary to make plans, but as briefly as possible. Tomorrow they could talk water, and rice, and terracing, and the mysterious ancient tanks of Malaikuppam, the whole day long. Tonight they must devote themselves to making the girls' stay here pleasant.

'And for you, Miss Galloway and Miss Madhavan, I think we can arrange something more interesting. I hope I have done the right thing. Dominic mentioned when he telephoned that you had originally intended going to Kuttalam. It's less than forty miles from here, so why should you miss it? My car will take you there tomorrow, if you would like that, and Lakshman will take care of you while we are busy. In the evening we shall all be together again.'

'It sounds perfect,' said Patti dutifully. Too perfect, she thought, exchanging a glance with Priya, we're being disposed of while the business men confer. And suddenly she would have liked to think of a way of piercing through that impregnable defence, that barrier of attentive politeness that fended them off so successfully and yet left them no ground for complaint. 'I don't suppose Inspector Raju would mind if we make a day trip, Priya, do you?'

'Inspector Raju?' said Purushottam, drawing his fine black brows together in a frown of inquiry.

'Oh! – I see Dominic didn't tell you everything on the phone. So he didn't explain how they came to acquire two girls as well as the original party. I'm sorry, I didn't realise.' But she had realised; how could Dominic possibly have put over that entire long story in the few minutes he had taken over his call from Thekady? 'It isn't such a pleasant story, I'm sorry now I spoke. We got mixed up with a police inquiry, that's all, and we're supposed to be on call if needed. But we shall be back here by evening. And I would like to go, very much.'

She knew, of course, that it could not rest there; once she had said so much, somebody had to tell all the rest, otherwise no one would have any peace of mind. It was Dominic who took on the job of filling the gaps, since Purushottam was primarily his concern.

'I didn't go into it on the phone because the inspector was waiting, and time was precious. But I should probably have told you tomorrow in any case.' Tomorrow again, when they would have got rid of the women, and have the whole day for their own concerns, thought Patti. But instead he told it now, briefly but accurately. Purushottam listened with close and shocked attention, and his brows levelled into a ruled line across his forehead. Once he looked at Priya, and not involuntarily or fleetingly, but a long, straight, piercing look, as though he saw her for the first time. In the face of his own overwhelming preoccupations, it was an achievement to have astonished Purushottam.

'And you think there may be other Naxalite agents active in these parts? It wouldn't be the first time, of course, there have been cases here before. A couple of them were picked up near the Nepalese border a week or so ago, so there doesn't seem to be much of a limit on their movements. I'm so sorry that you had to go through an ordeal like that.'

Patti asked, with wincing curiosity: 'It doesn't make you wish you hadn't come home? Or that you were in some different line, and not stuck with all this big estate? It's such a vulnerable position once you've got a revolutionary Left with members prepared to throw away their own lives for a cause – like this man Ajit Ghose.'

He gave a brief, almost scornful heave of his shoulders, and his mobile lips curled in what was not quite a smile. 'I've got work to do here, and I'm going to do it. I want to see this land twice as productive and twice as effectively run as ever before, and chalking up a substantial profit annually to prove it. I'm going to make two crops of rice grow where only one grew before, and where we're already getting a *thaladi* crop of sorts, I'm going to boost it by at least fifty per cent. And I don't want this to be a monoculture farm, either, I want banana plantations and some other crops, so that we can provide better than just casual work. I'm going to see this land paying and producing the way I want it to – or die trying. You know what it says in the Baghavadgita: Do what you must, and give no thought to the consequences. "But if thou wilt not wage this lawful battle, then wilt thou fail thine own law and thine own honour, and get sin." '

'The trouble is,' Patti said after a moment of silence, 'the Naxalites probably quote the Baghavadgita, too, and I bet Krishna says exactly the same to them.'

The three of them came slowly down the long hillside together, to where they had left the Land-Rover parked in the meal-white dust at the side of the track. Behind them the ground rose in broken folds, and there were the sparse beginnings of the forests that proliferated, far above, into dense jungle. Before them the open, rolling land lay outspread, fields and groves and villages, threads of shrunken water, standing crops and grazing cattle. They walked alongside the almost dry watercourse, marking at each decline the ridges in the ground where once the bunds of the irrigation tanks had been, mysterious hummocks under the grass.

They were talking hard enough now, with animation and point. The tanks could, Larry was positive, be put back into operation at comparatively little expense, given ample and willing labour. And much could be done at the same time to level some of these bordering fields, and conserve water and soil by discreet terracing.

'Ours isn't a delta economy, we're never going to get three crops off our ground. But we can get two, given these quick-maturing new hybrids the government are producing at Adutharai.'

'We've been doing some work along the same lines ourselves,' said Dominic, 'in our own laboratory. And our situation isn't very different from yours here. The Swami will probably bring Satyavan Kumar along to have a look at your land, as soon as he can. He's the man you want on seeds.'

'You know what we could do with most of all? Some sort of small, agriculturally-based industries. Something that will give a chance of steady employment, instead of casual. Capital isn't going to be a problem so much. My father left a great deal of money. And you've seen my place – what do I want with all that accommodation? It will make central stores and offices, and there's plenty of room to build more plant and workshops as we grow. And we've got plenty of skills, and some good, shrewd heads among the village councils. Three of the villages are bold enough and clever enough to come in from the start, two more will probably follow them in. The others will take a season or two to make up their minds, and all we've got to do to get them in is show an improved profit. Once they see their neighbours growing more prosperous, they'll want to come in, too.'

They had reached the road and the Land-Rover. Purushottam stooped and took up a few caked fragments of the brown earth, and crumbled them in his fingers, frowning down at them thoughtfully.

'I was very fond of my father, but I never did see eye to eye with him. That made me feel terribly guilty when he died, and I had to come home. Not that coming home is very easy, in any case, after living such a different life there in England. You feel a stranger here and an alien there. But I couldn't live anywhere else than in India, not permanently, so the thing to do seems to be to settle down as fast as possible. Not by following up what my father was trying to do, though. That would be a thumping lie for me. He tried to hang on to every acre, you know – he was a good landlord, mind you, and what he felt was partly out of loyalty to his tenants, but he didn't know how to change. He was a bit of a litigant by inclination, too, in his middle years, and there've been complications. Now I've got the clearing up to do, and I know what I want, and with the Swami's help we may be able to strike an agreement with the authorities.'

'His credit's high, in the state and centrally,' said Dominic, 'and he'll do everything he can, you can rely on that.'

'I've no ambition to be a landlord, none at all, but I do want to see all this land being put to the best possible use and paying good money to everybody who farms it, and it seemed to me that a co-operative grouping was the best way. And if the co-operative does get floated, and will find me a useful job, I'll be satisfied. I'm ready to plough as much as possible of my father's money into the funds.' He ran the fine brown dust through his fingers and let it sift to the ground. 'Water's the main need. Not much use looking for ground water here, though. Pity!'

'Those tanks can be brought back into service,' Larry assured him, 'and once you've got your fields levelled, contour channels will cost you very little. You'll get your water if you get your labour. And if they don't make you chairman of the co-operative, there's no gratitude or justice.'

Purushottom tilted his head back and laughed aloud. It was the first time they had heard him laugh, and it was a gay, impulsive, almost startling sound. Only now did they realise that something of the quality of defensive isolation had been banished from his eyes, and the pale, finely drawn tension had left his features as the formal self-consciousness had been shed from his gait and gestures. It was an unobtrusive transformation, but a complete one. For these two or three weeks, since his homecoming to perform the son's part at a funeral, he must have been the loneliest young man in India, and suddenly he had companions, even allies.

'I don't think I'm cut out for a chairman, somehow. I'll probably end up as general dog's-body and mechanic, like Dominic. Do you think I can keep up a household like mine on that? At least until we convert them all into agricultural workers?'

They drove back to the house in the early evening in high content, and the light grew rose coloured in the sky to westward. Patti and Priya and Lakshman were home before them from Kuttalam, and the servants were keeping watch on the dinner with one eye and the courtyard with the other, waiting for the last of the company to return before serving the meal.

During dinner Purushottam made a valiant effort to keep the conversation general, and defer to everything the girls had to say; but once the big table was cleared it was not long before the large-scale maps came out to cover it again, and the men gathered round with heads bent seriously together, tracing the fall of the land and the course of the meagre rivers, and marking out the possible immediate scope of the new farm.

'You cannot farm this land by smallholding, and that is what people here are still trying to do. The result is debt everywhere at the first monsoon failure, or the first blight, because there are never any reserves. It can only be made effective on a large scale.'

'And with a diversified economy.'

'Exactly. And we are not dealing with a silt-fertilised soil like the deltas, where even on a big scale hand labour pays off better than mechanical methods. We have less to lose and more to gain.'

They called in Lakshman to view the land they had surveyed during the day, and left the two girls to the newspapers and the radio. Patti watched the hands of the clock slip slowly past the hour of nine, and asked Purushottam resignedly: 'Have you got a typewritter, by any chance? If you wouldn't mind, I should like to write a letter home. What with all the trouble at Thekady, I haven't written for a while, and they do rather tend to expect them every few days.'

He jumped up remorsefully from the table. 'I'm so sorry, we're neglecting you terribly. Yes, there's a typewriter in the office, but it's a huge old table machine. I could have them bring it up here for you . . .'

'No, really, there's no need, if I can borrow the office for an hour or so. I won't disturb anything there. It's just that there really hasn't been a chance until now, and my mother is the worrying kind.'

'Of course, if you'll be comfortable enough there. It might be quieter for you, that's true, it's right across at the edge of the yard. I'll come down with you.'

She protested that she would find it, but he came, all the same. Above the beaten earth of the lower yard the sky arched immense and full of stars, the darkest of blues, and yet so clear that it seemed to have a luminous quality of its own. The low white buildings gathered out of the air whatever light remained, and shone faintly lambent, hollow-eyed with deep windows and doorways, with here and there the murmur of voices and the spark of a lamp. The office, as he had said, was the most remote of all the buildings, even its windows turned away from the yard which all through the day was the centre of activity in the household. It was thick walled and not very large, one wall stacked high with cupboards and filing cabinets, a big desk set near the window. Both it and the typewriter on it were littered with papers and folders.

'You were in the middle of something. I'm sorry!'

'No, I'm nearly straight now. When Mr Das Gupta gets here tomorrow morning I shall be ready for him.' He swept up the scattered papers and moved them out of her way, and whipped the current sheet out of the machine in such a hurry that he tore it. She exclaimed in regret, and he laughed. 'It doesn't matter. I left it so hurriedly this morning that I should have had to do it again in any case, I've completely lost the thread. It isn't more than a quarter of an hour's work, I'll do it early in the morning.'

'A lot of money certainly makes a lot of work,' she said, so gravely that there was no offence in it. 'Don't you ever want to drop the whole thing and just walk out?'

'I've never walked out on anything yet. You can't abdicate your responsibilities, whatever they are.'

'No,' she agreed, 'you can't do that. Krishna was right.'

Purushottam shook up the cushion to make the typing chair a little higher for her, and looked round to make sure the light was adequate on the carriage. 'My father hated figures so much – on paper, that is, he was clever enough with them in his head – that he made this office right away in the corner by the kitchen garden to be free from distractions while he struggled with them. I've had cause to be glad about that myself now. You're sure you have everything you need? There are stamps here, do take whatever you want.'

He left her to it; and only a few paces from the door she heard him break into a light, fleet run, so eager was he to get back to the plans for his super-farm. She sat down at the desk, and fed a clean sheet of paper into the machine, and began to type her letter home.

By the time Priya and Dominic came to look for her, more than an hour later, she had finished not one letter, but two, and was just folding the second into its envelope.

'One to my grandmother in Scotland, too. They're both

edited rather radically – I could hardly tell them we were so close to what happened in Thekady, could I, they'd be having fits! There,' she said, thumping down the flap of the envelope, 'that's duty done for the next two or three days.' And she reached into her big shoulder bag, which was slung over the arm of the chair, for her own store of stamps. She was glad it was not Purushottam who had come to fetch her back to the house; he might have been hurt at seeing her use her own stamps when he had offered her his, and she would have been sorry to hurt him.

Six

Malaikuppam: Wednesday Morning

They were up for breakfast at six, but Purushottam had been
up for an hour and more by that time, first superintending
the preparation of a supply of food for them to take with
them, then re-typing the memorandum he had spoiled the
previous day. He was a rapid but erratic typist, and by the
time he was called to breakfast he had finished the job,
and turned to arranging everything relevant in order, and
tidying away everything irrelevant from sight. A quarter
of an hour's strenuous work after the Land-Rover had
departed, and everything would be ready.

A dark brown maidservant, too shy to speak, brought
morning tea to Patti and Priya in their room. She drew the
curtains, and there on the table beside Patti's large bag were
the two letters, ready stamped and labelled for air mail.

'Purushottam will send them to the post for you,' said
Priya.

'Oh, I'll take them with me. We can drop them in a box
in the first town we pass through. You got on to first name
terms with him over the maps, did you?' she said carelessly.

'No,' said Priya composedly. 'I just thought of him so. I
have not called him so as yet.'

They dressed and packed briskly, forewarned by now of
Larry's strict time keeping. In four hours or so they would
be in Nagarcoil. Home, for Priya; and even for Patti, in a
sense, home.

India had not quite grasped the vital nature of time to a
western mind, and both the tea and coffee came rather late;
but in spite of that, it was only just after seven o'clock
when they all walked out to the terrace, and down the
steps to where the Land-Rover waited. The servants had
collected all the bags from their rooms, and waited to stow
them wherever Lakshman indicated. Larry had the bonnet
of the Land-Rover up, intent on the engine. Purushottam
and Dominic found themselves standing together in the soft
morning light, with nothing left to be done. They looked at
each other and smiled.

'Please give my reverences and regards to the Swami, if you should see him again before he finds time for me. Tell him I rely on him to smooth my passage with the state government. If they agree to let me do it this way, nobody in Delhi will raise any difficulties. I've thought about this ever since I got the news, in England . . .'

He had never felt alone or lonely in England until then; never until his widowed father died in his prime, and left to a virtual stranger – yes, however loving and bound, still a stranger – the estate he had tried to hold inviolate against the tide of events. Then in an instant he had known how Indian he was, and felt the tendons of his heart contracting and driving him back here, where he had been raised, where he knew every soul in the nearest three villages, every tenant for ten miles around, and felt for them as his father had felt, but had other means of expressing his membership.

'No, before then, really. Ever since I began to grow up and think for myself, and not just as I was taught. We could be almost self-supporting here. They all keep two or three buffalo, the women take care of them, they want them for milk, and labour, and manure. Give us time, and we might have a dairy, too – not a huge affair like Anand, just a small district Anand. And we have smiths, good workmen, we could be the district tool shop and repair station within a year. From that it isn't so far to a small factory for specialist tools – why not?'

'Why not?' agreed Dominic. In India there is one factor which is never missing and never in short supply: manual skill of all kinds, prepared to copy anything, prepared to improvise anything, given the idea. Something not to be found in repetitive processes, production belts and modern organistaion of labour.

The two girls stood a little apart, ready to get aboard when everything was loaded. They had done everything they had to do, and now there was nothing whatever to distract them from listening.

'Do you really think they'll buy the idea?'

'I don't see why not. They've been known to say that the co-operative is the hope of rural India, why should they back out on it in this case? And if the Swami and the Mission come in on it, that should clinch it.

'There'll be some tricky relationships to be settled, of course, what with hoping to bring in the small cultivators and the Harijan labourers on a fair footing, but that's for

399

the legal men to work out. It can be done all right, given the goodwill, and I do believe we shall have that. Just as long as they accept the idea in principle!'

'They'd be crazy if they didn't,' Dominic said, 'considering you're offering to give them the central base, a good deal of equipment, all your land and pretty well all the capital you possess.'

'Well, not quite all, you know. I've got some industrial stock and a bit of money my mother left me, I'm keeping that for insurance. But what do I need with a plantation establishment like this? My generation doesn't want to live this way. I don't really need any more, basically, than any man down there in the village – less than those who've got families to feed. I rather look forward to working my own passage on the same terms as the rest. Not that it will work out that way,' he added honestly. 'The name counts for a lot, and there's no way of altering that even if I wanted to. I shall be voted in there somewhere among the management, I know that. And I shall enjoy it, too, making this district work for every soul who lives in it, more efficiently than it's ever worked before. But at least I shall have to be *voted* in! If there'd been anyone left in the family but myself and one decrepit old great-aunt,' he admitted, 'it wouldn't have been so simple. But there's no one now to object if I choose to give away everything I've got.'

He would not have said that so simply if he had remembered that the girls were only a couple of yards away; but he had forgotten them utterly, he was speaking only to Dominic, who already knew his mind.

The luggage was all stowed. Lakshman opened the door for the girls to climb aboard, and Larry shut down the hood, and drew breath to make his farewells.

'You've been immensely kind to let us all descend on you like this—'

Patti, who had opened her shoulder bag and was rummaging frantically in its tangled interior, suddenly exclaimed: 'Damn! I knew I should leave something behind. Is the office open, Purushottam? I went and left my diary in there last night, I remember now . . . I must run and fetch it!'

'I'll go!' he offered immediately, but she was already in flight.

'No, I know exactly where I left it. I won't be a moment!' Back over her shoulder floated a long-drawn:

'Sorry, everybody!' She ran, the bag bobbing under her arm, all down the gently sloping court, little puffs of dust dancing at her heels.

'Just like a woman,' said Larry philosophically, and glanced at his watch. 'Oh, not so bad! Only eight minutes late.'

'After some months in my country that's extraordinarily good time keeping.'

'Look, you've got my address – let me know if you get started on the work here, and if I'm still around I'd like to be in on it.'

'I shall be glad if you can! In any case, come again before you leave India.' They stood and waited. Patti had vanished into the deep doorway of the distant office. Still they waited, and she did not reappear.

'So she knew exactly where she'd left it!' said Larry resignedly.

'I'll go and help her look,' Priya offered.

She had taken no more than two or three steps away from the Land-Rover when there was suddenly a curious quiver that shook the outlines of solid objects, and made the earth seem to heave with an imprisoned and contained life of its own. Then a muffled reverberation like a great, smothered gust of air caused the shape of the office to bulge and quiver, the thatch lifted and lurched drunkenly aside, borne on a wave of dust, the splintered door sagged outwards and fell from its upper hinge, and from the windows at the rear two clouds of dust and debris billowed, dissolving slowly into air. The sound of the explosion was strangely deadened and contained within the yard thick mud walls, but the blast came undulating like a snake across the earth, smoking with dust-devils, whipped at the folds of Priya's sari and slashed her ankles with gravel. Her eyes were blinded, and the wind pressed against her, holding her motionless. She felt someone's arm take her about the waist, and someone's body intervene between her and the tearing force that assaulted her; and she clung with closed eyes to this sheltering body until the ravaging wind had spent itself and left them still upright. She heard someone's voice saying, even before the sound of running feet began:

'Oh, my God, my God, not again!'

And another voice, her own voice, saying, not entreatingly, but with fierce professional authority, as she looked up into Purushottam's face:

'Let me go! Let me go to her! This is my job!'

The office, when they groped their way into it through the dense fog of dust and the particles of paper, wood splinters and debris from the burst thatch, was a scarred shell, windows and window frames blown out and scattered over the kitchen-garden at the rear, where three terrified but undamaged children crouched screaming hysterically, the door a tangle of sagging planks, the floor deep in wreckage. What was left of the typewriter, a skeleton of torn out keys and twisted metal, lay under the shattered windows. The desk, every joint ripped asunder, lolled against the wall.

They stumbled over the body of Patti Galloway as they fumbled their way blindly within, and at first they did not even realise what it was. Papers and dust covered her, she was a roll of matter powdered over with dissolution. Tatters of clothing draped her, once they brushed the dust aside, but she was ravaged and disrupted like a rag doll torn up in a temper. Dominic retrieved one sandal from the far corner of the little room. The tight enclosure of this place had magnified the effect of the explosive far beyond what they had seen in the open at Thekady. And yet there seemed to be some things that were almost untouched, the soft, pliable things that blew in the wind and made no resistance, like the long, straight fair hair that slid fluidly over Priya's arm as she raised the mangled head.

Patti was dead before they ever reached her.

Seven

Malaikuppam: Wednesday Evening

None of them, until some time afterwards, really got the events of that day into focus, or could link them into any significant sequence. They reacted rationally, answered questions coherently, even remembered abstruse and advisable precautions, and took them as a matter of course; but all in a haze, like automatons responding to automatic stimuli. Too shocked to feel, they could still think and reason, and do what the circumstances demanded of them.

So they left Patti lying where they had found her, because even her position might mean something to the trained observer, something to indicate where the explosive had been placed, and how fired. There was nothing they could do for her, except, as soon as it was bearable and time had allowed them to thaw out enough to recognise the necessity, to let her parents know what had happened to her, and perhaps, also, inform whoever had been more or less responsible for her in this country, her head teacher, or the business acquaintance of her father who had got her the job. No one could help Patti herself any more. If there is such a thing as instantaneous death, that was what had happened to her, and nobody could undo it.

So they set a guard on the doorway of the wrecked office, and another of Purushottam's servants in the garden at the rear; and Priya, still blindly following her own nature, retrieved the screaming children from among the vegetables, and made sure they had not a scratch upon them before she handed them over, now shaken only by hiccoughing sobs, to their distraught mothers. After that they went back to the house, all of them walking rapidly and mechanically like somnambulists, chilled of face and unnaturally wide and fixed of eye, and the telephoning began. First the local police; and they were not so far gone as not to realise that Purushottam's family name would count for a great deal there. Then to Mr Das Gupta in Koilpatti, to tell him that no car would be coming for him today, that no meeting was

Ellis Peters

possible today. Not the reason however; not yet. Later they might well feel that they needed his legal advice, but first they must let the police have their head. Touch nothing, alter nothing, inflect nothing. The loaded Land-Rover still stood below the terrace; they had forgotten it, until Purushottam sent out a servant to bring in the bags and remove the food before the heat of the day began. They all knew there would be no departure now.

'We ought,' said Dominic, expressing what they were all feeling, 'to let Inspector Raju know what has happened, too.'

For this could hardly be anything but a corollary of the affair at Thekady. Either one more in a series of outrages which had begun there, or else a move to eliminate witnesses of the first crime. The hovered between the two opinions, but the one thing they could not believe was that this was an unconnected incident. They had blundered into a labyrinth, perhaps merely by reason of being on the boat that discovered the murdered body of Mahendralal Bakhle; and now every move to find the way out might be the wrong move.

'It is a delicate matter,' said Purushottam. 'We are in Tamil Nadu, and the lake is in Kerala, and the state police can be jealous of their rights. We must wait until they come. But as it does seem to be a continuation of your Inspector Raju's case, they may even be glad to call him into consultation. We should be diplomatic.'

They could use such terms, and consider such niceties, while all the time within their shut minds the frantic thoughts kept running round and round in circles like shot animals trying to reach their own pain: 'Patti's dead. She left her diary in the office, and she remembered it and ran back for it, and the office blew up in her face and killed her. Ten minutes more, and the Land-Rover would have been on its way, and she would have been safe on board – but then Purushottam would have shut himself in there with his accounts – Patti delayed the departure, and it's Patti who's dead . . . *But which were they after?*'

'But we could call the Swami,' said Dominic.

'In Delhi?' It seemed almost as far away as America.

'Why not?' He wanted to hear the sanest, most reassuring and detached voice he knew. It had a way of settling things into a true perspective, even death. This was not the first time he had faced the Swami Permanathanand across a murdered

404

body, and perceived in consequence that death is only a part of the picture, however inevitable and omnipresent. 'He'll need to know what's happened, since he sent me here, and he's quite certainly concerned about you.'

'Yes,' agreed Purushottam, faintly encouraged. 'I suppose it might be a good idea at least to let him know what's happened.'

It took Dominic some little time to get his call through and even when he reached the number that belonged to the haphazard little central office of the Mission, buried in the narrow complexities of the Sadar Bazaar, it took him longer still to get hold of the Swami. There was a minor policy conference in progress over the projected purchase of some new agricultural machines, and the Swami could leave the council only for a few hurried minutes. Dominic could picture the earnest heads bent over coloured brochures, and all the ardent faces, young and old, so lit up with partisan enthusiasm that the sharp western mind would never recognise their angelic shrewdness and practicality until they had beaten down his prices and extracted from him his most effective lines. They had a small factory in Andhra where they were making their own, working them out to specification according to regional needs, but they couldn't yet do everything themselves. And angels need to be both practical and shrewd, in order to hold their own with fallible mankind.

The distant voice, gentle, courteous and abstracted, said in his ear: 'I have only a few moments, I am sorry. You are at Malaikuppam?'

'Yes, Swami, we're here. Since the day before yesterday . . .'

'And all is well with you and Purushottam?'

'No, nothing is well. We need your advice.'

'Tell me,' said the Swami alertly, and composed himself to listen in silence. When the brief but shattering recital was completed, he continued silent for a moment, and then he made utterance twice, with a thoughtful pause between, and very gently hung up the receiver.

Dominic came back into the room where the others waited; all their eyes were on him, and Priya at least seemed to see in his face something heartening, as though he had been given a promise, and carried the sheer relief and reassurance of it in his eyes.

'What did he say?'

'He said,' Dominic reported faithfully, ' "To the born

sure is death, to the dead sure is birth; so for an issue that may not be escaped thou dost not well to sorrow." '

'Helpful!' said Larry sourly, his New England mentality outraged.

'And then he said: "I will think what is best to be done." And hung up.'

'And is that all?'

'You don't know him,' said Dominic.

Strangely, as if a strangled spring had been released to gush freely, Priya bent her shining black head and began to cry, freely and quietly, not like a heart breaking but like a broken heart beginning to mend. And Purushottam, far too Indian to put an arm round her, nevertheless leaned forward with a gesture of fastidious delicacy, almost of fear, as though he had astonished himself, and took her hand in his.

The Tamil inspector of police from the district HQ was a strong contrast to Inspector Raju, a highly-strung, insecure man who made a fair amount of noise over his activities; but luckily his insecurity prompted him to accept a highly convenient let-out when it was offered. After lengthy discussion by telephone with his District Superintendent he gave it as their joint opinion that the Keralese authorities should certainly be called into consultation, since this appeared to belong to Inspector Raju's prior case. The probability must at least be examined. Meantime, all the witnesses were kept waiting in suspense inside the house, while Purushottam showed the police officers the scene of the tragedy. Then he, too, was dispatched to wait with the others.

It was no wonder that they had a long time to wait. They had seen the desolation of the office, every shard of which would have to be examined; for somewhere there were the fragments, such as remained, of the second bomb. And they had seen the violation of Patti, with which the police doctor was now engaged. What they had to tell was of secondary urgency. They waited now in a very slightly relaxed but still numbed quietness, chilled with shock for all the growing heat of the day. The servants brought food, but no one did more than play with it, if this helpless distaste could be described as play. Only late in the afternoon did Inspector Tilak get to them and even then it was to inform them that Inspector Raju had been notified several hours previously, and was on his way. The satisfaction in his voice was carefully suppressed but none the less present. The death of an English girl in a terrorist outrage was a very hot potato, which he was by no means sorry to be allowed to drop in the lap of the police of the next state. What he wanted to hear from them first, therefore, was the whole story of the events at Thekady; and they told them separately, each of them remembering in isolation. Their statements regarding the new outrage were left to wait until Inspector Raju arrived, as in the early evening he did, driven by Sergeant Gokhale in a rather unexpected Mercedes.

Mindful of his duties as a host, Purushottam had made provision for them. A meal was waiting, and there were rooms prepared, since clearly they could not return to their own state this same night. The two inspectors had a lengthy session together before they interviewed their witnesses, and it was past nine o'clock by the time they had all made their second statements, and were assembled again in conference. It seemed that Inspector Raju, in view of what they knew already, saw no point in concealing from them those aspects of this case which linked up only too surely with the previous one.

'Mr Bakhle was killed by a bomb, deliberately planted on board his boat. I can tell you now that the bomb that killed Miss Galloway, of which we have found fragments – more fragmentary, unfortunately, than in the last case – seems to have been manufactured in a similar way, with the same materials, probably by the same hand and at the same time. The connection is clear. We cannot reconstruct the dial of the firing device this time, and we don't know for what hour it was set, for there is a possibility that it may have gone off through some unexpected shock or vibration. So we can't deduce from the time of the explosion anything precise about the person for whom it was meant. But I'm sure you will not have missed the implications. In five or ten minutes more the party would have left, and it seems obvious from your statements that after your departure Mr Narayanan would have gone back to his work in the office, in preparation for his lawyer's intended visit.'

He looked round them all, and his lined face was a little grey and tired after his journey, but there was nothing wrong with the sharpness of his eyes.

'Yes, it is true, not everyone could have known that fact, though all this household could, as well as yourselves. But that is less significant than you may think, for the fact seems to be that ever since his father's funeral rites Mr Narayanan has spent much of his waking time in there, and that may be well known by now to most of the district. It could also very easily have been learned by anyone making a private study of Mr Narayanan's habits. I have seen for myself that though there may be a watchman during the night, this house is virtually open twenty-four hours a day. The gate is almost never closed, but even it it were, the wall would be very easy to scale. In short, the bomb could easily have been planted during the night by someone who had watched Mr Narayanan's routine for some days, but perhaps had not even realised that he now had guests. The necessary observations may well have been made before your arrival. But in any case another death, the death of an innocent bystander, quite uninvolved in any ideological struggles in India, would not worry the people who plant bombs to do their work. To them Miss Galloway, I'm afraid, merely represents the loss of a little explosive. They have more.'

Quietly and carefully Dominic said: 'You're saying, Inspector, that the attack was meant for Purushottam. Not for Patti.'

'I am saying that quite clearly that is the inference you have all drawn from the occurrence. It is, indeed, the inference anyone would draw. So much so, that now I am only wondering, and perhaps asking you to consider the possibility, too, whether that is not what we are all meant to think. Here is another landlord, a vulnerable target, obviously the bomb was meant for him.'

Purushottam's sombre face did not change; the idea was not new to him. Nor did it seem to impress him very much, after the day they had spent here together, and the sights they still carried burned within their eyes, and could not stop seeing.

'But,' said Inspector Raju, 'there are many landlords, some more obvious targets than our friend here. Here is a new bomb outrage, at the home of the land owner who *happens* to be entertaining the witnesses closest to the Bakhle killing at Thekady, and that bomb outrage just *happens* to wipe out one of those witnesses, instead of the host. I am not very fond of coincidences. I always tend to look round behind them – almost to believe that they are not coincidences at all. Therefore I would like you to consider the possibility that an agent of the Naxalites may very well have moved here from Thekady to Malaikuppam, not because his next victim had already been marked down here, but *because he was following you, the witnesses.*'

'But in that case,' said Larry, galvanised into speculation almost against his will, 'if he wanted to get rid of *us*, why not plant his bomb in the Land-Rover, and time it for when we were well away from here? It would be the safest method I can think of.'

'Because, Mr Preisinger, for the past two nights Mr Narayanan's watchman has been making your Land-Rover his base. He is a romantic, and to him a Land-Rover is an exotic wonder. You may be sure no one has had the opportunity of violating that sacred vehicle. Moreover, supposing there was a choice among witnesses – some, say, who knew virtually nothing, one who had some special knowledge – they would have preferred to aim, at least, at getting the vital one, and letting the others go. Many deaths are acceptable in a pinch, but need not be wastefully incurred where they are not necessary. And Miss Galloway had made use of the office yesterday evening. She may have been under observation then – even so closely that someone knew she had left her diary there. I do not say it is so. I say only that it is something to be considered, and I ask you to consider it.

'She wrote two letters,' said Priya suddenly, raising her heavy dark eyes. 'She had them sealed and stamped in her bag, ready to post. If she had any knowledge – if there was anything troubling her – may she not have put it into her letters home?'

'We had already thought of the same possibility, Miss Madhavan. The bag is virtually undamaged. We have opened the letters. They are exactly what would be expected of a young girl's letters home – quite straightforward accounts of her travels, only omitting, understandably, the ugly experience at Thekady. There is nothing there for us. Naturally they will be passed on to her family. But what made you think of that? Had she behaved as if she had some secret and dangerous knowledge? Her collapse at Thekady now almost suggests that she believed she knew something of perilous importance, and was frightened to confide it – frightened to a degree which cannot quite be accounted for by the shock of the discovery, which was common to you all. And under which, I must say, you yourself behaved with exemplary fortitude.'

She hardly heard the compliment, though if she had it

might have given her both pleasure and pain. She was peering into pure air before her, frowning anxiously.

'I don't know . . . She'd had such a sheltered life until she came to India, naturally she was very much upset by the manner of Mr Bakhle's death. She had never known anything like that. I don't know, it would be easy to misinterpret what was no more than the after effects of shock. What can I say? I hardly knew her. Surely you must have looked through all her belongings. Was there nothing?'

'Nothing. For of course you are right, we have looked.'

'And the diary!' Inspector Raju drew a long breath. 'What has become of that? Who will tell us? We have sifted through every scrap of paper that remains in that office, Miss Madhavan. But we have found no diary.'

In the hours before dawn, when at last he fell asleep after long contention with wakeful images that would not be shaken off, Dominic dreamed of hearing a car's engine climbing steadily up the track from the main road, endlessly climbing and climbing and refusing to give up or be discouraged, though every yard gained was replaced by an equal distance unrolling ahead. A part of his mind was still awake enough to realise that this was one of those frequent frustration dreams that come between waking and sleeping, usually in the last hours before arising, and go on for an eternity that turns out to have been contained in the twinkling of an eye. The frustration is there because the minuscule particle of time involved compresses the eternity too strictly for any fulfilment ever to be achieved. The car would never complete the climb, never arrive anywhere. He knew that as he slid away into deeper sleep.

But when he opened his eyes on the rose radiance of dawn, and his ears to the chattering of the sparrows on the verandah, and the passing scream of parakeets come and gone like a flash of light, he felt in his bones and blood that something was changed since yesterday. He showered and dressed, and went out through the quiet house, where nothing stirred but the distant soft movements of barefoot servants, to the terrace, and straight across it to the top of the steps.

Below him the Land-Rover still stood forlornly waiting; but beside it was parked, with almost pedantic neatness, an elderly black Morris. It seemed the car of his dream had completed the climb, after all, and arrived at its destination. He was not aware of ever having seen this car before. It had the discreetly old fashioned, anonymous, average look of a hired car, and betrayed nothing whatsoever about the man or woman who had recently driven it.

Dominic went looking for him. The terrace continued round the corner of the house and all along the north-east wall; and at an hour when everything that wakes turns its back on the chill of the night and looks eastward into the first rays of the sun, this jutting corner seemed to be the place where anyone already waking would naturally go. There was a stone seat just round the corner, draped with a hand-loomed rug. And there was a man sitting cross-legged on the seat, his hands cupped in his lap, his face upturned to the rising sun.

His colour was pale bronze, and in the reddish, gilding rays of dawn, launched horizontally like lances along the mist-blue and dust-amber land, he might have been indeed a bronze, made not so far away in Tanjore in the high period of the art, three centuries and more ago, for all his clothing melted into the same range of glossy metallic shades. Not even the darkness and texture of hair broke the unity, for his head, with close-set ears and beautiful, subtle shaping of the skull beneath the skin, was shaven naked as his face. Lofty, jutting bronze brows arched above large closed eyelids; the long lips were folded together peacefully in the faintest and purest of smiles, and the thin, straight nose inhaled so softly and tranquilly that not even the act of breathing seemed to inflect his charged stillness.

But he was not asleep. As soon as Dominic's advancing figure cast a shadow on his nearer shoulder, the bronze cups of his eyelids lifted from exceedingly bright, mild, knowing eyes, dark brown and deeply set; and when two more steps had projected the shadow across his body he dwindled magically but gracefully into a middle-sized elderly gentleman wearing a saffron robe with a frayed hem kilted comfortably round his loins, and a fawn coloured trench coat draped over his shoulders. His naked feet – his sandals lay beside the bench – were slim, bony and whitened with dust. He looked way-worn, but not tired. And he looked up at Dominic with a bright, gratified smile, and joined his palms gently under his chin in greeting.

'*Namaste*, my son!'

'*Namaste*, my father! I'm glad you are here.' His very presence resolved everything into a matter of serene understatements.

Ellis Peters

'You are not surprised?' remarked the Swami Premana-thanand, with a distinct suggestion of disappointment.

'Never surprised by you. But very glad of you.'

'I flew from Delhi to Madurai – it is a tedious business, though it is so quick. And from Madurai I have driven that hired car – quite unknown to me, I am used only to my own.' His own was a forty-year-old Rolls, visually reduced by sheer hard labour to a flying scarecrow, but mechanically nursed like an only child. He was slightly surprised by his successs with this modern degenerate, and a little proud. 'I arrived nearly an hour ago, but I did not wish to disturb anyone. I am afraid this is a house not well blessed at present with dreamless sleep.'

'I dreamed I heard you coming,' said Dominic.

'That was not a dream, I was thinking of you. As I promised,' he said, 'I gave thought to the problem of what might best be done. And I thought that my responsibility in this matter is very great, and that I ought to be here with you.'

He rose, and slipped his feet into his worn sandals, his long, prehensile toes gripping the leather thongs.

'Shall we go into the house?'

Eight

Malaikuppam: Thursday

Purushottam, puffy-eyed from want of sleep but eased and heartened at the sight of his visitor, made his ceremonial greeting, and bent to touch in veneration the Swami's hands and feet. Larry hovered, long and dubious and aggressively American where his scepticism was called into resistance, everything about him from his bristling crew-cut to his thick-soled travelling shoes making a point of its complete un-Indianness. Priya offered her *namaskar* shyly but with composure, and answered the grave smile with a pale, withdrawn smile of her own. Lakshman was respectful, dutiful and more obstinately the paid courier than at any time during the last few days, so that there should be no mistake as to where he stood, and how immovably he stood there.

And the police, after an hour or so of cagey assessment, maintained with scrupulous politeness and reverence, opened their ranks and let the newcomer in. That was perhaps the greatest compliment paid to the Swami Premanathanand that day.

It was Inspector Tilak who called the afternoon conference, and presided at the head of the table, with Inspector Raju tactfully on his right hand; though as officer in charge of the original case the direction of the discussion was smartly and gratefully handed over to the Keralese officer as soon as proceedings opened. The Swami took his place at the foot of the table; but Dominic, seated halfway between, found himself experiencing repeatedly the kind of optical illusion in which up becomes down, out becomes in, and the foot of a table is translated into its head. It did not disconcert him; he had seen it happen before where the Swami was concerned, even when, as now, that enigmatic person was doing his best to suppress the tendency. His face was attentive and respectful, his eyes mild, and his voice asked gently for guidance rather than making suggestions; and with his usual timeless but astute courtesy he listened carefully to everything everyone else had to say, as they went over once again the entire history of the case.

'So as I understand it,' he said diffidently, when he had absorbed everything, 'we have here two deaths which are certainly closely connected, and there are some facts about them which need not be questioned. That they are the work of experienced terrorists, most probably Naxalites. That the bombs were made by the same hand, almost certainly in Bengal, and therefore that someone brought them south to the agent chosen to use them. Now the agent at Thekady is known – unhappily after the event and after his own inadvertent death. Whether he was to be used again for the same role is something we do not know; but since he was killed by his own act, clearly he cannot be responsible for what has happened here. There remains the supplier. I am not so naive as to suppose that other Naxalite agents may not be available in the south; but they are unlikely to be experienced with such comparatively sophisticated weapons as these. And also it is wasteful to acquaint too many people with the plans for such an act. Even those who sympathise are safer knowing nothing. One person, the messenger who brought the bombs, was already in the secret, and is the most probable person to have pursued the intent to the end. Have I followed you correctly?'

'Perfectly,' said Inspector Raju.

'And is it established that this person must have brought the bombs south only recently?'

The two inspectors glanced at each other, and Inspector Raju said, after only a momentary hesitation: 'In the first one some folded sheets of newspaper had been used as wadding inside the case. We have identified a Calcutta newspaper, dated not quite four weeks ago.'

'So we are looking, in effect, for someone who has come from the north since that date. Someone who does not belong here. A stranger. It should not escape us, of course,' he said mildly, 'that there are several such in this room now, including myself. Naturally those of us who have known one another for some time will feel that that line is hardly worth pursuing, but we must not ignore it altogether. There were also, at Thekady, a number of such people, visitors to the wild life sanctuary. And those, I know, are being kept under observation since that time. But none of them, as far as we yet know, has been anywhere near Malaikuppam.'

'As far as we know,' agreed Inspector Raju drily. 'But

some were as close as forty to fifty miles on Tuesday night, and with cars it is not so difficult to move from one place to another. The Manis, for instance, decided after all to keep their hired car and driver rather than go by train over these last stages of their tour. They spent only one night at Rameshwaram. On Tuesday night they were at Virudhunagar, and last night at Tirunelveli. From either it would be no great journey here. Oh, they have reported their presence everywhere scrupulously. But there are still eight hours in the night. We shall check on everyone.'

'We are fortunate in having an officer who knows the district as Inspector Tilak does,' said the Swami warmly. He already knew from Purushottam's cook and watchman that the inspector was a native, born and raised not twenty miles away. 'So he will have everyone's goodwill and assistance in his inquiries about any strangers recently seen in these parts.' That hardly followed, Dominic thought, until he remembered that the stranger they were looking for was a Naxalite terrorist. In theory the extreme left-wing Marxist forces were on the side of the great suppressed majority; but in practice the members of that submerged class were the most likely of all to die in the ideological carnage, and nobody knew it better than they did, or resented it more bitterly.

'May I continue? I am talking chiefly to clarify matters in my own mind. Then we have the present outrage, and this unknown person who is responsible for it. It seems that we are confronted with two possible theories: one, that X was following up a pre-arranged pattern of events in attempting the murder of Purushottam, one more representative of "the chief class enemy": two, that he followed Miss Galloway here in order to wipe out what he had cause to believe might be a dangerous witness against him in the previous case. In short, in the first case the bomb was meant for Purushottam, in the second for the victim it actually claimed, Miss Galloway. Let us take the second case first.

'If it was Miss Galloway he wanted, then he must have followed the Land-Rover here, otherwise there would have been no way of tracking it afterwards on a cold scent to this particular place. Then again, X must have observed Miss Galloway using the office for her typing, and supposed – perhaps because of the diary she left behind? – that she was likely to do so again, or why plant the bomb there? But if he was there watching her during the evening, why risk the bomb at all? Why not a knife on the spot, or his hands? The office is one of the remotest buildings, with windows away from the court. Entry and exit would not be difficult, a cry could be cut off quickly, there was darkness to cover his retreat. He would have been a fool to take a more devious but extremely haphazard way. This militates against the theory, but does not altogether invalidate it, for we all know that sometimes men under pressure *are* fools, and *do* take the most inept ways of achieving their ends. And perhaps this one, previously merely the messenger, was too afraid of being personally responsible, too wary of ever actually showing his face. Better an inefficient attempt from a safe distance than a possibly disastrous direct confrontation. So let us still bear the theory in mind as a possibility. And what is in its favour? The matter of the diary, which Miss Galloway discovered she had left behind, but which was not in her handbag when she was found, nor anywhere in the office. So perhaps, after all, someone *was* watching, someone who wanted that diary removed and destroyed. Someone who both planted the bomb that night, and stole the diary. Miss Madhavan, did you ever notice this diary? Can you tell us what it looked like?'

'She had a little red leather address book and stampcase,' said Priya, 'and a big red leather writing-case. The diary could have belonged to the same set.'

'This we have found,' said Inspector Tilak. 'But no diary.'

'I don't actually recall seeing her writing up a regular entry in any book. But that needn't mean anything. It would be only a matter of a few lines, perhaps not even filled in each day. After all, I was with her for such a short time, only about ten days.'

'Nevertheless,' the Swami maintained, 'it remains a possibility that she had written down in it something of vital importance – perhaps something she did not even realise to be important at the time. If so, it can only have been something connected with the bomb outrage at Thekady. Now you were all together there, as we know. Even before the two parties joined, at the forestry bungalow, Miss Madhavan was with her, travelling with her, sharing a room with her. Now what can Miss Galloway have seen or realised that the rest of you did not?'

They could think of no possible juncture at which Patti's experience at Thekady had been different from theirs.

'And yet,' said Larry slowly, 'when we found the boat she

did come to pieces – to a rather surprising degree. I mean, it might be only a temperamental difference – I was knocked pretty useless myself at first. But she went down for the count, they had to give her a sedative and let her sleep through until next day.'

'Yet she had seen only what you saw. So it was not something *witnessed* then. Could it have been something *recognised and made sense of* then? Something that linked up with something else she already knew, and had not realised she knew? Go back, Miss Madhavan, to the journey up to Thekady. Go over it in detail in your mind, and see if there is not at some point something which she did, and you did not do, something she saw, and you did not see.'

Priya opened her tired eyes wide, and stared back into the recent past, and began to recount the whole commonplace detail of that bus trip into the hills, proceeding with a patience which expected no excitement on arrival.

'We got off at the bungalow, and took a room. No one else left the bus there The French couple were already there, and the Manis arrived just as we came out to walk down to the fruit-stall below. It was while we were at the stall that Larry's Land-Rover passed on its way up to the bungalow, but it was nearly dusk then, especially there among the trees, and they didn't notice us. Then we walked back. There was nothing else, I think – except that Patti looked to see if the sadhu was still sitting by the lingam, and then she went back and gave him some small coins. For luck, she said.'

For luck! Whatever force had been allotting Patti her luck had made sure that all of it was bad.

'Sadhu?' said Inspector Raju, taking his long, worrying fingers abruptly out of his tangled grey hair. 'What sadhu?'

'Just a sadhu. He was sitting by the Siva lingam, one bend of the road down from the bungalow. I don't remember noting him when we drove past in the bus, but we saw him as we went down to the stall, and then on the way back Patti turned back to give him some money. Suddenly she said: "Wait for me a moment!" and gave me her parcels to hold, and she walked back to him. I saw her reach in her bag for some coins, and heard her put them in his bowl.'

'Now this,' said Inspector Raju, unsheathing his pen, 'is interesting. I know that road as I know my hand, and never yet have I seen a sadhu choose that particular place to sit. Did your friends also see him?'

'No, he wasn't there when we drove back to Madurai,'

Lakshman said for them all. 'And we hadn't noticed him on the way up.'

'So only you two girls saw him face to face, and might know him again?'

Priya hesitated. 'I shouldn't know him again – I don't think I could ever be sure. He wore a devotional mark like this . . .' She drew the three lines and the small upright oval joining them. 'But he was sitting back among the trees, and it was getting dusk. I didn't go near, I just waited for Patti.'

'So she was the only one who got a close look at him?'

'Is he so significant?' Larry ventured. 'I thought they were liable to turn up pretty well anywhere, come when they chose and leave when they chose.'

'That is very true, but nonetheless this is curious. Consider this spot of which we are speaking! One bend of the road below the bungalow, where buses stop and a few people alight – one bend above the fruit-stall, where some at least of the passing cars might be expected to make a stop. But not *at* either of them. At a spot where no one is going to halt but the occasional archaeologist, and only if his attention has already been called to the meagre remains there. Those who live by alms must go where people are expected to be.'

'But there must be times when they're not concerned solely with extracting money from people,' said Larry.

'Those who sincerely desire a solitude where thought is possible will not be found sitting, from choice, beside a motor road. No, this is not a proof of anything, but it is a most curious detail.'

'It is also,' the Swami pointed out delicately, 'an apt occurrence of just what we were looking for – a stranger in the picture, however briefly. Someone who did not belong to the staff or the visitors at Thekady, or the bungalow, or the bus, or any part of that ordinary weekend excursion. Is it possible that she saw that face again elsewhere and recognised it? Perhaps at the lake, in quite a different connotation? He may be irrelevant, of course. But it would be no harm to inquire if such a Saivite devotee has also recently been seen near Malaikuppam.'

'We will see to that at once,' said Inspector Tilak, making notes with great vigour.

'Then, if I may, I would like to consider the other possibility. For in this case we must find the right course of action, in addition to taking thought. If the bomb was meant for Purushottam, and not for Miss Galloway, many things are simplified. The Land-Rover need not have been followed here. The terrorist came here because this was where his assignment awaited him, and the arrival of Mr Preisinger's party was merely coincidental. As we have said, a little reconnaissance would show that Purushottam has been spending his days in trying to make sense of his father's affairs. In short, a bomb planted in his office and timed to go off at almost any time during the day, between meals, would have an excellent chance of securing his death. It was meant for him, and only by reason of slight delay in the Land-Rover's departure, and perhaps also of this idiosyncrasy of exploding ahead of the fixed time, did it kill Miss Galloway instead.

'Those are the two theories. Either is possible. But the reason we must take this last one seriously has little to do with which will eventually turn out to be the right one. It is simply this: In the one case, if they meant to kill Miss Galloway, they have succeeded, therefore they will wish only to disappear into the landscape and not be traced. In the other case, if they intended to kill Purushottam, they have failed.

'Therefore,' said the Swami, calmly and distinctly, 'they will try again. So the question is, how are we going to ensure his protection?'

Purushottam, who had been all this time listening with only half his attention, and with the other half pondering some gnawing anxiety of his own, apparently in some way connected with Priya's clear profile, jerked up his head with a startled and almost derisive smile. As though, Dominic thought, he still doesn't altogether believe in the danger to himself, or, more perilously still, has no respect for it.

'My protection? What can one do except take all sensible precautions, and then simply go ahead with living? I shan't go looking for trouble, you can be sure. And we have a pretty large household, all of whom are to be trusted.'

'Yet still Miss Galloway is dead,' Inspector Raju reminded him austerely.

He flushed deeply. 'I'm sorry, you're right. I'd over-looked the fact that by attracting danger to myself I may have cost one life already. But that situation can easily be altered if you, sir, are prepared to let my guests proceed with their journey. Then I shall no longer be putting them in jeopardy.'

419

'How can we go?' Priya protested. 'We have sent a cable to Patti's parents, and we must be here to make arrangements – to do whatever they may wish. They may even fly over here to take her home. How can we abandon them now?'

'As far as the police are concerned,' Inspector Raju said, after a brief, consulting glance at his colleague, 'the party is at liberty to proceed on the old terms. Provided they will keep in touch, and be available at need, they may leave in the morning.'

'And I advise that they should,' said the Swami. 'I will remain here to receive Mr and Mrs Galloway, or their instructions, and will do whatever little can be done to make this loss easier for them. But that would not in itself solve the problem of Purushottam. No, don't refuse me yet, first listen to what I suggest.' He leaned forward, his linked hands quiet and still upon the table, and his brown, shrewd eyes surveyed them all at leisure, one by one. He had put on his wire-rimmed glasses, which sagged drunkenly to the right of his nose because the right lens was thicker and heavier than the left; and through the weighty pebble of glass his right eye put on its cosmic aspect, magnified out of reason and unnervingly wise. It lingered upon Priya, and passed on tranquilly enough; to Larry, on whom it pondered but briefly thoughtfully; to Lakshman, on whom it rested longer.

'We have here a party of guests expected to drive on to Nagarcoil and the Cape. It is only too well-known to our enemy by now, of course, that only one young lady will be going home to Nagarcoil. But three young men came, and three will leave. Now I admit that if a close watch has been kept on this household during the past few days, the probability is that Purushottam may now be known by sight to those who are seeking his death. But on the other hand, there is quite a good chance that he is not. He has been back in India only a very short time, and so deeply preoccupied during that time that he has hardly been out of the gates until Tuesday. Lakshman is about the same build and colouring.' The large, bright eye remained steadily trained upon Lakshman's face. 'Lakshman will remain here with me, in Purushottam's clothes. He will become Purushottam. And Purushottam will go with the party in Lakshman's place, as courier. Thus we can get him away safely from this house, on which the terrorist will be concentrating. It will gain us the time to take further measures, and allow the police to proceed more freely. And naturally,' he added, 'a very careful watch will be kept, twenty-four hours a day, upon Lakshman's safety.'

It was done with such gentle assurance that only Dominic, who knew him so well, realised what an astonishing suggestion it was to come from a man like the Swami, to whom the humblest of lives ranked in value equal to the loftiest, and indeed would probably take precedence in its claims on his protection and solicitude. Nor had it even the remotest hope of being accepted. He looked curiously at Purushottam, whose mouth had already opened with predictable hauteur, to veto the proposition. He was probably the last young man in the world to allow himself to be smuggled out of his own house because of a criminal threat to his life, especially if it meant leaving someone else to bait a police trap in his place. Dominic waited confidently for him to say so, and for some reason the words had halted on the very tip of his tongue. He cast one brief, piercing side-glance at Priya's profile, and another, as it seemed, back deep into his own mind, where he hid that private preoccupation which had been distracting him earlier. And he stopped to think before speaking. And then it was too late, for Lakshman had spoken first.

'I am quite willing,' he said, 'if you think it will be helpful.' His face was inscrutable, aloof and unsmiling, most markedly maintaining that ambivalence of his between servant and equal. There was even something of the proud forbearance of the servant assenting to something which should only be asked of an equal. And as though he had sensed it, Purushottam found his voice the next moment; a more subdued voice than anyone would have expected, and a more reasonable.

'You can hardly ask me to duck out now, if it means leaving one of my friends standing in for me here, where the danger is.'

His choice of phrase was not calculated; he was not, in fact, a person who ever did much calculating. Lakshman's face lost its chill of correctness. He repeated firmly: 'I am quite willing. I shall be well protected.'

'But whatever could be done to protect you could also be done to protect me. Why should not I be the bait to catch this agent? For I take it that's what you're hoping for?

Since I'm the one he's after, I could serve the same purpose, surely, and serve it better.'

But it would not serve the same purpose at all, Dominic realised in a sudden rush of enlightenment. Not the purpose the Swami had in mind, not the purpose Inspector Raju had instantly perceived and approved, though he kept his mouth shut. The Swami had looked round the entire party with a detached eye, excluded Dominic because he knew him, and Priya – yes, quite positively he had acquitted Priya – for reasons of his own. That left Larry and Lakshman, who had travelled down here from the north together. On balance he had considered Lakshman, as an Indian, more likely to be involved in political mysteries than Larry, and there was also the point that the suggestion he had made could apply reasonably only to Lakshman. How seriously he rated this possibility there was no knowing; but it could not be excluded. The suggestion had been made primarily to see how Lakshman responded to it; and he had settled that without delay by his proud assent. Did that let him out altogether? Not necessarily. There might be Naxalites here, too, who could be contacted and used, and need not, in the last resort, be confided in. So the Swami would persist in his proposition. His design was to get Purushottam away from this house without his departure being known, and to hold Lakshman here in this place; and then to mount constant guard on him night and day. If he was innocent, and exactly what he seemed, he should be protected from harm. If he was guilty, he should be so lovingly watched and guarded that he should have no chance to smuggle out a word or sign to any outside contact, to send other agents in pursuit of Purushottam. If he was innocent he would certainly be acting as bait for a police trap, and the few days' grace they would be buying by the exchange might produce a satisfactory capture. If he was guilty, and clever enough, they would have purchased nothing but stalemate. He would sit tight and take no action, and they would make no discoveries. But it was worth a try.

'And besides,' Purushottam went on reasonably, 'if they have decided on my execution, it's because I'm a land-owner. So my best defence is surely to go ahead as fast as I can with my plans to turn the estate into a co-operative farm, and stop *being* a land-owner.'

'You are making the mistake,' said Inspector Raju with a sour smile, 'of expecting logic and principle to have some part in your enemies' motivation. Fanatics recognise neither. They can decree hatreds; I doubt if they even know how to revoke one.'

'Moreover,' the Swami pointed out gently, 'even if your faith was justified and they called off the hunt in your case, this same killer of men and girls would be free to turn his attention elsewhere. We are asking you rather to help us to capture him, and save the next life, not merely to conserve your own.'

'Yes, I'm sorry, you're quite right. But if I stay, and Lakshman goes on, how will the position be different?' But he asked it as in duty bound, not vehemently; there was even a faint suggestion in his tone of reluctance to argue further.

It was Lakshman who provided the reasonable answer, and saved the Swami the trouble of finding plausible arguments to back his suggestion. Lakshman did it in the pure warmth of his response to being categorised ingenuously as a friend. Some answering gesture seemed called for, even if it had to be rather more self-conscious.

'I think,' he said, smiling, 'that the Swami feels he would have a more tractable subject in me, one more likely to obey orders and be cautious about his own life. Perhaps we should all breathe more freely in feeling that you are safely away from here.'

'In any case,' added the Swami smoothly, 'in a few days Lakshman also could be quietly dispatched to join you. It is simply a matter of covering your immediate retreat. The right number of people must be seen to leave, and someone must be seen to remain, to represent the master of the house. If no one is watching, well, we shall have taken pains to no purpose, but does that matter?'

'I will stay,' said Lakshman decisively.

Everyone looked at Purushottam, and Purushottam looked no less intently at the Swami, with a slightly baffled and curiously gratified expression, as if he had been conned into something he now realised he wanted to do.

'Very well, if that's what you wish, I will go.'

Inspector Tilak withdrew, no doubt gratefully, as soon as the conference broke up, and Inspector Raju departed with him, leaving two men under Sergeant Gokhale to spend the night on the premises. Dominic went down with them to their car.

'Manpower with us is as much a problem as with the police elsewhere,' said the inspector ruefully 'We can't do more. It would not be wise, in any case, to draw attention to your party by attaching a police guard to it, even if we had a man to spare.'

'We're warned,' said Dominic. 'We shall be keeping a sharp look-out, But it seems we shall be leaving the centre of action here with you.'

'If there is to be action. Too often the leopard withdraws into the jungle and is no more seen.'

'Do you know where the French couple are – the Bessancourts?'

'Last night, at Trivandrum. The night before they were at Quilon. Everyone appears to have done exactly what he proposed to do, and everyone has kept me informed.'

'And the boat-boy? The one who wouldn't stay at Thekady after the explosion? I think he expected to be the next!'

'Romesh Iyar? He has been reporting regularly to the police at Tenkasi. In any case, of all of you who left after that murder, he has been under the most constant observation, for he has been working at the junction there, portering on a casual basis. This evening he will be told – by now he *has* been told – that he can move on if he wishes, and need not report any longer. Why check on him further? He was working fifty miles away when the bomb that killed Miss Galloway was planted.'

'And the Manis are at Tirunelveli. Only we,' said Dominic sombrely, 'were here.' He thought of the Swami's practical and necessary realism, and wondered if they had really travelled in company with the murderer's accomplice who had now himself become a murderer. Useless pretending it was impossible, however hard it might be to believe. Useless to take it for granted that Lakshman's convincing display of innocence and co-operation could necessarily be accepted at its face value. He hoped fervently that there would be some move soon which would enable the police to produce the veritable culprit, alive, identifiable beyond question as guilty, and a total stranger.

Purushottam came in the dusk to where the Swami sat on his stone bench on the terrace quiet, rapt and alone. The young man brought a low stool and sat down at his feet. For a few minutes neither of them spoke. The very brevity of the twilight made it precious, a luminous moment held suspended in air, delicately coloured in gold and crimson and transparent green, soon to dissolve into the clear darkness of the night.

'And are you seriously interested in that young woman?' the Swami asked at length, in the same matter-of-fact tones and with the same aplomb as if he had been asking the time.

'How did you know that I wanted to go?' Purushottam demanded.

'I did not, until you showed me. I thought we might have considerable difficulty, my son, in persuading you to comply. You saved me a great deal of trouble.'

'I like her,' said Purushottam cautiously, and looked down frowningly at his linked hands, aware both of the inadequacy and the ambiguity of words. 'Swami, I am the classical Indian problem, and you must know it. I am the foreign-educated Indian youth coming home. I have two cultures, and none, two backgrounds and none, two countries, and none. You know the saying: He is homeless who has two homes. *I* am real, I am more real than ever I was, but nothing now has a real relationship with me. I am without parents now, without close family, and therefore, in a sense, freer than most young men coming home, but in many ways it is an illusory freedom, because it has to deal with the possible lack of freedom of others. And even in me there is still a great deal of respect for tradition, whether I like it or not. People in my situation come back agonisingly aware – almost morbidly aware – of the complexities and rigidities of Indian marriage. And I can see that any orthodox family might well hesitate at attempting to assimilate anything so bizarre as I have now become. And even worse, in this situation – in this shadow and uncertainty . . .'

'You need have no doubts concerning Miss Madhavan,' the Swami assured him tranquilly. 'I have known students, secretaries, clerks, cooks, housewives, artists, all manner of women who have at some juncture turned to terrorism. But never yet, in any country, have I known a case of a nurse who became a terrorist.'

'I didn't mean that. I haven't any doubts, of course. But if I am to continue as a target for assassins, how can I cause her to be involved with me? I have no right. Yet if I let her go now, I may never meet her again. And I know nothing at all about her family, the plans they may have for her, or what, for God's sake, they'll make of me!'

'There is a very simple cure for that,' said the Swami, watching the stars burst out, sharp and brittle as frost, in the distant sky, where the fading green of the afterglow ended. 'Go with her to Nagarcoil, and find out.'

'Three strange young men arriving out of nowhere? It will not be like that. We shall put her down a little way from the house, and she will take good care to wait for us to drive away before she goes in.'

'You will be making a very stupid mistake,' said the Swami reprovingly, 'if you begin by under-estimating the lady.'

Priya appeared in the doorway, the green of her sari outlined in silvery light from the room within.

'Purushottam, may I use the telephone?'

'Of course!' He was on his feet in a moment. 'You would like to call your home?'

Her white teeth showed in an amused smile. 'Ours is a very modest house, we have no telephone. But there is a silversmith at the corner of the street, a friend of my parents, he will take a message if I ask him. I want to let them know we are coming, so that they can prepare. I think we should be there by one o'clock? You are all invited to my home for lunch. My family will be very happy to welcome you.'

The Swami admired the stars, and said nothing.

Nine

Nagarcoil: Friday Morning

They drove out from the gate in the early morning, Priya between Dominic and Larry in the front seat, Purushottam among the luggage in the back, where Lakshman would be most likely to ride. Lakshman himself waved them away from the terrace, realistically enough. If there was a watcher, the picture was there for him to see. But it was hard to believe in it, except when the ruins of the office fell away on their left side, and the edge of desolation touched them afresh, and made the morning air seem suddenly preternaturally cold. They were all thinking of Patti, who had been so challengingly alive, and was now a mere broken body, not yet released from police custody. In a moment, in the twinkling of an eye. 'To the born sure is death, to the dead sure is birth; so for an issue that may not be escaped thou dost not well to sorrow.'

Priya had said earnestly to the Swami, before they climbed aboard the Land-Rover: 'They must not see her. It would be better to take home only her ashes and her belongings.'

And he had said: 'I will take care of everything.' For Priya had seen her, and Priya had strong feelings about what bereaved parents should and should not be asked to endure. It was a field in which he had some experience, too, but he respected hers.

To Dominic, and privately, he had said: 'Telephone me each evening until we meet again. And if anything occurs, *anything* that seems to you significant, or to have anything to do with this matter, then telephone me at any time, as soon as possible. We do not yet know whether the thread will stay here with us, or go there with you.'

But when they were through the gates, and Dominic was driving down the dirt road from the village, in the astonishing brightness of early morning, it was more than they could do not to turn their heads and their eyes away from the wreckage behind, and towards the world ahead, which was varied and beautiful, and had a welcome waiting for them.

They passed through Tirunelveli at about nine o'clock, and they were in the most Christianised district in the whole of India, though until they crossed the bridge over the Tambrapurni river, and saw the tall spire of the C.M.S. church soar in front of them, there was nothing to make them aware of the characteristic. From Palamkottai southwards they were on the main, unmetalled road to Cape Comorin, and the landscape was a sequence of palm groves deployed among rice paddies, thatched villages, the occasional gopuram of a minor temple, and always the accompanying shapes, misty and deeply blue-green under their jungle growth, of the Western Ghats on their right hand. Monkeys crouched under the trees along the road, unstartled, peering at them with their sad, wizened faces, and jack-fruit like huge, lumpy, holly-green Rugby footballs dangled on their thin, drooping stems from the branches.

'Soon,' said Priya, her face brighter now and her eyes wide with anticipation, 'we must turn off to the right for Nargarcoil.'

They were no more than eight or nine miles from the sea now in either direction, south-east or south-west. At the fork they took the more westerly road, as Priya directed. India had already demonstrated in its invariable manner the nearness of the ocean which its people, apart from a few fishing communities, do not love. The sky was almost an English sky, no more than half of it blue, the rest scudding cloud, driven fast, though there was no wind at ground level, and forming and re-forming in constantly-changing masses and temples and towers. The light had become a maritime light, moist and charged with melting colours, scintillating instead of glaring.

The road widened at the same time as it seemed to narrow, because lines of small houses had begun to frame it on either side. It acquired the texture of a street, and other and taller buildings sprang up behind the first, and became the beginnings of a town of more than a hundred thousand souls. A nondescript textile town, where among other things, they make hand-loomed towels of all kinds and sizes. A town with Jain associations, and Christian ones, too, of several persuasions; and in its way a pleasant place, more spacious than most of its kind, and with something of the air of a country market town, with energy and time to spare.

'Now we are coming into Nagarcoil,' said Priya.

Death to the Landlords!

* * *

The house lay off one of the quieter and narrower streets at the edge of the central shopping area. There was a space of beaten earth drawn back in an open square from the street, with a solitary tree at one front corner, and in its shade a patch of bleached grass. Each of the three closed sides of the square was a little, deep-eaved, whitewashed house one storey high and overhung by a red-tiled roof. They were as neat and clean as brand-new dolls' houses, and not much larger. Purushottam's ranch-like dwelling would have contained ten of them, and his compound at least fifty. And the children who came trumbling out of the house on the right, as soon as the Land-Rover turned into the yard, were as bright and spruce and petite as dolls. Little girls in minute cotton dresses, western style, little boys in cotton shorts and white shirts; all of them huge-eyed and smiling and excited, but perfectly silent, and all the girls wearing little crowns of flowers. The moment they had fully taken in the Land-Rover, and confirmed for themselves its veritable arrival, they shot back into the house as precipitately as they had frothed out of it, and the voices that had been mute outside were loosed in a torrent of shrill Tamil, speading the news. Before the travellers had all climbed out and shaken off the dust of their journey, Priya's parents appeared in the deep doorway at the head of the five shallow steps. They marshalled before them the three littlest girls, who held up at the full stretch of their short arms dewy garlands of lotus buds and roses and jasmine. With formidable solemnity they descended the steps, taking passionate care not to trip over their burdens, and advanced upon the visitors.

'Good God!' said Larry blankly, between consternation and delight. 'What *have* you got us into, Priya?'

'You have never been garlanded before?' she said innocently. 'In my family we do things properly.' And she went to meet the little girls, lifted the necklaces for them, and hoisted the first over Larry's head, and the second over Dominic's. But Purushottam, his face brighter than they had ever yet seen it, sat down on his heels to be on a level with the panting littlest, and let her hang her garland round his neck with her own hands. He had an unfair advantage, for he could talk to his hostess, who chattered back to him in high delight.

'All the ones who go to school know English,' Priya said

429

reassuringly. 'Come, I would like to introduce you to my parents.'

Mr Madhavan was probably in his late forties, no more; a short, square, muscular man with crisp hair just greying at the temples. His wife was plump and round, with a cheerful face that smiled even in repose. Their best festival wear was plain, practical cotton, whites for him and sensible wine-coloured sari for her, laundered many times but laundered superlatively. There was no wealth here, only a hard-won and shrewdly-planned living, and a great deal of good humour as oil for the machinery of making-do. There was a cheerful flurry of greetings, blessedly in English; and with ceremony which hardly seemed ceremonious because it was so exuberant in its warmth, the visitors were brought into the cool of the house.

'Not all the children,' Priya said, reading their minds, 'are ours. Two of the littlest belong to my eldest married brother, and two to my married sister – they both live quite close – and one or two from the neighbours seem to have joined the party, too. You are a great event, you mustn't grudge them gate-crashing.'

There was also a beautiful girl of about seventeen, a plain but engaging one of fifteen and two boys aged eleven and nine. They were so many and so colourful and the little ones so light and rapid in movement that it was like being surrounded by a cloud of butterflies.

How even the ones who belonged in the house ever found room there remained a mystery. So far as they saw, it consisted of only two rooms, though the kitchen was obviously elsewhere. The room into which they were brought was furnished very simply with a couple of cushioned benches which must also have done duty for beds, a large table and a few chairs, a chest of drawers against one wall, covered with an embroidered cloth and proudly presenting the parents' wedding photograph, two or three other family pictures, a carved box, and a bowl in which flowers floated. A curtained doorway led through into a second and smaller room with two charpoys draped with bright covers, and a little table loaded with family ornaments and souvenirs. The bright calendar hanging on one wall showed a blue, effeminate, mischievous Krishna leading a timorous Radha through the grove. But on another wall there was an unexpected reproduction of a modern Christian nativity, romantic and sugary-sweet, complete with ox and ass. Purushottam studied it with dazed interest, and turned to look wide-eyed at Priya.

As for Priya herself, she was perfectly at her ease, composed, even a little amused, certainly proud of her poor, prolific, hospitable and gracious family. She helped her mother to settle the guests comfortably, relieved them of their garlands, and brought, before everything else, glasses of cold water. Then the women vanished to the sacred and invisible kitchen. They also herded the small children out into the yard to play, though until their curiosity waned they tended to creep back and stand in a little rainbow cluster in the doorway, frankly and greedily staring.

'My daughter tells me,' said Mr Madhavan, sitting down with his guests, 'that you will go on to Cape Comorin. It is only about eight miles from here. But you are a South Indian yourself, Mr Narayanan, and doubless you already know it.' He was feeling his way towards a subject which must be mentioned, to set everything in clear order, but equally must not be allowed to cast too long a shadow upon this gathering. 'You will understand, we were expecting Priya to bring her friend with her. All my girls were looking forward very much to her visit. Priya has told us already, by courtesy of our good friend, Mr Achmed, who has a shop close by, what has happened. It is a terrible tragedy, and we are deeply sorry. For her parents especially. Such a dreadful loss for them. Death is not an ending, of course, but it is a separation.' It did not sound so far from the Swami's: 'To the born sure is death . . .' But it caused Purushottam to cast a fleeting glance at the pretty, Christmas-card Bethlehem on the wall.

Mr Madhavan followed the look, and smiled understandingly. 'Perhaps Priya did not explain us. We are Salvationists. Oh, yes, you will find we have quite a strong community here. Since my grandfather's day our family has belonged to the Salvation Army. There is an excellent Army school here, all our children attend it.'

It seemed utterly fitting that the good friend Mr Achmed, who took the telephone messages for the family, should be a Muslim, Purushottam breathed deeply, and warned himself, half-heartedly, not to expect too much; but so much had been lavished already that he found it difficult not to feel encouraged. Instead of the orthodox, narrow Hindu family he had feared, all the more insistent on the proper procedures because they were not rich, adamant about suitabilities of caste and background, here was this cheerful, exuberant, free-thinking tribe with a door wide open to friends of all creeds, and professing not merely Christianity – which after all might have been a disadvantage rather than otherwise in some of its manifestations – but the most down-to-earth, hearty and extrovert brand of Christianity possible. Exotics themselves in this conformist India, they were surely capable of assimilating even such an exotic as Purushottam Narayanan, half-westernised, a non-believer in caste, and about to beggar himself – comparatively speaking – by turning his lands into a co-operative farm, if the state authorities did not block his plans out of spite towards the central government, which was always a possibility. He had not admitted to himself until then how much he valued and wanted Priya, with all her quietness and her dignity, her courage and self-respect, the occasional spark of demure mischief in her eyes, and in particular, and most daunting of all, her sturdy ability to stand on her own feet and be independent even of him, in a world heavily weighted against feminine independence. Now he had qualms on only one score, that as yet he did not know whether she felt the same way about him. But one fence at a time!

'My middle son plays the trumpet in the Army band,' said Mr Madhavan, confirming with every word the good impression he had already made. 'My eldest son – he will probably come in for a coffee afterwards if he can get away from the shop where he works – has on the other hand reverted to his great-grandfather's Vaishnovite persuasion. It is a change without a difference, don't you think so? Largely a matter of what label one uses. But if a man feels more at home and more suited with one than with another, and finds the kind of help he needs, that is what matters. We get on very well together.'

Faced with so interesting a set-up, Larry came out of his shell and began to ask question after question, none apparently being barred, and none that he was likely to frame resented. It was not often he had such an opportunity, with someone at once as articulate and as artless as Mr Madhavan. And the children gazed and listened in fascination until the women reappeared in procession from some outhouse kitchen, and shooed them out again to play.

The fifteen-year-old spread the table with a cotton cloth, and the seventeen-year-old brought in four huge, glossy green banana leaves, delicately holding two, folded edge-to-edge, between thumb and forefinger of either hand, and laid them for plates. They were newly washed, and drops of water sparkled in the veins that ran down into the stems. Then Priya and her mother brought in the dishes, and stood and served as the men ate. There was rice, spiced and tinted with saffron, a variety of vegetables, and a chicken curry; and afterwards, some of the ultra-sweet Indian sweets made with coconut, which treacherously soak you with a fountain of syrup unless you know how to eat them. Forks had been thoughtfully provided for the foreign guests, but both of them chose to eat with the fingers, like the rest of the party. The two teenage daughters went off to feed the gaggle of hungry children in the kitchen, and the feast overflowed into the yard and into the street.

When everyone else was taken care of, Mrs Madhavan and Priya also helped themselves and sat down with the menfolk. And by the time the younger girls brought coffee Mr Achmed the silversmith had arrived, and the eldest son with his wife, and the married daughter with her husband, to meet the visitors and to reclaim their various children. The walls of the little house bulged.

Out in the centre of the open square the Land-Rover stood all this time, a magnet for the interest of the whole district. Word went round from one to another, and half the neighbourhood came to see.

Priya emerged from the kitchen with a new pot of coffee, and crossed to the steps of the house. The Land-Rover had nearly disappeared beneath a cloud of gaily-coloured children; but they were in pride and awe of it, more concerned with being seen to belong to it than anything else, and there seemed no need to call them away. It was because she was looking in their direction, however, that as she passed she looked beyond them, to where the solitary tree stood rooted in the baked earth, sheltering its little mat of grass.

There was a man in a yellow robe sitting cross-legged in the shade there, dappled with the sunlight filtering through the leaves over him. She saw the coils of wooden beads and coloured cords round his neck, the tangle of black hair, and the ash-smeared forehead with the cult mark of Siva. He was motionless, his body facing the street, but his head turned towards her father's house.

For one instant she had checked at sight of him; and though she resumed her purposeful walk at once, she could not be sure that he had not noticed and understood. She went on into the house, and poured fresh coffee; and then, without a word to anyone, and hardly missed among so many, she darted out again, down the steps and straight across towards the tree. For he could not be a coincidence, and she knew he was no illusion. She had no idea what she was going to say to him, or how he would answer her; but she must confront him, challenge him, and at least get a close look at him, face to face, so that in future she would be able to identify him wherever they met, and through whatever disguise he might put on. Here on the public street, among so many people, what could happen to her?

The grass-plot under the tree was empty, the scintillation of leaves quivered over the place where he had sat only a minute ago. The sadhu was gone.

She went on into the street, and searched in both directions for the flutter of saffron cloth, or a glimpse of the tangled, oily black hair; but he had vanished utterly.

She walked back slowly to the house. Now, she thought, I know that it was Purushottam they wanted, and not Patti, and having failed, they will try again. However he did it, this spy, he has found us. He is not wasting his time watching Lakshman from a distance at Malaikuppam; he is here, hard on our heels. And now, what are we to do?

He knows that I've seen him, this man. He went away because he didn't want me to see him more closely. So he knows we're warned. Would it be best to stay here, in a town, surrounded by people, where nothing can happen without instant detection, where action would be suicide? But no, we've seen already that they will contemplate suicide without a qualm, if they must. Death does not frighten them, not even their own. No, hundreds of innocent people passing by would be no protection, they would still toss a bomb in at the door and kill as many as need be, just to kill one . . .

A private part of her mind said, and she heard it and did not try to pretend deafness: '. . . ·*that one!*'

She had a family, parents, all those younger brothers and sisters and nephews and nieces . . .

No, she thought, we must go. Get out of here as soon as we can. The departure of the Land-Rover will be sign enough. If we can whip it away unobserved, now, while he is keeping out of my way for his own ends, I can guide it by a roundabout route, and not pass where we should pass on the direct road to the Cape. We may be able to lose them completely, and yet the fact that the Land-Rover is gone should leave my family undisturbed. All will be quiet here. The visitors gone – any neighbour will tell them. But not where! I must warn my father not to tell anyone where we are going.

All along, of course, it had been 'we'. She knew that she had never meant to remain here, and let him go on without her, still under that shadow. Not even before she had sighted the pursuit, much less now. Not until the threat had passed, once for all, would she part company with Purushottam.

She went back into the house, which was full of voices, and made her own quiet voice cut through them all, clapping her hands under her chin with a bright, apologetic smile. Purushottam had been trying for half an hour to raise his courage, and find the right words in which to request that she might be allowed to travel on to the Cape with them, and even in this liberating atmosphere he had found it a hard thing to do. Yet if he did not make some move now to continue the acquaintance, how could he hope to revive it later through the good offices of his one surviving aunt, who in any case would think the match most ill-advised? But Priya simply raised the pitch of her soft voice a couple of tones, and said deprecatingly: 'I am so sorry, but it is quite time that we should think of leaving now. Please forgive us!' and everything was resolved.

Ten

Cape Comorin: Friday Afternoon

On the last eight miles to Cape Comorin the Western Ghats had been left behind at last, the country opened level and green with paddy-fields and palms, broken only, here and there, by small, astonishingly abrupt, mole-hill-shaped mountains that erupted out of nowhere like the remains of old volcanic activity. Most of their area was bare, bluish rock; only in the scanty folds of their lowest slopes did trees and bushes cling.

'You didn't tell us,' said Parushottam, in the back of the Land-Rover with Priya, 'that you were a Christian.'

She did not take her eyes from the road unrolling dustily behind them; but she smiled. 'I'm not sure that I am. Not sure *what* I am. I think I am religious, but I am not very partisan. But I was brought up as a Christian, and I have never seen any point in changing, when calling myself something else will not really be any more appropriate to what I believe. I expect I don't think very logically about these things, but categories are so limiting, and so confusing.'

Still she watched their wake; she had been watching it ever since she had guided them out of the town by bewildering lanes and alleys, and round by cart-tracks to reach this southern highway at last. But there was no vehicle in sight behind them.

'What are you watching the-road so carefully?' he asked.

'To make sure that we're not followed.'

His mind had been too full of other thoughts to have any room for the consideration of his own safety. He had forgotten, temporarily, that it had ever been threatened. 'We shan't be followed now? Why should we?'

'I hope not,' she said. 'But there's no harm in keeping our eyes open.'

The tall gopuram of a temple showed ahead, rearing out of the palms. A large grove of trees surrounded it, but the tapering, gilded tower stood out far above the fronds of their crests, covered with carvings and alive with colours.

In five minutes more they reached the gates, and the broad, ceremonial path that led into its courts. There were several cars standing before the entrance, and at sight of the rear-most of them Dominic laughed, and slapped a hand lightly on the wheel.

'This is where we came in! What did we say? Provincial France has caught up with us again.'

There was no mistaking that old, sky-blue Ford, with the scratches of some ancient skirmish ripped across one door, and dabs of red retouching on the rear wing. The Bessancourts must be inside the temple enclosure with their box camera, doggedly making up the record of their travels. A tall, rangy young man in khaki shirt and shorts and a white headcloth sat on his heels, leaning back comfortably against the enclosure wall, his arms embracing his legs and his head pillowed on his knees, contentedly asleep, though they could only assume that his job was to guard the parked cars and discarded shoes.

'Shall we stop? Do you want to have a look at the temple?' asked Dominic, slowing down.

'No, let's go on,' said Larry. 'If everybody's going to be making for this hotel at the Cape, maybe we'd better get there ahead of the rest. Not much doubt we'll be seeing the Bessancourts this evening, is there?'

They could smell the sea, and trace the direction of the wind by the slant of the trees, before they came within sight of village, temple or cape. There were roofs of building ahead, more palmyra palms, and then a crossroads where a battered bus had just turned, clearly having reached its terminus. A few houses, small and modest, and a stall selling fruit and drinks, the cheerful stall-holder brandishing a machete to behead the coconuts, and slice a way through to the three pockets of sweet juice in the palmyra fruits for his customers. And that was all.

'Here we must turn to the right,' said Priya. 'Look, that big house – that is the hotel.'

A lane brought them to its gates, and to a parking-ground within. The house was quite un-Indian; it might have been more at home in any expensive Victorian suburb of any northern commercial town in England, and indeed it had once been a British Residency; but it had broad, grassy surroundings, and a few windswept flower-beds, and it looked solid, spacious and comfortable.

'The first chance I have had,' said Purushottam buoyantly,

'to be a proper courier for you.' And he led the way inside to book rooms for them all. They followed more slowly, and in the dimmer light within looked round them among the panelling and potted palms, glimpsing through open doors and rear windows a sudden dazzling vista of sand, flowing in undulating dunes along the edge of a half-buried road; and beyond that the glitter of water. The Indian Ocean, which had seemed still far away from them, was almost lipping at their back doorstep.

Their rooms were on the first floor. As usual they were all double rooms, but because of Priya's presence they needed three, so that one of the men was also privileged to enjoy a room to himself. 'You take that one,' Dominic said, and took Larry's bag from the room-boy and dumped it within.

'Suits me,' Larry agreed accommodatingly, and followed his belongings.

Purushottam caught Dominic's eye, and smiled. 'You feel responsible for me?'

'No sense in taking any unnecessary chances, you'd better share with one of us. Doesn't matter which.' But it did. He was the one who would feel answerable to the Swami for Purushottam's safety, and that mattered a great deal.

Priya's room and Larry's were neighbours, and faced east. The third room was approached by a small side-corridor of its own, and faced south. All three of them opened on a long balcony with railings of ornamental ironwork, supported on painted iron pillars from below. Purushottam tossed his bag on the left-hand bed, and unzipped it in search of a clean shirt. For verisimilitude he had brought away the bag which belonged to Lakshman, but he had put in his own toilet articles and pyjamas and a change of clothes. After the dusty journey he wanted a shower.

He was still revolving under the cool water when he heard, distantly through this splashing music, the shrill, peremptory shriek of a woman's voice, and then Dominic's resigned groan of: 'Oh, *no!*' from the balcony. In pure curiosity Purushottam emerged glistening and golden from the bathroom, trailing his towel over one shoulder and leaving moist footprints behind him.

'Why: Oh, *no!* – and so fervently? What was it?'

Dominic drew back a little from the railing, and pointed down into the garden.

The Manis, in all their glory, were just returning from a leisurely stroll along the coastal road from the village; Gopal

Krishna in immaculate beige linen and immense sun-glasses, with his expensive camera round his neck, Sudha in a lilac and blue sari woven in subtle stripes that changed shade with the light, her wrists laden with portable treasure of good bracelets, and her pale golden face plaintive with vexation. Sushil Dastur, harried as ever, trotted at her elbow bearing her bag, folding canvas chair, cushion and book. And what had occasioned the shriek of reproof was that he had let fall her bookmark, and lost her place in the book. Profuse and voluble in apology and reassurance, he was already feverishly hunting for it again, at the peril of dropping her cushion at any moment.

'*That* is what it was – the lady. You haven't encountered the Manis yet, but you will, the minute they set eyes on us. One of those cars outside must be theirs, but I never thought. All those black hire jobs look alike. And the devil of it is that they know Lakshman. In any case, they'll have read about Patti.' The mention of her name was like a stab, all the more because it was entirely possible, for brief periods, and on the tide of such crazy pleasure as they had experienced at Nagarcoil, to forget all about her. The reminder was still a crude shock when it came; and reality was treading on their heels even here.

'Do they matter?' Purushottam asked, watching the three figures advance towards the hotel.

'Do we know what matters? They were at Thekady. They'd seen us a couple of times before that. For that matter, the French people are surely on their way, too. The car we passed at the temple. A pity! As we were a couple of days behind schedule, I thought they might all have turned back northwards by now. Not that the Manis ever actually acknowledged Lakshman's existence,' he added scornfully. 'I don't believe they ever addressed a word to him. But the Bessancourts did. And in any case none of them can help noticing, at close quarters, that you're *not* Lakshman, whether they expect you to be introduced or not. Now how are we going to account for you?'

Purushottam wrapped the towel round him, massaged his slender body pleasurably and considered. 'Lakshman had to leave you, and I'm your new guide. My name's Narayanan. Why not? Supposing there is anyone here who already knows of me – the chap you're worrying about – then he knows my name. And for any others, Narayanan is a perfectly good name, common enough, you meet a few of us everywhere.

It will do for a guide as well as for anyone else. Who knows, they might even take me for a plainclothes policeman detailed off to escort you!'

'Good advice,' agreed Dominic, after a moment's reflection. 'Why complicate things unnecessarily? Hurry up and get dressed, and we'll go and brief the others.'

They had need of a united front; for the moment they appeared in the lounge, with its range of large windows giving on the coast road and the dunes, Sudha Mani rose with a small, melodious shriek of recognition and sympathy from her tea-tray, and bore down upon them in a gust of perfumed air, her sari fluttering.

'Oh, Miss Madhavan – Mr Preisinger – Mr Felse – Oh, we have been so anxious about you all! It was all in the papers – such a dreadful thing, that poor young lady! Ah, how we felt for her, and for her unhappy parents, so far away! Oh, how little we realised, when we said good-bye in Thekady, that in so short a time—' Her breath gave out; she held her swelling bosom, and heaved great sighs.

'My wife,' intoned Gopal Krishna, rolling ponderously up to her support, 'is so hypersensitive. Your bad news – such a shock to hear . . .'

'Yes, it is a wretched business,' Larry agreed rather forbiddingly.

'But why, I ask myself, should anyone wish to hurt a young English lady like Miss Galloway?' Gopal Krishna blinked behind his dark glasses, and shook his head heavily. 'The police have a theory? They did not detain you, I am so glad of that.'

'No, they didn't want us to stay put. Though of course we're in constant touch,' Dominic said. No harm to plant the idea that wherever they went the police might well have a shadow not far behind. 'As far as we could gather, they think that Miss Galloway may have seen something incriminating at Thekady, perhaps without even realising it, and someone wanted her silenced. But of course we may be wrong - it's just an impression. They haven't found it necessary to interfere with your movements, I hope?'

Sudha raised her fine black brows, a little disposed to be affronted by the suggestion, but her husband flowed on complacently enough: 'Oh, no, indeed no, we have not been troubled at all. But for such distressing happenings, it could have been a most pleasant trip. We spent two nights at Tirunelveli, and went out to the coast there to see the Subrahmanya temple at Tiruchendur, and the cave sculptures. We arrived here for lunch today. You are also staying overnight? That will be very nice, we shall see more of you.'

They withdrew, smiling their goodwill and shaking their heads over all that had proved regrettable and spoiled a perfect trip, and went back to their tea. Neither of them had given more than a faintly curious glance at Purushottam, who hovered in the background with a very fair imitation of Lakshman's ambiguous manner.

'Let's get out of here and have a look for the Cape we've heard so much about,' said Larry restively, and led the way out, straight through the lounge to an open door, and out into a narrow garden, a levelled waste-land of grass half silted over with the encroaching edges of the dunes. It was like Cornwall in many ways, the furtive wavelets of sand creeping towards the house, the sparse plantations of tamarisks, the smell of the sea.

A light, insinuating hand plucked gently at Dominic's arm as he passed through the doorway, last of the four. He looked down into the timid, apologetic dark eyes of Sushil Dastur.

'Mr Felse, I wanted only to say . . . I read in the papers yesterday, about Miss Galloway.' He shrank a little, drawing his large, bony head into his hunched shoulders. 'It is not for me – I am only a retainer . . . But I am so very sorry!'

Startled by the very simplicity of this direct approach, Dominic looked at him as if for the first time. The Manis made it difficult to view Sushil Dastur as anything but an adjunct of their passing, a kind of comic postscript. And the man himself made it no easier to see him clearly, since he saw himself in much the same manner, and would, in a sense, have preferred to be invisible. It was an act of courage and decision on his part to speak for himself. And even now he had in his other hand a silk scarf belonging to Sudha, and before he could break away she gave tongue in quest of it; 'Sushil Dastur, quickly! There is a draught here!'

'Thank you,' said Dominic hurriedly, and briefly touched the arresting hand with his own. 'We appreciate that very much. You're very kind.'

Sushil Dastur fled. And Dominic followed the others out into the seaward garden. It was from the right, from the west, that the sand was advancing, marching so softly, so insidiously, that for long months a broom might hold it at bay, and then suddenly one morning the broom would have to be exchanged for a spade. To the left the garden opened into an untroubled expanse of grass, and a few clumps of shrubs and trees. The drive wound round the building to this frontage, braving the rim of the dunes, and here, too, a few cars had found parking space, though that at the landward side of the hotel was higher by several feet, and quite free of sand. And there among the parked cars was the sky-blue Ford with the scratched door; and just hoisting out the bags and locking the boot again was the rangy young man in khaki shorts and bush shirt, who had been sleeping placidly under the temple wall on the road from Nagarcoil.

He lifted his head at the sound of their voices, staring for a moment in tension between delight and disbelief, and then his face split open in a broad and bountiful smile, and he dropped the Bessancourts' bags on the ground, and came gladly salaaming over the gravel pathway to meet them.

'Sahib . . . sahib! So I find you here also! You know me? You remember me? Romesh Iyar, boat-boy?'

'Romesh!' It was impossible not to be warmed by the reflection of his pleasure. Larry halted willingly. 'We never expected to see you here, you're way off your beat. I thought you had a job waiting on the railway at Tenkasi. What are you doing here?'

'Sahib, I stay in Tenkasi three days, work sometimes, but no regular job. My brother very poor man, I not stay there to live on him. Third day police say can go now, not report any more. In Tenkasi is not good, no jobs there. So I go try in Trivandrum, but there also I got no luck. Everywhere many men without jobs.'

'You'd have done better,' Dominic suggested ruefully, 'to stay in Thekady, where you had a job.'

The turbaned head shook violently. Anything rather than that. 'No, sahib, no stay there. No go there again. That was bad place, bad luck, must get away from that place.'

'But what will you do, then? Are you working for the Bessancourts now?' Self-contained and self-sufficient, those two elderly, invincible people seemed the last pair in the world to need or want a servant.

'I very lucky, sahib. Someone tell me, good jobs going in Dindigul, in tobacco factories, so I want to go there, but it is long way, cost too much money. But then I meet Bessancourt Sahib and lady, and they remember Romesh. They say they go from here to Pondicherry. Best road to

Pondicherry is through Dingigul. So I ask, please take me like servant, you not pay me anything, only food and let me ride with you, and I do for you everything. They very kind, tell me yes, can come.'

'Fine! And you think there really will be a job for you there?' asked Larry.

'Oh, yes, sahib, very good jobs in tobacco factories. I am good worker, can do all.'

'You drive a car, too?' Not that the Bessancourts seemed to need a relief driver, but there was little else for a travelling servant to do for them, they were so used to being self-supporting.

'Oh, yes, sahib, I drive anything with wheels, very good driver.' He went and picked up the discarded bags from where he had dropped them. 'Must go now, Bessancourt Sahib waiting for luggage. You stay here tonight, sahib?'

'Yes.' Dominic thought, as perhaps they were all thinking, it's Thekady all over again, but without Patti. The same cast, even a rather similar Victorian hotel, the same parked cars, the same – though very different – tourist spectacle long since formalised by strict custom. Here you don't go out to watch elephants from a boat; but the rules are no less firmly laid down. You go out in the evening towards the west, to watch the sun go down in the Arabian Sea, and in the morning you get up early and go out towards the east, and watch it come up again out of the Bay of Bengal, far away beyond invisible Ceylon.

Romesh Iyar had been an employee at Thekady for a matter of months, he remembered; and suddenly he asked on impulse: 'Romesh, all the time you were at the lake, did you ever see a sadhu begging by the Siva shrine, the one near the forestry bungalow? Wearing this cult sign?' he drew it with a stick in the gravel. Romesh had put down the bags again, and was gazing down at the scratched drawing with a face suddenly tight and wary. he took some moments for thought, though they could not escape the feeling that he had known the answer from the beginning. Finally he looked up into Dominic's face, and he was no longer smiling.

'Yes, sahib – once I see such a man. That is strange – it was that same time, same weekend when *that thing* happen. Day before you come to my boat, I go down to village with truck to bring flour, in afternoon I go. I see this sadhu then, sitting by lingam. I remember it because never before I see anyone sitting there. This once only I see him.' His face was clouded, even uneasy; something more was stirring in the back of his mind. 'Sahib, why you ask me this?'

'We saw him, too,' said Dominic, 'that same day. We wondered if perhaps he was often there.'

'No, never before I see him. Only that once. But, sahib – there is something else, now you have spoken of this man. Just such a man I see also today.'

'Today?' said Dominic sharply. 'Where?'

'Sahib, in Nagarcoil. Bessancourt Sahib stop there for midday meal, and I go look at the town. In Krishnancoil district I see this sadhu, sitting under a tree, in Jambukeshwar Lane. This same mark he had. Sahib, was this the same man? Was it he . . .' His voice foundered. The whites began to show in a widening band all round the pupils of his eyes. 'But, sahib, this was *a holy man* . . .'

'I shouldn't worry,' Dominic reassured him quickly. 'The police wanted to check on everyone who was in the area, that's all. Why should you be anxious about it now? You're with the Bessancourts, and in a day or so you'll be heading for Dindigul with them. You'll get your job, and never hear any more about this.'

'Yes,' said Romesh, but abstractedly, and as he picked up the bags for the third time his face was still taut and alert with something that did not quite amount to fear – wariness, uncertainty, disquiet. He would be glad when the sky-blue Ford headed north-east again. 'I go now, sahib, must go, got work to do.'

He set off round the corner of the house, and they stood looking after him until he vanished.

'You don't suppose,' Larry said tentatively, 'that he was making up today's sadhu, just to oblige?'

'No,' said Priya quietly, 'he is speaking the truth. The man was there. I know, because I saw him, too. Perhaps you did not notice – Jambukeshwar Lane is the name of the road where we live.'

She told them the whole story. 'If the Bessancourts were at lunch, that would be about the right time. I think Romesh must have passed by and seen him before I noticed him. When I went out again, he was gone. I think he knew I had seen him, and he did not wish to be seen at closer quarters. So I thought the best thing to do was to get you away from there at once, while he was keeping out of sight for his own sake. And that is what I did.'

'But why,' demanded Purushottam, aghast, '*why* did you

Death to the Landlords!

say nothing? If I'd known we were being followed – if I'd known they were watching us – I'd never have brought you with us into this danger.'

She looked at him with a pale but radiant smile, and said: 'But that *is* why. Now I am here, and there is nothing you can do about it. It was not only that I wanted to come with you, it was partly because there was no time for explanations, and I did not want to alarm my family. Also I did want to get you out of Nagarcoil by a roundabout way, in the hope of losing our shadow. And we may have done so, you know – I hope so. I feel sure no vehicle actually followed us. It seems that they know quite well who you are. But if they now know *where* you are, it's because they knew in advance where we were going, or at least were able to guess. Or because once again they have simply found us, as *he* found us in Nagarcoil. A Land-Rover is not so anonymous as one of those black hire-cars and taxis.'

Purushottam said, with eyes for no one but Priya, and in a hurt, reproachful voice, like a baffled child: 'You shouldn't have done this to me. Of all things in the world I wanted you safe.'

'Of all things in the world,' said Priya, almost crossly. 'I want you alive.'

It struck Dominic as being one of the oddest, as well as one of the briefest, love-scenes of all time, but it was exceedingly illuminating. Even Larry, whose perceptions were inordinately obtuse where women were concerned, looked astonished and enlightened. The retrospect of Nagarcoil acquired undreamed-of implications. That fantastic set-up knocked on the head all considerations of caste, and even of poverty and wealth. On the one hand this girl so extravagantly rich in relatives and so poor in terms of money, and on the other this lonely, aristocratic, voluntary exile from caste and class, with his head full of exalted ideas and his life empty of kin. An excellent arrangement, Dominic thought, the pooling of equal but different resources. I wouldn't mind betting the Swami saw this coming. For a life-long non-swimmer he is certainly pretty good at forecasting the tides.

'No point in arguing, anyhow,' he said reasonably, standing-in for his distant mentor, 'she's here now. Look, you go on out to the shore, and I'll join you in a few minutes. I've just remembered something I'd better do now, while I think of it.'

What he had remembered – though he had never actually

445

forgotten it, or detached his mind from it – was that he had promised to telephone the Swami whenever anything occurred that might be relevant to the matter in hand. And a Saivite sadhu seated in contemplation outside the little house in Jambukeshwar Lane seemed, in the light of past experience, alarmingly relevant.

'I see,' said the distant, meticulous voice, with evident concern, 'that I have miscalculated. I was afraid of it. Nothing has happened here. Lakshman is exemplary and immune – and I must say that I now feel every confidence in him – and no suspicious characters have been seen within a radius of miles. I am afraid no one is interested in us. The hunt has not been side-tracked. You understand what this means? Someone knew about that change of identities.'

There seemed no other explanation. From Koilpatti down to Nagarcoil they had seemed to have the road almost to themselves. If they had been followed – and they must have been – it had been at a most discreet distance. The pursuer had not had to depend on keeping his quarry in sight. And why set out to shadow the Land-Rover at all, unless someone had watched the embarkation, and observed and understood the change in the cast?

'It is a possibility,' admitted the Swami, 'that someone already knew Purushottam by sight, but it cannot be put higher than a possibility. Much more probable is that someone was watching *who knew Lakshman*. And now you tell me that there are no less than six people there who know Lakshman quite well, from the events at Thekady.'

'Seven,' said Dominic, reluctantly. 'There's Larry. I don't seriously believe he's anything but what he seems, but I daren't take it for granted. And if one of us was involved, there wouldn't have to be any watcher to find out the score, would there?'

The Swami blandly ignored the omission of Priya, even though the blanket phrase 'one of us' could have been interpreted as including her. He pointed out practically: 'But there *was* a watcher. At Nagarcoil, if not at Malaikuppam, he was seen. By two quite independent witnesses, whose evidence is mutually corroborative. However, I agree with you, we must lose sight of no one, of no possibility.'

'You do take this seriously, then?' He was dismayed but not surprised; he had known in his own heart that it must be taken seriously.

Death to the Landlords!

'I take it very seriously indeed. And since it is known to all these people that Purushottam is in the hotel, that is clearly the most dangerous place, and what I feel we must do is get him out of it as much as possible. Forgive me,' said the Swami with his habitual subtlety and courtesy, 'if I say "we", for of course in every case you will do as you see fit, and I have complete confidence that you will do rightly. But since it was I who sent you there into danger, in the belief that I was sending you out of it, I must take my share of the responsibility for your situation.'

'Give me your advice,' said Dominic. 'I need it.'

'It will be best if you behave exactly as visitors to Cape Comorin are supposed to behave, and take advantage of the possibilities that offers. It is nearly time now for the evening ritual. Go out loudly and noticeably in a party to the sand dunes to watch the sunset. In dispersed groups everyone will be doing the same. Out there you will soon find more company, the women and boys who sell shell necklaces and other souvenirs. It will be quite cheap to add them to your party – a little conversation, a few strings of shells, and they will gladly go with you for the evening, and hope to make a few more sales on the dunes. Surround Purushottam on all sides – go to the village and the temple afterwards if it is still too early to disperse of the night. No one will attempt the assassination of someone enclosed in a large, mobile group visible for miles around. And I do not think the enemy will be found among the humble people encountered there on the spot, the poorest of the poor who make shell necklaces to sell to tourists. In all their lives few of them travel more than twenty miles from home, or are acquainted with news from much farther afield than that. Also I do not think it will be advisable to eat at the hotel. At the temple and in the village there will be booths. Where there are pilgrims there are always people to supply their needs. And when you come back to the hotel – how are your rooms situated?'

Dominic told him.

'Good, that may simplify things. Then say good night to the others, lock your door, disarrange your beds as though you have slept in them, and leave by the balcony, taking the key with you. It should be a warm, gentle night, you can safely spend it out in the sands or in the village. Do not come back until the hotel begins to stir, then rouse your friends and go out to see the sun rise. And everything with care!'

'And not a word to Larry? – or even to Priya?'

447

'The innocent are safer knowing as little as possible,' said the Swami very seriously, after prolonged consideration. 'From tomorrow it may be necessary to improvise afresh, but let us first take care of tonight.'

'It seems crazy,' Dominic said in helpless protest, 'that four of us here should be virtually under siege from one miserable individual. Aren't we attaching too much importance to this threat?'

'The man without scruples,' said the Swami sadly, 'to whom every life but his own is expendable, always starts with an advantage worth a whole army over the man who regards life as holy. And the man who creeps in secret is more dangerous than armies. Never be ashamed of taking precautions against snakes. Though indeed,' he added remorsefully, 'not all snakes are vicious or treacherous, they want only to defend themselves. Men who should walk upright, but creep in the grass with poison like snakes, have no such justification.'

'And tomorrow?' Dominic asked. 'Do we pay our score and get out of here?'

The distant voice, after due thought, said gently and finally: 'Cape Comorin is the end of the world, where is there to go beyond? In the end one battlefield is as good as another.'

Dominic waited, but there was nothing more. And after a moment he heard the soft click of the distant receiver being replaced in its cradle.

Eleven

Cape Comorin: Friday Evening

Beyond the garden, all grass and sand, they stepped out on to a metalled road. To the left it wound away along the coast, growing more confident and freer of sand with every yard gained, to the village and the temple; but to the right, to westward, it struggled feebly along for only a few hundred yards, increasingly trammelled with sand, before the dunes swept over it, and rose in undulating waves of yellow and dun and grey to the skyline, unbroken to the very edge of the rocks. In that direction the coastline also rose, jutting in low but jagged cliffs; but in the sector where they stood the road was not very far above the level of beach and sea. They crossed it, and advanced into a zone of broken gunmetal rocks that slashed out into the ocean in oblique strata, knife-edge beyond knife-edge, laced with the froth of surf, and ripping every incoming wave to angry shreds. And behind this boiling filigree of black rocks and reefs and white foam, the Indian Ocean opened, sundrenched and cobalt blue, surging away due south without a break to the Antarctic.

Because of the stormy contention of the rocks against the incoming tide they had the impression that there was a fine gale blowing, but in fact it was no more than a fresh breeze that fluttered their hair, and the air was warm and clear. They scrambled out to the edge of the rocks, and looked down upon a narrow beach of smooth sand, up which the waves hissed and withdrew in steady rhythm; and to their left, perhaps half a mile away beyond an arc of troubled water, they saw the cape itself at last, the final promontory of rocks jutting far into the sea, with tidal foam washing round its feet.

Inland from it the roofs of the village began, and the temple of Kumari, the virgin aspect of Parvati, who gives Cape Comorin its name. And firmly planted on the outermost platform of rock, its *shikhara* tapering into the air to provide the vertical accent this largely horizontal and oblique land-and-seascape needed, stood the modern white memorial built on the spot where Mahatma Gandhi's ashes rested before they were committed to the Indian Ocean. All smooth white, touched with blue, rooted solidly into the dark rocks, with the cobalt sea beyond, and a scud of white cloud overhead.

'It's odd,' said Priya, 'but seen from here it fits in so well. And when you see it close to it's rather dreadful, like blue and white plastic.'

They turned westwards, following the road until it succumbed to the encroachments of the sand, and then began to climb up into the dunes. And presently there were small naked feet pattering alongside, and two little boys who had appeared out of nowhere were uttering soft blandishments in Malayalam and English, and holding out for their inspection long strings of pierced shells, some inch-long and oval-smooth in matt brown and white, some smaller and slimmer, textured like fine hoar-frost in several shades from white to fawn. The Swami had known this coast. Probably these bead-sellers were never far from the hotel, waiting for a well-disposed tourist to emerge on the evening pilgrimage. A young woman, wearing a faded red sari without a blouse, added herself to the group, proffering her own merchandise. The woman spoke a few words of English, one of the boys rather more, and Purushottam, at his most serene and sociable, spoke Malayalam with the other one. At the cost of a few *naye paise* they acquired three satisfied business contacts, who accompanied them cheerfully as they walked on up the heaving slope of the dunes. Soon other visitors would be making their way up here to watch the sun go down, and this was as good a spot for sales as any.

They reached the crest, and emerged upon an undulating plateau of fine sand, dappled only, here and there, by low clumps of tamarisks and wisps of dry grass in the slightly sheltered places, and little stars of sea plants. Here the coast rose in a jagged series of low cliffs embracing, with long, steely arms and granite talons, deeply indented coves into which the waves came seething at high speed, over sands fantastically coloured in shades of dark blackberry reds, and angry purples, and rusty black. These shades seemed to be laid down by the tides in a series of overlapping scallops, and in places the dark, sultry colours were varied by planes of yellow and grey-green. The necklace boys, amused by Larry's surprise and interest, shrugged their shoulders over this phenomenon; everyone knew that the sands at the Cape, and further up this western coast in Kerala, too, were coloured like this.

'It's ilmenite and monazite mostly,' said Purushottam. 'Quite valuable deposits. They get most of the world's thorium supply out of monazite sand. It occurs in this same form in other places, too.'

They slithered down a narrow, rocky path, and picked up handfuls of the copper-beech-red and crow-black sand, clean and fine and glittering, cool in the palm of the hand. For a while they walked along the beach, but the coastline was too deeply indented, and rocks and tide drove them up to the dunes again. Fold upon fold of sand, rolling in smooth curves from the broken coast more than a mile inland, to where the distant and scattered crests of trees showed like stains of green moss. The Swami had known what he was talking about. No one in his senses would dare to attempt to get within striking distance of a prospective victim here at this hour, where there was no cover at all, and no hope of withdrawal unseen.

There was only one thing to break the monotony, a squat little hut of timber and matting and thatch, perched on the neck of a long, narrow peninsula of rocks, tilted in knife-edged, striated layers. There was a small cove beneath it, the alluvial sand patterning it in dull green and sultry crimson. They crossed the neck of the peninsula behind the hut – it was only a few yards – and looked down into another bay, somewhat larger than the first and much more sheltered by the enfolding arm of rock; and here there were two fishing boats beached above the tide, and covered over with little gabled roofs of coconut fibre matting, and a net lay draped to dry in long serpentines across the sand, which here was clear and golden. The hut was evidently for the storage of nets and ropes and tackle, and had access by steep and difficult rock tracks to both little bays. It turned its back upon the weather and the sea, crouched into the last sheltering rise to the cliff-edge, and opened its narrow doorway and mat-screened window towards the land, scanning the miles of dunes with one blank dark eye beneath a coconut fibre eyebrow.

They sat down in the sand, in the lee of the hut on its blind side, facing westwards over the beach and the cobalt sea. Over the yellow of the sand the deep blue was transmuted into emerald green. The deserted boat below had a high prow like a gondola, and the net was a muted sand-brown, faint as a mist against the gold.

They saw when they looked back over the dunes that the solitude was beginning to be peopled. Several family parties of Indian pilgrims and tourists had streamed out from the village, and were making their way at leisure towards the sinking sun. And there among them came the Bessancourts, Madame thrusting indomitably through the sand in her sensible sandals and her black *shalwar* and *kameez*, her husband plodding tirelessly beside her with his box camera. And the Manis, immaculate and determined as ever, with Sushil Dastur labouring behind, this time with two small folding chairs in addition to Sudha's beach-bag. The sun was going to have a very respectable audience, in spite of the fact that it was already half-obscured by towering clouds, and more were driving up to join the accumulation.

'As a matter of fact,' Priya said almost apologetically, 'it almost always is cloudy. In the morning, too. Even if the day is very fine.'

The spectacle, nevertheless, was sufficiently arresting. The clouds changed and dissolved in a multiplicity of colours and shapes, and at the fieriest moment of the sunset, over that dazzling, dark sea, they ripped themselves away on either side, and let the crimson eye burn through and set fire to the miles of shadowy sand and the upturned, devout faces. For a few moments the dunes were molten. Then the great eye closed again, and the clouds banked low, touching the sea; and quite suddenly it was more than halfway to being night.

The bead-sellers had left them by then to go and tout for a few more sales among the pilgrims; but when they turned back towards the hotel and the village, one of the boys came trotting back and re-attached himself, making gay conversation with Purushottam all the way back to where the dunes dived headlong to the submerged road. Then he suddenly salaamed, and made off at a brisk trot towards the village, taking it for granted that his friends would turn aside into the hotel garden.

'Let's go on to the temple and the memorial,' Dominic suggested. 'There's plenty of time, no need to go in yet.'

It was very easy. They were ready to fall in with any plan that kept them outdoors in this mild, pleasant evening, and a part of this curious holiday scene. No one needed any persuading even when he proposed that they should forego dinner at the hotel, and eat like the pilgrims who thronged the forecourts of Kumari's temple. There were stalls selling every conceivable kind of spice, hot food, soft drinks, fruit, rice, various breads and in particular the highly-coloured and highly-sugared sweets that proliferate everywhere in India. After the dunes, the village was a revelation, crowded, busy, noisy and gay, a twilit fairground soon sparkling with little lanterns. Both village and temple stood on the levelled strata of the rocks, as near kin to ocean as to land. The sound of surf was a continuo to the sound of so many voices.

Afterwards they went, among many others, to the highly-polished blue-and-white plastic memorial, and climbed to the base of its white, lotus-bud-shaped tower to look out over the sea. A few child beggars came pestering, the first they had seen here; naturally they made their base where the foreign tourists were most likely to be found in profitable numbers. Purushottam bore with them for a while, and then gave them some small coins and ordered them crisply away, and they removed themselves without resentment, grinning.

'They do quite well here,' said Priya practically. 'Where there are pilgrims there must be some tender consciences, and the easiest way to peace of mind is to give. It is a fairly cheap way to acquire merit.'

The fairground showed no signs of closing down with nightfall. When they had walked themselves into a pleasant weariness, the village was as gay as ever; and when at last they turned back towards the hotel, the lighted stalls were still twinkling behind them like terrestrial stars.

Madame Bessancourt was installed in the foyer with her knitting, now a formidable roll of blue moss-stitch. She saw them come in from the night, and made them her invariable brisk bow over the flashing needles. Her smile was immemorial France, friendly but self-contained. The three who knew her halted to exchange the customary courtesies; Purushottam, after a quick glance, went on to the desk like a conscientious guide, and collected the keys.

'I saw in the newspapers,' she said, putting down her needles momentarily into her lap, 'about the death of your friend. I am very sorry. When Romesh told me you were here, I hoped to see you again, and at least express my sympathy. I know well there is no more one can do. The death of the young cannot be made good by anything the old may do or say. I have experienced it. But for my husband and myself, I offer you our sincere sorrow.'

There were no evasions about Madame Bessancourt. She looked them in the eyes, one by one, and her own eyes were as steady and dark as the rocks under Cape Comorin.

They told her she was very kind, and could find almost nothing else to say. To comment on the beauties of the Cape and the coast, after that direct assault, seemed meaningless. But she was not curious about their presence here, or about the new member they had acquired in place of Lakshman, or about any item of what was essentially their business. She had said her say and done her duty. After a few civil exchanges they said good night, and moved on to join Purushottam, who was waiting with the keys.

On impulse, Dominic turned back. There was never any harm in checking credentials.

'Madame – Romesh tells me you've taken him on to travel with you as far as Dindigul.'

'Yes,' she said, her needles clicking again. 'He asked us. And it is a very little thing to do for him. I only hope there will really be a job for him there, since we are not in a position to provide one. He seems a good boy.'

That was all he had had to ask, but for some reason he still lingered. 'You're going on to Pondicherry?'

'Yes. It is not so far now, we don't really need a third driver, but it satisfies him that he's doing something for his keep. Two days' drive, would you say?'

'Or three, as you feel inclined. I suppose it must be about three hundred and forty miles or so. Will you be making an early start tomorrow?'

'No, we want to have a look at the village and the temple in the morning. We have plenty of time.'

'And after Pondicherry?'

'Our tour ends with Pondicherry,' she said. Her fingers, broad and strong and brown, halted on the needles. She looked up at him with a shrewd smile. 'I think you must find it a little strange that two elderly people like my husband and myself should suddenly leave our provincial town and come here to India like this. No, no, please don't apologise, it is very natural. Sometimes I find it a little strange myself. Monsieur Bessancourt and I had a son, you see – our only child, and born rather late in our lives. He was a student of architecture. Three years ago he came out here to join the international team which is working on the first stages of Auroville. You have heard of Auroville?'

'Yes,' said Dominic. 'It's the ideal city of the future that they're hoping to build near Pondicherry. The people at the Sri Aurobindo ashram there started the idea, and I know a lot of the drive and talent is coming from France.'

'Raoul was an idealist. He believed in the future, and he wanted to have a hand in building it.' She folded her needles together with perfect composure, and began to roll the blue knitting round them. Her husband had just appeared in the doorway, returning from a last stroll before bed. 'Two days after he landed in Bombay,' said Madame, 'he was killed in a street accident.'

There was nothing he could say to her; she had herself made it impossible to offer her anything, nor did she need anything from him. She gave him a small, reassuring smile, well aware of everything that was happening within him. 'We were in any case near retirement. We sold our business, and came out here after him. And a part of the proceeds we have spent in travelling round India, where he wished to live and work. Is it very surprising that we should plan the tour to end at Pondicherry?'

'No,' he said in a low voice, 'not surprising at all. I can understand that very well.' He looked her in the eyes, and said, as she had said: 'I am very sorry.' And then, in delicate withdrawal: 'You will have a whole world of memories, when you get back to France.'

Madame Bessancourt tucked her knitting into her bag, and rose smilingly to meet her husband, who was crossing the hall.

'We are not going back to France,' she said. 'We are not young, we have not much to offer – yet still, perhaps something more than merely what remains of the price we got for the shop. When the time comes, we shall die in Auroville.'

They took Priya to her door and said good night there very quietly, for by the hush that had settled over the house they knew that most of the guests were already in bed. Larry let himself into the room next door, and Dominic and Purushottam went on, soft-footed, into their narrow side-corridor.

A dim light had been left burning at the turn. By its subdued gleam they saw, the moment they turned the corner, that the louvred outer door of their room was not closed. One leaf of it jutted into the passage, and a squat figure was leaning inside it, a hand on the door-handle, and an ear inclined against the upper panels, listening for any sound within.

Dominic came out of the haze in which Madame Bessancourt's confidences had left him, and leaped at the intruder. He made very little noise, but the rush of air alerted the listening man. He recoiled across the passage with a faint squeak of terror, turning to face the threat with shrinking shoulders and apprehensive eyes; but he did not run, for the corridor was a dead end, and there was nowhere to run to. The louvre swung back and forth, gently creaking; and they found themselves staring into the frightened and mortified face of Sushil Dastur.

Before they could utter a word he began to babble in a frantic whisper, excuse and apology tumbling over each other in their haste. 'Please, please, I beg you, Mr Felse, please don't rouse the house, please, I beg for silence. I can explain all . . . I was not trying to enter . . . I am not a thief, please believe me, I would not . . . It was a mistake, only a mistake. I thought this was Mr Preisinger's room . . . I wished to speak with Mr Preisinger . . .'

'At this time of night?' demanded Dominic disbelievingly.

'Hush!' pleaded Sushil Dastur in a frenzy of muted terror. 'Please, please keep your voice down! If Mr Mani should hear – Oh, I am so unlucky, so ashamed! What can you think of me? I wanted only to speak with Mr Preisinger privately . . . Mr Mani must not know about it, please, I beg you, don't tell him I came here . . .'

'What did you want with Mr Preisinger that Mr Mani mustn't know about?' Dominic asked in a milder tone, baffled by so sudden a manifestation of the devious in this hitherto predictable and inoffensive person. How could you tell, when it came to the point, who was capable of involved and circuitous evil, and who was not?

'I wanted to ask him – Mr Preisinger is an American, he travels with an Indian guide, he must surely be a person of importance. I wished to ask him,' whispered Sushil Dastur abjectly, 'if he does not need a good secretary during his stay in India. I should be glad to work for him if he can employ me . . .' No wonder he was trembling at his own daring and its ignominious ending. 'Or I thought that perhaps Mr Preisinger is connected with some firm which has business

456

interests here, and could get me a job with them if I asked him. Please, please, Mr Felse,' he begged piteously, 'don't tell Mr Mani about this . . . You understand, it would be very unpleasant for me . . . very difficult . . .'

It would indeed, Dominic thought, it would be a minor hell, especially if he really is a poor relation. They'd never let him forget it, life-long. And jobs in India are very, very hard to get, that's no lie.

'I am so unhappy . . . I have made you think ill of me, and I so much wanted your good opinion. Please do not think badly of me, I am telling you the truth – I had no other reason for coming here, none. It was a mistake about the room, please believe me . . .'

He was nearly in tears of mortification. It all sounded plausible enough, even probable. Many a time he must have toyed desperately with the idea of putting an end to the endless hectoring and harassment to which the Manis subjected him, and looked in vain for a way of setting about it. Small blame to him if he at least attempted it when an apparently well-to-do American came his way; and small blame to him if he did his best to keep the move secret from Gopal Krishna. All quite plausible. But then a story for an occasion like this would have to be plausible. And might it not be even a little too apposite? Thought out in advance to be used in the event of discovery?

'All right,' Dominic said. 'But better not disturb Mr Preisinger tonight. Mind you, I doubt very much if he wants or needs a secretary, or has any jobs to offer, but you can ask him tomorrow if you still want to.'

'Oh, no, I could not ask him now, I am so ashamed . . . But thank you, thank you . . . And you will not say anything to Mr Mani?'

'No, we won't say a word to Mr Mani.' What else could he do but accept it at face value and let the man go? There was no possible way of proving any ill intent on his part, and nothing to be done but go on keeping a close watch on Purushottam until morning. And then? The Swami had said no word of what was to happen afterwards.

'You are most kind, Mr Felse, I am grateful . . . So unfortunate, I'm sorry . . . I'm sorry . . . Good night! . . .'

Sushil Dastur scuttled away thankfully but still miserably, his big head drawn deep into his shoulders with shame and distress. They watched him creep round the corner, and heard the soft slur of his feet on the stairs. Without a word

Purushottam inserted the key into the lock of the inner door, and opened it. Nothing was said until he had locked it again carefully after them. Dominic switched on his bed-side light, and they looked at each other doubtfully.

'It could be true,' said Dominic fairly. 'You haven't seen as much of them as we have.'

'In any case, even if he was up to something, he seemed to be only just trying the door. It was double-locked, I doubt if he could have got in.'

Purushottam crossed to the window, which was open on the balcony. The filigree of the wrought-iron railings stood out blackly against the phosphorescence of the sea, and the lambent sky that seemed to reflect its glow.

'Come in,' said Dominic shortly. 'Leave the window open but draw the curtains. We've got our orders for the night, and we don't want to advertise the preparations. As far as the outside world's concerned we're now peaceably getting ready for bed.'

Purushottam turned back into the room obediently, though he did nothing about the curtains. 'And aren't we?'

'Not here, anyway.'

'Interesting! And when did we get our orders? And from whom?'

'From the Swami. I telephoned him this afternoon, before we went out.' He told him exactly what had been said. Purushottam stood attentive but frowning; his respect for the Swami Premanathanand was immense, but he still found it hard to credit that so much ingenuity was being spent either on hunting him or protecting him.

'Couldn't we have told the others? I don't like even the appearance of deceiving Priya.'

'As the Swami sees it, I think what you'll be doing is sparing her anxiety rather than deceiving her. He said, the less the innocent know, the safer they'll be.'

Dominic crossed to the window and attacked the curtains himself. They were opaque enough to hide all light, heavy, ancient velvet, perhaps from the days when this had been the district Residency. And they must have cost a great deal when they were new, for the room was exceedingly lofty, and the windows went right up to the ceiling. Dominic tugged at the dusty velvet, and found it weighty and obstinate, moving reluctantly on huge old wooden rings. The rail was a yard and more out of his reach. He was looking round for something to stand on, when he saw the long iron rod, with a blunted hook at one end, standing propped in the corner of the window. The answer had been provided along with the problem, many years ago. He reached up with the rod, inserting the hook among the rings, and drew them across until the curtains closed.

'All right,' said Purushottam, making up his mind. 'I agreed to come, so now I must keep the rules, I suppose. We'll need coats if we're going to sleep out. It won't be cold, exactly, but there'll be a chilly hour or two before dawn. And the beds . . . that's easy!'

Dominic turned back into the room with the rod still in his hand, swinging it experimentally like a player trying the weight of an unfamiliar golf club, just as Purushottam laid hands on the covers of his bed at the pillow, and stripped them down in one sweep of his arm, sending his discarded shirt of the morning billowing on to the floor.

Something else flashed from between the disturbed sheets, and flew in a writhing, spiralling arabesque through the air between the two beds. Dominic saw a lightning convulsion of black and white, slender and glistening from burnished scales; and in an inspired movement which was part nervous reflex and part conscious recognition, he lashed out with the long iron rod in his hand. It was thin, rigid and murderous, and he hit out with all his strength. The fluid thing and the unyielding thing met in mid-air with the lightest and most agonising of sounds, and the one coiled about the other with electrifying vehemence and rapidity, sound and motion all one indistinguishable reaction. Blackness and whiteness span so close to Dominic's hand that he dropped the rod in a frantic hurry, and leaped back as it fell.

On the dull brown carpet between the beds the snake lay threshing the quicksilver coils of its body and tail in feeble rage and helpless agony, tightening and relaxing about the rod, its head making only faint, jerky motions that did not move it from where it lay crippled. Its back was broken. Not quite three feet – but coiled and shrunken it looked even less than that – of black body banded with white rings, the scales on its back noticeably enlarged. Not a very big specimen, not a very spectacular species, nothing so impressive as the cobra with its spectacled hood. *Bungarus caerulius*, the common Indian krait, one of the most venomous snakes alive.

Twelve

Cape Comorin: Friday Night to Saturday Dawn

Purushottam had remained standing frozen in ludicrous astonishment, his hand still clutching the edge of the sheet, his face bright and blank, like a page not yet written on. But the page was rapidly, almost instantly, filled; with realisation and understanding, and a quality of horror that belonged to this death of all deaths. Everyone has his own private fears; snake-bite was Purushottam's, a dread aggravated rather than otherwise by the very thought that the luckless creature that could kill in such a frightful way was without malice, not even aggressive except when hunting food, rather a shy and retiring being, anxious to avoid conflict rather than to go looking for it. He stood rigid, staring at the wriggling thing that both horrified him and stirred him to pity. It was the first time he had seriously contemplated the creature behind this creature, the force that must pay for the krait's wretched end as well as for the attempt against him. He knew quite positively, at that moment, that the krait had been brought here to kill him. It could have been there by accident, having crept of its own will into a warm place to sleep; there was no way of proving the contrary. Nevertheless, he knew.

There are, of course, he thought with curious detachment, too many kraits in India, as there are too many cobras, and too many men. Their world is over-populated, like ours.

The krait still writhed feebly. A thread-like, forked tongue flickered in and out of its open mouth between the poison fangs. Its tight coils relaxed limply, quivering.

Purushottam reached out his hand almost stealthily, and slowly closed his fingers around the extreme end of the rod. With gingerly movements he eased it out of the flaccid coils until he could draw it free. He stood back and waited for the head to be clear of the contorted body, and then struck accurately at the neck. The carpet, old and good, absorbed the sound of the blow. The krait shuddered and jerked, twitched its tail once or twice, and was still. Over the dulling

460

body Purushottam and Dominic looked up rather dazedly at each other.

'That'll be twenty rupees, please,' Dominic said inanely.

'I'll give you an I.O.U.' said Purushottam, and meant it. His knees gave under him weakly, and he sat down abruptly on the edge of his bed, and as hastily picked himself up again the next moment and stood away from it, shivering with distaste. 'Another kind of explosvie this time,' he said grimly. 'If I'd simply undressed and gone to bed I should almost certainly have been bitten. They're not vicious, it takes quite a lot to make them bite, but having a great human oaf come plunging in on top of you when you're half asleep is a bit too much to take. And if you hadn't happened to have that thing in your hand, and lashed out with it like that, he'd have been away out of sight the instant he hit the floor, and he might have got one of us yet.' He held out the rod to Dominic. 'Here, use this to strip your sheets down, don't risk your hands . . . He may have brought two!'

'No need,' said Dominic, equally tense and pale, and pointed to the shirt now crumpled on the carpet, and the initialled bag at the foot of the bed. 'He knew which was yours. He knew who he wanted, all right.'

'Maybe, but don't take risks,' Purushottam insisted.

'But could it really have been planted deliberately? Would anyone use such a chancy method?' Dominic circled round the carcase warily, hooked the end of the rod in the neat covers of his own bed, and drew them down. 'In all the time I've been in India, this is the first time I've ever actually *seen* a krait, except in a zoo.'

'Plenty of people die of snake-bite in India,' said Purushottam soberly, 'who've never seen a snake – not even the one that bit them. But they're everywhere, all the same. Not as common down here as in Bengal, maybe, but there are plenty round Madurai if you look for them. Yes, it's quite a credible method of getting rid of someone you dislike. It's been used often enough before. There are people who make a study of handling these fellows. A stick with a noose, and the right sort of meal . . . Some people even used to keep them and breed them, in the days when there was a tally paid for killing them, just to be able to produce a constant supply of bodies. They make a profession of snakes. Looks as if your bed's clear, though. Two kraits in one room could hardly have been passed off as accidental. Do we still get out of here?'

'Faster than ever,' said Dominic, draping his bedclothes convincingly. 'Because whoever planted this chap will be standing by, expecting one of us – me! – to rouse the house any moment. Just to make sure everything's gone according to plan, and his job's done. He may even be watching our window . . .' The thought jolted him. Nothing would be gained if he withdrew Purushottam from this dangerous place only to draw the danger after him. But Purushottam reassured him instantly and confidently.

'He won't! That's the last thing he'll do if he's not just a thug from outside, but somebody known around the place, staff, guide, guests, whoever you like. He'll be with somebody else now, setting up all the alibis he can, preferably with three or four others – a card party, something like that.' He was thinking, perhaps, of the voluble and intent card party they had seen going on by lantern-light in the car-park, round a head-cloth spread out on the sand, with two of the room boys, an off-duty porter, and the Manis' sleepy, cynical hired driver, slapping down the cards like gauntlets. The Manis' driver – yes. A bored professional from Madurai, where kraits are common enough. They had never really looked at that driver; usually he seemed to be asleep. Dominic remembered him as an inanimate body curled up in the back seat at Thekady, while the whole place boiled with excitement round him.

'He'll be listening for the alarm,' Purushottam said with conviction, 'but round at the front, somewhere innocent, and in company, primed to be more surprised and shocked than anyone else. But if we delay, he may get anxious and come round to see if anything's happening.'

'Switch on the light in the shower-room,' said Dominic. 'As long as that's on, and a bedside light here, he won't wonder what's gone wrong, he'll just think we take the devil of a time to get to bed. That's it! We'll leave the curtains parted just a crack, to let the light show through.'

They took the wind-jackets they had luckily brought in with them, when they might just as easily have left them in the Land-Rover, and a torch which Dominic happened to have in his night kit, and cautiously parted the curtains to slip out on to the balcony and prospect the dark garden below. Everything was still. They stood tensed, listening, and there was no sound at all except from the distant sea, a muted, plangent, regular sound that had nothing of the spasmodic motivations of man in it, only the rhythmic motivations of man in it, only the rhythmic cadences of eternity, reassuring and terrifying, like the Swami's smile.

'Wait a minute, we'd better get rid of the krait.' Purushottam went back to hoist it carefully in the hook of the curtain rod, and carry it out to the balcony. 'Not even a big one,' he said in a whisper, 'They grow to four feet and more, this kind.' He slid the carcase through the railings, well aside from the iron pillar that held up the balcony, and let it slide dully into the thin grass below. 'All right, I've got the key. You go first.'

Dominic climbed over the railing, and let himself down to grip the pillar, and edge his way silently down to the ground. Purushottam propped the rod back in its place, and readjusted the curtain behind him so that a chink of subdued light showed through, and then followed him over. The balcony continued on round the corner, providing access to all the first-floor rooms, and at the far end on the eastern side, close to Priya's room, there was an iron stairway down into the garden; but the last thing they wanted was to run the risk of disturbing Priya. Purushottam lowered himself to the last decorative curlicues of wrought iron sprouting from the capital of the pillar, and then hung by his hands and dropped lightly into the sand below. They stood for a moment braced and listening, but the night was silent and still. The quickest way to cover was across the narrowest zone of the garden and out on to the road. They took it, moving carefully and quietly, the sand swallowing their footsteps; and once on the road, they turned towards the village.

The night was calm, mild and only moderately dark; after a brief period abroad in it they could distinguish each other's features clearly, and make out the shapes of land and sea as lucidly as by day, though through a pure veil of darkness. There was less cloud in the sky now than at the sunset, and the stars were huge and many, encrusted like jewelled inlays on a vault of ebony.

They spent the first part of the night in the village, fascinated by a life which had not ceased with darkness, but only slowed its tempo a little, and rested half its cast. There was something very comforting in moving among people who accepted them casually as a part of normality, and had no special interest in them, and certainly no design on them, except perhaps to extort the occasional coin. They even toyed with the idea of sleeping in the dormitory provided for the pilgrims, but discarded it finally in favour of a solitude. They were not the only ones sleeping outdoors that night, but in this dormitory there was room for all. They found themselves a hollow in a sheltered, sandy cove, not far from the village, high and dry above the tide-line, though the tide was well down now and still receding, and made themselves a comfortable nest there. The sand, at this higher level, felt warm to the touch, unlike the coolness of the alluvial deposits on the foreshore.

'I've slept in worse beds,' said Dominic.

Purushottam laughed rather hollowly, remembering the bed and the bed-fellow he had just escaped. Until now they had said not a word about that since leaving the hotel, but now he peered into the recent past and frowned, wondering.

'Dominic – was he really just trying the door, or just relocking it? — Sushil Dastur? They're old, big locks, maybe child's play to a professional, after all . . .'

'Do I know?' Dominic had wondered the same thing. 'But then there must have been a box, a bag, something – you don't walk in with a snake dangling from your hand. A rush basket – some sort of container . . .'

'That's true. And he didn't have anything.'

'All the same,' said Dominic very seriously, 'no one can logically be ruled out. There are six people here who were also at Thekady. Not counting our own party. Not forgetting myself,' he said firmly. 'From where you're standing . . .'

'Lying,' corrected Purushottam drowsily, working his shoulders comfortably into the sand.

'—you can't afford to rule out any possibility.'

Purushottam's tranquil face gazed up into the stars, and smiled, quite unshaken. 'I'll overlook that. Just so long as you don't ask me to suspect Priya.' He lay quiet for a moment, relaxed and still. 'Dominic! Are you . . . is there a girl somewhere belonging to you?'

'I'm engaged,' said Dominic. 'Tossa's still at Oxford, finishing her arts degree. After that we shall get married. We haven't made any further plans yet, but I think – I really think we may come back here together.'

'You make it sound so easy,' sighed Purushottam.

'Don't kid yourself, it's never easy. You have to work at it, like everything else. What are you worrying about?' he said reasonably to the silent, doubtful figure beside him. 'You've got virtually no family to make difficulties, and

she's got a family that could absorb half a dozen sons –
and daughters-in-law, and never turn a hair.'

'She has, hasn't she?' agreed Purushottam warmly,
remembering and taking heart. 'Not that I'm the best
bargain there ever was in the marriage market. Did you know
that even an ordinary close friendship with a fellow-student in
England – a girl, that is – could send a bridegroom's prospects
crashing to the very bottom of the scale? And having crazy
ideas about getting rid of your money, instead of making
more and more, wouldn't do a man's chances any good,
either. But *her* family – there ought to be enough Christian
charity there, don't you think? Even for someone as odd as
I am?'

'I wouldn't be surprised,' said Dominic encouragingly,
'if they're eccentric enough themselves positively to *like*
oddities.'

'Good, you hearten me.' He lay still for a few minutes,
his eyelids low over the dark, thoughtful eyes, his fingertips
playing gently in the sand. 'So now all we have to do is get
clear of this tangle. Alive.'

'That's all.'

Purushottam sighed, stretched, turned on his side and
scooped a hollow for his shoulder. In a few minutes he
was asleep. Dominic braced his back into the slope of the
ground, worked his heels comfortably into the sand and
settled down to stay awake through the night.

They worked their way back to the road opposite the hotel
at the first hint of daylight, some time before the sun began
to colour the eastern sky. From the garden they could see
the staff already stirring, and a light in one or two of the
guest-rooms, where visitors were rousing themselves in good
time to go out and see the sunrise. The timing appeared to be
good; even if they were seen strolling in from the road and
mounting the stairs to the balcony at this hour, they would
merely be written off as eccentric enough, or over-anxious
enough, to have got up an hour too early for the prescribed
spectacle. They looked under the balcony for the carcase of
the krait, and found it where Purushottam had let it fall, its
bright black and white dulled now to a dim greyness. It was
a reminder of a situation which was still with them, and still
unchanged, but in the first light of day it was difficult to
believe in it. The bedroom was as they had left it; no sign
of any further intrusion, though they tended to handle things

465

and move about the room with wincing care, and to watch every step they took.

'Better wake the others, if they're not up already,' Dominic judged.

'I think we're leading the field this morning.'

But they were not. When they walked along the corridor it was to see the Bessancourts just descending the stairs, almost certainly going out to watch the sunrise before breakfast, prior to making their planned tour of the temple and the village afterwards. Dominic watched the two straight, square backs marching steadily away towards the outer doorway, and suddenly saw for the first time the immensity of what they had done. Even for a middle-aged English couple, taking up their roots and committing themselves and all their capital to a new and unknown life at this stage would have been a daunting step; for these twin pillars of the solidity of France it was at once lunatic and heroic. Ideal undertakings like Auroville so often foundered for want of both faith and works, and they had made no preliminary inspection on the spot – though no doubt there had been correspondence – but simply realised everything they had, and set out. Auroville was to be the end of their journey; they were committed. He thought, the chances of one dream being realised will at any rate go up several notches when those two arrive.

They knocked on Larry's door, and elicited a sleepy grunt from within, and then a clearer utterance promising compliance. In a few minutes they heard him moving about, and the splash of the shower. They tapped on Priya's door and got no answer.

'Still asleep,' said Purushottam. 'Ought we to disturb her?'

They waited a little while, listening for any sound of activity from within. Then they knocked again, but still there was no answer. Larry opened his door to them, towelling his crew-cut vigorously, and still there was no reply from Priya.

'Perhaps she's dressed and gone out already, before we came,' said Purushottam, arguing with himself. His face had grown pale, and his eyes large. 'May I go through by the balcony, and see?'

They followed at his heels, across the room and out to the balcony beside the iron stairway. Priya's window stood open, the curtains half-drawn across it, just as when they had passed it quietly on coming in. The quietness began to seem ominous, the pre-dawn light inauspicious, though it had not seemed so then.

Purushottam tapped at the glass. 'Priya? Are you awake? Priya! . . .'

He knew she was not there; there was no sense of her presence, no lingering hint of her movements in the air, nothing. He opened the window wider, and went into the room.

The nearer of the two beds still bore the light imprint of her body, and was disarranged only as it would have been if she had recently risen from it in a perfectly normal way; but it was cold. The door was locked, and the key in the lock. Nothing seemed to be disturbed. But in the shower-room the film of water and the splashed drops from her overnight shower had already dried completely; the hand-basin, too, was dry, the towels were dry. The sari she had worn yesterday was draped neatly over the back of a chair in the bedroom, ready to put on again. Priya had neither washed nor dressed this morning. Of all her belongings, nothing was missing but her white night sari and her dark silk dressing-gown, and the sandals of light fawn leather she habitually wore.

'Look,' Larry said, hushed and uneasy, 'she was writing a letter last night.'

The letter, to her Punjabi room-mate in the Nurses' Home at Madras, was necessarily in English. It had reached one and a half pages, and then been tidily abandoned for the night, folded into her writing-case with the address and salutation protruding. And on top of the case was another sheet torn from her writing-pad and folded in two. 'There's a note here, addressed to someone – that's Tamil, isn't it?'

Purushottam came flashing anxiously across the room, and took it up with a soft cry of hope and relief. 'It's to me!' But even in the act of unfolding it he was shaken afresh by awful doubts, and looked again at his own name. He had never seen Priya's writing until now, in the neat, precise English of her letter; but these fiercely formed characters in Tamil gave him no sense of handling something which had come to him from her.

His hands were shaking as he began to read; they were like stone when he ended, and all the light was gone from his face, which for one moment was stunned and dead, until the dreadful certainty came.

'He's taken her – taken Priya.' He raised his eyes to their

faces. 'Because the krait was a failure . . . because I was out of reach when he came to see what had gone wrong. This time he meant to make sure. You want to know what he has to say to me?'

He read, translating slowly, freely and coldly, like a voice out of a computer:

' "It is you we want, not her. Now you shall come to us, and of your own will, if you want the girl to go free. You will come to the fisherman's hut on the dunes to take her place, *and come alone*. If I do not see you coming – *alone* – by seven o'clock, I cut her throat." '

The sheet of notepaper with its words carved deep like stabs dropped from his hand, done with. He was back on the balcony before they had wrenched themselves out of their appalled daze and realised what he was about. They started after him, Larry catching at his arm.

'The police – we must get them! They'll have to—'

'No police,' said Purushottam, biting off the word and shutting upon it lips drawn pale and thin. 'No police, no tricks, no anything. There isn't time.'

'But we've got to do something! They'll turn out all the forces they've got – they'll get her back—'

'Dead!' said Purushottam. 'You know what time it is? Well past six.'

'But the police have resources—'

'*No!* I say no police. Not a word to anyone, no hunt, nothing. If you try to be clever, Priya will simply be murdered at once. Do you doubt it?'

They did not doubt it. 'But the police are as capable as we are of moving discreetly, they have resources, they'll arrange it so that—'

'Fool!' said Purushottam without heat, his feet clattering on the iron staircase down which Priya had been dragged in the night. 'Have you forgotten how the hut lies? You could cover the whole sweep of the dunes from it. No one could approach without being seen long before. And Priya would die.'

Dominic said – it was the first thing he had found it needful to say, and it was no comfort at all, but it was the truth: 'At best she may – you know that. If she can identify him now.'

'Yes, I do know. But even such people as he *may* keep their word – I daren't stop hoping. If we start a hunt, then she will certainly die. To give him a better chance to get away. And to kill me by another way.'

'But a boat . . .' said Dominic.

Halfway across the garden, Purushottam spared him one quick glance, from very far away, and the brief ghost of a smile. 'Yes. If there was time, by water one might reach them. Even that would be a risk. But there's no time. It would be past seven before you got hold of a boat.'

It was true, and they knew it; the chances of beating that deadline were practically nil, without a motor-boat, and a motor-boat, even if one were to be had, might by its sound alert the kidnapper and precipitate what they most wished to prevent. Nevertheless, Larry suddenly swerved away from the hapless procession heading for the dunes, and turned and ran like a hare, not for the hotel, but for the village. At least to try – to make some sort of attempt to defeat what outraged him. Purushottam checked, and looked after him in exasperated distress.

'He's crazy! He'll only kill her!'

'No,' said Dominic with awful certainty. 'He won't have time.'

'No – that's true. He won't have time.' Purushottam sank his face between his palms for a moment, and shook his head from side to side helplessly. 'I did this to her. She never should have known me!'

'I don't believe she'd say so,' said Dominic, 'even now.'

They were motionless there in the garden for only a moment. But even so Dominic heard, shrill and indignant on the air, wafting from one of the first-floor balconies: 'Sushil Dastur! *Sushil Dastur!*' And Gopal Krishna's booming response, equally indignant but even more incredulous: 'He is not there! No one has seen him! Where can he have got to? What is he thinking of?' Mutually complaining, voices out of another world, they faded into the interior of the hotel.

But perhaps not another world, after all! Sushil Dastur, stooping at the doorway of a room where a krait had been introduced to do the dirty work for men . . .

Purushottam seemed not to have heard. He lifted a pale, set face out of his hands, and turned with determination towards the road, and the rising folds of sand.

'Don't go away! Come with me. As far as you can . . . You see I can't do anything else. There isn't any time left. I have to go. I have to do what he says, and hope he has a sort

of honour. There's nothing else I can do. One step wrong –
one foot out of place – and she will be the first to die.'

'I know,' said Dominic. 'I won't leave you. Not until you
give the word.'

Thirteen

Cape Comorin: Saturday Morning

Priya crouched in heavy darkness against the seaward wall of the hut, her back against the matting, the harsh coils of old fishing nets scoring her arms and shoulders. Her wrists were crossed behind her, and tethered uncomfortably tightly to a staple in one of the timbers of the wall. While her numbed fingers retained some sensitivity she could feel the grain of the wood with them, and touch the cold iron. Now that her eyes were more accustomed to the dark she could distinguish shapes and shades, the vague, formless monsters that were piles of coiled rope and cord, and stacked nets, and oars, and the heavy bamboo poles with which many of the boatmen steered their craft. But in particular nets; great coils of net, mesh within mesh. She sat upon a low mound of them, and the air she breathed was thick with the thready dust of coconut fibres, and their rank scent, and the smell of the many hauls of fish they had brought in in their time. The odour, too, of oil and joss and sweat, the irrational sweat of excitement and exultation.

She had drawn herself as far back against the wall as she could, and pulled in her feet and made herself small, to put as much distance as possible – whatever she did, it was all too little – between herself and the man. She saw him as two blurs of pallor in the darkness, one his head and one his loins. Here in the hut she could have sworn that the cotton cloths he wore were white, if she had not seen them in her own room at the hotel, and outside in the starry night, and known them for the faded peach-yellow that holy men wear. He had nothing on but those two lengths of thin cloth, and the oil with which his body was smeared. To make him hard to hold should anyone ever get to grips with him, and to enable him to withstand a long period in the water should he have to swim for it. He had his back to her now, but she knew better than to move a muscle; he could turn like a snake, and he still had the knife in his hand. He had made a horizontal slit in the matting shutter of the small window space, close to the door on the landward side, and he was watching the long expanse of the dunes through it, waiting for the light to come. Sometimes he talked to himself, low-voiced, forgetful of her. She did not exist for him except as a means to an end, she had realised that now. Sometimes he laughed, quite a sane laugh, contented, self-congratulatory, chilling her blood.

He was waiting for Purushottam. She knew that now; it was her sorrow that she had not realised it in time, and avoided the two fatal mistakes she had made. Now it was too late to redeem them; she had missed her chance.

She had started out of a dream to the awareness of someone in her room, and close to her bed, and in instant alarm for Purushottam she had opened her lips to cry out his name but never got beyond the first syllable before a hand was clamped over her mouth. That had been her first mistake, because it had told the intruder that she was indeed what he had come for, a sure and infallible bait for the man he wanted to trap. And then she had felt the cold fire of the knife against her throat, the fine prick of its tip deliberately biting under her ear, and a man's voice, muffled to a hoarse undertone, had told her to be silent or dead, as she chose. She should have taken the omen and grasped its full possibilities at once. Why had she come away with him so tamely?

But she had been half asleep and half in shock, incapable of connecting what her senses told her. A dance of fantastic details assaulted her eyes, her ears and her reason. The head that stooped over her was monstrous, swathed in saffron cotton wound twice over his face, muffling his features into a grave-mask. The hands that held the knife to her throat and covered her mouth were long and sinewy and strong. His body was naked but for the saffron loincloth, and glistened with oil. She was aware of the intent stare of his eyes through the cloth; though she could not see them, she knew that they could see well enough. The cotton was no thicker nor closer-woven than cheesecloth, it hardly hampered his vision at all, but it made him invisible.

Confused and disorientated as she was, it was no wonder that when he took away his hand, telling her flatly: 'Make one sound, and I kill you!' she lay mute and still, shrinking from the prick of the knife. No wonder that she rose from the bed at his orders, and put on her dressing-gown and sandals, and went down the iron staircase with him silently, the point of the knife pricking her onwards all the way. By then she had been aware that he was not solely dependent on the dagger. He made sure of being at the window before her, and from the place where he had propped it behind the curtain he retrieved a rifle, and slung it over his shoulder with a dexterity that told her he was well used to handling it. She had thought at first that she might be able to elude him, once in the garden, and escape in the darkness, but a rifle has a longer reach than a knife, and even in the dark, how can you be sure of evading it? And he had thought of the possibility, too, and made provision for it. She was no sooner on the ground than he had a hand twined in her hair, and dragged her back by it under the staircase, and there drew her hands behind her and knotted them fast with the girdle of her dressing-gown.

'Walk!' he ordered her, spitting the word almost soundlessly into her ear. 'Out to the road. And silently!'

And she had done it, had done everything he had ordered, his one hand always tight on the tether that bound her wrists, the other pricking her on with the ceaseless reminder of the knife. Up the undulating slope of the dunes, a moon-world in the lambent night, the smooth, dry sand sliding in and out of her sandals cool and light, like small silken hands stroking. A surrealist dream, austere and frightening. No wonder she had done everything she was told to do, and sought to keep the blade away from her throat at all costs.

But how she regretted now the slowness of her understanding! Not until they were well away from the house, from the road, from all listening ears, did she realise that she had mistaken her role and missed her one chance. She was nothing. What could this nocturnal assassin, in the saffron remnants of his old disguise as a holy man, want with her? She was accidental, simply an outsider who had blundered into a private war. Purushottam was still the quarry, must be the quarry. This man had come for Purushottam tonight. If he had taken her instead, it was because for some reason he could not reach Purushottam. She was only a second best, a second string – an alternative route to the prize.

So then, too late, she recognised her own mistakes. Her first waking thought had been for Purushottam; that must have been a gratifying confirmation of the enemy's thinking. What she should have done, as soon as the muffling hand was lifted from her mouth, was to scream and scream and arouse the entire house. She would probably have died, yes

– though not certainly, since nothing was ever certain – but she could not then have been used to induce Purushottam to venture his life for hers. She should have realised when she watched the invader fold the sheet he had torn from her writing pad, and score that savage superscription across it, and laugh silently, one eye always trained upon her as she fumbled stiffly into her sandals, one hand always ready on the knife. If only she had understood in time she might even have achieved the capture and arrest of her killer, and made the future safe for others. She thought 'others', but she meant Purushottam. And who knows, the killer might not even have killed. Petrified by the first tearing scream, he might have thought of his own life first, and run with no thought but to save it. The trouble is that one never has time to consider the issues fairly until it is too late.

Now she was here, bait for a trap, and there was nothing she could do.

'He will get my message,' crooned the man, self-congratulatory and exuberant, watching the bare, motionless sea of the starlit dunes, and stroking the butt of his rifle lovingly. 'He will come! Shall I let him see you, before I fire? Shall I let him come all the way, to find you here dead before I kill him?'

Priya said nothing. She had not uttered a sound since he thrust her in here before him, stumbling among the nets. There was no point in speaking with him, none in pleading or reasoning; that she knew. Whatever eloquence she had was being expanded inwardly, and directed towards whatever it was that she had made out of her odd, heritical heritage, something huge and approachable and not insensible to human outrage and anger; not necessarily just, but better, involved and indignant and compassionate, something that could be argued with, like Krishna enduring without offence the reproaches of Arjuna, and stooping to unravel for him the complexities of duty and compulsion and love.

'Listen, you,' thought Priya vehemently towards the anonymous power that hid itself from her but was patently there somewhere, too nearly palpable to be a figment of her imagination, 'I don't know what to call you, but since you must be everything in any case, what does it matter? You know all about us, all of us, I needn't tell you anything. *Don't let them win!* Not unless you're on the side of evil, and that's impossible. Don't let Purushottam come here tamely to be killed, as I've come. That's all that matters. If he survives, then *we have won*! There must be something one of us can do to unwind this wound-up machine, and break it. That's all I'm asking for. Then it wouldn't matter so much, dying . . . after all, everybody has to, in the end.'

She had begun to be aware, while she closed her eyes upon this emphatic wrestling with God, that the images were forming in her mind in a kind of insistent but disciplined rhythm, as though the tabla had just struck into the improvisations of the sitar for the first time, halfway into a raga; the key moment when the first acceleration begins, and the first formal excitement. It took her some moments to track this drum-note down, even after she opened her eyes; it was soft and private, felt rather than heard, like the tabla, a vibration rather than a sound. She sensed it throbbing in her spine, gently insistent, and sprang into full consciousness with a shock of wonder and disbelief.

It really existed, and deliberately it was hardly a sound at all, only a very soft, steady, rhythmic pressure, barely even a tapping, against the matting wall at her back. Once she had grasped its source, she began to trace it to its exact location; it had reached the thick, woven wall right behind her, and just above the level of her bound hands. When first she had become aware of it, it must have been approaching, slowly and stealthily, from her right side, testing and waiting all the way for a response. Someone was outside the hut, feeling his way to where she was, demanding an answer from her, while she had been demanding answer from whatever God was.

The mat wall pressed once, twice, against the small of her back. Painfully she hoisted her bound hands, grown prickly and numb from the tight cord, and thrust outwards with them, once, twice, three times, tapped with impotent fingers, scratched with her nails against the fibre.

Hard fingers pressed back against her fingers in recognition and reassurance. The rhythm of the tabla ceased. Whoever he was, he had found her.

'He will come,' whispered the man with the rifle, turning his featureless cotton face towards her for a moment. She saw light – already, even in this enclosed place, there was light of a kind – flow down his sinewy arms and long torso, and die into the pallor of the sadhu's cloth twisted round his loins. 'He will come, and this time he will be mine. You want to see him die, you, woman?'

Behind Priya's back, with aching, insinuating gentleness, the tip of a knife eased its way between the stitches that seamed the cocunut-matting wall. She felt the steel touch her arm, sliding by above the wrist without grazing. She heard the first fibre of the first stitch part, and thought it a terrible and wonderful sound, like the trumpets outside the walls of a city under siege. Very carefully she shifted her position a little, sitting forward on the coils of net, and posing her body steadily between her captor and the knife.

They reached the loftiest rise of the dunes, and Purushottam's headlong march wavered as soon as the ridge-thatch of the distant hut broke the suave undulations of the sand like a clump of stiff grass. He turned and looked at Dominic, seemed to be searching hopelessly for something to say by way of good-bye, and then would have walked on without a word, after all, because there was nothing left to say. But Dominic laid an arresting hand on his arm.

'No, not yet. Look, it's only just after half past six. Take every moment you safely can.' Safely! How could they be sure that the word had any longer a meaning for any of them? How did they know, even, that Priya was still alive? Dead hostages are quiet hostages, make no attempt at escape, identify no suspects. But in so far as there was still any hope at all, they had to preserve it as long as they could.

'He must see me coming before the deadline,' said Purushottam, in the level, low voice that had hardly varied its tone since they had found the note. 'Before seven, not at seven.'

'He'll see you the minute you go over that crest. Forty yards. Even if you go at ten to seven, you'll be nearly halfway to him by the hour. Wait till then.'

He shook his head, but he stayed. 'Does it matter?'

'Yes, it matters. The one moment we throw away may be the one that makes the difference. At least give it a chance.'

'You expect a miracle?' said Purushottam, with the most painful of smiles. 'I've been thinking – he must have a gun, don't you think so? I think a rifle. Because he's set me up as a target he can hardly miss, even at long range. The one thing moving in all this space, and no cover anywhere. Not that I'm looking for cover. And the sea right there at his back – that's the way he means to get away.'

If he's a poor enough shot to want me at short range before he can be sure of killing me, he thought, unable to break the habit of hope, I might be able to rush him yet. He wouldn't be able to take his eye off me then to turn on Priya, and inside a hut that size a rifle will be an unwieldy weapon. If I could reach him, hit or not hit, I might at least be able to give her the chance to get away.

The sun was already well above the horizon behind them, climbing with amazing speed. The dunes put on colour, and became a rippling sea of lights and shadows.

Dominic shook the arm he held. 'Give me until ten to seven. Promise!'

'What are you going to do?' he asked it indifferently, for he knew there was nothing his friend could do to help him. They were all bound hand and foot; for at the least wrong move, Priya would pay.

'Try and work round by the shore, if I can. I give you my word I'll keep out of sight.'

'Impossible. You've seen how indented the coast is. It would take you hours.'

It was true; he was only reaching out for something he could at least seem to be doing, to avoid the one thing he could not bear, having to stand here and watch Purushottam walk out to his death without raising a hand to help him. No Sidney Cartons here, even supposing one could be that sort of hero; whoever was in that hut knew very well the appearance of the young man for whom he was waiting. Nobody else would do; and the mere sight of another person approaching would mean the end of Priya. No, there was nothing at all left for him but to watch.

'Even if you swam every bay and climbed over every headland,' Purushottam said gently, 'you couldn't possibly get near by seven o'clock. You don't know these seas. It would be suicide to try it.'

Their eyes met, and improbable as it seemed, they both smiled pallidly. 'Coming from you at this moment,' said Dominic, 'that's good.'

'If Priya dies,' said Purushottam simply, 'I don't want to survive. But I shouldn't like to have to apologise to – what was her name? Tossa? – for you. No, don't go. Stay with me.'

Dominic stayed. A quarter to seven.

'If only we'd taken her with us . . .'

'No, don't! What's the use? We do the best we can.'

Twelve minutes to seven. 'I'm going now,' said Purushottam. 'Remember me to the Swami, and don't let him start saying: "If only . . .", either. I've got no complaints.'

He didn't wait for any reply, and he didn't look back. He walked over the crest of the dunes, set his course towards the distant dark speck of the hut, and marched straight towards it across the empty yellow expanse of sand.

A hand came through the growing slit in the fibre wall, and fingers felt their way carefully and blindly over Priya's swollen wrists, and singled out the spot where the cords crossed. The knife followed the guiding fingers, grazed her wrist lightly, and found the cords.

How long he had been working out there she had no means of reckoning, but it felt like an age. Even the parting of a thread seemed to produce a loud, commanding sound, the knife had to work with infinite quietness and delicacy, slowly, very slowly. She knew that it was growing light, she knew the sun was up, by the shafts of brightness that entered at the rifle-slit and through the chinks of the door. The man with the gun leaned devotedly at his spyhole, the barrel of the rifle thrust out towards the dawn; and he was humming to himself sometimes, and laughing gently, sure of his triumph.

Her numbed hands lurched apart suddenly as the cords parted, and she gripped her fingers together to hold her position, afraid even of the rustle of her own clothing. Pain seeped slowly back into her wrists, a live pain; she was no longer quite helpless. She held her place, covering her ally from sight; and with her reviving fingers she felt carefully at the slit in the matting wall behind her back. It ran upward from ground level - which was nearly at her waist, for the dune rose to the cliff's edge behind the hut - almost to the top of her head. To take it higher was more dangerous, though blessedly this was the dark side of the hut, no sun here to shine through the crack. Priya raised herself a little on the pile of coiled nets, to cover a few more inches of the wall. The gap was not yet quite long enough to allow her to slip out quietly and adroitly. The hand from outside took a moment to press her hand, warmly and quickly, before it went on with its work.

A long tremor of fulfilment and delight passed through the braced back turned towards her from the window, and a low, chuckling cry marked the moment when Purushottam came into sight. The hands that held the rifle calmed and grew still and competent upon the barrel and trigger. His whole body became a concentration of duty and efficiency.

Even when he addressed her now, he could not turn away his eyes from that solitary figure to look at the bait that was bringing it into his sights. She had served her turn; she was of no importance, first or last.

'He is coming! So quickly he is coming, he is in a hurry! Now I could drop him . . . no, not yet, yet him come nearer . . .'

It had become a race. The knife sawed away with feverish haste, ripping the slit in the matting higher. Purushottam walked rapidly, some corner of his mind still pondering the possibility – if it was a possibility – of getting just within range and then charging in like a madman, in an attempt to get to grips with his enemy. At least that would leave him no time to turn on Priya – if Priya still lived . . . Fatally, he let this half-hysterical hope in speed infect his pace as he approached. He was winning his race, and to win it was to lose it. There was no time left at all. The swathed head leaned lovingly to the rifle-stock, the long, muscular hand tightened its finger on the trigger and began to squeeze, slowly, slowly . . .

Two more minutes, and the hands of the rescuer would have been helping Priya out silently and swiftly through the matting. But there was not even one minute left, and no means of buying one.

Dominic had stood motionless all this time where Purushottam had left him, because there was nothing else for him to do; and even to stir from the spot, unless it was to follow, which he must not do, seemed like a kind of betrayal. But tension drew him, almost against his will, up the last few yards of the slope. He raised himself just far enough to see over the plain of sand, and could not turn his eyes away. He watched the lonely figure advancing upon the distant hut, more like an attacking army than a reluctant victim, very erect, moving in an unswerving and unrelenting line - a little more, thought Dominic helplessly, and he'd be running. And already so near! He felt the hairs in his neck rising with apprehension. The shot must come any moment . . .

Another figure emerged suddenly from behind the hut, a diminutive, fleshless figure in yellow robes that clung to his body wetly and glistened as he moved. He walked as rapdily as Purushottam, and on a converging course. Round the corner of the hut he came, and at a distance of a few feet from the shutter he stepped deliberately into the path between the levelled rifle and its target, blotting out Purushottam from view. There was nothing in the sights of the rifle now but his bony golden body and the saffron folds of his robe.

The Swami Premanathanand, to whom violence was impossible, was fighting this last engagement in his own way and with his own unique weapon, a finite body interposed at the last moment between death and its victim.

Fourteen

Cape Comorin: Saturday Morning, Continued

For the man peering through the sight of the rifle, the world dissolved suddenly into a blur of saffron cloth only a few feet away from the barrel of the gun. The lonely, advancing figure at whose heart he had been aiming had vanished in yellow light at the very moment when his trigger finger was tightening to squeeze gently home and put an end to it. The marksman uttered a curious, wailing cry of alarm and dread, and there was one instant when everything hung in the balance, when the finger almost completed its pressure and emptied the first round into that saffron cloud. It was superstitious shock that turned his hands feeble; the barrel of the gun lurched, and was lowered. He raised his cheek from the stock, to gaze with his own eyes, instead of with the automatic eye of the gun. And the cloud that blotted out the world condensed into the apparition – for what else could it be, here where he had deliberately created an empty solitude all round him? – of an elderly, venerable, composed personage in a yellow robe and a brown woollen shawl, standing perfectly still before him, almost within touch, though he saw it only through the slit he had made for firing.

Whether this was a god, a demon or a man, he had to stare it in the face and find a way past it, and instantly, or everything was lost. It stood so still that he dreaded it might not be human, after all. What man would take his stand there and wait, saying not a word? Ah, but the interloper was looking only at a blank wall! Did he even know that there was an armed man within? He could not know. No one who knew that would dare!

The man with the rifle flung out a long left arm and swept aside the shutter of fibre matting, gleefully expecting an ordinary man's predictable reactions of fright and retreat when suddenly confronted at short range with a loaded gun. The image remained undisturbed, serene and immovable, its mild eyes observing everything without alarm.

At the back of the hut Priya started up out of her nest of ropes and nets, stunned by the sudden burst of light from the window, and half-crazed with terror and exhaustion. Beyond her captor's shoulder she caught one glimpse of the Swami's composed, half-smiling face, but she could not believe in what she was seeing. A hand reached through the mat wall, plucking urgently and insistently at her arm.

'Come, come, please come . . .!'

'Get out of my way!' screamed the swathed head in its shroud of saffron cloth, choking with rage and hatred. 'Stand out of my way, or I'll kill you!'

The Swami, so impotent, so feeble a presence, merely moved a step or two nearer to the window-opening, to ensure that whatever was behind him should remain invisible. He did not say: 'Kill me, then!, but he did not move aside. Some way behind him he heard Purushottam's wildly running feet sliding and labouring in the sand. He could not hear Dominic, though Dominic was running, too, at his fastest, and straight for this spot. The Swami folded his hands before him, just out of reach from within the window, but so near that he eclipsed the world and covered his friends from harm.

'Come, quickly, come . . .' begged the voice outside the rear wall, and the timid, agitated hand tugged at Priya's wrist. She yielded to the pressure, drawn back towards the wall that gaped to let her through. And suddenly, above the Swami's golden shoulder, she saw Purushottam, running, stumbling, wild with anguish and hope; and then she could not move.

'Get out of my way!' howled the muffled head, almost inarticulate with fury. 'Now, or I will kill this girl!' He had remembered in time that he had at his disposal this more powerful persuasion, and at the recollection he swung upon her, levelling the rifle from his hip at point-blank range.

What he saw brought another thin shriek of rage out of him, for the wall at her back gaped, and a hand was holding it wide for her and urging her through the gap. He took one long, deliberate pace towards her, the rifle steadying with deadly intent on her breast. And Priya, tearing herself loose from the hand that held her for one inspired and desperate instant, scooped up in her arms the topmost coils of the pile of nets, and hurled them in his face.

She saw the closely-wound meshes open like a fantastic flower in mid-air, filling the lances of sunlight with dancing dust, and her nostrils with particles of fibre like musty pollen. Rifle and man lost their clarity of line, disintegrating into a tangled jigsaw-puzzle, as the flying lengths of net descended over both, and were carried by their weighted edges round elbows and hands, and the barrel and stock of the gun. The impact drove the man's body backwards, off-balance, and the shot went into the beaten earth at the foot of the wall, spattering Priya's feet with flecks of soil.

She turned, blindly and desperately, and clawed her way through the torn matting, the cut edges rasping her arms and her cheek. Hands reached out eagerly to help her, day-light flowed over her, clean sand filtered into her sandals. Her rescuer folded an arm protectively about her and hurried her away, across the narrow neck of land and into the first rocky defile of the path that led down into the second cove. In that maze of rocks they could hope to find safe cover even from a rifle.

The Swami stirred slowly, like a man coming out of a trance, and for once his face wore a look of immense surprise, though there was no one to witness the phenomenon. He was undoubtedly alive, and that was matter for profound surprise. He looked round, blinking at the sun. Purushottam was toiling through the last undulations of sand towards the hut, and some way behind him Dominic followed.

The Swami took the necessary three steps to the door of the hut, and pushed it open, letting in the sunlight over the heaving, trammelled form on the floor. The man had almost freed himself, slashing furiously at the folds of net with the knife he had kept in his loincloth. As the door flew open he dragged himself clear, snatched up the rifle as he rose, and charged head-down for the doorway and freedom. He had heard the pursuers drawing nearer; perhaps he thought they were more and better-armed than they were. This game, in any event, was already lost, for his hostage was gone, and if he stayed to fight he might be captured, and must be identified. He chose to run. And the Swami, to whom violence was impossible, stood courteously out of his path and gave him free passage.

It was the rifle that cheated him. A filament of the net had trapped the bolt, and as he rose and flung himself forward, grasping the stock, the net followed like a snake as far as the doorway, uncoiling until its weight became too great to be towed any further, and there ripped the rifle out of his hand. He checked for a fraction of a second, and then abandoned it and ran on, headlong for his life. He made for the nearer and smaller cove, plunged down the first steep drop into the

483

stones of the pathway, and continued in a series of strong, passionate deer-leaps halfway down to the beach.

Not until then had he raised his head or paused even for an instant to look beyond the next step. But there he did pause, and glanced down towards the sea, and uttered a sudden enraged and desolate cry. He looked from headland to headland, but the cove was empty, sunlit and serene. He turned wildly to look back, and Purushottam was already at the Swami's side, and Dominic not a hundred yards behind. There was no going back. He turned to the ocean again, and ran, plunged, glissaded onwards, across the yellow sand above the tide, into the fringes of the black sand now almost hidden, through the shallows that flashed at his heels as he ran, and still outwards until the surge lifted him from his feet, and he swam strongly and valiantly out to sea.

'I am afraid he was looking for his boat,' the Swami said in gentle, almost regretful explanation. 'That was where he left it, you see. We moved it in the night.'

'It is all right now, Miss Madhavan,' said an anxious, coaxing voice in Priya's ear, and the hand that held hers, and had been urging her along among the rocks, now checked her stumbling walk and quieted her into stillness. 'Quite all right now, we need not run any more. He has gone. Look, there are your friends, there on the headland. All quite safe. Everything is all right now.'

Her eyes had been open all the while, but so dazzled by daylight and blanketed by terror and tiredness that she had not truly seen even the stones among which her sandalled feet slipped and bruised themselves. Now she raised her head, and for the first time looked up, her vision and her mind clearing, into the roused, solicitous, almost unrecognisable face of Sushil Dastur.

There was no point in pursuit, no hope of overtaking him. They stood watching in helpless fascination as the swimmer sheered his way towards the headland between the coves, apparently bent on rounding it and reaching some point up-coast where he could come ashore unseen, and vanish once again into the landscape or the seascape of the south.

'He might get to one of the fishing boats,' said Dominic, looking down into the larger cove, where they lay high and dry in the sand under their thatched covers.

'He won't try,' Purushottam said, still panting from that

frantic race. 'He couldn't possibly get one of those into the water alone.'

'I fear,' said the Swami apologetically, 'that he may succeed in reaching his own.' He pointed into the lee of the headland, where they could just see the high prow of a smaller boat, almost hidden under the jutting rocks where Priya stood with Sushil Dastur, and by its slight, rhythmic motion riding to anchor. 'I could not beach it alone, either, I had to leave it afloat. Though of course,' he added reasonably, 'it may not be his own, it may very well be stolen.'

'Where is he now?' The swimmer was out of sight, concealed by the rocks. When he appeared again, it was off the point, in quieter water, and well clear of the saw-edged reefs.

'He's seen the boat,' cried Purushottam. 'He's coming in for it!' He turned to run across the narrow, grassy crest of the headland, with the intention of setting off down the path and reaching the shore first, but he halted before he had gone many yards, and Dominic checked with him. 'Not a chance! He'll be there long before we shall.'

Sushil Dastur had also marked the fugitive's change of course. He looked down into the blue, bright water beneath him, and saw the long, vigorous strokes carrying the swimmer steadily nearer; he saw a long arm stretched up to get a hold on the gunwale, and a brown shoulder heaving up out of the water. He had discarded the wrapping from round his head, or the surf had taken it, and streaming black hair half-covered his face. His hands gripped strongly; he rested for a moment, and then heaved himself steadily up to climb aboard.

It was too much for Sushil Dastur. He saw the enemy escaping, after all the evil he had done, after all they had risked in this one night to render him ineffective for ever. His sense of justice was outraged. He stooped to prise loose and hoist in his arms the largest stone he could lift, and hurled it down at the boat below. It seemed an endless while falling, before they saw it strike near the stern in a flurry of splinters and spray, causing the boat to plunge wildly and ship water; but it was a glancing blow, and the stone rebounded into the sea, though it took a length of shattered planking with it. The swimmer had clung tenaciously to his hold through the shock, and as soon as the boat righted, he hauled himself dripping over the side.

Silently they watched as he stooped to slash the riding line free, and leaned with all his weight on the heavy bamboo pole, thrusting off into deeper water. Slow though his progress upcoast might be, it would serve to get him out of sight, and ashore in some safer place, before they could do anything to prevent.

Sushil Dastur came clambering back to the headland, leading Priya with anxious solicitude. She came to Purushottam's side, and took her place there, but without a word as yet, her face drained and exhausted; and Purushottam, without a word, took her hand and held it. They watched the wake of the little boat stagger its way out to sea, and dwindle drunkenly up-coast; and already it seemed to them that it was settling a little in the water, and listing to one side like a limping man.

'I do not think,' said the Swami, between reassurance and concern, 'that he will get very far.'

The wreckage of the foundered boat did not begin to drift ashore for several days, and then most of it made its way to the Keralese beaches further to the north-west. But the boatman was brought in by the next tide, less than a mile up-coast.

The police took Dominic and Purushottam out by jeep to identify the body. Alone upon a brilliant expanse of dark crimson and jet-black sands, like an imperial pall, stripped of his last length of saffron cloth and naked as the day he was born, lay the muscular body and once agreeable and obliging face of Romesh Iyar, the boat-boy of Thekady.

Fifteen

Cape Comorin: Saturday Evening

They sat in one of the small, seaward lounges of the hotel that evening, after Priya had slept through most of the day, after the Manis had departed, stunned and incredulous, without Sushil Dastur, and the Bessancourts, grieved but unshaken, without Romesh Iyar, and after Larry had cruised his way in a local boat fruitlessly but gallantly up the coast and down again, only to hear that everything had happened without him, and that everything was over.

The hotel was very quiet, most of its guests out on the dunes or in the village, enjoying the cool of the evening after sundown. The police had completed their notes and interrogations, and departed, taking with them Romesh Iyar's rifle, stolen during the night from the belongings of one of the room-boys on duty, but strongly suspected of being the same one originally stolen from the baggage of a well-to-do guest more than a year previously. At Malaikuppam, tomorrow, Inspector Raju would be waiting to close his file on the case. Even the sad, repulsive carcase of the krait had been removed from under the balcony. The traces were being softly sponged away out of half a dozen lives, but only to make way for something new, which in its turn had arisen out of the old.

So they sat in the hotel lounge, Priya, the Swami, Purushottam, Larry, Dominic and Sushil Dastur, and told one another whatever remained to be told.

'After I had spoken with you,' said the Swami, 'I knew that I must come. The miscalculation that sent you here was mine. There at Malaikuppam it was already clear that no one was interested in us, and even more clear that Lakshman Ray is a very honest, estimable, though perhaps rather stiff-necked young man. He will accept any challenge if he thinks a reflection has been made upon him. And indeed I did, for a while, entertain the thought that he might be the person for whom we were looking, since it had to be someone, and apparently someone closely connected with your party. Lakshman is showing a marked interest in our programme for Malaikuppam, by the way. I hope you don't mind, Purushottam, that I discussed it with him. He is an intelligent boy. I think we must see that he completes his university course, he may be very useful in the future. Now where was I? Oh, yes! I thought I should join you here at once. So I took my hired car – if you had approached from the lane instead of the garden you would have seen and recognised it – and drove down here at once. Lakshman is in charge in Malaikuppam, should there be anything needing attention. I arrived here somewhat after midnight – no, later, it must have been nearly one o'clock – parked my car, and walked a little way towards the road and the dunes, in case I might be able to find you somewhere. So it happened that I was the first person to encounter Sushil Dastur. But Sushil will tell you.'

Sushil Dastur, in some celebratory exuberance, had put on his *achkan* tonight, and sat cross-legged, Indian to the backbone, in the cushioned settee along the wall. There was a hectic flush still perceptible on his prominent cheekbones, and a spark of excitement in his dark, vulnerable, once-apprehensive eyes. Sushil Dastur had lived through a night which transformed his life, a night he would never forget.

'You see, Mr Felse, Mr Narayanan, after I left you I was so upset, so ashamed, I could not possibly go to bed and sleep. I could not think how to make things right, and I was so restless, I went out to walk a little. I was among the trees at the edge of the garden, when I saw this man going out to the road, driving Miss Madhavan before him . . . It was terrible! He held her by a cord tied to her wrists, and he had a knife in his hand. You understand, I was afraid to call for help or make any sound, for fear he should kill her. So I followed them. It was the only thing I could think of to do . . .'

Sushil Dastur, who had been haunted and hounded all his life by his inadequacy and want of successs in trivial things, had astonished himself, when this genuine enormity confronted him, by being moved to immense indignation instead of fear, and boldness instead of caution. He had still not recovered from the shock.

'It was the right thing,' said Purushottam warmly. He had Priya close by his side, constantly and anxiously cherished with glances and attentions. Apart from that they did not touch each other, or anticipate by a word what they both knew to be inevitable and right. There are ways of doing these things, and theirs were Indian ways.

'If I followed, I thought, at least I should know where he had hidden her, and then I could bring help. Even in the darkness I had to take great care not to be seen or heard, but I saw him take her into the hut, and then I hurried back to get help.'

'And I was the first man he met,' said the Swami, 'and he was so good as to trust me at once with this story. I urged extreme caution, for Miss Madhavan's sake, for if we had raised a general alarm she would surely have been killed. But I had hopes that otherwise this criminal's interest was not in Priya herself, but rather in her value as a lure for Purushottam, in which case she might be safe for a while, provided there was no open hue and cry. That was why we examined her room and yours, Purushottam, and found the message which was left for you. You will forgive me if I left you no further message as to what we were about, but I had hopes that perhaps you need not know until all was over, if our efforts were rewarded. We knew now how much time we had, some hours of it blessedly in darkness still, and therefore we set of at once to act by stealth, trusting to bring her back, somehow, perhaps before you ever returned to the hotel. But the note we left where it was. We had no right to take from you, in the worst event, the choice that was there offered you.'

He looked from Priya to Purushottam, and his eyes were clear and calm. Those two knew more about each other, now, than most couples know who contemplate marriage, and had more reason to be confident and glad.

'We looked in my car's tool kit for whatever might be useful. I do not know why it should include so fine a knife, but we were very glad of it. We went mainly by the shore, climbing to the edge of the dunes when we had to, swimming when we were forced to. In the end the time we had was barely enough. In the first cove there we found a boat waiting. Obviously it was there to ensure his retreat after the shooting. So I went aboard, and poled it round the headland into the other bay, while Sushil Dastur climbed up to the rear of the hut with our knife, and began tapping his way along the walls to try to find out where Priya was, and make sure that she was alive and conscious, to be able to give us what help she could. And he found her, as she has told you, and she did help us, very substantially. When I had anchored the boat in the other bay, I climbed up from there to join him, and we began to cut our way through the wall to her. Though indeed Sushil Dastur was much more expert than I, and much more silent, and he did most of the work. And the rest you know.'

Yes, the rest they knew. Only the very simple part had been left for him to do at the end, when there was no other way of delaying Purushottam's execution by the two or three minutes necessary to complete the delivery of Priya. Without a weapon – and without the slightest intention of using one even if he had had one – to step in between the hunter and the hunted. That was all. Anyone could do that.

'How strange!' said Priya wonderingly. 'At Thekady we liked him, all of us. And yet he wore such a false face. Not just the crime itself, but all that manipulation of the other boat-boy – for it must have been Romesh who not only put those Maoist papers among Ajit Ghose's possessions, but also put it into his mind that Bakhle would be a profitable client and tip him well, so that he would want to exchange duties for the day. Perhaps he even suggested it, though he got Ajit to do the asking. It was all his evidence that turned the charge against the other boy. And I think – it is a terrible thing to say about any man, but truly I believe it of him – that he designed events so that we, in his boat, should be the ones to find the bodies. Because he *wanted* to be there. Because it gave him satisfaction to have contrived everything so cleverly, and to see his plans succeed.'

'It is a seductive delight,' said the Swami, for him almost sententiously, 'to excel at anything.'

'But a poor person like Ajit Ghose – as poor as himself – how was he the enemy? And to take not only his life, but even his good name!'

'Now at least he will get that back again,' said Purushottam. 'Everyone knows now that he was quite innocent, that it was Iyar who did everything.'

Dominic looked fixedly at the Swami, but the Swami sat silent, his face composed and tranquil

'And it seems that he himself was this sadhu we've heard so much about, and I've never seen,' said Larry. 'The one at Nagarcoil and at Thekady. In both places he claimed to have seen that sadhu himself, as soon as he was asked about him – and in the right spot, too. I suppose he threw in the sighting at Nagarcoil because he knew Priya had seen him casing the house.'

'And as it turns out,' said Dominic, 'it was only in Nagarcoil he managed to get himself taken on by the

Bessancourts. He gave the impression that that had happened earlier, in Trivandrum, but actually he never was in Trivandrum, he was following us. He only happened on the Bessancourts after he'd been checking up on us at Priya's house. Being with them made it possible for him to get to close quarters with us here.'

'But I confess I have not quite understood,' said Sushil Dastur humbly, 'the significance of this pose as a sadhu. I hope I am not being obtuse,' he said sadly, with a remote echo of his old uncertainty. It was important that he should not be obtuse. Purushottam had invited him back to Malaikuppam, in the passion of his gratitude, and offered him employment there, and the fear of being inadequate is not so easy to shake off in a moment.

'I have pondered on the same matter myself,' said the Swami considerately. 'I think he was there by the lingam at Thekady by arrangement, to receive from someone – someone possibly quite unimportant, and unaware of his role – the bomb which was planted in Mr Bakhle's boat. You will remember that he was seen there for only a short time, and that everyone testified to the fact that it was most unusual for any such person to find it worthwhile patronising that spot. It would have been unwise to have the messenger come and ask for him at the lake. Yet this place was within easy reach, and simple to find. And it is not so hard to become a sadhu in two minutes. A length of cloth, a handful of dust or ash, a touch of red or yellow paint, an oily hand passed through the hair – these are all you need. Having this small equipment with him, he used it whenever he had need to be other than his apparent self. The kit costs very little, also an advantage. Holiness is not an essential – though many may indeed be holy.'

Priya put out a hand with a sudden gesture of protest and pain, and Purushottam reached out rather shyly and took it in his, flushing and burning at the touch.

'Then is that what happened to Patti? I think and think of her – and they will come, her parents, and what are we to tell them? It was Patti who gave alms to the sadhu by the lingam. Only she saw him closely, no one else looked him in the face as she did. Surely she knew, or felt she knew, that face again, even seen so differently? In the dusk there, when we found the boat – the same hour of dusk, the same light – she suspected then. And that's why she died!'

491

There was a moment of silence, while the Swami gazed back at her with great gentleness and profound respect.

'It was surely by reason of her recognition or non-recognition of that face that she died. For surely *he* thought that she knew him. She was a victim of forces she could not possibly understand.'

'Patti is the thing I find hardest to forgive,' said Priya.

'I, too,' said the Swami, 'hardest of all.' He cast down his eyes, regarding with calm abstraction the cupped palms of his hands. In the half-lit room cross-legged with soles up-turned in the cushions of the couch against the wall, he looked more than ever like an antique bronze. He said mysteriously, and apparently as much to himself as to them: 'The Lord said: "He who at his last hour, when he casts off the body, goes hence remembering me, goes assuredly into my being." '

Epilogue

Malaikuppam

The police came and went at Malaikuppam, took statement after statement, congratulated the household and one another, even condescended to fill in a detail or two which had emerged later, such as Romesh Iyar's mode of transport on that last chase. It seemed that a motor cycle had been stolen, and later found abandoned at Nagarcoil, where he had rediscovered the Bessancourts through happening on their car, and had managed to get himself added to their party. And having completed all inquiries to their own satisfaction, Inspector Tilak and Inspector Raju closed the case, and departed. The terrorist was dead, the file completed, and this particular danger, at least, over for good.

The Galloways came and departed, also. During the three days that they stayed, every other person in the house walked delicately, tuned only to their needs and wishes. They were the essence of what Patti had once called suburban Cheltenham, unobtrusively well bred, well dressed and unadventurous. But they had also the advantages of their kind, reticence, consideration, honesty and fortitude, and the kind of durability which outlives empire. They would probably never do anything very big, very important, or very imaginative, but equally they were unlikely ever to do anything very mean, very cruel or crassly unimaginative. Their grief was contained but profound; they were not the kind to embarrass anyone with too intimate an insight into their troubles. Priya, who still had a week of leave, stayed and devoted herself to them until they left for the airport at Madurai, with Patti's ashes, en route for Bombay and home. And when they were driven away, Larry, who had also felt impelled to stay and see the affair out to its close, gazed after the departing car with a thoughtful frown, and said:

'The more I see of the New Left, the more I begin to value middle-class virtues.' To add the next moment, in case anyone had got the wrong idea: 'Virtues, I said. I know they've got their vices too.'

He and Lakshman were the next to leave, heading westward

493

over the Ghats to Trivandrum and up coast to Cochin; but when their tour ended, Lakshman was to return to his college with a grant guaranteed by the Mission, and Larry, too, had asked, noncommittally enough, to be informed if ever the work of restoring the old irrigation tanks should be seriously contemplated. They would both be back; at least to visit and remember, quite probably to stay.

Then Purushottam drove Priya home to Nagarcoil, to spend her last few days of leave with her family; not to broach the idea of marriage yet – that would be a job for someone else in the first instance – but surely to keep a sharp eye open for the quality of his own welcome, in the light of all that had happened. He came back cautiously elated, very thoughtful, but with a happy, hopeful thoughtfulness that looked forward, not back. And as for Sushil Dastur, turned loose on all the papers that had been salvaged from the office, dealing with abstract things like figures, which obeyed and never nagged him, he had never been so happy in his life.

And the next day Dominic drove the Swami to Madurai in the hired car, on their way back to Madras.

The whole household waved them away from the gates. As soon as they lost sight of the wall, and were threading the dusty centre of the village, the Swami sat back with a sigh in the front passenger seat, and turned his face to the future; but not yet his thoughts, not completely, for in a few moments he said, summing up: 'Well, it is over. Not, perhaps, without loss, but I think as economically as possible.'

'Except,' said Dominic, accelerating as they drew clear of the last fringe of the village, 'that justice has not been done. And you know it.'

The Swami gazed ahead, along the reddish-yellow, rutted ribbon of road, and pondered that without haste.

'In what particular?' he asked at length.

'Granted it was Romesh Iyar who planted the bomb in Bakhle's boat at Thekady, and set up the other boat-boy to take the rap, granted it was Romesh who hunted us to the Cape when he found Purushottam and Lakshman had changed places, and did everything that was done there – planting the krait, kidnapping Priya as bait, and setting the trap to shoot Purushottam – all that, yes. But not the second bomb, the one in the office. He had nothing to do with that. He couldn't have had. He was at Tenkasi, and the police were getting regular reports from him. He was there doing casual work around the junction until he was told on Thursday evening that he could go where he liked, and needn't report any more. He was fifty miles from Malaikuppam when that bomb was planted. And you know it. And so does Inspector Raju!'

'There is this matter of the stolen motor cycle. Fifty miles is not a great distance,' said the Swami experimentally.

'Yes, I noticed that Inspector Raju mentioned that the motor bike was found at Nagarcoil, abandoned after Romesh hit on the idea of attaching himself to the Bessancourts. But he never said where or when it was reported missing.' Dominic smiled along his shoulder, with affection, and even a little rueful amusement. 'Oh, no, I wasn't stupid enough to ask Inspector Raju, he might not have told me this time. But I did ask Sergeant Gokhale. Everyone got the desired impression that it was stolen in Tenkasi, at some unspecified time, and that he used it to commute up here by night. But actually it vanished right here in Koilpatti during Thursday night. After the police had told Romesh he needn't report any more. After Patti's death was in the papers. He didn't leave Tenkasi until then, and he left by train. He pinched the motor bike to get up to Malaikuppam from the station, and he kept it to follow us south when he saw us set off next morning without Lakshman – and with Purushottam.'

'The others,' said the Swami reasonably, having absorbed all this without apparent discomfiture, 'have not questioned the police conclusions.'

'The others don't happen to have that bit of information I got from Inspector Raju, as he was leaving on Thursday evening. I was asking about all the others, Romesh was only mentioned among the rest. But that's how I know he was still waiting in Tenkasi when Patti was killed in Malaikuppam.'

The Swami denied nothing of all this. He contemplated the road ahead, and looked a little tired, but not at all discomposed. 'And why have you said no word of this in front of everyone?'

'I suppose,' said Dominic gently, 'my reasons must be much the same as yours. I said justice hadn't been done – I didn't say I necessarily wanted it done.'

'And how long,' asked the Swami, after another considering silence, 'have you known?'

'Not long. Not even after we went to identify Romesh

Iyar's body. I only began to understand,' he said, 'when you evaded Priya's question about how and why Patti died. It was because of her recognition *or non-recognition* of the sadhu's face, you said, that Patti died. So it was. It was because she *didn't* recognise him again in Romesh, not because she did. If she'd known him when she met him again, she might have been alive today. Not,' he added honestly, 'that it would necessarily have been much better for her. But it was after you said that, that I began to put things together, and to remember everything that seemed insignificant at the time, and yet made absolute sense once I had the clue. Such as, for instance, that if only we'd taken the girls with us when we went to look over the estate and the old irrigation channels, again, Patti might have been alive today.'

They were out on the main road, turning left towards Koilpatti.

'As Purushottam said, at a moment when his every word merited attention,' the Swami remarked, 'we should not and must not turn to saying: "If only . . ." We do what we must, what seems right to us at the time, and none of us can do more.' He added with reserve, but with respect and resignation, too: 'Tell me, then, since you know so much—'

'Only because, in the first place, you told me! To see you confronted with the absolute necessity for telling a lie, and still managing not to tell one, is a revelation.'

'I see that you begin to know me too well, and to be as irreverent as a real son, my son,' lamented the Swami, with a sigh and a smile of detached affection. 'Tell me, then, if Romesh Iyar did not put the bomb in Purushottam's office – who did?'

'Patti did,' said Dominic. 'Of course!'

'Go on,' said the Swami, his face neither consenting nor denying.

'She came from England, already in rebellion against everything that represented her parents and the establishment. She came innocent, romantic, idealistic, silly if you like, a sucker for left-wing causes, and kidded into hoping to find the wonderful, easy, metaphysical way here in India. And India kicked her in the teeth, the way it does – in the belly, too, sometimes – showing her, as it shows to all silly idealists, its most deprived and venomous and ugly and venal side. She was absolutely ripe to be a fall guy. The obvious ills of India made her a sitting target for the Naxalite contacts I don't doubt she made in Calcutta – through the most vocal and articulate section of her society. It isn't any chore to sell the slogan of: "Death to the landlords!" to a girl like that, who'd never even seen anyone kick a kitten until she came here. To her violence was all abstract, until she had to see it with her own eyes, all the blood and mess that you can imagine away as long as it's still only in the mind. I don't know who got hold of her, there among the Bengali teachers and students, but someone did. And when she came on leave south, they got her to bring the two bombs from Calcutta. She had her orders about handing them over, and she knew the names of the parties for whom they were intended . . .'

'You are sure of that?' asked the Swami, pricking up his ears.

'Quite sure. In the boat she got the shock of her life when Romesh mentioned the name of Mahendralal Bakhle. Seeing him hadn't meant a thing to her, she hadn't known what he looked like; but she knew the name, all right. She passed it off by saying she'd read about his labour riots in the papers, but from then on she was dead quiet that day. Until then, I think, she'd sort of felt that she'd washed her hands of the first bomb, and nothing would really happen, nothing she would ever have to know about – and suddenly there was the man who was condemned to death, on the same lake with her, and she knew it was real. And again later, when we had to tell Inspector Raju where we could be contacted, and we said we were going to Purushottam Narayanan's house at Malaikuppam, she at once changed her plans and asked if she and Priya could travel with us. Oh, yes, Patti knew who the victims were. But the rest – her contact here – everything to do with the Naxalite organisation itself – no, they took good care she should know as little as possible about all that.'

'So the deliveries of those two bombs she carried, you think, were clearly laid down for her, in such a way as to prevent her from identifying the receiver?'

'It looks that way. The first – of course you know it – was dropped into the sadhu's begging bowl by the lingam shrine, along with her few *naye paise* . . .'

'Yes . . . the face only she saw, and by twilight, behind its ash and paint, and failed to know again in Romesh Iyar.'

'And the second, I think, was to have been delivered in exactly the same way to the sadhu at Tenkasi Junction,

when she and Priya de-trained there for Kuttalam. Why
else should he set off for there the next day, and wait there
three days? He thought she knew him, and had understood
everything – or perhaps he merely thought that she would
obey instructions, and use no initiative herself. Let's say, at
least, that it never entered his head that she would accept
the set-up at its face value, and believe absolutely that Ajit
Ghose was her contact, and that he'd sacrificed his own life
to fulfil his mission.'

'And therefore,' said the Swami sadly, 'that she was now
orphaned – bereft of her partner, and challenged to be as
selfless and as ruthless as he. That she was on her own –
with a bomb, and a known victim.'

'When we found that boat it hit her like a thunderbolt,'
said Dominic, sweating as he remembered the leaking hull
swaying sluggishly with its wash of water and blood among
the tall reeds. 'She'd never seen violence before – damn it, I
don't suppose she'd ever seen death before. You contemplate
it with heroic calm, yes – as long as it stays a thousand
miles away from you. When you see it, smell it, touch it,
that's another matter. Priya has never thought of violent
injury but with compassion and the urge to jump right in
and help. She's never willed it, and it doesn't frighten her.
Patti *had* willed it, and then she saw it, and it was sickening.
She collapsed, she was out of the reckoning all that night.
And in the morning, Priya said, she was very calm, and
talked of having to see Inspector Raju. Priya thought that
was only because she hadn't been fit the night before, and
felt a statement would be required from her. I think it was
more. I think she had slept on it, then, and made up her
mind to confess, and hand over the second bomb. Not
because of Bakhle, so much as because she thought that
her heroes, the activists, the Naxalites, had turned out to
be nothing but callous murderers, to whom an innocent,
incidental boat-boy was of no account, and could be wiped
out like swatting a fly. In a country, my God, where the
Jains won't even risk *inhaling* a fly! And she was right
then. But afterwards, when she did see Inspector Raju, it
was only to have it confirmed that so far from being an
innocent victim, Ajit Ghose was the assassin, and the martyr
for his cause, willing to die to carry out his assignment. And
it was then she changed course again. She didn't confess, she
didn't hand over the second bomb. On the contrary, when
she heard we were to be Purushottam's guests she hitched

a ride along with us. Poor Priya was shocked. One doesn't do such things, in a land where hospitality is in any case so instant, and so lavish. But Patti had risen to the occasion then, she was exalted. Ghose was dead, no longer able to take care of his second assignment. And she was confronted with his monstrous example. She was English, insubordinate, used to being allowed initiative. Romesh Iyar, who was sure she would just go ahead as planned, made off to Tenkasi to wait for her, never doubting she would come. Patti, believing she was left to hold up the world alone, and delivered from the ghastly thought that her heroes wrote off the humble as expendable – no, more than that, convinced that they regarded *themselves* as expendable – came with us to Malaikuppam dedicated to killing Purushottam.'

'You are very sure,' said the Swami, with sincere sorrow.

'Very sure. Aren't you? Who else was ever alone in Purushottam's office that day? She asked to use his typewriter to catch up with her letters, and she was in there, I suppose, an hour and a half before Priya and I went to see how she was getting on, and bring her back to the house. I don't know what she did with the bomb – taped it underneath the desk, maybe – I expect the police know. Anyhow, she left it there, set for somewhere around half past seven. You remember, we were to leave about seven, and the lawyer was to come at eight. She didn't want to kill the lawyer, she knew nothing about him. She knew nothing about Purushottam either – I blame all of us for that, but as you say, "If only . . ." has no meaning. We'd talked so much in front of her about farming on a big scale, and the uselessness of a small-holding economy here – but never, until the morning we were to leave, did we mention the word co-operative in her hearing, or let her into the secret that Purushottam was not setting out to enrich himself but to give away everything he had. Without realising it, we must have confirmed her ten times over in thinking she had the right to dispatch him out of the world. But in the morning, just when we were ready to set out – I remember almost every word now – we were talking as if she wasn't there, about the welfare of the villages, about how he was aiming at tranforming the district and financing the change himself . . . If we'd said it openly earlier – but how can you use it as a reproach against anyone that he doesn't talk a lot about his own good deeds? No, there was nothing we could have done.

'But Patti was standing there close beside us, and she

Ellis Peters

heard, then, and understood. It hit her like lightning-stroke.
She suddenly started rummaging in her bag, and then gasped
out something about having left her diary in the office, and
having to fetch it. There wasn't any diary, she wasn't the
diary type, but how did we know? We barely knew her at all,
even Priya. And she ran to undo what she'd done, to save
Purushottam, who wasn't what she'd thought he was. It was
her last change of course, it would have involved confession
– everything – though I don't suppose she thought of that at
all. But the bomb went off early, and killed her.

'And that's all,' he said sombrely, steering the car with
care through the narrow, chaotic streets of Koilpatti, and
out on the northward run to Sattur and Madurai.

'It is enough,' said the Swami. 'Do you not think so? Has
she not partially answered you? Do you think that justice
consists in revealing everything to everyone? I think not.
Why should we discomfort those two sad people by telling
them that their daughter became a dedicated terrorist, willing
to kill for a cause? And do you think it would redress that
balance if we also told them that afterwards she proved
herself, no less, a girl with the honesty and courage to
turn back just as vehemently when her eyes were opened?
To undo what she had done at the cost of her own life? No,
I think not. They would not be at home with either aspect.
Let them continue to believe in her as in an innocent victim,
too bland for either role. I believe they will be happier so.
And she . . .'

'And she?' said Dominic.

'Do not despair of Patti. Do not despair for her. She
accepted the evidence that refuted her. She ran without
hesitation or fear to undo what she had done, as soon as
she knew it to be unjustified – even by her own lights. By
mine no violence is justified. Think of it! Your departure
was already some minutes delayed, it was past seven o'clock,
but still she ran to prevent Purushotam's death. And having
detached the bomb – for I doubt if she knew how to stop the
clock mechanism once it was set – what do you suppose she
meant to do with it? How to dispose of it?'

Dominic watched the road, and kept his hands steady and
competent on the wheel. 'I had thought of that. The office
was turned away from the courtyard, with its windows on
the kitchen garden. It was quite big and empty out there. I
doubt if she'd thought about it at all in advance, but once
there, with the bomb in her hands due to go off in about

500

twenty minutes at the outside, I suppose her instinct would be to throw it out of the window as far as she could.'

'Yes,' said the Swami, 'so one supposes. And have you forgotten what you told me? There were three of the household children playing there in the kitchen garden. There were things Patti could not do, and that was one of them. She could not throw out the bomb where the innocents might be harmed, no, not for her own life. And then she did not know what to do. I think she was still holding it in her hands when it blew up and killed her.'

FUNERAL OF FIGARO
AN OPERATIC WHODUNNIT

When Figaro is killed in an aeroplane crash it seems that nothing can save the production of Mozart's well-loved opera at the Leander Theatre. But then world-class baritone Marc Chatrier arrives from Europe and the cast breathes a sigh of relief. Yet music is not all that is close to the handsome singer's heart, and when he sets his cap at young Hero, the teenage daughter of the Leander's owner, feathers are ruffled.

Somewhat seduced by the unexpected attention, Hero is baffled by the signs of upset among the group, and there seems to be more than petty jealousy afoot. Then Chatrier is killed in the middle of a performance, and it is clear that someone has a particularly vicious dislike of the man, but would anyone resort to murder?

A broken love affair, a wartime betrayal and the respect of a servant for his master are some of the fragments of the past unearthed by Detective Inspector Musgrave in his quest to discover just who is responsible for the funeral of Figaro.

MURDER AT PLUM'S
A Victorian Whodunnit
Amy Myers

Plum's in St James's Square in London, with its worn leather armchairs and cocoon of inviting warmth providing a refuge from the world, is the very acme of respectability. In short, everything an English gentleman's club should be. With one exception: excellent cuisine provided by master chef Auguste Didier. For food is the very reason the club first came into being – its founder believing that if men can enjoy food together they can get on and rule the world together. But the late Captain Plum was an incurable optimist.

The trouble really starts the day women are allowed, for the first time, within the hallowed portals to watch the time-honoured ceremony of Plum's Passing. A series of bizarre incidents has already plagued the club – a rat left upon a dining table, newspapers wantonly mutilated, death threats made to a member, even obscene letters sent to the doorman. And Auguste, having always maintained that cooking and sleuthing go naturally hand in hand, is persuaded by his friend and rival Emma Pryde to delve once more into the realms of mystery. But murder at Plum's? Impossible!

Abruptly, inevitably, however, Auguste's investigations with his friend Inspector Egbert Rose of Scotland Yard turn into a hunt for a demonically clever and ruthless killer . . .

'Reading like a cross between Hercule Poirot and Mrs Beeton, *Murder at Plum's* provides a third outing for one of fiction's most unusual detectives . . . This feast of entertainment is packed with splendid late-Victorian detail' *Evening Standard*

FICTION/CRIME   0 7472 3397 7   £3.50

Crown in Darkness

P·C·Doherty

**A medieval mystery
featuring Hugh Corbett**

Alexander III of Scotland was riding to meet
his beautiful French bride Yolande one dark,
storm-ridden night when he fell to his death.
He left the Scottish throne vacant of any real
heir, though the powerful nobles of his own
kingdom, as well as the great European
princes, immediately started to fight for the
glittering prize.

Hugh Corbett, a clerk in the English
Chancery, is sent to Scotland by his old
master, the Chancellor, Bishop Burnell, to
discover the truth behind Alexander's death
and report on the chaotic situation at the
Scottish court. Corbett is drawn into
malevolent intrigue, suspicion – and danger
– before truth and lies are separated, and the
mystery solved.

'Brings the harsh medieval landscape of
Scotland to vivid life, particularly its gritty
and malodorous cities, its wildly beautiful
countryside and its population of devout,
enigmatic or sinister characters'
Publishers Weekly

Also by PC Doherty from Headline featuring Hugh Corbett
SATAN IN ST MARY'S

FICTION/CRIME   0 7472 3505 8

A selection of bestsellers
from Headline

FICTION

ONE GOLDEN NIGHT	Elizabeth Villars	£4.99 ☐
HELL HATH NO FURY	M R O'Donnell	£4.99 ☐
CONQUEST	Elizabeth Walker	£4.99 ☐
HANNAH	Christine Thomas	£4.99 ☐
A WOMAN TO BE LOVED	James Mitchell	£4.99 ☐
GRACE	Jan Butlin	£4.99 ☐
THE STAKE	Richard Laymon	£4.99 ☐
THE RED DEFECTOR	Martin L Gross	£4.99 ☐
LIE TO ME	David Martin	£4.99 ☐
THE HORN OF ROLAND	Ellis Peters	£3.99 ☐

NON-FICTION

LITTLE GREGORY	Charles Penwarden	£4.99 ☐
PACIFIC DESTINY	Robert Elegant	£5.99 ☐

SCIENCE FICTION AND FANTASY

HERMETECH	Storm Constantine	£4.99 ☐
TARRA KHASH: HROSSAK!	Brian Lumley	£3.99 ☐
DEATH'S GREY LAND	Mike Shupp	£4.50 ☐
The Destiny Makers 4		

All Headline books are available at your local bookshop or newsagent, or can be ordered direct from the publisher. Just tick the titles you want and fill in the form below. Prices and availability subject to change without notice.

Headline Book Publishing PLC, Cash Sales Department, PO Box 11, Falmouth, Cornwall, TR10 9EN, England.

Please enclose a cheque or postal order to the value of the cover price and allow the following for postage and packing:
UK: 80p for the first book and 20p for each additional book ordered up to a maximum charge of £2.00
BFPO: 80p for the first book and 20p for each additional book
OVERSEAS & EIRE: £1.50 for the first book, £1.00 for the second book and 30p for each subsequent book.

Name ....

Address ....

....

....